The Affinity Theory - Edited Version

The Affinity Saga Book 1

Eddie Dee Williams

Contents

A Message for the Adults

This version of The Affinity Theory has been modified to be more suitable for younger readers by reducing the foul language and removing the explicit scene from the manuscript. Now, our kids have the opportunity to experience the world of Uri City and meet the Elite Defenders Unit of the Uri City Division of the Company! Happy reading!

Prologue

No, I don't! No one does! Not like this!

Malcolm's eyes popped wide as he sat up suddenly out of his sleep. Hyperventilating, Malcolm gasped and dug his fingers into his chest, his lungs squeezed tighter than a stress ball in full use. His chiseled, chestnut body, tinted silver by the moonlight streaming through his open windows, was basting with sweat. He planted his palms onto his forehead and gripped his dome, his textured hair the only protection from his death grip as he desperately struggled to formulate an explanation for nightmares that didn't resemble any past events from his life. He recalled the grounding techniques his therapist taught him and breathed deeply to begin regulating his breath. He scanned the room and stated to himself five things he saw.

White bed sheets tinted silver. The clock on my nightstand says 20:55. I haven't even gotten two cycles of sleep yet. The walls of my room. The skyline. My hands. He lifted the sheets and exposed his skin to the crisp air. He planted his feet on the floor and cupped his face once again to continue his grounding exercise. *Four things I feel. The carpet strands under my feet. My skin rubbing against my palms. My hair. How cold it is in this room.* He stood up and walked into his bathroom. *Three things I hear. The hovercraft outside whizzing past the building. Um...* He flipped the light switch. *The flipped light switch.* He twisted the faucet knob. *Running water.*

Malcolm felt more centered and put enough distance between himself and his visceral reaction to the nightmare he ruminated on. He cupped some of the lukewarm water. He bent forward and splashed himself repeatedly, hoping the water would wash his nightmares away. He twisted the knob and pulled a couple of sheets of paper towels from the dowel. As he dried his face, he stared into the mirror in front of him, peering into his reflection and studying his ripped form, worried that the nearly naked man in front of him was indeed the red and black assassin who continued to haunt him in the crevasses of his subconsciousness.

Am I okay? Am I that guy? Why do I keep seeing this stuff? I don't remember any of it, but it was like I was there. My body knows something, my soul knows something. But why won't my memories confirm any of it?

He twisted the faucet knob again, and as the water flowed, he slipped his hand slowly into the water. He dialed up his senses, and as the water dripped from his hands, he focused on every drop. He sensed the molecular structure of every molecule that slipped through the faucet filter, felt the way the droplets shaped themselves around his fingers, flowed across his palm, and disappeared down the drain. He summoned the molecules to obey his commands like a conductor to his orchestra. As he moved his fingers back and forth, the water stopped flowing downward and formed a ball surrounding his hand like a water balloon without the balloon. The ball slowly enlarged the longer he waved his fingers. He then closed his fist, and the water splashed into the sink, now a small pool disappearing in the drain. He twisted the knob once more, dried his hands, and yelled, "Beko!" before throwing the used paper towel balls away in the trash can next to the sink.

His senses still dialed up, he sensed the molecules that made up the drywall and the paint that formed his room. He identified the fibers in the carpeting that brushed his feet. He noticed the different molecular structures in the plywood and steel that formed the ceiling fan slowly swiveling above him. He detected the compounds that made up the glass he looked through, and for kicks, he summoned the glass to wobble slightly. *Still got it.*

He gazed at the city skyline through the transparent wall – many of the same skyscrapers that crumbled in his dreams – and observed hovercraft whizzing past to reach their varying destinations. Unlike the doom his nightmares suggested, Uri City was alive and well. Malcolm felt overwhelming relief wash over him. *I wish I could feel like this forever, this peace, right here. Look at this, everything working like it should. The city abuzz while most are sound asleep. Lucky jerks don't know how good they got it.*

A low, sudden rumble jolted his serenity. He noticed a sliver of red and black smoke rise along the horizon from somewhere in the neighboring district. "Hope it's just a blast," he mumbled as he ran his hand over his face and over his thick, textured hair. Malcolm felt a light vibration in his left arm as a bright red line strobed from his wrist to the bend of his forearm. "Spoke too soon."

He lifted his arm toward his face and read the words scrolling across his stripe, "ELITE: Explosion in Leicester District, armed robbery in progress, suspected Powered individuals involved. Assemble and prevent robbery. APPREHEND SUSPECTS." Malcolm took a deep breath, raised his arms over his head, locked his hands, and stretched his entire body. Upon release, he said, "Here we go."

He walked toward the wall opposite his bed and touched a white panel with his palm. A mechanism whirred and clicked to unlock the wall. It slid open, revealing a black shirt suspended by a hanger, black shorts, and two buttons sitting on a small shelf. Malcolm took the shorts and slipped into them, then took the two buttons – one his uniform, the other his cloak – and snapped them together. He placed the buttons in a tiny hole bored in his chest near his heart. The buttons quickly spun and clicked to lock themselves in place. Malcolm tapped the button once, and his stripe strobed yellow to initiate the docking sequence. A monotonic voice in his ear stated, "Malcolm Bennett, identity confirmed," and his stripe strobed white, the color for confirmation. Malcolm pulled the shirt from the hanger and dressed himself, the buttons exposed from the tiny hole in the middle of the shirt. He then double tapped the button on his chest, and tiny nanites exploded from the buttons like a mad army of frenzied ants marching from a mound. They swarmed from his chest and enveloped him from head to toe. They then melded to form a metallic, flexible skin. Shades of black and blue materialized on the sizzling, hardening, dragonscale-like shell. The nanites covered his face to create a helmet with a visor. A screen lit up before Malcolm's eyes, scanned his pupils, then revealed the words "Identity Confirmed."

A soft, slightly crackled female voice greeted, "Good evening, Malcolm. Looks like another night in paradise."

"Indeed, it is, Stephanie. Surprised you're awake right now," Malcolm responded.

"So am I. I couldn't sleep, and I guess this is the reason why," Stephanie revealed. The visor's graphics rushed to reveal the location of the blast in the Leicester district. Stephanie continued, "Your team has been assembled and is rendezvousing to the site of the blast. It appears that the suspects are trying to steal power core prototypes that are believed will revolutionize the cloaking game."

His suit completed the process and solidified at his feet to form protective boots. He told Stephanie, "Oh, for real? So much for the Company being on the cutting edge. How will these prototypes revolutionize cloaking?"

"The cores are designed to last longer and adapt to their environment and threat level, meaning..."

"...if these get into the wrong hands, battles with the powered may turn deadlier since they would be able to withstand powers longer," Malcolm inferred. "Can't have that."

"No, we cannot," Stephanie replied. "The DD Corporation cannot afford to have these prototypes exposed to the public, nor the schematics released on the black market. Furthermore, the Company wants these guys caught alive so we can find out who hired them for this job."

Malcolm sensed there might be a secondary motive to the Elite Unit being sent out on a routine armed robbery. *Seems like overkill to send the six of us out there to handle this. I almost guarantee this is a plan to win favor with the DD Corp to broker a partnership between them and the Company and upgrade our technology.*

Ever the good soldier, though, he chose not to question the Company's agenda. "Orders received. We got this," Malcolm complied. He double tapped his chest again. A second set of translucent nanites swarmed his body, shimmering bright yellow like sequins as they encapsulated him from his crown to his soles. They then hummed lowly three times, then turned transparent. His cloak monitored the environment, prepared to adapt at any given moment to protect him from multiple combinations of imminent threats of bodily harm he might face on the battlefield. His visor displayed in cyan the cloak's shield integrity holding at '100%.'

Stephanie summarized, "Get in, secure the prototypes, apprehend the suspects, and get out. Good luck, K.C. May Akan's favor rain down upon you."

K.C. breathed deeply, shaking off the last remnants of his horrible slumber, and declared, "Let's get it."

1

Some Assembly Required

K.C. stood atop the edge of his apartment complex and stared at the night skyline ablaze with glittering lights from the twin moons, stars, and hovercraft above and the buildings and cars below. His visor highlighted a bright spot from where the armed robbery was taking place in the Leicester District. K.C. waited for his team to pick him up.

"This is Eagle, we're thirty seconds out, K.C.," he heard through the comms in his helmet.

He replied, "Copy that. Ready to rock." A roaring engine zoomed closer to K.C., and a series of recessed lights got brighter and more defined above him. K.C. looked up and saw the Eagle's hovercraft, a black and purple winged vessel.

The plane slowed, and its bottom bay door slid open. The interior glowed and shone a spotlight where K.C. stood. K.C. felt lighter on his feet, and the light magnetically charged. He suddenly lifted from the rooftop and was retracted into the hovercraft. The door closed, and he landed atop it.

He saw four of his teammates in their usual seats along the sides of the craft. "How's everybody doing?" K.C. asked.

"Ready to get this super fun assignment over with," Alexia answered sarcastically as she heaved her arms, her green nanotech glittering in the light. "I was in the middle of an amazing night when here comes my arm lighting up with this foolishness." She squinted her deep brown eyes and pursed her rose-painted lips in frustration.

"I'm with her on this," Duncan reacted, pointing one of his silver and gold metal arm cannons at Alexia. "Like, armed robbery? Why couldn't a Super team handle this? Frimas, even a Powered team could have dealt with this."

"I'm with them, too," a voice from the cockpit chimed in. "This doesn't sound like something we should be responding to."

Good to know I'm not the only one who sees it. K.C. silently instructed his uniform to remove his helmet, and the nanotech obeyed. The helmet melted away and revealed Malcolm's head. He walked past the four to take his seat next to Alexia and said, "Not gonna lie, it kind of bothered me, too, Malaysia," he acknowledged his pilot. "However, the Company assigned this task to us for a reason, so we must respond to it. Besides, Duncan, haven't you been itching to get in the field? You've been complaining for weeks now," switching to a whining child voice, "'When are we gonna get to see some action again?'"

Everyone laughed as Daisy, sitting opposite Malcolm, Alexia, and Duncan, leaned forward to pile on Duncan, "Got that right! I've never seen somebody want to jump in the fray so badly, like you're missing out on something. I promise you it's not that serious, right, Karl?" she nudged Karl, sitting next to her, in his rugged tricep.

"Well, I'm just saying, sitting at the Company training all day is boring. There are only so many training bots I can light up before it just gets old. I want to beat down some actual bad guys and make them wish they never came out of their hiding places," Duncan complained while lifting his arm cannons in front of him and mimicking rifle cocking action, then sticking his black-gloved hands through them again.

"Such a soldier," Malcolm chuckled. "Well, let's just remember that the Company wants these people alive. So as much as you want to light them up, our objective is to stop the robbery and apprehend *all* the suspects. So be extra careful using your powers today."

"True that," Karl chimed in as his oversized biceps tightened through his black and gold-speckled nanotech. "We've been doing a good job the past year and a half with not causing an incident. We want to keep it that way."

Everyone nodded in agreement except Duncan, who asked, "Wait, what happened a year and a half ago?"

Alexia's eyes glowed green, and mist slowly flowed from her fingertips as she started narrating. "It was awful, we..."

Before Alexia could give a visual history of the event, Malaysia interrupted, "Prepare to drop."

Alexia's eyes returned to their normal hue, and everybody stood up. Malcolm said, "Okay, everyone, we know what we're here to do. Visors on. Cloaks up." Everybody silently summoned their visors and helmets to cover their heads according to their desired specifications. The nanotech for Enchantra, Blitz, and the Eagle's helmets created a mesh-like opening for their hair to flow out of, while the Mammoth, Ammo, and K.C.'s nanotech covered their heads completely. Everyone's visors were blackened. K.C. continued, "Intelligence, you online?"

At their base of operations, Stephanie sat at her desk at the front of the Intelligence auditorium. "Yes, we're here," she responded.

"Awesome, Stephanie, what do we know so far?"

"Patching into DD's security system now," Stephanie replied through their comms. A moment later, they could see the building's security plan on their visors. Stephanie zoomed in to the third floor.

"The cores are believed to be on the third floor, guarded by a nanite cloak that stretches wall-to-wall," Stephanie informed. "They have a head start on you. You need to hurry before the hostiles dismantle the cloak and retrieve the cores. We're breaking through DD's security system to alert you to the cloak's shield integrity percentage in real-time.

"Meanwhile, we have four hostiles on that floor, all of them powered." The camera showed four individuals, one shooting lightning bolts from his hands, another firing a white laser beam from his eyes. The third, gargantuan in size, pummeled the cloak with his massive arms, and the fourth stood watching the other three. The Elite's visors displayed the cloak's shield integrity falling steadily, reading 42% in the upper left corner.

K.C. issued orders. "Alright, Mammoth, you'll play anchor tonight. Stay outside and keep the area secure in case there are additional hostiles that come our way."

"I don't get to have any fun tonight? I could have stayed home," the Mammoth joked as he pounded his massive right fist into his left hand.

"Whatever," K.C. chuckled. "Blitz and Eagle, you're up first. Use your speed and vision to quickly get on the third floor and take down whoever you can before we're fully exposed."

"Nothing I can't handle," Blitz confirmed as she swiftly shuffled her red nanite-clad feet.

"Enchantra and Ammo, once the floor is clear, you two and I will back them up to get into the core room. Ammo, blast the door down. Eagle, at that point, leave and get the hovercraft ready. Once we're inside, the four of us will need to become a barrier between them and the cores long enough to take them down. Ammo," K.C. urged, "tactics, stay cool and take down whoever's shooting, but remember, we need everyone alive, so don't go overboard."

"I know, I got it," Ammo rolled his eyes, frustrated with K.C.'s big brotherly attitude toward him. *I wish he'd get off my back already.*

"If they get the barrier to come down, or if things get too messy for us, Blitz, grab the power cores and get out. Better to explain taking the cores than taking a life tonight. Understood?" K.C. asked.

"Understood," everyone returned.

"Alright, everyone," K.C. declared, "let's drop the Kingdom on them."

"Just as corny as the last million times you've tried that line, K.C.," the Eagle rolled her white eyes behind her purple and black helmet. She was laser-focused on the screens, her hands planted on the surface in front of her. The hovercraft responded to her hand movements and followed her instruction to land on the street just outside the facility.

"Really? Still?" K.C. asked.

"Let's just go already," the Eagle walked away from the cockpit and toward the team. She pushed a button on the ceiling of the hovercraft. The bay door in the back slowly opened.

One by one, the Elite Unit walked out of the hovercraft and onto the street. They stood in front of the four-story DD Corporation building with a staircase terraced in front of it. The windowpanes on the front of the building were all shattered, and a few plants were still smoldering from a blast.

"Everyone, move out," K.C. commanded.

The Mammoth stood behind and scanned the area through his visor. The street was dark and empty. The earlier blast knocked out the lights from the tall streetlamps about two hundred feet in either direction. *At least the civilians are following protocol and have either abandoned the block or hunkered inside. Nobody should be around when the show starts,* the Mammoth reasoned. All seven feet, six inches of his bulky frame stood guard and waited for any action to occur.

Blitz energized herself and instantly became a red blur, speeding past everyone, using her hyperkinesis to dash into the building at a hundred miles a cycle. She analyzed the space faster than a supercomputer as she warped through the first floor in less than five seconds, noting particularly the elevators and the staircase. She ran up the dark corridor's stairs to the third floor, and upon opening the door, she saw another long, dimly lit corridor, where hostiles armed with light blasters stood around aimlessly. Blitz reasoned that they were in place to stop them from reaching the powered hostiles and thwarting the robbery.

She quickly closed the door and alerted the team, "Guys, we got more company up here than we thought, armed with blasters." Blitz took a deep breath, opened the door, and as she ran through it, the hostiles barely noticed her before she slid to trip the first and flip him over, then pushed herself back up straight with her right leg and bear-hugged the next hostile, knocking him to the ground. She then jumped quickly off him to take down the third by punching him in his chest, using that momentum to back into the fourth and head-butted him with the back of her head into a wall. She stood and sped toward the fifth hostile, who was trying to understand what was going on, but not before she kicked him three times in his stomach and face, dropping him to the ground instantly. She stood above the fifth and missed the first hostile rise back up and charge his blaster. Just as he prepared his finger to pull the trigger, two daggers jabbed into that same finger and his hand, and he dropped the blaster and screamed in pain. Blitz looked back, swinging her gold braids, and saw the Eagle, who walked to the assailant she had just stabbed and punched him unconscious. The Eagle said, "Just couldn't wait, huh?"

"I got a little excited, what can I say?"

"Excited, alright." The Eagle reported in the comms, "Corridor secure, come on up."

"Alright, that's us," K.C. said to Ammo and Enchantra. They marched upstairs, and he relayed, "We're running out of time. Integrity is down to 24%, let's move."

The team ran down to the end of the corridor. K.C. lifted his fist to signal to the team to hold position. The Eagle energized herself, and her eyes shuffled through multiple lenses to adjust her eyesight to look through the walls in front of them. Using infrared, she detected more hostiles blocking the entrance to the cores room. "K.C., we got eight more ahead of us before we get to the entrance," she reported.

"Ammo and Enchantra, you're up," K.C. instructed.

Enchantra's eyes glowed bright green, and she walked forward and turned to her left, exposing herself to the hostiles. She told them, "Alright, everyone, I'll be taking those blasters now," then raised her hands. Green mist swiftly flowed from her fingertips, and she could feel the steel in the soldiers' grips. She telekinetically wrapped the green mist around their blasters and quickly stripped the henchmen of their weapons. The blasters floated in midair as if held by ghosts, then spun to point directly at each hostile. They stood in shock and fear. "Anyone make a move, and I blast away," Enchantra announced. "I'm in a bitchy mood, so please give me a reason."

Ammo, Blitz, K.C., and the Eagle emerged from their hiding spot. Ammo retracted his right hand and held his arm cannon with his left hand. He aimed at the entrance of the battery lab, and he fired a charge disc from his cannon, and it dug its cleats into the doorway. Enchantra took the blasters and hurled them out a window behind the team. Green mist swiftly surrounded the hostiles, and they suddenly floated in the corridor. She slammed them head-first into the corridor's walls, knocking all of them out, and they slid to the floor.

The charge beeped, and Ammo counted down, "3, 2, 1!" The charge obliterated the door. K.C. and his teammates entered the ransacked battery lab. The vast atrium had been raided in the thieves' search for the prototypes. The bright white lights constantly flickered as they tried to illuminate the damage the room had incurred from the Elite's opponents. Shelves of batteries of all shapes and sizes were scattered across the floor. Desks lay in shambles, torn in half. The glass from the storage containers and beakers lay shattered everywhere. Sparks shot from the blown electrical outlets.

In the back of the atrium, the powered hostiles were working feverishly to take down the cloak shielding them from their prize: a long, flat black box containing tiny power cores the size of watch batteries. Once they heard Ammo's blast dismantle the entry, they immediately stopped pummeling the cloak, its integrity down to 9%, and turned around to see what happened. The fourth hostile, a short, stubby, bald man with a bushy mustache, told the other three, "What are you doing? Keep going! We're almost there!"

While the Eagle jumped out of the window Enchantra previously shattered, Enchantra covered the debris in front of them in green mist and telekinetically parted it all to make a straight path between them and their opponents. Ammo said, "Nice!"

K.C. stared at the hostiles and declared, "Alright, this is your one and only chance to surrender peacefully."

Fear gripped their hearts like a bear trap. They had heard the stories of the legendary Elite Unit, the Company's most lethal defenders of Uri City. Everyone knew that the Elite were the ones called when no one else could handle the situation, the force that took on the most challenging tasks at the behest of the government. These mid-level robbers assumed they would have to fight through security, but they never fathomed ever coming face-to-face with the Elite Unit, not for mere batteries. The gargantuan cowered, "Frimas, it's them! Why them?! Jorge, what are we going to do?"

Jorge, their leader, grew irritated. "Sam, Mick, take them down. Bash, keep working on the cloak!"

K.C. smiled. "Elite, you know what to do."

Enchantra immediately picked up Bash – a tall, slender man covered from head-to-toe in a black leotard save a silver visor on his eyes – and threw him into a wall. Shimmering sequins rushed across his back on impact, and the team noticed it. K.C. noted, "They're cloaked." Enchantra attempted to lift their leader but was unable to move him away from the prototypes' weakened barrier. Meanwhile, Sam, the gargantuan whose physique and strength was comparable to the Mammoth's, ran toward the rest of the team and swung his arms at them, missing K.C. but knocking Ammo backward. Blitz raced toward Mick. Mick thrusted his hands toward Blitz, and as they lit up, he shot bolts of blue lightning from them. A bolt struck and tripped her, and she slid into a damaged desk. Although her cloak absorbed most of the impact, Blitz groaned from the awkward way she landed.

Ammo got up, and he retracted his black hand into his silver and gold arm cannon. He recalibrated his munition to fire pressurized air and aimed the barrel at Sam. He fired a shot at Sam's back, and the impact knocked Sam forward. K.C. had picked up a piece of a damaged metal shelf rod. He hovered his right hand from one end of the rod to the other and summoned it to quickly morph into a bat. As Sam fell forward, K.C. ran up to him, swung the bat like a tennis racket, and bashed Sam's jaw, dropping him to the ground despite Sam's cloak.

Jorge couldn't believe the mission was crumbling before his eyes. He pulled out a small holoscreen from his pants pocket and scrambled to scroll to a red button. He pushed the button and stood as K.C. held the bat in front of him with his left hand, put his right fist in between him and the bat, then expanded his fingers, which morphed the bat into a shield. He ran toward Mick while Ammo pointed the cannon at Mick and shot off another pulse of air toward him. Mick jump rolled to dodge the pulse, then sent a bolt toward Ammo and K.C. Ammo ducked while K.C. held the shield in place. The bolt deflected from the shield into the power cores' cloak. The team saw the integrity meter drop down to 2%.

Sam shook his head and placed both fists on the ground to lift himself up. K.C. took his shield and threw it toward Mick. As it hovered toward him, K.C. expanded his arms, which made the shield grow. He then bear-hugged himself, manipulating the shield into a wrap which, upon impact with Mick, covered him from neck to toe. Mick was shocked that he became mummified and tumbled to the floor. Ammo walked up to him and said, "Please try to shock your way out of there, I'd love to see that." Neither he nor Ammo saw Sam's arm coming their way, but Enchantra quickly wrapped Sam in green mist and froze him in place before he could attack them. She then flipped him but didn't pay attention to the direction she hurled him in. When he hit the cores' cloak, his massive size brought the cloak down to 0%.

The cloak shimmered and hummed, then dissipated, exposing the black box sitting on its home desk. Jorge immediately ran toward the cores. Just as he stretched his arm out, Blitz sped past him and grabbed the black box herself, remembering her leader's orders. "Not today!" she emphasized.

K.C. surveyed the room and said to the Elite, "Let's wrap this up and get everyone back to base. Blitz, take the cores to the hovercraft. Ammo, secure this guy. Enchantra, take Sam and Mick, and..."

"Um, K.C., we got a problem. A really big problem!" K.C. was interrupted by the Eagle, who stood outside with the Mammoth waiting for the team to exit the building. A minute earlier, she detected three blinking dots moving in battle formation approaching from the north. Her visor could only zoom in so far, so she used her eyesight to magnify her view. The three dots were hostile hovercrafts shaped like killer whales with wings, with oversized missiles attached to their sides. She surmised their position was blown and feared they might not make it out in time.

"What is it?" K.C. asked.

"Three hovercraft about three miles out are headed our way, and they're carrying enough explosives to level several blocks. I don't think they want anyone to survive this. The Mammoth and I will try to hold them off, but you have to get out of there now!" She ran toward her hovercraft and summoned its auto-start through her stripe. Her vessel obeyed her command. It lit up from the inside, its lights shone, and the engine roared.

"You heard her. Let's roll!" K.C. exclaimed.

Ammo attempted to lift Jorge from the ground, but he would not budge. He laughed and said, "Oh, so you thought this was gonna be easy? Try again!" Ammo tried to lift him again and still could not move him.

Enchantra said, "I knew something was off about him. I couldn't move him, no matter how hard I tried. He's got a body density that's solid as a moon."

"Yeah, good luck taking me in. You guys aren't going anywhere. My crew is about sixty seconds away, and you're done for. She's not going to let you live through this."

"She, who's she?" K.C. yelled.

"K.C., we gotta move now!" Blitz interrupted. She clutched the cores and ran down the corridors, through the staircase, and out the front door. She saw the three hovercrafts headed their way and yelled to the Eagle, "Are you in the craft now?"

"Yes," Eagle replied from her cockpit. She moved her hands on the panel she stood at and motioned the craft closer to the building entrance. "I'm coming your way now. This is gonna be a tight window, guys. Hurry up!"

Enchantra carried Sam with her telekinesis, and Ammo carted Mick. K.C. looked around and found just Jorge. "Guys, where's laser eyes?" he asked. "Has anyone seen Bash?"

Enchantra and Ammo were near the hovercraft. They quickly scanned the area and said, "No, we don't see anyone, just the three hovercrafts coming our way."

The Mammoth said, "I got them. Just get on the bus!" He stood in front of their escape craft, flexed his muscles, and ripped a light post from the sidewalk like a twig from a tree. He then ran to another post about fifteen feet away and wrenched it the same way. He faced the enemy aircraft and hurled one of the posts a staggering three hundred miles per cycle into one of the enemy vessels nearly a mile away, and it tore through the cockpit windshield and slammed into the control panel and a pilot like tissue paper. Onlookers ran into buildings for safety as the craft spiraled downward and crashed into parked hovercars on the street. The other two crafts diverted their course to circle back toward them.

K.C. meanwhile kept searching for Bash in the battery lab. He dialed up his senses to distinguish him from the debris scattered everywhere but couldn't pinpoint his location. *Enchantra pushing all this debris to the sides might not have been the best idea, I can't make out what's what in this mess.* A blast suddenly hit him in his back, and while his cloak shimmered at the contact point, the impact still knocked him forward, and he rolled on the ground.

Bash taunted, "You wanted me, here I am. You're not getting out of here."

K.C. immediately grabbed a metal mesh cup with his left hand. He then pulled his left arm into himself and rolled to his left onto his back. With his right fist, he rapidly expanded his fingers, which expanded the mesh cup. He clutched his fist, and it hardened the expansion into a shield.

Bash sent another blast from his visor toward K.C., and K.C. knelt and held the shield in place to deflect his beam into the ceiling above. The white beam blew a hole through the roof. Jorge realized that K.C. was distracted and ran through the pile of debris undetected. He exited the lab and made his way toward the window Enchantra shattered earlier. K.C. held one hand at his side and began flexing his fingers. The deflected portion of Bash's beam began to collect above K.C.'s head until it became a bright ball of energy. K.C. then jumped and rolled to dodge Bash's eye beam and smacked the beam ball in

Bash's direction with his shield. It struck Bash in his chest, and he flew across the room.

The two remaining hovercraft circled back and took aim at the Elite's vessel. They unleashed short pulses their way, and they damaged the street below and the craft's cloak. The Mammoth launched the other light post toward the two, and they evaded his javelin. Ammo switched both arms to beam cannons and fired back at them. They evaded as much as they could before one was hit with a blast and crashed into the side of a building. The remaining hovercraft launched a rocket in their direction. The Eagle, standing in the cockpit, commanded the windshield to slide apart. Her eyes zoomed and locked onto the rocket. She took out a dagger and hurled it toward the rocket. Her knife soared the length of a ballfield in front of them and struck the rocket, and it exploded.

"Get in, now!" she yelled.

"But, what about K.C.?" Ammo asked.

"He can take care of himself," the Eagle responded. "We have the cores. We need to leave before more backup arrives."

As Blitz, the Mammoth, and Enchantra ran into the back hatch with their various cargo, Ammo noticed a figure racing away from the building. "Wait, is that the fourth guy?" Ammo said. He scanned him, and Ammo's visor confirmed that it was the leader of the op. "No way he's getting out of here!"

"Ammo, wait, he's not gonna let you take him, just let him go!" Blitz pleaded. Ammo did not respond. Rather, he ran toward Jorge and attempted to apprehend him. *K.C. said apprehend them all, so that's what I'm going to do! Maybe then he'll get off my back!*

K.C. walked up to Bash, who lay flat on the floor. Bash lowered his head and fired a short beam toward K.C., who once again deflected it, sending it into a wall. K.C. then grabbed the shield with his hand and placed it on top of Bash's head. He then extended his fingers and palms to make a ball then brought his hands together. The shield molded into a helmet over Bash's head. "Just, don't. Let's go buddy," K.C. said. He took another piece of metal and fashioned it into handcuffs, placed Bash's hands behind his back, and escorted him out of the building. "How's it looking out there, guys?"

"We're still dealing with another hovercraft," the Eagle said as she fired her bus's cannons. "Could really use your help out here."

"I'm on my way down," K.C. responded. He dragged Bash down the stairs and out the building. He saw his team's craft hovering just above the street and looked out to see the other hovercraft headed their way again. The hostile shot another missile in their direction. The Eagle aimed and fired several flares, and as the missile exploded, K.C. swiftly raised his left arm and clenched his fingers to hold the blast in place. The enemy craft wasn't prepared, and as it flew closer toward the Elite, K.C. released the blast, and the intensity of the energy incinerated the enemy vessel.

K.C. walked toward the Eagle's ship, thinking the mission was accomplished, when suddenly, the team heard a loud explosion come from the building.

"Ammo!" Blitz yelled through the comms. "What happened? Where are you?"

Ammo sprinted from the blast zone toward the hovercraft. K.C. pushed Bash into the hovercraft. The Mammoth grabbed Bash and put him in one of the empty cages on the ship. K.C. then grabbed Ammo and said, "What did you do? What happened? Where's the fourth guy?"

Ammo quickly lamented, "He wouldn't move, now he's gone. Let's get out of here."

"What do you mean gone?" K.C. demanded as they walked into the craft. K.C.'s helmet dissipated as the back hatch door sealed shut. The Eagle flew them away from the site just as Uri City's emergency response units were arriving to do damage control.

"What was the mission, Ammo?" Malcolm screamed. "What was the mission?"

"Apprehend them all," Ammo groaned as he took his seat, "and I tried, but he did his whole 'not budge' thing, and I fired off a blast that was supposed to move him or at least knock him unconscious, and it was too much. My bad, K.C."

"Your bad?!" Malcolm retorted, standing over Ammo. "He was their leader! We were right there! We were in the clear! Even if you would have let him get away, we still had these three and the cores."

"And let him escape? No, no way, I wasn't going to let that happen," Ammo reacted.

"You made that abundantly clear, Ammo. And that was the wrong call. Absolutely unnecessary. The director is going to kill us! And you can be tried for this, not just suspended, not just fired, *tried!* You should have let him go."

Ammo sulked in his helmet, trying to come to terms with Malcolm's correct assessment. *He's right. And I know better. If I killed that man, the director could have me arrested. Why did I do that? Why didn't I just get on the bus?*

Why did they put him on this team?! Several doubts rolled through Malcolm's mind, and as the craft flew into the night sky toward the Company's Uri City Division Headquarters, he prepared for what he expected would be a very long week.

This. This is why I hate rookies. They always find a way to mess things up!

2

Icy

She stared at the oversized digital clock floating about fifty feet away and thirty feet high near the ceiling of the vast, open atrium. It read 01:57 in bold, neon blue highlights. She sat alone in the soft, orange lounge chair with her ankles crossed, her black dreads draped over her shoulders and resting across her chest. Her deep brown eyes scanned the massive hall, and she felt slightly overdressed compared to the people walking past her in their gym clothes. She adjusted her crimson jean jacket and pulled at her tight white and gold-speckled t-shirt. She listened intently as a duo discussed taking the elevator down to the training room for a sparring session. She also tried to comprehend the strategy a group of three was devising as they shared their ideas for executing their next mission.

Hmm, I've been here for several weeks now, and I haven't been assigned to a team yet. I wonder what I'm gonna be doing today. She leaned forward, elbows on her knees, thinking how much more observing she was going to do before she fell asleep in the chair. She looked at the clock again.

01:58.

"Ugh, I'm bored," she sighed. She rose from her chair and walked to the same reception desk she had approached every day since her orientation began at the Company. "Hi, great rising!"

A slender, dark-skinned man shifted his attention from the holoscreen in front of him and adjusted his glasses closer to his face. He fought the urge to gaze at her and replied, "Great rising, indeed."

"I was just curious," she began as she crossed her arms on the desk and leaned forward slightly, "do you have an assignment for me today?" she asked.

"Place your palm on the reader right here, and I will check for you," the receptionist replied. She put her hand on the reader on the countertop, and it hummed lowly. The receptionist's holoscreen displayed her picture and general information. "Okay, Symone Watson," he said, "looks like your assignment is to sit here and wait for someone to come get you and escort you to the director."

Symone looked stunned, and her plump, rosy lips made a perfect "O" from bewilderment. "The director? Does it say why?"

"No, it just says to sit and wait. Someone will be here soon to get you."

Symone peered at the clock again.

02:01.

"Okay, well, I'll just 'sit and wait,'" she said. She returned to her seat and hypothesized. *Why does the director want to see me? Maybe I'm getting a team today? Maybe I did something wrong during the training yesterday? Did I fail one of the exams? Did I embarrass the instructor? I knew I shouldn't have flexed my muscles like that the other day. I bet I pissed him off, and he reported me, the big baby. Well, we won't know until we meet, so don't worry about it.*

She leaned forward, focused on the clock, and waited.

02:05.

And sat.

02:12.

And waited.

02:17.

Just as she was about to cock her head backward and use her locs as a pillow to catch a mid-morning nap, a voluptuous, honey-skinned, curly-haired woman in a white lab coat and red stiletto heels appeared from her right and signaled, "Watson?"

Symone jumped up, "Yes, that's me!"

"Great, it's so nice to meet you," the woman said as she extended her hand to shake Symone's. "I'm Stephanie Banks. I'm here to escort you to the director."

"Oh, great!" Symone said in relief and shook Stephanie's hand. "I was about to pass out in that chair before you showed up."

"I understand. Sometimes these introductions can take forever to begin, especially on a day like this," Stephanie replied as they walked together past the reception desk, through the white-lit, translucent-glass atrium, and toward the elevators.

"What do you mean, 'a day like this?'" Symone pondered.

"Oh," Stephanie put a hand over her mouth, then continued, "you didn't hear about the incident yesterday. Well, the Elite fumbled an apprehend order, and no doubt the director is catching Frimas from Central."

"What's an apprehend order, and what is Central?" Symone asked as they stopped at the elevator at the end of the atrium.

Stephanie pressed the "Up" button on the wall. While they waited for the elevator to stop at their level, Stephanie answered, "Oh, an apprehend order is when the team is supposed to arrest the suspects and not kill them. And Central is the Company's HQ."

They heard a low hum. A black line in the wall lit white, and the wall separated to reveal the elevator, designed just like the glass atrium they were standing in. Symone recalled from orientation, "That's right, this is the Uri City Division, and no one knows where Central is." They stepped inside the elevator.

"Exactly," Stephanie said. She pushed the "E" button.

"Wait," Symone said, puzzled because Stephanie pushed "E," not "O" for Orientation or any of the other letters for lower-ranked defenders. "Where are we going?"

"We're going to the Elite Grand Hall," Stephanie said with a smile, carrying a secret she was dying to tell.

"Elite, what do you mean, Elite?" Symone inquired.

"We're going to the Elite Unit. That's where the director wants to meet you."

The suspense was killing Symone, and a nervous giddiness churned in her gut. She fought the urge to tug on Stephanie's arm. "Why does the director want to meet me *there*? You know something, Stephanie. Come on, tell me!"

"No, no," Stephanie giggled, "I've been instructed not to tell." The elevator stopped, and the doors opened, revealing the Elite Grand Hall. "I am only to escort you to the director, who should be in the conference room now."

They stepped off the elevator and faced the translucent windows and doors that constructed the wall and entry to the Intelligence Division. Symone's brown eyes beamed with joy and glowed fiery red as she marveled at the hallowed ground she stood on. *The Elite Grand Hall!*

Stephanie turned to her left and motioned with her hand for Symone to follow her. Symone walked with a little more enthusiasm, still unsure what the director wanted with her, but grateful to be able to take in the view of the Grand Hall. She admired the spaciousness of the hall compared to how tight the lower levels felt to her, with the ceiling at least twenty feet high and the corridor itself at least fifteen feet wide. Her feet slowly pranced from one side of the corridor to the other, and her eyes danced and took mental pictures of everything she passed by – busts of past Elite defenders, holographic news articles of past victories of the last three decades, and countless awards, certificates, commendations, medals, and plaques for the level of excellence demonstrated by the unit. Symone reasoned, *Akan, I pray that this is not the last time I'm up here for a while. I have to get back up here permanently! Just wait until I talk to my mom and dad!*

They turned right, and as they walked closer to the conference room at the end of the hall, she looked at the visuals beaming from the frosted glass walls, videos of battles featuring former Elite defenders, a chronicle of the defense of Uri City by the Company's best defenders. Just before reaching the door, she marveled at the current defenders of the legendary Elite Unit. Stephanie gave Symone a moment to take in the mural.

"Duncan Blake, Ammo," Symone read the marquee scrolling across his chest. Duncan's Ammo avatar's silver eyes stared confidently back at Symone with a wry smile, a moving photograph of him clad in his silver and black nanotech armor with his left hand holding up his right arm in cannon mode. *"Blake's cybernetic technology makes him the perfect combat weapon. Bringing his military prowess and vast knowledge of artillery weaponry with him, Blake has served with the Company for a year and defends Uri City with pride and precision."* Hmm, *I'd like to see that in action.*

She stepped to Alexia's avatar next, and a chill went down her spine as she gazed into the avatar's green-lit eyes, fair yet glowing skin, and luscious lips. *She's got to be the most beautiful woman I've ever laid eyes on.* *"Alexia Montague, Enchantra."* *Ah,* Enchantra, *makes so much sense.* Enchantra's long black hair floated slowly as if blown by a fan. Her hourglass-shaped body was clad in green nanotech with a blue stripe down the sides of her arms and legs. Her palms were sky-side up, and green mist swirled around her body. *"A master of the mystic arts, Montague's telekinesis and telepathy are unparalleled. With the Company three years, she proved herself an irreplaceable asset to the Elite and demonstrates her ability to defend Uri City with every incantation she casts."* She can sure cast a spell or two on me.

Hmm, this is interesting. "Daisy Parker, Blitz. *Did you catch her? Hyperkinesis is Parker's forte, and she is a formidable defender, able to disarm and disable threats long before they even know she's arrived on the scene. She's solved problems for five years with the Company, and the Elite Unit for three."* Daisy's Blitz avatar was clad in red nanotech slightly blurred for visual effect as she stood in a runner's stance. Symone admired her brown skin and gold braids and was slightly envious that she couldn't get braids anymore. Daisy zipped across her entire video montage, and Symone fought to not get dizzy herself from watching it.

Oh yes, Symone swooned as she ogled at Karl Luther's Mammoth avatar. *He can come get this anytime, look at those muscles, Akan!* "Gifted with the *power to heal rapidly, Luther pushed his athleticism to unheard limits. He is one of the strongest men on Uretha, and he has lent his strength to the Company in defense of Uri City for the past five years, Elite for the last four."* Symone barely read the words off the screen as she gazed at the Mammoth's avatar – his rugged, mountainous arms, his pecs poking through his black and gold speckled nanotech. She stared at his face and swore Akan chiseled him out of granite. Even his legs looked like tree trunks. She couldn't help but steal a glance at his pelvis and wonder whether the undercarriage matched the boulder it was attached to. *If he plays his cards right, I'll make him weaker than a worm. He can lend his strength to me. Akan, let me move on before I start dripping through my jeans.*

Oh wow, her eyes are gorgeous! So is her hair, another locked-in sister! "Malaysia Jones, The Eagle. *Blessed by Akan with the gift of superior eyesight, Jones can see anything and everything. She has taken advantage of her eagle eyes and become the most precise sniper-warrior in the Company. She has defended Uri City for six years, Elite for over five."* Malaysia's avatar donned a purple and black nanite uniform. Her dreads were bound in a ponytail, and she held a long gun in her left hand while holding her elbow up with her right. *I love her already!*

Finally, she arrived at Malcolm's avatar, dust swirling around him as he held his hands behind his back and stared almost cockily at Symone. "Malcolm *Bennett, Kingdom Come."* The video montage of his battles and trainings played near his head. While in orientation for the past several weeks, and throughout the news reports she watched years before her arrival at the Company, she had heard stories of the one who could reshape objects with ease, of the man who was of the few powered defenders to ever reach Expert level and still actively defend the city. *"Bennett is coined by Chancellor Croft as the 'greatest defender in a generation,' as he has successfully mastered molecular manipulation to defend the city for seven years. He has never faced an opponent he didn't defeat, a situation he didn't resolve, nor a battle he didn't win. His power and his leadership have earned him the title of Team Leader of the Elite Unit Division."* She was supremely impressed by the video montage of his personal and team successes in battle. She gazed intensely at every move he made, his flips, his object manipulations, his stare-downs with enemies and suspects. She felt butterflies in her stomach, her eyes bore red embers, her breathing became deeper, and her power surged within her veins. A strange attraction suddenly came over Symone. Her body began to aura, her lady parts tingled with excitement, and her hair started changing colors.

Her right eyebrow raised slightly, a wry smile draped across her face, Symone silently declared, *I wanna fight him.*

Stephanie was at the conference room door twenty feet away and looked at her stripe noting the time. "Watson," she called.

Symone snapped out of her trance and composed herself. "Yes, I'm sorry, I'm coming," she said to Stephanie as she scurried toward the conference room door.

"Are you ready?" Stephanie asked.

Symone adjusted her jacket, ran her ebony brown fingers through her locs, and answered, "Yes, let's do this." *I'm about to meet the Elite!* Stephanie placed her hand on the palm reader, and a mechanical lock spun to open the door.

The entrance revealed an empty room lit white with blue highlights. Symone noticed seven rolling chairs slid underneath a white oval table. Several holo-screen panels of various sizes covered the walls. Symone walked into the room and was instantly bummed that no one was there. She looked at the wall closest to the door and saw four empty rolling chairs facing the table. "Wait, where is the director?"

"She will be here shortly," Stephanie answered. "Good luck to you, Miss Watson."

"Please, Stephanie, call me 'Symone.'"

"Right, Symone." She shut the door. Symone slinked to the chair at the end farthest from the door, rolled it from the table and sat down. She looked at the digital clock in the middle of the wall.

02:23.

She sat. And waited. Again.

This is so annoying. She planted her head on the table.

Suddenly, she heard a commotion outside of the room. She lifted her head and focused. The commotion got closer to the room. She couldn't make out the voices, but she distinctively recognized the sound of fury. Intensity. Rage.

BOOM! The door swung wide open, and Symone jumped slightly in her chair.

"You mean to tell me that you couldn't just let him sit there?! You thought, 'Hey, let me just blow him to smithereens. That'll teach him!'" Malcolm entered first, yelling vehemently at Duncan.

The Elite Unit paraded in the room to Symone's excitement. They dressed like they had just left the gym or gotten out of bed. They filed in one at a time while not skipping a beat in their heated debate. Symone wanted to say something, but she dared not interrupt them. "It's not going to make a difference at this point, Malcolm," Malaysia replied. "Yelling at him louder isn't going to change anything."

"Right, so let me yell at the both of them instead." Director Mallack entered last. She was a dark-skinned woman wearing a light green business dress with textured, tapered hair about two inches from her head. Her dark, piercing eyes displayed the fury she was ready to unload on her team. Symone couldn't believe her eyes. Standing just a few feet from her were the members of the Elite Unit, the current who's who in Uri City's contract defense. Symone stared at Malcolm and internally fawned over him. She hoped that he would sit next to her, but instead, Alexia sat next to her, followed by Malaysia, Malcolm, Duncan, Daisy, and Karl, who held down the opposite end of the table.

Is it my birthday? Is it Jubilee? The Elite, they are right here! This is the best day of my life! Should I say something? No, I'll wait.

Alexia looked at Symone and said, "Hey."

"Hi," Symone eeked back. *She spoke to me! This goddess spoke to me!*

Director Mallack took one of the seats about ten feet in front of the table and crossed her legs and arms. "You all had an apprehend order, not a kill order. How do you justify what you did, Blake? What was going through your mind when you went off like that?" Mallack asked.

Duncan placed his elbows on the table and raised his hands. "I don't know, he wouldn't move," Duncan shook his head, "and I got mad because he was taunting me. Like, 'You're not going to get me to budge. I'll move when I feel like it, and you're gonna watch me escape and not be able to do anything about it.' I got pissed and..."

"...decided to blow the man's legs off so you could move him, was that it?" Malcolm slowly articulated while staring Duncan down. "Brother, you have to be smarter than that!"

"Malcolm's right, Duncan," Alexia had focused back on the conversation and sided with her leader. "Like, what if your charge had been bigger than that? You could have blown us all up. You're powerful as Frimas, just like all of us, an Elite powered."

"But if you constantly get angry every time you're provoked and retaliate with your powers, you're gonna get someone killed. Maybe even yourself," Karl said.

"Exactly!" Alexia agreed with Karl as she slid back from the table slightly and rested her palm on her forehead. "I should have just grabbed you and made you sit down in the bird."

"You should've just gotten on the plane. We were in the clear. All you had to do was get on the hovercraft," Daisy chimed in.

Mallack sensed the tension rising to the point of no return, so she stood up. "Listen, you guys are just lucky as Frimas that his shield integrity didn't reduce to zero. UPD and UFD were able to dig him out of the rubble, disable his cloak, and nullify him to get him placed in custody."

"So, he didn't die?" Malcolm's eyes widened from shock. Duncan breathed a sigh of relief.

"No," Mallack declared, "He didn't die by the skin of your teeth, Duncan. He did not die from your mishap. Not that it matters, because we still are no closer to figuring out who they're working for. Look, as bad as this was, you guys did get these four guys off the street." Mallack pressed her left wrist, and the wall-sized holoscreen in front of them displayed the demographics of Bash, Mick, Sam, and Jorge. "And we have possession of the cloak core prototypes." The screen changed to display the black box Daisy secured. "The DD Corporation is grateful for our work, and as a side benefit, they have agreed to work with us on building better cloaking for the Uri City Division. Something good has come from all of this, and that's because of you."

I knew it. I knew this mission was more than just stopping a robbery, Mallack confirmed Malcolm's suspicions, and he fully understood that the Company would trust no one but the Elite to secure that alliance.

"However," Mallack continued, "these lower-level henchmen don't have any information to provide to us. Intelligence wasn't able to pull any information from them. Whoever this shadow is, they're not giving their soldiers any information that will give them away, and they are scrubbing their entire identities off the grid. We have to work smarter, not harder, to get something on these jokers before they get the technology they need to beat us. Intelligence pulled your tape, and the most that we got was that their leader is a 'she.'"

The team sulked but listened intently. Alexia delivered an undetectable green mist from her eyes through Symone's ears and tapped into her synapses. *Symone Watson, still in orientation, former prizefighter? I remember watching some of her fights in the past. Those uniforms really do keep people's personas private.*

Mallack continued her verbal flogging. "We got lucky this time that they only sent a handful of soldiers and a few powered warriors to try to take those cores. But if they see that the Elite Unit is as sloppy as you all were at the end of this battle, and in this room a few seconds ago, next time around, they're gonna send everything they have at us, and it's gonna take more than the seven of you to take them down."

Malaysia instantly caught what Mallack said, and her head shook in perplexity. "Wait, you said 'seven.' You said, 'seven,' what do you mean 'seven,' there's only six of us." Malaysia looked around and saw Symone sitting next to Alexia. *How did I miss her?* "Who is she, and why is she in here?"

The other four turned in their chairs and finally paid attention to Symone sitting in her chair. She stared at them as they stared at her. Symone then looked at Director Mallack, slowly waved and softly saluted, "Hi."

Director Mallack replied, "Well, since your last mission almost went terribly wrong, and thank Akan it was not the disaster from a year and a half ago, the Company thought this team needed one more recruit on it, and they chose her. Elite, meet Symone Watson. Symone Watson, I am Director Catherine Mallack. To your immediate right is Alexia Montague, followed by Malaysia Jones, Malcolm Bennett, Duncan Blake, Daisy Parker, and Karl Luther. Welcome to the Elite Unit of the Uri City Division of the Company."

Symone's jaw tightened. Overwhelmed with emotion, she placed her hand on her chest but was only able to squeak out, "Me?"

"Yes, you," Mallack answered.

"Are you serious? I'm Elite?!"

"Yes," Mallack declared. "The Company made the decision a few cycles after the mission, and that's why you're here. The Company believes you are the missing piece this unit needs, and you are to start right away. So, Elite, get her up to speed. We've taken a major PR hit, and despite your good work overall, HQ is not happy, and neither am I. Do whatever you need to do to make this right. The Company is usually not this forgiving, so take the olive branch and run with it."

Symone sat stunned. *I'm Elite? Me? Symone Watson? How? This is unreal! This doesn't make any sense! Why me?*

Alexia jumped and squealed with excitement and Malaysia looked a little confused. Duncan stared at Symone like a smitten high school freshman, and Karl grinned. Daisy pushed her seat away from the table and sped in a flash to Symone, embodying the joy most of the team felt for the new member of their family.

Malcolm, however, was having none of that joy. He stared at Symone with a look of instant contempt. He could not understand why the Company felt the need to add another member to the team after last night's fiasco, let alone her. *What the Frimas? I gotta deal with two rookies now? This is some bull!*

Mallack looked at Malcolm and the angst written all over his face. She cracked a wry smile. "Elite, introduce yourselves and get her situated. I'm going to leave to handle the comms and try to put this fire out before the news reports try to paint us as powered killers again. Watson, I'll see you soon and talk to you one-on-one."

"Yes, Director," Symone acknowledged. Mallack stood up and walked out of the room as the team followed Daisy's suit and rose to introduce themselves to Symone. Symone stood up with glee as the team came over. One by one, they all told her who they were, and she shook all their hands. Malcolm walked toward the door to walk out. The team noticed that he was walking away, and Symone, eager to make her presence known to him specifically, ran up to him and said, "Hi, Bennett, I'm Symone, um, Symone Watson." She walked toward him and extended her hand to shake his.

Malcolm stopped short of opening the door, turned around and faced her. He looked in her eyes, looked at her hand, and looked into her eyes again. In a split second, Malcolm felt something odd about Symone. His senses widened, and he could feel something powerful flowing through her veins, unlike anything he ever recognized before. Her energy radiated through her pores and surrounded her like an invisible cloak. It coiled through every strand of her hair, every cell of her eyes, laced her rosy lips, and connected to the ground she stood on. Malcolm's curiosity was piqued, and he struggled to discern the difference between attraction, wonder, and desire. Her energy was a force he'd never felt before, and it made her beauty indescribable. He craved to know what he was feeling, yearned to get close to her, eager with childlike awe to ascertain what her energy was.

Yet, his anger struck down his curiosity as quickly as it surfaced. *Nope, this is not happening, not today.* Malcolm turned around, opened the door, and walked out, determined to find Mallack and give her a piece of his mind.

As the door sealed, Symone slowly retracted her hand and fought through the immediate rejection. Alexia walked to Symone and tapped her shoulder, "It's been a long ten cycles. And Malcolm is extremely pissed at the world right now."

"Yeah," Daisy chimed in as she and the rest of the team walked toward them, "probably not the best time to put a whole new member on the team, but that's the Company for you. So, here you are!"

"Right, here I am!" Symone immediately shook off feeling slighted and reveled in her new role. "Wow, I'm still shocked, like, I haven't been here that long, and I know my skills don't hold a candle to you guys. You are all legends! I am truly honored to be among you," Symone said.

Duncan adjusted his voice to sound suave as he broke through the pack and bellowed, "The honor is all ours, and if you need *anything*, please do not hesitate to ask me." He tilted his head slightly forward and raised his silver eyes.

Symone thought, *He's yummy, but coming on a little strong. Let me burst this bubble real quick.*

"Oh," Symone responded, crossing her arms, "so you're that guy, huh?"

Duncan didn't flinch. "Baby, I'll be whatever guy you need me to be."

"Glad to be working with you, but please spare me the 'knight in shining armor' routine." Everyone laughed as Duncan sulked.

"Good to see that she's gonna fit right in," Karl grinned as he patted Duncan on the shoulder.

Duncan quickly shook Karl's hand off him and said, "Whatever."

Alexia spoke through her laughter, "Alright, crew, so let's show her the goods."

3

Starburst

Symone couldn't contain herself. She knew she hit the jackpot, standing among and breathing the same air as these giants. A lifelong student of her fighting craft, Symone thanked Akan for granting her a front-row seat to a demonstration of the Elite's prowess. She craved to see her new teammates flex their powers in front of her, and they would not deny her.

Malaysia said, "Alexia, will you start us off, please?"

"Why, of course, darling!" she answered. They all moved to the middle of the room between the table and the Director's chair. Alexia's eyes glowed green. She slowly raised her hands, and green mist flowed from them and wrapped around the furniture. The chairs and table slowly rose from the floor and suspended midair. Symone marveled with deep fascination.

"So, I'm telekinetic. Can move things with my mind." She commanded the furniture to return to the floor. She then pointed her hands toward Karl and raised them again, and Karl, surrounded by the mist, began to float. His legs dangled in the air, and a look of shock and then disgust flashed on his face.

"I hate it when you do that. Put me down," he bellowed.

Alexia chuckled, and Symone snorted. "I have to show off, you know that." She slowly planted Karl back on the floor.

Symone recalled, "You're also a telepath, right?"

"That's right," Alexia smiled. "Someone's done her homework. I can manipulate people's thoughts. I can make them think what I want them to, peer in their minds, or make them," as she pointed at Symone, "visualize a fantasy." Green mist flowed from Alexia's hands and swiftly infiltrated Symone's eyes and ears. Alexia tapped once again into Symone's synapses and commanded Symone's mind to visualize something she desired.

Symone's eyes turned the same shade of green as Alexia's. Suddenly, Symone felt herself being whisked away from the conference room. Day turned to night, and she swiftly landed in a dark alleyway between tall, dark brick walls. She glanced down and examined the asphalt beneath her feet. *How did I get here? Where am I?* She noticed she was wearing one of her old gold and crimson prizefighting uniforms. *Wow, what did she do to me?*

At the end of the alley emerged Malcolm. He walked toward her, holding a dagger in his hand. The closer he got to her, the more excited she became. Her hair tinted red, and she felt a tingle travel up and down her spine. Without warning, Malcolm and the alley suddenly turned into a green mist and disappeared, and she immediately returned to the conference room.

Malaysia was monitoring Symone through infrared, and she noticed how her body temperature had risen from her baseline. Her eyes widened, and she inquired, "What did you see?"

Alexia's eyes had returned to normal, and she disconnected from Symone's synapses. She smiled and crossed her arms, "I know what she saw, very fascinating stuff."

Symone did not respond, slightly embarrassed, weirded out, and giddy all at once. She held her head down and ran her hand through her locs while she returned, "Hopefully I'll get to see the living manifestation of that."

"Indeed," Alexia's eyes flashed green once more.

"Well," Malaysia said, "while Alexia's messing with people's heads, I can see everything. My eyes are hypersensitive to light and energy and can adapt to see all spectrums."

Symone pressed, "What does it look like to see that way?"

"It's almost like having a visor on. It's like having a file of lenses, and I flip through which one I want to see through: radar, infrared, visible, invisible." Symone and the others watched Malaysia's eyes change multiple colors and shades, and her pupils and irises changed shapes and sizes. "Plus, my eyes can zoom in and out. Would you like to know exactly how many gray hairs you have right now?"

Symone said, "Oh my goodness, no, please don't share that info with me right now," laughing nervously as she ran her fingers through her locs again.

"Just messing with you. It took me a long time to figure out how to make the best use of my powers, and over the years, I've gotten really good at shooting at and hitting things. Quick, take something out of your pocket and throw it in the air."

Symone didn't hesitate. She dug through her pants pocket and pulled out a ball of blue lint. "This is all I have."

Malaysia said, "Perfect. Throw it."

"Okay." Symone launched the ball of lint in the air, and Malaysia pulled a tiny knife from her back pocket and threw it over Symone's head. Symone flinched as the blade pierced the ball and the blade embedded into the back wall. Symone turned to see the blade, then back at Malaysia. She rushed around the table to the back wall, and she examined the black blade. She saw the strands of the ball of lint stuck to the blade and the wall. Her insides gushed. *The level of precision that took is unreal!* She fawned over Malaysia, "My goodness! That was amazing!"

As she walked back around the table, Karl stepped in front of Symone. His massive frame towered over Symone, the crown of his head two feet from the crown of hers. Symone fought the urge to lean against him. *Don't do it, don't touch him. They'll have to scoop what's left of you off the ground when you turn into a puddle.*

He declared, "I'm strong for no reason," and she craned her head to see his eyes, then backed up.

Yeah, you are.

"But my strength I had to build over time. My real ability is to regenerate and heal fast as Frimas. Hand me a knife, Malaysia."

Symone was flabbergasted. "Wait, are you serious? Is he serious?"

Malaysia took another knife from her pocket and gave it to Karl. He then sliced open his left hand, and Symone winced while blood dripped from his hand. Symone looked around at everyone else and noticed their lack of shock. She then looked at Karl's hand and saw that the bleeding had stopped immediately, and the slice quickly closed almost as fast as Karl had sliced it open. All that remained was the fresh blood on his completely healed palm.

"I took advantage of that and hit every gym I could and got ripped. I now have the strength of ten men, so I've been told."

Duncan wanted to show off his chest, too, and interrupted Symone's ogling session. "Well, he may have arms, but I've got guns." He bent his arms at the elbows so that his hands were side-by-side to his face. He then retracted his hands, and his arms transformed into cannons. He cocked each one, then continued, "My body is cybernetic, and I've modified my arms to change into any weapon I can think of. I like to shoot things off..."

"...including your mouth," Malaysia couldn't help herself once she saw the opening Duncan created. Everyone chuckled again.

"Haha, very funny," Duncan fired back as he brought his hands back. "So, I deal mostly in artillery, air, and plasma weaponry."

Symone replied, "Yes, one of the wisest military minds the city's ever known. I've read the stories. You've accomplished a lot both here and abroad."

Duncan blushed, "You hear that, guys? She's read about me!"

"Alright, alright," Daisy burst his egotistical bubble, "don't get big-headed again." Daisy motioned for everyone to move to the edge of the table, then said, "Me, I love to go fast. Very, very fast." She started to run around the room. Daisy activated her hyperkinesis and sped up, faster, and faster, and faster, until she became a blur. Symone tried to keep up, but her eyes lost focus. She ran even faster, and bolts of lightning began to fire off from the blur. Without warning, Daisy stopped in front of everyone. She crossed her right leg in front of her left and pointed it to the ground. She crossed her arms, and her bronze braids flapped in the air before falling behind her back.

"Nice," Alexia cheered as everyone else clapped.

"I am hyperkinetic. So, everything I do is fast. I absorb information fast. My metabolism is fast. When I'm really excited, I can talk really, really fast."

"Don't get her started," Alexia interrupted, rolling her eyes, "she can really, really go when she wants to."

Symone jumped and squealed. "I can't believe this! Am I dreaming? I really get to work with you guys, for realz? I'm not about to be psyched out, am I? This is crazy! You're even more phenomenal than I pictured!"

"Okay, new girl," Malaysia responded as she turned to Symone. "So, you've met us: Enchantra, the Mammoth, Ammo, Blitz, and me, the Eagle. Who are you, what do you go by, and what do you do?"

The Elite turned to face Symone.

This is my moment. Okay, Symone. Show them who you are. You belong here. The Company invited you here for a reason. They chose you for a reason. Show them why.

Nervousness turned into confidence. She marched to the front of the room, then turned on a dime in her boots to face the Elite. She instructed them, "Go stand behind the table."

"Oh yeah!" Alexia got excited, having caught a glimpse of Symone's powers during the meeting with Director Mallack. They all obeyed and stood with eager anticipation.

She continued, "Well, I am Symone Watson." She closed her eyes and pointed her hands to the ground at her side. As she concentrated, energy churned through her veins. Her temperature spiked. Sparks began to flow from her hands like two upside-down spark fireworks machines. She then slowly levitated two feet off the ground. Her hair slowly glowed from the root, changing from jet black to red to orange to bright yellow. An aura matching her hair color radiated off her body like a cloak. She leveled her head and opened her now-glowing yellow eyes. The team marveled and shielded their eyes from Symone's radiance. The Eagle adjusted her eyes to capture Symone in all her shining glory.

She declared, "My codename is Starburst, and I create stars." She brought her hands closer together in front of her and shaped them to outline a ball. A bright yellow sphere of heat, light, and energy formed in front of her, contained in her hands. "And then I launch them wherever I want them to go," she declared, pushing her hands forward and launching the star toward the back of the room. The Elite quickly darted away to not get hit. On impact, the star exploded into a dazzling array of sparks and cracked some of the holoscreens.

Symone landed back on the ground, her hair returned to its color, and her eyes dialed down their brightness. She said, "Oops," as she chuckled slightly.

The team celebrated, hyped by her performance. Malaysia was supremely impressed. "The holoscreens will be fine. They fix themselves all the time. I think the Company outdid themselves this time, right, guys?"

Symone smiled as the team responded with nods and sounds of agreement. Symone, while overjoyed, couldn't help but be a little disappointed because Malcolm wasn't there to show off his powers nor witness her showcase hers. *I have to wait for the right time to get around him. It's okay that he's not here right now. I'm on the team. Their approval seals it for me. I have all the time in the world.*

Malaysia said, "Okay, Symone, let's give you a tour of the floor. This is going to be your new home away from home, or it could be your home if you want it to. This place is so swanky, it makes Meridian look like the Underbelly."

Everyone crossed the threshold of the conference room just as Symone said, "Wait, what about Bennett, is he coming back?"

Alexia replied, "No, I don't think he'll be back anytime soon. Next time we see him, I'm sure we'll have a mission to go on or something. Don't worry, you'll get your chance to show him what you got."

Symone raised her right eyebrow and thought, *Damn right, I will. Mmm, the sooner, the better.*

While the team was getting to know its newest addition, Malcolm had stormed the Elite Grand Hall and marched to Director Mallack's office. *Infuriated* could not fully describe his mood. He refused to comprehend the Company's decision to add another rookie to the Elite Unit. Between the near-miss of the last mission and the team's growth to seven, Malcolm's crummy week became crummier. He could tell he was on edge and struggled to keep his senses dialed down. With every step closer to Mallack's office, he could feel the grains of frost on the glass walls he walked past, the dust that kicked up with each step he took, the burning diodes in the light bulbs in the ceiling. He fought the urge to grab something and crunch it to let off some steam. He settled for playing with the steel charm on his necklace.

He remembered where he was going and understood that even the most experienced and decorated defender in Uri City's most exclusive contract defense corporation was expendable, so he would do well to walk into the office with poise and class. He chose a different direction, though, slid the door through its slit, and yelled, "What the Frimas, Director?!"

Catherine Mallack sat in her executive chair at her thin, white desk toward the back of her office near the window-laced wall exposing Uri City's skyline. Translucent glass walls – lit white with yellow highlights – held the room together. A wall-sized holoscreen was at her right, and a bookshelf stood at her left. His childish fury could be felt a mile away, and yet Mallack, unfazed and unconcerned about his feelings, continued typing on her keypad while she calmly articulated, "Malcolm Bennett, you know I love you like a son, but I will kick your disrespectful ass if you ever come in here like that again."

Malcolm walked into her office. The door closed behind him. "Boss, I'm sorry, but no, this does not make sense to me," he said as he crossed his hands in front of him twice.

"What, Watson? Listen, the Company made a decision—"

"—yes, a *stupid* decision that is going to get us all killed!" Malcolm exclaimed as he plopped in one of the three chairs in front of Mallack's desk.

"How do you figure that, Malcolm?" Mallack asked.

Malcolm grew more irritated. He leaned forward, elbows on his knees, hands animated as he explained, "You gotta be kidding me. Duncan almost cost us the mission last night. He's only got one year of experience here, and despite my pleading with you all against it, you all decided to put him on the team. He's a hothead, and he cannot be controlled. You tell him to do something simple, and it's like he goes out of his way to make things worse for everyone."

"Remind you of anyone, Malcolm?" Mallack asked as she stared intently at him.

He took offense to what she was insinuating, never recalling being a hothead in battle and going against directives with reckless abandon. "Oh no, no, no," he retorted, "he and I are not the same. At least I know how to follow orders, Director. You tell me to do something, I do it. Even if I hate it, I tell you, but I do it anyway. Duncan Blake is going to do things Duncan Blake's way, consequences be damned. And he's getting closer and closer to getting one of us, or even himself, decimated in the field."

Mallack leaned forward at her desk and decided to play a game of *de-escalate Malcolm's anger*. "Two questions, Malcolm. First, did your team really fail?"

Malcolm considered Mallack's question and analyzed the mission objective, especially given the Company's true purpose for sending the Elite to the DD Corporation in the first place. He growled lowly, "No, not *technically*."

"What was the mission, Malcolm?"

Malcolm replied, "The mission was to secure the prototypes."

"That's correct. Yes, there was an apprehend order attached to it, but the primary objective was the prototypes. And you and your team completed that mission. Right?"

Malcolm's eyes squinted, and he sulked like a pouty kid as he sank into the chair. "Yes," he mumbled.

"Okay, then, so here's my second question. What now? What do we do with Duncan?"

Malcolm's eyes beamed, and he quickly sat back up. "Easy, we cut Duncan loose," he replied as he pointed his left thumb behind him. "Send him to another team, a Super team, get a few more years under his belt, then maybe we can bring him back, and we can be a team of *six* again."

"You mean *seven*, right?" Mallack corrected Malcolm.

Malcolm shook his head. "No, I said it right the first time, boss, *six*."

"Malcolm, you know I won't override the Company."

Fuming, Malcolm rose from his chair and walked around it. "Oh Akan!"

"Look, Malcolm," Mallack calmly interrupted his pending eruption as she raised her hand, "we're not going to let Duncan go. He's too powerful for us to demote him to another unit. The Company determined that he is formidable in battle and gives us an edge in combat that our enemies cannot contain. Yes, he has some authority issues, but the Company believes that you and the others can guide him to be more decisive and controlled in battle. Eventually, he will become one of the best defenders in Uri City."

Aargh, why does she have to make sense?! Why doesn't she ever listen to me? How does she outwit me every single time? Malcolm leaned forward on the back of his chair and sighed, "You're putting way too much confidence in us, Mallack. We're good, but we're not flawless. One day, Ammo is going to make a mistake that he cannot take back, and it's going to cost us a price heavier than any of us can pay."

"First, who said that I have confidence in you, Malcolm?" Mallack returned as she motioned him to sit down.

Ouch, Malcolm's pride took a hit that he was ashamed to admit to, *she doesn't have confidence in me? What does that mean? Does she think I can't handle leading the Elite? Does she not believe I'm a great leader?*

As if she read his mind, Mallack continued, "Listen, I think you're amazing, Malcolm. But I don't think you're a miracle worker. *The Company* thinks you are, and I'm inclined to trust HQ more than I trust myself. Which brings us to your next assignment: Symone Watson."

"The Frimas you mean?" Malcolm asked.

"Symone Watson, the new girl that you don't want to play with, the one you don't want on your team. She's your next assignment from the Company."

Perplexed, Malcolm returned, "No, no, they don't. They don't want me to train her."

"Yes, yes, they do. They want you to train her, personally," Mallack mirrored him, "to be her mentor, to forge her into the defender they think she's meant to be."

Malcolm shook his head in utter disbelief. *You have got to be kidding me!* He quickly rubbed his hand through his textured hair trying to relieve the tension headache that was twisting through his temples like a knife. "No, nope, nope, not gonna happen! I'm not about to have two whole newbies on my team that I'm responsible for, especially one that I have to personally babysit!"

"You act like you have a choice in the matter, Malcolm," Mallack fired back. "Duncan is *still on the team*, Symone is *on the team*, and you're *going to train her*. It's that simple."

Malcolm scrambled to try to change her mind. He used his stripe to tap into the Uri City Division's personnel files. He requested Symone's file, then said, "Put Watson's demos and stats on the big screen." AI obeyed his request, and the personnel file displayed on the holoscreen on Mallack's wall. Symone's avatar floated on the left, while her demographic and statistical data appeared on the right. Malcolm was dismayed, "Boss, look at her stats! You see that?"

"Yes, I see 'Ability: Elite,' and 'Affinity: Dark +3,' what's the problem?" Mallack said, purposefully ignoring a piece of information that she knew Malcolm was about to throw on the table.

Malcolm rose from his seat again and walked to the holoscreen. He pointed and yelled, "'Skill, Standard!' She's not even Advanced, boss! She's a Standard! What is a *Standard* doing on the Elite Unit? And why am I training her? They have a whole division dedicated to training Standards to Advanced before even considering them for Elite! How on Uretha did she leapfrog half our defenders and land here, with us, the Elite Unit, and get me as a trainer? It doesn't make sense, Boss."

Mallack had grown tired of Malcolm's petulance, but ever the patient manager, she tried one final redirect. "Let me ask you something, and you be straight with me," Mallack retorted while slightly moving her chair. "When has the Company ever made a decision that made sense to you? Aren't you always telling me that you wish you were at HQ making the decisions, that you want to climb the ranks to get to a position where you can actually create change rather than be down here having to execute someone else's commands?"

Malcolm thought about his career aspirations and his intent to one day sit in his boss's chair. He didn't want to depose Mallack, but he longed to be the man in that seat. His desire was known only to a handful of people, and he would never reveal his aspirations in the face of his teammates obnoxiously, having been advised by his parents to keep his head down, do his job well, keep his nose clean, and at the right time, watch Akan elevate him to a position no one could take him down from. He recalled having the "what do you see yourself doing in ten years" conversation with Mallack and was surprised that she still remembered his goal so poignantly. He answered, "Well, yeah, but..."

Mallack interrupted again, "No, no buts. You said to me that you want to someday become a director, or even higher than that. To be the one inviting and planting the defenders throughout the eleven city states of Uretha. 'To run the Company,' that's what *you* said, right?"

In this moment, he regretted telling her everything. *That's what you get for talking too much.* "You're loving how you're making me eat my words right now, huh?" Malcolm sulked.

Mallack grinned. *Checkmate.* "No, I'm not enjoying this at all," she said sarcastically. "Seriously, Malcolm, you're better than this crybaby person you're presenting in front of me. Just train Symone. And keep showing Duncan tough love. This team needs you, and you need every single person on the team. Things are slightly getting worse in Uri City, and if this team falters, a newbie at your side will be the least of your concerns."

Malcolm realized he had no more moves. She indeed had him beaten. "Fine," he conceded.

"Good. You're dismissed, Malcolm," Mallack declared and resumed typing the keys on her desk.

Malcolm walked out of Mallack's chamber, disgusted with himself for being bested yet again by his boss. *It's like she knows what I'm going to say before I say it and has a counter for it. No wonder she's the director. So, now I have to play nice with this girl. This week just keeps getting better and better. We nearly failed the last mission, now they want me to train someone. What if I fail at this? What if I can't train her properly? I don't think they'll give me anymore rope before I straight-up hang myself. This is all too much.*

Malcolm took a deep breath and reasoned that if he wanted to get to where he wanted to be, and not lose his job, he would do what he's told and not question the Company's wishes. He walked the Grand Hall while he recalled the energy he felt through Symone's veins and reconciled, *At the very least, I gotta figure out what's driving her engine, because that power, I've never felt anything like that before.* Malcolm searched for his team, and despite his curiosity, he secretly hoped that Symone had gone home for the day.

4

The Collector

Symone had no plans to go home anytime soon. Wide-eyed with a joy-filled heart, she continued exploring the halls of the Elite Grand with Malaysia and Alexia guiding her tour. Malaysia chuckled, "Remember when you first got up here, Alexia?"

"Oh yes! Man, look at her go," Alexia recounted her first day as an Elite and how much she marveled the place. "We probably should have let Daisy give Symone the tour; she's moving so fast."

They laughed, but Symone paid them no mind and continued analyzing the place with childlike awe. They approached the corridor to Mallack's office. "To our left, Symone, is Director Mallack's office. She has an open-door policy, so anytime you need to speak to her, just knock on the door. She's more than likely in there, but in case she's not, just ping her with your stripe."

"Cool, and what's over here?" Symone asked, pointing at the door to their right.

"This is Weapons and Wardrobe, 'Double W' as we like to call it. Here is where they equip us with whatever weapons we want to bring on our missions. Wardrobe designs clothing and cloaks, all specially designed to withstand the various powers we face, including our own. If you ever need new clothes, Wardrobe is where you will go to get them."

"Right, I remember that from orientation. Talk about a money saver, right?" Symone commented.

"Amen to that," Malaysia agreed. "I remember that one time Daisy forgot she wasn't wearing standard-issued clothes during training, and she literally ran out of her outfit. Had she not had on the right sports bra and boxers, she would have given us a real peep show."

Alexia giggled, "Daisy was not happy about that."

"Sure wasn't. So go get a whole new set of clothes from Wardrobe so you don't burn through your outfits in case we're ever on a mission in street clothes." They walked forward as Malaysia continued. "Over here at the end of the hall is where the Elite's Analyst resides. Analysis is a whole department, as they told you in your orientation, and each team has an Analyst whose job is to monitor every team member individually and the team collectively."

They reached the end of the corridor. Alexia placed her hand on the palm reader affixed on the wall. The palm reader scanned her hand, and it lit white for approval. The door popped, and Alexia opened it, revealing a bright room bathed in white with yellow highlights. Multiple holoscreens arrayed the left wall. On the right wall, a desk sat in front of a bookshelf filled with a disorganized set of books, folders, and papers on each shelf. The back wall was made of one-way glass, and the three ladies could see the city skyline. In the middle of the room was another thin desk with two chairs facing the holoscreens.

An average-height, stocky, brown-skinned, pepper-afroed man turned in his chair and jumped, rocking his chair back and forth with joy, "Oh, hi everyone!"

Alexia stepped forward and said, "Analyst, this is…"

"…Symone Watson," the Analyst finished as he stood up to greet her, "yes, I've heard much about her from the orientation Analyst. It is so great to meet you in person!" He extended his right hand.

Symone squinted her eyes as she took his hand and shook it, looking puzzled. "Wait," Symone returned, "are y'all playing with me?" Malaysia and Alexia looked at each other and chuckled lightly, delighting in Symone's confusion. "Aren't you the same Analyst from orientation? Like, I remember you very well from the probe. I'm sure you remember *all of me*." Symone lifted her hands to her head and then pointed them downward, referencing her third day in orientation, when she had to strip naked and be scanned thoroughly by Diagnostics, operated by the Analyst.

The Analyst nodded his head and stated, "Yes, well, I can assure you, that wasn't me. At least, it wasn't *me*, me. Ladies, care to explain it to her?"

Alexia turned to Symone and responded, "The Analyst is a cybernetic algorithm, one person split into several people. It's him, but he's also them."

Symone's jaw dropped. "That's crazy! So, you all share the same mind? Have *you* seen me naked, too?"

"Well, we all have access to each other's minds, yes. But we don't go around sharing things with each other as if we're huddled up in a room together, swapping stories. Everything we share is need-to-know. I know everything about the Elite Unit, and very little about the other teams because they don't involve me. Now, since you're here, I have access to all pertinent information from orientation, but no, I have not seen you naked. If your nakedness becomes relevant, then I will access that part of your file and see what Orientation's Analyst saw."

"Good to know," Symone said.

Malaysia chimed in, "Analyst is tasked with updating our demos and stats, analyzing the evolutions of our powers, skill levels, and affinities. We're monitored twenty-eight cycles a day, nine days a week, through the Smart Stripes embedded in our arms." Malaysia lifted her left arm to reveal the black line streaked from her wrist to the bend of her forearm. "As you evolve, Analyst will talk with you about what he sees and provide feedback about what your next steps ought to be. So, the more you train, the more battles you're engaged in, the more feedback you will receive from him."

Symone's eyes glittered when she heard the word *train*. "Where exactly does training happen?" she asked.

"Oh, that happens on the floors underground. We'll get to those after we're finished with the tour. Thank you, Analyst!" Alexia said as they walked out of the room.

The Analyst waved and replied, "Anytime, ladies. Thank you for stopping by! Alexia, we need to talk about your stats, soon, by the way."

"I'll be back soon," she replied. They walked past Weapons and Wardrobe and the corridor to Mallack's office, then the elevator and Intelligence. As they got to the break leading to the conference room, Alexia pointed to a door to their left and said, "That's the Cafeteria. Some call it the lounge, but basically, that's where the food is."

They finally reached the west end of the hall, and Symone noticed the word "Quarters" on the sliding doors. Malaysia placed her hand on the palm reader on the wall left of the doors and said, "Welcome to your new home!"

The doors popped and slid open, and Symone's eyes gleamed as she entered the Elite Unit's living quarters. The quarters common space could swallow a studio apartment. Glass panes made up the left and right walls, the city skyline staring in. Recessed lights were scattered across the fifteen-foot-high ceiling. As Malaysia, Symone, and Alexia walked in, Symone admired the full kitchen to her right with an island bar that separated the kitchen from the common area. Lounge chairs and coffee tables faced the glass on both sides. They took three steps down at the edge of the kitchen to enter the commons, furnished with black modernized sofas, love seats, recliners, and coffee tables built for kings. A massive holoscreen that stretched from the floor to the ceiling stared at the commons.

An entryway stood on each side of the holoscreen. Symone walked past the left side and noted nine doors, each leading to an Elite's chosen residence.

Alexia stood in one of the walkways and said to Symone, "Now, you don't have to stay here. Most of us have our own homes in Uri City, but this space will always be available to you should you want to crash here."

Malaysia pointed to the rooms and said, "Each of us has a room back here, fully customizable to fit your needs."

Symone walked back to the commons in complete awe of her new home away from home. The quarters' entry opened, and Karl, Duncan, and Daisy walked through. "There they are," Daisy said. "For a minute, I thought we were going to have to send out a search party."

"Thought they might be stuck in the Analyst's office like you were?" Duncan fired off.

"You heard about that?" Daisy recalled her first day as an Elite and how she and the Analyst went back and forth for cycles.

"Of course, I did!"

"Well, what about you? We couldn't get you out of Double W, checking out all the weapons at your disposal," she shot back as they stepped into the commons.

"They tried to fight me to get me out of the cafeteria," Karl joked seriously. "I needed nutrients, and boy, does the cafeteria have them. Speaking of, anyone hungry?"

"Karl, it's only 2:48," Alexia said, looking at her wrist.

"Exactly, I'm starving!" Karl responded. The team laughed as they all took seats.

I can't believe it, Symone smiled. *They're all so, well, normal.*

"So, I was wondering, Symone, what were you doing before you got *the call?*" Daisy asked.

Alexia grinned, "Ooh, origin story time!"

Everyone turned toward Symone and awaited her tale. Symone sat up, adjusted herself, and said, "Well, before I got the call, I was a prizefighter."

The team marveled, but before they could follow up, the doors opened again, and Malcolm walked in. "Hey guys," Malcolm greeted his crew as he walked toward the kitchen and pushed a few buttons on the countertop. He noticed that Symone was among them. *She's still here. Shouldn't be surprised, I wouldn't have left, either.* The counter then opened, and a tall tumbler rose from the hole. He drank from it, then said, "Please, don't let me interrupt. What were you talking about?"

"Well, Symone was telling us that she was a prizefighter before she got the call from the Company," Alexia replied.

"Is that right?" Malcolm was intrigued.

Symone picked up on Malcolm's sudden curiosity. *Hmm, he cares?*

"But I'm more interested in what you and Mallack were fussing about," Malaysia fired.

"How do you know we were 'fussing'?" Malcolm tried to deflect.

"Malcolm, really? This is me you're talking to," Malaysia said, blinking slowly twice to change her white pupils to different color shades, reminding him of her abilities.

"I don't know why I still act surprised," Malcolm said as he walked to them and rested his arms on the back of the sofa, leaning forward. He stood directly behind Karl, with Symone seated to his left and Daisy on his right.

Malaysia pressed, "For real, what were you two talking about? What's happening?"

Everyone except Karl turned to face Malcolm. He stated, "Well, Duncan, you're safe, for now. Despite your screw up, the Company still wants you here."

Duncan sat in a recliner to Malcolm's left, the back of the recliner facing the glass panes. He breathed a sigh of relief. *Thank Akan, I still have a job, still have a career, still have a* life. *Don't be so stupid next time, Dunk. They might fire you for real.* He then cleared his throat, dusted his shoulders off, and said, "See, the

Company knows what's up. They know how much value I add to you losers. You're nothing without me." He crossed his arms.

Alexia rolled her eyes and leaned forward, elbows on her knees as her hair dangled over her shoulders. "Malcolm, permission to mind-wipe Duncan, please, before I throw up," she reacted as she rubbed the fingers of her left hand together and green mist began to swirl around them.

"If only I had a kill order," Malcolm responded. He walked to his right around the couch and sat next to Malaysia on the loveseat she occupied solo, facing the rest of the team. "Seriously, though, brother, get your act together. None of us is guaranteed a spot on this team, not even me, and city defense is not some game that you get to start over from whenever you make a mistake. Mallack is taking undeserved heat for what we did. Remember that there are real consequences for all our actions. Understood?"

"Yeah, yeah, I got it," Duncan acknowledged.

Symone leaned forward, anxious to learn of her fate. "What about me?" she asked.

Malcolm looked at Symone and fought the urge to drink in her subtle charm. He didn't skip a stoic beat. "Well, new girl, it appears that the Company has high expectations for you."

Symone couldn't read his face and was unsure if his statement was laced with seriousness or sarcasm. "High expectations? What does that mean?"

"Not only are you Elite, but you're also getting a personal mentor."

"Really?" Symone asked, taken aback, putting her hand to her chest. "Well, who is it?"

"Me. I will be mentoring you."

Symone couldn't believe the day she was having. *How do I go from being a trainee to being a member of the Elite Unit and getting personally mentored by the number one in-field defender in the Company? This is incredible!*

Symone stood up and said, "I'm at a loss. I don't know what to say. This is ridiculous, thank you!"

Malcolm was not amused. *You could be less giddy about it.*

The rest of the team reeled just a little bit, and Symone noticed their reaction to the news. "Wait," Symone, concerned, blurted as she sat back down. "Am I missing something? Why are y'all acting like that?"

Malaysia chuckled, "Well, we're all very happy for you," she then stretched her arms out very fast, "landing the *greatest mentor* in the Company," she finished sarcastically.

Everyone laughed. "Oh yes, the *greatest mentor ever*," Alexia fought through her laughter. "Tell me, Malaysia, how long was it before you asked the director for a switch?"

"Two quarters. Maybe less than that?" she responded.

Everyone recalled their memories of Malcolm's mentorship programs, how hard he pushed them, and how much he annoyed them to the point of not wanting to train under him for very long.

"I know it was one quarter for me," Karl grinned as he sat up.

"Are we counting the first time or the last time?" Daisy leaned forward, her left arm across her lap, as she rubbed her chin with her right hand. "Because the first time for me was about seven weeks in, and I asked every day for a whole quarter after that before giving up."

"The very next day," Duncan slowly articulated.

Everyone laughed and yelled as Symone sat confused. *What am I getting myself into?* "So, you guys are saying I should cut my losses now while I'm ahead?"

"No, no, don't do that," Malaysia answered. "Just know that, well, Malcolm is not going to 'mentor' you like you think he is. Accept your fate because the director is not going to change her mind. She's not going to fight the Company on that."

"You all make it sound like I'm drawing the short end of the stick," Symone lamented.

"You said it, not us," Daisy replied. "Malcolm, are we lying?"

Symone turned to look at Malcolm, hoping for a glimmer of hope to streak across his face. But his steely demeanor, as he sat next to Malaysia, did not change. Malcolm smirked and shrugged his shoulders, silently enjoying his team's recollections and the breaking points he pushed them to. He leaned back in his seat, "And you're all better for it, right?"

Malaysia replied, "Doesn't mean we enjoyed how you got us here."

Symone thought to herself, *Well, this is an interesting position I find myself in. But I bet I can break him long before he breaks me.*

Just then, their conversation was interrupted by the buzzing blue line on everyone's arms except Symone's that said, "ELITE: Report to Intelligence." Everyone rose from their chairs, walked out of the quarters, and followed Malcolm to Intelligence. Alexia and Symone were last in line.

Symone pulled Alexia's arm and asked, "So, tell me the truth, is Malcolm really that bad of a mentor?"

Alexia grimaced, "Well, the thing about Malcolm is that he kind of expects you to figure it out on your own. He doesn't really offer the 'mentoring' you'd expect from a mentor. You're going to figure yourself out very well, and you'll find your place on the team. Eventually, he'll come around to being a great leader to you. You might even call him a *friend* or *big brother* like we do. Just don't set your expectations too high because that is one wall you will struggle to break through, climb over, or go around. Even my telepathy can't penetrate Fort Bennett. Believe me, I've tried."

Symone's right eyebrow raised as she thought, *He's never dealt with me, though. Challenge accepted. I'll find a way to pick that lock.*

Malcolm unlocked the entrance to Intelligence with his palm. The doors popped and slid open. The Elite Unit walked into a vast auditorium. Seven cascading rows, each furnished with four long desks from end to end, with a staircase that split the room and the desks. Each desk had two holoscreens atop them, and most of them were being used by Intelligence personnel. In the back of the auditorium was a wall holoscreen that stretched from end to end. Recessed lights in the ceiling were dimmed, outshone by the holoscreens across the room. At the top of the room, several auditorium chairs were affixed to the back wall, and a rail divided those chairs from the first row of desks. Symone gazed at the technology arrayed before her.

Malcolm walked to the woman in the white lab coat who was staring at the wall holoscreen. "Hey, Stephanie, why'd you call us in?"

Stephanie turned around, and Symone realized it was the same Stephanie she had met earlier. "Oh, you're here, great! Hi Symone! Welcome to Intelligence!" Stephanie said.

"So, you work here?" Symone said to Stephanie.

"Works? No, she runs this place," a young, thin, bald, brown-skinned man sitting next to where Stephanie stood gently corrected her.

"This lovely gentleman is Dax, my right-hand man and the best Intelligence analyst I could ever ask for. Yes, I oversee the Intelligence Division of the Elite Unit. Everything involving your missions runs through here. We provide tactical support and information to aid your success in defense of the city."

Malcolm said, "Right. Stephanie, Dax, and this crew are the best in the business. We wouldn't be the Elite without them backing us up."

Stephanie pushed a lock of her hair behind her ear and blushed in gratitude. "Aww, thank you, Malcolm." Symone paid attention to Malcolm's sweet sincerity.

"So, what's up?" Malcolm shifted focus.

"Oh, right," Stephanie said. "You guys have a seat. Dax, pull it up."

Symone was the first to grab a seat, followed by Alexia, Daisy, Karl, and Duncan. Malcolm remained standing on the staircase, while Malaysia perched on an empty holoscreen desk chair. Dax tapped buttons on a keyboard embedded within the desk itself. The big screen mirrored Dax's holoscreen and displayed a gray avatar and a set of demographics with question marks littering most of the fields.

Malaysia asked, "Okay, what exactly are we looking at?"

"Yeah, looks to me like an empty dossier," Duncan tagged on.

"Don't focus on that just yet," Stephanie said. She urged, "Dax, pull up the map." Dax tapped again and displayed a map of Uri City with red dots scattered across it. "Over the past year, we have been working in collaboration with the Uri City Police Department to solve a string of murders involving powered individuals. At first, we thought that these murders were just random crimes, people in the wrong place and wrong time, or crimes of passion, you know, things that wouldn't necessarily need the assistance of even a Super unit."

Malcolm studied one dot hard. He snapped his finger, "Right, I remember that case, in the Leicester District, that was the murder of Madam Reila."

"Madam Reila," Symone said at the same time Malcolm said it.

Malcolm turned his head to look back at Symone, and their eyes locked. Malcolm's squinted eyes, tilted head, and half-smile asked, "What do you know about Madam Reila?" Malcolm's senses instinctively dialed up and focused on Symone's oddity again, and he noticed its intensity was slightly stronger than before.

She replied, "No, what do *you* know about Madam Reila?"

"Can somebody tell *me* who Madam Reila is?" Malaysia asked.

Malcolm gasped, then explained, "She was an incredible singer, had such incredible promise, but her life was cut short when she was randomly mugged outside of..."

"...Jackson's Pier," Symone continued as she stood up and leaned over the railing. She pointed at the map as she explained, "Everyone just assumed because it was in Leicester, near the edge of the Underbelly, that it was just another horrible night, and the case was never solved. Are you saying she was powered?"

Stephanie, excited by the intel, clapped her hands and replied, "That's precisely what we're saying. It took Intelligence quite some time to piece this together, but you're never going to believe what we discovered! Madam Reila was an underdeveloped powered person, and her power was her voice, and her ability was strong enough to carry a unique signature. By analyzing her past work, we were able to sample the signature. And we determined that her power has resurfaced."

"Wait, her power 'resurfaced?' How is that possible?" Daisy questioned.

Stephanie gestured to Dax to change the information on the screen. Madam Reila appeared on the left side of the screen, and another woman appeared on the right. "There's a new artist named Reign who has the exact same signature as Madam Reila. She emerged about eight weeks ago and has been climbing the music charts with her hits."

"Yes," Symone swooned, "Reign is so amazing! I love her music! But wait, you're telling us that she actually has Reila's vocal *power*, and that's why she's lighting up the charts?"

Stephanie beamed. "That's exactly what I'm saying! And because of that, we are convinced that these other murders were not coincidental. Every time someone was murdered, that person's ability was taken beforehand, and that power resurfaced in another person. Now, without proof, we cannot say for sure that these 'new' powered individuals didn't just come into their powers, but the signatures do not lie."

The holoscreen displayed the deceased and their powers, and then showed lines tracing to another list of individuals who allegedly owned the deceased's powers. Everyone's eyes widened in shock.

Malcolm, anger and vengeance coursing through his veins, walked a couple of steps down the staircase. "How is this possible? Transferring powers from one person to another?"

"That brings us to the dossier," Stephanie said. "The Company has been chasing this person for at least ten years. We have only known this individual by codename and what he does. We call him The Collector." The gray avatar and question mark-filled demographic fields reappeared. "We don't know who he is or where he's from. But we do know that his power involves draining the abilities of powered individuals. We believe that he is the mastermind behind these murders. In his early work, he would just take people's powers and vanish, devolving the powered into ordinary individuals."

Dax chimed in, "We thought that maybe he just didn't want people to have powers. But since these murders and the subsequent transfer of the deceased's powers, we have determined, with the help of Uri City Police and some under-cover work from our Super teams, that the Collector sells powers to the highest bidders at what are known in the Meridian District as Power Parties."

Stephanie continued. "Elite, the Collector has done an incredible job scrub-bing himself off the grid and hides behind a mercenary crew that we believe he may have created with transferred powers. Knowing that he sells powers, we can surmise that these murders are not just merely an escalation."

"No, they're a statement," Malcolm declared. "Look," he said, pointing at the map, "the last three murders were not just randomly powered individuals."

"No, they weren't," Dax stated. "The last three were Super powered, and they worked for other defense companies. Torch from Z Group, Mirage from the Cavalry, and Beast Mode from the Hunters Organization."

"The Collector is trying to provoke us."

"Well, if it's a fight he wants, let's give it to him," Karl pounded his left fist into his right palm.

"Damn right! You're going after the defenders now?" Duncan gritted his teeth.

"I'm with Duncan on that," Malaysia agreed. "You're killing people and sell-ing their powers? That's low, even for the powered. Not even the Underbelly's kind would do something like this."

"Good! I'm glad you all feel that way." Director Mallack's face appeared on the holoscreen. "This is priority one for the Elite Unit. This is the closest anyone, any organization in Uri City, has gotten to catching and eliminating the Collector. He is not to be trifled with, though. You have to be ten times smarter than him, else you will end up another casualty on his wall of collected powers. From our information, he has never collected an Elite, and if he does, that power will sell for an incalculable amount of money."

"Or give whoever he transfers it to the ability to begin an assault on this city unlike anything we've ever seen before," Karl stated.

"Malcolm, your team has to be ready for any attack that the Collector brings Uri City's way. Understood?"

"Yes, Director, we understand." Malcolm stared into the screen, locked onto the gray avatar with a deep-seated rage. *You won't get away with this. We're going to get you and make you pay for what you've done. I loved Madam Reila! Reign is straight trash by comparison. What does Symone know about Madam Reila?* Nobody *knows Madam Reila!*

Suddenly, the screens across the room glowed red, and the holoscreen at the end of the room read "HIGH ALERT," and a siren blared. Everyone looked around, then looked at each other, as their left arms buzzed and lit up red. The alert stated, "Midtown – Robbery at Sentinel Bank and Trust. Three powered individuals."

"Stephanie, show us the details on the board," Malaysia requested.

"Dax," Stephanie responded. Dax typed again, and the screen showed Sentinel Bank and Trust. "Sentinel Bank and Trust is currently being robbed by three powered individuals. Hostages have not been taken, but multiple normal individuals are in the building and cannot get out. If money is taken from the supercomputer, the building will go into self-destruct mode to ensure digital currency cannot be taken from the indestructible drive that houses it or any keys it may be transferred to. Three objectives: 1) evacuate everyone out of the building; 2) preserve the building and the drive; and 3) eliminate the suspects by any means necessary."

Malcolm turned to face the Elite. "Alright, team, let's suit up."

"What about me?" Symone asked.

Malcolm smirked and replied, "You stay here and monitor from Intelligence."

"Oh. Okay," Symone said arms crossed, disappointed that she wouldn't be able to tag along.

"She didn't notice it, did she?" Alexia asked, chuckling a little.

"Didn't notice what?" Symone said.

"Look at your arm, Symone," Daisy replied. Symone pulled up her jacket sleeve and saw the glowing red line across her arm. She gleefully patted her feet, then composed herself. "She's like a little kid at Jubilee! But I know now not to send her messages. She might not answer them," Daisy joked.

"I'm just so excited! I felt my arm buzz, but I just figured it was someone else sending me a message. I'm ready!"

Malcolm instructed, "Alexia, take Symone to Double W to get her uniform and cloak.

"Yes, sir," Alexia acknowledged.

"Elite," Malcolm smoldered, "let's get it."

As they exited Intelligence, Symone thought, *Did Malcolm just mess with me? Mmm hmm, hard to break down that wall, huh?*

5

Dazzling Debut

Symone sat strapped in the cargo bay of Malaysia's swiftly flying hoverbus beside Alexia near the back hatch. The cyan light strips illuminated the charcoal metal frame that held the ship together. Recessed cyan lights shone upon the crew. Symone looked around the craft and then looked at herself, marveling at her new uniform: a gold star centered between her breasts, with two gold lines running parallel on both sides of the star. The lines broke the crimson that covered her entire body, with gold stripes running down both sides down to her boots. Within the crimson, the nanotech scattered gold speckles all over. Symone had great difficulty containing her joy. She placed her arms in front of her and rotated them again and again.

Alexia noticed Symone staring at herself and smiled, saying, "Loving the new suit, huh?"

"I'm just still in a daze," Symone smiled. "The day isn't even halfway over yet, and I'm in a new suit with a new team on my first mission."

Duncan overheard Symone and replied, "Don't get used to the daze. Most of the time we're not doing a whole lot. Going out on missions this often is unusual."

"Don't mind Ammo," Karl responded. "He wants to blow something up every day, so he gets bored easily. You're going to love being on this team."

Malaysia, flying the hovercraft, acknowledged the ping on her navigation panel and said, "We're close to the drop point."

Malcolm tapped on a mini holoscreen and issued orders to everyone. "Okay, team, here's the situation. Sentinel Bank and Trust is one of the most secure buildings in the district, home to the city's treasury. So, we're talking about all the money that funds the operation of Uri City, and pays our bills. Our objectives are to evacuate the civilians safely, secure the building and the money, and eliminate the threats. No kill order has been given, but we are to do whatever we have to do to take down the suspects."

"Yes!" Duncan yelled. "Can't mess this one up."

Malcolm rolled his eyes. "Path of least resistance, don't forget that."

"I know, I know. Geez, take the fun out of everything."

"No, this will still be plenty of fun for us all, trust. The building's security is tight, so we can't see inside the building at all. We don't know where the supercomputer is, nor the threats. Mammoth, knock out the cloak of the building so the Eagle can see through it and give us a layout of where we're headed. Blitz, you will go ahead of everyone and get every person out of the building. Search every floor, every broom closet until there is just us in the building."

"Copy that," Daisy replied.

"Enchantra, you will create a barrier between onlookers and the building itself. In case we are too late, and the building goes off, we don't want anyone hit by debris. Use your telepathy to keep people away from the building, and when we have a location on the computer, rendezvous with us there."

"Sounds like a plan," Alexia responded.

"Ammo, Starburst, you're with me." Symone's face lit up as she stared intently at Malcolm, paying strict attention to every syllable that flowed from his lips. "We will get the supercomputer's location from one of the staffers in the building and get to that floor as fast as possible to take down the suspects. Remember, if they get the drive out of the computer or download the money to a key, the building will go into self-destruct mode, and at that point, we abort and get the Frimas out of there. Cloaks up. Everybody ready?"

"Let's do this," Daisy responded. Everyone double-tapped their chests, and their helmets enveloped their heads. Everyone's cloak shimmered gold from head to toe as a reaction to its activation, except Symone's. Neither she nor her team noticed that her cloak did not activate.

The Eagle hovered the aircraft about ten feet above the street. The circular bottom hatch of the hovercraft opened, and one by one, everyone dropped to the ground and walked toward the Sentinel Bank. It was three cycles before midday. The team noted that the Uri City Police Department set up wooden barriers on either side of the building's street and sidewalk to block ground traffic. As the Eagle piloted her hovercraft to the hoverpad atop the building across the street, the team noted that UPD blocked air traffic on that same street by placing two officers on hoverbikes on each end parallel to the street barrier. Behind them, UPD had ten officers on the opposite sidewalk standing at the ready. Onlookers and news crews were gathered along the perimeter UPD had set, defiant of the officers' orders for them to get back.

"Does anyone else find it strange that a robbery at a bank like this is happening in the middle of the day?" Blitz asked.

"Stranger things have happened, so I'm not really surprised," Enchantra responded.

K.C. wondered the same but stayed focused. "Alright, everyone has their assignments. Blitz, Mammoth, go! Enchantra, stay here and keep everybody back."

Blitz zoomed past everyone and entered through the broken atrium doors of the bank. She stopped suddenly and saw multiple innocent civilians huddled and shrieking in fright underneath the bank teller desk counters. She noted busted-up chairs and desks, damaged countertops, and broken glass scattered across the floor. She held her hands forward and said, "Don't worry, we're here to help you."

One of the shaken civilians stood up and stammered, "Oh, thank you, thank you! They told us if we tried to leave the building, they would kill us, and none of us are powered, so we couldn't stop them. They killed Barry, our security guard, with one blast." She pointed to her left, and Daisy saw a man lying on the ground with a gaping hole in his chest. She continued, weeping, "We're sure the other guards are dead, too, they just overwhelmed and overpowered everyone. We didn't know if anyone else was outside, so we waited for UPD to come in and tell us it was safe to come out. We had been telling him he needed to turn his cloak on, and he just never listened to us."

"It's okay. Hey, don't worry, help is here, and we're going to get you all out of here. How many floors are there, and how many people?" Blitz asked as K.C., Starburst, and Ammo walked up behind her.

"Um, we have ten floors, and dozens of personnel. There's a lot of people here processing money and trying to keep the supercomputer secure."

"Where is the supercomputer?" Starburst asked.

"It's on the seventh floor, and you'll need a key to get in."

"If they've already blasted their way up there, then a key probably won't matter," K.C. said. "Okay, everyone here, walk out of the building now. Hands raised so they know you're civilians. Do that now. Stephanie, alert UPD that civilians are evacuating the building now."

"Copy that, K.C.," Stephanie responded in his ears.

"Blitz, go through every floor and get everybody out of here now."

Blitz became a red blur through the crowd of people walking past K.C., Starburst, and Ammo with their hands raised as they exited Sentinel.

"Guys, let's get to the seventh floor."

Starburst replied, "I'll meet you guys there from the staircase." She levitated and flew left toward the stairs.

"Oh, so she flies?" K.C. gazed at Starburst, stunned by her graceful exit. *How did I miss her flight ability in her demos?*

"Yeah, you should have been there. She's got skills, my brother," Ammo replied as he, too, gazed at Starburst.

"Get your head in the game. Let's go," K.C. said to Ammo to shake off his own infatuation.

The Mammoth, meanwhile, was outside of the white-coated steel building looking for Sentinel's cloaking generator. "Eagle, do you have any idea where this thing could be? I didn't know Sentinel was this wide."

The Eagle walked to the edge of the roof of the building across the street. "I'm looking. I'm looking." She scanned the building, then changed her eyesight to look for heat signatures. She saw nothing. She then scanned for invisible wavelengths and noticed another cloak humming behind the bank. "Okay, I see it, about fifty feet of the northeast corner. You're on the wrong side. Turn around and turn to your left."

The Mammoth turned around and bolted upward, then turned to his left and ran toward a concrete pad with nothing on it. "I don't see anything, Eagle!"

"It's right in front of you," the Eagle reacted. "It's invisible because of its own cloak. You'll have to break it down."

The Mammoth found a small pebble on the ground. He picked it up and threw it in front of him. The rock stopped suddenly, surrounded by several yellow ripples that faded away as the rock slid down to the ground. He walked up to the cloak and lifted his hand to feel the cloak. His hand formed a yellow rippling outline on it. He then began banging on the cloak as hard as he could, throwing punches at the cloak repeatedly. Each time, the cloak responded by rippling around his fists. "This thing won't budge," the Mammoth said.

"You gotta keep going, Mammoth. We don't have much time. Can you get under it? Maybe the cloak doesn't totally surround the pad. See if you can get up under it somehow," the Eagle suggested.

The Mammoth saw a cable cover underneath the pad and reached under, thankful that the cloak didn't reach it. He ripped the cover's outer shell to reveal wires. *This must power the cloak. Let's see.* He ripped them, and the cloak shimmered and dissipated, revealing a black octagonal box that hung on the wall. *It's humming hard. That's gotta be the generator.* He cocked back his right fist and smashed the box as hard as he could. His hand tore through the metal casing like tissue paper. He pulled his fist back and tore as many wires as could fit in his grasp. Sparks flew out of the generator, and the humming stopped. The building itself shimmered gold from top to bottom, then its cloak dissipated before everyone's eyes.

"Cloak is down," the Mammoth said, "Eagle, you're up."

"Copy that," the Eagle answered. She peered through the walls of the bank and saw thermal activity on every floor except the seventh. "Okay, Blitz, I can see you on the second floor, currently clearing it out. You've got seven more floors to clear; there appear to be civilians on all of them except the seventh." The Eagle scanned the seventh floor again and noticed three thermal lines, all converging at a single point. "Ammo, Starburst, K.C., three powered individuals on the seventh floor. It looks like they've already gotten past security and are through the main door. The generator for the supercomputer's cloak is still intact, probably offsite somewhere. They appear to be emitting some type of heat energy to take the cloak down."

"Enchantra, how are we looking on the perimeter?" K.C. asked.

"Civilians are all walking away from the building, and I've added a little extra protection to keep them from getting over here," Enchantra said. Her eyes were lit green as she extended her arms outward. Her hands emitted a faint green mist that extended to the edges of the building and the surrounding streets. From that mist, a barrier rose about ten feet that no one could walk into but could escape from.

"Okay, get up here and help us. We're approaching the seventh floor now."

"Be right there," Enchantra answered. She whispered an incantation, and the green mist within the barrier shimmered and froze. *That should hold.* Her eyes stopped glowing, and her hands stopped emitting. She then ran inside Sentinel Bank.

K.C. and Ammo met Starburst who stood at the closed red entry to the seventh floor. Ammo opened the door, and K.C. led them down the darkened corridor to a break on their right. He stopped them, then said to the Eagle, "Okay, Eagle, what do you see?"

"Okay, the break to your right is a straight shot to the supercomputer. You should have the element of surprise because they are focused right now."

"Blitz, how are you looking?" K.C. asked.

"Right now, I'm on the fourth floor," she answered.

"Okay, keep moving. Mammoth, get to the front of the building just in case we need you."

"Copy that," the Mammoth answered and sped to the front of the bank.

"Alright," K.C. whispered. "You two ready?"

"Yes," Starburst said.

"Let's get it," Ammo mimicked his leader's catchphrase.

"That's right!" K.C. smiled. "3, 2, 1, go!" The three Elite turned the corner and ran as fast as they could toward the powered suspects. Starburst, positioned at K.C.'s left, charged her hands with light and heat. Ammo, positioned at K.C.'s right, retracted his hands into twin cannons. K.C. reshaped a piece of metal he picked up from the debris outside the bank into a heated whip.

As they rushed into the supercomputer room, K.C. yelled, "Power down now!" and threw his whip while Starburst launched a star and Ammo shot a blast from each arm toward their opponents. The three, all clad in black from head to toe, turned suddenly in shock. The first one was struck by Starburst's star and flew backward into the supercomputer's cloak. His body created a yellow chalk line on the cloak that trailed him downward as he fell to the ground. The second was lassoed into K.C.'s whip. He grimaced as the whip burned him and damaged the cloak. K.C. swiftly pulled the whip back, and he spun around and wobbled to the ground, landing on his belly. The third was hit by both blasts from Ammo's cannon fire. He, too, flew backward into the supercomputer's cloak.

K.C. quickly scanned the room and noted the one-way windows to his left, the dark marble flooring they stood on, the high vaulted ceiling about thirty feet above them, and the cloak about fifty feet in front of them that housed the supercomputer. K.C. declared, "This is your only warning. Stand down or be taken in by force."

The second lifted his face off the ground. He raised his right hand and shot a purple heat ray toward K.C. He rolled to his right to dodge the blasts, and they hit the back wall near the entrance. The other two got up and charged their hands, and they all rushed forward to engage the Elite. Starburst charged her hands and lunged toward her initial target. She exchanged punches and kicks with him, and his cloak responded with each block and deflection. Starburst connected with a right hook to the head, then kneed him in the stomach. She created a small star and pushed her hand into his chest. She released a blast and launched him backward, but while he flew back toward the supercomputer, he shot a heat ray toward her, and it singed her left shoulder. The impact hit her hard, and Starburst spiraled in the air, pummeled into the ground, and rolled several times before crashing into the back wall.

Meanwhile, Ammo exchanged his right cannon back into his hand and engaged his target. His target shot a couple of heat rays toward Ammo, which he deflected with his left arm cannon. Ammo spun on the ground and extended his right leg to trip his opponent. His foe jumped over his leg but didn't notice that Ammo, while lying on the ground, extended his left arm out. Ammo blasted his adversary with a cannon shot that shuttled him into the air. He crashed into the ceiling and then plummeted to the marble floor. Ammo then shot another blast at him, but his opponent rolled away from that blast, shot heat rays from his hands to lift himself off the ground, then turned and faced Ammo. He shot rays toward Ammo, landing one of them in his torso. The cloak lit bright yellow and took most of the damage, but the rays still launched Ammo a few feet off the ground. He took the hit and landed back on his feet. He then shot another cannon blast toward his enemy, which he dodged.

K.C. had his hands full as his enemy shot heat rays toward him. With nothing to build a shield from, K.C. raced toward his opponent while dodging the rays. When he got within ten feet of him, K.C. jumped and tangled his foe by the neck with his whip. K.C. flipped behind his adversary and jerked the whip forward. The target fell backward onto the ground. K.C. used his hands to manipulate the temperature of the whip to try to burn his target's cloak and his target's neck. He was choking despite the cloak's attempt to keep him protected. K.C.'s opponent shot K.C. in the leg with a heat ray, and it knocked him off balance. K.C. loosened the rope's grip while compensating for the stumble. While trying to regain his footing, K.C. saw that Starburst had fallen to the ground behind them at the back of the room. He sensed her energy rushing through her veins like a raging volcano. K.C. realized, though, *I can feel her energy! Oh snap, she's not cloaked!* Before he could warn his teammate, his adversary took advantage of the distraction, flipped backward, and kicked K.C. in the head, making him stumble backward. The foe then blasted him with heat rays, and he careened into the supercomputer's cloak. As K.C. struggled to recalibrate from the daze, his senses could not break focus from Starburst's energy.

Starburst winced from the blast she took in her left shoulder. She noticed that her uniform had taken some damage, and her skin was exposed and burned from the ray. *I got something for that.* She pushed herself off the ground and levitated quickly toward her target. As he realized she was on her way, he blasted a continuous stream of heat from his hands. Starburst quickly charged her hands and created a ball of heat and energy to shield herself from his assault. She began to feel a pushback from his rays and slowly floated in the opposite direction. While trying to figure out a way to outmatch her opponent, she noticed that K.C. had crashed into the supercomputer's cloak and was slowly recovering from his opponent's blast. She wondered whether he was okay and should do something to help him, but she also recognized that her hands were full.

Suddenly, she felt a churning sensation in the pit of her stomach that radiated through her veins. As she continued to push against her opponent's rays, the star between her hands abruptly changed colors from yellow to white. She was mesmerized but maintained her focus on the levitating ball. The longer she stared at the star, the more her eyes changed colors, from yellow to white. Her locs also responded to the shift and changed from yellow to white. Her floating slowed to a halt midair, and Starburst summoned her newfound strength to push herself, her star, and her adversary's rays toward him. He thought he had the upper hand and couldn't understand how he was now losing momentum. She then hurled the white-hot star toward him. The star cut through the heat rays and slammed into her foe. The momentum from the blast pushed him into the marble floor, his body cracking some of the tile under him. The star's massive energy shattered his cloak as his nanites shimmered, then dissipated in response to the damage it took. She walked over to him and punched him in the head to knock him unconscious. "One down," Starburst declared.

Ammo reached his adversary and exchanged punches and kicks with him, but he was overpowered by the target when his foe spun around, kicked Ammo in his back and knocked him to his knees, then grabbed both of his arms and pulled back with all his might trying to snap his arms out of place. Ammo's cloak responded in kind, lighting up near Ammo's armpits. Ammo resisted and tried to pull his arms forward. He screamed as he could feel the tendons in his rotator cuffs tearing. His adversary charged his hands and lit Ammo's cloak up to reduce its integrity rapidly. Suddenly, his opponent released Ammo's arms, stood stiff as a board, then shuttled and crashed headfirst into the ceiling again, then flipped upside-down and planted headfirst into the ground. He then launched into the wall opposite the windows. The impact knocked him unconscious despite the cloak holding up.

Ammo's hands fell to the ground to hold himself up, then he looked back at the corridor to see Enchantra, who finally made it up to the seventh floor to help. "You good?" she asked as she ran over to him.

"He almost ripped my arms off!" Ammo grimaced as he struggled to get back on his feet.

K.C. and his foe were not finished. K.C.'s opponent shot a continuous heat ray at him, and K.C. leveled his arms, palms out to stop the rays just short of his hands. The rays collected into a ball of energy that enlarged in front of him. K.C. could sense that this energy was unstable, and he knew he couldn't hold it for long before he would need to run to keep from incurring damage from the blast it would create. As he scrambled to figure out what to do, he looked forward and saw Starburst's hair change from yellow to white. As he sensed her energy surge, K.C. suddenly felt his hands tingle like the circulation had returned after going numb. He could sense the heat rays differently than he had before. As he moved one of his hands, the glowing ball of energy moved in sync.

What the Frimas is this? How am I doing this?!

K.C. couldn't believe it but also couldn't afford to give himself a chance to process what had just happened. He decided to try to end this battle and, while suspending the ball, spun around three times, the ball spinning with him. He then released his grip on the ball to launch it toward his adversary, who tried to dodge it but couldn't. He was hit by the blast and launched into the back wall.

The blast radiated a shockwave of heat toward everyone. Ammo, Enchantra, and K.C. absorbed the shockwave through their cloaks. Starburst, though, was not cloaked, and the shockwave launched her into the same wall as K.C.'s opponent while knocking out windows.

K.C. noticed it and yelled, "Starburst, are you alright?" as he ran toward her.

K.C., Ammo, and Enchantra could see steam rising from Starburst's uniform. She knelt on the ground with her palms planted and groaned while saying, "Yeah, I'm great, nothing I can't, ugh, handle." She attempted to push herself up. K.C. helped her up as Enchantra and Ammo walked their way.

"You're not cloaked," K.C. declared softly. He examined her uniform, which had been torn in several places across her body in defense of her well-being. He offered his hand to her.

"I don't know what happened," Starburst grabbed his hand and groaned as she endured the pain radiating from her shoulder. "I thought I was, and I didn't pay attention to it once we started fighting. That blast almost wiped me out. I must not have double-tapped it right."

"We can't afford mistakes like that. Don't want to lose you in battle on a technicality."

Starburst felt a ping in her heart. "Aww, you care about me?"

K.C. chuckled. "I care about everybody on my team. And I should have told you to double-tap again. I noticed you were not cloaked but got hit and was distracted. That's on me."

"Well, good news is we cleared the board," Ammo said.

"You're right, Ammo," K.C. refocused. "Blitz, how are you?" K.C. asked.

"I'm outside. Every civilian is accounted for. How's the supercomputer?"

"The cloak is still intact. Supercomputer is secure. No one's hitting the jackpot today. Mammoth, I'm sending you a package from above. You ready?"

"I'm ready, send it my way," the Mammoth replied, looking up at the broken windows from the seventh floor. Enchantra's eyes glowed green, and green mist emitted from her hands and quickly wrapped around the three would-be robbers. She raised the three targets off the ground and hurled them out of the windows toward the Mammoth. He waited until they were about halfway to the ground, then took three big steps and jumped about twenty feet into the air and caught all three of them, then landed back on the ground. He walked them over to the Uri City Police Department's detainee hoverbus and told the officers, "Open the door." One of the officers pushed a button that popped the bus's back hatch. Two officers stood up from their seats. The Mammoth said, "Special delivery."

"Alright team. Let's wrap this up and head back to base, I am tired and starving," K.C. said.

"I second that," Enchantra reacted.

A moment later, they walked out of the building, and they were met with cheers and applause from the awaiting onlookers, building staff, police, and news crews, all anxiously waiting for the battle's resolution. The Eagle landed the hoverbus in front of the bank's entrance and opened the back hatch to let the Elite Unit in. The team walked into the hoverbus, closed its door, and flew back to headquarters.

Malcolm and his teammates summoned their nanites to remove their helmets and visors. The nanites melted into the rest of the suit. Symone's head piece, however, stayed in place. She double-tapped her chest, and her cloak shimmered from head to toe. They all looked at her, and she looked at everyone and sighed, "Great, *now* you want to turn on? Ugh, they're going to put me back in Orientation."

Malcolm sat down across from her and replied, "At least you came out alive. You fought well today. Excellent job, all of you. We did great today." Symone clenched her shoulder while holding her head down in bashful delight. The rest of the crew cheered in agreement, slapping high-fives and whooping.

In his mind, Malcolm couldn't stop replaying what he just achieved in the supercomputer room. He looked down at his hands, balled his fingers into a fist, then flexed his fingers again. He turned his hands palms-down, then flipped them again and squeezed his fingers again. He did this several more times while thinking, *I've never been able to move energy before. I've always been able to stop it, contain it for a little while, but I've never been able to move it. This is new. And I felt it happening...*

...as I was doing it, Starburst thought as she stared at her hands. *I've never been able to raise my stars' temperatures that high that fast before, especially to knock out a cloak that fast. This is new. I don't know what happened, I don't know how it happened, but damn.* She rubbed her left shoulder with her right hand while rubbing her belly with her left. *What a day.* She thought about Malcolm's concern for her welfare and his commendation of her skills on the battlefield, and she stared at him through her visor and smiled, taking in his subtle, commanding physique perfectly accentuated by the black and blue shrouding his body.

Wonder what it would be like to make him yield to me.

6

A Conversation

The hoverbus touched down on the rooftop of the Company headquarters, and the team exited out of the back hatch. Malaysia followed Malcolm, Symone, Karl, Daisy, Duncan, and Alexia out, and as her feet touched the ground, four mechanical arms attached themselves to the hoverbus's wheels. The mechanical arms locked, and the pad itself made a grinding sound as it lowered the hoverpad into the garage below.

The Elite Unit of Uri City's Company walked the steps to dismount the hoverpad and motioned forward toward the elevator shaft. Director Mallack stood about fifteen feet in front of it. She wore sunglasses to block the three suns Uretha revolved around. She examined Symone's tattered nanites and inquired, "What happened to you out there, Symone?"

"Either equipment failure or a lapse in judgment on my part," Symone sighed. *She's going to think I'm an idiot and have me demoted.*

"I see. We'll address that in the debrief tomorrow. Still, great job, Elite. Glad to see everyone made it safely, and all the objectives were achieved."

They stopped in front of her. "Thank you, Director," Malcolm replied.

Mallack clasped her hands together and said, "Feel free to take the rest of the day, it's been a long seventeen cycles for you all, so get some rest and let's debrief in the morning."

"Yes!" Alexia reacted. "Maybe I can make up for last night's date that got interrupted!" Alexia quickly emitted a telekinetic mist from her right index finger to push the down button, then rushed to the elevator door.

"I just want to shut my eyes and see nothing for a while," Malaysia said as they passed Mallack to the elevator entry.

As Malcolm approached the elevator, the doors opened, and the seven entered. He noticed that the director was still on the rooftop. "You're not coming with us?"

"No, I'm waiting for another team to come back from a mission," she said.

"Okay, take care, Director."

"You, too, Malcolm," Mallack answered.

The doors to the elevator closed. As the elevator made its way to the Elite Grand Hall, Daisy asked, "So, Malcolm, what are you about to do?"

Malcolm sighed and crossed his arms. Symone listened intently, plotting to catch a moment with him alone without the others around. "I'm going to talk to the Analyst and check on my demos and stats, then get a training session in before I head home."

"Seriously?" Karl said. "After all we did, you're still trying to get some more action in? You're going to train yourself into an early grave."

"What can I say? I'm always in for another round or six."

Symone thought, *Oh really? You haven't gotten in the ring with me yet.* Symone's eyes smoldered red. *Bet I'd tire you out!*

"Overachiever," Malaysia said, rolling her eyes.

"Got that right," Duncan replied.

"Well, you have fun with that, Malcolm," Alexia said. "Just remember there's more to life than the Company. One day, you're gonna look up and wonder what all you could have done when you were doing all this extra training."

The elevator stopped at the Elite Grand Hall, and the doors opened. Malcolm proceeded to the right to visit the Analyst while everyone else motioned to the left toward the quarters. Symone felt torn. She wanted to follow Malcolm, but she also wasn't quite sure whether she should barge in on what might be a private conversation between the Analyst and him. She walked a few steps behind the group, wondering if she should dart away at an open corridor. Just then, Alexia interrupted her plans by saying to her, "Come on, Symone, you'll get to use your room for the first time!"

"Can't wait." Symone walked a little faster to catch up with everyone. Karl opened the quarters, and everyone went straight through the commons to their residences. The nine rooms were arranged in an oval, with four rooms on the left, four rooms on the right, and one room at the end of the corridor. Karl entered his room on the left, closest to the common area. Duncan walked to his room, located across from Karl's on the right.

Malaysia escorted Symone to hers, saying, "Here's where you'll room, on the right, sandwiched between Alexia and Daisy. Hopefully, they got it all right for you. If they didn't, just talk to AI, and they'll modify the room to match your specs."

"Hey, I noticed there are nine rooms, but only seven of us," Symone investigated.

"Yes," Malaysia explained. "The director said that Elite Unit maxes out at nine, supposedly, though she's never said why, and the team has never risen above six until today. So, the room at the end of the hall and the room to its left, Malcolm's right, are both empty."

"Think those rooms will ever be filled?"

"Only time will tell. Anyway, I'll leave you to it. Great job today, new girl!"

"Thank you, Malaysia," Symone said.

Malaysia turned around and walked away to her room.

Symone slid her door to the right and entered her room, and the lights automatically turned on to greet her. Symone canvassed her new accommodations and couldn't believe her eyes. *This is definitely a step-up from the Underbelly! My parents would love this!* Everything in the room was white. To her left was the living room. A sofa and loveseat faced the right, where a holoscreen resided on the wall floating above a skinny table. A recessed light was in each corner of the ceiling. Separating the living room and the bedroom was an island with barstools, with the kitchen to the left and a half-bathroom on the right. Three lamps hung from the ceiling about five feet above the island. The kitchen wrapped along the left wall and the bedroom wall.

As Symone walked through the living room, a male voice bellowed, "Hello, Symone Watson. I hope this room meets your expectations. I have yet to outfit the room to meet your favorite color scheme, which is why everything is a variation of white. What colors would you like me to paint the room with?"

"Well, you can't go wrong with crimson and gold," Symone replied.

"Very good combination. Watch me work!" AI responded. Suddenly, the room bled with variations of crimson and gold, like an artist painting on a blank canvas. Symone's heart filled with joy as she saw her symbol on the wall behind the sofa – a nine-pointed star with flares shooting off it, and sparkles dancing around it, bathed in crimson and gold. She fought back tears as she walked to the bedroom.

The bedroom housed a king-sized bed with two nightstands on either side, facing the right, with ample space to walk around. AI bathed it, too, with variations of crimson and gold. A lamp shone on each nightstand. Recessed lights were located in the corners of the ceiling. The back wall of the room was all glass, overlooking Uri City. To her right was the entry to a walk-in closet and the adjoining bathroom. Symone walked in, and to her left, clothes, shoes, and drawers lined both sides of the closet extending about fifteen feet, with a mirror at the end of the closet shining her reflection. She kept walking forward into the bathroom. She turned to her left and saw a full sink, a toilet next to it, followed by a stand-in shower, and a step-down bathtub that Symone was sure was meant to be a mini-swimming pool.

"I have died and gone to glory," she said. "Come on, girl, Malcolm can leave at any moment. I don't want to miss my opportunity." Symone shook off her kid-at-Jubilee feelings and continued her pursuit of locking horns in a one-on-one skirmish with Malcolm. She quickly double-tapped her ripped uniform at the star symbol. The remaining nanites slid off her body and fed themselves into the pins they called home. She then twisted the pins to unlock them from her chest and walked to the closet. She remembered in orientation that Weapons and Wardrobe instructed her to look for a shelf labeled "U" for uniform and to place the buttons inside it. She looked at each drawer and found the "U" in the middle of the left side. She opened the small drawer, placed the buttons inside, and closed it. A small white light glowed inside the box. Symone, wearing only a sports bra, quickly looked through the closet and found a pair of jeggings, a simple white t-shirt, and a light jacket to put on. She grimaced from her bruises yet wasted no time getting dressed. She reached for the first pair of shoes she could grab to cover her feet. *Hopefully I can sneak out of here without anyone seeing me.*

She ran to her door and slid it open. She peeked around and sighed in relief that the doors were closed and no noise came from the commons or the kitchen. She darted away from her room, out of the residences, through the commons, past the kitchen, and out of the quarters. Malaysia peeked out of her room and noticed her sneaking out. *Mmm, hmm,* Malaysia cracked a smile and slinked back into her room.

Malcolm pressed his palm on the Analyst's door reader, then opened the door. Malcolm saw the Analyst sitting at his back desk facing the wall. "Analyst, what do you have for me?"

The Analyst turned around in his chair with a beam in his eye and clapped his hands. "Loads, Malcolm! Loads!" he replied. "You have to see this!" The Analyst got out of his seat and hurried to the desk in the middle of the room. Malcolm walked up to the same desk and took a seat next to him. The Analyst placed his right hand on the holoscreen on the desk and waved his hand upward and outward at the same time. That move took the contents of the screen, a combination of Malcolm's statistics and demographics and video footage, to the massive holoscreen on the wall facing them.

"Okay, so we know that you have the ability to manipulate any object, shape it, twist it, bend it, turn it into just about anything you want it to be."

"Right," Malcolm answered.

"And, you even have the ability to collect energy which keeps you and others from being hit by attacks from enemy forces."

"Yeah, I can pool power to a certain point before it becomes unstable."

"Right, but you've never been able to change an energy's trajectory. That," the Analyst gasped with glee, "that is something new, Malcolm!" He pressed "PLAY" on his counter keyboard, and the wall holoscreen displayed the recording from Malcolm's uniform button. It had been cued to the moment in Malcolm's last battle when he was pooling the heat rays from his opponent at the Sentinel Bank. It played to the moment when Malcolm raised his hand, and the collection of heat rays rose with it. The Analyst pressed "PAUSE," then said, "Right there, Malcolm, that was the moment when the energy moved with your hand."

Malcolm sat up, dazed in amazement. "Right, I remember that moment, right there."

"What happened? Can you explain it?"

"I don't know," Malcolm shrugged his shoulders and started mimicking his combat techniques as he narrated, "I mean, I was fighting with him, he shot his rays, and I started collecting them to make sure I didn't get hit. I remember looking at Symone kicking ass, and then my hands got tingly like I had lost the feeling in them, and it was rushing back. I could feel the heat rays in a way I've never felt anything else before in my life. It was like I could, I don't know, direct the energy, like, tell it not just what to do, but where to go. That's never happened before."

"And you didn't do anything new, say anything different? No secret spells or special moves?" the Analyst inquired.

"Nothing, it was just a feeling I got, and I went with it. I didn't have time to process it since we were all in battle."

"It was so cool!" the Analyst replied, nearly jumping out of his seat. "Like, you have evolved! You're already Elite, but if you keep this up, they might have to create a separate category for you, Malcolm. You should try to recreate this moment and see if we can get a full diagnostic in the training room."

"That's a great idea, I'll do that now. I wanted to get a training session in before I left today, anyway," Malcolm agreed as he rose from his chair.

"Your usual room is open. I'll be recording from here," the Analyst declared.

"I'll be down there in five," Malcolm responded. He walked to the door and exited Analysis. *I evolved, huh? Wow! Didn't think I'd hear those words again. Last time I evolved was, what, two, maybe three years ago?* He walked eagerly to the elevator and pressed the down arrow. The elevator opened, he walked in, pressed "T" for the training floor, and the doors closed just as Symone walked out of the quarters. She passed the elevator and walked toward Analysis.

She got to the door and hovered her hand over the palm reader on the wall, wondering whether her palm print would open it. She placed her hand on the reader, and to her surprise, the reader scanned her palm and lit white for approval, and Analysis's door opened. She walked in and scanned the room, only to find the Analyst walking back to his back desk. She asked, "Where's Bennett?"

The Analyst turned around and said, "Oh, Malcolm, you just missed him. He just left here two minutes ago."

"Oh, okay, thank you," Symone's countenance changed.

Before she could turn to walk out of the office, the Analyst continued, "While I have you here, Symone, I'd like to talk to you about your demos and stats if you have time."

"What about them?" Symone asked.

"Well, come and have a seat next to me." The Analyst returned to the seat in the middle of the floor. Symone pulled the same chair Malcolm sat in next to the Analyst as he pulled up Symone's demos and stats. He then pushed his hand upward and outward again, and the data was displayed on the wall holoscreen.

"We have your stats here, and as you know, we perform a multi-tiered composite of a person's abilities and character. The more complicated version of this is called the EvoCreatura Project." Symone and the Analyst looked at the wall and saw a vast series of numbers and letters surrounding a 3-D model of Symone standing with her arms crossed in her crimson and gold uniform. The letters and numbers looked like gibberish to Symone. "But to make it simpler for us, we compile all these numbers and synthesize these factors into three categories: Power, Skill, and Affinity."

The numbers all swooshed by and filtered under the three categories. Symone said, "So all these stats are filtered and that's how you come up with the three big numbers above me."

"Yes. The Power level rises from 0 to 3.9, with 0 being Normal or no powers, 1 being Powered, 2 being Super, and 3 Elite. The Skill rises from 0 to 4.9, with 0 being Normal or no skill, 1 Standard, 2 Advanced, 3 Veteran, and 4 Expert. Then Affinity is measured along a spectrum from Dark to Light, measured from +5 to 0 to +5.

"Your numbers are 3.1, 1.4, Dark +3. Or, at least, those were your stats this morning," the Analyst said with glee.

"What do you mean?" Symone asked, puzzled. "Did something change?"

"Yes. As you were in battle today at Sentinel, your stats shifted dramatically. It's unlike anything we've ever seen before."

"How do you figure that?" Symone wondered out loud.

"I can show you better than I can tell you." The Analyst cued up the tape from the battle at Sentinel Bank and Trust, playing the moment when Symone created a star to block her opponent's heat rays. He pressed "PAUSE" then said, "Right here, your stats are relatively the same, not a lot of fluctuation." He showed the tape and the stats side by side, demonstrating that the numbers stayed relatively around 3, 1, and Dark +3. "But then, at this moment, when your star, your eyes, and your hair started changing colors from yellow to white, your stats started climbing rapidly! Watch!"

The Analyst pressed "PLAY," and Symone watched herself make the star hotter as her hair and eyes changed colors to match. Simultaneously, her stats rose in the Power and Skill levels, rising from 3.1 to 3.5 in Power and from 1 to 2.7 in Skill.

"You see, we have never seen someone's Skill level rise that high in a single battle, in a single moment in battle no less, from Standard to almost Veteran. This is an exponential growth, the likes of which we haven't seen in history! Can you tell me what happened in that moment?"

Symone scratched her head, then gently pulled on a loc of her hair and turned in her seat to face the Analyst, replying, "Um, well, I got up after getting hit by the ray – no thanks to me not having my cloak on like a dumbass – to give him a beat down, but then as I flew toward him, he shot rays at me, and I made the star to block them. The rays were too strong, and I was getting pushed backward. I glanced at Malcolm and wondered if I should help him but couldn't do it without getting hit again, and then I felt my body get hotter. My hands were burning up, and the hotter they got, the hotter and whiter the star became. It was enough to shift the momentum in my favor, and I pushed myself and then the star forward to knock out my guy's cloak."

"That's it? No hidden incantations, secret codes, nothing?" the Analyst inquired.

Symone shook her head. "No, nothing, I didn't do anything differently than I had done in the past. Wow, you're telling me that I..."

"...evolved, yes, Symone!" the Analyst leaped out of his chair. "Oops, sorry, I'm just so excited, this is such an amazing event to witness! I've sent this to the director, and I'm sure she'll want to speak to you about it soon."

"How about that! Did you tell Bennett?" Symone asked.

"No, I just talked to him about how his stats changed, and then he went to the training floor," the Analyst slipped.

"Wait, his stats changed, too?" Symone's eyes flickered yellow.

"Crap!" the Analyst lowered his head, realizing his mistake. "I wasn't supposed to say that. You can't say anything to him."

Symone's right eyebrow raised slightly, and she replied, "I have no idea what you're talking about, Analyst. Thank you for your time and wisdom." She placed her hand on his shoulder and rose from her chair and exited Analysis.

The Analyst tapped on his counter keyboard to lock the big holoscreen and the desk holoscreen while remarking, "I have to learn to stop talking so much."

Symone walked toward the elevator just as Malaysia and Karl were leaving the quarters and heading toward it as well.

"Oh, there she is," Karl said. "Where were you?"

Symone didn't want to give away her intentions. "I went to Analysis to get some insight on my stats," Symone answered.

"Oh, boy, we have another *Malcolm Bennett* on our hands," Karl quipped.

Malaysia nodded her head in agreement as she pressed the down button on the wall. The doors opened immediately. As they entered the elevator, Malaysia said, "We sure do. No wonder the Company wanted him to train her. They're practically the same person."

Symone giggled, "No, there's no way we're the same person. He's an ogre, I'm nothing like that."

"Oh, okay. Let me ask you, where is Malcolm right now, Karl?" Malaysia asked as she pressed the "G" button for the street-level floor.

"Oh, he's definitely on the training floor by now," Karl answered as he crossed his arms.

"Right, and, uh, Symone, where are you going right now?" Malaysia inquired.

Symone knew she was caught. She didn't say anything. Malaysia and Karl looked at Symone, waiting for her to reply. Symone pressed "T" for the training floor.

"Mmm hmm," Malaysia chuckled, "that's what I thought."

"Well, I obviously need the practice. Couldn't even get the cloak to act right," Symone deflected.

"Hey, it happens," Karl said. "Probably just a malfunction. Double W will take a look at it and fix it. But just in case, do get some practice turning it on and off before the next time we suit up. Don't want you to get hurt unnecessarily out there. I'm the only one on the team who can heal fast."

"Noted," Symone answered.

Symone, Karl, and Malaysia rode the elevator to the street level, then the elevator stopped, and the doors opened, revealing the reception desk at the far end of the atrium. Malaysia and Karl exited and said, "Have fun training, Starburst!"

The elevator doors closed, and Symone traveled down several floors underground to the training floor. *Are we really that much alike? I'm definitely about to find out right now!*

The elevator stopped, and the doors opened. Symone walked out of the elevator and saw two vast corridors, one in front of her and the other running across. The floors were marble black, the ceilings rising one hundred yards high. Small white circular lights were attached to the walls about ten feet high. The walls were all black, with three-inch red stripes running parallel to the floor about five feet apart. Symone walked down the main corridor, hoping to find some sign of Malcolm's training room. Each room was actually two rooms sitting side-by-side. The doors were opaque and had two palm readers in between them: one for the room itself, and the other for the observation room. Symone walked the corridor until she found a room that read "DEFENDER: Bennett, M." on a scrolling marquee above his room's doors. Symone decided to watch Malcolm train so she could study him before squaring up with him. She placed her hand on the observation palm reader. It glowed white for approval, and the observation door slid open. She walked into a low-lit room with one-way glass from the ceiling to the floor facing the training room. A table with two holoscreens sat at the back of the room across from the door. She saw Malcolm, pulled a chair from the table, and planted it as close to the glass as she could. She sat down and leaned forward, pushing her locs out of her face.

The training room was an atrium one hundred yards in every direction. The walls, ceiling, and floor of the training room were all cobalt gray, with light strips running vertically, spread ten feet apart. The strips mimicked the stripes on their arms and provided illumination for the entire room. The walls were also cloaked so as not to get destroyed by anyone's powers. Malcolm had several random shards, chunks, and shapes of metal around him. He picked up a metal pipe with his left hand, and he hovered his right hand over the pipe, causing it to bend into a curve. He continued to hover-stroke his hand across the pipe until it sharpened, transforming into an oversized sickle. He then swung the sickle around a few times, held it parallel to the floor close to his face, and used his right hand and powers to straighten and stretch the sword to a needle point. He then took the sword in his right hand, thrust the sword forward twice, then swiftly swung his wrist to perform a parry.

Symone gazed delightfully, analyzing how quickly he manipulated the metal from one weapon to another, and admiring his fighting skills with each weapon he created. Her mind vacillated between his techniques, his skills, and his physique. *It's so effortless, how he switches from one combat technique to another without hesitating. He's an absolute beast!*

Her eyes absorbed every inch of his toned body, admiring the way his chiseled chest popped out of his shirt, the subtle way his muscles flexed when he bent his arms when he extended the weapons he crafted. She kept shifting herself in her seat while her mind and body began playing a game of tug-of-war as to which would be stimulated more. A gnawing passion built up in the pit of her stomach and began to consume her heart. Every time Malcolm sliced the air, her nostrils flared. She examined him and paid close attention to how he breathed, the subtle ticks in his facial expressions, and the sweat dripping from his forehead. Watching him was like listening to a symphony, watching a dance, and Symone was tranced.

No one in my prizefighting days can compare to him.

"Okay," Malcolm said, "initiate Defense Exercise 208."

A female voice responded, "Initiating Defense Exercise 208."

Malcolm double-tapped the middle of his chest. The cloak shimmered and then turned transparent in response. Three slits about ten feet high emerged from the walls of the back side of the training room. The panels the slits created slid to the left, and three robots armed with simple laser cannons rolled onto the training floor. The panels then slid back and closed. Symone gazed on as Malcolm picked up a metal pipe from the floor, opened both palms face up with the pipe in both hands, and the pipe flattened and stretched, and two handles protruded from the flat surface. Malcolm slid his right arm into the handles and lifted the shield to his chest. *Alright, let's see what happens. Just make the lasers move.* "Fire when ready," he said as he stood directly in the robots' lines of fire.

The three robots began shooting continuous beams his way, and he lifted his left hand to pool the beams directly in front of him, just before the beams could touch the shield. Malcolm focused his mind on trying to move the beams but couldn't do it. They collected, and the ball got bigger and more unstable, setting off sparks and tiny lightning bolts. Malcolm took the shield and rammed it into the collection to send it hurling toward the wall. It exploded on impact. The robots did not stop shooting, so Malcolm spun to not get hit by the beams. Malcolm stepped closer to the observation room, unknowingly showing Symone his backside. *What am I doing wrong?*

The robots blasted him again. He pooled the rays a second time and tried to move them, and still could not reproduce what he had performed at Sentinel Bank. The rays grew unstable again, and he again took his shield and batted away the collection into the wall. He rolled toward the training room entrance and pooled laser beams once more, only to achieve the same result and garner the same response. Growing increasingly frustrated, he rolled away and tried again, but failed once more. In his agitation, he miscalculated a roll and was hit by one of the beams. It knocked him on his back. Symone's eyes widened, and she shot up out of the chair, placing her hand on the window as if she was trying to reach out to him. Fire flowed through her veins, her heart raced, and she gasped for air. *Get up,* she thought.

Malcolm rolled backward, landing on one knee, and rolled toward the ob-servation room, standing next to the wall. His back was to Symone, where her hand touched the window. The robots continued their assault, and Malcolm collected the beams. "Come on man, you can do this," he said to himself. Symone's pupils dilated and glowed yellow like the sun as her competing desires of wanting Malcolm and wanting him to succeed churned inside. Malcolm felt an unusual surge of energy near him. He recognized it as the same weird energy signature that Symone carried and wondered, *How am I feeling her energy right now? She's nowhere near me, and these rooms are cloaked. I shouldn't be feeling anything but what's inside this room. Where is it coming from?* Suddenly, Malcolm began to feel his hands tingle again. The senses in his left palm felt the rays differently, just like at Sentinel. He moved his left hand slightly to the left, and the pool of rays shifted in the same direction. Letting out a whoop while trying not to break his concentration due to excitement, he then flipped his hand palm-up and raised his arm. As he did so, he observed not only the ball of rays rising, but also the laser beams being redirected to the pool, despite the robots aiming their cannons at Malcolm. The collection enlarged but was contained and stabilizing the longer Malcolm held it in place.

Symone was caught up, not realizing that Malcolm was supercharging her energy as he drew power from her. She released control of her body and flowed with the compulsion to levitate. Her eyes glowed like stars, and her hair's color changed from jet black to yellow, and a yellow aura framed her petite body. Malcolm dropped his shield and raised his right hand in the air. He then swirled his arms while keeping his palms flat, and the lasers continued to collect and swirl in a big ball of beams. He then lowered his arms parallel to the ground, and the ball of beams lowered in front of him between him and the robots. He then took his arms and flattened his palms, left palm face up, right palm face down, hovered his hands over each other, then flattened his hands together. The ball of energy flattened into a single parallel beam. He then thrust his arms and hands forward, and the ray of energy launched forward. It sliced through the robots, dismantled their cannons, and crashed into the back wall, causing a large explosion. Malcolm roared with the sound of victory, pushing his chest up in the air, arms extended downward.

Symone didn't want to give her position away or destroy the observation room, but she had to release some of the tension she felt. She let a few sparks flow from her hands to release some of the pressure, hoping it would be enough to keep her from pouncing on Malcolm once he came out of the training room. She lowered herself back to the ground, the aura dissipated, her eyes returned to their original brown, and her hair returned to jet black. *Where the Frimas did this feeling come from? Do I want him that much? I don't even know him like that. But I want him. I have to figure out why! If he makes me feel this alive just standing near him, imagine what he can make me feel if he's entangled with me!*

Malcolm breathed with huffs of joy. He felt he successfully reproduced what happened at Sentinel. He looked up at the walls knowing the cameras were rolling and said, "Analyst, I hope you captured all of that!"

The Analyst replied, "Yes, I got all of it! Analyzing it now and should have some good insight for you in the next couple days."

"Okay," Malcolm said. He was so excited to have evolved, he couldn't wait to repeat it. "Again," Malcolm voiced.

Symone, listening to every word, belted, "Aww, Frimas naw!" She felt she would end up destroying the observation room if she watched Malcolm set the room on fire again. She decided to take a chance and go into the training room and turn her budding fantasy into reality, to release the tension longing to erupt and explode out of her by sinking her claws into him in a brawl.

She burst out the observation room and placed her palm on the training room reader. It glowed white for approval, and the door unsealed. AI responded, "Symone Watson, codename Starburst. Modifying room to meet powered state."

Malcolm turned and admired Symone's silhouette as his eyes adjusted to the contrast between the corridor and the training room. "Miss Watson, what are you doing here?"

Symone composed herself. She walked up to Malcolm. "I've been looking for you since you left to talk with the Analyst. Everybody said you would be down here, so I thought I'd come and see if we could talk, you know, mentor to mentee."

"Okay," Malcolm said, "what would you like to talk about?"

Symone didn't hesitate. "I want to spar with you!"

"Is that right?" Malcolm asked. Wanting to see where Symone's head was, he volleyed, "And why do you want to spar with me?" He expected a fanboy's answer, something along the lines of, *You're a legend, you're so amazing, I've heard stories about you, you're the best fighter I've ever seen,* answers that rarely fazed him.

"Why not?" she returned.

Slightly stunned, he said, "What?"

"I said, why not?"

Malcolm blinked twice to wake his brain up. "No. I don't spar with anyone."

Symone looked puzzled. "No? That doesn't make sense, 'I don't spar with anyone.' How do you expect to get better if you don't spar with anyone?"

"That's what the training room is for. I get better in here. And so will you. Just not while I'm in it."

"Bennett, that doesn't make sense."

"It doesn't have to. But, hey, if you want a sparring partner, you should ask Duncan or Alexia. Both could use a sidekick in the room with them." Malcolm walked toward the exit.

"Bennett," Symone slightly chuckled, "Come on. You're kidding right? Newbie hazing. You're going to spar with me, right, *mentor*?"

"No, you and I are not going to spar with each other. Great job today, though. I'm really proud of your performance at Sentinel. Next time, though, how about you turn on your cloak?" Malcolm winked at her.

Symone wouldn't let it go. "So, you're just not going to spar with me, ever?"

"Ever."

Malcolm walked out of the room, and AI responded, "Malcolm Bennett, codenamed Kingdom Come, left room. Modifying room to meet powered state." Symone looked perplexed.

Malcolm walked down the corridor to the elevator. He pressed up and waited for the elevator to meet him. He thought, *Symone is an interesting woman. No one has ever stepped to me and wanted to spar with me just because. What is it with her? Should I go back in there and say 'yes'? No, remember what your therapist said. You know full well what happens when you get close to somebody too soon, especially when sparring. Do what you were told and mentor her. Her skills on the battlefield are mesmerizing, she definitely has a gift. What is it about her power that is so alluring to me? I've never felt anything like it before. If she can channel it better, she'll make one Frim of an Elite Defender soon. Just focus on keeping her alive until the mission is complete.* The doors opened, and Malcolm walked in, pressed "E" for the Elite Grand Hall, and the doors closed, and the elevator launched toward its destination.

Symone stood in the training room, the pressurized energy still raging inside her with nowhere for it to go. Her mind fluctuated between her frustration with Malcolm's flippant response toward her, her desire to take him down in battle, and her growing crush on him. She couldn't shake the fire flowing in her veins.

What the Frimas is wrong with me? What's got me acting like this? This doesn't make sense! I've gotta let this out. I hope the room can handle this. She concentrated more than she had ever before. She levitated, her eyes glowed, and an aura surrounded her. Symone raised her hands in the air, and a fireball grew above them. It enlarged quickly to about thirty feet in diameter. Her hair shimmered yellow as the star raged. Lightning struck from the star as Symone began to scream. Her focus shifted her energy, and her eyes glowed from yellow to white, her hair changed from yellow to white, and the star above her changed from yellow to white. She unleashed the star above her head to the ceiling one hundred yards above, and it exploded into billions of glittering sparks as she fell to her knees and palms on the ground. Her locs dangled from her head and instantly changed back to jet black, her eyes back to brown, and she breathed rapidly and heavily.

She turned and lay flat on the ground as she recovered from the blast. Her frustration resolved to focus. As she rubbed her stomach and her neck, Symone reasoned to herself, *You're going to fight me, Malcolm Bennett.*

7

Second Day

The clock on Symone's wall read 27:59. The first sun was itching to make its grand appearance across the horizon. Symone peacefully slumbered in her bedroom as she lay under a thin blanket wearing a bra and pajama pants. Her subtle snores cut through the silence inside her small apartment as the rush of hovercraft and cars outside marked the start of a new day in Uri City. Flashes of the battle from the day before dominated Symone's dreams, a soothing fantasy to her soul. She was floating in the air on the seventh floor of the Sentinel Bank, having evolved as she blocked the heat ray from her target. She launched the whitened star toward her opponent and landed on the ground. Malcolm walked up to her from behind and disabled his visor, saying, "Who are you?"

"Your sweetest dream, and your worst nightmare," she replied as she spun to her right to face him and swung her left arm, fist aglow with energy, aimed at his face. He didn't fall for the ambush. He blocked her arm with his right arm, grabbed her wrist, swung her arm behind her, and pulled her in close, and they touched chest to chest. Their cloaks shimmered in response to their embrace.

He stared deeply into Symone's eyes and responded, "You don't know what you're getting yourself into, Miss Watson." He swiftly thrust his left palm into the star in the middle of her chest and launched her caving body into the air. She flipped midair and landed on her left knee and right toe, quickly composed herself with her right palm planted on the ground, then blasted herself off the ground and rushed toward him as he rushed toward her. They bear-hugged and barrel rolled until their momentum stopped, with Symone sitting on top of Malcolm's waist. She breathed with joy as she stared into the windows of his soul. He rose to embrace her. He pressed his hands against her back and gently pushed her toward him to kiss her.

00:00. Symone's alarm broke the silence in the room. The first sun broke the horizon and set the sky on fire. Daylight flooded Symone's room through the windows above her bed. Symone's eyes slowly cracked open, and she stretched to shake the sleep from her body, then pounded her fists in frustration that her dream was interrupted. She rose and planted her feet to the bed's right side, excited to start her second day as an Elite. She stood up, rushed out of her bedroom door and turned right to enter her bathroom. She showered, brushed her teeth, and picked out a pair of black denim jeggings, a spaghetti-strapped gold shirt, and a light crimson jacket from her closet across from the bathroom. She slid on some socks and a pair of tennis shoes, expecting to do a lot of walking around HQ. She then hauled out of the hallway, straight through her living room to her front door, and placed her hand on her door's palm reader, which lit white for approval. She walked out of her door and to the balcony of her apartment complex.

Today is going to be a great day! She shot into the sky like out of a cannon from her seventeenth-story balcony, flying from the Underbelly district to the Company in Highgarden.

Across the city in Genesis Landing, Malcolm sat up in his bed, performing his grounding techniques after waking from the same nightmare from the previous night. Like most mornings, he felt conflicted and struggled to trace any connection between yesterday's events and his nightmare. *Was it something I watched? Something someone said? Maybe the bank job, but it wasn't even that big of a fight. I didn't spend any time listening to anything. I don't know.* He looked around and saw the clock read 00:14 on his nightstand, and the first sun raced to dominate the sky. He shook his head and rose from the bed, exposing his near-naked body to the crisp air in the room. He walked to the bathroom, showered, then went to the kitchen and opened the refrigerator door, pulling out an egg carton and cheese. He lifted his left arm and triple-tapped his wrist to turn on the holoscreen in the living room to cut through the silence. He said, "Switch to UNN."

The holoscreen shimmered and displayed the Uri City News Network. He squatted and opened a cupboard and pulled out a frying pan. A woman's voice on the holoscreen said, "...where three suspects attempted to steal the city's currency before the Company's Elite Unit arrived on the scene, disarmed the suspects, and rescued every person in the building. Three security guards died in the robbery attempt."

Malcolm opened the egg carton to pull three eggs out. *We did good. I wish we could have saved those guards, though.* He cracked the eggs in the frying pan. He then held the pan with his left hand and extended his right hand, palm up, under the pan. He concentrated, and the frying pan started to heat up, sizzling the eggs within it.

Meanwhile, a fair-skinned woman in a red dress with long, black hair continued talking, "Uri City's Chancellor Croft announced yesterday that he intends to continue his push for powered individuals to hold city offices. He made a statement at a press conference at City Hall in Midtown."

The screen cut to Chancellor Croft, the leader of Uri City, standing behind a podium and in front of a blue sheet with the city seal, a circle with the letter "C" nestled inside the curve of the letter "U," embroidered on it. Croft was an older, tall, dark-skinned man with a silver afro a few inches above his scalp. Wearing a purple and red-striped robe and gold-rimmed glasses, he declared, "It has long been unfair for the unpowered to be the only ones eligible to hold office, when the powered make up nearly 70% of our population. To ensure fairer representation in government, we must allow the powered to be eligible for offices and let their voices not just be heard, but also felt within every fabric of Uri City. It's not fair that we ask the powered to entertain us, to fight wars for us, to work and pay fares and taxes, but then exclude them from making decisions that impact the world we share. I am working diligently with our officials to put an end to this nonsense and give them the opportunity to speak for themselves in these very halls I walk through every single day."

Malcolm's eggs finished cooking, and he slid them onto a plate as the show cut back to the woman in red. "Senator Dariuz, a staunch opponent against this move, had this to say in response."

A much older, bald, pruned-skinned man wearing a trench coat was displayed on the screen. He was talking outside a glass-paned building. "The last thing we need is for the powered to reenter our government system. How can we trust the powered to not use their powers to impose their will on the weak? We were barely successful in expelling the last powered Chancellor over 150 years ago when he and his minions tried to enslave Uri City. Why would we put our beloved city in jeopardy like that again? It is a slippery slope that we cannot afford to slide down. As long as I'm in the Senate," Dariuz pointed at himself, "Croft will never see legislation pass that will give the powered that right."

"Here is your weather forecast…," the woman continued as Malcolm grabbed two slices of bread and sandwiched a slice of cheese and the eggs between them. He walked back into his bedroom to stare outside while taking a huge bite out of his breakfast. He contemplated his agenda for the day, recalling the moment in the training room when he moved the ball of laser beams. *I have to debrief with the director about yesterday's bank job, then talk with the Analyst, train, eat something, talk with the team, train again, then roll out. Should be light. I probably should call my folks at some point today, too, check in on them.*

Once he finished his sandwich, Malcolm sat at the edge of his bed and recalled, *Wait, I forgot about Symone. I'll have to rethink my day. I think I'll put her in the training room today and get a sense of who I'm working with.* Malcolm walked over to his dresser and pulled on the drawers to find a pair of black jeans, an active blue shirt, and a black hoodie jacket. He slid into his clothes and laced up his sneakers that sat next to the dresser. He then pressed his left wrist and activated a voice in his head and made his stripe light up. "Yes, Malcolm?" the AI responded.

"Play 'Give Me More' by Madam Reila," Malcolm said.

"Playing 'Give Me More' by Madam Reila. Enjoy the rising of the suns, Malcolm!"

"I always do on days like this," Malcolm replied as he walked out of his apartment. He passed four doors and pushed the down arrow for the elevator at the end of the hall. The elevator ran up the shaft to meet him. The doors opened as Malcolm mouthed the words, "I know that this feels like a dream/tasty like the smoothest scoop of ice cream/baby it's you that I adore/won't you come over and give me more." The doors closed, and the elevator lowered Malcolm to ground level.

He walked off the elevator and out of the building, meeting a busy street of passersby and hovercraft of all shapes and sizes, zooming past to their destinations. He pressed his right index finger on his left wrist twice and waited while mouthing, "Where were you before me/can you even remember/what life was like before me/our time is forever." Just then, a black hoverbike pulled up next to Malcolm. He straddled the seat and double-tapped his chest, and his cloak shimmered, then disappeared. He grabbed the handlebars, revved up his bike, then quickly accelerated into the sky toward Highgarden.

Symone soared to get above the skyscrapers. She closed her eyes and basked in the radiance of the atmosphere as the first sun continued bathing the city with light. She leveled and plotted her course to Highgarden. She slowly spun around and admired the hovercraft and other people who had the ability to fly, all dominating the air. Symone joyfully breathed in and exhaled.

She heard a hum in her ear and looked at her left arm; it read: "Incoming call from 'Mom.'" She said, "Answer. Hi, Mom!"

"Symone!" her mom answered. "I just saw the morning news! They got a video of you fighting with the Elite?! Why didn't you call us yesterday and tell us?"

"I'm sorry, Mom, I was so overwhelmed yesterday with everything, when I got home, I just went to sleep. I haven't slept that long or hard in quarters."

"It's probably good you did. You've never been the best sleeper," Symone's mom replied. "Well, I know you're probably on your way to work. Your dad and I just wanted to tell you that we are so proud of you and look forward to seeing you on the screen more often."

"Our baby girl is an Elite! You did it, Symone! So proud!" a strong, bellowed voice was heard in the background of the call.

"You heard your dad?" Symone's mom asked.

"I did, tell him thank you!" Symone answered, holding back a tear.

"Be careful out there, Star. I love you!"

"Love you, too, Mom," Symone responded. "I'll call you soon. Bye!" The call disconnected, and Symone pushed herself harder to fly faster toward the Company, a yellow streak following behind her.

Symone suddenly felt a heavy presence following her. She tried to shake the feeling, but the closer she got to Highgarden, the heavier the presence became. She soon noticed the sun no longer shining down on her. She twisted her body to face the sky and examined a small hovercraft flying about fifteen feet above her.

Her stripe lit up and revealed a newly made friend calling her. Symone said, "Answer."

"Hi, Symone!"

"Malaysia?" Symone answered. "Girl, is that you above me? Frimas, you scared me, don't do that. Thought I was about to fight somebody."

Malaysia was sitting in the cockpit of a single-occupant hovercraft. "Well, maybe not fight. But do you want to race to the Company?" she asked.

"Frimas, why not? Let's go!" Symone's hair and eyes shone yellow, and she burst forward. Malaysia revved up her hovercraft's engine, and the boosters blasted her forward. They raced past hovercraft and other levitators, trying to outduel each other on their way to the Company. Symone noticed that the second sun began to break the horizon.

Malcolm noticed it, too, as he bobbed his head back and forth to his playlist. He whizzed past hovercraft and flyers, then descended toward the thirty-story glass building the Company called headquarters. He pressed a button on the left bike handle which opened a bay of windows on the twentieth floor of the tower. He flew into the bay and landed his bike on a circular concrete pad about twelve feet in diameter in the middle of the garage. He got off the bike. As he stepped off the pad, his bike guided itself into a parking spot along the wall. He walked toward the elevator and pressed the up arrow. The elevator doors opened, and he walked in and pressed "E". The doors closed, the elevator shot him to the Elite Grand Hall, and the doors opened. He walked out of the elevator and walked casually to the conference room. He met Daisy and Karl at the door outside of the room. "Don't let me interrupt, I'm just going to go in and take my seat," he said.

"Oh, it's no interruption," Daisy, wearing a blue crop top and white leggings, said as she turned to face Malcolm. "We were just talking about how the news captured Karl's massive guns catching those goons out of the window."

"I got a lot of muscle to capture," Karl joked as he slowly raised his arms and flexed his biceps through his tank top," so it's not surprising. But hey, all of us did great. Considering what happened the night before, we got ourselves a win."

"Yeah, we did," Malcolm agreed. "Hopefully, we can build on that momentum, or at least enjoy a few days of quiet."

"Oh, Frimas naw, no more quiet days," Duncan came around the corner, overhearing the conversation. "I loved yesterday! We need more missions to complete! I say bring on the noise!"

"Well," Karl said, "you could go back to a Super team. They stay busy."

"That actually wouldn't be a bad idea. We should mention that to the director!" Malcolm said sarcastically.

"Haha, very funny," Duncan said.

"Who said I was joking?" Malcolm asked as he patted Duncan's shoulder. Duncan swiftly pushed Malcom's hand off his shoulder.

"Oh, stop picking on Duncan, Mal," Daisy said. "You know he's a part of this team and isn't going anywhere. It will probably do you some good to cool it just a tad, Duncan, but you are right. Yesterday was fun."

"No, last night was fun," Alexia said as she opened the conference room door from the inside. "Had such an amazing time in Leicester." She closed her eyes and inhaled deeply as she reminisced on her experience the night before.

"I can imagine you had enough fun for all of us," Malcolm said, holding the door for everyone to walk inside the conference room. They all took their seats.

Symone and Malaysia continued their sky clash, descending toward the top of the Company tower and splitting between skyscrapers. Symone lost sight of Malaysia and focused on the tower. Out of nowhere, Malaysia cut Symone off on her right, causing Symone to stall and divert left to compensate. Malaysia pushed the gas and blasted toward the landing pad of the tower as Symone gritted her teeth in slight frustration while internally enjoying Malaysia's well-timed diversion. Malaysia landed her craft on the pad, and Symone planted her feet next to Malaysia's hovercraft.

Malaysia's windshield opened like a clam shell, and she hopped out of her craft saying, "Not bad, Symone, not bad."

Symone laughed, "I saw what you did there, that was a slick move at the end, wasn't expecting that."

They walked off the pad, and Malaysia's craft disappeared into the parking garage. Symone and Malaysia walked to the elevator and pushed the down arrow. Malaysia replied, "Gotta keep you on your toes. Being able to see everything has its advantages."

"Yes, so tell me how that works, Malaysia," Symone pondered. "What all can you see?"

As the elevator door opened, Malaysia responded, "Well, the simplest way to explain it is like wearing a pair of glasses with interchangeable lenses that I use to manipulate the way I see things. I can command my eyes to switch frequencies so that I can see different things in different ways. I can see in the dark. I can see through walls. I can see in between things, like the bra you're wearing behind your shirt. I can change between x-ray and infrared, zoom in and out, all with a flip of a command in my head."

The elevator rushed downward toward the Elite Grand Hall. "How have you been able to get your powers to evolve like that? That's really impressive!" Symone exclaimed.

"To be honest, it was the Company. When they brought me on board six years ago, my powers were severely underdeveloped. At most, I could see through walls, people, and in the dark. Malcolm truly pushed me to take my eyesight to another level, and he continues to challenge me to explore the full extent of my abilities. He's the reason I'm even on the Elite Unit."

"Seems like he's an amazing leader," Symone stated.

"He really is," Malaysia answered. "Every last person who has worked with him did not leave him the same."

"So, I'm curious," Symone inquired. "How did he get you to this level? Have you sparred with him in the training room?"

"Who? Malcolm?" Malaysia laughed. "Oh, no, that's one thing none of us has ever done with him. He does not train with anybody in the room with him. I asked him about it, and he said to me," Malaysia mimicked Malcolm's voice, "'The training room provides everything we need to be our best,' and suggested that we spar with others, but never with him."

The elevator stopped at the Elite Grand Hall, and the doors opened. They walked toward the conference room as Symone continued her investigation. "What is that all about? Do you think he's afraid of something?"

"You know, I never asked him. But I have my suspicions. There are layers to Malcolm that he does not want any of us to get up under, and even with my sight, I can't see everything he's got going on. I can't knock his method, though, because this brother is training the Frimas out of all of us, and we're getting stronger every day. And you're getting the special mentor treatment, so I can't wait to see what becomes of you when he's done with you."

"Neither can I," Symone reacted.

Malaysia noticed Symone's heart flutter just a little when she said that. *Mmm hmm, this is going to be interesting.*

They opened the conference room door and found the rest of the team chatting away to pass the time.

"The gang's all here," Duncan said with arms raised. Symone looked around the room and saw two empty chairs, one next to Malcolm – who sat in the middle of the table – on his right side, and another in between Duncan – who sat at the end of the right side of the table – and Alexis. She watched as Malaysia walked toward the right side of the table, and she moved toward the left to take the seat next to Malcolm. Malcolm had his hands propped on his head as he listened to the team banter on about nothing.

Symone eagerly sat down next to Malcolm and said, "Hello, Bennett."

"Good morning, Miss Watson," Malcolm responded, not moving an inch. "You ready for today?"

"Ready for what?" she asked.

He then turned to face her. "Well, we have a lot to run through over the next few days, so I'm just making sure you're prepared for a lot of long days at my hip."

"Sure it's nothing I can't handle," Symone quipped.

Malcolm chuckled softly, "I'm sure. After the meeting with the director, I'm going to talk to the Analyst, then we'll hit up the training room for a little bit." Symone's eyes slowly glowed yellow in excitement. Malcolm noticed it and said, "Don't get too excited. I'm going to watch you work and see exactly what you can do, establish a baseline."

Without skipping a beat, Symone locked eyes with Malcom and asked, "Is that all you're going to do? *Watch*?"

Malcolm immediately caught what Symone threw. *Was that a pass?* He smiled and bantered in kind, "I *might* take some notes."

He caught it! Symone's right eyebrow raised slightly. "You might have a hard time scribing them."

"Oh really? And..."

Just as Malcolm was about to deliver another line, the doors opened, and Director Mallack walked into the conference room. "Good morning, team, sorry I am late. Hope everyone had a great night. I can't stay long, so let's review yesterday's bank job."

Damn it, Director! What were you going to say, Malcolm?

Malcolm was equally frustrated. *Damn it, moment's gone now.*

Mallack walked to the holoscreen and tapped her finger, which made the holoscreen reveal three video shots of the Sentinel Bank. Symone focused on what everyone was talking about. She heard the director ask Malcolm what the plan was to resolve the emergency, and he answered her detailing what every person was responsible for. Mallack asked each person a series of questions, going back and forth between the screen and the defender.

Mallack enlarged the middle screen, which showed Symone, Malcolm, and Duncan engaging the three suspects. She fast-forwarded through the battle, then paused at the moment Symone was hit with the heat ray in her shoulder. "Symone, right here, you were hit with a beam, and it knocked you back hard. What happened with your cloak? The Analyst reported that it wasn't a malfunction. You never turned it on."

Oh Akan, here we go. Symone answered, "I thought I had turned it on, Director. When I tapped it, my visor came on, and I assumed the cloak came on with it. I tapped the buttons wrong. I was so excited to be in battle, I didn't check to make sure I was secure."

"That's on me, Director," Malcolm spoke up, to Symone's surprise. "I should have ensured everyone's equipment was secure."

"Well, make sure it doesn't happen again," Mallack said. "We can't afford to lose anyone in battle on a technicality like that. I'll make sure to tell Double W to check on the alert system because your uniform should have warned you that you were uncloaked."

"Right," Symone replied.

"It won't happen again, Director," Malcolm declared.

"It's fine. Mistakes happen. Just do better next time. Moving on...." Mallack continued to review the footage, and a few minutes later, finished her debrief on the bank job. Symone swooned slightly. *Did Malcolm just stand up for me? Hard to bring the wall down, huh?*

Mallack continued, "Again, great job, everyone. This was a good recovery mission, and everyone did well. A couple of things before we dismiss. One, we cannot forget the Collector is our top priority for this unit. If Intelligence gets any information regarding the Collector, stop what you are doing and report to them immediately. The Company and the city are counting on us hunting and taking him down.

"Second, I don't know if you're paying attention to the news, but tensions are rising in the city regarding Chancellor Croft's push for the powered holding offices in government. We are still unsure whether a proposition will get on the ballot during the election, but whatever the outcomes may be, it will affect us. Watch your backs when you are off duty. Any questions?" Silence filled the room. "Malcolm?"

Malcolm raised his head, "No, nothing, boss."

"Alright, have a good day, everyone. Stay alert," Mallack walked out of the room. Everyone rose from their chairs and exited the room. Malcolm and Symone walked out last. As they exited, Malaysia turned around in the hallway and approached Malcolm.

"If you're not busy later, I want to run something by you," she said to him.

"Sure thing. Everything alright?" Malcolm asked with a concerned look.

"Yes, everything's fine. It's not urgent. Just come find me when you have a chance."

"I'll call you when I'm free. Answer the call."

"I'm not the one who has a problem answering calls, Malcolm, you know that," Malaysia quipped.

Malcolm chuckled, "You're not wrong, I know." Malaysia turned around. The three turned the corner. Malaysia stopped at the elevator while Malcolm and Symone continued walking in the direction of the Analyst.

"So, Watson, I assume you've been here long enough to know just about everything there is to know about the Company, right?"

Symone replied, "I'm sure I don't know everything, but I know enough to make my way around here."

"Fair enough. So, rather than give you a whole rundown all over again, I'm going to let you ask me questions, and I'll answer them. No question is off-limits, so don't hesitate to ask me whatever you want to know."

"Are you sure about that?" Symone asked.

Malcolm responded, "Yes. As I'm mentoring you, I'm going to make mental notes of what I'm observing and determine what I can do to make you the best defender you can be. I'll teach you everything I can until they believe we're done. Once that happens, the Company will decide what's next for you."

Symone squinted and smirked. "All business, huh? Sounds so cut and dry, 'the Company will decide what's next.'"

Malcolm shrugged his shoulders. "Well, yeah, that's pretty much how it goes. Whatever the Company wants, the Company gets. I'm your mentor because they asked for it. You're Elite because they said you are."

They arrived at the Analyst's lab. Malcolm placed his palm on the reader to unlock the door as Symone responded, "Something doesn't sit well on my heart with that. They 'said,' I'm Elite? What does that even mean, 'they said?'"

"Well, I don't know how else to put it except, 'they said.' HQ decides just about everything that goes on here. The Company is bigger than just us, this unit, this city."

The door slid open. The Analyst turned his chair as Malcolm and Symone entered and continued their discussion. "I get that. The Company is in every city on Uretha. Clearly, city defense is bigger and more complex than anything I can wrap my mind around. I just don't like that someone's making choices about me, about any of us, and we don't get a say in the matters."

"I never said we don't get a say," Malcolm rebutted.

"It doesn't sound like you had a say in mentoring me, Bennett," Symone challenged.

"Um, hi there!" the Analyst interrupted.

Malcolm silenced his mind, wanting to respond to Symone's keen observation, but believing that arguing with her would slow them down, and he was anxious to get to the training room. "Right, sorry, Analyst. I wanted to talk to you about what happened in the training room yesterday."

Symone looked frustrated, thinking to herself, *So, we're just gonna not finish our conversation?* She determined to stick a mental pin in that issue and to return to it soon while focusing on Malcolm and the Analyst's discussion.

"Right," the Analyst answered to Malcolm. "Is it okay that Symone is in here?"

"Yes, it's okay." Malcolm and Symone grabbed chairs and sat at the desk in the middle of the room as the Analyst walked from his back desk to meet them.

"Alright, so yesterday, as you fought through 208, your cloak analyzed your biorhythms to deduce the moment when you were able to activate this next level to your abilities. At first," the Analyst changed the holoscreen displaying footage of Malcolm's training, "you didn't change at all. Everything held steady. When you rolled toward the left side of the room, your biorhythms began to shift. When you rolled away toward the entrance, your biorhythms dialed down. You're hit at that point, and the biorhythms calculated an increase in adrenaline, but no change that would suggest that getting hit would make your powers evolve. You rolled toward the left side of the room again, and it's here," the Analyst paused the footage, "where your biorhythms changed again."

Malcolm and Symone looked at Malcolm's position in the room, directly behind the observation room. They were unable to see that Symone stood in the room directly behind Malcolm. "So, wait, you're saying that standing next to this specific wall is what makes my biorhythms change?" Malcolm inquired. "What's so special about this wall?"

"I can't say, Malcolm," the Analyst shrugged his shoulders and raised his hands. "I'm trying to understand it myself. There is nothing in the room, nor anything in the walls themselves, that would have made you change. We're not sure if it's environmental, tactile, or psychological, but the tape doesn't lie. Whenever you're in this spot, right here," the Analyst typed keys on the counter keyboard. He displayed an enhanced floor plan of the training room and circled the spot where Malcolm stood, "your powers evolved. We will want to study it again soon to see if we can further understand what's happening."

Symone quickly reported, "I watched you training, Bennett, and I saw when you made the change. I don't know how you did it, but it happened."

"You were watching me?" Malcolm said as he turned to face her.

The Analyst leaned forward to see Symone's face and chimed in, "What did you see?"

Symone got slightly flustered, "Well, um, just that once he rolled away from that wall," she pointed to the screen, "he started pooling the lasers together and didn't move them with his hands, so he slapped the beams away, but then misjudged his position and got hit. He did this sick move to recover his footing, then rolled back to the wall you're talking about, and somehow, he was able to pool and move the beams. It was awesome!"

"Did you see anything in the room, anything with him, anything that might be a clue?"

Symone searched her mind, then replied, "No, I can't think of a thing that was different. One moment he couldn't move them, and the next, he could. You saw the footage."

"Okay," Malcolm said as he clasped his knees and stood up. "Well, I'll just have to run it again. We're not going to figure it out in here today." Symone mimicked Malcolm and stood up, too.

"True, true, true," the Analyst replied as he typed on the keyboard and powered down the holoscreen. "When will you go back in the room?"

"Sometime today. Right now, it's Miss Watson's turn."

Symone's eyes flickered yellow. "Fantastic!" she said.

"We'll talk again soon, Analyst," Malcolm said, and he and Symone walked out of the lab.

Once the door closed, the Analyst walked to his back desk and sat in his chair. He rolled over to a small filing cabinet under his desk and pulled out the top drawer. He retrieved a small holoscreen and powered it up. He swiped through the applications and pressed "NOTES" on the screen. He then scribed, "Malcolm + Symone = AT???" He then powered down the holoscreen and placed it back in the cabinet, then rolled it back to the center of his desk.

Symone pressed the down arrow at the elevator and asked Malcolm, "Okay, so what do you want me to do today?"

Malcolm crossed his arms. "Well, I've seen your body of work from your orientation and our op at the bank. But I still don't understand what you do. I figured let's put you in target practice, and you show me who Starburst is."

They entered the elevator and Malcolm pushed "T." Symone didn't hesitate and replied, "I could show you much better who I am if you were in the room with me."

You don't know how to quit, do you? Malcolm thought. *Don't respond. Keep it profesh.*

"So, you were watching me before you came into the room yesterday?" Malcolm asked.

"Yeah, I was," Symone admitted. "I was looking for you after leaving the quarters but showed up too late at the Analyst's office. So, I came down to training to talk to you."

Malcolm pondered, *So, it was her energy I felt in the room! But how is that possible? The room is cloaked, and even the Analyst didn't detect her energy radiating anywhere in the room. How did I sense her, and nothing else did?* He quickly dialed up his senses and picked up Symone's energy signature surging through her. *Yep, that was it.*

Symone could feel something shifting in her slightly and tried to shake it off. *Akan, stop, Symone! You're going to tackle this man!*

The elevator stopped and the door opened. "I got you. This way, Miss Watson." He led her to the right, and they passed a few training rooms and heard muffled bangs, booms, and rattles coming from them. They stopped at Symone's training room, as indicated by her name above the door. "You can do the honors. I'll be watching from the observation room."

Symone suddenly realized that she had not equipped herself with her uniform or cloak. "Let me ask, should I cloak, Bennett?" Symone laughed.

Malcolm chuckled and said, "I'll let you decide that for yourself, Watson. Although, if you think the targets are going to hurt you, you might be in worse shape than the Company initially thought." Malcolm pressed his hand on the observation room's palm reader, it lit white for approval, and he walked into the room. The door was sealed shut.

Symone inhaled deeply, then exhaled deeply and said, "Alright, Symone, let's give him a show." She placed her palm on the reader, and it lit white for approval. She entered the training room, and the door closed behind her. A woman's voice reported, "Symone Watson, codename Starburst. Modifying room to meet powered state."

Malcolm sat at the holoscreen at the back of the observation room and powered it up. It displayed a live feed of Symone in the room on the left side and information on Symone and the targets on the right. Malcolm pressed a button on the tabletop, then typed the command "TARGETS." Symone looked around her as white floating circles the size of dinner plates appeared around the room. A door opened, and a black, sticky substance launched at and attached to Symone. She gasped for air as she watched the nanites stretch to cover her from neck to toe and turn into a uniform that conformed to her body.

"Wasn't expecting that," she remarked as she turned her arms twice, "but it works. Hey, Bennett, next time, can you warn me about the weird costume change?"

Malcolm pressed "INTERCOM" on the counter keyboard and spoke to Symone, "And take the fun out of it? No way! Okay, Miss Watson, I'm going to give you five minutes to destroy as many targets as you can. Let's see what you got."

Symone raised her right hand and requested, "Um, before we start, can you play a song for me?"

"Sure, what are you thinking?"

"How about 'Give Me More' by Madam Reila," Symone answered.

No way! "I'm surprised you know about that song! No one knows about that song!"

"You'd be surprised by what I know, Bennett," Symone smiled.

"One Madam Reila masterpiece coming up." Malcolm searched for and played the deceased songstress's ballad, and the beat dropped almost instantly.

Symone nearly lost herself in a trance as she tapped her foot to the beat of Madam Reila's song, slightly rolled her neck from side to side, then closed her eyes. Suddenly, her eyes popped open, lit yellow. Her hair slowly transformed from jet black to yellow, and Symone levitated off the floor. Her hands glowed as fire flowed through her veins, and sparks began to fly from her fingertips.

Malcolm said, "Your five minutes start now."

The targets flew upward away from Symone, and though they surprised her, she was unfazed and hunted the targets down as she began to mouth the words to "Give Me More." She built small balls of light and heat in her palms and threw them one by one repeatedly at several of the targets, destroying each of them. The remaining targets reached the ceiling nearly one hundred yards in the air, then split into two groups as they descended to the ground. Symone took her hands and stretched them to her maximum wingspan, then created two stars the diameter of her body. The targets couldn't compensate for the size of her stars and crashed into them. Small explosions floated off her stars.

She continued to sing the words to Madam Reila's song as Malcolm deployed another set of targets from bays in the ceiling. This time, the targets circled around Symone about twenty feet away. Symone descended toward the ground, and the targets descended with her. *Okay, straight shots, I'll have to use a gatling approach,* she reasoned. She held her right hand forward and shot multiple stars the size of golf balls from her hands, destroying each target without missing a single shot. Symone began flipping herself midair as she continued to descend to the ground. Malcolm was awestruck and quickly fought off the daze and sent more targets in. Saucers entered and exited the walls in a single-file line. Without skipping a lyric, Symone rotated her body horizontally and continued spinning her body like a propellor while shooting stars from her hands, destroying target after target without flinching.

Malcolm said, "Okay, let's make things interesting. Can you see a smaller target?" The next series of targets were the size of cup saucers.

Is this supposed to be a challenge, Bennett? Still singing the lyrics, Symone flew away from the targets that were suspended closer to the ceiling. She planted her feet on the ground, then twisted her arms upward and created a large star above her head. She launched it to the ceiling, reducing the smaller targets to dust. Malcolm then tapped several buttons on the countertop. Golf ball-shaped targets rose from the ground and rolled around Symone. As she levitated slightly, she employed a gatling-like approach to destroy each target, successfully hitting every single one without missing.

Malcolm then said to Symone, "How well can you handle the dark?" He then tapped on a few buttons that reduced the illumination from the light strips in the walls to nothing, leaving Symone's hair, eyes, and glowing hands as the only things visible in the room. He then tapped a few more keys to send an array of targets levitating in random places across the training room. Symone continued singing Madam Reila's melody as she created a star and held it in place on the ground, then rushed straight up in the air, stopping about twenty yards to create another star and holding it in place. She repeated the pattern at forty, sixty, eighty, and finally, the ceiling. She then descended to about midway between the ceiling and the ground, then hovered close to the back wall so she could see all the stars she had created. She then focused her mind, still singing song lyrics, and turned her body parallel to the ground so that the stars ran crossway to her. She then placed her hands in front of her, and as her eyes lit up even more intensely yellow, she shot a concentrated burst smaller than the stars she created earlier at each of them, which caused them to explode into smaller bursts of energy.

The bursts scattered across the room, destroying every target in the room while creating a light show that stopped Malcolm in his mental tracks. He slowly stood from his chair and looked in the room, staring in awe of what Symone just accomplished. His eyes peered beyond the sparks arrayed across the training room and absorbed every detail of Symone – each strand of her hair hovering around and shining from her head, her silhouette glowing from the aura around her, her eyes shimmering like fire bellowing from within. Symone's light show left him confounded.

Symone rotated right-side up and slowly descended to the ground, singing the final lyrics to Madam Reila's song, "Why are you still standing there/you know that no one else compares/baby it's you that I adore/won't you come over and give me more." Symone slowly planted her feet on the ground. She powered down, her hair changed back to black, the aura around her body and hands disappeared, and her eyes returned to their natural color. As the lights turned back on, she lifted her head to breathe in deeply, then let out a victorious exhale and smiled.

She lowered her head to face the observation room. "Is that all you want to see?"

Malcolm was tranced. He couldn't stop staring at Symone. Malcolm tried to snap back to reality, but he felt a tug in his heart that he couldn't ignore. He felt knocked off balance, drawn closer to the window. His senses heightened uncontrollably, the room's brightness intensified in his eyes, and the energy he felt once before surrounded him again. Malcolm could feel Symone's presence in the observation room with him.

Symone said, "Bennett?"

Malcolm heard Symone's voice reverberate in his ears. *Watson is incredible! That was sexy as Frimas! What a display of power and grace! What is happening right now? Why am I feeling like this? Why does it feel like she's standing right next to me? How is she doing this to me? She's in a cloaked room, there's no way I should be able to sense her right now. Come on, brother, get it together!*

"Um," he stammered, "I think we got what we need for a first run. Come in here and let me show you what the suit captured."

Malcolm shook his head several times and banged it with his palm a few more to regain his composure. Symone began to walk out of the training room, and the black nanites melted off her and levitated to the wall they came from. The door opened, and she walked out. She pressed the palm reader for the observation room and entered. Malcolm stood at the computer desk. He looked at Symone and began, "Okay, so these are your demos and stats which the Analyst showed you before. Using this desk here, you can go back and forth between your training exercises. You can replay your training, look at what you did in the training, and so forth here."

Symone stood next to Malcolm while looking at the holoscreen's data. She said, "Okay, so what's next?"

Malcolm replied, "Well, I wasn't expecting you to put on a concert and destroy all the targets that fast."

Symone turned to face Malcolm. "I really didn't do anything."

Malcolm turned to her. "Oh, so the targets just destroyed themselves? Okay," he answered with a smile.

"So, are you going to suit up and show me some moves?" Symone asked.

"What, you want to watch me train?"

"Well, you won't spar with me, so I guess watching you will have to be the closest I can get. I want to watch you fight something in the room."

Malcolm scratched his head as he responded, "Well, maybe not now. I need to go back up and see what Malaysia wanted before she gets busy and can't be found. What I will do, though, is show you how to modify the room through the computer so that maybe this afternoon you can give me a training session worth my time."

"Okay, teach me something," Symone said. Malcolm pulled a chair and gave it to Symone. He then pulled another chair, and they sat next to each other as Malcolm tapped on the countertop and shared his knowledge of how to make modifications to the room's parameters and training objectives.

"See, the room is set up to match whoever is in it. The walls are protected by cloaks that increase and decrease in integrity so that we don't bring the building down while blasting everything to bits." As he showed her the details, Symone stored as much information as she could, tapping on the keys that Malcolm pointed out so she could make alterations to different training exercises, view videos of past training, and take notes of what she would want to work on at later points in time.

"Well, this is a lot," Symone said. "Do you mind if I work on this until you come down here later today?"

"Oh, not at all. Take all the time you want. You know your way around the facility, so make yourself at home. If you need me, just call me." Malcolm got up from his seat and began to leave the observation room.

Symone told him, "I'll see you soon." He left the room, and Symone looked at the screen, thinking to herself, "Okay, let's get to work." She tapped on keys and accessed past training. She saw a file marked, "Bennett, M." She tapped the countertop to access Malcolm's file, and the holoscreen displayed several files of past training room exercises. She hovered over and accessed the last training Malcolm completed, and the holoscreen played the footage. Symone's eyes slightly glowed with excitement as she reveled in the treasure trove she had just uncovered. *This is going to be fun! Since I can't fight with him yet, I'll just learn everything I can about him this way instead.* She tapped on the keys and opened a command prompt. She typed, "copy all to Watson, S., stripe." All of Malcolm's training and battle footage began to download to Symone's stripe in her arm. Her stripe-filled blue from her bend to her wrist.

Symone's face then lit up as she discovered, *I can have the whole team's training!* "YES!" She eagerly accessed the files of the entire Elite Unit and copied them to her stripe. Her motivation to crush Malcolm in the battle arena germinated a seed in her imagination. *I'll spar with everyone else and destroy them. I'll study all of their moves and take them down one by one. I'll convince him that I'm a worthy challenger and unafraid to take him on. Malcolm will have no choice but to fight me, then! I'm gonna "King of the Mountain" him!* Symone tapped the keyboard to return to Malcolm's file and played footage of another previous training and studied intently with a resolve to train herself to become the greatest fighter Malcolm ever faced.

Malcolm entered the elevator, replaying his last encounter with Symone. He could feel his heart slightly tightening like prey grappled by the talons of a hawk. He had never sensed an intensity like this before, and the echoes pulled at the strands of his consciousness. The walls of the elevator suddenly glowed. Malcolm's chest tightened, his breaths shortened, the glass and steel box painted with streaks of red and black, and Malcolm felt trapped. Screams rang through his ears. Malcolm scanned his surroundings and couldn't gain his bearings. He clutched the chain around his neck and expected an adversary to reveal himself.

A black, slender figure stood next to him and whispered in his ear, "We are destined for this."

He spun to take the figure down, and it disappeared as quickly as it had arrived. Black and red smoke engulfed the elevator. Malcolm could barely breathe. He reached his hands out but couldn't sense the smoke. Malcolm dropped to one knee.

Okay, okay. Um, five things I can see. Smoke, smoke. Wait, no, um, my hands, my arms, my shirt, the elevator door. The smoke slowly disappeared. *The buttons on the side of the door. The ground underneath me. My shoe. Wait, that's seven things.* The elevator stopped. He breathed heavily. Sweat beaded on his forehead. His soul shuddered. *What just happened? This has never happened before. I thought they were just dreams, nightmares. What is happening to me? Did Symone's powers do this?*

The elevator opened, and Daisy appeared on the other side. She saw Malcolm on his knee. "Malcolm, are you okay?"

Oh crud. Malcolm raised his head and said, "Yes, I'm okay, I was just tying my shoe."

"I don't remember tying a shoe requiring so much *deep breathing*, but okay. I'll see you later?"

Malcolm stood up and walked out of the elevator as Daisy walked in, replying, "Yes, I'll see you later. Hey, have you seen Malaysia?"

"Oh, yes, the last I saw her was with the director. I think they're still meeting in her office."

"Okay, thanks. I'll talk to you soon," Malcolm said.

"Sure. Next time, slow down with the shoelaces so you don't run out of breath," Daisy joked while twirling one of her braids. The elevator doors closed.

Malcolm walked to the director's office while trying to sort out his thoughts, wavering between his budding feelings toward Symone, his sudden change in his powers, and his nightmares showing up in the middle of the day. He sat in a chair next to Mallack's office entrance and waited for Malaysia and Mallack to finish their meeting and compartmentalized his feelings and thoughts. *You have got to get a grip on yourself. The last thing you need is to be distracted by anything, even by me.* He ran his hands across his hair and patted himself on the head twice.

Mallack's doors opened. Malcolm's head popped up, and he saw Malaysia walk out. She saw Malcolm and said, "Oh, hey, Mal, I wasn't expecting to see you so soon."

Malcolm stood up and said, "Yeah, well, it seemed like you had something important to tell me, so I figured I'd talk to you now rather than later."

"Oh, right," Malaysia recalled. Her eyes narrowed, then widened. "I just want you to be careful with Symone."

"What do you mean, Malaysia?"

Malaysia stood next to Malcolm. "Symone is not like the rest of us, Malcolm. I can see it. And you know how you are. I can't understand why the Company put you and her together any more than you can. But there is something different about her beyond what's on paper, and you've been entrusted with her. So don't screw this up."

"Malaysia," Malcolm responded as they walked away from Mallack's office, "when have I ever screwed anything up?"

"I'm only going to say this one more time, don't screw this up. I know how I survived you, but I can't speak for the others. Symone is built differently. Just, for once, please don't do what you usually do. She's remarkably gifted, and the team feels more complete with her on it."

Malcolm folded his arms and slowly growled before saying, "Fine, I'll try to do better with Watson."

"You'd better. You know I got my eyes on you."

8

Three Weeks

Symone admired her reflection in the mirror while binding her locs into pigtails and prepared for bed. It had been about three weeks since her first training exercise, and despite all her efforts, Malcolm still would not spar with her. She joyfully reminded herself that her time in the ring with him was coming if she continued to exercise patience. As she thought more about Malcolm, her eyes flickered, and the urge to fight him coursed through her veins hotter than the fire that powered her stars.

She finished tying her hair, then walked into her bedroom. She lifted her arm and pressed her left wrist. Her stripe lit up, and a voice in her ear said, "What can I do for you, Symone?"

"Replay my journal entries dating back to my second day of training." Symone was a student of her craft. She desired to examine her progression and was grateful she remembered to log in, just like in her prizefighting days. She sat in her bed, legs crossed, as a hologram of her from three weeks prior materialized in front of her, standing where she was when she recorded her entry.

The AI responded, "Entry log 02-17-5723, 20:15."

Symone watched her holographic past prance around the room in excitement as she narrated, "I cannot believe it! I had the best day ever! I had no idea that being a part of the Company would be this much fun. Today, I got a really good taste of training with Malcolm. I still don't understand why he calls me by my last name. I call him by his in kind, though, maybe it's just a training thing. He's much more personable than I originally thought he'd be. Anyway, he put me in the training room today, and I put on a show for him that I hope will inspire him to get in the room with me soon. That, though, wasn't the best part for me. Malcolm has given me access to a treasure chest of fighter files that I didn't know we could view on our own like this. I spent cycles watching these tapes of Malcolm, Malaysia, Karl, Daisy, Alexia, and even Duncan, and just getting to know how they all fight. I even watched some of the Analyst's reactions to them. This is like getting the cheat codes for a prizefight! I miss those days, wow. I'm going to study them a little more tonight and try to emulate their styles. Malcolm won't fight me, so I'm going to do what he suggested and spar with the others. I figure if I can demonstrate just how awesome I am by defeating all of them, then he will have no choice but to spar with me. Actually, now that I think about it, he was supposed to meet up with me later so I could put him through a training session. I guess we both let time get the better of us. Regardless, I have a lot of homework to do tonight, so I'm going to study hard and then decide who I should ask to spar with first. Probably Alexia. She seems the easiest of everyone to get along with, so I'll ask her tomorrow."

AI said, "Entry ended. Entry log 02-18-5723, 21:21."

The first hologram disappeared and was replaced with the following night, and this Symone sat in a chair pinning her hair up, narrating, "Today we met for a brief meeting; nothing really was said today. I went to Malcolm and asked him why he didn't come back yesterday, and he told me that something came up and he had to take care of it. I could tell something was off with him. But I didn't know if it was my place to press him. I just asked again, 'Are you okay,' and he answered that he was, so I left it alone. After the meeting ended, I went to Alexia, who is such a bubble of joy and energy, and I asked her if she would like to spar with me. She almost pounced on me when she said, 'Yes!' I asked her when she wanted to do it, and she said in three days, so that gave me a little more time to do my homework. I asked Malcolm afterward if there was anything he and I were doing today, and he said no. I said to him that I would be in the observation room studying film, and he asked me of what. I said, 'The team.' He said, 'Really? Why?' And I said, 'Well, you said the only way to get better is by training? This is how I do it.' He looked at me as if he knew I was going to say that, but he didn't say anything back to me. He just smiled. I said, 'What?' And he said, 'Nothing, it's just, it's like looking in a mirror. Anyway, I've got some things to take care of up here today, but maybe if I have some free time, we can watch tape together.' I said, 'Sure, I'll be here pretty much all day.' I can tell I'm growing on him. There's something about him, I don't know what it is, but I feel this weird yet strong connection to him. Not that it mattered today, anyway, because sure enough, I watched a film of Alexia all day long, learned her moves and everything, and never saw Malcolm the rest of the day. I even went up for lunch and spent time with Karl and Duncan – with his smooth operator self – hoping that I would catch Malcolm, but he never showed. I still have a lot of studying to do to get ready for this spar with Alexia, so I'm going to bear down and study hard today, then hit the training room tomorrow and see what I can do."

AI loaded the next day's entry. This time, Symone stood at the window looking outside at the cityscape.

"So, I am all in my feelings today, because even though he's still so standoff-ish with me, I feel like Malcolm gets me. Today, he asked me to train for him again, and I figured I'd use this as an opportunity to prep for my fight with Alexia. I asked Malcolm to load an Alexia simulation. He asked, 'Alexia? What for?' And I told him, 'Well, if you would have been here yesterday, maybe I would have told you.' I didn't realize what I had said, considering he's my boss, but he didn't seem fazed, instead just saying, 'You're right, that's on me. Loading the Alexia simulation now. Is there a song you'd like to listen to while you're training?' I wanted to see where his head was, so I said to him, 'How about you choose a song for me.' Malcolm then chose this song that set my soul on fire! It's like he knew exactly what I needed to get the sauce flowing in my veins. The simulator ran, and I beat the crap out of it! Little did I know that Malcolm wanted me to train for a long time in the simulator, though, because before I realized it, one song had turned into seven. And though I was tired, Malcolm said, 'You got about 20 more minutes before the simulation ends. Keep going.' Another Alexia showed up. And another, and another, and another! And, not gonna lie, I was exhausted. Especially since this was just a simulation." Symone banged her fist on the window. "I wanted the real thing, not just a machine. I wanted flesh and blood in the room with me, real hands, real fists, real grabs, real throws, real power, a real battle. I finished and got plenty of reps in, but the whole time I just wanted Malcolm to surprise me, to come in the room and be like, 'Okay, enough games, take me on.' Just to go to blows with me. But that never happened. Oh well, I guess a girl can dream. Alexia's simulator is difficult, but you know, I think I got her handled when we spar in two days."

Symone lay in the bed with her hands behind her head as she continued listening to her journal entries.

The next entry displayed Symone in a different location than her apartment. "So today, I decided I would camp out in my quarters for the first time. I found out that Malaysia, Karl, and Duncan spend a lot of their week here while the others choose to go home. I didn't spend much time with Malcolm today; just a routine check-in. He did say that I should talk to the Analyst soon, but nothing much beyond that. There are these moments where he can seem so distant, like his mind is somewhere else. Anyway, I went to my room and locked the door, and I gotta say, my room is rather swanky. I asked AI to convert it into a workout space, and the room and kitchen literally transformed into a mini gym. I turned on Alexia's training exercises and spent the rest of the day studying film and matching her rhythms. She has this childlike fury that she fights with, like an uncontrollable tantrum. I wonder if there's a way I can exploit that, especially since she can move things with her mind. She might try to crush me, but I think maybe if her emotions are all over the place, I can throw her off her game. She has a hidden strength and agility that you wouldn't think exists on the surface. I memorized her cadences and footwork all day. I then looked on the Forum, found one of my old prizefights, and listened to a few commentators reacting to my fight for motivation. Karl was in the commons as I was leaving, and he asked if I was okay since I was locked in the room all day, and I told him that I was just preparing for my spar with Alexia tomorrow. He said, 'Oh yeah? That I gotta see!' And I told him, 'Well, come on then! Invite the rest of the crew if you want.' So we might have an audience for this. Sheesh!"

"Next entry," AI said.

"OH AKAN!!! I can't believe I won!" the holographic Symone yelled. "Alexia tried her hardest to take me down, but she didn't realize how much work I put in to understand how she fights. Let me tell you, when she threw stuff at me, I thought she was gonna knock me out cold. I couldn't see what she was doing behind me. Even when I was above her, she knew how to psych me out. My dumbass thought I cloaked – in fact, I know I cloaked – but somehow, I didn't cloak, and she took advantage of that, tapping into my mind and projecting this weird image in my head where I was out in space and couldn't see her. She kicked the snot out of me, then clutched me with her kinesis, pulled me back to her, then punched the crap out of me, then clutched me again, then went to kick me again, but I managed to compose myself just enough to grab her leg, throw her sideways and hit her with a star that spun her into a wall. I then landed on the ground to try to shake off the doozy feeling in my head and turn my cloak on, but not before she pushed herself off the wall and grabbed me again kinetically. She squeezed the Frimas out of me, and I swear my insides were being crushed, and she was going to snap me like a twig. I tried to push myself upward and could barely move. She said, 'Yield, Symone!' And that just pissed me off, like, the Frimas you mean 'yield'? I pushed all the energy I had in me to raise my arms, but before I could get my arms pointed in her direction, she knocked me into one wall, then knocked me into another wall, raised me up close to the ceiling, then sent me straight down. I remembered from one of her trainings that she released her grip just before her previous opponent landed on the ground, so I knew if I timed it just right, when she released me, I could push myself back up and not be knocked out cold by the impact. And about half a second before impact, I felt her let me go, and I pushed myself with a burst of my hands, then twisted myself and shot off a gatling of stars in her direction. She was not ready for them, and they knocked her to the ground. I then sent a large star in her direction, anticipating that she would try to deflect it, thereby not seeing me behind it. She deflected it and didn't see me, and I punched the out of her, then kicked her in her stomach twice, then tomahawked her in her skull. She fell to the ground face first, and I sat on top of her back with my knees on her arms and lit my hands up next to her head. I then told her, 'Yield.'

"Alexia snapped her fingers, and suddenly I got smacked in the head with some stuff in the room with us, and it knocked me off her. She then threw more at me, and I covered myself in a star as I tried to remember that I had to knock her off balance somehow. I blasted the star off me, then launched myself at Alexia, and we traded punches and kicks. I remembered her cadence as our fight became a dance in my head. She couldn't land anything on me, and I could tell she was getting frustrated that nothing was working. As she would try to punch me, I would dodge and grab her arm, then swing away from her. Her kicks were hitting air, jabs were landing in the wind. She even tried to do a kinesis, but I blasted a star into her arm, and it messed with her concentration. Eventually, she got so frustrated that she threw a bunch of objects at me from behind, and I fi-na-lly caught on and fell flat to the ground, and those objects hit her instead. I knew then that this was my moment to take her down. I grabbed her legs and flipped her to the ground, then jumped on top of her, straddling her torso, and hit her with the biggest series of hand smacks to the head I've ever launched on someone in my life. I even lit my hands up for extra pain. I then punched her one good time in the head, flew up in the air, then created the biggest star I could make in a three-second span, then sent it into her. The boom it set off scared even me. Alexia's cloak failed, and I flew straight down and put my feet on Alexia's hands and hovered a star over her face. I then said, 'Yield.' Alexia nodded her head and said, 'Okay, I yield. You win.'

"We then heard this loud, 'Ohhhhhhhhhhhhhhhh' from the observation room. Then, the training room door opened, and Duncan, Malaysia, Karl, and Daisy ran in like kids in a candy store. Karl was like, 'Yo, that was incredible! Alexia, Symone, that was next level! Who knew you had moves like that!' Daisy said, 'Where'd you learn how to fight like that?' While I was so happy at how they reacted to Alexia and my fight, I couldn't help but wonder whether Malcolm had been there. I told everyone, 'I'll be right back,' and walked out of the training room. I caught Malcolm's backside as he was about to hit the elevator and said, 'Hey, Bennett, where are you going?' And he turned around and said to me, 'I'm going up to get something to eat, then I've got to see the Analyst.' I walked up to him, kind of confused, and asked, 'So, you're just going to leave?' And he said, 'Well, yeah. You fought well. I knew you would.' And I said, 'And how did you know that?' And he said, 'Because I know you.' Just then, the elevator rang, and he walked in. I knew he wanted to tell me something, so I pressed him. 'What, Malcolm?' He said, 'You should come with me. The Analyst and I are going to watch your fight.' He had no idea what that did to me! I almost fell apart! I said, 'Let me check on Alexia, and you get something to eat. Meet with you in a cycle?' The elevator closed as he said, 'See you soon, Miss Watson.'

"I went back to the team, and they had gotten Alexia up and were all talking, and we went back up to the quarters. I cleaned myself up and went to the Analyst, and there Malcolm was sitting with the Analyst waiting for me. But before I could even get a word out, his stripe lit up, and he said, 'I have to go. You can stay here and watch your fight.' I wanted to ask him if he really had to leave, but I just said, 'Okay,' and tried not to show my disappointment. I didn't see him for the rest of the day. Gah! It was an amazing day, but I really wanted to watch his reaction to my fight. I can't get that moment back. Ugh. Oh well, one down, five more to go."

Symone sat up in the bed and walked toward the window to watch the night skyline as the AI continued with the next entry.

"Late this morning, Malcolm asked me to walk the streets with him. We walked out of the Company and went on our trip to nowhere. Malcolm wasn't saying much to me initially. I didn't know what to say to him, even though I had a billion questions I wanted to ask and a ton of things to get off my chest. About ten minutes of walking later, I was about to break the ice myself, but then he asked me a question. 'Why did you say "yes" to the Company?' And I told him, 'Why not? It's the Company! Every powered person on the planet wants to be a part of this organization. When I got my invitation, I would have been a fool to say no.' He chuckled, and I said, 'What's so funny?' He said, 'I didn't ask you why it was a good idea to join. I asked you, Miss Watson, why did *you* say yes?' I said, 'Well, I've been fighting a long time, and I've beaten just about every person I thought was a worthy opponent, and I have been bored. It was time for the next challenge, you know? I want to reach another level of my powers, and I can't do that fighting people lesser than me for creds.' He then asked me a question that I never really thought about before. He said, 'How will you know when you've reached your maximum potential?' I responded, 'I honestly don't know. No one has ever asked me that before.'

"I then said, 'But what about you? Why did you say "yes?"' He said, '"It's the Company!"' mocking me. I gave him a puzzled look, and then he smiled and said, 'Honestly, I've always wanted to help people. My powers are strange and difficult for even me to understand, but I've learned to use them to help others when they need defense or protection. When you think about it, this city is full of powered people, and most of them want to use their powers for good reasons – make money, buy homes, live well, take care of their families, all that stuff. But there's always that group of people who wants to use their powers for selfish reasons and will resort to hurting people to get what they want. The laws are in place to keep us in check, but they only do so much. So that's why I do it, to do my part to make sure that everyone can live free and without fear.' I couldn't help but marvel at how sweet he sounded, but also dumb and idealistic. I said to him, 'That was a lovely speech, did you read that off the Company brochure?' He said, 'Shut up,' and nudged my shoulder with his hand. We talked a lot, more than I expected us to. Three cycles must have gone by because before I realized it, we had entered Midtown. I don't know what it is, I still can't wrap my head around it, but Malcolm makes me feel, I don't know, safe?" The holographic Symone looked at the stripe in her arm and said, "Oh, I gotta go, scribe over."

The next entry began. "I didn't get a chance to journal yesterday because I had to cram for my next spar that happened today. I challenged Daisy, and she said yes and we should do it today. I was not expecting that and spent all of yesterday watching all her film. I was really surprised at what she is capable of with her speed. She's not just fast. She's able to create all sorts of issues for an opponent and gave me a run for my money in the ring. I don't think I got any sleep last night trying to find a weak spot that I could exploit. I realized after watching her that wherever Daisy travels, she sparks the air around her and leaves a trail behind her that can be ignited if it's hit at the right moment. I said I'd keep that secret in my back pocket until after we fought. And man, did we fight!

"We went into the ring, and the rest of the team went into the observation room. And sure enough, Daisy came at me so fast I could not keep up with her. She knocked me out so many times, I for sure thought I was done. I couldn't fly high enough away from her because the girl runs so fast. She can climb walls! When I burst to the ceiling as high as I could, she ran up the wall and kicked me back to the ground, then met me on the ground and kicked me in my chest so hard I thought my tits were gonna fall off. She then spun around me so fast that a dust storm full of lightning surrounded me. I was like, 'Where the Frimas did all this dust come from in this sterile room?' She kept slapping me and punching me and kicking me. And at that point, I had to summon the quickest burst I could release from me and surround myself with that energy long enough to get my bearings straight. At that point, I flew up as high as I could. She chased me, and I fell underneath her to catch her trail behind her, then sent gatling bursts of energy in her trail, hoping I released them fast enough. Sure enough, I did, and the trail caught fire! The trail followed her and eventually popped her in the ass, and it shocked her so badly that she crashed into the wall and bounced and rolled on the wall until gravity took control and sent her spiraling to the ground. I then hit her with several stars to try to disable her some more before she regained her bearings. It didn't take long for her to crash to the ground. I flew as quickly as I could to catch her before she sped away, straddling her back, squeezing her with my thighs, and holding my hands to her face, prepared to light her up. I demanded, 'Yield,' and she responded, 'How did you do that?' I repeated, 'Yield, and I'll tell you.' She conceded, 'I yield.'

"The rest of the team then arrived, except for Malcolm, of course, and we discussed how great the fight was, even though I didn't contribute much this time around. Afterwards, I went to see where Malcolm was, and I saw him in the observation room, replaying the tape. I asked him, 'You enjoying the show?' He looked at me, then looked back at the holoscreen, and said, 'I'm just taking notes.' I asked him why, and he didn't answer me. He just kinda looked at me in the corner of his eye and gave me this half-smile. He turned the holoscreen off, then said, 'I'll see you later, Miss Watson.' I said, 'Where are you going?' He said, 'I'm hungry.' And I was like, 'Um, I could eat, too,' and to my surprise, he said, 'Well, what do you want?' Malaysia and Karl overheard us, and Karl said, 'True that, I could eat, too. Where are we going?' So, after I cleaned up, we all went to this spot about two blocks away from the Company. While we were eating, I asked, 'So, is this mostly what we do, as a team? Like, we haven't done anything for a while,' and Malaysia said, 'Yeah, this is pretty much what we do. We do a lot of waiting, and I mean a lot of waiting.' Malcolm said, 'If you're looking for some action in between time, you are always welcome to join a Super team when they're out on missions. Just have to clear it with the director first. Well, for right now, me first, then the director.' I was like, 'When were you going to tell me this?' to which he said, 'It's not like I'm following some script or manual of information to give you. So, I guess when the time called for it, or when your stripe lit up to tell you your help is needed?' Malaysia laughed and said, 'If there's something you want to know, Symone, you are going to have to just ask Malcolm or any of us. Otherwise, Malcolm is going to tell you things as they come up.' I didn't know if I should be mad at him because I really don't like it when people keep stuff from me, especially if I'm being denied a chance to fight of all things. But I didn't let it get the better of me at that moment. I just said, 'So if I want, I can just join another team and assist them?' Karl said, 'That's one of the perks of being an Elite.' I said, 'Okay.' Malaysia looked at me, and I could tell she was examining me. I said, 'Don't look at me like that,' and she said, 'Sorry, force of habit.'

"I then got up to go to the bathroom to shake the irritation I was feeling. I didn't want them to know how frustrated I was becoming by feeling like people were doing things pertaining to me without my permission. I gathered myself, then walked out of the bathroom. Malaysia was waiting for me, and she said that she was really sorry for making me feel uncomfortable, and I said it was okay. I don't know, I know being a part of this team, the Company, is an amazing opportunity, but something about being here feels wrong sometimes, like I'm being directed, like someone is making me do things without telling me. I feel like I'm here by choice, and I want to believe I am here because I choose to be here. But I don't know. I'm going to turn some music on and decompress for the night."

Symone shook her head. She got out of her bed and walked through her living room to the kitchen. She opened the refrigerator, and the cold draft in it blasted her near-naked body with a chill that produced goosebumps. She pulled out a pitcher of water with lemons and limes floating in it, grabbed a glass from a cupboard next to the refrigerator, poured the glass full, then put the pitcher back in the refrigerator. She quenched her thirst with the crisp, fruit-infused water while the next entry played.

"Today, Director Mallack called me into her office. It's been about fourteen days since I've been an Elite, and the director told me that she has been watching my progress with the team and is impressed with what I have done so far. I told her thank you for giving me the opportunity, and that I hadn't really been doing anything but talking, training, and observing. She said that that's exactly what I should be doing, just getting ready for the next mission when it comes up. I asked her about being able to go out in the field with Supers, and she said that she sees no problem with that so long as Malcolm approves it first since he's my supervisor for now.

"She then said, 'Speaking of, how are things going with your training?' I said, 'Well, I think things are going great. He doesn't really tell me much other than he's watching my progress and to keep training.' She said, 'One thing about

Malcolm, he knows what he's doing, even when it doesn't seem like it makes a lot of sense. So, if he tells you you're on the right track, trust him.' I asked her, 'Have you ever seen him in the training room with someone else? Like, sparring?' Mallack smiled and said, 'Me, no, I haven't seen it since his first year.' I said, 'Oh, okay. Well, do you think it will ever happen again?' She said back, 'I can't tell you whether it will or won't, but – and don't tell him I told you this – I think if it does happen again, it will be against you.' I looked at her and asked why she felt that way. She said, 'Because I've been monitoring your stats and demos, and you are evolving at a rate that only one other person has been able to attain. I'll give you one guess as to who that other person is.' I said, 'You're kidding,' and she said, 'No. Malcolm has told me that he's told you several times that you should see the Analyst.' I looked stunned. I know that I have been growing, but I really had no idea that I've been growing this much in such a short time." The holographic Symone's stripe lit up, and she said, "Oh, I gotta go. Stop scribing."

As the next entry played, Symone returned to her bed and sat up.

"So, I talked to the Analyst, and he showed me how my stats and demos have dramatically increased in the past week and a half, and he said that the sparring I've done with the team has greatly enhanced my abilities, but that there was also something else that was causing my evolution. He couldn't pinpoint exactly what it was, but he promised to keep an eye on it and let me know if he could identify it. I had a weird suspicion that he wasn't telling me everything. I asked him if he was sure he didn't know what it was, and his response was, 'Well, I just think that you're getting close to your teammates, and the closer you guys all get, the stronger you all become, and since they've all reached their limits, you're catching up to them.' I said, 'Okay, that makes sense.' I walked out of there feeling like that wasn't it, and I should have pushed him. I knew I could get him to talk to me, but I didn't push. I didn't want to take that from him. If he wanted to tell me, he would. I decided to come home early and turn on tape of Malcolm, trying to find any footage of him sparring with someone in training.

"I shouldn't have done that.

"It started innocently enough, you know. It was purely for research. But the more I watched Malcolm and his training tapes, the more I just got lost in him. His raw strength, yet his incredible control and restraint. He's an absolute monster, truly unpredictable. His power seems to make sense to me, but I feel like he could do so much more with what he has. He can manipulate any object into something completely different, making weapons and stuff, sure. But it seems so elementary. I watched him as he took down dummy after dummy. He's just like me, turning on a song that I've trained or fought to a million times and turning his fight into a dance. I found myself dancing right along with every video I watched, replaying them five times over and matching his moves as best as I could. His agility, his skill, his defense, his attack. I just imagined myself being in the room with him, blocking his punches, grabbing him and throwing him up against a wall, him pinning me to the ground, the two of us rolling back and forth, shuttling in the air, arm in arm. Every video imprinted in my head. Then I saw this one video of him with his shirt off, and I was like, 'Oh Akan!' Malcolm has this hidden physique that you wouldn't expect to see hidden with all his garb, even in uniform. His ripped pecs, abs, arms, mmm, I was in a daze, and my veins were on fire. My eyes wouldn't stop flickering, my hair was slowly glowing, and, not gonna lie, my body was begging for some much-needed attention."

Symone chuckled a little as she closed her eyes and slightly shuddered.

"Ever since I stopped prizefighting, no one I've ever fought or wanted to fight has made me feel like this. Man, let me stop lying to myself, no one has ever made me feel like this. Watching him fight, watching him train, hearing his voice, being near him, I don't know what this is. But I feel something happening within me, and somehow, he is the reason why. After watching the last video, I ran outside and flew as high as I could, all this energy churning inside of me. I raised my hands and created the largest star I could muster, yelling so loudly that I'm certain someone must have heard me and wondered what on Uretha was happening. As I released the star, I knew it lit up the city for a brief moment. That star wasn't enough, though, and I kept yelling, and all this energy just shot out of me, like, out of my entire body! That had never happened before, and it felt so good, and sapped my energy so bad that plummeted. I didn't care, though, and I fell for a good thirty seconds before I finally course-corrected and slowed myself down to a safer speed, returned to my rooftop, and lay on the ground, staring at the sky above me. I said to myself, 'If just watching Malcolm makes me do all of this, I have to make him fight me.' And that's exactly what I'm going to do. I'm going to make him fight me. I want it. I want *him*." The holographic Symone paused for a moment. She then ended the transmission when she said, "But I have to fight Karl tomorrow, and the rest of the crew first."

Symone said to herself as she lay back in her bed, "Keep going."

The AI said, "Entry log 02-31-5723, 16:37."

"I fought Karl today and won, of course! Karl is more than just brute strength. Karl is intelligent as Frimas, and though I knew that, you wouldn't expect it fighting him blindly. From my studying, he basically wants to beat you senseless, and you can't just beat him senseless because the man barely gets hurt himself. I nearly had to blast him a billion times just to make him move an inch. But I'm getting ahead of myself. I looked at the tape and learned that if I could stay above him, then the most that he could do is try to either climb up to reach me, which in our training room, unless you call for the environment to change like that, climbing is out of the question, or throw a bunch of stuff at me. But even staying above him is just a fool's errand because you still gotta find a way to hurt the man. So, agility had to be my best friend to subdue him.

"We entered the training room, and right on cue, this dude charged at me, and I did not know how fast this man could run. I told you, you cannot underestimate him at all. Imagine the fastest track runner with the weight of a wrestler and the physique of a basketball center, and you've captured maybe half of what he is capable of. He is so fast, so when he came at me, it surprised me. He knocked the Frimas out of me with his right fist, and it sent me flying into the wall. Before I knew it, this man jumped in the sky, had to be about twenty feet, and was crashing down, about to tomahawk the crap out of me. I barrel-rolled just in time, then shuttled in the air out of reach just to give my mind a chance to catch up to the pain in my face. I was sure I was almost concussed, thanking Akan that the cloak worked for me! I sent a few stars his way, knowing they weren't going to do a thing, but I had to do something to keep him occupied while I thought of my plan of how to take him down. I figured since I was faster than him, I will have to hit him with a barrage of energy all at once but from every direction to overload his senses. But I would also have to get low enough to set these stars everywhere, otherwise, it won't do any good.

"Once the pain slightly subsided, I hovered low to the ground and started placing stars everywhere as he chased me, throwing things at me that the room had prepared for him. He was landing some of those things at me, not gonna lie, and they hurt like Frimas. I was blasting some of the objects while still laying stars in as many places as I could. But then, I noticed that he stopped throwing things at me, and started throwing things at the stars. I was like, 'No way!' He had figured out what I was trying to do! So, as I lay more stars around the training room, I also threw stars at him to distract him from my stars. So, we ended up hurling stars and debris at each other while he was trying to hurl debris at my stars. It got so exhausting. I eventually landed on the ground, and he saw that I was trying to catch my breath and charged at me. When he came at me, I hit him with as many gatling stars as I could just to slow him down, for what good that did, though, because he just batted every star away as he continued to charge. I flew backward until my back hit the wall. I waited until the last minute when he came at me with his fist and slid under him as his fist hit the wall. I grabbed his leg, and with every ounce of energy I had I tried to trip this man. I lit my hands up with everything in me, but it was like trying to rip a tree trunk out of the ground. Nevertheless, the star I popped his leg with was enough for him to at least jump in pain, I guess? He jumped and hopped on one leg, and I slid and flew backward away from him while laying more stars around him and the room as he tried to regain balance.

"I said it was either now or never, and I tried to recreate what I had done the night before and burst energy from my body in hopes of igniting the stars all at once rather than shooting them in a gatling way. I thought about it, but I couldn't produce it. I tried again, and still nothing. Karl was regaining his composure. And I said, 'What is it?' And I thought about Malcolm and our walk to Midtown, and I don't know what to say except thinking about him set me off. All of a sudden, I got super-hot within my body, and the more I thought about him, the hotter I got. And right before Karl turned to get ready to charge at me, I felt the rush of energy I had felt that night, and I yelled, and although the burst from my body wasn't as strong as it was that night, it was strong enough when it burst from my body to set off every star I released, and the explosions did exactly what I wanted them to do. Karl was completely discombobulated, dazed from the light show and the explosions. I then hit his head with a barrage of gatling stars as the explosions continued all over the room, and his mind couldn't take the physical, visual, or auditory overload he was bombarded with. He hobbled as he tried to regain a sense of direction and balance, and I flew over to him and hit his head with a star and finally toppled the giant. He fell to the ground, and I stood over his face, hands lit, and said, 'Yield.' He was asleep, so he couldn't answer me.

"Everyone came into the room as always, and after we carted Karl out of the room and sent him to his quarters to recuperate, Alexia asked me if I wanted to go out tonight in Leicester, and I immediately said, 'Frimas yeah!' I'm actually getting ready to meet up with her now, this is going to be so fun; it's like the first time I've had a chance to have fun with somebody in almost two years. Before I left the quarters, I asked Duncan if he wanted to spar with me next, and he told me, 'Well, I do, but not yet. I'd be kidding myself if I said I'm ready for you. You'd easily hand me an "L," so fighting me right now will be a waste of time.' Anyway, I'm excited for tonight, I gotta go."

Next entry. "I was shocked today. As I was in the cafeteria, Malaysia came and sat with me. She said she had been meaning to talk with me but just hadn't had a chance to get with me with everything she's had going on. I asked her if everything was okay, and she said, 'Oh yes, I just do a lot of simulator training since I am a pilot, and I rest my eyes a lot. Anyway, I just wanted to know how you're doing.' I joked with her and said, 'What, you don't know? You see everything, right?' She laughed and said, 'I know, I know, I got my eye on everything. But for real, how are you?' I told her that I'm doing great and really glad to be a part of the team. She said that she was happy that I am here. She then asked, 'So, how are things with you and Malcolm?' I told her, 'As good as I can expect, I guess. He is so hard to read. Let me ask you, why won't he fight anybody in the training room?' She said, 'I knew you were going to ask me that. Malcolm's power is incredibly strong and incredibly unstable. So, his true strength is in his ability to restrain himself. But he also does not like to lose. I remember when I asked him to fight me, and he said that he didn't want to hurt me, and after all I had seen of him prior to me being on the Elite Unit, I believed him and never questioned him about it. Let me ask you, why do you want to fight him so badly?' I told her, 'Why not?' She said, 'Come on, Symone, why do you want to fight him? You might as well tell me. I see how you are when he's around you.' She did this weird eye thing that still annoys me, but I said, 'You know, it's just something about him, I don't know what it is, but it's like I'm drawn to him. His energy, his attitude, I mean, you've seen him fight. Bennett is unlike any other person I've ever faced. It feels like I'm destined to kick his ass.' Malaysia laughed at me and said, 'Well, I don't know what you're going to have to do to convince him to join you in the room. Just be aware that all your hard work might prove unfruitful, despite how he may feel about you.' I stopped her and said, 'Wait, what do you mean?' She said, 'Remember, I see everything. And I see that he's feeling some type of way about you.' I asked her if she really felt that was true, and she said yes. I asked, 'Well, what should I do?' Her answer was, 'Just be careful.' I told her I would be, then we talked about nothing for about another cycle. At the end of it all, she said to me, 'So, I'm guessing it's my turn to fight you, right?' And I said to her, 'You already know! When are we doing this?' She answered, 'How much time do you need to study me?' I looked at her like, 'Wait, how do... never mind. The real question is, how much time do *you* need?' She answered me, 'Let's give it two days.'

"Later that day, I ran into Malcolm and asked him if he was training at all today, and he said that he was going down in about a cycle. I told him that I had a training session prepared for him if he was interested, and he said sure. So, I went with him to the training room about a cycle later, surprised that he actually kept the appointment. The day before, I went to the Analyst and asked him how I could load myself into a training program so that I could fight someone remotely, a trick I had learned from my prizefighting days when my old partners and I wanted to practice fighting opponents without fighting them directly. And he told me that it was really simple, so long as the same program was running in both rooms. I asked the Analyst if he would create a program that would pit Malcolm and me against each other, and he created the program and taught me how to upload it. So, before Malcolm was ready today, I went to the training rooms and reserved one for me and had the program already loaded. After Malcolm went in his room, I loaded the program to his room, then left and went to my room. I then said, 'Load program,' and as the training suit latched onto me, a dummy-Malcolm appeared in the room. I made sure that the dummies didn't look like us so that Malcolm wouldn't know what I had done. But I was finally about to get a taste of what it felt like to fight with Malcolm. I made the program simple – beat me.

"I turned on a song that I knew both he and I would love, which set the mood perfectly. However, before I could get lost in a trance, Malcolm interjected, 'So, just beat the dummy? That's it?' I responded, 'Yes, it's that simple. Good luck!' Malcolm then took the chain from his neck and stretched it, causing the dummy in my room to do the same. I assumed a battle stance, and I guess Malcolm's dummy mirrored my actions as well. Malcolm spun the stretched chain like a whip and sent it my way, and I blasted in the air, then hurled a few stars at him. He barrel-rolled away from my barrage, then pressed his arm, which opened a door in the training room and released several scraps of metal for him to use. He grabbed one and turned it into a bat with spikes at the end of it. I was thinking, 'YES, this is what I want!' I rushed down to meet him, and he swung the bat at me, which I dodged, then tried to smack him with my hands lit up, and he dodged my swing, rolled to the ground and tried to trip me with his foot, but I jumped over it and sent a star his way, but he swung the bat at it, and the star shattered the bat. He flipped back up, then grabbed another piece of metal and changed it into a dagger, then rushed toward me and swiped at me several times, and I returned a series of jabs and punches his way, which he ducked and dodged before finally landing a punch to my face, and damn did he wallop a punch! I rolled to the ground but quickly regained my composure and rushed him, grabbing him by the torso, and tried to launch him into the wall before he grabbed my arms, released my grip and kneed me in the chest, then punched me in the face again.

"I lost my momentum while he – and I don't even know how the Frimas he did this – planted himself on the wall like he was about to get ready for a 100-yard dash, then pushed himself off the wall and stood straight up. He then picked up several pieces of metal and shaped them into these ninja star, boomerang-looking frisbee discs and somehow lit them up like they could set something on fire and threw them at me, my vulnerable self lying on the ground trying to stand back up. I saw them coming and shot them out of the sky before they could reach me. He rushed toward me and threw a bunch of haymakers at me, and I blasted him with a star that sent him flying across the room. I then grew a bigger star and hurled it his way, but he was so smart, he took another metal shard and turned it into a shield that the star obliterated on impact. He then took another shard and turned it into a shield and charged at me, anticipating that I would throw another star his way. I rose as high as I could, then sent multiple stars his way. It's like he could anticipate my movements and my aim, because he ran through the maze like a lab rat.

"Malcolm began singing the words to the song I had on, 'If I was blind/you'd be my eyes/If I'm the walking dead/bring me back to life' as the last star I threw he stopped near his face. He then used the shield in his hand, and somehow his shield's density was stronger than the star to where he batted the star away, blasting the wall. He then took a few more pieces of metal and manipulated them to become a large staff. I think he knew what to do to match my stars' intensity at that point because he spun that staff like he knew what to do with a stick." The holographic Symone shivered, just as Symone herself shivered thinking about what she just said and the thought she had regarding staffs and sticks. "I started sending more stars his way, and he blocked every star, sending them all over the room, exploding left and right. I sent another one his way, and he swung that staff with such accuracy that he almost hit me with the star. Malcolm, being *Malcolm*, was learning on the fly, reminding me of my ex. I came down to meet him again, and he threw the staff at me. That mess hit me in my head and sent me barreling into the ground, I just didn't see it coming. He then picked the staff up and jumped about fifteen feet in the air, and proceeded to try to pin me, but not before I sent a star his way. The density of the staff split the star in two but slowed its velocity enough for me to roll away from him, blast myself upward, and catch him in the sky. I dragged him upward, but he immediately broke from my grip and started falling from the sky. With the staff in his hand, he quickly shifted it into a slide, and upon impacting the ground, he somehow slid to the ground, landing on his feet! He ran, then slid and picked up another shard which he turned into a sickle on a chain. I sent more stars his way, which he dodged and sliced with his sickle.

"Unlike any other person I had fought so far, he had indeed been the most unpredictable, and it felt like nothing I could do would make a difference. I flew higher into the sky, and he launched the sickle and chain my way. I tried to stop the chain via stars and it did not work, but he also did not hit me; the chain actually flew past me. What I didn't notice, however, was that he manipulated the sickle to turn into this flat surface, and as he pulled the chain back to him, the flat surface slammed into me and pulled me back toward him. His hands heated the chain, which heated the flat surface, and started burning me. I rolled away in time before the flat surface met him and his fist could meet my face again. I then built the biggest star I could and hurled it his way. But he stopped it with his power. I hadn't seen anything like this before, someone stopping me from doing what I wanted to do, not like this. It was turning me on, and I could feel my veins boiling from the intensity in my body, much like that night and that time I fought Karl.

"I felt like the only thing I could do at this point to try to win this fight was to burst again, and so while he played with the star, I charged up, thinking about Malcolm and what he made me feel, and with every fiber of my being, I would charge to the point of exploding, then calm myself, then charge up again right to the edge, then calm myself then as Malcolm still tried to do something with that star, I flew behind him, then landed near him and said, 'Surprise!' Malcolm turned around, and I released all that tension I was feeling, bursting a wave of heat and energy all around me! I had never felt such a surge of release leave my body like that before; Akan, it was so intense, so gratifying! It left me in a daze, which was not good for me at all, because as I lost my composure, I didn't realize that Malcolm had actually stopped the burst from hurting him at all, catching the part of the burst that should have unloaded on him and walking out of its path before releasing it to crash into the wall. He then rushed me and pinned me to the ground. Before I knew it, Malcolm was going for the kill, and just as he was about to slice my head clean off, I said, 'Kill program,' and my dummy shattered into dust.

"I lay there on the ground recovering from that energy surge, realizing at that point that, 'Oh, crap, I gotta get back to the observation room!' I got off the ground and flew as fast as I could to the observation room. Malcolm was asking what happened to the program, and I said, 'I believe you won, Malcolm,' and I got back in time before Malcolm could get more suspicious and try to walk into the observation room. I sat down and said, 'What do you think?' He responded, 'Definitely gave me a bit of a run for my money. You modeled this after you, didn't you?' I said, 'Figured I'd give you a sample of what it's like to be in the room with me,' to which he said, 'Okay, then. I'm impressed, Miss

Watson. Run it again!' I was like, 'Malcolm, what are you doing to me?' But I was not about to turn down another round with him. So, I mustered up the energy to turn the program back on, went back into my training room, and we ran the program again.

"We fought for what had to be two cycles, and Akan, he's everything I expected him to be and more. It was so unfair because I was fighting a dummy and not him, but this was as close as I could get to being in the room with him, and it felt so good. He is the challenge I've been waiting for my entire life, and there's no other person I'd rather get in the ring with.

"When it was all said and done, I had to make sure he didn't realize that I was completely out of breath and in need of an oxygen tank. He came into the observation room and was like, 'Did you enjoy the show?' And I told him, 'Oh, you have no idea. Still, I'd much prefer to be the leading lady in your movie rather than just watch. Come on, Bennett, when are you going to let me in?' He answered, 'You're persistent, I'll give you that. But no, not gonna happen.' I said, 'What are you afraid of?' And he finally revealed to me, 'Of losing a team member.' I was like, 'So, you're afraid of losing me?' He said, 'Of anyone, and that includes you.' He then walked out of the room, saying, 'You're a star, Miss Watson, in more ways than one.' I didn't know how to take that. I wanted to ask him, 'In what way,' but I was just stunned that he said it. Stunned and shocked."

"Two more," Symone whispered.

"Malaysia, wow, she is one of the fiercest opponents I've ever faced in my entire life! With just her and Malcolm alone on our side, I don't know how anyone can beat us in the field. She beat me down all fight!

"I've obviously watched the tape, and the girl literally has no weaknesses outside of sensory overload. But she's been training herself on how to cope with that for so long, none of the tapes were of any help to me. The best I could think to do was to beat her with brute strength. We entered the room, and once we started, Malaysia took out these daggers and just started hurling them at me. I was reminded of my first training with Malcolm, and I threw stars at each of the daggers to deflect them, only to realize that the daggers had been tipped to withstand the heat of my stars and were piercing through them and, subsequently, two of them hit me, one on my left arm and another on my right hand! Had it not been for the cloak, my hands would have been done for. Malaysia must have figured that if she can disable my hands, then that's pretty much a wrap. She charged at me, throwing more daggers my way, and I rolled past them, and she compensated by throwing daggers ahead of me. I didn't catch it, and another dagger hit me in the head, bouncing off the cloak, but knocking me off course.

"She threw another barrage of daggers my way, and I flew up in the air. She compensated by throwing daggers ahead of me and almost hit me in the head again before I stopped. But I stopped too soon, and she anticipated it, because more daggers came and hit me three times in the chest. Those daggers hurt, too. I understood then why she called herself the Eagle. I sent stars to the ground, trying to surround her and restrict her movement, but without hesitation, she ran away from where I was sending them. I created a star as bright as the damn sun, hoping to blind her and keep her from seeing me throw something at her. But nope, she was prepared for that, too, and not only still saw me, but threw more daggers at me, curving the stars themselves!

"She then switched up on me and went from throwing daggers to whipping out a bow and started shooting arrows at me! I was like, the Frimas, when did she start doing this? Not only did I not anticipate them, but I also didn't think the arrows would be tipped with explosives, so when two of those bitches hit me, they blew me back and into the wall. She shot more arrows at me, and I threw stars at them to set the explosives off. This bitch had the arrows tipped so that even when the explosives went off, the arrows still shot at me, and one hit me in the head! I'm just like, this bitch is going to kill me! I was pissed, and I flew down to meet her. She saw me coming and waited until I was near her face to then smack me upside the head with the bow, then grabbed an arrow from her quiver and shot me from behind in my butt of all places, and of course, it was rigged with an explosive, so I literally got popped in the butt! It sent me tumbling to the ground. Malaysia said to me, arrow taught in the bow, 'Yield, Starburst.' I said, 'Damn that!' and got up from the ground. I then tried to do something different. I knew performing a burst like I did with Karl and Malcolm would probably knock her out, but I couldn't risk being completely winded since I hadn't practiced the move enough times to maintain stamina afterwards. I decided this time that, since her daggers were molded to withstand the heat of my stars, I had to make my stars hotter.

"So, I flew all the way to the ceiling, and with all the might I had in me, I focused my energy on making a hotter star. First, I created an energy barrier that would at least keep the explosions on the arrows Malaysia would keep shooting at me from reaching me. I knew the arrows would get through, and I could only hope that by scattering myself, she wouldn't be able to hit me. I then concentrated on going from yellow to white hot. At first, I got nothing. And the arrows kept coming through. One hit my shoulder, and I said, 'Okay, if thinking about Malcolm makes me burst, maybe if I calm myself enough, I can just get hotter.' So, I thought about Malcolm, and just as sure as my attraction to him is, the heat in me began to rise, and I saw the strands of my locs intensify from yellow to white. In fact, I could have sworn one of my locs started burning my shoulder, but I couldn't worry about that because I then felt a sharp pain in my left leg. Then my right breast, I'm talking about the nipple part. Then my abdomen, then my left thigh!

"Suddenly, I realized that Malaysia had switched from arrows to bullets! She whipped out a rifle and was hunting me like a buck! Once I realized that I was hot enough, instead of throwing stars, I decided to go hand-to-hand with her. She needed a smackdown, if I could get close enough to smack her. I dove down to meet her, and as she kept shooting, I zig-zagged to finally reach down to her. I grabbed the rifle and melted it down with my hand, and she tried to trip me, but I dodged it. Then we traded punches and kicks before I finally smacked her hard in the face, grabbed her arm, and swung her into the wall, then punched her as hard as I could in her abs. She doubled over but grabbed my head by my locs and slammed my head into the wall, then flipped onto the wall to elbow me in the head, then grabbed me by my shoulders and pinned me to the ground. She threw a couple of haymakers at my head, and I blocked them, then grabbed her arms and blasted a star into her chest, which sent her back into the wall again. She then whipped out a couple of daggers from Akan-knows-where and pushed herself off the wall and lunged toward me. I sent another white star her way, and she threw the daggers, but the daggers disintegrated within the star, and the star hit her and sent her back into the wall again. I knew at that point I had the upper hand but did not know how much longer I could hold the heat.

I flew as far back as I could, and I created the biggest star my focus could muster, watching Malaysia whip out her bow again and pull out an arrow. But then I said to myself, 'No, that's what she wants,' and I flew in the air, and I put a white star on the ground in each corner of the room, and then as she let her arrow fly, I shot a star at the arrow, and it exploded, and at the same time, I blew each star up into sparks. The show dazed Malaysia, who I could only assume was trying to find me with all the explosions going off and trying to switch to a vision that would best help her. Whether she did or didn't, I met her and smacked her with the hardest heat smack I could muster and sent her flying into a wall again, then shot her with a barrage of white stars that she could not get back up from. She slid to the ground.

"I hovered over her, standing on both her hands, star-loaded above her head. I breathed so hard, so exhausted, I could barely get the words out. But I said, 'Yield, Eagle.' In my head, I said, 'Please yield, I can't fight any longer.' She looked at me like she wanted to do something to me, like she wasn't done yet, like she wanted to go another round or two. But she couldn't move. She said, 'I yield. Good work, Symone.' I crumbled to the ground next to her, writhing in pain. Everybody came into the room. I nearly fell asleep and was gonna ask somebody to carry me to the quarters, but to my surprise, Malcolm came into the room after everyone else! I could barely lift myself up, but I mustered up the energy to say, 'Bennett!' Everyone turned around and seemed just as shocked to see him come in. I slumped back down and went to sleep.

"I woke up in my bed in my quarters, with Alexia waiting for me to wake up. She asked me if I was okay, and I said yeah. She then said she was so proud of me and surprised that I took Malaysia down after all she put me through. I said I was just as surprised and glad she yielded because I literally had no more energy in me to fight her. Alexia then said that Malcolm carried me to my room, then had her clean me up and lay me down. I thought to myself, 'I would, I would miss that, damn it!' Alexia asked me, 'So, are you going to fight him next? I mean, Duncan already told us he's sitting a battle with you out because he's not taking an "L," so that just leaves him on your list.' I told her, 'Well, I can't make him fight me. Can I?' She told me, 'From what I can tell, you can do whatever you want to do, Symone. You sometimes have to make someone do what you want. It's not always that you can wait on the other person to just do it. If you want something bad enough, sometimes you have to just take it. And if I know Malcolm like I do, just like I know you like I do, he wants to fight you just as badly as you want to fight him. He just doesn't know it yet. Or maybe he does, via a training program a certain person built for him?' I looked at her and said, 'How do you – know what, never mind. This team seems to know everything, I'm beginning to understand now. So, you really think he wants to fight me?' She answered, 'Trust me, he wants to do so much more than just fight you.'"

The holographic Symone's stripe lit up. "Gotta go. Stop scribe."

Symone slid to the top of her bed and pulled the covers over her body and got ready to go to sleep. She said, "Last one."

The last entry began to play. "After a long day of recuperating from getting my rear kicked by Malaysia, I decided to take it easy on myself. I had no plans of going anywhere, just staying in the quarters under the covers. The rest of the team was gone. I got up in a crop top and workout shorts to make myself a glass of water in the kitchen. Malcolm knocked on my door and I let him in. He said to me, 'Wanna go for a walk?' I wanted to tell him, 'The Frimas? A walk? I want an infirmary worth of drugs in me right now.' But I said, 'Sure, just let me get dressed.' He said, 'Actually, what you're wearing is fine. We're just going to walk around the building. Barely anyone is here. Just put some shoes on.' I said, 'Okay.' I didn't see him, but I was pretty sure he was checking me out because when I looked back at him, he kinda darted his eyes away. So, I kept the shorts on to be his eye candy and slid into some shoes. While I was internally grimacing from time to time, I walked with Malcolm around the building. I asked him why he was here, and he said it was because I had been asleep for the past forty-two cycles, and he wanted to make sure I was okay. 'I was really surprised that you handled yourself so well against Malaysia,' he said, 'because those rifle bullets were designed to destroy cloaks.' I said, 'Listen, I thought she killed me about ten times in there, not even gonna lie. Malaysia is *that* bitch!' Malcolm laughed and said, 'That's why I'm glad she's on my side, my best friend and right hand.' I said, 'You two go way back?' He answered, 'No, not that far back, but since she's been an Elite, she's been one of the best people I've ever worked with, and I wouldn't trade her for anyone on the unit. Frimas, that's how I feel about all of you.'

"I said, 'Even me?' He smirked and said, 'Yes, even you. I don't think you realize just how special you are, Miss Watson. This entire team cannot stop talking to me about you.' I said, 'Wait, they talk about me?' He laughed, 'Yes, they talk about you. I cannot stop hearing everybody talking about Symone. "Did you see Symone do this?" "Did you hear that Symone did that?" "Symone is amazing!" "Symone, Symone, Symone!" It's all I've been hearing since you got here.' I said back to him, 'I don't believe you, you're making that up.' He responded, 'Oh, you think I'm kidding?' He then whipped out a recording on his stripe of a conversation between Karl, Daisy, and him. It played Karl saying to Malcolm, 'Man, did you see how Symone lit up like a star on a Jubilee tree?! It was the most spectacular thing I've seen in training ever!'

"'See,' Malcolm said, 'whether you realize it or not, you've made an impression on this team in such a short amount of time. And everyone adores you.' I didn't know what to say. I hadn't felt like I've had a strong connection with a set of people like this since my prizefighting days, and I just felt this warm feeling inside my heart. 'Well, thank you, Bennett, I don't know what to say.' 'Just accept it,' he said back to me. 'You're part of the team, the family. And we're not letting you go.'

"I asked Malcolm, 'What about you? What do you think of me?' Malcolm stopped walking and turned to face me. I stared into those eyes, and it was like this man could see my soul when he said, 'I think you're the brightest star in the damn galaxy.'

"I froze, then said to him, 'Wait, what does that mean?' And he said, 'Well, in the short time that you have been around us, you've done nothing but grow and evolve. But it's more than that. I can't speak for you, but I feel this deep connection with you. I don't know if it's the energy flowing through your veins, or just your charisma, but it feels like we're bonded somehow. I can't describe it, nor I can't explain it. Watching you fight is like watching a symphony. And being around you, I don't know, feels...' And I finished his statement, '...safe.' 'Yeah, safe,' he echoed back to me.

"I asked him one more time, 'Malcolm, why won't you fight me? Are you that afraid of hurting little ol' me?' He smiled and said, 'You saw what I did to your dummy program. Frimas, you saw what Malaysia just unleashed on you. What do you think I'm going to do to you?' I got close to him, raised an eyebrow, and said, 'I want to know everything you're gonna do to me, everything you want to do to me, Malcolm. Haven't you figured that out by now?' Malcolm looked stunned, but answered, 'I've been wondering the same thing about you, Miss Watson. Maybe one day soon, we'll both get the answers we're looking for.' We arrived back at the quarters, and as I walked in, I asked Malcolm, 'Are you coming in?' He caught what I was throwing, and he answered, 'Much as I want to, not yet, not until I'm no longer your supervisor.' I told him, 'I won't tell if you won't.' And he said, 'You won't, and Frimas, neither will I, but the Company sees and knows everything. So, if you can wait long enough for your mentorship to end, I'll wait for you.' I said, 'Okay, but that means you're going to have to sign off on me being your mentee quickly. And you're definitely about to miss out on all of this. Unless you fight me.' He said the words I had been longing to hear, kinda. 'Soon, Miss Watson.' I told him, 'Just say my name already, *Malcolm.*' 'Good night, Miss Watson.' He walked away from the quarters, and I walked to my room, jumping up and down like a little kid at Jubilee! Then my body reminded me of how much pain I was in again, and I hobbled back to bed.

"After tonight, I definitely know that I'm nudging him closer to getting in the ring with me. But I'm not gonna lie, I like him. Like, *like him,* like him. And I know he likes me, too. Tonight wasn't just some playful banter between colleagues, and I don't know what to do about that. He's right, we shouldn't do anything with each other until he's not my supervisor anymore. But he's made not liking him difficult as Frimas. Regardless, I want to fight him, real bad. What Alexia said to me makes sense, and I think he's finally warming up to the idea that it's okay to square up with me. I wish he would have just said, 'Hey, let's fight in three days,' or something. He did say 'soon' though, so I can only hope that soon really means *sooner,* and not three years from now when he's retired or promoted or something.

"I just want to fight him. Is that too much to ask?"

The AI in the room said, "End of journal entries. Would you like to playback an entry?"

Symone, with one eye barely open, said, "No, I'm good. Thank you." She closed her eyes and instantly fell asleep.

9
Conflict

H e stood with his back to the wall next to an entryway on his left. He scanned the dark, narrow alley and could barely see anything around, just the building across the alley and the lit street about fifty yards to his left. *The perfect place to hide a hostage, and on a night where the moons are both in crescent phase. Can't see a thing.* He double tapped his chest, and the cloak shimmered, then disappeared. He breathed deeply twice, then whispered, "Okay, let's do this."

He turned the corner and entered the years-abandoned warehouse. The outside streetlamps dimly shone through the silt-covered windows across the walls. The building was about thirty feet high, with cobwebs and dust wrapped around columns that ran through the middle to hold the ceiling in place. His footsteps echoed on the tile paneling he walked on. *This place is completely abandoned. There's no one here. Where's the hostage? Wait, where's the rest of my team? Why am I the only one here?* A terrible feeling sank deep into his gut. The farther into the warehouse he crept, the emptier and darker the atrium became.

He attempted to contact his team, "This is the Crawler, does anybody copy?" Silence.

"This is the Crawler. Does anyone copy? Matchstick? Wolfbane? Anyone copy?"

He looked down at his stripe, and it streaked gray. The scrolling marquee reported, "Lost connection. No signal." Anxiety riddled down his spine. *Abort.* Before he could perform an about-face, he noticed a bright yellow dot on his chest. Then another on his right leg. A third on his left arm, then another on his right arm. A fifth on his left leg. Silently, five armed assailants dressed in all-black nanotech emerged from the deep shadows of the warehouse and surrounded him, blocking his exit. The Crawler closed his eyes and breathed in deeply twice to still his trepidation. He placed his hands behind his back inside his trench coat, handling a small ball attached to the back of his belt. He then declared, "Okay, I'll give you all one chance to drop your weapons and let me leave without incident."

"Drop to your knees and put your hands behind your back," one of the assailants calmly replied. They drew to within ten feet from him.

"Hard pass," the Crawler said. He spun, knelt to the ground while lifting his left arm in the air, and smashed the small ball into the tile. Smoke filled the room and clouded the assailants' sight. They adjusted their visors to smoke-resistant, but the Crawler wasted no time and pounced on one of the assailants with a bear hug to tackle him to the ground. He punched him twice in the head, then took his cannon. He then did a one-handed handstand while blasting the second assailant in the leg. The shot was blocked by the cloak but landed with enough force to trip his opponent. The Crawler took the blaster and threw it at the third assailant, then bent forward and planted his heels into the chest of the fourth to launch him into the air. He pushed himself off his foe with his feet, grabbed the fifth combatant by the neck, and with all his might, forced him onto the ground. He punched the fifth in the head a few times, then spun up. The first assailant got back up and whipped out a machete.

The Crawler ran to a column. He activated his power, and thousands of microscopic hooks protruded from his hands and feet, and the nanotech he wore thinned itself enough for the hooks to break through. He effortlessly scaled the pillar and jumped onto the upper scaffolding. The other assailants got back up and aimed their weapons to try to take him down. The Crawler threw another smoke bomb and a flash grenade to distract them. The Crawler swung from one beam to the next to get to the exit. One of the assailants regained his eyesight and shot his cannon toward the Crawler. It missed him but damaged the beam he was about to swing to, causing the Crawler to lose his momentum. He fell with the beam, caught the beam with his arm, then pushed himself off the beam and caught the next one still attached to the warehouse. He made it to the end of the building, then scaled down the wall to land on the ground. The assailants shot cannons his way, and he clung to the ground, dodging each shot, then rolled a final grenade toward them. When it went off, it delivered bolts of electricity at them designed to temporarily disable their cloaks and zap them. The assailants shook uncontrollably, then fell to the ground.

The Crawler let out a sigh and said, "HQ, does anybody copy? I'm in trouble and need exfil immediately!" The stripe remained gray. Just as the Crawler thought he could get up and leave, three silhouettes blocked his exit. "Man!" he exclaimed.

The figure to the right was juggling letters, numbers, and symbols lit up in purple and gold. The figure to the left wore a mask resembling a sound speaker. The middle figure's hands were palms down with small bolts of electricity shooting from them.

The Crawler got up and said, "Listen, I don't want any trouble from you three. Just let me leave. Nobody has to get hurt today."

The middle figure said, "You're absolutely right. Nobody has to get hurt. But you will, if you don't come with us." Her hair protruded from her helmet like a mohawk, and as she charged herself, her hair shone brilliant silver. Current spiraled around her and illuminated her white and neon blue uniform, and sparks of electricity popped from the strands. Her voice sounded eerily familiar to the Crawler. "You're late for your date."

"The Frimas you mean?" the Crawler volleyed. "The only thing I'm late for is my bedtime, dealing with you fools."

"Don't worry," a voice from the sound speaker mask sarcastically assured. "This won't take long, and you'll be able to relax in your bed in no time."

"Sorry," the Crawler said as the AI from his visor scanned them and attempted to upload who his opponents were. He slowly took a couple steps backward while he placed his right hand in his right jacket pocket to find flash grenades to create a diversion. "I'd rather travel alone at this point. Let me guess; you guys set all this up. Very impressive how you disabled my stripe, but how the Frimas did you set up a hostage situation and patch it through to me? That's impossible to do."

"All in due time. For right now, you're coming with us. Hex, will you do the honors?" the middle figure said.

"My pleasure, Streak," Hex, the right figure, said to the middle.

"Nope, gotta run guys," the Crawler said as he dropped three balls on the ground to release flashes of disorienting light and smoke. The three were temporarily stunned and adjusted their visors to compensate. The Crawler, by then, had blitzed past them and made his way out of the door, then crawled up the outer warehouse wall to get away from them.

"Sonic! Get rid of this smoke!" Streak yelled.

Sonic let out a screech, and the sound wave pushed the smoke away from them. They ran out of the warehouse and could not see the Crawler. Streak released a bolt of lightning from her right hand into the sky. Her flare didn't help. She then advised her AI, "Scan the area for the Crawler's signature." Their visors switched to a view of their area that revealed the Crawler's path based on the adhesive his body's hooks secreted to stick to objects. They noted his path up the warehouse wall.

"Looks like we're headed up. Let's go hunting!" Hex said. Symbols swirled around him, and he rose in the air. Sonic bellowed a howl to the ground, and it pushed him upward to the roof of the warehouse. Streak propelled herself by blasting lightning into the ground. They followed the Crawler's tracks. "Hurry," Hex said, "his signature is decaying fast. We'll lose him if we're not quick."

The Crawler raced as fast as he could, jumping from one rooftop to another, monitoring his stripe and pleading that its gray hue would finally change back to white. He could feel the hunters gaining ground on him. He jumped from a rooftop to a wall, sticking to it with his hands, then catapulting himself to the roof of the next building. He did this for five more buildings when finally, the stripe changed to white. Midair, he screamed, "This is the Crawler to HQ, I've been ambushed and need help at once! Three supers are pursuing me in Genesis Landing. I need an ex-fil at once! Get me out of here! I don't have much time!"

Back at Intelligence, Stephanie stood at the holoscreen and said to Dax, "Did you get that?"

Dax, sitting at his usual desk, responded, "Yes, I'm pulling it up now." Dax rushed the data entry, then pulled up the Crawler's location. The holoscreen displayed Dax's coordinates on a map of Uri City.

Stephanie then responded, "Crawler, this is Intelligence. We're sending a team your way. Can you give us any intel on who's chasing you or why you're in Genesis Landing?"

Running on a rooftop, the Crawler said, "I was given a distress signal from who I thought was you guys of a hostage situation. I responded, but when I got to the location –" the Crawler jumped to the next building, then landed on a wall, "oof – I was alone without my team. They jammed my signal, so I couldn't escape the ambush. I disabled five assailants. Then these three hunters, whose powers are sound wave manipulation, lightning strikes, and spellcasting, tried to take me down, saying I'm late for a date."

Stephanie's eyes widened and her skin grew pale. Dread filled her heart, and her jaw opened slightly. She quickly turned to face Dax and with urgency yelled, "Dax, it's the Collector. Send in the Elite Unit now!" She then told the Crawler, "Do you think you can get to the safe house?"

"Negative," the Crawler answered. "They're tracking me somehow and are too close for me to get to the house safely. If I get there too soon, our house will be compromised."

"Okay. Get somewhere safe, Crawler. We're sending in the Elite to come get you. Stay as far away from them as you can. Chances are they're going to jam your beacon again if they get close to you."

Dax tapped on the countertop, then hit "EXECUTE" to dispatch the Elite Unit.

Malcolm sat on the roof of his complex, watching the night skyline. Hovercraft and people in flight danced in the grid of the cityscape. The light breeze kissed his face. His legs slowly dangled from the edge. He reflected on blurred memories of his childhood when he swung on the swing set at the park with his parents. "Much easier times," he reminisced. His uneasy mind wrestled with this newfound insight regarding Symone's desire for him and his emotions toward her. He thought about the times he watched her in the training room taking down some of the best warriors he ever fought alongside, how he could not keep his focus on her skills and admired her body, beauty, ferocity, grace, and her subtle, awkward charm. Despite already admitting it to Symone, Malcolm still did not want to accept that he was drawn to her. Staring into the bright lights shimmering in the darkness, reminded of the sparks that flew in the training room her first time in, he flashed back to that night when Symone invited him into the quarters. His vivid memory would not let go of how ravishing Symone looked in her shorts. He slightly chuckled at how strong Symone tried to appear to him, knowing she struggled to walk with him. But it was that same show of strength that made him admire her more.

He recognized her brilliance in training and thought about a few things she should begin working on to improve her in-battle tactics, trying to keep his thoughts about her professional. But just as he would make a mental scribe, his focus would drift all over again. Malcolm heavily sighed. *Man, I just made life tougher on myself. Frimas, I shouldn't have said what I said to her the other night. All I had to do is just get through these next few weeks, then sign off on her mentorship. But nooooo, you had to go and start liking the girl. Great job, Malcolm. Some mentor you're turning out to be.*

He scratched his fingers through his textured fade. His mind zeroed on Symone's persistent request to fight him in the training room. He worried that he would seriously hurt her, knowing how competitive he was and how he sometimes pushed his power too far, sending teammates to the infirmary. *I shouldn't fight her. Right? I mean, Malaysia already banged her up pretty good, and she's nothing compared to me. But,* Malcolm reasoned, *maybe she can actually take me. Maybe she should have a chance. After all, she's beaten the rest of them. And I honestly wouldn't mind the challenge. I haven't sparred with anybody in the training room in years.*

Malcolm vacillated between calling Symone and leaving her be for the night. "Screw it, I'm gonna call her."

Malcolm summoned a call through his stripe, and he contacted Symone. A low hum rang in his ear.

Symone was sitting on her couch in her mid-lit living room in a black spaghetti-strapped shirt and white gym shorts. She munched on chocolate-covered pecans while watching a prize fight on her holoscreen. Her arm buzzed, and she was going to ignore it, but she recalled Daisy's quip about missing calls three weeks back. She looked at her stripe and saw that it was Malcolm calling her. Butterflies fluttered in her stomach. She quickly finished chewing and swallowed her candy, then cleared her throat and answered the call, making her voice sultry.

"Hello?"

Malcolm stood up. *Even her phone voice is hot!* "Hi, Miss Watson."

Oh, goodness, his nighttime phone voice is so smooth. "Um, hi, Malcolm. You know, you can call me by my *first name*, especially if you're calling me this late."

"I know, Miss Watson. And I'm sorry I'm calling you this late."

"No, don't be sorry," Symone responded. "I don't mind that you called."

Malcolm nervously said, "Oh, okay, good."

A moment of awkward silence filled the air between their lines. "So, what's up?" Symone broke the ice as she played with a loc.

"Right, well, I've been doing a lot of thinking the past couple of days."

"Oh yeah? What about?"

Malcolm slowly started pacing the rooftop. "Well, about you, really."

I'm surprised you're actually thinking about me. Thought I shouldn't because, come on, this is me *we're talking about.* "Me? What about me?"

"Just this whole sparring mountain you're climbing."

Symone sat up straight. He had her full attention. "What about it?"

"Well, I seriously believe this is a terrible, terrible idea, but I accept your challenge, Miss Watson." Symone's jaw dropped. Another moment of awkward silence consumed the airwaves as Symone's brain shorted and rebooted. Malcolm said, "You still there?"

Symone regained her composure and cleared her throat again. "Um, yeah, yes, I'm still here. Are you serious? You're not messing with me, are you?"

"I'm for real. I will spar with you, Symone. I mean, someone has to put this new girl in her place, thinking she can go undefeated in the Elite ring and everything."

"Oh, so you think you got what it takes to take down the champ?" Symone quipped.

"'The champ'? You must have forgotten who owns the belt and the crown. Last I remembered, that was me!" Malcolm returned.

"Oh, okay, I see what it is. Well, just remember that I've taken down every single person in your unit. You gonna wind up getting your feelings hurt real bad."

Malcolm laughed and said, "Oh, Miss Watson, I am going to enjoy kicking your pretty little butt up and down the training room."

You think I'm pretty? Symone's eyes flickered as she felt a sensual tingle roll down her spine and churn in her stomach. "You promise?" Symone inquired.

Malcolm's pride filled his chest, and his ego wasn't the only thing rising to the occasion. He allowed himself to enjoy the banter between them. "You have no idea what you are getting yourself into."

"Please keep underestimating me, Malcolm. It will make destroying you that much more satisfying."

"Oh, trust –" Malcolm was interrupted by a buzz and the red stripe across his left arm. Symone was summoned by the same. He looked at his arm and saw: "PRIORITY ALERT: Genesis Landing. Company Defender has been ambushed and is under attack. Pattern matches M.O. of The Collector. Elite Unit assigned. Authorized to use lethal force."

"Do you see this?" Malcolm asked Symone.

Symone stood up from her couch. "Yes. We gotta move."

"Suit up, we gotta get to him before the Collector does." Malcolm switched his communication to speak directly to every Elite Defender at once. "Elite Unit, this is K.C. Intelligence is going to send us the coordinates. Everyone, converge to the midpoint, and let's roll together on the Eagle's craft. We'll brief on the mission from there." Malcolm pulled his suit-cloak buttons from his pocket and pulled his shirt from the collar and fitted the buttons to his chest. They screwed and locked in. Malcolm double-tapped his chest, and his uniform enveloped his body and the cloak shimmered. In his visor appeared a map to show everyone's location, the team's convergence point, and the quickest paths to get there. He then slid down the ladder of his complex as he summoned his hoverbike to rise to meet them. He saddled his ride and pulled on the handlebars, racing to the convergence.

Symone ran to her room and grabbed her buttons from her dresser. She locked them, then fitted them in her chest. Once they locked, she said, "Okay, let's get this right the first time." She double tapped her chest, and her uniform enveloped her body, and her cloak shimmered, confirming that she got the tap cadence right. She screamed, "Yes!" She ran out of her apartment, rushed down the open corridor, and blasted into the sky.

Moments later, Malcolm saw Daisy lighting up the ground below, convinced she would arrive first to the point as usual. He looked beside him and saw Duncan meeting up with him on his hoverbike, then Alexia on hers. Karl was not too far ahead, meeting in the opposite direction alongside Symone. They began to hear an increasingly loud roar coming from above them. Malaysia caught up with all of them and opened the back hatch of the hoverbus she was piloting. One by one, the Elite entered the craft, and they docked their bikes as Daisy whizzed past everyone and Symone landed. The hatch closed.

Malcolm asked, "What's our ETA?"

Malaysia responded, "Two minutes."

"Make it one, we don't want to miss this guy!"

"You got it! Everyone, hold onto something!" Malaysia pressed "HYPER" on the control dock. The bus shuttled toward their destination in the middle of the abandoned sector of Genesis Landing.

K.C. faced the team and said through his visor, "Okay, listen up everyone, this is our first chance to see whether we can get anything on this Collector if not catch him altogether. Let's stay alert and sharp. But remember, the priority is this super's safety. Any information on who he is?"

Blitz stood up and walked to the holoscreen. "According to the dossier, the super is the Crawler, one of the members of Super Team V. He can attach himself to any surface on command. He's responsible for several rescue missions over the past two years since he can reach spaces that few others can."

"I remember working with him," the Mammoth said, "The guy got me out of a jam one time. Owe my life to him."

"Alright, well, let's make sure we get this right. Collector or not, we want to secure his safety. His beacon has him here," K.C. said as he pointed to the map on the screen, "so let's rendezvous with him and get him on the hoverbus..."

"His signal just cut out," the Eagle interrupted, "So that is his last location. We're gonna have to track him using his signature once we get there."

"Damn it," K.C. responded, "okay, Blitz, once we get to the drop point, canvas the area to see if you can find his signature. Eagle, scan the area above. Crawler could literally be anywhere, so your eyes are critical to his survival."

"Copy that," the Eagle responded.

As the bus closed in on his last location, the Crawler clung to the side of a metal warehouse three stories up, breathing heavily and trying to think of what his next move should be. He saw the stripe in his arm turn gray again. "Gotta keep moving," he sighed. The Crawler slowly slid down the wall and jumped from his spot, then rolled on the ground and ran as fast as his legs could carry him. He heard steps behind him but kept moving forward. The lights that illuminated the street guided him to a small opening that led to an underground parking deck where he hoped he could disappear from his hunters. Still looking forward, he slid underneath the crawl space, clutching the edge of the street to bend his body, then letting go of the edge, holding onto the wall again to catch himself from falling to his doom. He repeated this for about thirty feet until he made it to the ground.

About a minute later, back on the street, the three hunters followed his signature and finally caught up to the opening but couldn't fit in the crawl space. Sonic said, "Let's find a way inside. We're running out of time."

"Step aside," Streak replied. The two moved over as she raised her arms parallel to the ground and charged her hands with electricity, then streaked bolts of lightning from her hands and blew a huge hole in the wall, exposing the parking deck below.

"That'll work," Hex answered while looking into the hole.

The predators jumped through the hole and continued their hunt. The garage was a square concrete slab about three hundred feet wide and long with yellow dimmed lights suspended from above. They peered through the spaces created by the hovercars and bikes. Then Streak said, "Since he wants to play hide and seek, let's shock the Frimas out of these cars."

"Oh, this is going to be fun, I love watching you work, Streak!"

"Why, thank you, Sonic," Streak replied. She charged her hands again and delivered bolts of lightning from them. Like magnets, they attached themselves to every hovercraft on the floor, and alarms blared across the garage. She unleashed her storm, and suddenly one hovercraft after another exploded. The Crawler could no longer hide in his spot and revealed himself before a craft could flatten him.

K.C. and the Elite arrived at the drop point. "Alright team. Before we lost the signal, the Crawler was headed in that direction. Once they can get a read on his location, Enchantra, Mammoth, secure him and get him back to the bus. The rest of us will watch for any signs of the Collector or his team. Don't try to be a hero today. These supers Stephanie was told about by the Crawler seem to be on their A-game. Electricity, sound, and spells. Let's get this right."

"Understood," everyone said.

"Opening the hatch now. Everyone, keep your visors on and move as the information updates," The Eagle instructed.

The Eagle lowered the hoverbus to the street, and Blitz zipped out of the bus to begin canvassing. Starburst flew out of the hatch, while everyone else jumped back on their hoverbikes and rode out, all in search of the Crawler through the maze of warehouses, parking decks, and loading docks that defined this section of Genesis Landing.

Blitz quickly canvassed the location and said, "K.C., we're too late, the signature decayed beyond visibility."

"I've struck out, too," the Eagle said, "we got here too late."

"Alright, everyone fan out. Any sign, any trace, alert us all at once!" K.C. demanded.

"Hex, would you do the honors?" Streak asked.

"It's about time. Haven't had the chance to do much in a while," Hex responded with glee. He waved his hands across his face, then said, "Omree, matrox, unidesh, akjoni!" A series of purple and gold sparkles in the shapes of letters and symbols suddenly surrounded him. He pushed his arms out, directing those symbols in the Crawler's direction. The Crawler didn't skip a beat, rolling past the symbols, jumping onto pillars and parts of the destroyed craft to avoid getting caught in Hex's spellcasting. Sonic stood and let out a screech that shook the garage and set off more alarms. His attack stopped the Crawler in his tracks. He clutched his head to deafen the piercing sound that neither his suit accounted for, nor his cloak could dampen. Hex continued the chant, and the symbols began to swarm the Crawler. Slowly, the Crawler's speed diminished. Streak charged her hands, and bolts began to pop from them as she savored the moment. She then delivered a powerful, continuous wave of electric current to the Crawler. The Crawler's cloak shined yellow as it tried to deflect the energy, but Streak's extremely effective strike damaged the cloak's integrity rapidly. He was too slowed by Hex's spell to move, and within seconds, his cloak's integrity reached zero, and it shimmered and disintegrated. Streak charged up again and delivered five potent strikes, and each bolt lit him up. The Crawler's suit sizzled, some of the nanites were burned off and charred, and he lay paralyzed and unconscious by the assault.

"Excellent work," a dark, altered voice said. "Streak, Hex, you know what to do next."

Streak walked to a pillar and charged her hands. She then touched the pillar, and electricity flowed through her. The current surrounded the outer perimeter of the garage and solidified into an electric fence. Hex lifted his hands up and chanted, "Omree, matrox, unidesh, akjoni!" Purple and gold symbols then flowed from his body across the building and transformed into a barrier between the hunters and the outside.

Sonic declared, "You're good, boss."

Sonic, Streak, and Hex scanned the opposite side of the garage. A dark, thin figure dressed in an all-black hooded coat, a black mask covering the entire face, and black combat pants emerged from smoldering hovercraft and garage rubble. Sonic used a low roar to lift the Crawler's lifeless body off the ground. The dark figure came up to Sonic and the Crawler and said, "This is good. This will get us closer to our goal. Getting the Crawler's power will make the statement we need to get their attention."

Sonic pondered, "Wait, shouldn't the Elite be here by now?"

"Yes, they should be arriving right about now. I assume the one they call Blitz will show up first."

The Elite Unit received intel that a garage was experiencing a series of explosions. The Mammoth said, "It looks like a garage just exploded about three blocks from where we are. Also getting reports of the same garage lit up like a Jubilee tree."

K.C. said, "Blitz, get to that location now!"

"I'm on my way," she responded. Blitz picked up her already hyper pace to get to the garage. Blitz noticed the building shining like a neon sign. "Um, guys, I don't think getting in here is going to be an easy task. There's an electric field and what looks like some type of cloaking barrier that's keeping us from getting inside. I'm going to run around to see if there's a way in, but you guys need to hurry here!"

K.C. said, "We're about 90 seconds out. Eagle, are you already there?"

"About thirty seconds away," the Eagle replied. "I can try to find a way to blast through."

"Whatever it takes. We can't let them take the Crawler."

Blitz ran around the building and could not find a way in without touching the electrified spell barrier. Soon, the Eagle arrived with the hoverbus and scanned the building and the barriers. She said, "This thing looks impenetrable, K.C. I don't know how we're going to get through this. Enchantra, this looks like a job for you if you can find who's casting the spell or creating the fence."

"We're almost there. Land the bus, Eagle. We're gonna need you on the ground this time," Enchantra replied.

"I agree with Enchantra," K.C. said, "get in this fight with us."

The dark figure looked up and said, "Oh good, they're here. Let's get this over with, then provide me with cover to get out of here." The dark figure pulled a small box from a jacket pocket and dropped it on the floor. The box unfolded itself several times and became two black stands about four feet tall – one with a thin, open black ring about six inches in diameter atop it, and another with a gold circular disk about three inches wide with a thin slit in the middle around its perimeter, also six inches in diameter. The two stands were connected by a thin black tube with a button in the middle.

Sonic hovered the Crawler to the machine and lay his body next to it. Hex then spun the Crawler to stand straight up. The dark figure walked to the machine. The figure placed one arm inside the black ring. Sonic walked to the machine and bent down and pushed the button to turn the machine on. Sonic said, "Ready."

"Excellent, let's start the transfer." The Collector took one hand and touched the Crawler's pale face, then began absorbing the Crawler's power. The Crawler was powerless to do anything, all the fight having been sapped from him between the shocks and the hex. The Collector painlessly drained the Crawler's powers from him. His essence flowed from her wrist inside the black ring and through the tube. The gold disk began to separate, and as the Collector drained the Crawler, the parted disc widened with a white, glowing substance in between them. The canister grew to the size of a wine bottle.

Sonic said, "Collection complete."

The Elite Unit arrived and stared at the building. K.C. said, "I'm going to try to bend a hole through the barrier. When I do, Eagle, see if you can find the prick who's doing this, and you and Enchantra, take him down. If I can make the hole big enough before then, Starburst, Ammo, get in there and lay them to waste, Blitz, find our Defender and get him out of there. Mammoth, get under us and see if you can get below them and take them out from their belly. Everyone got their assignments?"

The Collector said, "Okay, it's time for me to go. Give them a good show!" The stands began to dismantle and fold back into the box. The Collector knelt, picked it up, and placed it back in a jacket pocket.

Sonic said, "Your detail is waiting for you out back. We'll keep them at bay in plenty of time for you to get out of here. We'll also keep the cameras rolling for later." Sonic grabbed the cannister and handed it to the Collector.

"We are one step closer. This is our destiny!"

The Collector executed the escape plan as the three hunters turned around and prepared for a fight.

K.C. stretched his hands out as he began to feel the energy of the electricity and the spell barrier. He closed his eyes and visualized the particles in front of him in the shape of a circle. He then put his fingers together and created a ball shape. The team stared at him, especially Starburst, who was keenly interested in how his powers were going to manipulate a different type of material. K.C.'s muscles strained. Suddenly, a small hole began to rip through the barrier. K.C. slowly separated his fingers as if he was physically separating two boulders. The hole grew and exposed the hunters and debris below. K.C. struggled to hold the barrier open but continued to enlarge the hole as the team got ready. Starburst shook her awe and got ready as well. K.C. said, "Okay, 3, 2, 1, go!"

The Eagle and Enchantra ran through the hole first and were immediately hit by Sonic's screech that pinned them against the wall. The Eagle fought the grip of Sonic's screech to reach her firearm at her side. Blitz zipped into the building nearly undetected and scanned the room quickly to find the Crawler's lifeless body on the ground, several feet behind the hunters. She reached him and knelt next to him. She scanned for signs of life. Starburst and Ammo jumped into the hole next, and Starburst immediately launched a series of stars toward the hunters, and Ammo fired plasma rounds from his arms. Enchantra snapped her fingers, and suddenly Sonic tripped and fell over himself. Enchantra and the Eagle slid to the ground. Starburst's stars and Ammo's cannon shots were obliterated by Streak's lightning strikes. Hex raced through his chant, but before he could finish it, Blitz swiftly kicked him in the head and launched him toward Enchantra and the Eagle. Blitz then ran back to the Crawler, picked him up, then ran to a concealed location in the garage and waited for the barrier to finally come down. The Eagle pulled out a pistol and fired a tranquilizer dart at Hex's neck. The serum within it made Hex drowsy almost instantly, and he crumpled to the ground.

K.C. told the Mammoth, "Get under them now!" The Mammoth began to pound on the ground underneath him. He tore through the street and made his way one level below the hunters and the Elite. K.C. jumped through the hole and released his grip on the barrier. He observed Sonic continuing his barrage of high-intensity sounds and Streak shooting lightning bolts at the team. Enchantra lifted Sonic off the ground and launched him into a wall. He screeched at the wall to prevent making contact with it, then sent a sound shockwave toward Enchantra. She couldn't dodge it and was knocked on her back. Meantime, Starburst and Ammo continued their assault on Streak, who matched them shot for shot. Starburst flew to the ceiling, then dashed down and tried to kick Streak, but she missed her head and struck the ground instead. Streak supercharged herself, and she kicked Starburst in the head, sending a shockwave through her body to Starburst that flipped her airborne. Ammo tried to shoot Streak, but Streak didn't fall for his blindside. She blasted Ammo's shots and then delivered a bolt from her hand. She then held the bolt like a whip and grappled onto Ammo's arm. She supercharged the bolt to shock Ammo, then blasted him into a pillar twenty feet behind him.

K.C. picked up a pipe that had been blasted off the roof and manipulated the tip to have several spikes on its end. He wound up the mace, rushed toward Streak, and jumped. Streak launched a bolt toward him. He stopped the bolt with his hand, then landed underneath it, standing within striking distance to Streak, and swung the bat at her, landing a swift blow to her head and spinning her like a top.

He followed her to continue his barrage, but then felt his arms tighten and stiffen toward his body. Letters and symbols surrounded him, gripped him like a vise, then raised him in the air and shuttled him into the back wall. The Eagle looked shocked because she remembered she had shot Hex with a dart. She scanned the garage and noticed that *that* Hex was still on the ground. "Oh, you jerk!" she yelled as she realized he had duplicated himself.

The ground shook underneath them all. Everyone tried to regain their composure but shook again. After a third tremor, the Mammoth emerged from the pavement under them. Blitz saw this as her opportunity to escape with the Crawler and made good on it. She raced out of the hole the Mammoth created with the Crawler draped over her shoulder, through the dark, dank sewer underneath the parking garage, upward through the entrance the Mammoth created, out onto the street, and into the Eagle's hoverbus.

Enchantra paid close attention to Hex. She launched a telepathic assault on Hex by pointing her palms toward the ground and latched her green mist onto his purple and gold swirls to reverse his vise spell. He felt his grip on K.C. loosening and followed the green mist trail. He whispered a doppelganger spell. Another copy of himself snuck behind Enchantra and touched her cloak. Her cloak's nanites' signals scrambled and reversed direction, and they delivered pinpricks across her body. She could not resist the pain signals her body was receiving, and she dropped her grip on Hex's vise as her body twitched all over.

Sonic said, "Okay, I'm ending this!" Sonic stood tall and tilted his head upward. He unleashed a howl that shook the garage. Ammo tried to blast Sonic, but every shot was obliterated by Sonic's audio pulses by the time they reached him. Starburst rose from the ground and launched stars toward him, and they disintegrated well out of range. The Eagle's mind was splitting from sensory overload, so she hid behind a pillar. Streak then charged her hands and unleashed a storm of lightning all around her. The sound waves and bolts turned the garage into an electric maze. The Elite were getting zapped left and right, and their cloaks responded to absorb the damage, shimmering each time they were hit. The Mammoth pushed with all his might toward Streak and Sonic. K.C. stood up and began collecting as much electricity as he could while his eardrums split. The entire team received signals that their cloaks were losing shielding integrity from the hunters' assault.

The Eagle glanced from her position to scan for a weakness between the sound waves and lightning strikes. She discovered a weak spot in between pulses that, if she could shoot through it, could stop Sonic from crushing them for good. As she prepped her cannon, she felt her arms tighten, as did the rest of the team. Enchantra, the Eagle, K.C., the Mammoth, Ammo, and Starburst were all vised by Hex, shocked by Streak's lightning bolts, and losing their sanity from the barrage of noise from Sonic.

"Keep it up, drain their cloaks, and let's take them down! We can take these trophies home to the Collector, too!" Streak exclaimed in victorious praise.

"K.C., we gotta do something!" The Eagle screamed.

K.C. could barely think straight, and as he tried to keep it together, his mind flashed between reality and his subconscious, as his nightmares began flashing before his eyes. The Mammoth noticed him fall to his knees. "K.C., get up man!"

K.C. saw the garage bathe in hints of red and black. Lightning turned into fire. The screams of a thousand kills replaced Sonic's howl. A sharp, intense pain pierced deep within K.C.'s brain. K.C. put his left hand toward his left ear while barely holding onto the collection of lightning strikes in front of him.

A soft voice whispered, *We are destined for this.*

Blitz blasted from the hole she escaped from earlier, and she rapidly assessed the situation, scanning the room and processing her options faster than a supercomputer. *Okay, everybody's lying on the ground, the sound waves and electricity are radiating from those two over there. Looks like my team's constricted. They can't move! It's not the sound or the electricity. Something's got them tied up. Purple and gold, purple and gold. Those look like symbols and letters and numbers, like Enchantra's powers maybe? The third guy. Yeah, him! Alright, if I take him, then that should free them up.*

Blitz ducked Streak's electricity and dodged Sonic's sound waves to get to Hex. She rushed and bear-hugged him, then pushed him with all her might into a car head-first. The speed at which his head crashed through the hovercar's window knocked him out cold despite the cloak he wore. The team immediately felt relief as they regained their ability to move. The Eagle drew her cannon and shot a laser through the sound waves and lightning strikes and dealt a devastating load of damage at Sonic. He blasted into the electric fence Streak had created earlier and slid onto a ledge on the garage that met the street level outside. Starburst then quickly assembled a star in front of her. K.C. was still shaken up from the visions but held tightly to the collection of lightning strikes in front of him. K.C. said to Enchantra, "Enchantra, do something with this lightning ball!" As Enchantra concentrated on the ball of lightning, Ammo cocked his cannons, and he, Starburst, and Enchantra delivered their barrage toward Streak. Streak, however, did not fold and intensified her assault and destroyed their strikes.

Streak stood ready to destroy the Elite when suddenly, she heard the Collector's voice in her visor say, "End this now. We need them alive."

Streak then announced, "Well, this has been fun, but it's time for us to go." She electrified herself even more, and as the Mammoth charged at her, she unleashed a wave of electricity that gripped the entire team and blasted them upward and out of the garage itself. Streak's blast was so strong, the entire parking garage's roof disintegrated into dust. The Elite Unit careened onto the street they started from.

A moment later, K.C. opened his rolling, hazy eyes. He lay on his back. He shook his head and noticed a faint red and black haze floating above him. He could smell smoke. He shook his head again, and his body began to wake up. He groaned in pain and coughed. He bent off his back and surveyed the damage. The parking garage was gone, smoldering from the blast. He panned and saw his team was all lying on the ground, groaning and writhing in pain along with him.

"Is everyone okay?"

"No, K.C.," the Eagle groaned. "We are not okay." She coughed and continued scanning the area. The team could hear sirens and turbines headed their way.

Starburst struggled but lifted herself up and said, "That ended terribly."

"No crap," Ammo replied. "We got our asses kicked. What the Frimas?"

"K.C., we've never come up against a Super that strong. There's no way she's a Super, any of them are Supers," Blitz reacted.

The Mammoth coughed. "Blitz is right, whatever intel we got on them was dead wrong. They have to be Elites. How the Frimas did they beat us like that?"

"Just like that, and I'm pissed," Enchantra coughed as she fought to get up. "We were not prepared for this."

"No, no, we weren't," K.C. resigned. "Come on, let's get back to the bus. We at least got the Crawler out alive, so all is not lost."

"Um, about that," Blitz began, "The Crawler might be alive, but the Crawler is not the Crawler anymore."

"No, what the Frimas does that mean?" Ammo exclaimed.

"I connected him to the recovery unit on the bus, and although his vitals are returning, all his demos are completely changed. He's not a Super anymore. He's not powered anymore. The Collector got his powers."

"Damn it!" The Mammoth screamed and pounded the ground, splitting the street below his fist.

K.C.'s heart dropped. He simply said, "Okay. Everyone, let's just get in the bus and head back to HQ. Mallack, Intelligence, and Analysis are going to need all our data to see what they can make of what just happened tonight."

The Elite Unit, wounded physically, mentally, and emotionally, walked to the bus. They didn't say it out loud, but they all were trying to make peace with the fact that they had just met their match.

Under the cover of smoke and fire, Streak, holding Hex over her shoulder, walked up to Sonic, who was barely standing on the opposite end of the parking garage, shaking off the daze from The Eagle's bullseye. "Come on, Sonic. We gotta head back to base."

"Right," he returned. "How's Hex?"

"No telling. Blitz knocked him out cold. Still breathing, though. Think the boss is gonna be pleased?"

Sonic replied, "Of course. We, well, you just took down the Elite. Everything is going according to plan. This is our destiny, right?"

She answered, "Right. This is our destiny. Let's move." They ran to their hoverbikes and swiftly mounted them. They sped off into the distant night before UPD could reach them, and they returned to their base deep in the Underbelly.

The Elite dragged themselves into the hoverbus as emergency personnel raced toward the eviscerated parking garage. They plopped and slumped in their seats, despondent and dejected, struggling to make sense of what they just experienced. Malcolm walked up to the Crawler, who lay on a stretcher. He was hooked to the recovery unit. Malcolm asked AI, "What's his real name?"

The AI responded, "Steven Boyd."

Symone noticed Malcolm's steely, hurt demeanor. She wondered just how badly this loss affected him and wanted to say something to him. "Malcolm," she said as she walked up to him. "Hey, are you okay?"

Malcolm kept staring at the Crawler, not knowing what to say. "I don't know. Probably no, right?"

Symone stood next to Malcolm and looked at the Crawler, then at Malcolm. "I know this goes without saying, but we did everything we could. And we got him out alive." She touched his back with her left hand.

"I know," he said in agreement. "I guess I'm just trying to process all this." He stared blankly through Symone's eyes as he thought about how vivid his nightmares felt while Sonic's sound waves were blasting his mind apart.

Symone could tell his mind sent him someplace else. She waved her hand in front of his face and said, "Hey, where'd you go?"

"Um, nowhere. I'm gonna go to the cockpit with Malaysia and get ready for the debrief."

"Oh, okay. Hey, Malcolm, I'm here if you need me, okay?" Symone said.

"Thanks, Miss Watson," he answered. Symone watched Malcolm walk to the cockpit and stand next to Malaysia. She walked to her seat and strapped herself in.

Karl looked at Symone and noticed her concern. "He gets like that after a loss."

"I don't blame him," Symone sighed. "This sucks."

"Yeah, it does," Duncan said, sitting across from Symone.

In the cockpit, Malaysia tapped a few buttons to power the bus and grabbed the yoke to launch it. She looked over at Malcolm and started to say something but knew nothing would make him feel better, no silver lining she could point out. "Headed back to HQ," she announced to the team. The bus rose into the night sky and sailed into the distance of the long night. The roar of the engine was their soundtrack.

10

The Competition

The Elite dragged themselves out of the elevator and onto the Grand Hall floor. Director Mallack stood waiting for them at their quarters. She sensed their heavy countenances, bruised egos, and shaken confidences. This was their first major loss in six quarters, and she chose to respond empathetically. "Is everyone okay? Anyone hurt?"

The team reacted in the affirmative. Malcolm spoke for them, "We're okay, ma'am."

She nodded. "I can imagine you're all struggling right now. Clean yourselves up, please visit the Infirmary if necessary, and crash here for the night. We'll debrief and analyze come morning. Rest well." She patted Malcolm on the shoulder and said, "A word?"

Malcolm walked with Mallack as the rest of the team went inside their quarters. Symone, entering last, looked at Malcolm and Mallack, then exited the hallway while leaving the door slightly cracked and standing near it to hear what they were saying. Mallack turned to look at Malcolm and said, "So, tell me what happened."

"Boss, they beat us down, plain and simple," Malcolm was deflated. He crossed his arms. "We were ill-prepared. We couldn't have been ready for that."

"What do you mean?"

"Those were not Supers, Director. Lightning girl has mastered her powers. We've only dealt with someone as powerful as her a handful of times, and we dealt with them six-to-one. Sound boy almost broke my mind, literally. And the spellcaster could have easily trapped us in that garage long enough for our cloaks to be disabled and our bodies obliterated. It was just *three* of them. Had it not been for Blitz, we would have been toast. None of them are the Collector, but we have to assume that his army is full of Elites."

"Not only that, Malcolm, but we also have to assume that they are resourceful, too. They were able to mimic a distress signal and target the specific person they wanted to extract power from. And they obviously do not care about putting on a show."

Malcolm shook his head. "No, they don't. This was a statement. They should have killed us. But they wanted us to size us up. They took Steven Boyd's powers, and they wanted Steven Boyd to be there, and for us to show up. They knew we were coming. You're right, to orchestrate something like this, the Collector's had somebody doing some serious work behind the scenes."

"The question is 'why'? What is the Collector's endgame?" Symone said instinctively, creeping from behind the door. Mallack and Malcolm looked at her. *Oh no.* Symone realized she butted into their private conversation and was concerned she'd be accosted for it.

Mallack, however, just sighed and said, "We don't know."

Whew, okay, Symone winced slightly from the tension in her muscles she used to walk to them. She followed her mind trail. "My best guess? She wants one of us, an Elite."

Malcolm was taken aback and replied, "You might be right."

"Okay, Symone, explain," Mallack said.

"Like Malcolm said, they easily could have killed us tonight because of how ill-prepped we were. Boyd's powers are sticking to walls. It's a great power, sure, but compared to lightning strikes, spellcasting, and sound waves? Let's be honest, sticking to walls really isn't high on anyone's list of powers to possess. The Collector's dossier said that he's been climbing the powered charts. I don't know if it's a specific power he's looking for or just wants to get an Elite-level power altogether. But seeing how we almost got decimated a cycle ago, I don't think the Collector wanted Boyd's power. He wants one of ours, or Frimas, all of ours."

Mallack was impressed by Symone's quick assessment. "So, what, then? Do I sideline you and send another team to take the Collector down?"

"Screw that!" Malcolm roared ferociously.

Oh boy, Symone fought her eyes' urge to flicker from the bass in Malcolm's voice. *Talk, then!*

"*We're* going to take the Collector down. He doesn't get to walk away from this, and we're not backing down. After what we faced, there is no other team in Uri City that can handle them and survive."

"Okay, Malcolm," Mallack responded. "So, what are you going to do?"

"Well, first, we're going to go to sleep, and then tomorrow, we're going to analyze, watch film, train, and get ready for the next fight. It's that simple."

Symone's eyes glowed slightly as she recalled the conversation Malcolm and she had earlier about their imminent sparring match. Director Mallack said, "Okay. Get some rest, you two. We've got some long days ahead of us. I already know my stripe is not going to stop lighting up, so make these debates I'm about to engage in with the chancellor worth it." Malcolm and Symone limped into the quarters while Mallack walked away toward her office. She said, "Hello? Yes, Chancellor, I know, I just spoke with the team. Yes, I am aware...," her voice trailed off as Malcolm closed the door to the quarter's entrance.

Malcolm watched Symone walk toward her residence. Malaysia was in the kitchen, leaning over the counter, finishing off a glass of water. Karl sat on the couch in the commons with his head tilted back, and his snores could be heard in the Analyst's office on the other side of the building. Symone grimaced as she walked. She turned around to see if Malcolm was still following her. Noticing that he stopped in the kitchen, she walked toward her door and slid it open.

Malcolm said to Malaysia, "See you in the morning."

"Good night, Malcolm," Malaysia responded.

Malcolm walked through the commons toward his residence and passed Symone's closed door. He wondered whether he should knock. He didn't know that Symone was on the other side of her door, having slid to the floor, clinging to what little consciousness she had, hoping he would walk into her room. He lifted his hand to tap the door, but then he changed his mind and kept walking toward his own door and limped inside.

Malcolm slumped on his couch. His mind continued to ruminate over the visions he saw and the battle they just lost. He tapped and held his suit button, and the nanotech slid off his body and into the buttons. He then detached the buttons from his chest and laid them on the armrest. He was too exhausted and mentally deflated to keep his eyes open any longer. He stretched out on the couch. Both Malcolm and Symone drifted to sleep.

The next rising, the team gathered in the conference room. Mallack, Stephanie, and the Analyst were in the room waiting for them. Mallack greeted them with the same steely demeanor she had given off the night before. They sat down, and Mallack started, "Okay, team. Take me through what happened." One by one, the team talked about the battle itself, recounting the events that led to their defeat. The Analyst and Stephanie chimed in at times to give their insights but held back much of what they wanted to say from the team.

"Once lightning girl hit us and the garage with that last blast, it was pretty much over," Malcolm said. "I thought we had her. If not for our cloaks, we would have been cooked."

Mallack said, "Right. Okay, I had Stephanie and the Analyst pull all the video footage we could from the Crawler, the garage, and you, and they pieced together the timeline of events. Everything is consistent with how you described everything. Stephanie?"

Stephanie walked up to the holoscreen and began, "So the Crawler received the distress signal while he was in the Highgarden district. We haven't been able to trace where the original signal came from. Somehow, they managed to hack our transmission frequency in the area and deliver their distress call specifically to him. We can only assume that a signal like that had to be transmitted at close range, so they knew exactly who Boyd was and where he resided. He suited up and traveled to Genesis Landing. At this point here," she said as the map highlighted the general area where the Crawler was ambushed, "his stripe cuts out, so we're unable to track his location or communicate with him, neither him with us. His video, audio, and location were disabled. We're assuming he was ambushed somewhere within this five-block radius. Once he escapes the ambush, he then moves further away from Genesis, where his stripe goes back online here. Based on his movements, we believe he was trying to get to the safe house in the district. In hindsight, Director, we should have just told him to go to the safe house."

"There's nothing we can do about that now, Stephanie. Don't beat yourself up over that," Mallack tried to console her.

"You're right, boss. Anyway, his video and audio at this point are all working, and he contacts us, and we dispatch you guys. His last location is found here, a few blocks from the parking garage, before the signal cuts out again. However, his video was still active. No audio, just video."

"Which gives credence to your 'making a statement' theory, Malcolm," Mallack said. "Continue, Stephanie."

"Yes, Director. The Crawler is seen here engaging the three as they're using their powers to disable him." The holoscreen displayed the Crawler's battle from his visor's point of view. "The three henchmen – Sonic, Hex, and Streak – finally subdue him using a combination of sound, spell, and electric shocks. The fields interfere with the quality of the video, so we can't get a good enough shot to recognize anyone with biometrics beyond this point, which would have been helpful when who we can only assume is the Collector shows up and engages Sonic and the Crawler. We can see some type of machine being used to extract his powers, but his camera points forward at this point, and we don't see how the machine works or where the Collector goes afterward."

"Wait," Malaysia said, "Don't we have the parking garage footage?"

"We did, but once Streak fired up her lightning bolts, she shorted the cameras. The footage prior to her lighting the place up trying to disable the Crawler is the only footage we could use to physically identify them, which wasn't worth anything because it appears they have all been scrubbed from existence."

"Are you serious? We got nothing?" Daisy asked.

"Oh, it gets worse. Analyst?"

Everyone's eyes converged on the Analyst. The Analyst cleared his throat. "Oh, yes, well, using your cameras and analyzing your engagements with your opponents, we were able to gather a ton of metadata that we never expected in a single battle. Between your biometrics and their biometrics, it was a data mine, unlike anything I've ever had the chance to analyze in such a—"

"Analyst," Alexia interrupted, "short version."

"Right, I'm sorry," the Analyst said, scratching his head. "So, Malcolm, the director said that you felt like your team engaged a team of Elites, not Supers. Your assumption is correct. In fact, based on the data we pulled, we believe you were fighting Elites who were not fighting you at full strength."

"Wait, what?" Symone exasperatedly let out.

"The Frimas you mean, 'not fighting at full strength?'" Malaysia inquired furiously.

"Um," the Analyst cleared his throat, "well, I ran numbers through our demographics and statistics analyzer five times. And each time, when Sonic is blasting you with his sonic waves, his potential/kinetic ratio is at 70/30, meaning that—"

"He was beating us with 30% of his power," Malcolm finished.

"Yes. Hex was at 62/38. And Streak, well, uh, she was at an unprecedented level of 88/12."

Duncan stood up and yelled, "You're serious?!"

"The numbers don't lie," Mallack responded. "You were right, Malcolm. The Collector's team, this 'army' you talked about, they were toying with you last night. You got a couple of hits in, especially at the end when Daisy stopped Hex and Malaysia shot Sonic. But they could have easily gotten back up and done far worse to you. The Collector does not want to kill you, not yet."

Karl leaned forward on the table. "You said 'unprecedented,' Analyst. Why did you say that?"

The Analyst looked at Mallack, and Mallack lifted her hand and directed the Analyst to answer Karl's question. "Um, well, look at the holoscreen." He pushed a button on his mini-holoscreen, and the data table on the big holoscreen changed to display each team member's potential/kinetic ratio. "I ran the data for each of your battles, practices, and spars since your time here at the Company. I looked at your battles, balanced them with the opponents you've faced, and determined that none of you have ever fought and won a battle with someone at your level without using at least 40% of your power. Now, you all have evolved since these moments in raw power, intelligence, agility, and all the other demos—"

"But these Elites can beat us down without even blinking or breaking a sweat. That's what you're saying, right? Brilliant," Malcolm sighed.

"Yes, Malcolm," Mallack said, "but they won't. What did you tell me last night? 'We're going to analyze, watch film, train, and get ready for the next fight.' So, that's what you're all going to do. This, the Collector and his team, is what you have been preparing for your entire career. He means to make a mockery of us and sell off powers to get rich. We're not going to let that happen. Take this information, get in the training rooms, and prepare for the literal fight of your lives. We will not let the Collector nor the rich decide who gets to have powers. And we're for sure not going to let him take one of you to further his agenda."

"But Director," Daisy attempted to rebut.

"No 'buts,' Daisy. You are the Elite, hand-picked by the Hub to defend this city when no one else can. You, at this point, are the only thing that stands in the Collector's path. Find him and remind him why you, not his crew, are the Elite. Dismissed."

Mallack, Stephanie, and the Analyst walked out of the conference room as the team sat in their seats. Everyone looked at each other with concern, stunned and not knowing how to process the information they just received. Alexia finally cut through the silence when she said, "So, how are we going to take the Collector down?" No one said anything, to which she replied, "No one? Nothing? Malcolm?"

Everyone turned to him, looking for him to say something, anything that would counter what Stephanie and the Analyst revealed to them and give them hope. He stood up and said, "I'm not going to lie to you guys. Mallack is right. This is the fight of our lives, *for* our lives. The Collector wants to take us out, but we're not going to let him nor his team defeat any of us. You know what this calls for: train. Get in the rooms, study film, whatever you got to do to get better. We are the Elite, and Uri City is our city. Let's defend it and defend each other with everything we've got."

Everyone stood and walked out of the conference room, leaving Malaysia, Symone, and Malcolm behind. Malaysia flashed her eyes and remarked, "You don't sound so convincing to me, Malcolm."

Malcolm crossed his arms and shrugged his shoulders, then said, "I don't know what else to say. You saw the numbers, and you were in the fight with us, too. The only thing we can do is train and hope that the next time we cross paths with the Collector and his crew, we're strong enough to take them down. Or at least survive to the next fight."

"I mean, you're right, but remember, this team is your team, Malcolm. If you don't believe in us, in yourself, then you cannot expect us to function when we're out there in battle. You are the best of us. If you stand, we will stand with you. But you have to be ready, too. Whatever *you* have to do to get better, do it."

"Understood, *Director*," Malcolm joked.

"Whatever, you just better have your head all in. I've got your back, and I have to know you have mine, one hundred percent."

Malaysia walked out of the room, leaving Symone and Malcolm alone. Malcolm looked at Symone and said, "So, what are you going to do?"

Symone looked puzzled, expecting Malcolm to give her an order, not ask her a question. "Um, well, I honestly don't know. What do you think I should do?"

"I'd suggest seeing the Infirmary to make sure you're in tip-top, then get in the training room and put in work. You're evolving the fastest, according to the Analyst, and there's not much information to go on for why that's the case. The sooner you get in the room, the more data he can pull and figure some things out. Frimas, for all we know, your power might be exactly what we need to pull this off."

"Okay, then that's what I'll do."

Malcolm and Symone walked out of the conference room and walked silently to the break in the hallway. As Malcolm turned in the direction of the quarters, Symone figured it was a good time to inquire about their sparring match. "So, Malcolm, when do you want to spar with me? Maybe it could help us get stronger faster."

Again with this? He stopped, then turned to face Symone. Symone stared into his piercing eyes and felt like a little child about to be scolded for asking for candy before dinner. Malcolm wanted to dig into her and demolish her soul, but he remembered the order Malaysia gave him to handle her with care, and to not screw this up, whatever *this* was. He tamed the fury in himself, recognizing that it wasn't her he was upset with, and he softened the blow.

"First things first, Miss Watson," his voice was less alarming, his tenor giving off big-brother-concerned-about-the-safety-of-his-siblings vibes, and he placed his hands on her shoulders. She struggled not to tremble in delight of his controlled, firm touch. "Let's get ready for the next bout with the Collector, and *afterwards*, we'll see where things stand."

Symone's countenance dropped as all the joy she had felt just the night before dissipated in an instant. She answered, "Okay," and turned and walked in the direction of the Infirmary, convinced that her hopes of fighting Malcolm had been dashed by a red stripe glowing from their arms. *Damn Collector! Had to go and mess everything up!*

11

Spar-k

D^{*amn.*}

The clock Symone stared at read 03:43. Three days had passed since the Elite's loss against the Collector. And in those three days, Symone, from a distance, watched Malcolm become a shell of himself. He didn't spend much time with her. He didn't spend much time with anyone, maximizing every minute of his day burrowed in his training room. She barely caught glimpses of him when he got off the elevator or walked in and out of the Analyst's office. He hadn't shown his face in the quarters at all. Just when she thought she was beginning to understand him, he completely flipped on her. Symone wracked her brain to understand what his wall of silence was founded on.

A part of her wanted to leave it alone and let him exist in his own little world. But she also remembered what Mallack said to the team during their last debrief. She recalled a piece of advice one of her prizefighting trainers gave her over a decade ago:

"Listen, Watts, the only way you're going to be the best is if you beat the best. You can't fight simulators forever. You gotta get in the ring with real fighters. And not just second-rate wannabes. No, you gotta train with people stronger than you to get stronger. It's the only way to know for sure you're getting better."

She also remembered what Malaysia and Alexia told her about Malcolm's training method, but then thought about the Analyst's conclusions regarding them fighting well below their opponents' potential. Her instincts advised her to overcome the wall Malcolm built, not just for her own personal appeasement, but for the sake of the team and the mission. And the only way to get over it was to climb it and kick it down brick by brick.

I have to talk to him. But I have to use tact. Usually, when I confront somebody, I end up throwing stars, and it never ends well. I gotta try, though. He has to at least tell me why he's acting like this. Not wanting to fight me is one thing. Completing icing us out, this is something different entirely. And I'm gonna do something about it. If he doesn't talk to me, if I don't break him out of his shell, I'm gonna give him the fight of his life. I'm gonna find him, I'm gonna beat him down, I'm gonna get fired, then I'll go home.

She raised her right eyebrow, cracked a wry smile, banged her hand on the table, and got up from her seat and proceeded out of the conference room. She marched to the cafeteria. Karl, Daisy, and Duncan sat at one of the tables about ten feet away chatting about nothing. Symone walked in and asked, "Has anyone seen Bennett?"

Daisy turned to face Symone. "Last I saw, he was headed to the training room again."

"Thought so." Symone's pupils burned yellow. She clenched her fists and caused sparks to fly from her hands.

Duncan noticed it and reacted, "Whoa, you alright?"

"I'll let you know when I get back."

She turned around to walk out. Daisy's eyes widened, "Wait, what are you about to do?"

"Kick his ass." Symone opened the door and left. Daisy rose up to catch her, but Karl gently grabbed her arm, and Daisy turned to Karl and saw him shaking his head.

"Let her go," he commanded.

"But Karl, Symone's going to spar Malcolm."

"I know," he declared. "And it's about time."

"Why do you say it like that?" Duncan inquired.

"We all have been waiting for somebody to give Malcolm a run for his money," Karl reasoned. "If anyone is going to do it, might as well be her."

"Karl, you can't be serious," Daisy rebutted. "Malcolm isn't going to lose to her."

"Well, we definitely won't know sitting here, will we? Let's go!" Duncan shot out of his seat. "Let's find the others and get a front-row seat to the fight!"

"I'm with him," Karl agreed as he stood up.

"This is a bad idea," Daisy argued. "But okay, let's get Alexia and Malaysia."

Symone turned and marched to the elevators. She took in the view one last time in case it was the last time she'd see the Grand Hall. Symone pressed the down button and waited impatiently. The elevator bellowed a low hum, and Malaysia came out of the elevator as Symone crossed her walking in.

"Hey, Symone! Where are you headed?" Malaysia asked.

"To find Bennett," Symone spoke with the voice of a Divine. She pressed "T" for the training floor. Malaysia noticed Symone's eyes through her sensitive lenses and noticed that she was literally heated. Malaysia raised her right finger and started to say something just as the doors closed. She watched the elevator speed down the shaft, then shrugged her shoulders and headed to the quarters.

About ten seconds later, Karl, Daisy, and Duncan walked out of the cafeteria and headed to the quarters. They saw Malaysia, and Karl yelled, "Malaysia! What are you about to do?"

Malaysia turned around and said, "About to run a flight simulator in my room. You all look like you're about to get into some trouble."

"We're about to watch a fight," Duncan said.

"Ooh, between who?"

"Malcolm and Symone," Daisy chimed in.

Malaysia's jaw dropped. "You're kidding! For real? Malcolm's going to fight Symone?"

"Well, more like Symone's about to fight him," Karl reasoned.

"We can't miss this. Where's Alexia?" Malaysia asked as she motioned them to head to the quarters.

"Probably inside. Let's get her and head down there!" Duncan exclaimed.

Okay, Symone rationalized, *when you get down there, don't do anything stupid, okay? Just ask him what's going on with him, let him answer, and then you're good.*

Remember, you've fought your whole life to get on this team, and they chose YOU.

I want to fight him so badly. But maybe I shouldn't do this, not yet.

I should just ask Mallack to be transferred to another team, another supervisor. If he's not willing to train me the best way I know to be, then maybe he's just not the one. I should just fall back.

I want all that energy, all his energy. He'll never forget me once I'm done with him.

The elevator hummed. Symone breathed deeply. The doors opened, and she marched down the hallway to Malcolm's training room.

Malcolm was running through his basic forging exercises, bending metal into a variety of weapons. He held a small metal plate in his flat left palm and slightly flexed his fingers, concentrating on the molecules and energy the plate contained, and he molded the plate into a throwing knife. Completely transformed, he grabbed the handle of the knife with his right hand and threw it toward the training room entry, just as Symone opened the door. The knife whizzed past the right side of her face and pierced the wall behind her.

Malcolm saw Symone's silhouette and sensed her energy, noting that she was a bit warmer than usual. Symone walked into the training room. The AI advised, "Symone Watson, codename Starburst. Modifying room to meet powered state." The walls hummed as the door sealed them inside.

With a low tone, she said, "Hello, Bennett."

Malcolm shook his attraction to her body and maintained his steely-eyed, straight-faced, resolve. "Miss Watson, what are you doing here?"

"I'm here to train," Symone responded.

"What do you mean?"

"Exactly what I said. I'm here to train. If I'm going to get better, I have to train, right?"

Malcolm walked toward her, "Yes, but why in here? With me?"

Symone planted her feet and balanced her weight on her right heel. "The only way I know how to get better is by fighting against fighters, the best fighters, not stupid simulators. You ought to know that about me by now, but you've completely shut me out, so I guess I shouldn't be surprised."

Akan, can't you give it a rest?! Malcolm wanted to say.

Instead, he retorted, "I haven't shut anyone out. I've been training, just like you and everybody else should be." He noticed Symone shifting her weight and sensed her charging up.

"Prove it, Malcolm. What is going on with you?" Symone slowly lit one of her hands, tiny sparks flowing from it. Symone calmly explained, "Since that night with the Collector's team, you've given me the cold shoulder. You barely talk to me, and you haven't said two words to anyone else here. Frimas, Duncan's swooning is better treatment than this! What's really going on with you?"

Malcolm started feeling ambushed. But there was something comforting to him about her confrontation. *I got a lot going on, but I don't want to talk to you about it. Except, I do.* Her presence and her defiant concern made him want to bare his whole soul, to describe to her the nightmares and the visions he couldn't shake, to reveal how vulnerable he felt since that night when he put his feelings out there to her, to share how embarrassed he felt after he had his ass handed to him by an opponent with an 88/12 ratio.

But he also had a sudden urge to crawl into a hole and disappear from the room. *Symone won't move, she's standing in my way!*

Symone sensed that Malcolm was near the edge but couldn't bring himself to jump into her arms. Her eyes smoldered yellow, and she declared, "You're not leaving this room until you talk to me, Malcolm. So, either start talking," suddenly, white nanites shot out of the right side of the wall and enveloped Symone from neck to toe, and the cloak shimmered yellow around her, "or suit up."

She charged her hand, and an energy star hovered below it. She then flicked her hand, and the ball surged toward Malcolm and hit him in his chest. The blast shocked his cloak while he grimaced and took two steps backward to catch himself from falling.

"What the Frimas?" Malcolm yelled, shocked that she attacked him.

She hurled another star at him, and he planted his feet and crossed his arms to brace for impact. The star knocked him onto his back. Symone stepped toward him. "You gonna talk to me now?"

"What the Frimas are you doing, Watson?" Malcolm swiftly got back on his feet.

"Whatever I have to do to get you to say whatever is on your mind. Or, you can try to dodge my stars, just like you keep dodging my question." She volleyed another star toward him. He timed the delivery, sensed the star, and deflected its trajectory from him to the wall.

Karl, Daisy, Duncan, and Malaysia ran into the quarters to find Alexia. She sat on the couch watching a reality show on the holoscreen. "Alexia, come with us to the training rooms!" Karl summoned.

"Oh Akan, I don't want to train today," Alexia sighed.

"No, not you," Karl said. "Symone went down to fight Malcolm!"

"Are you serious?" Alexia leaped from her seat in excitement and raced toward them. They all ran out of the room and toward the elevators. Alexia pressed the down button on the elevator and waited excitedly. "Oh, Malcolm is about to get the business! She listened to me! I can't believe it!"

"Wait, you encouraged this?" Daisy asked. "You should have stopped her! She could get hurt!"

"Daisy, you worry way too much," Alexia retorted. "Symone is a grown woman and can do whatever she wants to do. And she can take him, I know it!"

"Yeah, Malcolm's met his match in there," Duncan said. "And I need a front-row seat for this!"

"Malcolm isn't going to fight her. I bet he's already left the room," Daisy said.

"No, not this time. Symone isn't going to let him leave. She's built differently than the rest of us. And Malcolm knows it," Malaysia responded.

Malcolm got frustrated with Symone's barrage. She said to him, "I won't let you keep ignoring me, Malcolm." She volleyed another star toward him, and he deflected it the same as the last. "So, what are you going to do?" She created a bigger star than the last, and Malcolm woke up. "You accepted my challenge to fight you, only to disappear on all of us like we have the plague. Why?" Symone hurled the star at him.

Malcolm ached inside, knowing fully that she was right. Unless he was going to reveal his heart to her, the only option left was to fight. He charged toward Symone and slid under the star, barely escaping its size and energy. As he slid across the floor, his head craned to watch the star barrel into the wall and explode. He didn't notice Symone rallying toward him, both hands lit and ready to strike him. He exploded onto his feet suddenly, and just as Symone lunged forward, he jumped and flipped over her. She barrel-rolled on the floor, regained her footing, and turned around, only to realize she had lost her position in front of the door.

I fell for it. He better not reach for that door. I'll blast his arm off! She quickly blasted upward and arced above him, determined not to let him escape.

To her surprise, Malcolm ripped a black metal chain from around his neck and quickly morphed it into a thin rope the size of a charging cord. *Alright, Watson, you asked for it.* He then held onto one end of the rope and launched the other end toward Symone. The rope spun around her and seized her immediately.

She gasped gleefully. *He didn't leave?! Yes!* The rope then began to glow, and Symone slightly moaned as the nanites took on the damage. She stared ravenously at Malcolm, who was staring back intensely while pulling on the rope and slowly drawing her closer to him.

Malcolm expressed, "I accepted your challenge because I believe you are amazingly gifted. You might be the only fighter here that can handle me. But I choose not to spar with anyone because I always end up hurting people. And I don't want to risk hurting anyone under my direct supervision."

Symone was irritated by his good soldier schtick. "Such textbook bull! That may be how you feel. But you don't get to make that choice for me." Symone's body auraed, and the heat eviscerated his lasso. Symone lit her hands, and a bright yellow ball of fire grew in front of her. With a ferocious calm, Symone declared, "I decide whether I want to fight. I decide who I want to fight. I decide when I want to fight. I knew the risks when I signed up for this. I knew the risks when I met you. We have to make that decision *together*. You don't get to take my choice away from me." She launched the star at Malcolm, and the impact blasted him into the wall.

The Analyst sat in his lab running calculations on his holoscreen. An alert appeared on his holoscreen. He tapped it, and it displayed Symone and Malcolm battling in the training room. Exhilarated, his face beamed like one of Symone's stars. He cried, "Yes! Yes! Yes! This is what I've been waiting for!" The Analyst activated his stripe and connected the line to Director Mallack. "Director, take a look at the shot I'm sending you now."

Seated at her desk, Mallack saw the alert on her holoscreen. She tapped her keypad, and it opened the live feed of Symone and Malcolm in the training room. She smiled and declared, "About time. Okay, let's see if we were right about you, Symone Watson." She swiped her hand upward, and the display moved to the big holoscreen on her wall. She turned her chair and watched intently.

Alexia wailed, "Come on, come on! We're missing it!"

The elevator finally stopped, and the doors opened. Daisy beat everyone to the observation room while the others sprinted to get there. They pulled out the chairs from the desk in the back and glued their eyes beyond the glass.

Malcolm groaned as he picked himself slowly off the floor. Symone's hair and eyes glowed bright yellow. Malcolm swore he was staring into the face of a Divine. *Frimas, who is she?*

Symone said, "How can you expect any of us to get better if you isolate yourself from us? You heard Mallack. We have to get stronger, faster. But you will not get as good as the Collector's Elite doing the same stuff you've always done, expecting different results. We are a team, Malcolm, and if we ever expect to beat them, you have to learn to trust us and fight us. Just like this." Symone charged her hands again, and Malcolm picked up a metal sword he previously created and flattened it to make a shield. He then charged at her, and she threw another star at him. The star obliterated the shield, and Malcolm continued his charge, launched himself at her, and kicked her in her abdomen. She flew ten feet and slid on the floor. *Damn, he kicks hard.*

He took another weapon and morphed it into an oversized hammer and swung it at Symone. She rolled away from him as the hammer struck the ground, then kicked Malcolm in the face with all her might. Malcolm rolled to the ground, then rolled back up, kneeling in fighter's stance. Symone stood up, and they traded punches, jabs, kicks, blocks, and grabs before Symone lit her hand and smacked Malcolm with a hot left slap to his face, just as Malcolm grabbed her right shoulder and hurled her to his right, where some loose metal plates were on the ground, spinning her twice before she could regain her footing. Malcolm quickly flexed his senses and used the metal plates to construct a metal dome around her, and before Symone could understand what Malcolm did, she was sealed shut. Malcolm piled on the plates to give the impenetrable crypt more strength and density. Malcolm then pushed his hands toward each other to shrink the dome's size, making it more difficult for Symone to stand. As he shrank the dome, he piled on more plates.

Symone knelt as the walls caved in. *How the Frimas does he do this? No time to get curious, how do we get out of here?* She charged her hands and touched the walls. The dome began to glow, and Symone began to yell.

Director Mallack leaned onto her desk, marveling at the screen like she was watching a prizefight. Her stomach was a bundle of nerves churning inside her. "Come on, Watson, what are you going to do?" she mumbled, glad no one heard her rooting for Symone.

Stephanie entered her office and said, "Here's the quarterly report you asked for, Director."

"Great," Mallack responded without taking her eyes off the screen. "Copy it to my holoscreen."

Stephanie noticed Mallack's gaze and pondered, "Everything okay, Director?"

"Oh, yes. Just watching Malcolm and Symone sparring in the training room."

"Malcolm?" Stephanie's eyes widened. "*Malcolm,* Malcolm? As in Malcolm 'don't train with anybody' Bennett?"

Mallack chuckled, "That's the one."

Stephanie's lips parted. "Wow, I never thought I'd live to see the day." Stephanie took her mini holoscreen out her white coat pocket and placed it on Mallack's desk. The report copied to Mallack's holoscreen. She then retrieved her holoscreen and swiped and tapped to get the live feed of Malcolm and Symone in training. She smiled and said, "Let me know if there's anything else you need, ma'am."

"You got it," Mallack waited for Symone's counter to Malcolm's strategy.

Daisy stared at Malcolm and thought, *He's gonna kill her!* She attempted to run out of the room, but Karl grabbed her before she could speed away. "No, she's got this," he said.

"He's gonna kill her, Karl!" Daisy said.

"No, no he won't. She won't let him. Stop being dramatic and sit down." Daisy pouted and crossed her arms.

Symone supercharged, and the dome glowed from red to yellow to white to blue. The dome burst into billions of lights like several fireworks all set off at once. The training room shook from the explosion.

Symone stood up, her entire body aglow with a dizzying light display that kept Malcolm mesmerized as he stared at her like a deer caught in headlights. Her intensity and fervor caused Malcolm to unravel. The walls he had feverishly fought to maintain turned brittle and imploded in response to the captivating light show Symone put on for him. She raised her hands above the white locs glowing from her head, and a white star the diameter of her body hovered over her. Malcolm came to his senses and ran toward Symone, both hands in front of him. Symone launched the star at Malcolm, and Malcolm suspended the star in midair. He then began to manipulate the star, holding his hands and mashing them slowly together out in front of him, trying to flatten the star. Symone then reached out one hand and pushed star power to make the fireball denser, more intense, and unstable, hoping the star would be more challenging and time-consuming for Malcolm to manipulate.

An invisible force began compelling her to reach out her other hand toward Malcolm, pulling her arm like a magnet. *What's this? What's going on? Get it together!* She resisted the pull and locked in, simultaneously feeling a surge of energy rush through her fiery veins. Malcolm experienced a similar compulsion to draw power from Symone, to draw Symone closer to him, as if he sensed Symone's presence inside him. He detected the same energy signature he felt in Symone's veins and her stars now flowing through his own veins. Symone had tripled the size and intensity of the star, and Malcolm's senses dialed up uncontrollably. The ball of fire morphed in response – the fire extinguished, and the ball solidified to a rock. Lush green and yellow grass sprouted all over. Water flowed from the rock and filled some of the spaces on it.

Malcolm and Symone were stupefied, knocked out of concentration. Their release from the rock, and each other, unlatched the rock's in-air suspension, and it crashed onto the floor, the cloak on the ground keeping it from breaking the floor beneath it.

Malaysia stood up and said, "What the Frimas?" The rest of the team marveled at what they achieved and debated internally over what this meant for the future of their squad.

Malcolm could not ascertain how his power evolved, nor how he transformed the star into a planet. Symone did not care, though, her heart filled with euphoria, ecstasy, and passion, unlike anything she had ever felt before, a joy pumping from her heart like a flame ablaze. All logic thrown to the corners of her subconscious, she charged at Malcolm and grabbed him by the shoulders, pinning him to the floor. She straddled Malcolm's lap and squeezed his sides with her thighs tightly, silently wishing she could feel something bulging through his nanotech underneath her. She latched to his shoulders again and slammed his back into the ground three times. She then threw haymakers at his face. He blocked as many of them as he could, then took her arms and swung them around her and behind her back, then sat up, with her still sitting in his lap, bear hugging her.

His manhood was fighting his logic for control of his will. He threw her to his left and rolled on top of her between her legs, now having her pinned, and the internal struggle only intensified. She yelled in passionate fury, taking her legs and wrapping them around his body. *Damn, she feels so good.* She squeezed with all her might, but he wouldn't let her go. She twisted, trying to regain the upper hand, but he only held her down tighter. He stared into her eyes as she stared into his, still struggling to get free from his grip. They both breathed heavily from exhaustion and lust.

"So, what are you going to do?" Malcolm inquired, slightly raising his right eyebrow, quick not to admit he was talking to himself more than to Symone.

She wriggled just a little longer, relishing this moment, having not felt this invigorated in years. She wouldn't give this moment up. Her hands gave off sparks. His touch, his strength, his power, his control, she would not admit it, but she was putty in his hands.

Alexia yelled, "Come on, Symone, get up!" Duncan nodded in agreement.

Malcolm could not stop staring at Symone, seeing something he felt he had never seen before, but feeling déjà vu, an echo of a lifetime ago. He sensed Symone's soul. He *knew* it. She awakened him, brought something dead in him to life. He wanted her more than anything else in the world at this moment. She sparked his engine somehow, and the boulder in the middle of the floor was the proof.

But before Malcolm could give into his emotions, his legs suddenly dangled in the air. Symone levitated, carrying him with her thighs still wrapped tightly around his waist. He struggled to get his bearings straight and not be entangled by how perfect her body felt connected to his, nanites be damned. Symone shuttled them upward, then swiftly unwrapped her legs. Malcolm bear hugged her from the small of her back.

Symone struggled to contain her lust. *Screw it.* She reasoned to kill two zintols with one stone. She hugged him from his shoulders and pulled him into her. Their cloaks instinctively responded to her action and moved away from their faces. She pressed her lips into his and gave him a kiss that sent a shock down his spine and engulfed their veins with a heat they hadn't felt in ages. Her eyes shone white behind her eyelids while she reveled in the passion she ignited.

She then whispered to Malcolm, "Gotcha." She released him, then pushed against his chest with her palms, forcing him flat before blasting an energy beam into his chest. Malcolm plummeted. Snapping out of his blissful state, Malcolm braced himself for imminent impact. He twisted his body, preparing his feet and cloak to absorb the blow. He hit the floor, and he flexed his knees. *Frim of a move, Watson!*

He gathered scattered metal shards from the floor and sharpened them with his senses. He then launched them upward toward Symone. Symone destroyed the shards with small stars, then rushed toward Malcolm. She dropped stars on the ground near Malcolm and attempted to blow them up, but Malcolm grabbed them and threw them back at her. She raised an energy shield to block the stars. As she drew closer to the ground and dropped the shield, she didn't see Malcolm rising to meet her with a bat in his hand. He swung it and slammed her in her left shoulder. He knocked her off balance, and she crashed into the ground. Malcolm landed on the ground and split the bat into two pieces.

Symone got up and noticed Malcolm with two short swords in his hands. He ran up to her and swung them. She dodged them and created an energy shield to block his swords, hoping they would shatter in his hands. But he forged the swords to endure her intense heat, making the swords burn with each swing into the shield. She quickly launched three stars at Malcolm. He dodged two of them, but the third struck his leg and tripped him. He dropped one of the swords as he fell. She then opened her lit fist and tried to land a palm plant into the back of Malcolm's skull, but he rolled and stood up, then swung the remaining sword at Symone's arm. He barely missed, and Symone countered with another star that hit Malcolm's side. He flew backward, anticipating Symone's next move to launch another star at him. He grabbed it, spun, and hurled it back at her. It hit her chest, and she careened into the wall.

The Elite were watching an instant classic, high-stakes prizefight that should have been televised. Director Mallack marveled and took mental notes. Stephanie, Dax, and the analysts in Intelligence ate popcorn and chips and stared at the big holoscreen after they placed bets on who would claim victory. And the Analyst canceled all his appointments and prepared to spend the rest of the day analyzing the data collected from their contest.

Malcolm waved his arms, and every sword in the room rose and circled in front of him. He concentrated on their shapes and their molecular make-up, and he summoned them to heat up. The swords glowed red. Symone shook off her daze and analyzed Malcolm's latest tactic. Malcolm took those same swords and made them spin around his waist. He then assembled a disc that surrounded his waist and stretched the disc to become a cylindrical tube, capped with a platform he stood on. The swords spun faster, and they propelled Malcolm off the floor. He made a beeline toward Symone.

Okay, now damn, man! How am I supposed to beat this? Symone winced, lit her hands again, and launched into the air to defend against Malcolm's pursuit. She launched stars at him trying to knock the swords off, but having compensated for her heat, Malcolm's swords sliced through her stars unscathed. She moved toward the floor, and Malcolm took other shards of metal and launched them at Symone. She dodged some and shot others out of the sky. *I can't outfly him?! How is he doing this?!*

She stopped midair and built a large star in front of her. Malcolm flexed his senses with his hands and split her star in two. She felt her arms slowly being pushed backward by Malcolm's might. She concentrated and pushed her arms forward, pushing the star back together and making it more intense. Malcolm was dissatisfied and split the star again. They tugged back and forth for thirty seconds before she finally launched the right half toward him. He held it while not losing grip on the left half or his flight contraption.

Symone then said, "Surprise, Malcolm!" Malcolm didn't realize that Symone had carefully placed tiny stars around the room while he was chasing her around. She released her grip on the big star, then lowered herself swiftly to the ground.

Okay, Symone. It's now or never.

As fast as she could, she unleashed an aura burst from her body, and it set off every star in the room. Malcolm was unfazed. He grabbed all the energy that exploded from across the room and swirled his hands to concentrate the energy. He then flattened his hands and forged the star power into an energy whip. *It's time to end this.*

Symone had run out of options. Malcolm lowered himself toward the floor and threw the whip in her direction. It coiled around her, and he tightened its grip. She attempted to fly away, but he yanked her toward him, and her struggles only caused the whip to constrict her even more. Then, he intensified the whip, causing its temperature to soar. Symone, drained from the relentless fight, was devoid of strength. Malcolm then squeezed the whip, and it exploded. Symone crashed into and slid down the wall onto the floor. Her cloak was dealt massive damage, rendered down to just 3% integrity.

Malcolm landed and dismantled his contraption. He grabbed one of his swords and held the tip of the blade toward Symone's neck. The nanites shimmered at the blade's point.

"Yield."

While trying to catch her breath, Symone defiantly said, "Screw you, Malcolm." She stubbornly tried to get back up. Malcolm's eyes widened, and he growled, dropped the sword, and picked Symone up from her armpits and pushed her up against the wall.

"Yield, Miss Watson!"

Symone had no more fight in her. She tried to swing at Malcolm, but her arms would not cooperate. She tried to kick him, but she could barely move them. Still, she would not give Malcolm the satisfaction.

"The only way I'm going to yield is if you kill me. I never yield." She raised an eyebrow with the tiny spark of energy she had left. Malcolm stared into her eyes again. "What are you going to do to me, Malcolm?"

Their breaths matched. Symone gazed into his eyes, then drank in the tall glass of man he was, taking in the way the black nanites accentuated every part of his chiseled frame. She loved the way his hands held her so firmly, yet gently, like he was afraid of hurting her for real. She recalled how her butt bounced and pressed against the wall when he pinned her, and the only thing keeping her from running her fingers through his hair and wrapping her legs around him in that moment was the weakness that possessed them all. She wanted him to use that controlled strength on her right then, realizing that the mantra he defended the city with was a mantra for life, and she craved to experience *him* in his rawest, purest form.

Malcolm was frazzled internally, and he analyzed every single inch of Symone's body, from the locs of her hair to the soles of her feet, the way her chest moved as she struggled to catch her breath, the way her lips parted and quivered in weakness. He could sense *and* feel her vulnerability in his hands. He craved to tend to her, to care for her, to *love* her.

Damn it, Watson. You are so fine, and stubborn as Frimas! What am I going to do with you? What have you done to me? Malcolm's attraction to Symone was undeniable, and he wanted to order the nanites off them and meld their bodies together. But he couldn't bring himself to make the same move she made on him earlier, his righteous logic overtaking his instinctual craving. As he recognized the battle was over, regardless of Symone's desire to fight to her literal death, he surmised a moral victory would be his prize instead of a literal concession.

He slowly released her from his grip, softly lowering her to the floor. He stared at her a few seconds more, then turned and walked toward the door.

What the Frimas? Symone sighed, "Don't stop." Symone slumped to her knees and looked up at him. "Where are you going, Malcolm?"

As he touched the exit, he replied, "I'm not going to kill you, Miss Watson. That'd be a bad look for both of us. The Analyst is going to want to talk soon, so I'm cleaning up then talking to him about what happened in here."

Symone shook her head, her hair dangling from her scalp as she looked down. Her body screamed for a release of the tension and passion she felt all over her body despite the agony her same body was begging to be numbed away. *Come back here! Please come back! Pin me back to the wall. Do something to me.* She finally got her fight fix, but she desired more. Her body was on fire, and she wanted him to put her out, but she wouldn't tell him that, not now. She instead sank in defeat, sitting on her feet, struggling to keep her torso straight, while the maintenance droids emerged from the walls and began to clean up the mess Malcolm and she made.

Malcolm then said to her, "I try to train twice a day, once in the rising, and once sometime after midday just before I go home."

"Wait, what?" Symone gasped.

"You know when I'll be here. I won't come looking for you, so either be here, or don't."

Malcolm left the room, and Symone breathed a sigh of relief, falling to her side and rolling onto her back as the machines whizzed by resetting the room. She chuckled a little, a tear falling from her right eye. *This dramatic bastard. He might have won the game, but I won the match!*

Malcolm walked toward the elevator. He couldn't stop thinking about that midair kiss, the way she felt when she straddled him on the ground, the tiny planet they created, and his new enhancements and his instant mastery of them. His heart couldn't stop pounding from the adrenaline and dopamine coursing through his veins. The doors opened, and he walked in and wondered, *Aww Frimas, they got this on camera. Mallack is going to have a field day with this.*

Meanwhile, Alexia, Duncan, Malaysia, Daisy, and Karl waited for the elevator to take Malcolm up to the Grand Hall before leaving the observation room and entering the swiftly repairing training room to check on Symone. Malaysia and Alexia knelt and asked, "You okay?"

Symone laughed and admitted, "I've never felt better."

"I don't know if that's sarcasm or real, but you did your thing for sure, Symone," Daisy reacted. "I can't believe you survived!"

Symone tried to get up, but Alexia signaled to her to stay on the floor. "You guys were watching?"

"Of course! We weren't going to miss this! You and Malcolm fighting? Girl, y'all were legendary!" Duncan exclaimed.

"But, I lost," Symone answered.

"You didn't yield," Alexia countered, "so technically, the battle is still on. I see you took my advice. How did it feel?"

"I can't begin to explain it to you all. Right now, though, I'm just tired and need like three days of sleep."

"Well," Karl reasoned, "how about I carry you to the quarters and you sleep it off there."

Symone nodded, "I'd like that very much, please and thank you."

While the team helped Symone off the floor, the Analyst backed up all the data from Malcolm and Symone's fight. He slid open the drawer where a small holoscreen sat, took it out, and laid it flat on the countertop. He tapped a few buttons on it, and it began downloading a copy of all the data to it. The Analyst called Director Mallack and said, "Director, did you watch the whole battle?"

Mallack stood looking at the skyline. "Yes, I did. What can you tell me, Analyst?"

"Well, from what I can gather, both Malcolm and Symone experienced a colossal shift in their powers just by being near each other. I can't tell whether it was rage or what, but Symone's heat signature intensified significantly. Meanwhile, Malcolm manipulated molecular structures at a much more rapid pace and seemed to have gained a new power of telekinesis, though I don't think that's what's happening."

"What about the star that turned into a planet?" Mallack inquired.

"Malcolm tapped into molecular structures in a brand-new way. He doesn't just manipulate them. He transforms them. Again, this is all preliminary stuff. I haven't even begun data mining to give any credence to what I'm speculating."

Mallack got impatient. "Well, tell me what you're speculating. Help me understand what you think is happening to them."

The Analyst sat down at his desk, cleared his throat, and asked, "Director, have you ever heard of the Affinity Theory?"

12
Reflections

“So, let's talk about yesterday."

Malcolm sat in his usual chair in Director Mallack's office, legs crossed with his right arm on the armrest and his left hand holding his head and covering his mouth. He stared at his boss, preparing for this conversation the past twenty-five cycles, just as nervous as he was when he rode the elevator after leaving Symone in the training room. Mallack stared back at him, seated with her hands at her side and back against her seat, and waited for him to say something back.

"What do you want to know?"

"Where's your mind at?"

Malcolm danced around the question. "What do you mean?"

Mallack sat up, planted her elbows on the desk, and clasped her hands together. *Why is he always like this? I mean, I know why, but* why?

"Malcolm, a lot has happened in the past few weeks. And it's clear to me that you've been affected by much of it. You've changed, and yesterday's spar between you and Symone is proof of that."

Malcolm rubbed his middle finger across his nose. He then shrugged his shoulders, "I can't argue with you on that, boss. A lot has changed within me, and I don't understand it, how it's happening, or why."

"Malcolm, the Analyst said you evolved again yesterday, utilizing your powers in ways you never have before, with a level of mastery that defies logic. You're flying. You're stopping energy and sending it back. You're creating planets, now!"

"Yeah," Malcolm returned as he slightly chuckled, "the planet part kind of surprised me, too."

"How do you explain it, Malcolm? What's going on with you?"

Malcolm scratched his head and adjusted himself in his seat while replying, "To be honest, I really don't know. I've been training and practicing, and I've only been able to reproduce this *change* twice since the Analyst told me about it happening at Sentinel. And both times, I didn't tell myself, 'Evolve.' I just did. And here we are."

Mallack decided to push the issue and addressed what Malcolm wanted to avoid. "This evolution, it wouldn't have anything to do with Watson, would it?"

Malcolm wasn't shocked by her question, but he didn't want Mallack to know that, so he adjusted his face to appear puzzled. "What do you mean, Director?"

Akan, he is really making me work for it! Mallack pushed her chair back and stood up while saying, "Exactly what I asked, Malcolm. I'm looking at all possible explanations, and since Symone has been here, you have been different. And so has she. The Analyst noted that both your demos and stats are changing at an accelerated rate. None of your previous trainees have recorded such changes, and none of them have changed you this much this far into the process. Do you think she has something to do with it?"

Malcolm recalled his interactions with Symone and tried to piece together Mallack's theory. He was certain that Symone was a significant factor, especially since he was beginning to unpack the connection between what he sensed with Symone and the stars she produced. But to what degree, he was unsure. "Well, boss, I can't say for sure whether she is the common denominator. I talked to the Analyst about it yesterday, and he said he would look into it more since he needs to do more data processing. So, I don't know if it's her powers doing something to me or what."

"Well, if not that, what else could it be?"

I don't want to tell you, boss! It's embarrassing as Frimas! Malcolm backed off again, "I don't have a clue."

"You're being coy with me, Malcolm," Mallack observed as she walked toward the seat next to Malcolm. "Talk to me about how things are going with you and Symone. We're about halfway through this quarter. How is she faring in your eyes? Is she Elite? Do you think she understands her role on the team?"

Malcolm sat up, then leaned forward, elbows on knees. "I mean, she's great. The team adores her, she's intelligent and insightful. She has a killer instinct that she needs to work on, but that same instinct makes her dangerous in the field in a good way. She wants to be better, if not the best, at what she does. She wants this team to succeed, she wants to be on this team, and I think she makes us better. As much as I didn't agree with it at first, I think putting her on the team was for the best. Especially given what we're up against now."

Mallack stared at Malcolm for about five seconds, then leaned forward and said, chuckling, "Malcolm, that's the biggest load of bull you've ever tried to unload on me."

Malcolm said, "Director?"

"Malcolm, cut the crap! Do you remember what you said to me about Malaysia after her first four weeks?" She mimicked Malcolm's voice, "'I think she is an absolute waste of time and needs to spend more time down in the Powered Academy before ever considering her for a Super team, let alone the Elite.' Or even Karl, who aced every single test you gave him, 'The Mammoth would be better off handling demolition projects than serving on this team. He has a lot to learn about being a team player and honing his skills for the sake of defending Uri City.'"

"You called Daisy a 'know-it-all' who you thought was more interested in running the unit than being on it. Told me that Alexia would never get over her past mistakes to graduate from the Academy. And need I remind you about Duncan at the beginning of the quarter?"

Malcolm looked to the side and resigned, "You remember that?"

Mallack's eyes widened. "Malcolm, I remember *everything*! You're one of my right hands in this building. Are you going to be honest with me now? Or do I have to do you like Symone did you yesterday to get the truth out of you?"

Malcolm slowly rolled his eyes and tilted his head upward, then let out a sigh while he said, "I can't get anything past you, can I?"

"Please stop trying and talk to me," Mallack pleaded. "What the Frimas is going on with you and Symone?"

So much! She's a dream! And I'm struggling between keeping things professional between her and me, fanboying over her, and begging her to have her way with me! But I'm not going to tell you that!

"Director, there's nothing going on as far as I can tell," Malcolm lied. "She is my mentee; I am her mentor. I'm training her, and once training is complete, it'll be on you and HQ to decide whether she stays or moves on or whatever. I can only tell you what I see, and she's doing remarkably well. She could work on her desire to fight every person she comes into contact with, though."

"Right, and what else?" Mallack said.

Malcolm scrambled, feeling and resisting the pressure to reveal his heart. "I don't know, boss. She reminds me a lot of me."

"Is that what it is? You see you in her?"

"Kinda."

Mallack cut her eyes and took a deep breath. She knew trying to get more out of him was moot. "Okay, Malcolm. I'll leave you alone, for now. Whatever this evolution is, keep honing it. I have a feeling we're going to need it, going to need you, to take down the Collector and his plans."

"I know, boss. I'm counting on it and looking forward to the next challenge."

"Well, Malcolm, is there anything else you want to say?" Mallack asked.

Malcolm wanted to express his fears about the nightmares in his head showing up as visions in real time, but he withdrew because he didn't want to cause more concern for Mallack. He simply replied, "No, boss, I'm good."

"Very well, then you're dismissed."

Malcolm rose from his chair and walked toward Mallack's door when she said, "Malcolm, I want you to know that you can talk to me about anything."

"I know, Director. Thank you." Malcolm exited Mallack's office. Once the door sealed, she rose from her seat and returned to her desk. She then typed a few keys on her countertop, and a notepad appeared on her holoscreen. She typed, "Bennett and Watson's connection □ Affinity Theory? Push them together and observe further evolution of their demos and stats. Revisit in two weeks with the Analyst." She then hit SAVE, and the notepad disappeared. She sat still, ruminating on the future and Malcolm and Symone's potential role in securing it. *Gotta stay the course. They are the key.* Her stripe lit up, and she answered the call, "This is Mallack. Thank you for calling me back. I need to meet with you as soon as possible. I need to discuss something with you. Really, I have a favor to ask of you."

Symone and Alexia were taking advantage of the beautiful, sunny day by walking to a small eatery a couple of blocks away from the Company. Alexia was extremely curious about Symone's fight with Malcolm and her thoughts on the outcome, but she did not want to just read her mind and extract that information from her. She wanted the story from Symone's mouth. "Okay, so tell me everything. Like, how did you two end up fighting each other?"

Symone grinned and said, "Well, first, he actually called me and told me he accepted my challenge!"

Alexia's jaw dropped, and she shook her head and batted her eyes in disbelief. "Wait, he did what?!"

"Yes, he called me and was like, 'I want to accept your challenge and put you in your place,' talking all kinds of bravado."

Alexia rolled her body around in a sensual motion while saying, "Ayeee, you got inside his head, Symone! Look at you!"

"No, it wasn't like that," Symone downplayed that interaction, "but I was definitely excited about it."

"So, did you two decide yesterday would be the day?"

Symone narrated, "Actually, no. He accepted my challenge right before we had that battle with the Collector's goons. After we lost, Malcolm was super reserved and closed off, you remember? He wouldn't talk to me. He wouldn't even look at me. Losing the Crawler's powers like that pissed him off so badly that he became a shell of himself. And it pissed me off how he was treating all of us, so yesterday I marched down there and basically told him, 'You're either going to talk to me or fight me, but you're not going to keep treating us like crap,' and he didn't say much, but we finally fought, finally!"

"And?" Alexia asked.

Symone's eyes beamed with glee. She jumped a couple of times as she commented, "It was *everything*! Oh Akan, I've never faced anyone like him before. He was so powerful, so strong, and yet so reserved. It's like he didn't want to hurt me, but he flirted with killing me so many times."

Alexia's eyes closed as she breathed in deeply. She responded, "Mmm hmm, that's the sweet spot for you right there, I can tell."

"What do you mean?" Symone asked as Alexia motioned for her to stop. They arrived at Seigel's Restaurant, and Alexia opened the door. The aroma of fresh bread and savory meats filled their nostrils. Symone walked through, and Alexia behind her. The white tile flooring and silver chrome beamed brightly under the white lights above them. The counter, seats, and tables were all covered with royal blue. The bar and the stools stretched the left wall where a single cashier stood waiting for them.

"Well, it's no secret among the team that you're looking for a real fight. You beat all of us down to get Malcolm to notice you. And you took my advice to finally get in the room with him. And, well, it worked!"

"True, but he withdrew. There's something deeper going on with Malcolm than just dealing with me, the team, and defending the city. He's got something inside his mind that he's not sharing with any of us. You'd probably do well to do your mind-reading thing on him to see what exactly is going on with him because he's definitely keeping some stuff to himself that might affect us all."

They stopped at the bar. "Hi, welcome to Seigel's! What can I get you today?" the cashier asked them.

"I'll take the Chef's Mystery Meal," Alexia said. "Symone, what do you want?"

"Oh, you don't have to..."

"I'm going to, though," Alexia interrupted. "Besides, I'm not going to eat by myself. What do you want?"

Symone smiled and said, "Thank you, um, I'll get the Mystery Meal also."

"That's two Chef's Mysteries, that'll come to seventeen creds," the cashier said.

Alexia raised her stripe up to the credit reader, a small, black box on the bar in front of the cashier. The box pulled credits from Alexia's digital wallet. Alexia's stripe turned green, then read, "17 Creds to Seigel's Restaurant."

"Great! The chef will prepare those for you shortly, feel free to have a seat anywhere in the restaurant."

"Thank you!" Alexia said. "Now, you were saying I should read Malcolm's mind?"

"Well, I was joking-serious about it," Symone said.

"It's not like I haven't read it before. But Malcolm's mind is incredibly resistant to my powers because of his powers."

They chose their table toward the front of the restaurant. Symone chose the seat closest to the entrance, and they slid their chairs to sit down as Symone grew curious. "That's interesting. What do you mean by that?"

"Well, Malcolm's power is 'molecular manipulation,' right? So, he can literally take anything and change it into something else."

"Right, but I thought that only applied to stuff like metals and energy, like bending and shape-shifting."

"Oh, Symone, Malcolm hasn't told you what he can really do? Bending metal barely scratches the surface. Malcolm has an incredible power that he barely taps into when he's out in the field, or even training with you. Like, his fight with you yesterday was a sight to see because he's never done that in the field before, and even that barely scratched the surface! But I've always known that he could do that."

Symone's eyes flashed in excitement. "Tell me more!"

"Okay, so, how my powers work, right?" Alexia began to move her hands around, and green mist swirled around them. "The Analyst explained to me that, scientifically, I tap into and bend radio frequencies and electrical signals that give me access to the images in people's heads. I can move back and forth through a person's mind. I can place images in people's minds, turn people's minds off, wipe them blank, all through these different frequencies. But it takes an incredible amount of concentration to do some of these things depending on the mind I'm bending. Same with telekinesis, but it's more about using those waves like ropes to pull things from one place to another. What I call mysticism, the Analyst calls frequency manipulation. Anyway, that's unimportant."

"No, no, I love this, keep going!" Symone said.

"Well, Malcolm can take those same radio frequencies and turn them into things if he wants to. He can block me (or anyone else for that matter) from invading his headspace. He could turn those frequencies into weapons of some kind and probably mess my mind up for a week."

Symone looked shocked. "You're kidding me! Has he ever done that before?"

"Well, he says he hasn't because it takes an incredible amount of concentration on his part to grab frequencies and particles that small. He can feel them, but he said the most he can do is block them. To transform something that small and unstable would probably wipe him out."

Symone tilted her head slightly and squared her eyebrows as she pondered, "So, then, how was he able to do all that he did in the room with me?"

"Girl, I do not know. He made a planet out of your star." Alexia planted both her hands on the table. "That was some next-level stuff he pulled off while still giving you the business."

"Hey," Symone felt a little offended, "I got a few licks in, too, don't forget. I almost had him with that surprise flight."

"Sure, you did," Alexia laughed. "I honestly thought that kiss was going to seal it for you."

Symone chuckled and stuck her tongue out, "I thought it would, too."

"We all did! Was it worth it?"

Symone's voice dropped a few notes as she leaned in, "Not gonna lie, it wasn't because I still lost the fight, but Frimas, yeah, it was! Akan, his lips were so soft for him to be so rugged. I almost didn't want to fight anymore and just wrap my legs around him."

"I was surprised, too, well, not really. I mean, I've seen how you two have been around each other."

Suddenly, a drone appeared in front of them and landed on the table with their meals in plastic containers. "Enjoy!" the cashier said.

"Thank you!" they said as the drone whizzed away.

Symone continued, "So, you're saying that Malcolm literally can manipulate anything?"

"Anything," Alexia summed, "if he has the time to do it. Speaking of doing it, what's going to happen with you and Malcolm?"

"What do you mean?" Symone asked.

"I mean, you two fought, which amounts to you two basically screwing each other, right?" Alexia quipped.

Symone laughed nervously, realizing she was caught red-handed. "I can't get anything past you, can I?"

Alexia's eyes glowed. "Nope, accept your fate. So, what's next?"

"I honestly don't know. We haven't spoken since he left the training room yesterday, and he's still my mentor. I mean," Symone popped her container and looked inside to see pasta noodles lightly soaked in cream and cheese with sliced grilled meat on top, "we did have this one moment after I got beat down by Malaysia when I thought we might hook up, but he said, 'After our mentorship is finished, let's see where things stand,' so I don't know."

Okay, Malcolm! I see you! "Well," Alexia returned as she popped open her container and saw three mini-sub sandwiches, "one thing is for sure, you've got an effect on him. It can't hurt to see it through."

"Unless HQ decides to fire us for doing something stupid. Frimas, I'm surprised Director Mallack didn't cuss me out for kissing Malcolm."

"Mallack doesn't care about that. Malcolm lives by that stupid rule he made up himself. We're all grown, and as long as everyone consents to everything (and nobody's abusing or taking advantage of anybody), no one cares. Director Mallack has let far worse go on before interfering or getting HQ involved, trust me."

Well, Symone pondered, *that's good to know. I wonder why he's so stuck on being Mr. Righteous?*

As the two began scarfing down their Chef's Mysteries, Symone circled back to Malcolm's powers. "Wait a minute, so Malcolm manipulates molecules. Why, exactly, does he need us? He could literally kill everything on site, including the very people he's assigned to capture or kill."

Alexia swallowed what she was chewing on and replied, "Well, between the concentration it takes and his restraint, I think he genuinely doesn't want to just wipe out the world. He's the best of us, for real. He preaches restraint to all of us, 'Remember, we're not out here just using our powers because we can. We're here to help people and defend this city.' He knows that we are all more powerful than we could ever imagine, but he wants us to channel that power into being incredible defenders, not just powered people with a license to kill, you know?"

"That makes sense."

"So, when are you and Malcolm going to fu-, I mean, fight again?"

I'm working on both. "Whenever I can get him alone again," Symone raised her right eyebrow, then they both laughed.

She and Alexia continued eating their meal and sharing stories and laughs. Sometime after finishing their meal, Symone asked Alexia, "So, how did you find yourself here with the Company?"

"Oh, well, before I got here, I was doing odd jobs here and there. My ability to read minds made me a lot of money for people who needed to extract intel from people and who needed things moved from one place to another. I did some terrible things in the Underbelly, so kind of as a way to right my wrongs, I managed to get a job with the Uri City Police in the Highgarden District, doing the same thing but for the good guys. I cracked safes, pulled information from bad guys, that sort of thing. I did that for about four years until I had a freak-out moment where my powers kinda got out of hand."

"What do you mean?" Symone asked.

An idea popped into Alexia's head. "I can show you better than I can tell you." Alexia's eyes turned green, and she lifted her hands. Green mist trailed from her hands to Symone's eyes and ears, and suddenly, Seigel's Restaurant pixelated. Alexia and Symone sat in their chairs under the cover of darkness. Alexia began, "The last job I went on with them. There I am with UPD, those three hovercrafts right there."

Symone observed three UPD hovercrafts parked along a driveway in front of a vast yard. A three-story mansion stood about two hundred feet off. Symone overheard UPD officers dressed in full-tactical gear discussing the plan with a younger Alexia dressed in black and green.

One officer said to her, "Okay, our intel says that he's in there. All we need is for you to take control of the guards, and we'll move in and apprehend him. Should be a quick extraction."

"No problem," Alexia returned to the officer. "Ready when you are."

Alexia narrated to Symone, "The last job I went on with them, we were after a crime boss and closed in on one of the top henchmen that had actually seen the boss's face and home base. This was a top priority, and they wanted me on site, nothing out of the ordinary."

The past Alexia suddenly started wobbling and took four steps backward. She reached for the back of her neck and felt a pin sticking out of it. She pulled it out, examined it, and wondered aloud, "What the Frimas?"

"I didn't own a cloak, and I got hit with a hallucinogenic dart. No one knew where it came from, but man, I was seeing all types of stuff."

The younger Alexia's eyes widened and glowed with the deepest, brightest green. She screamed, and before any of the officers could attempt to help her, they, their hovercraft, the house, and the street they stood on lifted off the ground and then slammed back down forcefully. Alexia unleashed a wave of mental energy, causing the officers to scream in pain. The sirens blared, and some of the security team for the crime boss's henchman started running out of the leveled mansion. Alexia delivered green mist toward them, and one UPD officer tried to subdue Alexia to slow her down. But before he could, Alexia twisted his mind to think that bugs were crawling all over him, and he screamed and wiggled. The security team rose in the air, and Alexia launched them through the sky over half a mile away.

"It was awful. I ended up ripping half the unit apart. It was the worst day of my life, and they had to let me go, else risk the department being exposed for using a powered person to solve crimes."

"Right, because of the ban on the powered in government positions," Symone recalled.

"Exactly."

Light suddenly pierced the darkness. The yard pixelated, and Symone and Alexia returned to Seigel's Restaurant.

Symone rubbed her eyes. "I remember seeing something about that in the underground news wire. The UPD claimed it was a training op gone wrong. I'm so sorry," Symone sympathized.

Alexia sighed. "It was horrible. It took me two years to get over that incident. I spiraled hard. Returned to the Underbelly and channeled my anger and sadness into one-night stands, orgies, and heavy drinking, all while being consumed by non-stop self-rage and -anguish. Because of that and my powers, it was a really bad time for anyone to be close to me. I would put all sorts of thoughts in peoples' heads just to mess with them, get what I wanted from them, and hurt them. I was an absolute wreck."

Symone leaned in and asked, "So, how did you get out of it?"

"Honestly, the Company called me while I was in the middle of another wild night. I was so out of it, I didn't even realize they had called me. They left me a message on my stripe. I woke up the next morning in some rando's bed, and I was in total disbelief when I heard the message. I thought they had made a mistake, but when I called them back, they said, 'Come to this address in two cycles,' and I grabbed my bags and made my way here, hangover and all, and, well, here I am!"

"Did they start you in the Elite?"

Alexia burst into laughter. "Oh, Frimas, no, girl, are you kidding? They put me through the Powered Academy first. I had to get sober, get therapy, get over my sex vices, learn healthier coping skills, *and* relearn how to use my powers more effectively. It took me a whole year to get out of the Academy and make my first Super team. When I got my shot, though, girl, I killed it! I was so determined not to screw it up. I knew this was my last chance, and I made the most of it. I met Malcolm and Karl, who were Elite at that point, and Karl convinced Malcolm to train me."

"Really? How did *that* happen?" Symone was shocked.

"Karl is a really cool guy, you know that. From what I could tell between him and Malcolm, Karl has a way of convincing him to do things he doesn't necessarily want to do. If you ever want Malcolm to do something, Karl is the guy to persuade, to persuade Malcolm. Anyway, so Malcolm takes me to the training room and puts me through pure Frimas. Talking about this man understood my powers and my pain, and he pushed me not only to use my powers better, but to use my pain as my true source of the power."

Symone put her hand in front of her. "Wait, explain that," she nudged, taking mental notes, soaking up everything Alexia was telling her.

"You have to ask Malcolm how he breaks powers down. He says to us all the time, 'Talk to the Analyst,' and he tells us that because the Analyst is on a-whole-nother level with this power/affinity stuff. Malcolm realizes that all of us have a source where our powers come from. It's more than just biology, being born or imbued with power. The source of our powers is connected to our minds, our hearts, and our souls. Whether we're on the Light side or the Dark side of the Affinity scale, we can only become who we're meant to be if we embrace it. So, Malcolm used the darkness in me and taught me to take advantage of it.

"He said, 'It doesn't matter whether you're Dark or Light. Being Dark doesn't make you a bad guy, no more than being Light makes you good. It's just the source. You decide whether you're good or bad, not what you did, not who you were, not where you came from. You decide, here and now, who you choose to be. And with that choice, you use your powers and trust that your team will have you back no matter what.' That broke me, and I never looked back."

Symone's eyes flashed. "He really said that?"

"Yes, Malcolm said that. And I tell you, it's not just words. He believes it, and so do all of us. Malcolm is *the reason* I'm Elite. Even though he didn't believe in me initially, he pushed me, anyway. I owe my life to him."

Symone's heart swooned. "He really has an effect on people."

"Yeah, that he does. And you're getting an up-close-and-personal exclusive of just how effective he can be."

"I don't know," Symone doubted as she shrugged her shoulders. "I still feel like he's got a wall up with me that keeps growing as the days go by. But the only way to bring it down is to climb it."

Alexia reasoned, "Trust me, you're a lot closer to him than he's letting on. He's only acting like that because you're his mentee. I don't think he's going to let that be a barrier for much longer."

"Well, you haven't been wrong yet, so we'll–"

Symone and Alexia's stripes lit yellow with the following message: "ELITE UNIT: Meet in Intelligence with Director Mallack in 30 minutes."

Alexia sighed, "Well, that's us. Let's get going."

"Yep, let's get going." Symone and Alexia rose from their table, and Alexia summoned mist to telepathically lift their trash from the table to the waste bin. "Thank you!" Symone said to the cashier.

"Thank you for coming! Enjoy the rest of your day!"

They walked out of the restaurant as Malaysia called Alexia through the stripe. "Hey Malaysia!" Alexia said.

"Hey, you get the message?" Malaysia wondered.

"Yes, I got it. I'm here with Symone, and we're walking to the Company now."

"Oh, good, I'm going to three-way her. Symone, can you hear me?"

"Yes, I can hear you," Symone answered.

"Okay, good. I don't know what this week is going to bring us. Clearly, though, we need a breather, so I was wondering if you wanted to hang with me sometime."

Alexia jumped with surprise and glee. "Malaysia, are you kidding me? I've been wanting to hang with you like forever! You're always so off to yourself. I can't remember the last time we got to go out! Yes, just let me know, us know. Symone, you're game, right?"

"Frimas yes!" Symone said.

"Good deal, ladies. See you in a few minutes." Malaysia signed off.

Alexia grinned, "This is going to be great, I'm so excited, mmm hmm!"

"Me, too!"

13

Playing Dress-up

Alexia and Symone arrived at Intelligence in the Elite Grand Hall first. "There seem to be a lot more people in here than usual," Alexia noticed a larger group of analysts seated at holoscreens.

Stephanie, standing in the middle of the room, wearing a blue lab coat over an orange pencil dress, turned around and greeted Alexia and Symone. "Hi there! You're early."

"I expected to see Daisy here first, so I'm just as surprised as you are," Alexia replied as she and Symone stepped down and stood next to her.

Stephanie laughed and responded, "That's true. She's always scared she's going to miss something."

"She can't help it," Dax added. He typed on his keypad while he continued, "Even when we try to tell her to relax, she can't. Mind's always racing trying to piece things together. It's her nature."

"Yeah, her gift and curse," Alexia agreed while sitting down immediately to Stephanie's right.

Symone walked farther down the steps of Intelligence to the big holoscreen. Her eyes took in the room and the multiple views on the big wall for the first time. "I never noticed how amazing this room is," she pondered on how she could host a fight night someday in the auditorium.

Dax walked up to Symone and responded, "Yeah, Intelligence is the most advanced data analysis center on Uretha. We literally have access to everything in Uri City and can get access to anything worldwide. Every camera, every holoscreen, anything connected to a network, we can get into it. We're constantly data mining to get every shred of intel we can to help you guys defend the city. That's one of the reasons the bad guys are working feverishly to block us, and why we have spies everywhere trying to knock down their firewalls so we can get what we need to help you guys do your jobs efficiently and effectively."

"That's really good to know," Symone said.

"Sorry I'm late," Daisy suddenly appeared through the door with a gust of wind following behind her.

"Daisy, you're ten minutes early," Alexia reminded her.

"Oh," Daisy chuckled, "you're right, I am. Did I miss anything?"

"You already know you didn't, Daisy. We do this every meeting."

"Just making sure, I don't want anyone to have to repeat anything on account of me."

"You have the worst case of FOMOW ever," Stephanie joked.

"Sure does," Alexia agreed.

Intelligence's doors opened again, and Karl entered the room with Duncan right behind him. "Is Daisy okay?" Karl laughed. "Would hate for her to miss anything that happened *before* the meeting started."

"See, you guys get it," Alexia laughed.

"Alright, alright," Daisy quipped.

"I mean, it's great. You really want to be in the know of everything and not miss an ounce of information," Duncan said. "Do you ever take a break? Slow down, literally? Your mind is already running a million miles a minute."

"There's plenty that can slow my mind down, but not long enough to make a difference. Frimas, you all know I burn so many calories just by sitting down. Can't tell you how much I thank the Analyst for fixing that problem for me."

Symone turned around, her curiosity piqued. "Wait, fixing what problem now?"

"My metabolism problem," Daisy replied.

"Oh boy, you got Daisy started with her metabolism story?" Malaysia said as she entered with Malcolm behind her.

Malcolm's head tilted upward, then back down as he joked, "Get ready for a cycle-long soliloquy from the great scholar, Master Daisy Parker!" Malcolm's eyes locked onto Symone's.

"Haha, very funny, Malcolm," Daisy said. "Anyway, the short version is that as my powers evolved, so did my metabolism. My digestive system kicked into hyperdrive, and I looked and felt awful. My muscles started atrophying, and my bones became incredibly brittle from a lack of nutrients. The Analyst had to literally put my body in a coma and supercool me for a third of a quarter before he found a way to constantly keep me fed through my stripe. So now, I only eat for enjoyment, not for survival."

"That's neat. Think he can hook me up with something like that?" Symone asked.

"You should pay a visit to the Analyst and ask him yourself, Miss Watson," Malcolm met her. "He'd love to see you and share some things with you."

Symone raised two fingers to her forehead and saluted Malcolm. "Aye, aye, captain. How are you, by the way?"

"I think the better question is, 'How are *you*?'" Malcolm volleyed.

Malaysia, sitting behind Alexia, leaned and tapped Alexia's shoulder. Alexia turned around, and Malaysia pointed at Malcolm and Symone and widened her eyes with her mouth slightly agape. The others got quiet to pay attention to their interaction.

"You want the truth?" she said.

"Whatever that truth is, it'll have to wait," Director Mallack interrupted with her usual low, steely tone as she walked in. "Everyone, take a seat. Stephanie, bring us up to speed." Mallack leaned on the railing in the back of the room.

"Just when things were about to get interesting," Duncan said under his breath.

"Yes, Director," Stephanie followed orders as Malcolm and Symone took open seats next to each other in the front. "Dax, let's begin."

"Right away, Stephanie," Dax tapped keys on his countertop, and the holo-screen followed Dax's commands to display the demos of the Collector and his henchmen Streak, Hex, and Sonic. The team viewed the screen with disdain and fury. Malcolm sighed heavily.

Stephanie began. "Since your last encounter with the Collector and his team, we've attempted to find any scrap of intel we can on them. The Collector works tirelessly to keep himself and his team off the grid, so we have come up with very little. We grabbed what little biometrics we could from this little snippet of the Crawler's video, but the video is so generic that we don't have any clear indicator as to who he is. Streak, Hex, and Sonic have also been scrubbed from the grid, but we have our best people on this information, including voice recognition, power demographics, biometrics, all of it. We're hoping to yield something promising by the week's end."

"This means that we still have to keep our guards up. We don't know when or how the Collector will strike again, or who else he has recruited in his army. There's no telling who may be next on his radar or who he may use to fight us again," Director Mallack added.

"Right. Fortunately for us, we have a lead," Stephanie cheered.

"Wait, a lead?" Malaysia's eyes widened.

"How is that possible?" Daisy chimed in.

"This is Intelligence. This is what we do," Dax reminded the Elite.

Okay, Dax, Alexia loved Dax's bravado. *Stand up for your unit, your sexy self.*

He continued, "Two of our spies have given us a piece of information that may get us another crack at the Collector."

"No way," Symone's eyes flickered. "Talk to us, what's this lead?"

The holoscreen displayed three separate videos of people partying at a night rave. "The Collector hosts what's known in the underground as 'Power Parties,' where people who are interested in buying powers come together under the guise of a costume ball/night rave hybrid to bid on powers the Collector is auctioning off." The screen showed pictures of entertainers, political leaders, and crime bosses on the sides of the party videos. "The who's who will be there, talking mega-ballers who have a ton of creds to blow and plenty of reason to get their hands on the latest power the Collector's extracted. These parties attract everyone from the unpowered, the crooked, politicians, celebrities, to even mob bosses – all who want to get a leg up on their rivals. This is one place a Defender does not want to show up unannounced.

"Until now, we've only heard about the parties after they happened, once the powers are sold and they show up in somebody else's body, you know?" Dax displayed a list of powers and their previous owners, and the parties where they were sold. "So, this is a huge deal to know about the party beforehand."

"Not only that," Stephanie walked to the front and turned around to face the team, "but we also know what they're selling: the Crawler's power."

The screen displayed the Crawler's full-body avatar.

"You're kidding me!" Karl yelled.

"Not at all. We have both a shot at the Collector *and* getting the Crawler's abilities back. There's still the matter of transferring said powers to him, but we will cross that bridge when we get to it."

Alexia dropped an elbow and rotated her hand, asking, "Okay, so what's the play? We go in, lay waste to everyone there because they're all scum, then get the Crawler's powers, kill the Collector, and call it a day?"

"Although I really love that idea, Alexia," Mallack answered, "going scorched Uretha isn't the best option. You all would end up dead, and the Company would be out of commission in Uri City for a decade. No, this time we'll use stealth to pull this off. Stephanie?"

Dax tapped on his keypad while Stephanie instructed, "The primary objective is to *win the auction* and secure the Crawler's powers. The unit will be split into four teams." The holoscreen displayed seven black avatars split by red lines to designate their teams. "Team 1 is the Primary Buyer, who will win the auction; Team 2 is the Secondary Buyer, who will drive up the price to prevent other buyers from making the purchase; Team 3 will be our Eyes in the Sky, tasked with gathering as much biometric information from the partiers and the participants; and Team 4 will provide tactical support in the bus and backup when necessary.

"Once the auction is complete, the winners will be taken to a private room where the transaction will be made. Team 1 will give the Collector this briefcase," Stephanie walked up to her desk and pulled a silver briefcase off the tabletop, "which houses a holoscreen loaded with digital creds. Once the sale is complete, the Collector will be traceable from anywhere, having downloaded not money, but a tracker undetectable by even the most secure tracing systems. Team 1 will then take the Crawler's powers and walk away like it's Jubilee morning!"

"And when exactly is this Power Party supposed to happen?" Daisy asked Stephanie.

Stephanie stammered. "Right. So, the bad news, the party is *tonight*."

"You're joking!"

"No, and it gets worse before it gets better. Each of you will be fitted with a security code downloaded in your stripes that will get you into the party. But that code will not match your biometrics. So, once you're in, you will have approximately forty-five minutes to win the auction, upload the tracker, retrieve the Crawler's power, and leave the party before their security scanner determines that you are all uninvited guests and tracks you down."

"What time is the auction supposed to go down?"

"About a cycle into the party, so if the party starts at 19:00, I'd say you'd need to enter the Party at 19:50, and leave by 20:35," Dax instructed the team.

The Elite looked at each other with exasperated faces. Director Mallack could tell that even Malcolm felt like the plan was too rushed and risky. She said, "Listen, I know all of you are worried that this might go wrong."

"Might? With all due respect, Director," Alexia said, "but this is a bad plan, a really bad plan. We're going in nearly blind, just about powerless because we can't reveal who we are or what we can do, and without backup if something goes wrong. It's literally just us, and like you said, we can't just blow the place to kingdom come, no offense Malcolm."

"None taken," Malcolm responded.

Daisy interjected. "Director, this is a logistical, tactical nightmare. Alexia's right. If this place is the cesspool our UC's say it is, we could end up losing more than just the Crawler's powers. This just feels wrong."

"Okay," Mallack crossed her arms. "So, does anyone have a better idea? I'm all ears."

Everyone got quiet and turned to Malcolm, who was staring at the screen, puzzled. He noticed the silence and turned around to see everyone staring at him. *Is there any other way to do this? Think, Malcolm. Can you see another way? If they sell his powers, that's game. He's never going to get them back, no matter who they end up in. No way anyone would give up powers they paid top dollar for.*

Unfazed, he answered, "I got nothing. I'm with Mallack, Stephanie, and Dax. This is probably the only shot we're going to get at getting the Crawler's powers back. So, I say we go with Stephanie and Dax's plan."

"Wow, okay," Alexia reacted, slamming her hands on the countertop.

"Hey, I get it, okay? We got beat down last time, and we don't know what we're walking into. But we're the Elite. These are the exact circumstances we signed up for. We take the assignments no one else can complete and go the places no one else dares to. We're going to have each other's backs and make sure we all walk out of there alive and in one piece, with the Crawler's powers intact and the Collector tracked. He will not walk away from this unscathed."

Everyone nodded, then turned their chairs back toward Mallack.

"Okay, team, so here are the assignments. Team 1 will be Malcolm and Symone, Team 2 will be Karl and Alexia, Team 3 will be Daisy and Malaysia, and Duncan will remain in the bus," Mallack said.

"Man, I am so upset that I have to hang back in the bus while you guys take on such a hard mission," Duncan sarcastically quipped.

Symone asked, "So does this mean I need to buy a dress?"

"Me, too?" Malaysia volleyed.

"I guess we all are. If this is going to be our last night alive, we might as well look good doing it. Let's head down to Weapons and Wardrobe and make sure we blend in well." Alexia responded.

Mallack saw a look of concern on Malcolm's face again and probed, "Malcolm, join us, what's going on in your head?"

I want to throw all the weight of the Company on the Collector, make him pay for every person he ever killed and stole power from. But I feel like we're walking into a trap. Something doesn't feel right about this to me. This feels wrong. I should say something. Tell Mallack to call this off. We'll lose Boyd's powers, but we'll be able to game plan better. We're not ready to take them yet.

"Nothing, boss. We got this," he replied.

Mallack sighed. "Okay, Elite, you all have your assignments. You have nine cycles to get ready. Your stripes will be updated with your temporary ID's. Learn them well, and make this mission count. We'll debrief tomorrow morning, and if all goes well, we'll have a location on the Collector by week's end and take him and his forces down once and for all. Dismissed."

Alexia, Daisy, Malaysia, and Symone got up and huddled together near the front of the room. They began chatting about sleeve options, colors, splits, heels, and accessories, while Malcolm, Duncan, and Karl slowly rose from their chairs and proceeded to leave the room. Alexia saw them and used her telepathy to seize them in place. She yelled, "Oh, hold on, boys, you're not escaping from this!"

"Oh, no, we were just going to go do *any*thing else," Malcolm replied.

"Yeah, we just figured Wardrobe will outfit us for tonight," Karl added.

"Right, it's not like we're going to party for real," Malcolm agreed.

"Oh, come on now, guys," Alexia countered as she released them from her grasp. "This is the first mission in a while where we get to play spy and not just blow stuff up. I think it's a stupid idea, but since we're here, let's at least enjoy it a little?"

"Alexia's right, gentlemen," Malaysia chimed in. "Let's at least get the costumes right so we blend in."

Malcolm responded, "Okay, well, you ladies do what you gotta do. Talk with Double W about what Karl and I should look like to match you and our profiles, and let's meet back at the quarters afterwards."

"You guys are no fun, but fine. Ladies, to Double W we go," Alexia resigned.

As the men left, Symone recalled she wanted to chat briefly with Malcolm and said, "Ladies, I'll meet you at Double W, I gotta handle something really quickly." She raced out of Intelligence and yelled, "Bennett!"

Malcolm turned around and told Karl and Duncan, "I'll see you guys in the quarters." He walked toward Symone. "Miss Watson?"

She began, "So, we really haven't had a chance to talk since yesterday."

"No, we haven't," Malcolm replied with his hands behind his back. "Everything okay?"

"Yeah. Why?" Symone asked. They started walking aimlessly through the hallway.

"Well, I just handed you your first loss, so I kinda figured you wouldn't be okay."

Symone giggled a little, then as she fiddled with a loc, she said, "Um, last I checked, I did not yield, so that would mean that our battle isn't over yet."

"Oh, so what, we pressed 'pause' and will restart another day?" Malcolm inquired.

"You said it, not me. Besides, you left on your own. I didn't force you to walk out of the room."

"Miss Watson," Malcolm slightly turned to face Symone and smiled, "I wasn't going to kill you just to say I won."

"That's on you," Symone countered, pressing her right finger into his chest. "I never yield. It's win or die."

Malcolm stopped their pace and stared into Symone's deep, brown eyes and said, "You are a strange being, Symone Watson."

"Perhaps," Symone slowly shrugged her shoulders, staring just as intensely. She raised an eyebrow, "But you gotta admit, you're intrigued by me."

Malcolm answered, "Maybe I am. You're definitely more than what's seen on the surface."

"Oh? Tell me, Malcolm, what do you see?" Symone longed to hear more of his thoughts of her.

Malcolm gently locked his hands onto Symone's shoulders and answered, "In due time, Miss Watson. Right now, we have a mission to prepare for." Symone shuddered as she felt pleasurable tension flow through her veins. Malcolm sensed the fire in her veins slowly intensifying. Without skipping a beat, he continued, "But always know, I see you, can *feel* you, in ways you can't even imagine."

Symone's eyes flickered, her body shivered in delight, and her curious mind raced about what Malcolm meant by his words. "You can't tell me now?"

Malcolm leaned forward, stopped just short of her ear, and parted his lips to whisper, "Not yet." Malcolm let her go, then began walking toward the quarters.

Symone's mind raced as she fought to dial down the erotic tension winding up in her gut while relishing in and ascertaining Malcolm's impactful words. She ran her fingers through her locs. *I wonder what he feels. I wish he would tell me what he feels. I know what he makes me feel right now. Is it really going to take him not being my mentor anymore to stop holding back from me? Because Akan, I want to jump him!*

Symone shook off the sensual tension she felt down her spine and walked to Weapons and Wardrobe.

Malcolm thought to himself, *You should just tell her how you're feeling. It's obvious you have a thing for Symone. Does anyone else see what's happening between her and me? I bet Malaysia sees it. Probably Alexia, too, and her can't-stay-out-of-peoples'-heads self. No matter. We have a mission to get ready for, and I cannot afford any distractions. I'll tell her when it's the right time.* He walked into the quarters and said, "AI, boot up the ID dossier for my mission."

As the dossier loaded up and began showing Malcolm information about his fake ID before his eyes, Karl, sitting in the commons, turned toward him. "Is everything okay with Symone?"

"Oh yeah, everything's fine. She just wanted to talk about our fight yesterday."

Perfect. Now's my chance to address this. Thank you for the alley-oop. "I'm glad you brought that up," Karl said.

"Wait, why?" Malcolm asked as he signaled to AI silently to hide the dossier information from his sight.

"Well, for starters, you fought her! Malcolm, I've known you for a while, brother, and you've never, ever fought anyone in the room since you've been an Elite. Frimas, we're lucky to fight with you, but never against you. Why'd you fight her?"

"Well, she asked for it!" Malcolm replied. "She wasn't going to stop asking, and she had proven herself among all of you, so I figured she could handle her own."

"Malcolm, that's bull, you know that, right?" Karl said.

Malcolm sat adjacent to Karl. "You know what? You're the second person to say that to me today. So, lay it on me. How is this bull?"

Duncan overheard the two of them talking. He walked from his residence into the commons and started laying out the argument. "Malcolm, all I've wanted to do is train in the room with you. You remember what you told me? 'You're not strong enough. Even the training exercises are too much for you.' I trained for two whole quarters and beat every single training op like it was a video game, and still got nothing but 'keep training' from you."

"You remember what you told Director Mallack about me?" Karl asked.

Malcolm sighed, "Yes, I was reminded of that earlier by Mallack."

"Well, Malcolm, that's how you've treated every single person you've trained or fought alongside. You always found some lame excuse as to why you wouldn't let us get in the ring with you. We fight well together as a team, as teammates, no doubt about it. But brother, you've never let anyone close enough to you fight you. Not until Symone."

"That's for sure," Duncan cracked as he sat adjacent to Malcolm. "What, are you two screwing or something?"

"What?! No! Frimas, naw! The Company would have my job for that!"

Wait, they would? Why? Duncan wondered.

"Well, what is it then, Malcolm?" Karl asked. "Because Symone obviously has drawn something out of you that has you treating her differently than the rest of us."

"Are you jealous?" Malcolm countered, begging for a subject change.

"Not at all. I'm just reading the terrain, Malcolm. And so is everyone else. We're not complaining, not judging you. We just want to understand it."

"Especially given that fight yesterday," Duncan remembered. "Bro, that was legendary! We've never seen anybody do the things we saw happen in that room. You made a planet, controlled Symone's stars. She tried to blow the room up, and still didn't yield after you had her dead-to-rights. Frimas, that's the kind of fight I'm working my way up to."

"Fellas, I don't know what to tell you," Malcolm resigned. "I guess if I had to pin down a reason, it would be because I was assigned by the Company to mentor her, unlike the rest of you, who I just 'trained' because you were on the team or asked for training. I don't know."

"Malcolm, until you're honest with us about Symone, we're not going to stop asking you about it. For the sake of the team, Frimas, for yourself and her, figure it out so that one of us isn't killed by a misstep of judgment on either of your parts," Karl advised.

"Damn, Karl," Duncan said.

"I'm just saying. Don't blast the messenger."

"You're right, Karl. I'll figure it out," Malcolm agreed, but only to switch the conversation, not because he wanted to figure anything out. "Right now, though, we need to focus on this semi-suicide mission we're about to go on. We don't have a lot of time to get our covers straight for tonight, and we gotta get this right if we're going to stop the Collector."

Karl looked at Malcolm and said, "Alright, brother, I can take a hint. Let's focus up and get this right."

"Well, gentlemen, I'll leave you to it. I'm going back to my room to learn how to be productive on the bus," Duncan replied.

"Wait," Malcolm noticed the change in Duncan's attitude and decided to press the issue, "you're rather chipper about being sidelined, Mr.

'Shoot-first-ask-questions-later.' What's going on with you? So worried about me and all."

Pensive, Duncan answered, "Well, look, after the last battle, I feel like I could use a break for a bit. I've been thinking a lot about what you've been saying to me this whole quarter about needing to get my head on straight, and though I'm always down for a fight, a night in the bus sounded quite nice, and I wasn't about to turn it down."

"Okay, why now?" Malcolm perked up.

"Truth is, when I was in the military, I *always* put my team before the mission. I always made sure my teammates had my back, and I theirs. I don't know why it's been different here. And that's something I need to work on and figure out. You're right. I need to get my head on straight."

"Wait, run that back? You said what?"

"That I need to get—"

"No, before that, you said, 'You're right.' I just want to hear you say it one more time," Malcolm poked at Duncan's admission.

"Man, shut up!" Duncan threw a pillow at Malcolm as his brothers laughed.

Karl slowly shrugged his shoulders, and Malcolm tilted his head and declared, "Well, I'm glad I didn't speak up when Mallack paired Symone and me off."

"Why?"

"Well, I was going to tell Mallack that it might be better for you and Alexia to be Team 2 while Karl and Symone go in as Team 1, or even you and Symone be Team 1, but I held off because I could already foresee that Mallack wasn't going to go for it."

"Akan, Malcolm!" Duncan yelled and flailed his arms in the air. "Why wouldn't you say what you were thinking?"

"Oh, now don't get mad, Dunk," Karl slightly chuckled. "Besides, it looks like you got what you asked for anyway."

Duncan grunted and growled, then responded, "Fine, yeah, whatever."

Malcolm walked over to Duncan and patted him on the back. "Akan always finds a way to give us what we really want, right? So, in essence, I was only doing what Akan was guiding me to do on your behalf."

"Screw Akan, and screw you," Duncan shot out of his seat. As Malcolm and Karl both laughed, he walked back to his residence, leaving them alone again.

"You sure you don't want to get it off your chest, Malcolm?"

"I got nothing else for you, brother," Malcolm responded. "Let's get to work."

"Okay," Karl answered as he thought to himself, *I've never seen him like this before. It's good to see him directing his energy on something other than work. Malcolm and Symone. Hmm, I always bet my money on Malaysia, but this works, too.*

Symone pressed her hand against the palm reader, and it lit white for approval. The door to Weapons and Wardrobe slid open, and Symone walked through.

Weapons and Wardrobe was a white-lit room with white paneling covering the floor, the walls, and the ceiling. The room itself was the size of two tennis courts. Each side had several tables perpendicular to the wall that had holoscreens on it to enter data. Each table sat next to a holoscreen the size of a wall mirror. Malaysia, Alexia, and Daisy were sitting at the third table on the left side. Malaysia noticed Symone enter the room and said, "Symone, come on!"

Symone walked over to the group. Alexia asked, "Everything okay?"

"Yes, everything's good," Symone answered. She took her seat next to Malaysia and said, "How's it going here?"

"We're just getting started," Daisy replied.

"Yes, and we're starting with you," Alexia interrupted, "because I've been waiting forever to play dress up with you!"

"Really?" Daisy asked.

"Yes! You have way too much body not to show off, especially tonight!"

"I'd like to think that I am very stylish," Daisy remarked.

"Sure, but I want you to give off 'do me' vibes tonight," Alexia declared.

"What she means is," Malaysia interjected before Alexia could do more damage, "we're going to help you accentuate your appeal so that you don't stand out like a sore thumb tonight. You don't have to walk out of there with a date, but you can't look like a chaperone." She nudged Alexia and said, "Let's get started. Put Daisy on the holoscreen and throw some options up there for her."

Alexia typed keys on the countertop, and the wall holoscreen displayed Daisy's petite physique in a black leotard. Alexia said, "Okay, so let's start with the basics. Daisy, what's your favorite color?"

"I'm partial to red, hence my uniform."

"Of course, so we'll just put that as the primary color, then we want to do a tapered dress," she continued as she typed. "We'll one sleeve it, low-cut coming across your breast and around the shoulder like this."

As she typed, Daisy's black leotard conformed to Alexia's modifications. Daisy looked at herself and said, "Wow, I didn't think I could look like this!"

"What did I tell you?" Alexia reacted. "Now, we'll take the end of the dress to just above the knee, then split it on your left side to oppose your revealed arm and voila!" The holoscreen revealed Daisy in a shimmering red dress with the modifications Alexia asked for. "Now, I know you need the right kind of shoes to make a break for it if need be, so we'll put you in wedges, but ask for them to be modified to turn into shoes designed for you to haul ass."

"You already know!" Daisy replied.

"You sure you didn't miss your calling?" Malaysia said.

"Oh, no, no, this would get boring for me. It's fun, but not what I'm made to do. Malaysia, you're up next." Alexia prepared to perform the same magic for Malaysia.

"Okay, for me, I need to be able to bend my legs in any position in case I need to shoot somebody, so I want a dress that exposes one of my legs and covers the other. And I gotta give everybody some eye candy, so I want the dress to drape from my neck and cover my goodies, exposing my arms and back. And I want to be in sandals that strap in a crossed string pattern."

Everybody stared at Malaysia as Alexia asked, "Who are you?"

"What? I'm a girl, I like clothing!"

"So many questions, but okay. Color?"

"Purple," Malaysia answered.

Alexia completed the modifications, and Malaysia's avatar transformed to display her in a purple dress and black sandals. Alexia said, "Malaysia, we definitely have to hang out more."

"Once this mission is complete, we will."

"Alright, Symone, you ready?"

"I sure am! Crimson and gold me, please!" Symone said.

"With pleasure! Anything specific you want this dress to look like?"

Symone thought carefully, then answered, "I want it to shimmer in the light, rise above my knee, the sleeves tight on my arms, give me some cleavage, you know, show the girls off but keep a little mystery. Simple."

Alexia finished her work, and the screen displayed Symone in her desired look. She saw herself and thought, *I look incredible!*

"Symone, what do you think?" Alexia asked.

"I think we're gonna cause problems at this party," Symone answered.

"You got that right," Daisy laughed. "Alexia, what are you wearing?"

"Oh, so my outfit will be similar to Malaysia's, except my legs will be exposed through pants slit from waist to ankle, and I'll be wearing sandals. Symone's right. We're about to be a real problem at this party. We should go to Leicester afterwards, not let these clothes go to waste."

Everybody laughed. "Okay, so all that's left is to get the guys suited up, and then we can go," Daisy said.

Symone stood up to leave. Malaysia asked, "Hey, where you headed?"

"I'm going to the quarters to get ready. Gonna study my dossier and make sure I got my cover straight in my head."

Malaysia stared at Symone and smiled. "Okay. Your dress will be ready in fifteen minutes and will be in your closet. In case you don't know, it will be built to withstand your powers, so in case you need to go ham, you don't have to worry about changing. Just make sure to equip your cloak."

Symone chuckled and said, "Maybe I should be wearing pants to this thing, you know, in case I need to crush somebody with my legs?"

"I don't think that would matter to the one you'd have to crush," Alexia responded.

Malaysia's stripe lit up, alerting her that she was receiving a call from Director Mallack. She lifted a finger to tell everyone to quiet down. "Yes, Director?" Silence. "Yes, ma'am, I'm on my way." She disconnected the call.

Daisy chimed, "Everything alright?"

"Yes, the director just wants to talk to me about something in her office. Symone, let's go."

"Sure, let's go."

As Malaysia and Symone walked out of Wardrobe, Daisy pondered out loud, "Wonder what that's all about."

Alexia agreed, "Yeah, that's kind of strange. But it's none of our business. Let's get these guys outfitted."

Symone saw an opportunity to talk to Malaysia about wanting a chance to get to know her a little better. "So, Malaysia, before you head off to Mallack's, um, we haven't really had a chance to talk to each other after we sparred."

Malaysia turned to face Symone, her back in the direction of Mallack's office. "No, we haven't," Malaysia answered. "When are we going to change that?"

Symone was stunned. "Oh, well, you said earlier that we should get together after this mission, but in case that doesn't happen, I was thinking we should just grab something to eat sometime and chat."

"Or you can just call me, or we can hang out in your residence, or mine," Malaysia said. "I know you are slightly intimidated by me."

"What, no, it's not that," Symone reacted.

"Symone, this is me you're talking to. I know you are, and I know why. But I promise I don't bite. You ever want to talk to me about anything, even Malcolm, I'm here. I'm gonna go see what the director wants and see you back in the quarters." Malaysia turned around and walked to Mallack's chambers.

Symone walked to the quarters thinking, *What did she mean by "I know you are, and I know why?" Between her and Malcolm seeing and feeling me, I'm gonna need them to share their top-secret info with me already. Are they talking about me behind closed doors? Speaking of, I wonder why the director wanted to meet with Malaysia. Okay, Symone. Focus, let's go memorize this dossier and get ready for tonight.*

Symone opened the quarters and saw Malcolm and Karl in the commons reviewing their dossiers. They looked up and saw her walking through the door. "Miss Watson, how are you?" Malcolm asked.

"I'm good, just finished at Wardrobe. The girls stayed behind to finish your suits for tonight. They should be here any minute now. I'm going to my room to study my dossier."

"Okay," Malcolm replied. "While you're studying yours, you should study mine as well."

"In case they ask us questions about each other, that makes sense," Symone reasoned.

"That's right. I'll meet you in two cycles to quiz you?"

"You know where I'll be."

Symone walked past the commons to her residence. Karl looked at Malcolm as Malcolm watched Symone walk. "Mmm hmm," Karl said.

He caught me. "Focus up, Karl," Malcolm quipped.

"I am focused. Are you?" Karl said.

"Yes, I'm focused. Let's continue."

Two cycles went by. Malaysia and Duncan sat in the commons watching the holoscreen. Karl, Daisy, Symone, and Alexia were in their residences. Malcolm was in the kitchen. He looked at the clock suspended on the wall in the commons and remembered that Symone and he needed to review their covers to make sure they knew everything about each other's roles. He took a last swig of his drink, sat the glass down, then walked to Symone's residence. He knocked on the door, and Symone responded, "Come in, it's open."

Malcolm opened Symone's door and walked in. He saw her in her living room, standing next to her mirror as she examined and admired herself in her crimson and gold dress that shimmered in the light. He marveled at how the dress contoured her physique, dazed by every curve of her supple form. "Oh, I'm sorry, I didn't—"

"Malcolm, it's okay," Symone said without turning around to face him, sensing Malcolm's hesitance and embarrassment. "What do you think?"

"Oh, well, I think you will definitely blend in at the party," Malcolm said as he crossed his arms and stood in the doorway, trying to stay on mission. "No way they'll mistake you for a Defender."

Symone smiled and shrugged as she adjusted the dress around her sleeves and her thighs. "Is that all you're thinking?"

"I think you already know the answer to that," Malcolm answered.

"I'd rather hear your answer," Symone said while she twisted around, making sure she felt right in the dress, and gave Malcolm an extended look at every inch of her ravishing body. *That's right, keep gazing. Take me all in.*

"You look spectacular as Frimas, Miss Watson. Or should I say 'Emma Leslie,'" Malcolm admitted while trying to divert his attention away from her.

"Oh, I see what you did there," Symone quipped. *He's trying to distract himself from me. Not going to work.* "Well, 'Jackson Santana,' should I keep this dress at its current length, or should I hike it up a couple more inches?"

"Well, seeing as you don't like to bring too much attention to yourself, I suggest hiking up so that you don't stick out like a sore thumb. Flash isn't really your style," Malcolm closed the door and moved toward Symone.

Still staring in the mirror, Symone noticed Malcolm inch closer to her. *Come here, Malcolm.* "Right, while you, Jackson, love the spotlight, making as much noise as possible, but having a bite that matches the bark."

"You'd be right, Emma," Malcolm bellowed. "I can still remember the first time I met you, this unimposing, shy, delicate flower at a poker game."

"Yes, a poker game that decided the shift in the power balance in the Underbelly. You were showing a pair of aces, while all I had were two unconnected cards. I beat you on the river with a full house. You were fuming mad with me."

"I was," Malcolm responded as he stood behind Symone and gazed at the two of them in the mirror, "but I'd like to think that I won something much better than a seat of power that night." *Damn, we look good together. Akan! What am I doing? Don't think about it. Just do it.*

Malcolm wrapped his arms around Symone's belly, pulling her close to him. He stood about four inches taller than her. Symone thought, *Akan, he feels so right.*

"You most certainly did, that was the luckiest night of your life," Symone said as she slowly lifted her right arm to caress Malcolm's head and face. "Somehow, my panties weren't the only thing you finessed me out of. Our combined forces made us one of the most unstoppable forces in the Underbelly as we carved out most of the territories there. All that studying at Brandt University paid off for you." She could feel Malcolm's package bulging beneath his jeans and pressing against her butt.

"Mmm hmm," Malcolm continued in her ear, "while your military experience gave you an insight into weapons technology that dwarfs the intelligence any government has possessed. And now, we just need a few Super-powered soldiers in our ranks, and we will finally be able to take the entire Underbelly, Frimas, Uri City."

Symone shivered from his voice reverberating in her ears and his strong arms covering her like a coat. She turned her body, pulled herself into him, and stared him in his eyes while he held her by the small of her back. "There's very little standing in our way, Jackson. Are you ready to take us to the next level?" Symone asked as she took her left hand and slid Malcolm's right hand from the small of her back to her butt cheek. *Are you ready to take me?*

Malcolm sensed the tension in Symone's body rising, the fire within her lit and smoldering. His senses dialed up, and he desired to add dynamite to it and cause an explosion that would satisfy their wet, demanding, frenzying appetites. He thought, *I want her so badly right now. She feels so good in my hands.*

"Careful, Emma, might start something we can't finish," Malcolm quipped.

Symone stared deeply into Malcolm's eyes. She could feel that same magnetic draw locking her into him, an inescapable vise that she didn't want to be free from. Without missing a beat, she softly delivered, "You should have thought about that when you played poker with me. Or fought me in the training room. Your eyes are telling on you."

Malcolm was powerless to resist Symone, and all he could think about at that moment was kissing her, touching her most intimate places, and becoming one flesh as he satisfied himself by satisfying her craving. His senses expanded uncontrollably, and he felt everything, everywhere, all at once within a quarter-mile radius. Still, all he could focus on was Symone. He closed his eyes, and she closed hers. He leaned in to press his lips against hers, when suddenly, their arms buzzed, and their stripes lit red. Symone, slightly frustrated, said, "Ignore it, Malcolm."

Malcolm sighed while looking up in the air, feeling the bulge in his pants. But the red stripe knocked his focus completely off. His senses dialed down, and the interlock between their powers and their passion disconnected. He looked at his stripe and saw the words, "ELITE UNIT: Meet immediately in Intelligence."

"Malcolm, what do you want right now?" Symone whispered.

"I want you," Malcolm answered as he began to loosen his grip on Symone.

"So, what are you waiting for?" Symone countered, feeling his grasp loosen.

"Time," he resigned. He let her go, and she dropped her arms to her side. "You might want to change out of that dress, don't want to stick out like a sore thumb, Emma."

"Screw you, Malcolm," Symone said. Malcolm walked out of her room to round up the rest of the team. *I should take a cold shower first. Akan! Why did*

I leave? They could have waited another fifteen minutes. But then they would know something's up between us. I can't let that happen.

Symone turned and looked at herself once more in the mirror, adrenaline and fire traveling through her veins like a bullet train. *Time,* she thought. *How much more do you need?!*

14

The Power Party

Symone stared through the window of the hover-limousine. The heavenly lights sparkled in the sky, competing with the cityscape below them. *If you only knew what the stars above really looked like, you'd all turn this city off and bask in their radiance.* She revisited the times she soared as high as the air would allow and how amazed she would be each time she reached the divine summit. She reminisced on standing on the spires of the tallest buildings in Uri City, looking straight up and wishing she could live among the stars.

Her mind recalled her mother and her younger self lying on towels on the rooftop of their home, staring at the night. Her mom held her hand as Symone sucked on a lollipop. The longer they stared into the darkness, the more intense the luminaries shone. Her mother's voice echoed, "One day, the world will look at you the way we marvel at the moons." The younger Symone smiled, just as present-day Symone remembered and smiled.

Malcolm, sitting next to her, noticed her lips curve and inquired, "Miss Watson, something on your mind?"

"Just admiring the view."

"Yeah, it is pretty spectacular," Malcolm responded, though he wasn't talking about the skyline. He couldn't stop staring at Symone, admiring how well-put-together she was, from the way her locs lay on her shoulders and draped over her chest, to the way her smooth-shaven legs crossed one on top of the other. He prayed she wouldn't look back at him.

Symone, still staring out the window, asked Malcolm, "What exactly is your superpower?"

"That's a random question to ask," Malcolm said.

"Well, I haven't really asked you what it is you do or how you do it. I've asked others, and now I want to hear it from you. With this possibly being our last night alive, I figured, why not get that mystery solved."

"Of all the mysteries you have, *that's* the one you want solved?" Malcolm quipped.

Symone turned and faced him. Malcolm quickly darted his eyes so he wouldn't get caught gawking as she replied, "Well, I didn't want to make it too difficult for you...wait, wait, stop stalling and answer the question."

Malcolm chuckled. "My bad, okay. Well, the technical answer is molecular manipulation. In its simplest form, I can take anything and reshape it into anything I want it to be. So, like this glass," Malcolm picked up a drinking glass from the console across from him, "if I want to turn it into, say, a glass snowflake, I just think it, and—." The glass morphed into a snowflake the same height as the glass was before.

Symone gazed at the snowflake. "Okay, but it's more than just morphing things from one shape to another, right? I mean, the person I fought in training wasn't just morphing metals."

"Right. Everything in the universe, known and unknown, seen and unseen, is made of atoms, molecules, the whole science thing."

"Uh huh," Symone replied, gazing at Malcolm as he continued to explain, trying to contain her enchantment.

"Well, I literally *feel* everything."

Symone remembered Malcolm saying to her, "can *feel* you," earlier that day. She pressed on that. "What does that mean?"

"Exactly what I said. I *feel* everything. Every molecule around me, every molecule I am within reach of, every atom, even the spaces between the atoms, the wavelengths beyond our eyesight and earshot, I can feel them. And with the right push, I can command them to do what I want them to do."

"Oh yeah?"

"Yes. It's like moving pieces on a board, or weaving string together to make clothes. I can tell whatever I want around me to do what I want it to do."

"So," Symone commented as she waved her hands around, "you literally have control of the universe in the palm of your hand."

Malcolm was taken aback as he tilted his head, pursed his lips, and squinted his eyes. "When you put it that way, yeah, that's kinda what I have."

"Malcolm," Symone's eyes widened, "that is literally the most amazing ability ever. You can literally be anything, do anything, control anything that you want. Frimas, you could rule this city, the world, Frimas, worlds! Why the Frimas are you working as a Defender? Why are you working for the Company?"

"Well, for one, I can do anything, but I can't do everything for very long. The more complicated the transformation, the longer and more energy it takes to do it. Morphing things is easy to do because I'm just bending shapes. But true transformation, like changing the molecular structure of a thing, takes deep concentration. I don't do it much in the field because if it takes too long, the bad guys will have popped me in the head or something."

Symone chuckled, "True, you'd definitely need to be well-guarded to pull off something truly spectacular, like creating a planet, in the middle of a battle. But you *can* pull off something truly spectacular! So that doesn't explain why you're defending the city."

"I mean, I love my city," Malcolm reasoned. "I love the people in it, and I want them to live freely. Most of us are born with abilities, and some of the powered decide they want to use their powers to hurt people, to take from them, to oppress, you know, all that 'blah blah blah' you referred to weeks before. I decided a long time ago that I didn't want to be *that* guy. It'd be easy for me to be a monster, to use my powers selfishly and hurt people along the way. But I'd rather help people and be at peace knowing that I did everything I could to make a difference in others' lives."

Man, the way he speaks. His words are like poetry, and he's not even trying. I could listen to him speak all day. Fire and blood sparked in Symone's veins, and Symone's chest tightened. Despite sitting inches away from him, she longed to draw nearer, to be entangled with him, their bodies to meld together, and their hearts to intertwine. *I know we have a mission to focus on, but Akan...*

"Malcolm, have you ever thought that you could be making a difference some other way?" Symone asked.

Malcolm looked at Symone and replied, "To be honest, no, I haven't. Being a Defender has been my sole focus for such a long time. I haven't really considered doing or being anything else."

"Malcolm," Symone called to him while slowly placing her right hand on his left and locking their fingers together, "you are so much more than just a Defender, you know that, right? Your power alone makes you one of the supreme beings on Uretha. I'm not suggesting you hang up the cape and live a life of philanthropy like some retiree. But you should really think about what else you could do with your power beyond fighting for the Company and Uri City."

Malcolm played with Symone's fingers and palm, "This coming from the one itching to fight all day, every day?"

Symone pointed her left index finger at Malcolm, then at herself, repeatedly as she answered, "See, we're two different people." She then pointed at him, "You fight because you have to." She then pointed at herself, "I fight because I want to."

"Okay, so why do you *want* to fight?"

Symone took a risk and turned her body, her back facing him, then backed into Malcolm to be spooned. She lay her head on his chest and grabbed his arm and lay his hands on her stomach. The feel of his chest against her head, his arms around her body like a cloak, Symone felt safe and adored. *Akan, can we just stay like this? Can we tell the limo driver to turn around? Take us away from here?*

Malcolm smelled the sweet fragrance of her hair gel mingled with the fruity aroma of her perfume, and his senses amplified. Malcolm thought, *Geez, what are we doing? I'm so not focused on the mission right now. We're going to fail. Should I push her off me? But Akan, she feels so good on my body, she fits me like a glove. Her energy is surging, I can feel it. And I want it, want her. The director will have my head if she finds out about this, about us. Us, did I just call Symone and me "us"? This is crazy!* Malcolm held Symone softly as she answered his question.

"I fight because there is very, very little in this world that makes me feel more alive than the arena. I've been fighting since I was a little girl, and the rush I feel when I'm trading blows with another person," Symone's eyes flickered, "mmm, I can think of only three other things that make me feel like that."

Malcolm's senses dilated, and he felt more connected to Symone's energy. He resisted the sudden urge to squeeze Symone's body while inquiring, "Is that right? What are those three things?"

"K.C., Blitz and I are about two minutes from approaching the party," Malaysia stated.

"Copy that," Malcolm answered. Symone thought she should get up, but she noticed that Malcolm did not shift his body in any way nor take his arms off her. "Alright, team, according to the plan laid out by Intelligence, the Eagle and Blitz will enter the party first and find their perches. They will scan as many people as they can so that Intelligence can have a running list of potential future threats to the city. Mammoth, Enchantra, you two will arrive exactly three minutes after Blitz and the Eagle check in and make your way to the Auction Room. Starburst and I will arrive exactly four minutes after the Mammoth and Enchantra check-in. At that point, we will have thirty-eight minutes to do what we gotta do if we're going to leave together at the same time. At the five-minute mark, if Starburst and I don't have the Crawler's power and the tracker downloaded, Eagle and Blitz proceed to exit the party and meet with Ammo in the bus parked atop the building across the street. Mammoth, Enchantra, same goes for you two. If things go south, Starburst and I will blow out the windows of the prize room and make our escape from there. Everyone understand the plan?"

"Understood," Blitz said.

"Copy," Mammoth responded.

"Yes sir," Ammo agreed.

"Loud and clear," Enchantra said.

"Everyone be careful. Clean entry, clean exit," Eagle assured.

"I copy," Starburst said, looking up at K.C. She then said just to him, "Are you ready, Jackson?"

"As ready as I'll ever be, Emma."

Starburst lifted off K.C. and said, "Let's hope the auction starts on time. Otherwise, we're gonna be cutting it even closer."

"No kidding," K.C. replied.

The Eagle and Blitz's hovercar arrived at the Hi-Fi Hotel entrance. The Eagle opened the door and stepped out of the hovercar with Blitz right behind her. They stared at the sixty-story high-rise: a fully glass-paned structure striped with lights that made the building glow like a Jubilee tree. Music played loudly, and several people were gathered around the entrance talking, laughing, and dancing with one another as spotlights panned in the sky from one side to the other. The Eagle and Blitz pranced to the hotel door about thirty feet away and met the security guard who said, "Stripes, please."

The Eagle handed her arm to the guard, and he scanned her stripe with a reader. The reader glowed white signaling granted access, and the Eagle walked forward. Blitz did the same, and the reader glowed white again.

They walked through the revolving door, and the Eagle reported, "Start the clock now. It is 19:51, we now have forty-five minutes. Blitz and I will separate. I'll take my post on the fifth-floor balcony while Blitz walks the ground floor and makes her way up to me."

"Copy that," the Mammoth acknowledged. "T-minus three minutes until our arrival."

"I gotta say, Karl, your outfit really suits you. Maybe I am missing my calling," Enchantra admired her handiwork, having designed the Mammoth's green crocodile-skinned suit with a black V-neck shirt slightly exposing his large chest.

"Well, you have always had a great eye for making yourself look good. Only makes sense that you would enhance my incredible physique," the Mammoth agreed.

"Incredible indeed, mmm hmm. Here we go, Aron Vance."

"Let's do this, Cherie Vance."

19:53, the Mammoth and Enchantra's craft arrived at the entrance, and Enchantra stepped out first, followed by the Mammoth. She locked arms with him as they followed the same protocol as the Eagle and Blitz. The reader acknowledged them both, and they entered the Power Party. Inside the hotel, the vast lobby had been turned into a dance floor. The ceiling of the lobby was ten stories high. The lights were dimmed, and people were littered across the floor, some dancing, some sitting at tables and the bars along the walls talking, laughing, making out, eating and drinking, and jamming to the music. A DJ was staged at the back of the lobby floor. Flying dancers paraded mid-air across the open atrium. Music pulsed through the speakers and reverbed in everyone's bodies. The Mammoth and Enchantra marveled at how elaborate and exquisite the party appeared.

"Guys, this is lux," Enchantra declared as she bounced her shoulders to the beat of the music.

"Focus up, guys, make your way to the fourth floor, the auction starts in five minutes," the Eagle said. She was on the fourth floor as she slinked through the crowds to get to her post.

"Copy that, we're on the staircase now," the Mammoth answered.

19:57, K.C. and Starburst's hover-limo arrived at the entrance, and Starburst stepped out first, followed by K.C., who donned a white and red tux with a white shirt and bow tie striped black and red. K.C. and Starburst walked arm-in-arm to the entrance. K.C. held the silver briefcase that housed the digital creds and tracking device. K.C. said loudly, "Alright, let's get this show on the road! Time is money, and I don't have either to waste."

As they got scanned, the Mammoth and Enchantra arrived at the Auction Room door. Greeted by security guards, they were handed black face masks to wear. They each took a mask and put them on their faces. The guards opened the doors, and they walked into a dark corridor dimly lit by tiny lights arrayed on the wall near the ceiling. About fifty feet later, the corridor opened to a dark room with several desks arranged in a circle. Each seat was lit by a spotlight and paneled so no one could see who was to the left or right of him. The desk was pushed up against a one-way mirror in front of it so no one could see anyone in front of them. The Mammoth whispered, "Okay, guys, we are in a dark room. Everyone has masks on, seated in cubicles arranged in a circle." Enchantra and he walked around until they found an empty cubicle.

"Copy that. We're making our way up now," Starburst said as she and K.C. climbed the staircase.

"I'm in position, beginning facial recognitions now," the Eagle announced.

"Same here," Blitz said. "Working my way through the crowd." Blitz shimmied and twirled around the dance floor as her AI used her eyes to scan as many people as she observed. The Eagle leaned over the fifth-floor railing to scan the dance floor below and the walkways of each floor. She utilized her enhanced eyesight and assisted Blitz while watching the clock.

Blitz couldn't believe her eyes. "Guys, I am in utter shock at who is here. Seriously, Intelligence, are you getting this?"

"Focus, Blitz. Don't editorialize right now. Just scan. 19:59, thirty-seven minutes left, team," Eagle reminded the Elite.

"We're at the Auction Room. Security's about to let us in," K.C. said. The security team gave K.C. and Starburst their masks and opened the door. They then walked through the corridor to an empty cubicle in the Auction Room. K.C. sat down in the chair and placed the briefcase under the desk as Starburst placed her hands on K.C.'s shoulders. K.C. breathed in two deep breaths. *Okay, here we go. Let's get it.*

20:00. The auctioneer, a monotonic, automated voice, announced over a speaker in the cubicles, "Good evening, patrons. Welcome to the Power Auction, where tonight, you may be able to walk out of here with an incredible prize: the ability to climb on walls and stick to objects."

Groans and murmurs echoed across the room as some patrons felt cheated and slightly disappointed. "Now, before you get bent out of shape," the speaker continued, "we've put together a compilation of the power at its peak, wielded by one of the Company's Super-powered Defenders. This footage features the Crawler, from whom we extracted his power, which granted him the ability to perform these feats."

A holoscreen projected images of the Crawler utilizing his powers in the middle of the room. K.C., Starburst, the Mammoth, and Enchantra looked at the display with blank stares hiding their rage. The Crawler had been recorded climbing buildings, grasping columns and quickly spinning around them, sliding into difficult spaces, and taking objects from assailants by sticking to them. The recordings also showed him in the training room completing similar exercises to elevate his skills.

"How the Frimas did they get this footage?" K.C. whispered angrily as he clenched his fists.

"Stay in character, K.C.," the Eagle reminded K.C. Starburst squeezed K. C.'s shoulders to calm him down.

"Can you imagine if one of your strongest soldiers had this ability? Think of the safes he could break. Or the smallest soldier, the impossible locations he could easily slip through and access. This power has evolved to Super level and will instantly make one of your soldiers one of the strongest warriors the city has ever seen, thereby making you superior to your enemies and allowing you to maintain or even expand your territories within the city."

The patrons' reservations subsided. The four Elite heard them making calls to banks and their associates to determine their available cash on hand. Starburst said, "Jack, you ready?"

"I was born ready. Let's do this," K.C. said, staying in character.

"To make your bid, simply tap your amount on the holoscreen in front of you. From the starting bid, you will have seven minutes to be the highest bidder."

"Wait, what?" Enchantra said before catching herself and clearing her throat.

"Silent auction," the Mammoth whispered to her nervously. "We won't know whether K.C. is atop the board without giving ourselves away."

"Relax, guys," the Eagle said to them. "Remember what we went over at Intelligence. Key phrases to signal where you're at. Just don't yell 'Boo-yah' or whatever."

"But I wanted to yell 'Boo-yah' tonight," K.C. joked.

"Ladies and gentlemen, we will start the bidding at one million creds," the auctioneer declared. The holoscreen in front of them displayed the starting bid in big white numbers and a clock above it in green that read 7:00:00. The display floated above the ground and rotated slowly. "Let the auction begin!" The countdown began.

Immediately, several of the patrons began entering bids, and within thirty seconds, the price increased to seven million. The Elite could feel a bundle of nerves in their stomachs, but K.C. and the Mammoth stayed their hands. The bidding continued, and with six minutes to go, the price for the Crawler's powers jumped to twelve million creds.

"Wow, bunch of amateurs, watch this," K.C. declared. He typed in a price, then pressed "BID." The price jumped to twenty million with his bid. Some of the patrons grumbled. A few of them got up and left the room. K.C. looked up at Starburst, and she gave his shoulders a good squeeze as she planted her chin on the crown of his head. "That's how we do it!"

5:15 to go, and someone bid twenty-two million creds. The Mammoth was about to place a bid, but Enchantra stayed his hand, saying, "Not yet. We still have a lot of time left."

The Eagle continued scanning the people at the party, just as surprised as Blitz to see who was attending the party. *We might as well be in the Underbelly,* she thought.

The Eagle heard someone yell, "Malaysia?" She tried to ignore it, thinking someone else at the party must be named Malaysia. But then the voice cried out again, "Malaysia Jones?"

"Guys, I think I just got made," she said. "Gonna try to shake him off." She turned around to see a tall, dark-skinned, curly-haired, incredibly good-looking man. A wave of memories and emotions suddenly flooded the Eagle's mind and body. Goosebumps flashed all over her body, her eyes dilated, her nostrils flared, and her lips parted. Her lungs pushed all the air from her body, and a sudden jolt of ecstasy engulfed her veins.

It can't be. She froze for a second and marveled at the blast from the past walking up to her. She mustered up, "Oh my goodness, Jack-son?"

Enchantra perked up and whispered, "Wait, did she just say Jackson?"

Starburst perked up and squeezed K.C.'s shoulders a little harder, "Jack-son," she stammered, trying to calm herself down, "San-tan-a."

Blitz lifted her head out of the pile of dancers she was immersed in to see if she could get a visual on the Eagle. "She's out of my range, guys, I can't see her or who she's with."

"*Jackson Santana,*" the Eagle barely got the name out of her mouth, dread and shock piercing her stomach like her daggers through an enemy. "What a surprise!"

"I'm surprised to see you here, too," Jackson responded, projecting his voice low and flirty, as he stepped closer to the Eagle, "it's been way too long, like, what, six years?"

"More like seven, yes," the Eagle responded as she slowly motioned her body to her right to give herself unobstructed access to the staircase. "How have things been with you?"

Santana lifted his arms and replied, "Things have been going great for me, you know the city never sleeps, and work is still being done."

The Eagle crossed her arms and stared intensely at Santana. "If by work you mean building a criminal empire—"

"I know," Jackson interrupted as he turned his hands upward, tilted his head, and slightly shrugged his shoulders, "you don't have to remind me of the scum you think I am. Though, as I recall it, you were right there building it with me in the beginning. You were always my best set of eyes."

"That was before I found out what you were actually doing, or have you forgotten the lie you tried to sell me?" The Eagle, her back pointed in her desired trajectory, turned around and started walking toward the staircase.

"True, true, you got me on that. But look at me now, I'm sitting on top of the world with the resources and the men I need to make all my dreams come true. Just missing a few more pieces and I'll be able to run this town my way."

The Eagle stopped walking, suspecting that Jackson was trying to make a play for the Crawler's power. She turned around and asked him, "What are you doing here exactly? Dance parties aren't really your style."

Jackson knew he had caught her attention and walked up to the Eagle again. He tried to turn up the charm. "I was going to ask you the same thing, Malaysia."

"I asked first."

Hands behind his back, Santana responded, "Well, I'm close to making my army the strongest it's ever been. Once I've secured this auction, I'm convinced the Underbelly will be mine."

The Eagle played dumb. "What do you mean 'auction'?"

3:45 left, and suddenly, a bid was made for thirty-five million creds. K.C., Starburst, the Mammoth, and Enchantra immediately realized that the real Jackson Santana sent a proxy to bid for him.

"Guys, between him and Emma Leslie, they have unlimited buying power. There isn't a number they cannot reach," Daisy reported. "What are you going to do?"

"I'm not supposed to say anything, but I'm gonna win anyway, so, this isn't a dance party. It's actually a Power Party, and in about three minutes, I will have secured a Superpower. Once I win, one of my strongest muscles will get injected with the juice, and then we'll see who is king of the Underbelly."

"Aron, make a bid?" Enchantra, feeling a sense of desperation in her chest, whispered her plea in the Mammoth's ear with 2:20 to go. The Mammoth rapidly pressed the keys on the console and placed a bid for fifty million creds.

Santana's proxy said under his breath, "Sir, the bid is at fifty million."

Jackson lifted a finger and said, "Excuse me, Malaysia." He turned away from her. The Eagle took advantage and darted away from him. As she proceeded down the stairs, the Eagle fought to shake off the tension corked in her and the sensations her body vividly remembered Santana made her feel many moons ago. Santana's voice switched quickly from low and flirty to gruffly and anxious. "So bid fifty-one."

The proxy typed on the holoscreen and hit "BID" for fifty-one million creds with 1:57 to go. Starburst said, "We can't break him, but we can beat him. Shoot it up to seventy-five million."

"Now?" K.C. asked.

"Trust me," Starburst assured her. K.C. quickly typed in seventy-five million and hit "BID," leaving 1:34 on the clock.

"Sir, the bid is at seventy-five million," the proxy told Jackson.

Jackson grumbled, and the real Emma Leslie chimed in his ear, "I told you this was a bad idea. What are you going to do?"

"Shut up, Em! Eighty million," he answered.

The proxy typed in eighty million and hit "BID" with 0:55 to go.

Starburst had been counting the time it took for Jackson's proxy to counter their offer and knew how to win the auction. "Do exactly what I say when I say it, Jackson," Starburst said. "Type in one hundred million and wait for me to say 'go.'"

K.C. instinctively trusted Starburst and typed in one hundred million, then hovered his right hand over the "BID" button. Starburst, K.C., and the proxy sat and looked at the clock counting down.

"Now, where were we Ma—" Jackson said, not realizing that the Eagle disappeared. "Malaysia?"

"If you hadn't been reminiscing on old girlfriends," Emma commented, "maybe you wouldn't have lost control of this auction."

With 0:20 to go, Starburst said, "Wait until seven seconds are left."

"Seven, why seven?" K.C. asked.

"Just trust me, we got this," Starburst calmly assured him.

K.C.'s hand froze, ready to strike, as the clock ticked down, :17, :16, :15, :14, :13, :12, :11, :10, :09, :08.

:07, K.C. hit "BID." The proxy said, "Sir, the price has jumped to one hundred million creds."

"Aargh!" Jackson said. "101 million!"

The proxy typed in 101 million, and he attempted to hit "BID," but the "BID" button disappeared on the keypad, and the holoscreen's timer landed on 0:00:00 with 100,000,000 creds spinning in all white. K.C. and Starburst's cubicle spotlight shined brighter while the others' turned off completely. Starburst cheered and hugged K.C. from behind while K.C. screamed, "Oh yeah, oh yeah! That's how Daddy does it!"

Meanwhile, the real Emma said to the real Jackson, "Great work, Daddy. Looks like your luck ran out. And lucky you, because you know good and well you don't have 101 million creds."

"I don't understand," Jackson said. "Who on Uretha has one hundred million creds to burn? There's no way. Is there a new player on the scene we don't know about?"

"I don't know," Emma answered. "But what I do know is that we have a lot to worry about, because not only does this new character have a ton of money. But he also has a Superpower. And I'm certain this won't be the last power he tries to acquire. Come home, darling."

"No, I want to meet this guy first," Jackson furiously replied.

"You know that's not how these meetings work. Stop being so emotional and get back here before you cause a scene."

"Ugh, fine," Jackson resigned. He began walking down the staircase. When he got to the fourth floor, he saw his proxy and walked over to him.

Meantime, the Eagle walked the lobby floor and caught up with Blitz. "That was weird, there was no intel on him being here tonight, and he didn't show up on any of the facial recognition scans for us to be aware of," Blitz said.

"You're right. He was already at the party before any of us, so he must have already been on the fifth floor behind me or in a bathroom somewhere."

"You know we're gonna have to talk about how you know him, and why you didn't say anything about knowing him earlier, right?"

"Ugh, yes. Not looking forward to the debrief. Mallack's going to kill me," the Eagle sighed.

K.C. and Starburst were the only ones left in the room. K.C. said, "Okay, everyone, proceed to the lobby floor. We have about twenty-four minutes left."

K.C. stood up and picked up the silver briefcase as the auctioneer stated, "Congratulations on winning tonight's auction. Proceed to the Prize Room to acquire your lot and make your transaction." A second door opened, flooding the room with light. K.C. took Starburst's hand as they walked together toward the entrance to the Prize Room. Starburst, surprised by K.C.'s gentle clasp, felt a slight tingle flow down her spine.

"You and I are going to make love all the way home tonight, Jack!" Starburst said.

I wish. "Ooh, I'm getting lucky twice on the same night!" K.C. played along. *You could if you want. I don't mind.*

The Prize Room was a vast corner office about fifty feet in width and length, with glass panels covering the back and the left side of the room. The floor was red marble, the ceiling was fifteen feet high, black with recessed white lights arrayed, and the walls were covered with decorative art splashing color around their white bases.

K.C. and Starburst entered. "Well, well," a voice said from a seat at a desk at the back of the room. "Looks like you two will be quite the insatiable pair all night long. All the money you're spending and sex you're about to have—"

"It's been a good night for us, that's for sure," Starburst responded.

"That it has, and it'll be even better once we have this power, haha!" K.C. reacted. "Do we get to meet the person in the chair?"

"Yes," the voice said as he spun the chair around. K.C. and Starburst hid their shock, fury, and dread as they finally came face-to-face with their nemesis, donning the same all-black attire as before. "I am the Collector, and I am simply delighted to meet you two, Jackson Santana and Emma Leslie. I hear you two are collectors yourselves, of the Underbelly's subsects, that is."

"Yeah, well, when you're building an empire, you gotta be able to take it over piece by piece, know what I'm saying?" K.C. said. He could feel Starburst's hand get hotter and massaged it to remind her to calm down.

The rest of the team could hear their conversation. The Mammoth asked Ammo, "Are you getting this recorded, Ammo?"

Back in the bus, Ammo was seated near the holoscreens, watching his teammates' views. Ammo tapped on the keypad and made sure the screens were recording. He responded, "Yes, I am getting it. And I am pissed right now."

The Collector sat calmly with his hands pressed together in a prayer stance. "Well, you two are certainly doing a remarkable job of taking the Underbelly. You have almost half the territories now. Though I think you'd agree that your alliances are quite shaky. It's good you came to me. You are in serious need of major firepower, and this Superpower is a great start."

The right-side wall split apart, and several white-clad henchmen walked onto the Prize Room floor. The Collector pointed at them. "I brought some of my people along to watch the process, and some of my best fighters for you to meet, Streak and Mygalo."

Streak and Mygalo entered last. K.C. and Starburst gripped one another's hands tightly. Mygalo stood about six feet tall and had tentacles protruding from his back, covered in red-coated steel. His suit was green with black vertical stripes from his visor to his boots.

Ammo announced to Enchantra, the Mammoth, the Eagle, and Blitz, "Guys, Streak is in the prize room with K.C. and Starburst."

"Your best fighters?" Starburst said. "What, pray tell, do they do?"

"Emma, darling," K.C. attempted to deflect, thinking about their time constraints, "I'm sure we all have better things to do than to waste time on introductions, right?"

"Oh, it's quite fine, I'll be quick, I know you two have a power to collect and love to make. Streak shocks things, and Mygalo is a man-spider. Very simple." The Collector pressed a button, and a hole opened in the middle of the floor. The Collector's power transfer machine rose from the hole and locked in place. The Collector slid open a drawer at his desk, and picked up the Crawler's power, which still glowed white within the tube. "Now, who is the lucky person I'm transferring this power to?"

"Oh, so the transfer is happening now?" K.C. asked.

"Why, yes, Mr. Santana. What were you expecting?" the Collector asked.

"Oh, well, I was expecting us to pick a date and time to get together to make the transfer, but by all means, we can do it now." K.C. placed emphasis on his next statement, "My *biggest, strongest* man is ready to become a crawler like my man Mygalo, right?"

"Roger that, K.C., I'm on my way up now," the Mammoth understood the message.

"Guys, this isn't how it's supposed to go down," Blitz said.

"We don't have a choice. We're running out of time, we gotta get out of here. Mammoth, get in there and, I guess, get injected with the Crawler's power? Frimas, this doesn't feel good, guys," the Eagle said.

The Mammoth made his way up the stairs to the fourth floor, passing Jackson Santana and his proxy walking down along the way.

"Meantime, should you get your money? We can at least get that out of the way while we wait for our man outside to make his way here," Starburst suggested.

"Most definitely. I assume that the creds are in the briefcase?"

"Yes. Let me just walk this over to your desk—"

"I'll take that," Mygalo said as he walked over to K.C. and Starburst. He used a tentacle to grab the briefcase from K.C. and walked over to the Collector's desk.

"The combination is 397," K.C. revealed.

"Thank you," Mygalo responded. He entered 397 in the keypad, and the briefcase opened, revealing a flash drive the size of a finger. The Collector picked up the flash drive and inserted it into a slot on the countertop. The Collector then typed keys to begin the cred transfer. When he hit, "Start," the digital currency moved from the drive to the Collector's banks. K.C. and Starburst looked at each other and smiled as they successfully completed part two of their mission.

"Guys, we have sixteen minutes left," the Eagle reported.

"I'm at the door," the Mammoth reported.

Security signaled to Streak that the Mammoth arrived, and Streak said, "Santana's man is at the door."

"Great, send him in," the Collector said. Security opened the door, and the Mammoth walked through the hallway, circled the desks, and walked through to the Prize Room.

"Good, just waiting for the funds to finish transferring, and then I can get strapped in and make this gargantuan more powerful than he's ever been," the Collector said.

The Mammoth stared down the Collector, reminding himself not to say a word or to act out of character and blow their covers.

Outside of the hotel, two vehicles rolled toward the entrance, and five assailants dressed in dark red suits stepped out of them. Jackson Santana and his proxy walked outside to meet them, and he huddled them up and whispered, "We're going upstairs to take that power from the auctioneer. Everyone, cover up your weapons, act natural, and once we get in, let's make our way to the fourth floor."

"Boss, how are we going to get in? We need passes, right?" one of the goons asked.

"Don't worry about that. Already taken care of. Just follow me." Jackson Santana and his five henchmen all walked up to the security team and, to the henchmen's surprise, got scanned and approved to come into the building.

The Eagle observed Santana and noticed his five henchmen behind him. "Guys, we got a problem, a really big problem. Santana is back, and he's brought guys with him. They are packing a lot of heat. I think he's gonna make a play for the power. If the Collector finds out he's here, we're done."

"So, ah, how much longer before the transfer's complete? I'm ready to get sauced up and wax my lady across some leather seats!" K.C. declared as he tried to hide his nervousness. He began doing a cost-benefit analysis in his head and considered the collateral damage should they power up and blast their way out of the party.

"We're at 67% so far. Just a little while longer. Meanwhile, your man can go ahead and sit down."

"Twelve minutes," Blitz said.

The Eagle made a beeline to Jackson, hoping to throw him off course. "Jackson?" she yelled to him.

Jackson turned around and said, "Malaysia, where'd you go?"

"When you got on the phone, I had to use the bathroom real bad and I didn't want to interrupt you."

"Well, now is not a good time for us to catch up."

She pressed into his chest gently. "You look worried about something, is everything alright?"

"Oh, yeah, everything's alright. Just gotta tie up a loose end with the auction, and then I'll be on my way."

"What do you mean?" the Eagle tried to tie him up, but he signaled to his henchmen to make their way upstairs, and he followed suit.

"Guys, he's headed up to the Auction Room. You gotta get out of there somehow," the Eagle declared.

"I can take them and divert them," Enchantra said.

"That's not a good idea, Enchantra, you might get made," Blitz warned.

"We don't have a choice. Move. Get close to them and be careful. We've got eleven minutes before they know we're not supposed to be here."

Enchantra hurried up the stairs to catch Jackson and his henchmen and prayed they were not cloaked. She strategized to discreetly make them turn around one at a time. As she got behind them, she charged herself, and her eyes slowly glowed green. She flicked her right hand. As green mist swiftly rose from her hand, she whispered to the first henchman, "Turn around and walk out the door." The henchman's eyes turned green, and he instantly turned around and walked down the stairs. She flicked her hand again and said the same to the second henchman, and he followed suit. One by one, all five henchmen walked away from Jackson and went out the door, leaving him alone.

"82% transfer. Mr., I'm sorry, I did not catch your name," the Collector said to the Mammoth.

"Big, Mr. Big," the Mammoth replied.

Streak, her hair slowly giving off sparkles as strands flowed from her visor, examined the Mammoth and thought, *Why does he look so familiar to me?* She began trying to recount any memory of him but came up short.

"Mr. Big, then. Just stand in the middle of the room, and we'll get started very soon."

Starburst grabbed K.C.'s hand and said, "We should think about lighting up the sky once this is over, break open bottles of champagne, and blast off into the darkness."

K.C. immediately recognized Starburst's coded message and continued his analysis. "You always get poetic when we're on the cusp of something great. I'd have to agree. We'll paint the town red and ride out on the best craft money can buy," K.C. responded as he took Starburst's hand and twirled her around.

"You two are quite entertaining," the Collector observed.

Enchantra walked behind Jackson just as he was about to approach Security at the Auction Room and flicked her finger while saying, "Turn around and walk out the door."

Jackson stopped moving, his eyes turned green, and he instantly reversed and began walking in the opposite direction. Security already saw him, though, and scanned his face. The scan was reported to Streak and Mygalo. Streak looked at the scan, then looked at K.C. She walked up to the Collector's desk and lay her left hand on the countertop to download the scan to the holoscreen. She instructed the holoscreen to display the image flat on the countertop out of eyesight to K.C., Starburst, and the Mammoth.

The Collector looked down at the countertop, which displayed Jackson Santana at the Auction Room entrance just before turning away, then at the data log of his entries and exits from the Hi-Fi Hotel. They noticed that Jackson Santana entered the building twice more than he exited. The Collector then said, "Mr. Santana, you and Ms. Leslie are extremely lucky to be getting this power from me."

"Certainly, and you, to be getting a load of money from us for it! I'd say we're all lucky tonight!" K.C. said.

Starburst recognized a slight shift in the Collector's tone of voice and sensed that something was wrong. "Is everything alright, Collector?"

"Well, I'm just curious as to how you were able to come up with one hundred million creds to spend on this power when, according to all my scouting, you're only worth about forty million."

"Well, when you're as resourceful as we are, you can cash in on many, many favors. You can trust that we are good for it," Starburst challenged.

"Once this transfer is complete, we shall see whether those favors truly turn into cash," the Collector countered.

"No reason why they shouldn't," K.C. tried to reassure the Collector. "We went through a lot of trouble to get here."

"I see, so much so that you arrived twice without leaving once?" the Collector said.

Crud, K.C. thought, *we're blown.*

Ammo said, "Guys, this isn't good. The Collector knows K.C., Starburst, and the Mammoth are imposters."

"We can't leave them behind. We stay and stick to the plan," the Eagle said.

"Eight minutes," Blitz said.

"Call it an assurance measure," K.C. answered the Collector's question. "We've been to several of these Power Parties and come up short, which I'm sure your scouting will support. Mr. Santana and Miss Leslie wanted to ensure that they won this time, which is why we are serving as their proxies. I told Mr. Santana that your team would never fall for a doppelganger, but he's such a hothead, he was sure this plan would work, and you wouldn't be the wiser. Miss Leslie told him to stay home. Well, as you can see, he didn't listen."

Starburst stared at K.C. and couldn't help but find him more attractive at that moment. *How the Frimas did he come up with that?*

The Collector stood up from his seat. "Seems like a lot of overkill to try to procure power. Your boss must be desperate," the Collector laughed.

"He and Leslie are this close to cementing their grip on the Underbelly, so, yes, I'd call them desperate. And smart," Starburst commented.

"I can't argue with that logic," the Collector agreed. "And right on time because the transfer is complete! One hundred million creds are now in my possession. So, let me just strap myself into this machine, and Mr. Big will get to crawl all over buildings and whatnot."

"We have a problem," Mygalo said. "It appears that Mr. Santana and five of his men are standing outside of the hotel and just, well, standing there."

"What do you mean 'standing there?'" the Collector said.

"Literally, just standing there, doing nothing."

"Five minutes, guys, we gotta get out of here now," Blitz announced.

"Okay, now I'm getting mad. Get Security to bring Santana up here, we'll get it all sorted out," the Collector gritted his teeth.

"Baby," Starburst whined as she put her hands on K.C.'s shoulders, "I really wanna break champagne bottles now."

K.C. concluded they would need to utilize the element of surprise to get the Mammoth, Starburst, and him out of the windows. He said, "Yes, I think I want to blast off into the sky, too. Let's just smash everything." He leaned in close to Starburst's ear and said, "3, 2, 1, go!"

15

The Great Escape

K.C. double-tapped Starburst's chest while double-tapping his own, and their cloaks shimmered and enveloped them. He summoned his energy and concentrated on the windows in the room. With a surge of energy flowing from his hands, all the windows on the left side of the room shook violently and exploded into pieces, bouncing onto some of the henchmen and causing them to fall forward. The shards revealed the henchmen's activated cloaks. Starburst raised her hands and quickly launched small stars at the henchmen still standing in front of the windows and knocked them to the ground. The Mammoth double-tapped his chest with his right hand. He instinctively smashed the Collector's transfer machine, grabbed a piece of it in each hand, and threw them at Streak and the Collector. The Collector ducked behind the desk as Streak blew those parts away with lightning strikes from her hands. The three Defenders immediately ran toward the windows to make their escape.

Mygalo saw them about to jump and said, "Oh, no you don't." His four metal-coated tentacles stretched then locked in battle position. He aimed them at K.C., Starburst, and the Mammoth, and shot webbing at each of them. The webbing hit their targets and stuck to them. Mygalo then pulled his arms back, and K.C., Starburst, and the Mammoth all jerked backward and fell on their butts. He then somersaulted between them and the open windows as some of the henchmen recovered and stood up.

"Get out of here," Streak told the Collector. "We'll clean up this mess."

"Lock this building down. No one in or out. I have a feeling they're not the only uninvited guests here tonight," the Collector said as he sat in his chair. He pressed a button underneath the right armrest, and a shaft opened underneath. The chair strapped the Collector in and launched him downward through the escape hatch leading to the parking garage underneath the hotel.

Streak then charged up. Bolts lit up her hair, and an electric current flowed around her entire body. Her visor lit bluish white from inside the helmet. K.C., Starburst, and the Mammoth rose from the ground. They stared at each other, at their opponents, and at their way out. K.C. said, "Team, get out of the building, we're blown."

"I knew I remembered you from somewhere. Came back for seconds, I see," Streak said. She planted her right hand on the holoscreen console on the Collector's desk. She unleashed a powerful electrical surge. Suddenly, the building trembled, and Streak's current raced up and down the exterior of the building's glass panes, becoming an electrified barrier that no one could walk through.

Ammo quickly noticed the electric fence. He placed both hands on his head, leaned back and forth, and declared, "Guys, this isn't good. That's the same fence we faced before."

"I'd suggest giving up now," Mygalo persuaded the three.

"I disagree," Starburst declared as she charged her hands. K.C. picked up a metal rod from the wrecked transfer machine, and the Mammoth pounded his fists.

"Have it your way," Streak said. "Kill them."

The crowd in the lobby was unaware of the battle happening above them or the fence surrounding them. As they continued their revelry, Blitz, the Eagle, and Enchantra stood in the middle of the dance floor, scrambling to figure out what to do.

"One minute before security knows we're not supposed to be here. What do we do?" Blitz asked.

"We head underground. Chances are the fence doesn't cover the garage. We can get past it and find a tunnel to get around the fence underneath," the Eagle said. "I already see our best exit is behind the DJ booth. Blitz, scout ahead and take out the security guards there. Enchantra, build us a team to block their path to us. And let's get the Frimas out of here."

"Let's do it," Enchantra confirmed.

Starburst launched stars at Mygalo and a few of the henchmen. Mygalo blocked her star with one of his tentacles while the henchmen were knocked back. The Mammoth grabbed one henchman and threw him into two others.

K.C. turned the metal rod into a staff and ran toward Streak. As he spun the bo with his hands, Streak launched several lightning strikes his way. He blocked all of them, then grabbed the staff with his right hand and knocked Streak in her side. She flew to her left, halting her momentum with a lightning pulse she sent toward the Mammoth, then landed a punch with the same hand on K.C.'s face. He and the Mammoth stumbled backward. Starburst launched herself toward Mygalo, and Mygalo shot webbing at her. She quickly created a heat shield to burn the webbing, then pushed it into Mygalo and knocked him to the ground. Two henchmen grabbed her arms. She then flew to the ceiling about twenty feet above them, cracking their skulls with the ceiling. They let go of her and plummeted to the floor. Mygalo quickly regained his footing and shot a web to the ceiling and pulled himself upward to meet Starburst, but not before the Mammoth grabbed his foot and threw him into the wall.

K.C. and Streak exchanged a series of punches, blocks, staff swings, and kicks. Streak hit K.C.'s chest with a lightning bolt, and he lost his footing and stumbled. Two henchmen grabbed the staff he was holding from behind him on each side and tried to pin him to the wall by his neck, choking him. He bent the staff on each end to wrap around their bodies, then split the staff in two to free his throat. He kicked them in their kneecaps to put them on the ground, but before he could recover his staff, Streak launched three lightning strikes at him, each dealing damage to his cloak and pinning him to the wall.

Starburst launched two stars at Streak from behind, and Streak stumbled forward. Streak turned around and launched lightning strikes at Starburst. They missed her, and Starburst shuttled down to meet Streak. She tried to kick Streak in the head, but Streak calculated her attack and maneuvered away. Starburst hit the ground with her foot, bent her knee, and launched from that foot to deliver an array of attacks on Streak. The Mammoth raced to help, but before he could swing a left hook, Mygalo shot webbing at the Mammoth's massive left arm and pulled him backward, then shot more webbing at the Mammoth to mummify him. His massive body hit the floor hard, and everyone shook from the tremor.

K.C. saw that the Mammoth was in trouble, recovered his staff, and ran toward Mygalo. One of Mygalo's tentacles unsheathed a dagger, and just as he was about to jab the Mammoth in the face, K.C. morphed his staff into a bat and smashed Mygalo like a fly ball over left field. The Mammoth pulled with all his might, and his strength, plus the cloak's resistance, broke him free of the webbing. The Mammoth told K.C., "Thanks, brother."

K.C. replied, "Don't mention it," and grabbed his right hand to lift him up.

As they struggled to get out of the Prize Room, Ammo's patience wore thin. He watched K.C., Starburst, and the Mammoth trying to escape and thought, *I should be doing something. Maybe I can break through the electric fence and blow a way out of there for them. I don't know how to control the bus like that, though. I knew I shouldn't have skipped the trainings on this. But I do have two arms full of bullets. But they said to stay in the bus. Ugh, what do I do? I can't just sit here and watch them struggle like this.*

The struggles continued as the Eagle and Blitz's forty-five-minute window expired. Security guards across the building were alerted by their stripes that they were unauthorized guests at the Hi-Fi. One of the managers signaled to the guards, "These two individuals are unauthorized to be here. They may have something to do with the lockdown. Find and neutralize them immediately."

A wave of armed guards marched from the doors, the perimeter of the lobby, and the perimeter of the dance floor. They weaved through the floors of the Hi-Fi. The Eagle saw them and warned, "Our time is up, Blitz, go, now!" Blitz bolted past everyone on the dance floor and past the DJ stage. Three guards stood in front of the exit for the stairs. Blitz swiftly pushed her hands into the first guard and launched him into the other two guards. All three of them hit their heads on the tile flooring, knocked out cold. As Blitz was about to make her escape through the door, her stripe turned electric blue, and a piercing, intense pain coursed from her arm through her entire body. She groaned loudly and planted both hands on the ground as she knelt.

The Eagle's stripe turned blue, also, and delivered a shockwave of pain through her body. She groaned, and Enchantra immediately recognized what was happening. "They're trying to shut you down so you can't escape. Come on, I got you." Enchantra laid the Eagle's right arm across her neck and held her by her side. She then flicked her hand, and her eyes turned green as she said, "Protect my friends and me from the security team." She delivered her message to multiple people at once and tranced them. They stopped dancing and created a wall between the incoming security team and them.

The Eagle gritted her teeth while saying, "Blitz, how are you holding up?"

"Ugh," she moaned, "not great, but I'm here. At the stairs now, waiting on you."

"We're a minute out," Enchantra responded as she and the Eagle pushed through the crowd. The security team ran into Enchantra's wall of support and struggled to get past them.

"This stupid stripe is like a beacon now. We gotta hurry," the Eagle winced.

Ammo's impatience took over, and he couldn't wait anymore. He opened the bus's hatch. He ran out and scurried to the elevator shaft on the side of the building. He double tapped his chest, and his uniform and cloak enveloped him. On the ground floor, he ran to the sidewalk and perched himself behind a hovercar. He looked up to see the open windows K.C. shattered that were still sealed by Streak's electric fence. He charged himself, and his hands slid into his cannon barrels. He aimed them at the fence and began firing cannon shots to try to knock it down. The booms were muffled inside by the music pulsating throughout the lobby, but several security guards outside noticed the plasma fire and communicated to management that something was wrong.

Inside the Prize Room, the Mammoth and K.C. charged toward Mygalo and traded punches and kicks. Mygalo countered their moves with his arms, legs, and tentacles. The Mammoth grabbed one of the tentacles and swung Mygalo over his head, and K.C. took his bat and took a swing at Mygalo. However, Mygalo latched his tentacle onto the Mammoth's hand, and he lay prostrate midair to miss the swing of K.C.'s bat, then lay on the ground and threw the Mammoth over his body and into K.C., sending them both to the ground. K.C. and the Mammoth groaned while feeling the shocks of the barrier hit by Ammo's cannon fire.

Starburst threw several stars at Streak, and Streak deflected them all with her bolts, then threw bolts at Starburst, which she deflected with heat shields from her hands. Streak grew frustrated and stomped the ground, sending a lightning bolt through the ground and upward to Starburst. It popped her feet and launched her slightly in the air. Streak took advantage and grabbed Starburst's arms. She then surged electricity through her hands, overloading Starburst's cloak trying to break its defensive integrity. Starburst felt some of the electricity stinging her body like a tattoo gun. She grabbed Streak's arms and responded in kind, charging her hands and sending waves of heat through them to break Streak's cloak. Their energy created a burst that separated them and sent Streak into a wall while throwing Starburst into the electric fence, shocking her even more before she tumbled back to the floor.

K.C. and the Mammoth lifted themselves off the ground. K.C. said, "Help Star with Streak. We gotta get that fence down and get the Frimas out of here."

The Mammoth shook his daze and ran toward Streak, who was still recovering from the blast. He neared her but did not see three of the henchmen who had recovered from their previous beatings. They ganged up on him, each delivering a series of unimpressive punches and kicks that proved to annoy him. He grabbed one and threw him into the other two. That, however, gave Streak enough time to regain her composure and lift her arm to deliver a powerful wave of electricity to the Mammoth. He planted one foot in front of him to withstand the barrage and pushed himself one step at a time to try to get to Streak and pummel her.

K.C. focused his attention on Mygalo, who was battle-ready. He separated his bat and changed his weapons to batons. He rushed toward Mygalo, and he swung the batons repeatedly at Mygalo while Mygalo dodged each swing. Mygalo spun behind K.C. and grabbed both his arms and legs with his tentacles and began bending all four of K.C.'s limbs backward, trying to break them from his body. K.C. screamed in pain as he fought to regain ground but lost in that effort. Mygalo said, "Consider this your fate; your end has come."

"Man, shut the Frimas up!" K.C. turned his hands upward and pulled down a huge piece of the ceiling that crashed into Mygalo's head. He crumpled, releasing K.C. in the process. K.C. tumbled forward in pain and took several seconds to recover. He then turned around to assess the damage. Mygalo had swiftly crawled away and was not underneath the rubble. K.C. couldn't sense that Mygalo was above and behind him, tentacle drawn with a dagger, poised to strike K.C. in his skull.

Starburst's eyes widened, and she instinctively launched herself and bear hugged K.C. She waved her arm and delivered a blast at Mygalo. It cut Mygalo from his webbing and hurled him into the electric fence, shocking him, and he slid to the floor. Starburst and K.C. hit the tile, and she lay on top of him, their cloaks responding to their positioning.

Starburst lifted herself up, hovering over K.C. He stared into Starburst's eyes, and his nervous system was flooded with infatuation, adrenaline, shock, joy, and lust. At that moment, K.C.'s heart, mind, and body unraveled all at once, turned on by Starburst's salvific response to the imminent threat to his life. Time froze, and in that space, with their bodies pressed against each other's, nothing else mattered. His instincts told him to grab her, embrace her, and have his way with her, to show her just how much he appreciated her, *craved* her.

Focus, boy!

"Thank you, Star," he said to her.

Starburst stared into K.C.'s eyes and could tell that he was feeling something for her. *You like me on top, huh?* But she knew they didn't have time to revel in it, recognizing the clear and present danger still in front of them. "Come on. We gotta get out of here."

Enchantra and the Eagle met with Blitz, and the three of them struggled to descend the staircase. Blitz and the Eagle continued to groan in searing pain. They arrived at the parking garage, and Blitz said, "Daylight, yes, let's get out of here." Blitz sped toward the tunnel when she hit an invisible wall and bounced off it. The Eagle saw Blitz bounce and shifted the frequency in her eyesight. The wall became a series of ascending and descending purple and gold symbols that formed a barrier.

"Oh no," the Eagle grimaced, "ugh, Hex is here."

"How do you know?" Enchantra inquired.

"The symbols, I remember them from the last mission. He's in here, and he's keeping us trapped," the Eagle replied while dragging her body closer to the exit, hurting worse with each passing second.

Hex revealed himself behind the barrier and said, "That's right, and you three aren't going anywhere."

"Enchantra, you gotta get us out of here. Break the barrier down, and we'll take care of Hex at that point," the Eagle instructed.

Enchantra's eyes turned green, and she attempted telekinesis to throw something at Hex, but her mist hit Hex's wall and could not break through. She then concentrated on the wall itself. The Eagle doubled over and fell to her knees as the pain continued to course through her.

Blitz limped toward the Eagle and Enchantra, then fell to the ground and said, "I can't control my legs. This hurts so much."

Enchantra began to see the symbols within the wall and started to decode them, then her stripe lit blue. She started to writhe in pain. "Frimas, my time ended. They know I'm not supposed to be here. That means they know the Mammoth isn't supposed to be here, too. We're about to be useless."

Ammo, meanwhile, was still blasting the fence to no avail. He kept trying nonetheless, hoping eventually, it would make a difference. He noticed that people were running away from the building while several black-suited men and women slowly walked toward him, with a familiar figure approaching from the middle. "Oh no," Ammo said.

"We meet again, I see," Sonic said. "And it looks like you're outnumbered. Where's the rest of your team?"

"I don't need the team to take you down," Ammo oversold. He aimed his cannons at everyone and fired as many shots off as he could. Sonic immediately belted a piercing, focused screech that shattered every window of every hovercraft within a hundred yards of its path. Ammo couldn't bear the sound. He planted his hands on his helmet and screamed in pain. He crumpled to the ground and lay on his side, his mind splitting apart from the noise rattling in his ears and scrambling his brain. Sonic continued to screech until Ammo lay motionless.

Sonic and the remaining henchmen walked to him. Sonic then placed a small circular medallion on his chest. The circle made Ammo's cloak shimmer. The medallion glowed red, and the nanites that made up Ammo's cloak began to glow brightly for about thirty seconds. Suddenly, the cloak overloaded, and its integrity fell to zero. The medallion then planted itself on top of Ammo's uniform/cloak buttons and latched on, permanently disabling the cloak.

Sonic instructed, "Tie him up, make sure to put disablers on his cannons, and put him in the craft. The boss is going to love this! Jubilee came early! One step closer to destiny!" The henchmen picked him up and carted him off into the darkness behind the Hi-Fi.

Starburst rolled off K.C., and the two of them stood. K.C. looked around and realized they had been playing the wrong game. He surmised, "The desk, Streak powered up the fence using that console."

"Destroy the desk, destroy the fence," Starburst immediately put together.

They gathered themselves. Starburst blitzed toward the desk, and Mygalo, who also quickly recovered, shot webbing and pulled her down to the ground, then dragged her toward him. K.C. sensed broken shards of glass and pushed them into the web's path to cut it, separating Mygalo from Starburst.

The Mammoth was still trying to get to Streak, and while his cloak was drastically reduced in integrity, he had dragged himself to within six feet of her when suddenly, his stripe turned electric blue, and a pain signal shot through his body, wrecking his concentration by the tiniest bit, and Streak's surge pushed him halfway across the room. Starburst rolled backward toward K.C., and the Mammoth walked back toward them.

"Okay, team. Star, distract Streak. I got Mygalo. Mr. Big, tear that desk apart!" K.C. ordered.

Starburst launched toward Streak again and hurled stars at her. Streak delivered another wave of electricity toward Starburst. K.C. turned his batons into a hammer and jumped high and tried to deliver a strike at Mygalo. Mygalo rolled on the ground so that K.C. wouldn't make contact with him, which K.C. anticipated. K.C. took advantage of the roll and used his power to pull the ground up. Mygalo rolled into the wall. Mygalo was shocked, and K.C. landed a huge blow to Mygalo's head, launching him once again into the electric fence. Both K.C. and Starburst's distractions were enough for the Mammoth to take several huge steps and jump as high as he could to bellyflop on the desk. His massive body crushed the console. The electric barrier disappeared. Mygalo, with nothing to support him, fell out of the building. K.C. quickly created a lasso out of the hammer and saved Mygalo from meeting his doom by gluing the lasso to the floor. He then picked up a piece of glass and morphed it into a glass mallet and threw it at Streak, who wasn't paying attention. She took a shot to the chest that sent her into the wall.

"Star, Mammoth, let's get out of here!"

The three finally jumped out of the window. The Mammoth's stripe stopped glowing. Their cloaks broke their fall while they groaned from their four-story plummet.

Enchantra screamed as she fought to decode Hex's barrier. The Eagle twitched and Blitz wriggled. Enchantra feverishly scanned through the symbols and noticed a pattern that she remembered from one of her spell books. *I just need to move one symbol to switch the barrier from "closed" to "open." Where is it?* She knelt, her vision severely blurred. She lifted a hand, and green mist floated to the wall, and she gripped a symbol and shifted it to the left. The barrier shimmered, and she announced, "Blitz, Eagle, it's coming down." When enough of the barrier was broken, Enchantra used telepathy to pull two hovercrafts from Hex's left and slammed them into him. They careened into the left wall.

Some of the security team opened the door to the parking garage, having fought through Enchantra's blockade.

"Come on, guys, ah, this hurts. Let's go." Enchantra summoned up as much energy as she could to place Hex into a temporary spell that would keep him from doing anything to them. She then lifted Blitz and the Eagle up, and they floated past the point of Hex's wall. She then threw a few more hovercraft toward the Security team to buy them time to get through the tunnel.

Once they passed the threshold, their stripes stopped glowing, and the security team's pain signal instantly ceased.

"Ah, okay, give me a minute," the Eagle sighed in relief. They all rested for about thirty seconds. They then gathered themselves together and sprinted to the first ladder they saw. They climbed it and lifted themselves out of the sewer manhole cover and onto the street.

"K.C., do you copy?" Enchantra signaled.

"Yeah, I copy. How is everyone?" K.C. asked as he, Starburst, and the Mammoth ran toward the building across the street where the bus was perched.

"Eagle, Blitz, and I are hobbled but we're all clear."

"Star, Mammoth, and I are alright. Ammo, get the bus ready to get us out of here."

Silence.

"Ammo, do you copy?" K.C. asked.

Silence.

"Ammo, come in!" K.C. demanded.

Nothing.

"Does anybody have eyes on Ammo?"

"No," Eagle said, "I don't see him anywhere. We gotta get up to the roof now."

They mustered the last of their energy to get to the elevator while Starburst and Enchantra levitated to the roof. They reached the hoverpad, opened the bus hatch, and found it empty. "K.C., he's not here. Ammo's not in the bus."

"The Frimas?! Where did he go? He wasn't supposed to get off the bus!"

"I don't know. He's not here. He's not answering his stripe. You think he got off and tried to help us?" Starburst asked.

"Why would he do that?!"

"The plan went to Frimas, and he doesn't know how to fly the bus. My guess is he tried to bust you three out," the Eagle said.

The other four got off the elevator and got on the bus. K.C. looked mortified. He said, "Eagle, get us home. Blitz, pull up Ammo's tracker, let's see if we can get a read on where he is."

Blitz sat at the holoscreen and typed keys to pull up locations on the team. She highlighted Ammo's location and said, "Nothing, K.C. His tracker has been disabled."

"What was his last location?" he asked.

"Last location," she looked up tracking history, "was about half a block from here. Nothing after that."

"Pull up footage from his cloak."

"Okay," she responded. She typed keys to look for video footage from Ammo. She played it on the holoscreen. "Okay, this is the last video received from his cloak. He was half a block from here and was shooting at the fence where the Prize Room is. He is then surrounded by a bunch of guys from Security and this guy. This guy, he looks familiar. That's Sonic!"

The team rose to look at the holoscreen as the Eagle launched the bus into the air. They observed Sonic, Ammo attempting to take everyone down, and Sonic releasing the supersonic sound that eventually debilitated their teammate. The camera feed cut out about ten seconds after Sonic placed the medallion on Ammo's chest.

"That's the last we have of him, K.C.," Blitz reported.

"Intelligence, can you read me?" K.C. called into HQ.

"We're here, K.C. Everyone okay?" Dax confirmed.

"No, we are most certainly not. Can you pull up camera footage from outside the Hi-Fi about eight minutes ago?"

"Pulling up the footage now, what are you looking for?"

"Ammo."

"What do you mean, Ammo? He's not with you?"

"No. He got out of the bus," K.C. reacted, banging his fist on the side.

"Why did he get out of the bus?" Dax interrogated.

"Hey, focus up, Dax, get the footage, dammit!" K.C. insisted.

"Right, pulling it up now. Um, there's no footage, everything's been blacked out. Probably because of the party, anonymity," Dax resigned.

"Okay, thanks Dax. We'll see you back at HQ."

K.C. turned around and found his seat. He sat down, fuming. *Great. Just great. First, he nearly kills a dude. Now he disobeys an order and gets himself captured?! So, not only did we fail this mission. One of the Elite got caught in the process, which is exactly what the Collector wanted! We're so done. We're so done. Mallack is going to kill us all!*

Starburst walked over and sat next to him. "We're gonna find him, okay? The Collector won't get away with this."

"I just wish he would have stayed on the bus. How hard was that?" K.C. countered.

"Yeah, but he didn't, and you know why. We will respond in kind."

16

The Collector's Mission

S he sat silently as the hovercar autopiloted through the night sky. She slowly closed her eyes, listening to the music reverberating through the speakers, and breathed a sigh of joy, relief, wonder, and fear. As the slow beats and rhythmic melodies of the music group Armada infiltrated her ears, she fell into a slight trance and quietly celebrated her victory while agonizing over the lengths she had to go to accomplish it. She recalled the number of bodies she compiled while on her quest to achieve her mission, the people she killed, the hits she ordered, and the lives she destroyed in the process. She wondered how much more she would have to sacrifice before finally claiming her prize.

The hovercar rose higher to escape the skyscraper jungle. A tear escaped her left eye and rolled down her cheek, hidden behind the mask that shielded her identity from the world. She pressed her hand to her chest and felt herself choke up. She held tightly onto the belief that her destiny was once again within her grasp. If what she felt was indeed reality, not just a fantasy, she believed that she was realigned to her life's mission.

She whispered to herself, "It was him. It really was him."

She smiled and started to chuckle. She took in several deep, heavy breaths and fought the urge to break out into sheer joy. Tears escaped her controlled resolve as her glee mingled with overwhelming sadness, burning anger, and unstoppable rage that fueled her ambition to finish what she started decades ago.

The hovercar's AI said, "One minute to your destination."

"Acknowledged," she replied, her voice heavily distorted through the mask.

The hovercar descended to the streets and floated over an abandoned, unlit parking lot. She pressed a button in front of her, and the parking lot's hydraulics hissed then clanged. The pavement dropped about a foot then split and separated, exposing a hoverpad bay about one hundred yards below. The hovercar lowered into the bay and landed on an empty hoverpad. The parking lot entrance reversed and closed, and spotlights flooded the bay with luminance. The hovercar docked, and she opened the door and exited, making note of the completely grayed-out walls and floor. She walked across the parking deck filled with hovercars, hoverbikes, and a couple of hoverbuses. She walked up a series of steps toward a red door. She placed her hand on the palm reader, and it lit white for approval.

The door opened, revealing a long corridor about twenty feet wide lit aquamarine across the moldings of the wall at the top and bottom. Every ten feet, a cutout was framed, covered with glass, and within it contained a glowing cannister. Underneath each cutout was a name scribed on a holoscreen nameplate. She admired each frame as she walked down the hall to her residence at the end of the corridor.

She placed her hand on the palm reader. The lights turned on and revealed her living area converted to an office with a large desk toward the back of the room, several chairs arrayed around the walls, and more trophies embedded in the walls. The lights glowed from the ceiling and floor moldings to create her preferred calming ambience. She walked to the back of the desk, pulled the chair out, and sat down. She tapped on a few keys to wake her holoscreen up, then took out her left arm and laid it on the desk. She laid her head back and stared at the ceiling while the holoscreen began downloading information from her stripe.

Two minutes went by, and the download completed. She got up and proceeded to walk to the bedroom of her residence and clean herself up when she received a call. She answered, voice still distorted from the mask, "Yes?"

"Come to the pad. We have a surprise for you. Although, with you, I don't think you'll be that surprised," a very familiar voice said on the other side of the call.

"I'm on my way," she responded. She walked out of her residence, down the corridor once more, and out to the pad. Waiting for her were Sonic, several henchmen, and a bound Ammo, hands covered with mini-cloaks, and kneeling, still severely dazed from Sonic's attack. She clasped her hands and pranced down the steps to Sonic while declaring, "Well, well, well, Sonic, you have truly outdone yourself this time!"

Sonic stepped forward and decreed, "Consider this an early Jubilee present, boss! This is—"

"—Ammo, yes," she responded as she leaned forward to see him close-up. "I've heard so much about you and witnessed your prowess on the holoscreen news reports. I knew we were entangling with the Company's Elite Unit, but I never thought I'd get to meet one of you so soon!"

"Somehow, I don't believe you," Sonic said.

She stood straight. "Well, I must say that I saw this coming." She then placed her right hand on Sonic's left shoulder as she continued, "But you, Sonic, you executed a flawless plan. You knew that separating the Elite would get us a one-on-one session with at least one of the seven, and it happened just like you said. Did you doubt yourself?"

"Not at all, boss," Sonic cleared his throat as he twisted his left arm to pat her right arm in affirmation.

"Good, so you should celebrate this incredible accomplishment! You have achieved an important objective of our mission." She let him go. "Trust me, your hard work in this endeavor does not go overlooked. For any of you."

The hatch above them opened again, and a hoverbus came down and landed next to Sonic's. The back hatch of the bus opened. Hex escorted a hobbled and wounded Mygalo out first, while Streak exited last appearing unscathed.

"Ah," she said, "look who decided to join the celebration! Welcome, you three! Um, where's the rest of your crew?"

"Oh, they're all still at the Hi-Fi, either unconscious or critically injured. Figured it best to leave them there to be attended to than bring them here," Streak said.

"Probably should have left Mygalo there, too, geez, you look an absolute mess!" she sympathized as she gently stroked and petted one of his tentacles.

"The morphing guy, I swear he was going to rip the coatings off my tentacles despite being cloaked. I've never fought anyone, anything, like him and the others," Mygalo said.

She agreed. "Yes, you just had a run-in with the Company's Elite, judging from who we have in our midst today," she deduced. She waved her hand to direct Streak, Hex, and Mygalo's eyes toward Ammo.

"No way," Hex bellowed in disbelief.

"You really did it?" Streak asked as she walked to Sonic and patted him on the shoulder.

"Of course he did! Why is everyone so surprised? Last I recalled, this was my team we put together, right?"

"Right," Hex agreed. "It's just, he's an Elite!"

"Yes, that he is, and now he belongs to us," the masked woman declared. "But before we get into all of that, mission reports, you three."

"Right here, boss?" Mygalo said.

"I didn't stutter, tell me what happened up there."

"Well, Streak put the fence up, and we tried, we really tried to take them down. But they outsmarted us, boss. They refuse to fight as individuals. They moved as a unit, and they adapted to everything we did. But they didn't want to kill us. They just wanted out of the room. Once they destroyed the console, they were out of there."

The masked woman tapped her chin with her right index finger. "I see. Hex, what about you?"

"I held them with the barrier, but Enchantra was able to decode it and knocked me down with some of the hovercars there. Before I could get up, they were already gone," Hex reported.

She tapped her chin with her finger and sighed, "I understand. Well, we weren't expecting you to kill anyone tonight, although that would have been a treat. They exposed themselves, and they gave us information that will prove valuable for the next leg of our mission. I'm proud of your efforts tonight, and I am even more grateful that they didn't kill you tonight. We cannot reach destiny without each other."

"Wait," Streak countered, pride slightly bruised, "what does that mean? You make it sound like they should have killed us, like they're stronger than us, like they're better than us."

Geez, let me stroke her ego. "Is that what you *think*, Streak?" She turned to face Streak. "I *never* said that. I just know that we are poking the bear in ways we never have before. After taking the Crawler's powers, the Elite have gotten emotional. May account for why they were noticeably sloppy tonight, lacking the poise and precision we're accustomed to seeing from them when they execute a plan. Now, I suspect they want our heads on platters and stakes. Do I believe they're stronger than you? Mathematically, no. But they possess weapons that we need on our side, weapons that make them a formidable challenge whether fighting solo or as a team. Now that they're pissed with us, they're more volatile than ever. And that might make them dangerous.

"Still, I wouldn't worry. Everything is going exactly as planned."

She walked over to Ammo, leaned forward, and slapped his face. "Wake up, Ammo. Come on, now, wakey, wakey. We have some things to discuss."

Ammo battled to regain full consciousness. His eyes fluttered, and his head spun. He looked around to get his bearings straight. His vision sharpened, and he made out Sonic and his henchmen to his right and the familiar shadowy figure in front of him. He shook himself and tried to break free from his bonds.

She chuckled. "Nah, now, come on, you're not going anywhere, so don't fight," she said, raising his face. "Now, tell me, do you know who I am?"

Ammo groaned a little, then lifted his head and answered, "You're the Collector."

"Yes, that's right. It is so nice to finally meet an Elite in an official capacity. I take it you know some of the other members of my team – Streak, Hex, and Sonic – who you fought valiantly and foolishly against tonight. There's also Mygalo, who you haven't met yet, but I'm sure you two will get well acquainted soon."

Ammo calculated that he was outgunned and outmanned 20-to-1. "What do you want with me? You know the Company is tracking you right now, right?"

The Collector laughed and reached out her hand to palm Ammo's chin. "Oh, you mean with your trackers? Oh, don't worry. We made sure to disable those before you got here. You're completely off the grid. No one is coming for you right now." The Collector's team chuckled softly.

"What about those creds you deposited? Might wanna double check your bank accounts," Ammo said as he snatched his head away.

"Ammo, you know what I love about you?" The Collector stood up and pointed at Ammo. "You're always so overconfident, willing to show your cards and hold nothing back, including that mouth of yours, which I'd love for you to put to use in different, more pleasurable ways. But one thing you'll learn about me is that I'm always, *always* three steps ahead of you. I figured your team would try some kind of digital currency trace, so as your viral creds flowed to my various accounts, I 'washed' them of any anomalies that would cause problems for my team and me. So now, you've made me very, very rich, so even if the creds are fake to you and me, the banks will never know it."

Ammo looked despondent within his helmet and visor, bowing his head down. "Oh, I'm so sorry. Did we cause a wrinkle in your otherwise flawless plan to recover the Crawler's power? You and the other Elite made a righteous effort. I was really impressed with you guys tonight. But you came up short, and, well, this is *me* you're fighting against."

The Collector glided a few paces toward her lair's entrance, then turned around to face him again. "Anyway, so do you want anything, need anything?"

"Just your face planted on the ground," Ammo shot at her.

She laughed again. "Mmm, a delightful idea, but Ammo, come on, you don't have any other loftier goals than seeing me on the ground? Ugh, so simple-minded. This is almost a waste of my time. We should just kill him now, get this over with."

She's going to take my powers and kill me. This is what we were afraid of. And my stupid self got caught! This is not how it's supposed to end! What can I do? What can I do?! Why didn't I just stay on the Akan-damned bus?!

Ammo struggled, and two henchmen placed each arm on his shoulders to keep him down. "Wait, what are you going to do with me? My powers? Are you going to take them from me?"

"Your powers?" The Collector snapped her fingers. "That's a great idea, actually! We *should* take your powers from you. But that shouldn't be your concern, to be honest."

"What should it be, then?" Ammo asked.

"You should be worried about staying alive," the Collector responded. The team all laughed.

"So, you're going to kill me?" Ammo deduced.

"I haven't yet decided what I'm going to do with you, Ammo. But one thing is certain. Your arrival here has ensured that I will achieve my goal. And I couldn't be happier. Team, place him in lock-up, and make him comfortable. I do not want him harmed. I'm a great host when I want to be, and I want to be with him."

Ammo was lifted by a couple of henchmen, one on each side, and they and the other henchmen walked him out of the hoverpad area and escorted him to a holding cell within the halls of the Collector's lair.

Ammo couldn't wrap his head around the Collector's plan for him. *What kind of sick mess is this? Unharmed? Comfortable? A great host?! What's she going to do? Fatten me up so she can sacrifice me to Bashko or something? I should have stayed on the bus, should have just sat right there until the team got out. Did they make it out?!*

The Collector walked out and was followed by Streak, Hex, Sonic, and Mygalo. The Collector said, "Mygalo, go to Medical and get checked out. Make sure you're not badly hurt. The rest of you, into my residence."

Mygalo turned to the right while everyone else kept straight down the green-lit hallway. They entered the Collector's residence and shut the door.

Streak began, "So, for real, are we on track?"

"Are you kidding right now? We are most definitely on track!" the Collector spun around. "We are insanely on track. Can you not see it?"

"Um, no, that's why we're asking," Hex retorted, pulling a chair from the wall and sitting down. "The Elites are not going to take this lying down, you know that, right?"

"Of course I do," said the Collector calmly, taking a seat behind her desk. She propped her feet up on the desk and continued, "I fully anticipate them to unleash the full weight of the Company upon us. After all, we have just kidnapped an Elite, and in a rather spectacular manner, if I may say so myself."

Streak began to worry that the Collector was getting ahead of herself and selling the team pipe dreams. Unafraid, she pleaded, "Please, tell us, how is *this* part of your plan?"

"Wait, first, let's all take these ridiculous masks off," the Collector said. She popped two clasps on her neck and a third clasp on the back of her head, then pulled the mask off. The three saw her dark brown eyes, dark brown skin, rose-colored lips, and pixie-cut midnight-colored hair.

Meanwhile, the three summoned their nanites to remove their visors. Streak's silver hair fell behind her shoulders. Her caramel skin and light-brown eyes shimmered in the ambient light. Hex's face was slightly disfigured, scarred, and charred on the left side, his eyes like that of a dragon, red piercing irises and permanently purple sclerae. Sonic's clean-shaven head contrasted with the goatee that surrounded his lips. He had dark brown skin and black eyes.

The Collector took a deep breath and said, "Ah, Akan, much better," in her normal voice.

"Side note, you're gonna have to tell me how you keep your hair so perfect in that helmet you wear," Streak said.

"You're one to talk, dear. Have you looked in the mirror?" the Collector reacted as she air-clawed around her head, symbolizing Streak's perfectly flowing mane. "Now, how is kidnapping an Elite a part of the plan, you asked."

"Yes, because you know us, boss," Sonic stepped forward and chimed in. "We're not in it for the money. You are very generous with it, don't get me wrong. But I want to win, not just get paid. This all just seems rushed, like we're taking on more and bigger risks than we should be."

"And now that we have Ammo with us," Hex added, "I just worry that this 'whole weight of the Company' will undo all you have accomplished."

The Collector looked up, took another deep breath, and said, "Listen, lady and gentlemen, you have been on my side for years. We have been on this mission for a very long time, and I know it's taken us to some strange, dark places, and there have been more close calls than I want to remember. But when I tell you that we are this close, oh so close, to achieving destiny, I can feel it in my bones, can taste it on my lips. I guarantee, taking Ammo tonight will get us the next piece to the puzzle and one step closer to giving us the return on investment we have longed for. Do you trust me?"

"With my life," Streak said.

"Absolutely," Hex declared.

"There's no one else I trust more," Sonic promised.

"Then trust me now. I don't question your loyalty, so don't question my dedication. We've got this. And I've got you. For tonight, just celebrate and rest well. I have a drive I need to build. Once it's done, we will meet again to talk about how we're going to use it."

"What about Ammo's powers? Are you going to collect them?" Sonic asked.

"If it's necessary, Sonic. Right now, go, have fun, and go paint the town red! That's what I'm about to do, sort of."

"What do you mean?" Hex asked.

"Well, my stripe just revealed that I have a date tonight," the Collector referenced a buzzing she felt from her left arm. "And I can't be late. Her power is too great, and this will be my only shot at getting it from her," the Collector said with a smirk on her face.

"Wait, you're not about to screw somebody out of their power again, are you?" Streak asked.

"Yeah, well, the great thing about being me is that I will always have the power of anonymity on my side. So, no matter what I do, as long as people are left satisfied, they will never, ever know it was me. She'll be paralyzed from the waist down, and I'll be one power stronger with the perfect recruit to transfer it to. She won't even realize her power's gone until well after I've left for the night."

"Wait, how does that work exactly? This is news to me," Sonic asked, highly intrigued by this new piece of information about the Collector.

"I mean, isn't it obvious? I can absorb power from anywhere on me. *Anywhere*. That's why no one should ever touch me. No telling what I might snatch. Souls, hearts, powers, really depends on what kind of mood I'm in. And right now, it's just business. Too bad she doesn't know that. Now, it's time for you all to leave so I can get ready. Great work tonight, again, all of you. To destiny!"

"To destiny," they all agreed. Streak and Hex rose from their chairs, and they all turned to leave and sealed the door shut.

Streak still wasn't convinced. *Something doesn't feel right to me. I hate it when she's this cavalier, this giddy. I know I shouldn't question her. She has been leading us this entire time, and she's right. This is the closest we've ever gotten to our ultimate end. But we are moving too fast, taking on too much. Especially with these Elite we're fighting against. I don't think we can outlast them on our own, Ammo be damned.*

Hex noticed Streak's shifted demeanor and quickly probed her mind. He captured everything she thought, then gently clutched her arm and looked deep into her eyes. "What is it you're not saying?"

"You know I hate it when you do that, right?" Streak answered as Sonic turned around.

"That's irrelevant. Talk to us," Hex demanded.

"I don't know," Streak crossed her arms. "We've never had a reason to question her before. And I don't want to start now."

"But?" Sonic pressed.

"I just wonder whether she's really telling us the truth or just playing us. I don't want to believe the latter, so I won't question it."

Hex responded, "I understand. I've been with her longer than you all, so trust me when I say she knows what she's doing. When she's close to achieving something this big, it seems like she's overshooting her shot, but she sees and knows things beyond our comprehension. So, if we've trusted her this long, let's not doubt her now. We're running the gauntlet now, and the Elite are our target. Let's remember what we're fighting for and keep our heads in the game."

Streak sighed heavily. "Right. To destiny. Let's rest up, you two."

The Collector, meanwhile, sat in her chair for a minute more, her soul still rattling from the mayhem in the Prize Room. She said, "Am I crazy? That wasn't him, was it? Yes, yes it was. You know it was. It's really him."

She leaned forward and typed several keys on her holoscreen, and a dialogue box opened. A line appeared in the dialogue, "What would you like this drive to do?"

She typed underneath it, "I need it to retrieve information."

"What kind?" the next line read.

"All kinds," she responded.

She typed several keys and continued communicating her instructions for her operative to create the next puzzle piece to further her success.

17

Visions

Malcolm lay restless in his bed, staring at the ceiling of his quarters' residence that glowed from the silver light of the moons outside his windows. The faint sounds of the roars of hovercraft zooming past the building couldn't lull him to sleep this night. He ruminated on the last conversation he had with Duncan, when Duncan said that he felt like he should step down from being an Elite, that he felt a night in the bus would do him some good.

Why, why didn't he just stay on the bus? Why didn't he listen to me? Am I losing control of the unit? I just know Mallack's going to have my head tomorrow. This is my third failure in four missions. No way she's going to let me off the hook for that.

He started losing control of his senses, and he felt every molecule in his residence, including the cloak that protected the perimeter of his room from powers. His heartbeat raced, and his breaths shortened. The waves crashed through his mind. The more he internally beat himself up, the more intense his senses dialed. Shades of red flashed before him, and the threads between reality and fantasy tore. A stinging pain pierced his brain, echoing the same feeling triggered by Sonic. He rolled out of bed and planted on all fours, his forehead kissed the carpet, and he grasped his skull. Malcolm cried out, begging for the torture to stop. His fears engulfed him, and he drowned in a sea of fury and wrath.

A sweet, encouraging, soft voice whispered, "We are destined for this."

Malcolm's room crumbled into dust. Tall, decayed, cracked, and shattered buildings surrounded him as he stood in the middle of the fissured, empty street. Dust and tiny shards of glass, concrete, and metal slowly fell from the sky. Peering through the light green haze, he made out three people about thirty feet in front of him. One was a fair-skinned lady with reddish-brown hair dangling from her head, her clothes tattered and dirty. She knelt, holding her hands up, and stared with dread in her eyes and apprehension gripping her breath. A dark-skinned man of average height with a backward cap covering his skull stood in front of the woman with his legs parted, one arm stretched toward her, and the other stretched toward Malcolm. His hand glowed brightly as it suspended a fireball pointed directly at him. The third, much shorter, stood in front of the second. A bush of black hair sprouted from his face, and his head was clean-shaven. A pot belly protruded from his orange shirt and blue pants. He wielded a short blade in each hand, connected by a black metal chain that dangled to the ground.

Malcolm noticed that the woman bled heavily from the left side of her abdomen, her white shirt stained by a deep wound. Malcolm looked to his left and saw that he was holding a blade, and its tip had blood dripping from it. As he stared closer at the weapon, he could sense the grittiness of the blade, comparing how it felt to grains of a beach. He noticed the dust swirling in the air and realized that the weapon was constructed from the same dust. The terrain they stood on shook as the sky's hue changed to gray.

The sweet, encouraging, soft voice echoed to Malcolm, "You deserve this power."

Resolve sprang in Malcolm's heart, but he could barely discern where the desire for justice and retribution originated. The fireball-wielding combatant yelled, "Why are you doing this?! Let us go! We've done nothing wrong!"

Malcolm struggled to remember what they possessed and why he had to retrieve it, but he could not stop himself from trying. Malcolm dropped the sand weapon, then raised his hands above his head, and the skyscrapers around him vibrated violently. Shards of glass, steel, concrete, and wood flaked from the rumblings, then suddenly suspended in midair. He craned his face upward. The debris rushed toward Malcolm and began to revolve around him as though he was the center of gravity. He shot his hands in front of himself and noted his red and black nanotech covering his body. He rotated his hands and forged the debris into three lances. He screamed, "Don't make me do this!"

Wait, what? No, Malcolm, you don't do this!

As the lady yelled in pain and fear, Malcolm hurled the blades toward the three. The fireball in the dark-skinned man's possession grew suddenly, and he launched the fireball toward Malcolm. Malcolm diverted the blades, and they pierced the still-crumbling buildings. He then stuck out his arm to stop the fireball inches from his body. He flipped his right hand, stuck out his left, and brought both hands together to flatten the fireball into a thick, smoldering orange and white lasso.

The sweet, encouraging, soft voice whispered in his visor, "They don't deserve this power."

What power? Who is talking to me?

He grabbed the rope and cracked it like a whip. Malcolm then ran toward his opponents, swung the rope, and hurled it toward them. Like a snake wrapping around its prey, the cord broke the chain of the smaller one's weapon, and bound them, burning them on contact. They screamed in pain, aware that their time was running out. In agonizing pain, they mustered up what little strength they had left to endure Malcolm's assault, but they knew they were done for.

Malcolm clenched his fists, and the rope glowed from red to orange, orange to white, white to blue. Their screams were only muffled by the continuous shaking of the crumbling edifices around them. The heat from the lasso burned them alive. Malcolm then snapped his fingers, and the lasso exploded, eviscerating them and the asphalt under them.

The blast catapulted Malcolm and transported him to a dimly lit back-alley miles away from the explosion. He saw a man in red and black nanotech and recognized he was standing thirty feet away from himself. He observed himself struggling physically with a person of the same height dressed in all black near a brick wall. *What the Frimas is this?!*

He witnessed himself use his left hand to grab his adversary's arm by the wrist and press his right hand into his opponent's chest to thrust him against the brick wall. He whipped out a blade and swiftly stabbed the man in black in his heart. The stranger gasped for air as he felt his life slowly drain away from his body. The man in red and black calmly said to the man in black, "You don't deserve this power."

The sweet, encouraging, soft voice whispered, "You deserve this power."

Who is this? Who keeps talking to me?! Come on, Malcolm, think! Think!

The sky turned pitch black, and Malcolm teleported to another combat zone. This time, he observed himself struggling with a woman in nanotech in a plaza surrounded by tall, thick bushes. A yellow aura surrounded his foe. *Is that Symone?* She had him pinned to the ground, sitting atop his torso. She punched him in his helmet several times, trying to knock him unconscious. He stretched his arms out and tightened his fingers. Malcolm sensed and removed two cinder blocks from the walls surrounding the plaza and slung them into her skull, knocking her out cold. Her aura instantly dissipated, revealing her yellow-tinted white uniform and helmet to match. Her thin, lifeless body slumped atop the man, and he immediately pushed her off him, rolling her on her back.

The sweet, encouraging, soft voice whispered, "We are destined for this."

Destined for what?!

Red lightning cracked the sky, and an intensely shining red meteor raced from the heavens and shuttled toward Uri City. Everything shone like a photography development room. Screams and cries saturated the air in every direction, and dread filled Malcolm's heart. He heard grunts and shouting behind him, and he swiftly turned around. Malcolm saw himself in the same red and black, fighting against an older man. The older man's grey beard reached his stomach, his bald head shining red from the doom star looming over them. The older man launched himself away from the red and black assassin, hurdling 150 feet of lake to distance himself from Malcolm. The wizard raised his hands in front of him, and water from the lake rose in response. He then thrust his hands forward, and the water obeyed his command and shot forward like a geyser at the assassin.

Malcolm stretched his hands out to stop himself from hurting the old man, but he was powerless. He watched his red and black doppelganger bend forward with his right arm covering his face to withstand the pressure of the water blast. He then raised his hands slowly, and the water obeyed his command and accumulated into a wall. He instructed some of the droplets to reshape into tiny pins and protrude the wall. He rolled to his left, bringing the wall with him, then pushed his hands forward, launching the water pin wall toward the old man. The pins stabbed the old man all at once, dropping him and the water to the pavement.

The red meteor's luminance shone even brighter. Its acceleration was so swift, its size so massive, that it broke through the cloak that covered the city about five miles above the surface, dismantling parts of the metal frame and shattering the nanites that held the cloak in place without decelerating. The sky burned crimson and black as smoke from the cloak's destruction engulfed the air.

The sweet, encouraging, soft voice whispered, "You deserve this power."

No, I don't! Stop saying that! No one does! Not like this!

He looked forward again and witnessed himself in the middle of the splintering street, suspending another stranger in midair. With arms outstretched, he stared into his opponent's eyes and echoed the soft voice's sentiment, "You don't deserve this power," and stretched his fingers wide. His victim screamed in agony as he disintegrated little by little, the dust of his skin, muscles, and clothes glittering red from the glow of the star above.

Malcolm knelt and buried his head in his hands, agonizing in disbelief that he was capable of such carnage. The meteor slammed into the heart of the city, and a mind-splitting boom silenced the screams. The force of the impact eradicated the Midtown district, and its impact blast rapidly annihilated everything in its path. Fire and radiation swiftly raced closer to Malcolm, and he stood ready to meet Akan, knowing that the end had come, and no one could escape this fate.

As the blast decimated him from flesh to bone, the sweet, encouraging, soft voice emphatically declared, "We are destined for this."

Malcolm came out of the trance, back on all fours, his chest heaving, lungs gasping for air, his clothes sweat-soaked. Unlike the other times, his mind didn't spin. He didn't have to wonder what this or that meant. Malcolm had resolved some of the biggest mysteries that dreaming alone would not allow.

It's me. I'm the man in red and black. No doubt about it. These can't be just random nightmares. But what are they? Memories or visions? Who is the woman who keeps whispering to me? And why me? Why is this stuff in my head?

He picked himself off the carpet. With no resolution in sight, he chose to reexamine his last battle with Streak and Mygalo. He recalled searching for Mygalo after dropping the ceiling on him and not realizing that he was right behind him. He remembered Symone had blasted from nowhere and rescued him from Mygalo's deathblow. His senses replayed her grip on his body. Her sudden salvation felt firm, her body so soft when she landed on top of him. He snapped from there to the ride to the Hi-Fi when she turned her body and pulled his arms over her to be spooned.

She feels, she feels, right. Just being in her air sends chills down my spine. Touching her, feeling her body pressed against mine, it feels like I've known her forever. I don't understand what she's doing to me. Is it her power source, her energy, that's got me like this? She feels too right, too perfect. But man, she's so hot, and she knows it. That dress, her flawless look, if only we were at the Power Party to actually party, not work. Ugh! I don't want to be her mentor anymore.

Malcolm continued to trace his infatuation with Symone, thinking about how close they got when quizzing each other on their cover stories, placing his hands on her shoulders in the hall, walking with her after her battle with Malaysia, her kiss in their spar, her telling him, "Screw you, Malcolm," as their spar ended. The more he thought about her, the less real estate his nightmarish trance took up in his mind.

It's like, the more I try to resist her, the more she invades my space. The more she invades my space, the more I can't resist her.

He went to his drawers and pulled out an A-shirt and a pair of sweatpants to change into. Once dressed, he walked out of his bedroom, through his living room, and stood at his door. He grabbed the slot but stopped short of sliding the door and second-guessed himself. *No, no, we can't do this, I can't do this. Be patient, Malcolm. You hooking up with your mentee in the middle of this is the* worst thing *you could do right now. Back the Frimas up and think about what you're doing. Sit down somewhere.* He slowly placed his head on the door.

Symone stood on the other side of Malcolm's door, clad in a black sports bra and crimson leggings, hand pressed against the door, contemplating whether to knock. She felt an incredible desire to be near him, connect with him, and get physically entangled with him. She rationalized that she should check on Malcolm and provide support to him, then see where things led. She hesitated, thought, unsure whether tonight was the right time to try.

No, she reasoned, *I shouldn't do that to him. I want him, Akan knows, but I don't want him to second-guess wanting me. I'll just go back to my residence.* She backed away from the door and turned around to walk away. Malcolm then slid the door open and was shocked to see Symone's backside. He took a mental snapshot at how alluring her body appeared, her dreads draped behind her shoulders like arrows pointing at her bubble butt and signaling *come get this!*

Symone turned around and stared back at him, mesmerized at how his A-shirt accentuated his chiseled chest, broad shoulders, and toned, milk-chocolate arms. *Mmm.*

"Miss Watson," Malcolm said as he stepped outside and closed his door. "Everything alright?"

Symone couldn't help but admire Malcolm's physique, allowing her eyes to soak in the milk chocolate, incredibly toned figure before her. She shook off the shock and returned his volley. "I was wondering the same thing about you."

"I'm alright," Malcolm lied.

"Are you sure?" Symone asked as she stepped closer to him, staring into Malcolm's deep brown eyes.

"Well," Malcolm succumbed, "I mean, I have to be, right? No sense in staying angry about everything."

"Malcolm," Symone placed her right hand on the side of Malcolm's left shoulder, "you don't have to pretend that everything is okay."

"I know," Malcolm replied.

"So, talk to me. What's going on?"

"Walk with me," Malcolm responded and motioned Symone to travel the corridors of the Grand Hall by pressing gently on the small of her back. Symone closed her eyes to hide the embers glowing from them. *I wish he was inviting me in.*

They walked out of the quarters, and Malcolm admitted, "I'm just pissed that he got off the bus."

Symone nodded her head. "Yeah, you're not the only one. But you know why he got off the bus."

"I know," Malcolm growled, "he's such a hothead."

Symone chuckled, "True, but he meant well. Had he blown the fence open, we'd all be calling him a hero."

"Naw, I still would have chewed him out for getting out the bus," Malcolm countered, and Symone made a *stop lying* face with one eyebrow raised, "*but* still would have thought that was a bold move on his part."

"There it is," Symone lowered her head and smiled. "See, underneath all that 'steely supervisor' armor you put out," she waved her hands around his face, "you like a little spontaneous action every once in a while."

"I mean, it's not that I don't like to be surprised," Malcolm volleyed. "It's just that if we stick to the plan, everything will go the way it's supposed to go." Malcolm heard his words and immediately clarified his comment. "I mean, *usually,* things will go the way they're supposed to go. At least we'd all still be here and not worried that he's out there somewhere."

They stopped near the entrance of the cafeteria. Malcolm used the palm reader and opened the door. They walked in as Symone replied, "That's the key word, though. *Usually.* If you continue living in your head like that, you're going to miss all the life you could be living out here with the rest of us."

Malcolm stood silent as he pondered on her poignant response. She continued, "Malcolm, clearly, you're not one to take defeat lying down. And we've taken a lot of L's lately from this Collector person. Since I've been on the team, we're what, 1-2, and I hate that. We all are just as pissed as you are with him. We'll figure out how to take him and his squad down."

"That's just the thing, S-Miss Watson," Malcolm quickly corrected himself, "I'm trying to understand what his game is."

Symone caught that Malcolm almost said her first name and smirked gleefully. "What do you mean?"

Malcolm and Symone walked up to a drink-making holoscreen in the middle of the cafeteria floor. He selected a berry punch, then asked Symone, "Do you want anything?"

"No, I'm fine, thanks," Symone said.

Yeah, you are. He grabbed his beverage from a slot in the countertop. He motioned them to sit at a table near the holoscreen. He took a sip of his drink and began, "I'm sitting here thinking about the Collector's patterns. I remember a while back when you, Mallack, and I were talking about the Collector, and you had said that you think he wants one of us."

"Yes, I remember that. What, you think that's not what he wants?" Symone inquired.

"At first, I did, and I kind of still do. But check this. Now, I'm not an analyst, so Intelligence will probably take my thoughts, and—anyway, the Collector's main objective has been stealing and selling powers. In the last few murders, he stole their powers first, then killed them. But this time, we stopped him from killing the Crawler. We got to the Power Party, and the Collector escaped us but took Ammo."

"Because he wants to take an Elite power, right?" Symone reasoned.

"Yeah, maybe," Malcolm said as he ran his palm across his hair.

"Maybe? What do you see that I'm not?"

"Well, remember what the Analyst said about Streak, Sonic, and Hex? They haven't used their full strength on us. If I were the Collector and had the strength of these three Elite assassins on my side, I would do what Sonic did to Ammo, to all of us, then simply strip us all of our powers and call it a day."

"Maybe we got stronger and could take them down," Symone pondered.

"In such a short amount of time, no way. None of us would have evolved that quickly to take them down, especially Streak. Besides, our objective wasn't to kill them but to escape the party. We only cared about taking down the desk and getting the Frimas out of there."

"I don't know, Malcolm. What would the Collector's endgame be if not to take powers and sell them? It sounds like you're implying that he doesn't even care about building an army of his own."

Malcolm shrugged his shoulders, "That's what I'm saying, Symone. I think we're severely underestimating the Collector. Like, we really don't know what the Collector wants or what lengths he's willing to go to get it. Somehow, I feel like we're being directed, and I'm concerned that we're playing right into the Collector's hands."

Symone looked away from Malcolm and crossed her arms, then looked back at him and asked, "So, what do we do about it?"

Malcolm shrugged his shoulders quickly. "I honestly don't know. I mean, we have a debriefing in the rising, so I'll bring it up with Mallack and Intelligence. This has become a straight-up clusterbiff, and there's no telling what Mallack's going to think or say or do after this." Malcolm sat back and sighed.

Symone sensed that Malcolm was beating himself up over Duncan again. She leaned forward. "Malcolm, don't think the worst," Symone said as she gently pressed her hand on top of Malcolm's on the table. "We did everything we could to make the situation work. When you came up with that proxy cover on the fly, I was like, 'How did he do that?' We did everything we could."

"Yeah, I don't know. I just got an awful feeling about all of this."

"Well, whatever we're about to face, we will face it together," Symone said. "I, for one, am not going anywhere."

"You sure?" Malcolm asked, turning his hand palm up to gently scratch his fingers on Symone's palm.

She did the same as she said, "Sorry to disappoint you, Malcolm, but you're stuck with me."

"And how do you know that?" Malcolm tilted his head downward and smiled as he peered into Symone's eyes.

"Because you called me by my first name, finally," Symone said, raising her eyebrow with a full smile across her lips.

Malcolm looked up and replayed the conversation in his head. *"That's what I'm saying,* Symone."

"Wow, I did say your name, didn't I?"

"It's about time, *Mr. Bennett,*" Symone joked.

"Well, that'll be the last time you hear me say your name for a long time, so hold onto the memory," Malcolm chuckled.

"I seriously doubt that. You said it so effortlessly, it was only the natural thing to do. Stop fighting it."

"Seems like putting up a fight against you is an exercise in futility," Malcolm reviewed, still playing with Symone's hand.

"Yeah, I'm getting a similar sense with you, Malcolm."

"What do you mean?" Malcolm's antennas felt Symone was about to reveal something that would give him clarity over something he had thought about not even twenty minutes prior.

Symone's anxiety piqued. She knew what she wanted. *Ew, feelings! Well, here we go. This might bite me in the rear but go for it.*

Symone's chest tightened, and she lay her heart bare. "Well, I know that you're my 'supervisor,' and what this is, what we are, what we're becoming, people are going to think that I'm scoring points with my boss to get a leg up in the Company or whatever. And I can only imagine what you're going through, trying to keep your distance from me for the sake of the team, your reputation, and the Company."

"But?" Malcolm said, still holding onto Symone's hand, his eyes not flinching.

"But," Symone sighed, "I can't deny what I'm feeling for you. And I am certain that you feel the same way for me. And I am convinced," she said as she locked her fingers with his, "that we're not going to be able to fight this for much longer." She warmed her hands, igniting a tiny spark between them, as her eyes flickered red.

Malcolm leaned forward and concentrated on the tiny spark from her hand. Two strands flowed from the glowing spark and began wrapping themselves around their hands. Symone's hair began to glow red from the excitement and passion churning in her stomach as she watched Malcolm manipulate the string. The string morphed from a strand of light and heat to a crimson-colored fabric ribbon entangling their interlocked hands.

As a wave of tension, fire, and passion flowed through and intensified within them, Malcolm surrendered, "You're right, Symone. We're not going to be able to. I've resisted the urge time and time again, and I've grown tired of fighting this, fighting 'us.' So, we'll cross that bridge, or burn it down, when we get to it."

"Malcolm," Symone softly spoke as she marveled at the transformation, then gazed with awe into Malcolm's eyes, "how did you just do that?"

"I honestly have no idea. It's something about you, about your energy, that just makes this effortless," Malcolm replied.

Tell me more. Keep talking. What do you mean by that?

Before she could voice her thoughts, the cafeteria door slid open, and Alexia walked in, dressed in a green sports bra and white gym shorts. They saw her and let go of each other's hands. Symone's hair instantly stopped glowing and returned to its natural color. Malcolm swiftly unraveled the ribbon and released their hands from it. It lay in the middle of the table. Alexia locked eyes with them and walked in their direction, saying, "Can't sleep, either, huh?"

"Nope, Team 'No Sleep' in full effect," Malcolm answered. "I'm dreading the debriefing."

"Aren't we all? What are you guys doing, just talking?" Alexia asked.

"Yeah, just processing everything, trying not to get mad all over again," Symone backed into her chair as she responded. "What about you?"

"Oh, I was just gonna grab something to drink from here, sit around for a bit, and try to clear my head. I told y'all it was a bad plan, and I'm just so angry," Alexia revealed.

"Yeah, you're right. We should have listened," Malcolm sighed. He finished his drink, then got up from his seat. "I'm gonna head back to my room and try to get some sleep. Thanks for keeping me company, Miss Watson. I'll see you both in the rising."

"See you tomorrow, *Malcolm*."

Malcolm smiled, and as Malcolm walked away, Alexia sensed something happened between them. "Did I interrupt something?"

"Um, no, you didn't," Symone gave her. "We were just digging through our thoughts trying to figure all this out."

"Indeed," Alexia responded. "Let me get something from the bar, I'll be back."

As Alexia walked away, Symone noticed the ribbon lying on the table. She held it, balled it up, and placed it in her pocket, wondering what she wanted to do with it, determined to never let it, or Malcolm, go.

18

Failing Forward

"Rough night I assume," Malaysia said to Malcolm.

Malcolm looked like he had been hit by a hoverbus. It was the following rising, and Malcolm sat on a stool, wearing a hoodie and the same sweatpants from the evening prior, while Malaysia cooked breakfast. His eyes were red. Bags resided under them. His head hurt from the tension still radiating from his brain.

Malcolm answered Malaysia, "Yeah, very rough."

"Thinking about Duncan, right?"

"Duncan, the mission, the team, Mallack, Miss Watson, everything. It's just a big, jumbled mess in my head right now," Malcolm revealed as he placed his elbows on the countertop and his head in his palms.

"That's a lot, Malcolm. Hopefully, after the meeting today, you can release some of that. Or you can talk to me about it right now." Malaysia's locs dangled to the small of her back and swiped left to right as she moved from one end of the kitchen to the other.

"Ugh, I don't want to," Malcolm said.

"Yes, you do," Malaysia countered. "You wouldn't be sitting here if you didn't."

"Ask your questions, Malaysia," Malcolm resigned.

"Ooh, testy, I see. Just one, Malcolm," Malaysia said as she flipped the pancakes in the pan. "How have your nightmares been?"

Malcolm was stunned. He miscalculated Malaysia's topic of interest, thinking for sure she was going to ask about Symone. He lifted his head, "Um, the nightmares? I haven't had one in a while, perhaps not for the past four weeks or so."

"They're still affecting you, aren't they?" Malaysia stared intensely.

"Yes," Malcolm released slowly from his lips.

"How so?"

"Well, they're not just dreams anymore," Malcolm admitted to her.

"What do you mean?"

"You can't tell this to anyone, not to Mallack, not even your diary."

"Tell me," Malaysia said, switching from the pancakes to the eggs and bacon.

"Well, I'm beginning to see these dreams in the middle of the day when I'm wide awake. Like, when Sonic unleashed his screech on us in the parking garage, he scrambled my brain. I saw everything I've ever seen in my dreams in real-time – the fire, the destruction, the pain, the death. I thought maybe it was just a part of his attack, pulling from our subconscious or something. But last night, I couldn't sleep, and I fell into a trance, and everything showed up again. It scared the mess out of me."

"Malcolm, what do you think that means?" Malaysia asked, not skipping a beat as she switched to slicing pineapples, strawberries, oranges, kiwi, and grapefruit.

Malcolm rose from his chair and responded, "I honestly don't know. I thought they were just dreams, but they feel so real, I don't know if they are memories or visions. Maybe I'm just super stressed and need a break from everything for a little while."

"Maybe. Or you need to get laid."

Malcolm laughed and said, "Or that."

Malaysia shrugged her shoulders and tilted her head to the side, "Just saying, maybe you're pent up and need a release. I think Symone's available. What do you think?"

Malcolm jumped up, "Huh?"

Malaysia looked at Malcolm with a smirk, then said, "Malcolm, do you think I'm blind? I see the way you two get when you're around each other. If you guys aren't screwing, you're close."

"Unbelievable, it's that obvious?" Malcolm said.

"So you two *are...*"

"No! No, we're not screwing."

"But you want to," Malaysia smiled, "Frimas, I know she wants to."

"I mean, you're not wrong, but come on, Malaysia, you know I can't do that."

"Frimas, why not? There's no rule against it, nowhere."

"I'm her mentor. That would be such a bad look."

"True, but who cares? Not us, not Mallack, not the Company. She's gorgeous as Frimas, you're fine as Frimas. She's single, *you're* single," Malaysia finished cooking the breakfast buffet and began turning off the oven.

"Malaysia, you're tripping," Malcolm laughed.

"Listen, all I'm saying is that anyone with a bit of sense can see that you two want each other. She might not say anything to us, but she is picking up whatever it is you're throwing at her. This aversion you have about getting with her, I'd suggest throwing it in the trash. Maybe then you can get some, let Symone knock you out cold, and get a good night's sleep."

"Hey, if anybody's getting knocked out, it'd definitely be her," Malcolm let his pride get the better of him.

"Mmm hmm, see? Handle your business, Malcolm," Malaysia laughed.

"I guess." Malcolm swiped a slice of bacon and began chomping on it. "You know, Karl said something similar, except for him, he was afraid that I might lose focus in the field," Malcolm revealed to Malaysia.

"Is he wrong? Do you feel like you're losing focus?"

"Not at all. I mean, I don't think I am. Frimas, this last mission should be proof of that. But I guess Mallack and Intelligence will decide that for me."

"I wouldn't worry about Mallack and Intelligence," Malaysia responded as she tapped keys on the countertop, and different flavored juices, milk, and coffee appeared through slots on the countertop. "If anything, I'd worry about Alexia. She's the one who's going to give them the business. She was right, and we got beat down because we didn't listen to her."

Malcolm sighed. "She said the same thing last night. It's one of the few times where I wish I could skip a meeting."

"Naw, naw! Get your popcorn ready. Sparks are going to fly all over the place." Malaysia used her stripe to send a message to the team: "Breakfast is ready for whoever wants some. Better hurry before we're called to Intelligence for the debrief."

Malaysia put a little bit of everything she had prepared on a plate and said, "Here, Malcolm. Something tells me you're gonna need it and a ton of caffeine to make it through the next eighteen cycles."

"Mmm, it smells amazing in here!" Symone declared behind them. Malcolm turned around and saw Symone standing in the entryway between the commons and the residences wearing the same black sports bra and crimson leggings, with the ribbon he had crafted tied around her exposed, toned waistline. Malcolm cracked a smile at Symone. She saw him, looked down at the ribbon, then looked back at him and smiled. Malcolm then looked back at Malaysia, who looked at him, flashed her eyes, and cracked a smile too.

About two cycles later, the Elite assembled in the conference room. Mallack was joined by Stephanie, Dax, and the Analyst. They all sat in their respective seats. Malcolm sat in between Alexia and Symone. Malaysia sat at the left end of the table, while Karl and Daisy sat at the opposite end. They were all fully aware of the empty seat that Duncan typically occupied in between Malaysia and Alexia.

Mallack could sense the overwhelming apprehension in the room. She looked at each Elite, then at Stephanie, Dax, and the Analyst. She cleared her throat, stood up from her seat, stepped forward, and said, "Okay, Elite, I don't want a rundown of what happened. I think we all can see that the plan was a colossal failure. Rather, I want to know where the breakdown occurred and why."

Alexia was chomping on the bit. Without hesitation, she replied, "The breakdown occurred when we said 'yes' to this mission, Director. I told you all that this was a mistake, and we should never have agreed to it in the first place."

"You're right, Alexia. We shouldn't have."

"Now Duncan's gone, and we have no idea where he is or what they will do to him, and for what? We didn't get the Crawler's powers back, and I can almost guarantee Dax will say that the trackers failed, right? They failed, didn't they?"

Dax looked down, then back at Alexia and answered, "Yes, they failed, were scrubbed on upload."

Alexia growled. "Why doesn't anyone ever listen to me? This plan was bogus from the jump. We should have waited a little longer. And we still have no clue who the Collector is, but I guarantee you we made him richer, and no telling when he will take Duncan's power from him!"

Mallack calmly returned the volley, "You're right."

Alexia's eyes glowed brighter than they'd ever beamed before, and she clenched her fists and gritted her teeth. "That's all you have to say, Director?!"

"What do you want me to say, Alexia? You're not wrong. We messed up. That's why we're here, to figure out, aside from making the decision in the first place, how we messed this up."

"Aargh," she yelled, and green mist puffed from her body as she slammed her hands on the table.

Mallack continued. "I know you're pissed. We all are. And there's plenty of blame to throw around. I'm sure everyone will get their share of it at some point. So, while we're in this room, let's get it all out. Where did we mess up?"

The room got quiet.

"Anyone?"

Malaysia offered the first guess, ready to throw herself on her dagger, "Jackson Santana."

"Yes, Jackson Santana," Daisy echoed. "Who the Frimas is he, and why did he show up at the party? That's the point where the plan went completely south."

Symone agreed. "Right. We were on track to get the power from the Collector, even if the trackers did fail. Then the Collector started asking us about our identities, both Santana and Leslie. These IDs were supposed to be bullet-proof."

"I don't know what happened," Stephanie took ownership as she uncrossed her legs and leaned forward. "From all the intel we collected, there was no reason for Santana or any of his associates to show up at the party. It's why we used him. Our intel told us that the Collector never sees his patrons' faces, and Santana did not have the capital to engage in a sale this high."

Malcolm chimed in, "True. The Collector said that it didn't make sense for Santana to make a one hundred million cred purchase when his entire net worth is only forty million. He was essentially out of his league."

"Which may mean that Santana and Leslie have somehow put themselves in a position to take the Underbelly with just a few more pieces of whatever puzzle they're assembling," Mallack added. "Stephanie, Dax, look into their histories in the Underbelly and see what you can come up with regarding their dealings. We can't be directly involved without UPD approval. But maybe if we can provide UPD with intel, they will give us permission to put a Super team on it and find out what Santana and Leslie are up to, and how close they are to achieving it."

"Yes, Director," Stephanie answered.

"Okay, so we had bad intel about who would be at the party, which led to faulty IDs. What else?"

Malaysia silently let out a sigh of relief. *Thank Akan, I thought they would ask me how I knew him.*

"Wait, not yet," Alexia piped in again. "Those IDs, the intel, from whom did we get that intel? Why aren't they in here?"

"Our undercovers? They're still undercover. They don't come to the Company until their missions are complete," Dax reported.

"Well, what happens to them? Like, we went in because of their information. Shouldn't they have to answer for this mistake?"

"They will, Alexia, at the appropriate time," Mallack replied. "But we also have to keep in mind that to get the intel we received, they put themselves in incredible danger and took steep risks to pass this information along. Rolling their heads on silver platters will not solve the problem nor make any of us feel better."

That wasn't good enough for Alexia. She shot back, "It might." Malaysia looked at Malcolm, and Malcolm looked back at her, both understanding that they should get their popcorn ready.

"Alexia, don't be unreasonable," Daisy chimed in. "It sucks, yes, but they did their jobs, just like we all do, and we went in with what we had."

"Don't be unreasonable? If Duncan loses his power, or worse still, he dies, what should be the reasonable thing for us to think or do?"

"Avenge him," Karl's scruffy, deep voice boomed across the room. "Just like we would for anyone here."

"We shouldn't have to avenge him," Alexia snapped, her eyes glowing green again.

"You're right, Alexia," Malaysia added. "But who's fault is that, really? Not any of us here, not Intelligence, not Mallack. Duncan made a choice. A choice to save us, his friends, his family."

"Exactly," Malcolm had enough and was ready to move on. Everyone faced him. "Bogus plan or not, we chose to go to the Hi-Fi. None of us have guns pointed at our heads saying, 'Go or die.' Mallack isn't a dictator, and the Company isn't controlling us like mindless drones. Any of us could have said we wanted out and gone home. But we decided to fight for our ally the Crawler, for the Company, and for those the Collector stole from and murdered. And we got beat down again. Duncan made his choice to help us get out of the hotel. Was it foolish, Frimas yeah, it was! He couldn't blast that fence down. But he was willing to try. And that's all we could ask of any of us. Be willing to try. Now the Collector wants us to get angry and fall apart over this. We can't let him win. For Duncan, we *will* not."

Alexia simmered, sulked in her chair, and cut her eyes. "I hate it when you do that."

"Do what?" Malcolm asked.

"Make sense."

Malcolm shrugged his shoulders and said, "Just speaking the truth. Duncan did what any of us would have done: whatever it takes. So, let's figure it out, stop looking for who to throw our anger at, and focus all that energy on the one person who truly deserves it: the Collector."

Underneath the table, Symone slid her hand on Malcolm's and locked fingers with his, enamored by his speech. Mallack was impressed and said, "So, now that we got all that out, let's continue. What else?"

Daisy was sitting at the ready. "Duncan was isolated, and Sonic was able to beat him that way, compared to the rest of us who were all teamed up. There were three of us in the Prize Room and three in the parking garage. They isolated him just like they isolated the Crawler, just like they isolated the others they've stolen from," she analyzed.

"So, they won't fight us as a team in an attempt to steal powers because, as a team, we can overpower them, even if barely, right, Analyst?" Malcolm asked.

As the Analyst began to answer the question, Malcolm felt a buzz in his left arm and turned it to see that Symone slipped him a message. He read, "Your words, how do you know exactly what to say?"

"Right, well, I did a preliminary analysis on the powers being used by Streak, Hex, and Mygalo. While Mygalo was at near full strength, Streak and Hex were well under their potential, using similar numbers from before to hold you guys down. It's like they don't want to kill you," the Analyst gave them.

"I'd imagine they don't want to kill you but rather want to debilitate you so they can get your powers stripped from you," Stephanie said.

"I mean, I'm not a master of the language or anything, but..." Malcolm returned to Symone.

"Yeah, but if that's the case, Stephanie," Karl thought, "why not debilitate us? Analyst, that's the second time you've told us that Streak and Hex severely outmatch us, and I'd assume Sonic, too. And yet, outside of Duncan being taken, we've walked away from two battles with them. The Collector had all seven of us, twice, and only took Duncan?"

Malaysia noticed that Symone looked at her stripe and smiled. Symone thought about a witty response, then refocused on the meeting, remembering that Malcolm had a theory about the Collector's intentions. She whispered, "Malcolm." He glanced at her with a puzzled look. She said again, "Malcolm," eyes widened, then motioned her head to offer his insight to the situation.

Mallack noticed their exchange and said, "Something you two would like to share with the rest of us?"

Symone released Malcolm's hand and blasted, "Yes, I believe Malcolm has a theory that would be great for us all to hear. Malcolm, would you like to share with the class what you thought last night?"

Malcolm cut his eyes at Symone, and Symone grinned.

"Well, Malcolm?" Mallack said.

Malcolm responded, "Well, what if the Collector is after something different entirely? What if 'stealing power' is a cover?"

"A cover?" Stephanie inquired.

"Think about it. Karl just said it himself. If the Collector was really about that 'build an army' life, you just squandered not one, but two opportunities to construct it with some of the most impressive powers on Uretha. You settle for a relatively new Elite when you can have Uri City's Company's entire Elite Unit? You don't even use your own 'Elite' – who haven't even gone full strength yet – to eliminate your only threat to your goal?"

Everyone nodded.

"What are you saying, Malcolm?" Daisy asked.

"I'm saying we're playing checkers while the Collector's playing chess. I'm saying, what if the Collector is directing us, making sure that we're in the right place at the right time to do whatever he wants us to do for a bigger purpose than just taking people's powers? What if power is not what the Collector is after, and we're distracted because of the powers he's stolen and the people he's kidnapped and killed?"

"So, what do we do, then? We can't just sit and do nothing while the Collector's out there collecting people's powers," Alexia railed.

"I'm not saying we don't do anything. But I honestly don't know, Alexia," Malcolm returned. "That's what makes the Collector one of the most dangerous opponents we've ever faced."

Mallack stared at Malcolm, then said, "That makes sense, Malcolm. Well, I think this has been helpful. Everyone, take the day. Right now, the Collector is in the wind, and until we get a signal flare from Duncan or some intel from our undercovers, we are back to square one. Rest, train, stay sharp, and when the time comes, be ready. Dismissed." Everyone rose to leave, and Mallack said, "Malcolm, Symone, a word?" They were stunned but didn't show it, sitting back down, poker faces on, unsure what Mallack would want with them together. Malcolm was worried that he was about to get reprimanded for losing Duncan, or worse, for getting too close, too soon, to Symone.

Everyone else left the room, and it was just the three of them. Mallack walked up to them and said, "Symone, I asked you to stay while I talk with Malcolm since you're being mentored by him. Feel free to chime in if you feel like you have anything to add to the conversation, though."

"Oh, okay," Symone replied, confused.

"What's up, boss?" Malcolm asked.

"I just wanted to tell you how proud of you I am."

"Wait, what?" Malcolm was taken aback.

"Well, yeah, Malcolm, this was an incredibly stressful situation, and you handled it very well. I saw the tapes. You tried to salvage the situation in the Prize Room when the Collector found out your IDs were fake. And just now, with Alexia, you defused her volatility before she accidentally used her powers to snap a holoscreen or worse."

"I mean, I didn't do anything. I just read the situations for what they were and did what needed to be done," Malcolm returned.

"Malcolm, don't be modest," Symone said. "You were a straight-up boss in the Prize Room, and you know it."

"Whatever," Malcolm chuckled, "I just wanted to get the power and get us out of there alive. I got one without the other."

"Listen, Malcolm, you've taken some losses lately, but you've kept your composure and bounced back every time. Trust me when I say the Company is taking notice. Regardless of how this Collector situation ends, you're putting yourself in position to become a director someday," Mallack cheered.

"Wait, what are you not saying, Director?" Malcolm asked.

"Nothing, Malcolm. I'm just calling it as I see it. And the conversations I'm having with HQ look very promising for you. Keep doing the work, keep leading this team the way you're leading it, and when the time comes, you'll be directing a city defense of your own."

Symone looked at Malcolm and said, "I mean, you've got the makings of one, that's for sure."

"Thank you, Director," Malcolm couldn't believe his ears. *Wow! Maybe I'm not screwing up as badly as I thought.*

"Okay, you two, dismissed. Get some rest."

Mallack left the conference room as Malcolm and Symone rose from their seats. After a short time, they, too, walked out of the conference room. Symone asked Malcolm, "So, what do you want to do?"

You.

Malcolm turned to Symone and said, "Honestly?"

"Yes," Symone answered.

"I want to train."

Symone's eyes burned brightly. "Music to my ears."

19

First Date

Malcolm's black training uniform enveloped him, and the cloak shimmered and disappeared in response. Symone's white training uniform did the same. She activated her hands, and sparks began to flow from them to the floor. Malcolm picked up a couple of scraps of metal pipe, forged them into twin maces, and heated them up. They stood about fifty feet apart. Symone stared at Malcolm's visor, and he at hers.

She declared, "Don't you go easy on me now."

Malcolm pointed the left mace at Symone and reacted, "Funny, I was going to say the same thing to you." He then locked both of his arms in battle position, quickly shifted his right foot, and charged forward.

Symone launched herself to meet him. She quickly crafted a star and threw it at him. He used his right mace to knock the star away, then used that momentum to spin around once and swing his left mace at Symone. She grabbed the mace mid-flight and dragged Malcolm with her. She stopped suddenly and jerked the mace with all her might. Malcolm wouldn't let go, so he flipped over her head. He released the left mace as he made a couple of cartwheels in the air, then threw his right mace at Symone. She created a heat shield, and the mace bounced off it.

Malcolm's senses surged, and he summoned the mace to his hand. To his surprise, the mace obeyed him and flew to him. He grasped the mace as he planted his feet on the ground. *It's happening again!*

Symone paid the move no mind, rushed toward him, and threw several yellow stars at Malcolm. He hardened the mace and played baseball with each one, hitting grounders and fly balls back-to-back. Malcolm then ran up to Symone, and she planted her feet on the ground and dealt a series of punches and kicks. Malcolm blocked and dodged them, then launched a series of his own. Finally,

Symone grabbed Malcolm's arm and flew upward. Malcolm kicked her in her abdomen, and she let him go. She launched another star. He caught it, turned his body, and speedily morphed the star into a stability ball, bounced onto the ground and flipped right-side up.

Symone got frustrated and charged up, her hair and eyes changing from yellow to white. She raced upward, floated about fifty feet in the air, thrusted her hands downward, and blasted the floor with several heat rays. Malcolm was knocked onto his knees by a few of them. He rolled onto his back to miss another ray, then raised his legs up to flip himself back upright as another ray missed him by a half-second. Another ray came down, and he raised his right hand to stop it and flatten it into a disc. He stopped another and another until he disappeared from Symone's sight under a white glowing ceiling. Malcolm rotated his hands parallel to the walls, palm-side pointed at himself, then stretched his fingers, and the rays collected into a superstar. He pushed it toward Symone, and Symone quickly blasted the superstar with a continuous heat ray. Malcolm countered her defense by pooling her heat ray into the superstar, and it got larger and more unstable. Suddenly, the superstar exploded, and the impact knocked Symone into the ceiling and Malcolm into the wall. Their cloaks shimmered, absorbing the blows they dealt.

Symone thought, *Malcolm's changed. I thought he said it takes him too long to do things like this.* Symone thought about her next wave. But before she could launch an attack, she noticed little flickers of light around her like grains of sand. She wondered whether she was tripping, if her powers had changed or malfunctioned. Then the flickers popped. The grains got closer to her and popped her cloak. She felt tiny stings and wondered, "What the Frimas is this?" She looked around to see if she was doing this and reasoned that it wasn't her. She looked down, though she could barely see Malcolm doing anything. As she flew closer to him, she saw his fingers snapping, and with each snap, particles around her would pop. Malcolm was activating the residue in the air from the exploded superstar to attack her. She got closer and heated her palms, getting ready to throw haymakers at him, but before she could reach him, he clapped his hands, and a pop turned into a boom! It knocked Symone off course, and she crashed into the ground, rolling several times before coming to a stop.

Symone was dazed, and fury pumped through her veins. *How the Frimas is he doing this?* She wondered how far her cloak's integrity percentage had fallen. She saw 67% in the corner of her visor's view.

The Analyst, getting readings and signals from every holoscreen in his lab, recorded every strand of data he witnessed. He couldn't believe his eyes as Malcolm and Symone's demographics rapidly evolved like a mutation. *They're doing it!*

Malcolm said, "Had enough?"

Malcolm pissed Symone off, but Symone didn't know what she could do to catch Malcolm off guard. *I have to trap him with my powers when he uses mine against me somehow.*

She pushed herself off the ground and turned to face Malcolm. She summoned all her energy and ran at Malcolm. Malcolm charged at her. At the last second, Symone created a heat shield in front of her and slammed it into Malcolm. He stumbled backward, and Symone took advantage, heated her hands, planted them hard into his chest, and blasted a heat wave that shuttled Malcolm across the room. She blitzed him with a gatling of stars, pummeling Malcolm into the wall. He gathered himself as he was being assaulted and started collecting the stars in front of him. Before he could do anything with them, Symone ascertained his plot, grabbed the mace off the floor, and heated it up. She slid on her knees onto the ground and knocked Malcolm in his left leg with a right swing, and he tumbled, releasing the star he developed, which Symone then caught and pressed into his stomach, sandwiching him. She burst backward off the ground and levied a continuous heat wave into Malcolm's chest, intensifying in her heat and energy, and her eyes, hair, and the wave changed colors from white to blue.

Whoa! I'm blue! Let's go! Kick his ass, Symone!

Malcolm's cloak's integrity degraded to 58%. He tried to pool Symone's heat wave but couldn't catch the particles she was outputting. He focused his attention on the metal shards in the room and raised several of them off the ground. He hurled them at Symone, but once they reached her, they disintegrated in her blue, much more intense aura surrounding her body.

I'm running out of options. This girl went blue on me! Um, maybe I can change her energy, but how? Think, Malcolm, think!

Symone yelled, "Yield!"

Malcolm volleyed, "Not a chance, Symone!"

He called me by my first name again!

Malaysia, meanwhile, was sitting in the commons of the quarters catching up on an episode of her favorite show, laughing as the characters delivered a punchline. She picked up her drink off the tabletop and took a swig of it. She lay back on the couch, soaking in the rest time, recovering from the night before and happy to get a chance to relax her body, especially her eyes. Malaysia closed them, and she vividly recalled her chance encounter with Jackson Santana. She reminisced on how fine he looked and how great he smelled. A part of her wished he had touched her the way he used to.

Mmm, he was so good, so bad, my goodness.

She rubbed her belly softly and toyed with a loc as she recalled their time together in the Underbelly, the bed they shared, their adventures, and how good they were together.

Why did he have to be such a jerk? Maybe that's what I loved about him. Before I found out about him doing shady things, he was a jerk, but he was my jerk. Girl, stop before you need to go to your residence and take a different, much more pleasurable stroll down memory lane.

Just as she was falling into a trance starring Santana and her, daydreaming about what he used to do to her and vice-versa, her stripe lit red. She noticed the buzz and looked down. "Aww, come on, man!" she yelled.

The stripe read, "ELITE: URGENT MESSAGE FROM INTELLI-GENCE. THE COLLECTOR IS UPLOADING A MESSAGE TO US THROUGH THE SHADOWNET. MEET IN INTELLIGENCE AT ONCE."

Malaysia sighed, "We can't catch a break." All her horniness dried up immediately. She rose, turned the holoscreen off, and headed out the door. Alexia and Karl came out of their residences and followed behind her. They arrived in the red-bathed Intelligence auditorium and noticed Daisy, Stephanie, and Dax on the floor.

"How much longer before the upload is ready?" Malaysia asked.

"About five minutes before the scrub is complete," Dax announced.

"Okay. Man, the hits keep coming, don't they?"

"The Collector's trying to blitz us, no offense, Daisy," Karl reasoned.

Daisy turned around and faced Malaysia, Karl, and Alexia who were leaning against the top rail. "None taken. You're right. The Collector isn't backing off. He's taking advantage of his position in his game."

About a minute afterward, Malaysia noticed that Malcolm and Symone were missing from the crew. "Has anybody seen Malcolm or Symone?"

"No," Karl responded. "Probably down in the training room. He usually turns his stripe off when he's down there. Probably taught Symone to do the same."

"You're right. I'm gonna go down there and get them," Malaysia said. She backed up and walked out of Intelligence.

Malcolm pressed his hands into Symone's wave and focused with all his might on the particles. His cloak had fallen to 42%, but he wouldn't back down. The intensity of Symone's heat and light flooded his cloak and flowed past his hands. Rather than try to volley them back, he decided to cool them down. He grabbed every molecule in the air and mixed them with the wave. Steam rose from the impact point of her wave on his hands. The more she shot, the more water flowed from his hands. He began pushing the water wave her way.

Malcolm could feel his senses surging in his bones. He drove his water wave's temperature down farther and faster, and the water suddenly switched to frost. Symone swore her eyes deceived her. Fire and ice collided in between them. She refused to lose and kept pushing the fire. Malcolm wouldn't back down and kept pushing the glacial blast.

After thirty seconds, Symone said, "Screw it," and spun out of the blast zone. She watched the glacial blast shoot past her face while she zoomed past it hoping to catch Malcolm off guard. She motored toward him, and before he could notice that she had let her heat wave go, she faceplanted him with a smack from her open palm.

Malcolm grabbed her hand, lifted her arm up, and punched her in her stomach. She doubled over and flipped herself to knock Malcolm in the head with her foot. They tumbled to the floor. Symone trapped Malcolm's head between her thighs. With her right fist clasped tightly in her left hand, she tomahawked Malcolm's head several times, attempting to render him unconscious. Malcolm struggled to free himself from Symone's inescapable grip. They rolled on the ground twice, and Symone said, "No, no, not with these thighs, you won't." Malcolm grabbed Symone's clasped fist and pulled her forward, slightly startling her, then punched her in her stomach, which released her grip on his head. Symone fell backward, and Malcolm lay between her legs for a few seconds, coughing as he struggled to catch his breath. He rolled forward and tried to stand up, but not before Symone jumped on his back.

Malcolm stumbled forward, then grabbed her thighs, spun around and jumped backward, laying Symone flat on her back as he crushed her and lay on top of her. She released him, and he rolled off her while summoning a shard his way. He shaped it into a hammer, clasped it in his hand, and swung around to hit Symone in the chest. She quickly motioned her hands to create a heat shield, noticing that her heat was dying down, her hair and eyes changing from blue to white. He beat the hammer down on her shield before she spun herself on the floor and tripped him. He fell on his back, but he recalled the last time she did something like this. As Symone proceeded to jump him, he flipped himself up and landed a punch to her head. She stumbled back, heated her hands and punched Malcolm in the shoulder. Malcolm put his arms up and defended himself against her barrage, then performed a roundhouse kick. She caught his foot, spun him around, and released him. He landed on his feet, then as Symone prepared to shoot another star at him, Malcolm rushed at her, grabbed her hand, raised her arm in the air, and rushed her into the wall with a knife in his hand to her throat.

"Yield," he declared.

Both Malcolm and Symone were breathing heavily, exhausted from the intensity of the attacks they delivered to each other. Neither one of them wanted to give up, and neither one of them knew what to do next. Symone stared deeply into Malcolm's visor. She decided that she had had enough waiting, consequences be damned.

Symone summoned her cloak to power down and her visor to be removed from her head. Malcolm stared deeply into Symone's eyes and noticed her breathing rapidly and deeply, her lips slightly parted and quivering, longing for him to quench her thirst. He summoned his cloak to power down and the visor to be removed from his head. Symone looked downward at his lips, then back to his eyes, then his lips again.

Symone lowered her arms, leaned her head forward, and pressed her soft lips against his. A wave of passion rushed her entire body. The last of Malcolm's defenses came tumbling down. Malcolm tilted his head slightly and locked lips with Symone, fulfilling a fantasy that had been playing on repeat in his head. His mind then snapped back to the reality of what-ifs, and he dropped the knife and released Symone, backing two steps away from her. He stared deeply into her eyes, and she into his. He wondered whether this was a ploy from Symone to catch him off guard like during their first spar, but his lust for her overrode his battle tactics. He only thought about how supple her lips were and how much he yearned to feel her body pressed against his.

Symone looked at him and chagrined, *Akan, I hope I didn't just make another mistake. What is he going to do?*

He then gently rushed her into the wall again and kissed her passionately. They traded kisses as they locked arms, rubbing each other's backs and squeezing each other tightly. The tension they had been holding onto for so long finally erupted as they lifted off the wall. Symone spun Malcolm around, then pinned him to the wall and continued kissing him. She cheered internally, *Finally, this, him, this is what I've wanted!*

Malcolm, meanwhile, struggled between, *What are we doing?* and *Why didn't I do this sooner?*

Malcolm double-tapped his uniform, then double-tapped Symone's. Their uniforms melted off them and returned to their homes, ridding Malcolm of any restriction to touching her soft skin against his. He spun and grabbed her legs, lifting and pinning her to the wall. She let out an ecstatic moan, and they locked lips again as he rubbed on her thighs and butt, and she wrapped her arms around his neck. She adored the way his hair felt as she rubbed her hands through it. She swapped from his taut neck to his strong shoulders. Her thighs held on tightly as their bodies begged to unite for the first time.

Their desire for each other would no longer be denied, and the more they tasted each other, the more they craved from each other. Malcolm sensed Symone's energy flowing through her veins like molten lava, and he squeezed her tightly, engulfed by her energy. Malcolm finally surrendered to her in his heart, no longer willing to resist Symone as they bathed in the throes of their lust and affection. Her hair glowed white, and her body and energy were fully submerged in the fire. She pulled at Malcolm's A-shirt, daring him to take the risk, pull it off, and expose his body to her.

Just then, the training room door opened, and Malaysia stood in the doorway silhouetted by the brighter light outside. Malaysia looked at them, and Malcolm turned his head while Symone stared back at her. Malcolm unpinned Symone and slid her down the wall until she caught herself with her feet. Symone's hair changed back to its normal color. They quickly adjusted themselves, looked downward, slightly embarrassed, and looked at each other before turning their bodies to face Malaysia. AI said, "Malaysia Jones, codename The Eagle, entering the room. Adjusting room to meet specifications."

Malaysia thought, *Alright now! About time! Get her, Malcolm!*

With an unfazed look, Malaysia said to them, "Wow, should I come back?"

"Um, no, ah, you're good. Um, what's up?" Malcolm replied, struggling to find letters to create words to construct a statement.

"Right, we got a message from the Collector. Intelligence is downloading and scrubbing it now, and we're needed upstairs to hear it."

"Okay, we'll be up in a few minutes," Malcolm responded.

"I bet," Malaysia said with a smirk, silently cheering Malcolm and Symone on. "Don't take too long." She left the room. AI responded in kind.

Malaysia walked to the elevator, and as she summoned her ride back up to the Grand Hall, she silently chuckled, *They deserve each other. My boy Malcolm deserves this win! Good for him! Good for them!*

Symone looked at Malcolm, and he back at her. They both smiled and laughed. Symone said, "So, now what?"

Malcolm walked up to Symone, grabbed her by the small of her back, pulled her into him, and kissed her again. He pulled his head away and said, "I don't know. But there's no turning back now. We should head upstairs."

As they walked out the training room door, Symone said, "I bet the Analyst is having a field day with this."

Malcolm laughed and said, "Man. Well, that footage will live on forever."

"Ooh, that's exciting! You think he'll grade our performance?" Symone beamed.

Malcolm laughed again, "With him, anything's possible."

They entered the elevator. Symone said, "You think Malaysia is going to say anything?"

Malcolm quickly answered, "Nah, she's a fortress. If she has something to say, she'll come straight to us."

Symone saw they were close to arriving at the Grand Hall and thought, *Crap. Crap!* She pulled Malcolm's arm, and asked, "Malcolm, are you okay? Are you sure about this?"

Frimas naw! This was a mistake. The best *mistake I've ever made.* He gently grasped her hand. "I'm not sure about anything, except this, except *you*. I don't know why, but it's just you. I am sure about you."

The elevator stopped, and the doors opened. They released hands, and they walked across the hall and stopped at Intelligence's door. Malcolm asked, "Symone, you ready?"

Akan, say my name again.

Symone echoed her mentor's countdown, "3, 2, 1, go."

20

The Affinity Theory

Malcolm slid the door open, and Symone and he walked in. They both gritted their teeth, trying to contain their delight, their hearts still abuzz from their physical confirmation of their emotional attachment. Karl, Alexia, Malaysia, and Daisy were sitting in their usual seats across the room. Alexia saw them and said, "There they are, Player One and Player Two."

"What did we miss?" Malcolm asked to quickly deflect any other comments or questions about what took them so long to get there. They stepped down to their usual row. He glanced at Malaysia to see if her demeanor would change.

Dax answered, "We just finished the scrub about thirty seconds ago. The message is cued up and ready."

"Alright," Malcolm said as he and Symone sat down next to each other. "Boot it up."

Dax pressed "PLAY," and the holoscreen in front of them displayed a dark room with the Collector, clad in her complete uniform, sitting at her desk barely outlined enough to distinguish her from anything else.

She began, "I am still so elated to have finally gotten the opportunity to meet some of the Company's Elite face-to-face last evening. I must admit, I was not expecting such a spectacle to unfold. Before I digress, I just wanted to let you know that, as of today, our guest of honor who calls himself Ammo – which, by the way, is a horrible name that I hope he changes – is alive and well and sends his regards."

"This bitch," Alexia's eyes glowed, and green mist swirled around her.

"I haven't decided whether to kill him yet, but rest assured he will not be harmed unless and until it is necessary. Still, the clock doth tick, and at some point, blood will be spilled."

"He's twisted," Symone denounced.

"I decided, against my team's better judgment, to offer you one chance, just one, to rescue him from my diabolical clutches, I guess," the Collector sarcastically pronounced as she lifted her arm and raised one finger. "The two pretending to be Jackson Santana and Emma Leslie, they, and only they, must retrieve a drive I created that will reveal his secret location to you all. I'm sure you're all itching to save him from my death blow, so if you want him alive, that drive is the key to his survival. Oh geez, I'm making this sound so creepy, dramatic, and sinister," she laughed.

"Permission to scissor-kick him in the face until his head falls off?" Daisy remarked.

"Get in line," Malaysia's lenses shifted.

"Oh, and you'd better hurry up because the one who has the drive told me he will sell the drive to the highest bidder in two days. So, you'd better get to him before he gets antsy and finds some dummy to trade it to. Oh, and another thing, before I forget, if more than just fake Santana and fake Leslie show up, Ammo dies. If the drive is somehow sold because you didn't get it, he dies. If the drive is destroyed, he dies. I hope you see where I'm going with this. Good luck, and happy hunting!" The tape continued, "So, what do you think? Was that too much? I think it could have been better. We should try it again, drama it up a little more, add some—"

"He's so smug, aargh!" Alexia cried, banging her hands on the desk.

"Something's off about the Collector, that's for sure," Malaysia noticed.

"What's up Malaysia?" Malcolm asked.

"It's his mannerisms. Something just doesn't seem right to me. He's not giving me 'super slayer' vibes, you know?"

"Yeah, he's a twisted psycho," Symone retorted.

"Yeah, nah, that's not a 'he.'"

The team paused to consider what she said. Dax spoke up, "That's not something we ever considered. In all the reports dating back the last ten years, it was always assumed that the Collector was biologically male, and we've never had any data to confirm or deny that."

"Trust me, that's not a guy," Malaysia said. "The vocal distorter can't take the mannerisms away. That's not a man. But let's not get sidetracked. Right now, the priority is Duncan."

"Right," Malcolm agreed. "Who is this 'guy' the Collector referred to?"

Dax tapped keys to minimize the video and pull up the dossier the Collector sent. "The Collector calls him Dredge." The holoscreen in front of them displayed a portrait of a short, stocky, dark-skinned man with beady eyes and spiky, textured black hair, and a goatee. "A low-level guy who mostly trades random black-market items for creds. Never stays in one location for very long but bounces mostly between Leicester and Genesis Landing. There's not a whole lot of information to go on. We do have an address, though, not sure if this is his home address. But it borders the Leicester and Underbelly districts." Dax continued to tap on keys. "The address isn't registered to anyone or any companies. The street looks like a bazaar." Dax displayed a street view of the address and pulled the video of the day and nightlife of the address.

"Leicester gets crazy every night, especially there. It's the perfect place to do something in secret," Malaysia quipped. Symone turned and glanced at Malaysia. Malaysia didn't lock eyes, and Symone turned back around. Malaysia then looked at Symone and smiled.

"Alright, team, I'm going to run this by Mallack and see what she wants us to do. I don't like the idea of just Watson and me facing off against one of the Collector's goons," Malcolm advised.

"No need, Malcolm, I've been listening in," Mallack showed up on the holoscreen. "And though I'm not a big fan of it either, you two are more than capable of handling this."

Malcolm pondered silently. Alexia, however, spoke for him, "For real? You're sidelining us? You can't be serious!"

"Yes, I'm sidelining you all. Listen, trust me when I say this. You all need a break. And before you give me the 'we were built for this' spiel, remember who gives the orders and who receives them. Everyone is ordered to stand down except for Malcolm and Symone, who are tasked with retrieving this drive. When they return, then you can all gear up and beat the Collector down.

Right now, stand down and rest up. Malcolm, Symone, your stripes are being uploaded by Stephanie with the intel on Dredge, and as they get more data, you will get more. Get that drive, whatever it takes."

Malcolm thought, *No way, something isn't adding up, Mallack. This is unusual, even for you. You never send someone out without backup. What are you up to? Why are you doing this?*

But he answered, "Message received, boss."

Malaysia's stripe lit blue with the message, "From Mallack: Meet me in my office now." *Oh, Akan. What does she want? Bet she wants to finally talk to me about Jackson.* She rose from her chair and said, "Well, you heard her. Malcolm, Symone, good luck. I'm going to take her advice and rest because my eyes feel like Frimas."

"But Malaysia—" Malcolm tried to interject.

"No, no, I was watching my favorite screenshow before the Collector decided to interrupt my day with her bull, so now that I have permission to sit down, that's what I'm going to do. I'm tired."

Karl agreed as Malaysia walked out of the room hoping to not do so weirdly and be followed. "That's true, we just need a minute to catch our collective breath. Let's all just chill – well, we'll chill, you and Symone go do what you gotta do – and be ready for what's next."

Alexia disagreed but assumed fighting any longer would prove moot. "This is some bull," Alexia remarked.

"You stripe us if you need anything, Malcolm and Symone," Daisy offered.

"Thank you, Daisy," Symone responded.

"Okay, so Dax, give us anything else you got on this guy," Malcolm declared.

Meanwhile, Malaysia hurried to Mallack's office before anyone from Intelligence could spot her on her way there. *Either she wants to talk to me about me, or about them.* She hoped Mallack was seeking a status report on her secret mission and found herself torn between keeping everything to herself or revealing all she knew. Malaysia knocked on Mallack's door and heard a response, "Come in."

Upon entering, she found the director seated behind her desk, accompanied by the Analyst who occupied one of the office chairs. "What's going on?" Malaysia inquired. "What's the Analyst doing here?"

"Malaysia, have a seat. The Analyst and I need to share something with you that I think will answer some questions you may have had for me regarding the recon mission I assigned you."

"Okay," Malaysia silently took a huge sigh of relief. *Thank Akan!*

"Analyst, please begin."

The Analyst's eyes beamed as he started, "Okay, pay attention to the holo-screen." As he mirrored his mini-holoscreen to Mallack's wall holoscreen, they displayed two gray silhouettes and the big three stat numbers aside each of them. "I'll try to be as brief yet thorough as possible. There are several debates among asheologists about the origins and evolutions of our powers. Some believe that our ancestors were imbued with power from Akan and the Divines. Others theorize that the powered are part of the natural evolutionary process. Regardless of how we got them, how we become stronger has been debated by many disciplines for centuries. The overwhelming majority believes that our ability to evolve is strictly based on how often we use our powers and how hard we push ourselves beyond our limits. We eventually evolve because of the time we put into becoming better, stronger.

"However, there are some who believe that evolution goes beyond mere training. They argue that our evolution can be influenced by our connection to others. By reaching a level of synchronicity, we can mutually enhance and improve each other's abilities in a way that training alone cannot."

The Analyst tapped his screen, and numbers displayed underneath the big three descriptors. "Take these two, for instance. Before interacting with each other, their demos and stats read like this. Person 1, Power Level: 3, Skill Level: 1, Affinity Dark +3; Person 2, Power Level 3.5, Skill Level: 4.2, Affinity: Light +4. Typically, numbers like these take time to move up and down, and we don't see much change, especially in someone like Person 2. However, when the two of them are together, their numbers change dramatically over an incredibly short time." The Analyst pressed a button, and the two silhouettes' demos changed, with Person 1's demos shifting to Power Level: 3.7, Skill Level 3.4, and Affinity Dark +1, while Person 2's shifted to Power Level 4.98, Skill Level 4.7, and Affinity Light +2.

"The asheologists call this the Affinity Theory, which posits that when two powered individuals are biorhythmically synched to each other holistically –

spiritually, mentally, emotionally, and physically – they will enhance, alter, morph, and transform each other's powers exponentially."

"So, the closer they become, the stronger they will be," Malaysia surmised.

"Yes, that's the Affinity Theory," the Analyst smiled.

"I don't understand. Why the science lesson? What does that have to do with my mission?"

"Malaysia, you don't see it?" Mallack said.

Malaysia pondered on the mission Mallack assigned her. *Keep your eagle eyes on Malcolm and Symone and let me know how things are going with them.* She looked at the screen, thought about the silhouettes, and then it clicked! "Malcolm. Symone? Aww crap!"

Mallack's eyes beamed. "Ever since the day you stepped in my office to tell me that you were concerned about Malcolm and how he would treat Symone, I've kept my eye on them and noticed their increasing interactions with each other. Since then, and Analyst, play the highlight reel, I've been watching as keenly as you have how they are with each other and how they're affecting one another's abilities. At Sentinel, they both changed. When Malcolm reproduced his ability to grab and push powers, Symone was in the observation room. We pulled tape from there and noticed that she was doing crazy things at the same time. When they sparred the first time, Malcolm created a planet! And just today, their powers registered through the roof again. And each time something like that happened, their demos and stats settled at a higher resting rate than before."

Malaysia stared at the screen and felt hopeful and gleeful. Mallack pressed, "I had you watch them and notice how they have been toward each other. Tell me now, how close are they?"

She admitted, "Director, they're close as Frimas. We've talked about how Symone crushed on him, how they've been dancing around each other, the things I've seen in their heartbeats, and all that. And now," Malaysia was almost embarrassed to say like a little kid telling on her friends at school, "I caught them making out in the training room. I think they're falling in love. All due respect, they're going to have sex soon, if not tonight."

"Okay, didn't ask for *all of that*," Mallack pumped Malaysia's brakes and chuckled, "but that's my point, and the Analyst's. They have become remarkably and significantly stronger than ever before. So, logic tells us that the closer their connection, the more powerful they will become." The Analyst revealed the silhouettes on the screen to be Symone on the left and Malcolm on the right. "Though I frown upon supervisors and trainers hooking up with their mentees, we cannot deny that their evolution is the breakthrough we have been looking for to tip the scales in defense of this city."

Malaysia stared at the screen with wonder, then turned back to the Director. "It's incredible, Director!" Malaysia replied. "We should tell them what's going on. I think they would be just as excited to know!"

"Well, I don't think that would be wise," the Analyst countered.

"Why not?" Malaysia interrogated.

"Well, from all my studies on the Affinity Theory, the asheologists all said that they tried 'manufacturing' the results we're witnessing. The theorists concur that if the subjects have prior knowledge of them transforming each other's powers, it will adversely affect them because their focus will be to become more powerful instead of improving their connection to one another. That will stunt the process, if not halt it entirely. Telling them would *not* be advantageous for them or the Company."

Malaysia disagreed. "So, you're saying we should keep them in the dark? To what end, Analyst, Director?" Malaysia asked.

"I believe we should wait until after we've beaten the Collector to allow their powers to reach their maximum limit, even if there is such a thing."

"The asheologists believe that their powers will reach their maximum potential once they're both balanced in their affinities when they're neither light nor dark. But again, it's just a theory," the Analyst provided.

"Right. Further, we know that Streak, Hex, and Sonic are Elite. Who knows who else the Collector has recruited for his army! You all got lucky to walk out with your lives the last couple of battles. But that wasn't because of a lack of skill on your part, but because of restraint on theirs. No, they can't know. We cannot tell them anything. Is that understood?"

"As long as you understand that I believe that is a *stupid* decision, Director. They have the right to know and deserve to hear from you, from us, what we know is happening to them," Malaysia reasoned.

"And they will, at the right time. For now, your recon mission will continue as planned. I'm sending you on mission with Malcolm and Symone, but as an observer only. Keep an eye on them and what they do on this mission. Report to me any pertinent information. I don't need to know if they have sex, so please keep that to yourself."

"Message received, Director. But if they get into serious trouble, I will expose myself to them. Wait, that didn't come out right. I meant I would help them fight their way out of their situation. Wait, you know what, you know what I mean! Bye!"

Mallack stood up and said, "Malaysia, thank you. Seriously, this is the breakthrough we've been looking for, and if we're right, this could be the game-changer for the citizens and defenders of Uri City."

"Understood." Malaysia got up and walked out of the Director's office.

"Analyst, thank you, you're dismissed as well."

"Thank you, Director. This is so exciting! I can't wait to see what develops!" The Analyst got out of his seat and walked out of the office.

Director Mallack stared at the screen, at Symone and Malcolm.

"K.C. and Starburst. Everything is coming together."

Malaysia wrestled with keeping the secret. *Malcolm and Symone really like each other, right? Like, I didn't push them together, did I? I don't think I did. They liked each other from the jump; they didn't need my help. All I did was observe and report. But I did tell Malcolm to get the sticks out of his butt and let the girl know how he feels. Crap, if I tell them about the Affinity Theory, they will think I tried to make them like each other, and that will blow this whole plan of Mallack's apart. Follow orders, Malaysia. Don't say a thing.*

She walked to the elevator and pressed down to go to the parking garage. The elevator doors opened, revealing an empty box. She went in and hurriedly pressed the garage button. The doors closed, and she breathed a sigh of relief, thankful she had time to herself to swallow the secret deep in her soul.

21

Going Rogue-ish

"**M**alcolm, I don't like this."

A cycle had passed. Malcolm and Symone stood side by side in the conference room, studying dossiers and the plan drawn up by Intelligence. Symone stared at a map of the drop point on a holoscreen while Malcolm looked at a picture of Dredge and a still shot of the Collector during her last video message. A sinking feeling resided in Symone's gut since the briefing in Intelligence. She did not believe they could walk out of a meeting with one of the Collector's contacts unscathed.

Malcolm felt similarly, still reeling from losing Duncan to the Collector. He questioned his own decision not to protest Mallack's plan in the meeting, wrestling between whether he should have spoken up and believing that this was the only option.

"Yeah, I don't like this either," he agreed. "We're doing this wrong."

Symone turned to face Malcolm. "We should have said something, Malcolm. We should have spoken up and told Mallack this was a bad idea. This feels like déjà vu."

Malcolm backed away from the holoscreen and faced Symone. "I was just thinking the same thing. I had so much to say then but couldn't fix my mouth to say it," he admitted as he looked to the side in slight dismay.

"You do that a lot, Malcolm," Symone acknowledged. "I notice in our meetings you look like you have a ton of things to say but don't."

Malcolm agreed. He turned around to find a chair to sit in. "Well, we're paying for that now. This is a crummy approach. Going in blind again? This isn't right." Malcolm pulled a chair from the back of the table, planted the chair in front of it, and plopped into it.

Symone turned to face the holoscreen, then turned around and walked toward Malcolm while asking, "So, what do we do? Better yet, what *should* we do?"

Malcolm folded his arms and leaned back in the chair. He said, "Well, ideally, we'd pull in the whole team. Have one team on the street and two teams running observation – one in a bus and another on the street a safe distance away."

Symone squatted and placed her hands on Malcolm's knees. "Yeah, but the director benched everyone else." *Mmm, yeah, this feels like a great place to cause some trouble.*

Malcolm internally shivered from Symone's touch. *Girl, get up from there before I lay you out on this table!* Malcolm placed his hands on top of Symone's while his gears grinded, "And we can't pull in anyone else from other teams without alerting Mallack. We can't risk pulling the whole team out of here. That will only get them in trouble. Daisy would make too much noise, and since Karl basically lives here, being away too long might cause concern to the trained eye."

Symone nodded her head. "That leaves Malaysia and Alexia. Alexia is for sure down for whatever. You think Malaysia will help us, though?" Symone asked.

"Without question." Malcolm held onto Symone's hands, slid the chair back, and stood up, pulling Symone up from squatting. Symone hid her shiver of pleasure as Malcolm slowly dropped her arms and let her hands go. Malcolm walked to the holoscreen again. "We just need only ask. We can use them both to observe from a distance and provide backup if we find ourselves in a jam."

"What's your plan?" Symone walked next to Malcolm.

Malcolm pointed at the map of the location provided by the Collector. "We will have Malaysia and Alexia set up posts above and on the street. Malaysia should perch here on this rooftop about half a block from the meeting point. Alexia should sit across the street from that same point here. Once we make contact with Dredge, we should get Alexia to see if she can get inside his mind."

"Hopefully, he's not cloaked. We should have Malaysia scan him prior to us trying him like that, else he might split," Symone thought out loud.

He turned to face Symone. "That makes sense. Once we have the drive, we should have Alexia take the drive via telekinesis and then make our exit without incident."

"Sounds good, but what if this is a trap? What if Streak or Hex or Sonic, or all three show up? Or worse, the Collector?"

"This drive seems too important to the Collector for her to risk exposure. It's too public a location for the Collector to try something like that. But if she does, the four of us together have enough firepower to escape."

"We'll be ready. So, okay, how do we get Malaysia and Alexia to help us without raising any alarms?"

Malcolm rubbed his chin and then immediately had an idea. Lifting his hand off his face, he asked, "Hey, are you hungry?"

Symone shook her head, "Not really, no, my stomach is acting like a real bitch right now."

"Really? Because I could eat, and I bet you could, too," Malcolm stared at Symone.

"How can you be thinking about food at a time—" Symone caught Malcolm's widened eyes and immediately changed her tone, "Oh, you know what, now that you mention it, I am *starving* and could really use a bite to eat."

"Mmm hmm, and there's a spot I know about in the Leicester district that I think you would love," Malcolm strategized as he pointed to a location on the map a couple blocks away from their target location.

"You do?" Symone responded sarcastically. "What all do they have at this spot?"

"Oh, just about everything, a real smorgasbord," Malcolm playfully returned.

"Oh, I can't wait for you to take me! In fact, we should invite—"

"—Malaysia and Alexia!" Malcolm clasped Symone's shoulders. "Symone, that's a fantastic idea! How about you call Alexia, and I'll call Malaysia, and they can meet us there!"

"Sounds like a wonderful idea to me!"

They shut down the holoscreens. Malcolm held the door and followed Symone out of the conference room. They walked casually to the quarters and went to their residences to change into street gear and grab their uniform and cloak buttons. Malcolm finished first, walked out of his residence, and waited in the kitchen, leaning on the countertop. Karl was watching the holoscreen in the commons on the couch, and after about a minute of silence, said to Malcolm, "Hey man, everything alright?"

"Yeah, man," Malcolm answered. "Just getting ready for this meeting."

"Listen, brother, like Daisy said earlier, if you need anything, you call us. No hero stuff, okay?"

"No doubt, my brother. I got you on speed dial. But this should be an open and shut case, so just sit back and wait for us to return," Malcolm offered, remembering that Symone and he wanted Karl to remain in the Grand Hall.

"Alright, my man," Karl said as Symone made her way through the commons. "Symone, you be careful out there. Keep our man safe."

"Oh, you didn't know they hired me as his bodyguard?" Symone joked.

"Ah, that's why you stay at his hip, roger that!" Karl reacted as they all laughed.

"Oh, then we have nothing to worry about. I feel so secure already!" Malcolm responded. "Alright, we'll see you later, Karl. Symone, let's get it."

Symone and Malcolm walked out of the quarters and to the elevator. Once on, Symone said, "Okay, so—"

"Shh, not yet," Malcolm quickly hushed her, then pointed upward at the ceiling and made a small circular motion with his finger, reminding Symone of the building's surveillance. Symone slowly nodded and held her head down, then back up, looking straight at the elevator doors.

The elevator revealed the parking garage, and Symone followed Malcolm as he double tapped his left wrist, then dragged his finger up his arm. An engine roared, and a hoverbike zipped toward them. Malcolm straddled the bike, then told Symone, "Hop on."

She thought about it for a second and was about to jump on the bike, but then she double tapped her left wrist and dragged her finger up her arm, and a second engine roared. Symone's hoverbike presented itself to her. Malcolm looked at her, then at her bike. She said, "Just got him about two weeks ago."

Malcolm thought, *I've never been more attracted to anyone before in my life.*

He said, "Okay, patching you the coordinates right now." He sent the restaurant address to Symone's stripe. She straddled her ride, and the two rushed out of the parking garage glass gate and into the midday skyline.

Malcolm double tapped his chest, and his cloak enveloped him. He called Symone and said, "Okay, you call Alexia, and I'll call Malaysia and tell them where to meet us for lunch."

"Okay," Symone confirmed. She double tapped her chest, and her cloak enveloped her. She called Alexia.

Alexia walked past the stores of Uri City's Mega Mall trying to get her mind off the past few failures. She was frustrated, tired of being overlooked when her instincts were dead-on. She stopped walking and looked up at the diamond-faceted glass enclosure that covered the mall from the elements while flooding it with light. Her left arm buzzed. She looked down and saw it was an incoming call from Symone. She immediately responded, "Hey girl, what's up?"

"Hey, Alexia! So, Malcolm and I are going to get something to eat and wanted to know if you wanted to come along."

"Oh?" Alexia questioned, skeptical of Malcolm and Symone's request. Snippy, she continued, "Are you sure you two want me to tag along? I mean, as quickly as he agreed to the mission, I suspected you two would want this time to yourselves."

Symone could tell that Alexia was still frustrated with the way the briefing had gone but would not let Alexia's feelings get in the way of their plan. "Yeah, we are sure. In fact, he said he's buying. He wants us to get together in Leicester. He said he knows a spot there that we'd all enjoy."

"All the way in Leicester? Why would he want—" Alexia stopped and immediately pieced the puzzle together, "Oh, Leic—yes, I'd love to! Just stripe me the address, and I'll meet you guys there soon!"

Symone breathed a sigh of relief and answered, "Great, see you there!"

Malcolm, meanwhile, called Malaysia. She was already in Leicester, walking the block of the street address provided by the Collector in preparation for her recon mission. She blended in with the bustling crowd of patrons and merchants, dressed in a purple hoodie, black jeans, sneakers, a hat, and shades. She examined the buildings, the openings, entry and exit points, and other intel she needed to ensure she could have an unobstructed view of Malcolm and Symone wherever they would be.

She looked at her stripe and saw it was Malcolm calling her. *Oh no, what if he asks me something about Mallack? I shouldn't answer.*

"Hello?" Malaysia answered.

"Hey Malaysia, how you doing?"

"I'm good, what's up?"

"Miss Watson and I are about to grab something to eat and wondered if you wanted to tag along," Malcolm presented.

"Oh, for real? Well, I am hungry. But are you sure you want me there? I mean, I don't want to cut in on your alone time with Symone. Speaking of, you two in the training room? Nice!" she laughed.

Malcolm played along, trying to steer her to say yes. "Yeah, well, what can I say? It felt like the right time, and I turned out to be right until the Collector decided to mess everything up."

Malaysia continued her recon on the street. "Yeah, what else is new these days."

"But anyway, yes, we want you there. We're meeting at this spot I know in Leicester, and we really want you there."

Malaysia choked up. *Play it cool, Malaysia.*

"Leicester? Surprised you know anything about Leicester, Malcolm."

"Hey now, I know a thing or two about Leicester," Malcolm assured, "come through and let me show you. My treat!"

Malaysia's mind scrambled. She looked around and replied, "Oh, and you're paying? Well, count me in, then! But, just so I'm clear, you're sure this is okay? You and Symone could really use some time alone right now, between this morning and your mission."

"Trust us," Malcolm pleaded, "we could use some good company right now."

Malaysia reacted, "Okay, I'll be there. Send me the address."

"Okay, see you soon!" Malcolm killed the call, then sent Malaysia the address in Leicester.

Malaysia received it and saw that the address was two blocks away from her current position. *I gotta get out of here. If they see me here before them, they're going to think something's up. Or will they? I just need to have a good cover if they see me and arrive at the restaurant after them if they don't.*

Malaysia ran into the brick-and-mortar shop behind her. She turned and marveled at the walls, shelves, and tables filled with every type of knife, gun, spear, sword, and ammunition imaginable. Malaysia's eyes beamed. *I couldn't have found a better place to perch.*

A floating holoscreen hovered near her. An all-green face displayed on the screen and started talking. "Welcome to The Armory! Can I help you with anything?"

"Most definitely," Malaysia moaned. "Take me on a tour. Show me *everything.*"

Malcolm and Symone rode parallel through the busy skies toward their destination. Malcolm turned his head to his left and caught a glimpse of Symone singing a song. He couldn't help but smile while thinking to himself, *Wow, she is me in female form.* He asked her, "What are you riding to?"

She turned to look at him, then set her stripe to sync the song she was vibing to with his stripe. To Malcolm's surprise, it was a song from Ashera, another artist he didn't think anyone else on Uretha knew about. They sang the melodies and harmonies while whizzing past the skyscrapers, hovercars, bikes, buses, and others in flight. Malcolm added this song to the soundtrack of this next chapter of their ripening bond.

Symone thought, *This man gets me.*

"We're almost there," Malcolm pointed out a few minutes later. They descended closer to the street and looked for a place to park, finding an open lot about half a block away from the restaurant. They landed at the entrance of the lot and hopped off their bikes. The bikes drove off and parked themselves.

As they walked together, Symone asked Malcolm, "Truth moment?"

Malcolm said, "Sure, what's up?"

"When Mallack wanted to talk to us alone earlier today, I thought she was going to say something about you and me," Symone giggled.

Malcolm laughed, "Listen, I thought she was about to give us a whole lecture about mentors and mentees. I spaced out a little bit when she was talking about being proud of me."

"How come?"

"I've known Mallack a long time, and one thing about her, she says things on purpose. It's like she always knows the right thing to say or do to get people to say or do what she wants. That's why I asked her what is she *not* saying to me."

Symone raised an eyebrow of suspicion. "It's funny, she does give off 'reverse psychology' vibes."

"How so?" Malcolm looked at her.

"Well, it's just when she asks questions and says such pointed things. It's like she is probing for something but just won't come right out and say what she's thinking. Until now, though, I never thought about it. I'm starting to wonder what's behind all that now."

"I can't be rubbing off on you already," Malcolm reasoned.

"Why do you say that?"

They stopped walking. "Well, it was just today, for instance. It's not like Mallack to rush into plans like this, at least not to me. It was bad enough we rushed the Power Party plan. But then we rush this plan, too? So quick to agree with the Collector's plan and give no thought to an alternative? Sideline the rest of the team? It just doesn't seem like something Mallack would do."

"Malcolm, what are you implying?"

Malcolm knew exactly what he was implying, but he wouldn't fix his mouth to say it. "I don't know. I'm just looking at the situation and saying that something doesn't seem right."

"No," Symone grabbed Malcolm's arm and turned in front of him while shaking her head. "Don't do that. Don't back down. Don't shy away." Symone urged him, "Finish your thought. Tell me what you're implying."

Malcolm sighed heavily, looked up, then faced Symone again. "What if Mallack is being directed? What if she's being pushed to do something she doesn't want to do, but can't or won't say anything about it? Or worse—"

She let go of Malcolm's arm and backed up a step. "You think she could be working with the Collector, don't you?" Symone interjected.

"Akan, I pray not. But she's not being herself."

Symone shook her head, wishing she could unhear Malcolm's theory. "We have to give her credit. We didn't speak up ourselves like we should have, so we didn't give her an alternative to consider. Still, if what you're thinking has any shred of truth to it, how would we be able to stop her without raising suspicion?"

Malcolm shook his head and trashed his theory. "You're right. We should have spoken up. That's probably what she wanted from us, and we didn't do it. Let's not focus on that. Our priority right now is getting Duncan back." They continued walking slowly to the restaurant.

"You're right. And I thought the craziest thing that happened today was you kissing me in the training room," Symone admitted.

"Frimas, being with me, kissing will be a walk in the park compared to whatever else we have to deal with. Definitely not the craziest."

Her heart swooned. "'*With* me?'" Symone volleyed, walking a couple of steps ahead of Malcolm and turning backward to face him. "Malcolm, are you implying that we are together?"

Malcolm's face froze, and he blinked twice, then quickly recovered as he raised his hands up and said, "I mean, I'm not saying we're *together*, together, but I'd like to think we got something good going on here."

"Careful, Malcolm," Symone sarcastically and softly articulated, "you just might admit you're falling for me." She turned around and continued walking, prancing her legs like she was on a runway.

Malcolm couldn't help but stare at her shoulder-blade-length dreadlocks flowing from her head, and his eyes followed their pointed direction to her butt. "I thought we'd already established that."

Thirty seconds later, Malcolm said, "We're here." They stopped at the entrance to Draygo's. Malcolm pressed gently on the small of Symone's back to guide her to the entrance. He pushed the door open, and Symone walked in with Malcolm, following closely behind him.

Draygo's was a dim-lit restaurant and bar. There wasn't a customer in sight. The bar sat on the left wall, booths hugged the right, and tables were in the middle. The walls were all blacked out.

"Welcome," the bartender, cleaning glasses on the left, greeted them. "Find a seat anywhere. We're slow right now."

"Thanks," Malcolm greeted the bartender back. They picked the booth in the back of the restaurant. Symone sat first, choosing to sit facing the entrance.

Malcolm motioned her to slide over and sat next to her. "Let's hope they get here soon."

Or not, Symone secretly hoped.

"Yeah," Symone said. She looked at her stripe to see what time it was, then put her hands on the table.

Malcolm looked at her and asked, "So, Symone—"

"You said my first name again, *Mr. Bennett*!" Symone caught him.

Malcolm laughed, "Shut up! Anyway, you had mentioned before that you've been fighting since you were a little girl."

Symone sat up with glee. "Yes, I have!" she exclaimed.

Malcolm chuckled. "Look at you all lit up like Jubilee!"

Symone put her hands up to her face to hide for a moment. "I'm sorry, I just get so excited when I think about my fighting days."

"Please share. How did Symone Watson become *Starburst*?"

Symone took a deep breath as her fighting history flashed before her eyes. The skills she learned, the people she fought, battles won and lost all washed over her like a flood. "So, I was an early bloomer, got my powers around six years old. I burned so many beds in my sleep and destroyed so many things that I held in my hands. It scared the Frimas out of me, and my parents. For a while, they thought they would have to seal me in a water tank forever or send me to the Asylum for the Uncontrollable just to keep me from destroying the house and spending money on repair after repair."

Malcolm, a sucker for a glorious origin story, placed his right elbow on the table and his head in his right hand as Symone continued. "I remember one night when I was about eight, I snuck out of bed and went into our living room. My dad was watching a prize fight between Midas and Stinger. Watching them in the ring battling it out was so legendary. My hair started glowing, and my dad saw the room get brighter. He turned around and saw me. I thought I was in trouble, but instead, he lifted his finger to his mouth, then told me to come sit next to him. With my hair all red, I was glued to the holoscreen. My eyes soaked up every punch, kick, lightning bolt, and gold bar being thrown. It was insane, and I loved every minute of it.

"At some point, I got up and was mimicking their moves, and my dad saw me, and a light bulb went off in his head. He touched my shoulder and said,

'Hey, you think you can be like them?' And I forgot to stay quiet and yelled, 'Yes, Daddy!' Next thing I knew, he downloaded a ton of books and charts and videos of fighting skills and styles."

Malcolm stared into Symone's eyes, his heart captivated by her story. She continued, "For about three quarters, my dad and I would go to the roof and practice things. My mom was concerned at first. She told me that she had questioned my dad about it, and he told her that as I got better, I was slowly gaining control of my powers, too, noting how long it had been since my last bed burned. She agreed and decided that this would be good for me, even encouraged it. Eventually, I got too strong for my dad and almost blasted his head off. So, he quickly enrolled me in a fighter's gym."

"Real quick, are your parents powered?" Malcolm inquired.

"My parents? Well, my mom mostly gardens, can control plants. My dad's powers have faded over the years, but he is a pure telekinetic."

"That's so cool. So, wait, a fighter's gym? I thought you were going to say that your parents enrolled you into an academy or something."

"Yeah, well, there weren't a lot of academies to enroll in, in the Underbelly. And my parents weren't about to move. But they also weren't about to squander my skills. Plus, they didn't want the house to burn down on account of me and couldn't afford to fireproof the place. You know how expensive cloaking is," she chuckled. "So, I trained in the gym. I worked my tail off for years, and at sixteen, my trainer signed me up for my first fight. And Malcolm, when I tell you, I got my behind kicked! Sheesh, that was the worst night of my life."

"Not 'win or die!'" Malcolm laughed. "You lost big?"

"My Akan, yes! And I then proceeded to lose seven more times after that. I wanted to quit and be like, 'Nope, I'm just gonna use my powers to be a human firework.' But my trainer wasn't having that. One night during training, he told me, 'You know why you keep losing?' I was like, 'Because I'm not good enough,' and he said, 'Bull, Watts! You're stronger than most of the people I train in here and can take any of these punks in this ring. You're losing because you're afraid of dying.' And I was like, 'Frimas, yeah, I'm terrified of it!' He then pinned me down on the ground and choked the crap out of me! Like, literally, I was turning blue. He told me, and I'll never forget this, he said, 'Until you're no longer afraid of dying, you'll never know how it feels to truly live. And for damn sure, you'll never win a fight. I'm going to keep telling you this until you get it – in this ring, it's—'"

"—Win or die," Malcolm finished her statement.

Symone grabbed Malcolm's hand. "Malcolm, when I tell you, even though I was literally fading away, dying in his hands, when I surrendered to it and stopped squirming, lay my hands flat on the mat, and said to myself, 'Don't be afraid,' I never felt more alive. It's like all this rush of power lying dormant inside me finally woke up. My eyes were closed, and I couldn't see anything, and I swear I lost consciousness, but my trainer told me that he saw me start glowing all over my body like never before. And in that moment, he said, I started floating off the mat. He released me from his grip, and my body naturally turned right-side up on its own, my arms straight to my side, my hair glowing. My trainer said when I opened my eyes, he swore he saw the eyes of a Divine. He then said, 'Everybody take cover!' and ran as fast as he could out of the ring. He said that they all ran into the office that had windows so they could see everything, and I yelled out of nowhere, then, suddenly, I released my first burst of fire across the entire gym! Then I crumpled back to the ground.

"When I woke up two days later, my dad asked if I was okay, and I told him, 'I've never felt more alive in my life.' Later, my trainer told me, 'Now you're ready to return to the ring.' I returned to the gym a few days later, and they showed me the tape. I couldn't believe it, and I was motivated as Frimas. My next fight was four weeks later, and I won. And next thing you know, I won and won, and kept winning, and kept winning. Fight after fight, I was amazing! At eighteen, I had made it to the Underbelly's majors, the youngest female to do it. My trainer said, 'Now that you're here, we gotta get you a name.' He thought I should be called Lightshow, and some of my training partners thought Firework or Boom or Knockout, but I could tell most of them were thinking more about strippers in Leicester than a real fighter's name. I thought back to something my mom used to tell me all the time. She said, 'One day, the world will look at you the way we marvel at the moons,' and I would tell her back, 'the way we marvel at the stars!' And between that and my first burst, I decided, 'Starburst.'"

Malcolm gazed at Symone with wonder. He declared, "So, since then, you've been out here straight slaying folks, daring them to give you their worst and conquering them all."

"Yeah, and no lie, I've had some amazing fights that gave me such a rush. Then others were so dismal that I would literally try to find somebody else to fight that night just to scratch the itch. Fighting, literally, is a drug to me, and for about six years it took me a while to control the monster inside me. As I told you, only about three other things make me feel the way fighting does. And thank Akan the Company found me and recruited me because it's the perfect way to get a healthy fix for my thirst for violence."

Malcolm laughed and said, "I knew something was a little twisted in you when you scaled the Elite mountain. Now I understand where it comes from."

Symone revealed, "It's not something I try to hide. It's me. It's who I am. And I feel like if I can't embrace myself, then what's the point of living?"

"That was incredibly insightful," Malcolm was taken aback. "So, wait, you were fighting in the Underbelly. Did you ever consider fighting in the other districts? As good as you are now, I'm sure you could have done some damage in the Highgarden."

Symone recalled, "Highgarden had too many restrictions and rules. I mean, I fought a couple of times there when I was twenty-three. But they wanted too much from me and didn't put out enough, and they were super sneaky about things that rubbed me the wrong way. My ex-boyfriend and I found out that many of my requests to fight people were being thrown out for no reason, and some of the fighters I wanted to square up with never received them."

"Oh, they were taking your choice away from you," Malcolm rationalized.

Symone's eyes glowed, *Oh Akan, how does he know me so well?!*

"Yes, Malcolm! You get it! I was pissed, and I almost burned the Highgarden down. Instead, I took my talents back to the Underbelly and never looked back. And some of the fighters in Highgarden found out and came with me. I'm telling you, man, my crew, my people, they had my back in ways I could never have imagined. Those were some of the best years of my life."

"I'm so glad I got to hear this," Malcolm professed.

"I'm glad I got to share it with you, Malcolm." She grabbed Malcolm's arm and rested her head on his shoulder. He laid his head on top of hers, and they sat there for a minute.

"Okay, I gotta pee. I'm gonna go use the restroom, and I'll be right back," Malcolm said.

Symone let go of Malcolm and said, "Okay, I'll be here." Malcolm went to the restroom while Symone pondered, *Gosh, I want him so much. I hope I didn't reveal too much to him. Do I sound like a psycho? No, plenty of fighters have moved over to the Company.*

The restaurant door opened, and Alexia ran through it, saying, "Hi, I'm looking for—oh, there she is. Symone!" Alexia hurried to the back of the restaurant and sat across from Symone.

Symone lifted her arms and rested her hands on the table as she declared, "Alexia! I'm so glad you're here."

"Where's Malcolm?"

"Oh, he went to the restroom. He'll be back in a second."

"Okay," Alexia said. "So, what are we doing? What's the play?"

"Girl, I can't wait to tell you."

"We're being so bad, but I'm so glad you called me. I've been walking around the mall fuming, knowing you two were going into the fire. Not this time."

"Aww, you were worried about me?" Symone raised an eyebrow and smiled.

"Frimas, yeah! Mallack was wrong about the Power Party, and she was wrong about this meeting. I know you can handle yourself, but I couldn't live with myself if something happened to you or Malcolm, and I was out buying clothes or, like Malaysia, sitting at home watching the holoscreen."

"Oh, well, Malaysia's coming, too," Symone corrected her.

"Oh, so we really getting into some trouble!" Alexia shouted and danced in her seat. "What about Karl and Daisy? Are they coming, too?"

"Malcolm and I thought it'd be good for them to sit this one out so their absence doesn't attract negative attention."

Alexia agreed, "Smart. Karl lives in the quarters, and Daisy basically wants to run the Grand Hall. If they're not around, people will think something's up."

Malcolm returned and sat beside Symone, "Good, you're here, Alexia. Did Symone catch you up?"

"Not entirely. Glad you thought to bring me along. You had me worried for a minute," Alexia shared.

"Well, we both agreed that we couldn't nor shouldn't do this by ourselves. We're just waiting on Malaysia, and then we'll get started."

A couple of minutes later, Malaysia walked into Draygo's. She saw Malcolm and Symone and thought, *Okay, just be calm, don't say anything stupid. It's just lunch.* When she arrived at the booth and saw Alexia, too, she said, "What's going on?"

"Sit with us, Malaysia," Malcolm said, motioning his hand to point to her seat next to Alexia. "We couldn't ask you two for your help without raising suspicion in the building, so we asked you two to lunch as a cover."

"Ask for help? Oh!" Malaysia breathed a sigh of relief and sat down.

"The fact is, we don't know what we're walking into, and we won't let the Collector isolate us and take us, too."

"So, where's Karl and Daisy?" Malaysia asked and looked around.

"We don't want to cause alarm, so we didn't ask them to join us for this."

"Smart, Daisy would just run and tell Mallack, and ruin everything," Malaysia said. "So, I'm guessing lunch is not on the table?"

"Oh, girl, if you're hungry, grab the menu and order something. I got you!"

Malaysia, kidding, chuckled and shook her head. She then wondered, "Malcolm, are you sure about this? Mallack is going to have your head!"

"Listen, at this point, I care more about us staying alive than my relationship with Mallack. Whatever it takes, remember? We screwed up already once before," Malcolm looked at Alexia with widened eyes, and she smiled, grateful that somebody finally listened to her. "We're not going to do that again. The real question is, are you sure you want in? You can say no."

Malaysia looked at Malcolm with a stare of disgust. "How dare you! What kind of question is that? Of course I'm in! What's the play, Malcolm?"

Malcolm leaned in, and Symone, Alexia, and Malaysia did the same. "Okay, here's what we're going to do. Dredge is supposed to arrive about two cycles after sunset."

Malaysia interjected, "Malcolm, just say, '16:00.'"

"Okay, fine, *16:00*, he'll arrive about half a block from here. Malaysia, we want you to cover surveillance atop a perch two buildings southward. Alexia, you'll be across the street at the drink shop, keeping an eye on us from there. We'll keep comms on so that you can hear everything we hear.

"Once he arrives, Malaysia, scan him to see if he's got a cloak on. Alexia, try to read his mind and extract any information on him and his ties to the Collector.

Frimas, we might even get some idea of who the Collector is through him. Once he gives us the drive, Alexia, take it from us using your telekinesis. Then we all walk away. Easy peasy."

"If something goes wrong, or additional folk show up…" Alexia brought up.

"…then we fight until backup arrives. If the Collector wants a show, we'll give her one she'll never forget," Symone declared.

"That's what I'm talking about!" Alexia rallied. "Whatever it takes!"

"Damn right," Malcolm agreed. "A while back, we agreed that we are in the fight for our lives. I don't know what to expect tonight, but from now on, we have to assume that the Collector is out for blood and fight like it's our last. We're going make sure that we win every single time from now on."

Symone swooned. *This guy, I see why everybody wants to work with him. He could lead a crowd off a cliff, and they wouldn't think twice about it.*

"Did you practice that, or did that just come off the top of your head?" Malaysia joked.

"Every rising in the mirror, just before breakfast," Malcolm returned to her.

"Alright, so 16:00, that gives us about eight cycles until showtime. What do you guys want to do until then?" Alexia pondered.

"For real, though, can I get some food?" Malaysia asked.

Malcolm laughed as he raised his hand up and said, "Bartender? Whatever the ladies want. I'm going to step outside for a minute." Malcolm got up and walked outside the restaurant.

Symone was concerned and said, "Excuse me, y'all," and followed him out. Alexia and Malaysia looked at each other and grinned.

Malcolm stood on the sidewalk, his head pounding as thoughts of Duncan and the Collector bounced from one side of his cranium to the next. *I need this mission to end well.*

Symone came out of the restaurant, placed her right hand on his back, and asked, "Hey, you alright?"

Malcolm turned around and said, "Oh, yeah, I'm good. Just in my head."

"Can I help you get out of it?" Symone offered.

"Oh? And how do you propose to do that?"

"Well, like they said, we have about eight cycles before we meet. Let's eat with them for about, say, two of those cycles, and then let's get out of here, whether with them or by ourselves."

"And do what, exactly?" Malcolm asked, highly intrigued.

"We'll figure that out when we get to that point."

Malcolm agreed, "Alright. I think I can get on board with that."

22
Dredge

Leicester's nightly festivities were swinging into gear. Malaysia looked at the street below and noticed the sights and sounds of the bazaar. Music pulsed seven stories high to reach her ears, and Malaysia found herself grooving a little to the beat and wished she could be down there enjoying herself along with the street dancers, onlookers, bazaar owners, and passersby. She stared once again at the corner and saw no sign of the team's target. She looked at her stripe that read 15:58. She thought about her recon mission and wrestled with her feelings, her desire to share all she knew about the Affinity Theory and what that may mean for Malcolm and Symone, and her wish to end the Collector's life and mission by any means necessary. She looked at her stripe and vacillated between calling Malcolm and telling him everything and leaving it alone.

"Okay, I'm walking over to the shop now," Alexia communicated.

"I have eyes on you," Malaysia responded. She saw Alexia walk out of the drink shop with a cup in her hand. Alexia saw tables near the corner of the street and made her way through a small crowd of people who were admiring a powered person making shapes out of fire from his hands. She pushed past them and sat facing the target corner.

"I have a perfect line of sight from here." Alexia took a sip from her cup and locked eyes on the corner.

"Okay, we're making our way to the corner now," Malcolm relayed, Symone walking next to him. They passed Alexia's table and crossed the street. They stood at the corner, scanned the area, and Malcolm reported, "No sign of Dredge. Malaysia?"

Malaysia widened her search. "No, I don't see him yet. The area appears clear, no anomalies detected, mostly normal and low-powered people."

"I wonder how long he's going to make us wait for him," Symone questioned.

Malcolm and Symone waltzed around each other and looked harder for Dredge. Symone looked at her stripe again, and it read 16:01. They began to worry but wouldn't show it. Malaysia stared at them for a moment, thinking to herself how happy she was for Malcolm. He seemed to have finally found something outside of the Company worth enjoying.

Just then, a figure matching Dredge's description popped up from the north, fighting his way through the crowd, headed toward the target corner.

"Okay, guys, I think we're getting action. Dredge is on his way, walking from the north," Malaysia informed them. Symone and Malcolm turned to their north and waited.

Dredge wore a dingy t-shirt, a slightly tattered tan vest, and light-colored ripped jeans. Malcolm thought, *He doesn't seem intimidating at all.* Malcolm noticed a nervousness in Dredge's eyes and shakiness in his boots. Dredge crept toward them and said, "You two must be fake Jackson and fake Emma, right?"

"That's right," Malcolm began. "And you must be Dredge."

Malaysia began scanning Dredge as he continued, "Yes, that's right. I was told to meet you guys here to talk about a drive," Dredge said nervously.

"Guys, he's wearing a cloak, next-gen, too," Malaysia discovered. "Alexia, see what you can do?"

Alexia began using telepathy to try to break through the cloak while Symone said, "Okay, Dredge, so where's the drive?"

"Right, so I don't have the drive on me," Dredge stammered.

"What do you mean?" Malcolm instinctively blurted, slightly enraged. He squinted his eyes and thought, *Here we go!*

"I mean, I don't have it on me. I actually need your help with something," Dredge said.

"Hold on, hold on, first, how do you know the Collector? What's your power? Who else is with you?" Malcolm flashed.

"Me, power? No, no, I don't have any powers," Dredge admitted. "I just know how to use holoscreens and build drives for people. My *power* is in making holoscreens do what people want them to do, nothing more, nothing less. People pay me money, and I make drives. That's how I know the Collector. I've done jobs for her, and she's paid me well."

"Doesn't seem like it, given, well, your look," Symone said, noting how old and worn his clothes appeared.

"Oh, well," Dredge said as he wiped his shirt twice, "just because people pay me well doesn't mean I know how to keep my creds. I have a slight addiction to prizefight bets and a really bad betting track record."

The three walked slowly eastward. "So, what are you and the Collector planning right now? Why did she bring you into this?" Malcolm interrogated.

"I can't break that cloak, guys," Alexia regretfully revealed. "That cloak is too powerful. Either he's lying about his money, or he's got some big-time help."

"Oh, she didn't bring me into anything," Dredge admitted. "I asked her for help, and she told me to build her a drive and meet you guys here to make a trade."

Symone was confused. "A trade? What kind of trade?"

They stopped at a well-lit alleyway in between two stores. "Well, I've done a ton of work for the Collector, but I've also worked for other people between here and Genesis Landing. I did this one job for an underground group called Dust that operates from here in Leicester, and they paid me my money, and I gave them their drive. An easy gig for me, build-and-go. But they botched their job, then blamed *me* for their screw-up. They want their money back, but like I said, I'm not good with money, so I don't have it."

Malcolm shook his head and couldn't believe his ears. "So, what, you want us to pay you the money you need to come from up under Dust? You gotta be kidding me!"

"What? Screw that! No, I don't care about Dust! I want you to help me rescue my daughter!" Dredge pleaded. He pressed his wrist and flipped his left palm sky-side. A holographic video of a little girl floated from his hand. Symone and Malcolm slightly bent forward and noticed the girl with two small, black puffs crowning her head, twirling around and smiling. Tears welled up in Dredge's eyes as he tried to continue, "See, I didn't know that Dust is a people-trafficking network, and when I told them that I didn't have their money a week ago, they said to me that one way or another, I would pay. So about five days ago, I woke up, and she wasn't in her bed. I saw this message that said, 'She will suffice.' I scrambled, trying to find anyone who would give me money to get her back. I ran traces on top of traces and came up empty. When I thought I had run out of options, suddenly, the Collector buzzed my stripe three days ago, and she asked me what I wanted as payment. I told her about my daughter, and she said she wouldn't pay me the money, but she would send me help, provided that I make a drive for her."

"And?" While feeling sorry for the little girl, Symone was growing increasingly aggravated. "Where is this help?"

"Um, you, you're the help," Dredge nervously responded as he pointed to Malcolm and Symone. "That's why I'm here."

Malcolm huffed and rolled his eyes. Malaysia said, "The Frimas?"

Malcolm bent his head back straight and reacted, "So, you're telling me that the Collector sent you here to recruit us to help you get your daughter back?"

"Yes."

Malcolm had had enough and shifted his weight. "No way, no, I don't believe you," Malcolm said. He grabbed Dredge and rushed him up against the wall of the building they stood next to. Dredge's cloak responded to the slam. "Tell us the truth! What are you here for? What does the Collector want? Where is the drive?"

Symone placed her hand on Malcolm's shoulder and said, "Malcolm, wait."

Dredge lifted his hands and cried, "I promise, that's what she told me. If I build her a drive and come to this spot, she would ensure I would receive help to get her back."

"This doesn't make any sense, Malcolm," Alexia said.

"Okay, if this is true, if what you're saying is true, then let one of my people scan your mind," Malcolm rashly disclosed.

"Malcolm, what are you doing?" Symone bellowed.

Malcolm faced Symone, "Look, if he's telling the truth," then turned to face Dredge again, "which I'm not completely convinced, by the way, then we should probe him and see," he angrily proposed.

"Malcolm, that's a bad idea. That'll give our position away," Alexia countered.

"I'm telling the truth, I'm telling the truth! Please don't probe me, man!" Dredge was afraid his mind would get scrambled, and he would end up a mindless body in someone's assisted living center. He ruffled through his pocket and said, "Here, here's the drive!" Dredge pulled out of his pocket a black flash drive the size of a finger. He continued, "Listen, I don't care about this, whatever beef you got with the Collector. All I want is my daughter. You can have the drive. I'll find another way to get my daughter back. World's best warriors, my ass."

Malcolm put him down. Dredge straightened his clothes and wiped his backside off any dirt from the wall he was pressed up against. Dredge then gave Malcolm the drive and said, "I'm a dead man anyway, regardless of whether they get their money from me or not. I just want my daughter alive and safe. Thanks for nothing." Dredge walked away.

Malcolm looked at the drive. Symone tugged Malcolm's arm and motioned her head in the Dredge's direction. Malcolm couldn't believe what he was about to do, but his conscience would not drop the urge to help. Dredge had made it out of the alleyway and was headed in the direction he came from. Malcolm growled and huffed then ran with Symone following toward Dredge and said, "Hey, wait!"

Dredge stopped and turned around. Malcolm reasoned, "Look, I don't know you, and I don't trust you. Anyone who does work for the Collector can hump a goat. But your daughter didn't ask to get caught up in your mess, and we want to help."

"Malcolm, what are you doing?" Malaysia was concerned.

Dredge hugged Malcolm, tears welling up in his eyes again, and choked up, "Oh, thank you, thank you!"

"Okay, alright," Malcolm slightly seized up and squirmed. "So, how do you make contact with this Dust crew?"

Dredge let go of Malcolm, rubbed his thighs, then replied, "Um, okay, so I got this message from them. They said that when I'm ready to make a trade, to call them, and they would give me a location and time to meet them."

"Okay," Malcolm quickly plotted. "Here's what going to happen. You're going to call them. Tell them you have their money and are ready to make the trade. Once they give you the address, you're coming with us, and then we'll take it from there."

"Wait, that's it? That's all I gotta do, just get their address and give it to you?" Dredge asked.

"You want your daughter back, right?" Malcolm rationalized.

"Well, yeah," Dredge agreed.

"Then this is how we're going to do it. Make the call now."

"Now?"

"Did he stutter?" Symone aggressively chimed in.

"Okay, okay, I'm calling them now." Symone looked at Malcolm, and he nodded in agreement with her aggressive push. "Yeah, this is Dredge. I-I-I got your money, and I'm ready to make a trade. But first, I want to know that my daughter Lana is okay." Silence, then, "Baby, are you alright? Have they hurt you? Listen, Daddy's coming to bring you home, okay?! Lana?" Silence again. "They hung up." Tears began to fall from Dredge's eyes as Malcolm and Symone looked on. Dredge's stripe lit up yellow. He lifted his arm to read his stripe, "Mission Pier, Port 217, Genesis Landing. 20:00."

Dredge lifted his arm to show Malcolm and Symone the message. They looked, and Symone said, "That's less than four cycles."

"Okay, Dredge, come with us," Malcolm said. "Malaysia, Alexia, stand down. We're going to the safe house."

"Wait, there were others?" Dredge asked.

"I wouldn't worry about that right now. We gotta save your daughter," Malcolm quickly countered. Malaysia came down from her roof post via the elevator, and Alexia got up from her table and walked toward Malcolm, Symone, and Dredge. Malaysia came out of the building and met up with them, and they traveled five blocks through the busy streets and bright lights of Leicester to the Company safe house in silence.

Alexia sent a message to Malaysia, "Are we seriously going to help this guy?"

Malaysia returned, "Malcolm's convinced that we should. I'm sure he will talk to us about it once we get to the house."

Alexia sent, "He'd better because this is bull! We HAVE THE DRIVE "

Malaysia replied, "For real, it's so suspect."

About twenty minutes later, they finally arrived at the safe house, a condominium behind a clothing store. They went inside the store. Symone noticed the clothes arrayed across the walls and racks of the store and said, "I didn't think we were going to buy something. What is this for, disguises?"

"Just watch," Malaysia answered her.

A few seconds later, a petite teenage girl with a pixie cut greeted them, wearing a black crop top and tan leggings. She said, "Welcome. Can we help you find anything?"

Malcolm responded, "Yes, something that I can see myself wearing for a while."

The girl recognized the verbal command prompt and reacted, "Oh yeah? Silk?"

Malcolm heard the word silk and answered, "Satin."

"Red?" she volleyed.

"Orange," he volleyed back.

"What is going on?" Symone pondered.

"Forty-four?" she asked.

"Thirty-eight," Malcolm delivered.

The girl smiled and said, "You're in luck! A set just came in last night. Follow me, everyone."

As they walked toward the back of the store, Symone leaned over to Malcolm and asked, "And when were you gonna tell me about this?"

"We usually don't deal with safe houses until well after training is over," Malcolm whispered.

They followed the girl to the dressing room area. She said, "Okay, your outfits are in the dressing rooms. Just enter and try them on."

They each entered a dressing room and closed the door. The dressing room door was locked behind each of them. Symone looked back when she heard the click. The back of each dressing room opened, revealing a hidden entrance to the safe house about thirty yards back. It mimicked the entrance to the quarters of the Elite Grand Hall.

They walked down the low-lit corridor. Malcolm placed his hand on the palm reader. It scanned his hand and lit white for approval. The entrance opened to the commons, with the kitchen to the right and the residences to the left.

"Okay, Dredge, go take one of the residences on the left and crash for a bit while I talk to my team," Malcolm insisted.

"I will. Wow, this is lush!" he admired. He walked to one of the residences, entered, and sealed himself in.

Once Dredge entered, Malcolm said, "AI, disable all holoscreens, network connections, and stripe communications."

The AI responded, "Acknowledged."

"Be damned if he connects to anything while he's here," Malcolm explained.

"Smart," Malaysia agreed.

They walked to the couches and chairs in the commons while Symone said, "Malcolm, what was all that back there, about to get Alexia to scan his mind?"

Malcolm admitted, "Not gonna lie, he pissed me off. All I could think about was Duncan, and I felt like he was lying to us. He still might be."

Malcolm and Symone sat on a loveseat while Alexia sat to the right of it on the couch and Malaysia to its left in a chair. Alexia retorted, "Exactly, Malcolm, so why would you agree to help him?"

Malcolm palmed his face and responded, "Because it's a little girl. She didn't ask for this and doesn't deserve this. This Dust crew sounds like bad news, and I can only imagine what kind of life she's about to endure if we don't do something."

Malaysia said, "Malcolm, are we really going to do this?"

"Why not?" he asked.

"Malcolm, what if this is a trap? What if he's playing us?"

"Yeah, he might be, but we owe it to her to at least try, right?"

Alexia sighed, "Malcolm, we have the drive! We should just walk away and let him deal with the decisions he made on his own. Nobody put a gun to his head and told him to make a deal with Bashko. And we're just supposed to clean up his mess?"

Symone countered, "True, you're right, Alexia, he did make this deal." She paused for a few seconds, and everyone looked at her intently. "But," she paused again, "Lana didn't ask for this. It doesn't sound like Dredge makes the best business decisions when it comes to who he chooses to work with, but we can agree that he was obviously making a living to take care of his family."

"Yeah, that and his debts," Malaysia quipped.

"Yeah, but even still, a host of folk make silly decisions and work questionable jobs all the time to make it in this city. His kid shouldn't be collateral damage for his mistakes, right? No matter how messed up his connections are. Both things can be true at the same time."

"Speaking of," Alexia brought up, "Can we talk about how the Collector is wrapped up in all this?"

"Yeah, Akan," Malaysia perked up. "So, the Collector recruits us to help somebody? Make that make sense! Is she going to owe us a favor now? She got him to build a drive we need and make a trade for our services? To save his daughter by stopping a people-trafficking gang? Who the Frimas is this chick?"

"I don't know who *she* is," Malcolm caught Malaysia holding onto her theory of the Collector's anatomy, "and like I've been wondering since the beginning, we don't know what she's trying to do or why she's doing any of this. I'm just as confused as you all are. Like, if we help her, which we have to for Lana's sake, what does this mean?"

"Malcolm, you said before that you feel like we're being directed," Symone recalled.

"Yeah, Malcolm," Malaysia remembered, "back at the debrief after the Power Party. So, where is she directing us? Is this how she recruits her soldiers? She sends people on random missions, retrieving items they need while lying to waste all her enemies and leaving her on the board as the last woman standing?"

"That's really a good point, Malaysia," Alexia declared as she pointed at Malaysia.

Malcolm agreed. "The Collector is resourceful and a master manipulator. It's like she knows what it will take to get us to do whatever it is she wants us to do," Malcolm reasoned.

"The Collector is a sociopath," Symone believed, "and she is intelligent as Frimas. And no matter how we slice this, we don't have a choice but to help Dredge get his kid back and stop those monsters from trafficking anyone else. I mean, this is what we do. This is what we signed up for when we became a part of the Company, right? What's the point of having all these powers if we won't use them when they're needed the most?"

Alexia sighed again. "Akan, you sound just like him!"

"Like whom?"

"Like Malcolm!" She looked at him, and he looked at her and slowly shrugged his shoulders. Alexia breathed heavily, then continued, "So, what do we do with the drive? I mean, we can't just walk out there with it on us. We have to take it back to base. For sure, we can't give it to Dredge, and right now, I don't trust anybody here at the safe house to keep it secure."

"Right," Malcolm agreed. He pondered for a few seconds, then responded, "Okay, if we give the drive to Intelligence, then the mission is considered complete, which means that you're no longer benched, right?"

"That's right, we're benched until this mission is over," Alexia answered.

"Okay, Symone and I will take the—"

"Wait, *Symone*? You're on a first-name basis now?" Malaysia caught on and teased Malcolm.

"Aw Frimas," Malcolm blurted out as he rolled his eyes and tilted his head backward.

Symone chuckled as she tapped his left hand twice with her right, "Mmm hmm, been doing it all day. I told him he might as well stop fighting it. My name rolls off his tongue so effortlessly."

Malcolm rolled his eyes and crossed his arms. "Ugh, fine, *Symone* and I will take the drive to the base. While I take the drive to Intelligence, Symone, you get Karl and let him know what's going on. Malaysia, once the mission is declared completed by Intelligence, call Daisy and let her know, too. We'll all assemble at Port 210, get Dredge's daughter back, and round up Dust for UPD. Assuming they're not powered, this should be open and shut."

"I like it. Let's do this," Alexia concurred.

Malcolm lifted a finger and issued a warning, "Now, ladies, this will be an unsanctioned mission. The law does not allow us to do missions without government approval, and the cost is high for anyone who does. So be aware that regardless of how this goes, we will get in trouble for this, and we could be kicked off Elite or, worse, placed in the Asylum."

"I'm not afraid," Symone assured.

"We're in, Malcolm, all the way, whatever it takes," Malaysia voted in the affirmative.

"Y'all aren't leaving me out," Alexia declared.

Malcolm smiled. "Okay, Symone, get Dredge."

Symone got up from her seat and walked past Malcolm. Malcolm snuck a peek at Symone's bubble butt as she walked to the back and knocked on Dredge's door. He opened the door and said, "Yes?"

"Malcolm wants you. Let's go."

"Okay," he followed Symone to the commons.

Malcolm, Malaysia, and Alexia stood up. Malcolm said, "Okay, Dredge, we're going to leave you here until the mission is complete and your daughter is secured. You won't be able to leave, and we've blocked everything against your hacker self, so don't try anything or swear to Akan, Symone will fry you when we get back and make sure you never see your daughter again, understood?"

"Okay, I understand," Dredge acknowledged as he sat down in the commons.

"Help yourself to as much food and drink as you'd like," Malaysia said.

"I will. Thank you for the offer," Dredge's eyes lit up.

"Ladies, let's get it," Malcolm instructed.

The four walked out of the safe house entrance, down the corridor, and through the dressing rooms. As they exited the dressing room area, the sales associate asked them, "Did you find everything to your liking?"

Malcolm returned the code, "We left one behind, but everything else was wonderful. Can't wait to return to make up our minds and make a final purchase."

"Okay, come back and see us!"

"Okay, but seriously, Malcolm, you're going to have to teach me all that," Symone pinpointed.

"All in due time, Symone," Malcolm answered as they walked outside. "Okay, everybody, meet at Port 210 at 19:45."

"Copy that," Malaysia said.

"See you guys soon," Alexia agreed.

Malaysia and Alexia walked in the opposite direction from Symone and Malcolm, who both made a circle on their left wrists with their right index fingers and then dragged them up their left arms. They walked as they waited for their hoverbikes to meet them. Symone said to Malcolm, "Okay, so we're headed to base."

"Yep, that's where we're headed."

"Bet you I get there before you do," Symone raised an eyebrow and cracked a smile.

"Girl, you don't want these problems," Malcolm considered her proposal.

"I'll make it interesting," she said as she turned to face him. "Loser has to do whatever the winner wants him to do."

"You're talking like you already know who's going to win," Malcolm teased as she caught where she placed *him* in her sentence.

"Just confident that you will definitely lose. What do you say?" she asked just as their bikes parked near the sidewalk next to them.

"If you have to ask, you're already a second behind, which is all I need to smoke you," Malcolm grinned.

"See you in my rearview," Symone reacted. They jumped on their bikes and raced across the deepening black sky toward the base in Highgarden.

23

Time

At about 17:20, the door of the Company's parking garage opened, and Malcolm breezed in with at least twenty seconds to spare. He landed his hoverbike as Symone rushed in, highly upset that she had lost to Malcolm, *again*. Her pride was bruised, but she worked to regain her composure to not take her anger out on Malcolm. *He won fair and square, ugh, whatever.*

Malcolm hopped off his bike and his bike drove off to park as Symone landed her bike. She unsaddled her seat, cut her eyes at Malcolm, and said, "Nice job." She rolled her eyes and slowly sashayed away from him.

Malcolm couldn't help but stare while replying, "Your losing streak is growing, Symone. You good?"

Symone answered playfully, "Maybe I'm letting you win. Ever thought about that?"

Malcolm followed her to the elevator. "Nah, nah, I don't wanna hear that, 'win or die.'"

Symone snorted, then said, "Don't do that, don't make me laugh. I'm trying to be mad at you."

Malcolm grinned, "And why is that?"

"Because now I'm in your debt. No telling what you're going to make me do. Probably visit the Analyst for fourteen cycles straight, beat up some bots in the training room, or something else lame," Symone rolled her eyes again as she pressed the down button.

"No, I actually have something a little more," Malcolm paused, "challenging in mind."

"Oh?" Symone perked up. "How so?"

"You'll have to wait until the right time," Malcolm said while they entered the elevator. Malcolm pressed "E" for the Grand Hall.

"There you go with that word *time* again," Symone sighed.

"Trust me, it'll be worth it," Malcolm assured Symone.

He touched the small of her back, slowly sliding his hand from one side of her torso to the other, noticing the small dip where her spine lay and wondering how soft her skin must feel underneath her shirt. Malcolm thought, *I love how she dials my senses up the way she does. Touching her makes me feel so alive.*

A chill traversed Symone's spine from where his hand caressed her to her neck and back down. She closed her eyes as they smoldered, and she shuddered. *Please don't stop. Touch me more.*

He dropped his hand and clasped them both behind his back. They arrived at the Grand Hall. Malcolm said, "Okay, tell Karl the situation and stay in the quarters until I get there. Let him know he should leave immediately and to not waste any time. Malaysia will give him more information once he leaves and calls her. Tell him to make sure to take his suit and cloak."

Symone shook the dopamine that he set off in her and accepted her assignment. "Okay. I'll see you soon."

Malcolm walked to Intelligence and opened the door. He saw Dax and several analysts at their holoscreens communicating with themselves. "Dax!" Malcolm got his attention.

"Oh, hey, Malcolm," Dax walked up the steps to meet Malcolm. "You're back. I'm glad to see you in one piece. How's Symone?"

"She's good," Malcolm returned. He was anxious to finish the mission but tried not to show it.

"How was the mission? Any issues?"

"Surprisingly, the mission was a success. We got the drive," Malcolm revealed the flash drive, holding it up next to his face. "Here you go."

"That's great news! I know we were all worried the Collector was going to do something random, so this is good." He took the drive from Malcolm.

"Good, so you'll scan this and declare the mission completed," Malcolm declared.

Dax walked down to the table in front of the holoscreen while he said, "Yes, we'll just lay this on the counter and...," the holoscreen in front of everyone booted up an auto-scan command prompt and began scanning the drive. Next to the prompt displayed a message, "Mission: Retrieve the Drive from Dredge. Status: Complete."

Dax turned back to Malcolm. He said, "So we'll scan this, look for any abnormalities, and get back to you guys in the rising to let you know when we have Duncan's location."

"My man," Malcolm reacted while patting Dax's right shoulder with his left hand. "Hey, Dax, listen, thank you for everything you do, man, you and Stephanie. I know we don't really get a chance to say it often—"

"It's all good, Malcolm," Dax replied. "I appreciate you. We value all you do out there. It's good to know we're valued, too."

"Without question, we couldn't do our jobs without you. Run the scan, and we'll see you in the rising."

"Get some rest, my man. You look like a shell of yourself."

"Rest?" Malcolm quipped. "What's that?" Malcolm walked out of Intelligence and messaged Malaysia, "Drive has been delivered. Mission declared complete. You guys are off the bench. Get everybody ready. See you at Port 210 at 19:45."

A moment later, Malaysia replied, "Great! Letting Karl and Daisy know. See you at the port."

Symone, meanwhile, entered the quarters and found the holoscreen watching Karl half-asleep in the commons. Symone walked up to Karl and shook his shoulder. "Karl?" she whispered. "Karl?! Karl!"

Karl jumped and yelled, "What just happened?!"

"Karl, it's me, Symone," she patted his shoulders to calm him down.

"Oh," Karl's breathing slowed, "you scared me, Symone. Everything okay? Where's Malcolm?"

"He's fine; he's in Intelligence. Everything's fine, but not. We got the drive, but we have another problem. We need you to grab your suit and cloak and leave the base. Malaysia will contact you in about seven minutes to give you instructions on what to do from there."

"Okay," Karl got up from his seat and turned to face Symone. "But what about the bench order?"

"Once Malcolm gives Intelligence the flash drive, the order will be lifted. At least, that's what Malcolm said."

"Makes sense. The mission was the drive. Something must have happened while you were there?"

"Did," Symone answered. "Malaysia will fill you in. We don't want to catch attention here or sound any alarms." Symone instinctually made the same spinning finger sign Malcolm made earlier in the elevator to remind him of the cameras and microphones in the building.

"Right. Okay, let's go."

Symone countered, "No, Malcolm said he'd meet back here with me after he left Intelligence."

"Right, that will make the all-clear real," Karl reasoned. "Alright, we'll see you two in a little while, I guess." Karl walked away to his residence, grabbed his cloak and uniform buttons from his countertop, then walked out and passed by Symone in the kitchen and said, "See you soon."

"Be safe. See you soon." Karl left the quarters, and Symone walked to her residence.

Karl marched toward an anxiously calm Malcolm. "Hey brother, Symone brought me up to speed. I'll see you in a little while."

"Alright," he stuck out his fist, and Karl pounded it with a fist bump. "Malaysia just messaged me back. She's going to call you in a few minutes. We'll meet up with you soon."

"Okay, see you soon, brother." Karl walked away.

Malcolm looked at his stripe that read 17:39. He asked AI, "What's the ETA to Port 210 on Mission in Genesis Landing?"

"At your typical speed, it shouldn't take longer than a half-cycle," AI responded.

"Good, okay," Malcolm thought. "Plenty of time."

Symone sat in her residence, antsy as she thought about the mission in Genesis Landing. She asked AI, "How far is Port 210 from here?"

"About half a cycle, given how fast you fly," AI reported.

Symone answered, "Okay, thanks." She nervously trembled her legs, then stood up and paced the floor. *What's taking Malcolm so long? I thought it was just going to be a drop-and-go. They're probably holding him up, asking all sorts of questions. By the time he gets out of that meeting with them, it'll be 19:10, and we're going to be cutting it so close, I can feel it. I should go and help him get out of*

Intelligence. What kind of excuse can I come up with? But he said to wait here, and I should just listen to him. She rubbed her hands, ran them through her locs, stretched her arms upward, holding her stretch for about three seconds, and released, though it didn't ease the tension she felt. She looked at her stripe, which read 17:41. She determined, *Know what, I'm going to Intelligence.*

She walked to her door and opened it, and Malcolm stood outside her door, arm lifted as he was about to knock on it. "Hey, Symone," Malcolm said.

"Oh, hey!" Symone nervously answered. "I was just about to go to the commons to wait for you there," she fabricated. "Um, how did it go with Intelligence?" She backed away from the door.

"Everything went without a hitch," Malcolm reported as he walked into her room. "Dax has the drive and is doing his deep scan thing. He said we'll have what we need in the rising, so we're good. The bench order is lifted."

"Good, Malaysia knows?" Symone walked into the kitchen, with Malcolm slowly following her.

"Yes, sent the message to her stripe. She's getting in touch with Karl and Daisy, and everyone knows to meet at the port," Malcolm sat on the island while Symone went to one of the cupboards and grabbed a glass from it.

"Good, good. So, are we ready? What's next? What do we do?"

Malcolm had been thinking about the answer to that question long before Symone asked it, ever since Symone saved him from Mygalo. While he didn't say his answer as bluntly as he was thinking it, he stood up from his seat and responded, "Well, I figured we have well over a cycle before we have to get out of here."

"Uh huh," Symone wondered where Malcolm's mind was going as she turned on the faucet to fill her glass with water.

He slowly made his way over to her side of the island like a hunter locked onto his prey. "And there's the issue of you having to do whatever it is that I want you to do."

Symone felt a tingle ride up and down her spine again. She turned the faucet off and turned around. She drank some of the water out of the glass, then reacted, "Yes, and you said that we needed the *right time* to do something *challenging.* Are you saying that *this* is the right time?"

Malcolm reached for the glass in her left hand. She gave it to him, and he laid it on the countertop next to the sink. He then faced Symone and gently grabbed her with his right arm by the small of her back – which had become one of his favorite spots on her body – and turned her back toward the island and pushed her up against it.

"It's definitely the right time," he declared. He pressed his lips against hers, and they shared a deep kiss. Symone's eyes and hair bathed in red. The intensity she felt within her ignited into a raging fire. Symone wrapped her arms around Malcolm and squeezed him tightly as her lips opened and locked onto his. Malcolm slid his left hand onto Symone's butt and gently gripped her cheek.

Symone slowly backed her face away from Malcolm's and hissed. As they held each other, she bellowed, "So, what is the challenge? What do you want me to do?"

Malcolm swiftly picked Symone up and smoothly planted her on the island. As if her butt was a button, her legs popped open, and he stood between them, his right palm on her soft left thigh and his left hand on the island top, and he kissed her again. Their soft kisses turned instinctual as they locked lips, and their tongues tasted each other. Malcolm thought to himself, *She even tastes different, my Akan!*

In between kisses, he declared, "Yield to me."

Symone's arms wrapped around Malcolm's strong shoulders, and she rubbed her hands across his jacket, ready to tear through his clothes and feel his body. Malcolm rubbed his hand up and down Symone's thigh, took his other hand, and felt up and down her back.

I thought you said this was going to be a challenge. Holy crap, I'll yield to you any day. You feel so damn good! Symone's breathing intensified. She let out a moan as Malcolm's hands continued to rub her back and thigh simultaneously. He dialed his senses up, and he molecularly felt Symone's bodily responses to his actions, enjoying the pleasure he brought to her. She pulled at Malcolm's jacket, and he slipped his arms out of their sleeves and dropped the jacket to the floor. She felt the shirt he was wearing and started pulling it over him. He helped her help him out of his shirt. All that was left was the A-shirt he had on. Malcolm then mirrored her by pulling at Symone's shirt. Symone lifted her arms up to help him help her out of it. She was now wearing a black sports bra.

Malcolm looked at her toned belly and noticed the ribbon he made from her star tied around her waist. He smiled, then looked into Symone's eyes and said, "Are you sure about this?"

"What do you mean?" Symone whispered.

"I know I won the bet. But I don't want you just because I won. If you don't want to do this—"

Symone pressed her finger against his lips and smiled. "Forget the stupid bet. I want you." Malcolm smiled again, then pulled her into him as they kissed again. He pulled his lips off her lips and started kissing her neck. She moaned excitedly, ecstasy churning through her veins. She longed for him to give her the release she'd been craving for weeks. He massaged her back with his strong, gentle hands, his fingers sliding up and down her spine as he intricately explored every inch of her.

He picked her up, and her thighs instinctively locked onto his waist. He escorted them into her bedroom. Malcolm himself was overjoyed and mission-bound, paying attention to Symone's body while also feeling deep pleasure from Symone's energy and essence. Malcolm and Symone had made love with others in the past, but they had never experienced this level of entanglement with another person. With every touch, Malcolm's senses attached to Symone's starpower flowing through her veins. The physical satisfaction they felt from one another intensified as their powers intertwined, causing eruptions of ecstasy that they had never experienced before.

After an eternal several minutes, they fought to catch their collective breaths, giggling as Malcolm pulled them both onto the bed, and lay on his back next to her. She turned her body to face him as her hair's color changed from white to yellow to red to black. She kissed his lips and then slowly pulled away to stare at her man. She could not believe what had just happened and grasped for words to describe how perfect he felt to her. *What was that? My Akan!*

Malcolm gazed into Symone's eyes, wondering how he had become so fortunate and why it had taken him so long to express the deep, inexplicable passion he had felt for her since that fateful day in the conference room.

She stared at Malcolm's incredibly toned physique, her eyes drinking in the chocolatey delight he was. She lay next to him, placing her hands and her chin on his chest. Symone smiled at him and said, "What are you thinking right now?"

Malcolm was dazed. He pulled one of Symone's pillows and scooted it under his head to lift himself up, looking Symone up and down and admiring Akan's handiwork, his eyes lapping up every detail of her supple form. Malcolm professed, "I can't believe how amazing you are to me."

"Why can't you believe it, Malcolm?"

He took his finger and ran it from Symone's forehead down her cheek, moving a loc. "Because you are *amazing*, and I can't help but want you. I've never felt like this with anyone before."

Symone chuckled and replied, "You're just saying that because you're in your feelings."

"No," Malcolm said confidently, "I'm for real. Symone, I don't know what you've done to me. You've changed me."

"I've changed you? How?"

"Well, I don't get close to people this fast, least of all to women I'm attracted to. I'm much, much slower to react to my emotions and my desires. You're different, and as much as I've tried, I can't stay away from you."

Symone pushed herself up and sat cross-legged. "Malcolm, why do you wall up the way you do? Do you not want to get close to people?"

Malcolm joked, "Are we about to get real with each other? Wow, we really did give each other the business, huh?"

Symone remarked playfully, "I'm serious, Mal. What's so bad about you connecting to others?"

"I don't know. I guess I just got tired of letting people into my world only to get let down or hurt or disappointed, or worse, hurt them."

"What do you mean?"

Malcolm lifted and pulled Symone into him, and they laid her head on his chest, and she turned her body on her side. He laid his hand on her shoulder. He grew awkward in his head, trying to find the words to express what he was feeling. "It's just that, geez, I don't even know how to explain it."

"Never had to, I'd suspect?" Symone questioned, grabbing his right hand and gently stroking it.

"To be honest, many have tried, and I've given them all the same response."

"Mind if I try to explain it to you?"

Malcolm was taken aback. "Um, sure."

"So, you've got this incredible superpower, right? Probably the most dangerous power on Uretha. And with that power, I can imagine it isn't easy to trust people. You're useful, and people have probably tried using you to do things for them, taking advantage of your desire to help people and weaponizing it for their selfish intentions. You never said anything or probably didn't see it coming, either. But when you felt that way, you wouldn't know who to trust to say you felt like that. Friends, partners, teammates, bosses, women, men, Frimas, even your family. I can imagine you probably have sabotaged some of your relationships to break from them before they could hurt you, right?"

Malcolm was stunned at her precision. His memory was a blur, but he could recount moments when he felt exactly what she described. Staring at Symone's ceiling, he reacted, "Wow, um, yeah, that's quite accurate, Symone."

"It probably wasn't just your powers, either. Your kindness, willingness to try, and selflessness, you've guarded it all with the full fury of your powers and your ferocious heart."

"Yeah, yeah, you're right."

"And yet, with all that steel and brick and mortar you erected around your heart, here you are, lying next to me in my bed," Symone poignantly explained.

"Right," Malcolm squeezed Symone, still surprised at how soft and smooth her body felt against his, and she gasped. "I can't help myself. I crave you."

Symone raised an eyebrow. "And to think, you tried to resist me. That first day, in the conference room, when I came up to shake your hand," Symone laughed. "Mal, you glanced at me, then my hand, then back at me, and essentially told me, 'Screw you,' and walked out of the room."

Malcolm chuckled, recalling that day and how angry he was regarding her addition to the team. "Frimas, yeah, I was pissed. I own that."

"Well, lucky for you, I'm persistent. Wasn't gonna let your negativity get in my way."

"Oh-ho-ho," Malcolm grabbed Symone and rolled on top of her. She gleefully shrieked as he continued, "So this was your plan all along, to get me in bed and have your way with me?"

"Well, perhaps not *in bed*, though this was certainly a very, very delicious, added bonus. But no, my intention was to get closer to you and make you like me. I won't lie, Malcolm, I never expected to fall for you as hard as I have. If anything, I just wanted to fight you. I never could have imagined you would be interested in me like this.

"But I've never felt this safe with anyone in my life, and although I know this was an amazing moment between you and me, I know we haven't gotten to know each other well enough to make any claims about what we are. Still, you matter to me more than I expected and more than I've been comfortable admitting to you.

"I care about you. And I want you." Symone couldn't believe her ears as the words escaped her lips.

"Well, Symone Watson," Malcolm grinned, then moved downward and kissed Symone, "I am right here. I want and crave you, and I'm not going anywhere. It looks like you're, how'd you put it, 'stuck with me.'"

Symone stared into Malcolm's eyes and recalled, "You remember that day in the corridor when you held me by my shoulders, and you said to me, 'You're more than what's on the surface,' and 'I see you in ways you can't even imagine?'"

"I do," Malcolm replied.

"Tell me, Malcolm. What do you see in me?"

Malcolm suddenly had a dictionary's worth of words to say and didn't hesitate to answer her as if he had been saving these words for her since their battle at Sentinel Bank. "I see eternity. It's like, I've only known you a quarter, but it's like my soul remembers you beyond time. I see someone who longs for glory, to be seen, to be known for something, to make an impact, to be valued and treasured. And you are *glorious*. I see you. I know you. I value you. And I treasure you. I feel someone who, gosh, you make me *better*. I didn't realize what I was missing in my life until you came along. You, your power, I feel you inside my soul. The first time I sensed you, I can't believe I'm saying this, I felt something I've never felt before, and the closer we've become, the more intense the feeling has become, and it's transformed my entire being.

"Like you said, whatever this is, I don't want it to end. You are amazing, and I'm alright," he joked, "but together, we're destiny."

Symone's heart burst into song, the melody of Malcolm's surprising out-pouring of emotions hitting her like a wave of the ocean. His expressions put her in a spotlight she didn't realize she needed, and her soul glowed with excitement and joy as she felt seen for the first time in ages. She pulled Malcolm down and hugged him, then turned her head in his direction and kissed him on his cheek. He responded by turning his head her way, and they kissed each other once again.

Malcolm looked at his stripe. It read 18:07. "So, we still have a whole cycle before we have to get ready."

Symone grabbed hold of Malcolm, rolled him on his back, and straddled him. "Say less. It's your turn to yield to me." She mirrored Malcolm's words back to him, "I want you, I crave you, and I'm not going anywhere."

Malcolm and Symone spent the next cycle deep in the throes of passion between one another, the physical, mental, emotional, and spiritual tension between them finally unleashed onto each other, fantasy colliding with reality. They had become one.

The Analyst, meanwhile, documented and analyzed their biorhythms recorded on their stripes. The Analyst, with every fiber of his synthesized being, believed that their freshly materialized passion had awakened a force in them that would prove invaluable, unparalleled, and nearly unmatched by anyone in Uretha. In his mind, they could not fathom how important this one moment in time would be for them and the world. He looked forward to their next battle, ready to determine just how powerfully they would evolve. He tapped on his holoscreen, "02-43-5723, Malcolm and Symone holistic connections are complete. Monitor changes in demographics and statistics. Report findings to Director Mallack after the next battle."

24

Port 217

Daisy was the first to arrive at Port 210. She stood at the thin, white, seven-foot-tall marker on the street corner. She noticed the dimly lit buildings of Genesis Landing that sandwiched a small restaurant where two hovercrafts were parked. Daisy was concerned that someone could suddenly emerge from a dark corner somewhere. Then she reminded herself that she was one of the fastest people on Uretha and should be confident that she could get out of any situation.

She pondered why Malcolm had the team on this unauthorized mission. *This isn't right. Malcolm should have told Mallack what we're about to do. I don't like this. I should call Mallack.* She stared at her stripe, then looked up in confusion. *I know the bench order is lifted, but this is wrong. This is a capital offense in contract defense – only authorized missions, no vigilante work. Once the city finds out we did this, I know I won't be able to work again. This is my fourth contract, and I can't afford to screw this up, else I'll have to move out of Uri City. But I don't want to be disloyal to Malcolm, either. Frimas.* She stared at her stripe again, sighed, and then put her arm down.

Alexia rode toward Daisy on her hoverbike, landed next to her, and unsaddled her ride. "Daisy, you ready?"

Daisy shook her head and admitted, "I don't have a good feeling about this, Alexia. Mallack really doesn't know what we're about to do?"

"Of course not," Alexia shook her head. "She wouldn't have approved it if we told her."

"You don't think we should be doing this, do you?" Daisy asked.

"I don't. I think this is stupid. But Malcolm and Symone are right, and I don't want that little girl or anyone else to be trafficked. We have to help them."

"Yeah, but we could still let the director know. She's already taken enough heat as it is from our past missions," Daisy reasoned.

"Well, then, let's not mess this one up. We can deal with it afterward."

Just then, Malaysia appeared above them. She landed her hoverbike and unsaddled her ride. "You ladies ready?"

"I guess so," Daisy reacted with a gloomy look.

"I know, Daisy. This isn't by the book, but we're gonna make this work and get Lana back," Malaysia reasoned.

"I know, I know. Still doesn't make it right." She crossed her arms.

Pointing upward, Alexia interrupted, "I think I see Symone."

Symone descended from the starry night, landing next to Malaysia. Malcolm was not too far behind, landing his hoverbike and walking up to them shortly afterward. He said, "Alright, looks like Karl is all we're waiting on."

"Malcolm, I really think we should loop the director in on this," Daisy reasoned once more.

"Daisy, I know your stance on things like this. If you want out," he looked to everyone, "any of you want out, I understand. I said this earlier, this is more than likely going to get us in deep Frimas with the director and HQ, but I can't sit this out. Lana's life is at stake, and we can't afford to waste another minute. So, what do you want to do?"

Karl's massive presence walked up on the Elite just as Malcolm made his plea. "I want to stomp this Dust into the ground."

"I'm with Karl. Let's kick some ass," Alexia responded.

"No arguments from me. I'm in," Symone concurred.

"Somebody has to watch over all y'all," Malaysia reminded them.

"Well, Daisy, what's it gonna be?" Malcolm asked.

Daisy looked at the team and said, "I'm in. But if Mallack asks, I'm blaming you for this."

"Wouldn't have it any other way," Malcolm responded.

"Okay, so what's the play?" Malaysia inquired.

Malcolm reported, "Port 217 is about three blocks away." Malcolm reached his left hand out, palm face up, and his hand revealed a hologram of Port 217. The team circled his hand and leaned in to view the map. "I'm assuming they're going to meet with Dredge outside, between these two buildings."

"The perfect bottleneck," Symone chimed in.

"Exactly. We split into two teams. Symone and I will distract the crew they use outside. Malaysia, Daisy, you two will scan and search the buildings to determine where the captives are. Once you do, you two and Karl and Alexia will get them out unharmed as we all take down the suspects. Treat this like a no-kill order."

"I will call UPD and report suspicious activity happening near here. Hopefully, it will be enough to bring half the force in Genesis Landing this way to round everybody up and get the captives to their people," Symone added.

Malaysia noticed how Malcolm and Symone seemed to know more about the plan and were in sync with their responses. *Interesting.*

Malcolm continued. "The target is Lana. When you find her, get her out of the building, no questions asked. We will hand-deliver her to Dredge when we leave from here."

"We should be in and out in fifteen minutes tops," Symone returned.

"We'll need to be. UPD's rapid response units strike like lightning. We don't want to be around once they arrive," Malcolm answered.

Karl perked up, watching the volley between the two. "Well, look at you two finishing each other's sentences and all. You'd think y'all discussed this before meeting with us."

"Well, we had no choice. We couldn't bring you all in while we were still at base. Suit up, we got this," Malcolm deflected.

Symone declared, "Lana's in there. Let's get her out."

Malcolm saluted, "Elite, let's get it."

The Elite double-tapped their chests to get battle ready and silently marched to Port 217. They passed several closed buildings and open lots. They adjusted their visors to compensate for the darkness to ensure no one blitzed them from the shadows. The Eagle switched her eyesight to sense heat. They reached the 216 marker, and K.C. lifted his right fist to signal the team to stop moving. "Okay, across the street is Port 217. Eagle, Blitz, fan out and start the search."

"Copy that," the Eagle responded. She moved ahead of the team and shifted to the left. She perched behind a hovercar parked a building down and scanned the buildings. She said to the team, "Okay, so far, the buildings are not cloaked, so easy access in and out. It looks like there are four levels in each building. Guys with guns and blasters patrolling the floors. I'm reading four vault-looking rooms in each building with who might be our captives inside."

Blitz did a quick run around the buildings. She reported, "No issue with the outer perimeter. Just low-level guys with guns and blasters. No security on the rooftops. We should be able to get in and out of here without problems."

"Alright, it is now 19:55. We should be getting some action right about now," Enchantra accurately projected. A door on the side of the right building opened, and ten men draped in an array of dark colors, materials, and accessories proceeded to the end of the street. Some were armed with blasters. They scanned the street for Dredge.

One of the men said, "I don't see anyone."

"Dredge?" another yelled as he stepped forward.

"Star, make the call," K.C. instructed Starburst.

Starburst connected with Uri City Police Department. "Yes, this is UPD. What's your emergency?" the dispatcher inquired.

Starburst changed her voice to sound like she was panicked. She whispered, "Yes, I'm at Port 217 in Genesis Landing, and I see a bunch of folk outside fighting right now. It doesn't look good. Can you please send someone here? Oh Akan, they got blasters!"

"Okay, miss, where are you again? You said Port 217?" the dispatcher stated calmly.

Starburst continued, more frantic than before, "Yes, Genesis Landing, at Mission, please hurry, someone's going to—" Starburst immediately disconnected.

"Alright, Mammoth, Enchantra, Starburst, and I will distract them while you group with Blitz and the Eagle and rescue the hostages. When you're clear, make your move," K.C. commanded. "Star, you ready?"

"Ready," Starburst replied.

"3, 2, 1, go."

K.C. and Starburst revealed themselves from behind the wall of a building on Port 216 and walked forward toward the group. Their uniforms shined in the light from the lampposts. The man who stepped forward said, "Hey, who are you two? Get out of here now!"

K.C. volleyed, "We'd love to, but we were told by one of our friends that this is the spot to meet up with some locals to make a deal."

The same man squinted his beady eyes and stepped closer to them, cradling his blaster. "I'm gonna give you 'til the count of five for you and your little bitch to take a hike, else we will blast you to pieces and feed you to our dogs."

"Look, we don't want any trouble from you guys," Starburst declared. "We just want the little girl, and then we'll be on our way."

"That's right, give us Dredge's daughter Lana, and we'll walk away."

The man assumed Dredge sent proxies in his place. "Oh, I see, so you're here to make the trade for Dredge? Very well, then. I assume you have our money?"

Malcolm shook his hand while saying, "No, no, you misunderstand. There is no trade. We're here for the girl, and you get nothing but the satisfaction of walking out of here with your lives." They had Dust's full attention. The Mammoth and Enchantra took advantage and met up with Blitz and the Eagle undetected. They proceeded to the back of the left building.

"Oh, I think you're the one with the misunderstanding. It's simple, see? No money, no girl. So, if you don't have the creds, this is your last warning. Leave, now." Some of the gang members raised their blasters, while others raised their hands and charged them.

Oh, crud, K.C. thought, *we got powered in the field,* but he couldn't say anything without giving his team's position away.

"K.C., we're entering the left building now. Keep them busy," the Eagle checked in.

"Okay, you leave us no choice then," K.C. stated. Malcolm concentrated his mind on the blasters in the assailants' hands, and they all flattened and exploded in their hands, knocking them all to the ground. The powered Dust crew members stared in disbelief for a moment, then gathered their thoughts and threw energy balls of various colors at K.C. and Starburst. Starburst quickly threw up a heat shield to protect them from their blasts and hurled a star in the air that exploded about thirty feet above them. The assailants were distracted by the light show. K.C. saw a piece of metal on the ground, rolled from the heat shield while picking it up, and swiftly morphed it into a staff. He knocked a crew member in the head and onto the pavement. A thug saw him and launched an energy ball his way. K.C. stopped it with his hand and threw it into another's chest, thrusting him fifteen feet from where he stood and onto the ground. Starburst rose from the shield and started launching stars at the crew's feet, causing them to scatter and scramble to regroup and launch a counterattack.

The Eagle, Enchantra, the Mammoth, and Blitz entered the left building. The warehouse was four stories tall, with scaffolding on each floor along the walls and doors leading to different rooms. Dim lights dangled from the ceiling, making it a little tricky to see without assistance from their visors. The Mammoth ran to the middle of the floor to cause a distraction. He yelled and beat his chest, attracting the attention of every thug on the warehouse floor and scaffolds. As they leaned on the sides of the scaffolds, Enchantra concentrated her energy and lifted every crook off the ground, shocking them all and crippling their efforts to figure out who the Mammoth was and why he was there.

Blitz ran through each floor to find the hostages while the Eagle met the Mammoth in the middle of the floor. She pulled out a rifle and said to the Mammoth, "Target practice." She shot each gang member with a tranquilizer dart that ensured they would be asleep long enough for UPD to round them all up. Once they were all hit, Enchantra released them, and they crumpled to the ground.

Blitz opened one of the hostage rooms on the ground floor, and men, women, and children screamed in fear. She assured them, "It's okay, we're with the Company, come with me, let's get you guys out of here. This way!"

Everyone scrambled out of the room and down the scaffolding to leave the back of the building. Enchantra assisted as Blitz arrived at the second room and could not open the door. "Mammoth, come knock this door down," Blitz requested.

The Mammoth leaped onto the second-floor scaffolding and banged on the vault door several times, then pulled with all his might until the door broke off its hinges. He threw the door over the scaffold. More men, women, and children came out of the vault and followed Blitz's command to leave the building. Blitz ran to the third floor and easily opened the first room, directing everyone down, then ran to another vaulted room and called on the Mammoth, who pulled himself up from the second to the third-floor scaffold and broke the door the same as the other.

As the hostages walked down and out of the building, the Eagle scanned their faces, and none of them matched Lana. "Okay, team, none of these is Lana. She must be in the other building. Let's get over there and finish the job."

K.C. recognized that some of the crew were retreating toward the right building. He quickly lifted the pavement from the ground and created a wall between them and the door of the right building they came from. "No, no, you're not going anywhere," he declared.

"What do we do?" one of the gang members asked in a panic.

"Somebody shoot them already!" another one demanded.

"With what?" he asked again.

At that point, Starburst crafted a star above her head. K.C. took that star and flattened it into a strong, heated rope. He commanded it to corral them. They sat down and grimaced in pain.

The Mammoth, Enchantra, Blitz, and the Eagle barged into the second building, and they were met with a blaster assault that pelted their cloaks. They fell back and hid behind the wall. "Crap," the Eagle reacted. "We've been ambushed on the other side, K.C. They must have been signaled by someone that we're here."

"Copy that. We'll cover you," K.C. answered. "Star, come with me."

Sirens wailed in the distance. "We're running out of time, guys. We gotta hurry," Blitz announced.

K.C. and Starburst walked to the front service door. Starburst blasted it apart, and K.C. she walked through the hole. The blaster-armed thugs turned around and began shooting at them. K.C. pooled the blaster energy into a ball that Starburst then channeled her energy into, creating a bright, white mega star. K.C. then morphed the ball into a wall of white fire and pushed it in their direction. They shot at the wall to no avail. The other Elite ran into the building. With their opponents distracted, the Eagle shot them all with tranquilizers, and they fell.

Blitz, Enchantra, and the Mammoth quickly ran through the building and helped the other hostages escape the same way they had in the left building. As they ran out, the Eagle scanned them and found a little girl with two puffs crowning her head. She ran up to Lana, bent down, grabbed her hand, and said,

"Hi, Lana, my name is the Eagle. I know your daddy. He told me to come and get you and bring you to him."

Lana was crying and fought to ask, "How do I know you won't try to hurt me like the other guys?"

"Because I'm one of the good guys. I know you're scared, and you're good not to trust me. But my friends and I will not hurt you. We want to take you back to your dad, okay?"

Lana sobbed and responded, "Okay." She grabbed the Eagle's hand, and they walked out of the building together.

K.C. sandwiched the firewall, flattened it to a box, sat it in the middle of the floor, and cooled it down, reducing it to a box of coal. "Alright, team, let's get out of here. The sirens are getting closer."

Once outside, K.C. instructed the hostages, "Okay, everyone, run on this side of the building toward Mission Pier. When UPD asks, tell them the truth about what happened here. Team, let's roll."

The hostages ran to the main street. The Elite ran in the opposite direction, summoning their hoverbikes to converge at their covert location. UPD arrived at Port 217. Officers got out of their hovercars and couldn't believe the number of hostages standing outside of the buildings. They scratched their heads. One officer contacted Genesis Landing's UPD Division, "Yeah, we're going to need detectives, ambo's, the works. We got a whole situation on our hands. It looks like a trafficking ring just got busted."

As Genesis Landing's UPD prepared for a night of questions and puzzle solving, the Elite silently rode into the starry night, having pulled off their clandestine operation without a single death and with every hostage accounted for. K.C. praised the team, "Great job. You all are free to leave. The Eagle and I will deliver the package to Leicester."

"Fat chance," Blitz countered. "We're in this together, and we're all going to see this through together."

"I'm with her," the Mammoth agreed. "All the way, together."

K.C. smiled. "Very well."

The Eagle asked the little girl, "Lana, how are you?"

"I'm great, and this is wicked!" Lana screamed gleefully as she reveled in her first hoverbike ride, clenching to the Eagle with all her might while enjoying the glittering lights above, below, and beside her.

The Elite boosted their hoverbikes and blasted their way to Leicester to return Lana to her father.

About twenty minutes later, they landed as close to the safe house as possible. Leicester's nightlife had swung into full gear, with music blaring from every corner of the street, people crowding the streets watching others put on shows and demonstrations with their powers, dancing on the sidewalks, making out in the alleyways and on the walls of the buildings, everyone enjoying another night of spirited debauchery. The Elite turned their cloaks off and came out of their uniforms to blend in with the street life in Leicester. Lana gripped Malaysia's hand as they made their way to the safe house. When the Elite entered, they met the same teenager from before.

"Hi there! Can we help you find anything?"

Malcolm started to relay the code, but Symone stopped him and said without flinching, "Yes, that's something I can see myself wearing for a while."

The girl didn't skip a beat as she recognized the verbal command prompt as before and delivered the first part of the password, "Oh yeah? Silk?"

"Satin," Symone replied. Malaysia looked at Symone with amazement.

"Red?"

"Orange," Symone answered as Alexia looked dumbfounded.

"44?"

"38," Symone volleyed back as Malcolm stood dazed with wonder.

"You're in luck," the girl confirmed Symone's password, "a set just came in last night. Follow me, everyone."

Malcolm held back his fandom, everything within him wanting to jump Symone and show her how much he admired her at that moment. They walked into the dressing room. The girl said, "Okay, your outfits are in the dressing rooms, just enter and try them on."

Lana followed Malaysia into her room as the others all entered theirs. The backs of the rooms revealed the entrance to the hidden quarters. They entered and saw Dredge sitting on a couch covered with food wrappers in the commons.

"Looks like somebody made the most of room service, huh?" Alexia examined.

Dredge sat up and tried to clean himself off, "Um, yeah, well—"

He recognized Lana standing next to Malaysia and jumped out of his seat, "Lana?! Lana, come here, baby!"

Lana and Dredge ran toward each other. As Dredge knelt, Lana leapt into her father's arms and bear-hugged him. Tears ran down their faces as they embraced each other for what felt like forever.

Daisy looked at them, and her eyes welled up with tears. Karl looked at her and said, "Daisy, stop, man, you're going to make me cry, too."

"It's okay to cry, y'all. This is why we did this tonight," Symone responded, eyes glistening.

Malcolm said, "Let's let them have their moment. I'll be in one of the residences if anyone needs me." Malcolm walked behind the holoscreen to one of the residences. One by one, the team followed suit, listening to Lana and Dredge's exchange of love, adoration, and affection.

"I'm so sorry, baby. I promise I will never let anything bad like that happen to you ever, ever again!"

"You promise, Daddy?" Lana pleaded.

"Absolutely, I promise, baby girl. Nothing like this will happen ever, ever again. Daddy will keep you safe always. I am so sorry I let this happen to you. Thankfully, I had my friends to come and help me find you and bring you back to me."

"They were amazing, Daddy! And the Eagle, she let me ride on the back of her hoverbike, and I could see the stars!"

"That's awesome! I'll get a bike one day, and we can do that every night!"

"Daddy, I love you!"

"I love you, too, Lana, so very much!"

Malcolm chuckled and grinned as he listened to them from his doorway. Symone noticed his grin as she was about to walk to her residence and said, "I see that! Well, well, a smile! Look at you all happy and stuff."

Malcolm rolled his eyes playfully and responded, "I mean, it's not like I don't have a heart for the babies. We did good tonight."

"So good, this felt good, Mal, right?"

"So good," Malcolm agreed as Malaysia walked past them without saying a word. Malaysia took note of their closeness and pressed on to her residence to clean up.

"I can only hope this is the start of some really good momentum for us all," Symone projected.

"Same here. I feel like this might get us back on track. Well, come on, we gotta clean up and get Dredge and Lana out of here," Malcolm motioned Symone in.

"Wait, you don't mind me coming in?" Symone asked.

"I mean, there's no point in us trying to hide."

"But what about the team and what everybody might think?"

"Let's be honest, everybody on the team knows about us, so I don't think they really care what we do at this point. And I don't have anything to hide. No pressure, though. I'm gonna leave the door open." Malcolm backed up and walked toward the bathroom. Symone raised an eyebrow and smirked, then followed Malcolm into the residence and closed the door.

About ten minutes later, everyone walked out of the residences and back to the commons, where Dredge and Lana were on the couch talking. Malcolm said, "Okay, everyone, ready to go?"

"Yes!" Lana jumped off the couch with excitement.

"Most definitely," Dredge said. "Listen, everyone, I cannot thank you enough for coming through for me. It means a lot to me that you went out of your way to save my little girl."

"Dredge, we were happy to do it. But listen, you gotta make better choices, my brother," Alexia advised.

"For real, next time you decide to do some work for somebody, do a better job of screening them so you don't end up in a situation like this again. Just like you said to us," Malaysia pointed to Lana, "she didn't deserve this."

"You're absolutely right, guys," Dredge said. "From now on, I'll do better at taking the right jobs."

"And listen, if you need help trying to kick your gambling habits so you can keep your creds, we can point you in the right direction with that," Karl offered. "You got skills, as we're discovering with this drive you built for the Collector, I'm assuming."

"Speaking of," Dredge said, "that drive, it's designed to challenge you. I'm not supposed to say anything, and the Collector could probably kill me, so I'm not going to risk my daughter for you all any more than this. It's not just going to give up the coordinates to your boy. When your team finally cracks it, prepare yourself. The Collector wants to play a game with you. To what end, I do not know. But aesthetically speaking, this drive is a masterpiece."

The Elite sighed. "Great. Well, given that Lana was our highest concern, we will let you slide with this and take your word for it. Don't let us see you again, Dredge. I want to like you, but you just put a sour taste in my mouth again," Malcolm reacted.

"Say no more. I'm out of your hair. Lana, let's go, baby!"

"Thank you, Eagle, everybody!" Lana yelled. "Bye!"

Everyone walked out of the safe house and through the dressing rooms. They met the girl one last time, and she asked, "Did you find everything you like?"

Malcolm looked at Symone to see if she knew what to say. Symone silently shook her head, and Malcolm responded. "Everything was wonderful, but we will go elsewhere for what we're looking for."

"Okay, come back and see us!"

They walked onto the crowded sidewalk. Dredge pressed his left wrist twice and dragged his finger up his arm. Moments later, his hovercar appeared. The doors opened, and Lana jumped in first. "Again, thank you all. I won't forget this. The Collector was right about you all."

The Elite watched as Dredge's hovercar jetted away into the night sky. Malcolm wondered what he meant by *the Collector was right about you?*

"Well, what do we do now, guys?" Alexia asked.

"I'm sure I'm about to get a call from the Director soon, so I'm waiting for her to call me," Malcolm answered.

"Oh yeah, you're going to get cussed all the way out!" Malaysia agreed.

"Why would he get cussed out?" Symone wondered.

"Because UPD is going to cuss Mallack out, and afterwards—" Daisy started.

"I am going to get cussed out," Malcolm finished. "It's all good, though. I knew this was coming. You guys should go home, go out, celebrate, whatever you want. I'm incredibly proud of all of you. We did great tonight, regardless of whatever hit we take. This is why we do this, and I'm so glad you all stood by us. Lana is alive and with her dad because of us, and I have no regrets."

"100%, Malcolm," Malaysia returned. "We got your back, no matter what."

Karl gave Malcolm a fist bump as he walked away. Alexia patted his shoulder and summoned her hoverbike. Malaysia walked with Alexia.

Daisy said, "Good luck, Malcolm. And remember, this could have all been avoided had you told her first."

"You're such a mom," Malcolm retorted, "but you're right. Thank you for riding with us regardless."

"I'm always going to have your back, Malcolm, even when we disagree. I'll see you tomorrow." Daisy disappeared into the crowd in the blink of an eye.

Symone stood next to Malcolm and was about to say something to him, but his stripe lit up. He answered Director Mallack's call. "Director?"

"Don't 'Director' me, Malcolm," Mallack said furiously. "What the Frimas happened in Genesis Landing tonight? Why do I have the UPD lighting fire up my butt right now?"

Malcolm fed his conversation to Symone, and she listened as Malcolm didn't flinch. "Director, I don't know what to tell you. We were all in Genesis Landing, celebrating the fact that we got the drive from Dredge without incident. We decided to go somewhere quiet and went to Port 210 to hit up a restaurant there. On our way, we saw some suspicious activity and investigated, and we got mixed up with some thugs. We heard a scream, and Blitz ran inside the warehouse and saw hostages. So, we did what we had to do. We honestly didn't know what we were stumbling upon tonight."

Symone thought, *Wait, I don't remember us going to a restaurant.* She tried to recall everything she saw at Port 210 when she landed next to Malaysia.

Mallack, meanwhile, didn't buy it. "You mean to tell me you just happened to stumble upon an entire trafficking ring by dumb luck on the same night that you retrieved a drive built under the direction of the Collector? That's what you're telling me right now, Malcolm?"

"That's *exactly* what I'm telling you, boss," Malcolm replied as Symone stared at him, noticing his steely demeanor as he delivered his lines as if he had rehearsed them for weeks. "We stood down after we turned in the drive to Intelligence. Then we got together in Genesis Landing. There was no way we could have known that a trafficking ring would be in the same spot as we would. But we couldn't do nothing, either."

Just then, Symone's eyes widened as she remembered the dimly lit restaurant with two cars parked in front of it at Port 210. *Malcolm, you slick son of a bitch! I never would have thought of that. I wondered why you told everyone to meet at Port 210. I thought it was just a good spot to gather at. You are incredible!*

Mallack gritted her teeth as she reacted, "Malcolm, I ought to suspend you, the whole Elite. This is gross insubordination on so many levels. You had no jurisdiction here, no orders from the Company, not UPD, no one. But if what you tell me is true, I shouldn't be angry with you. You busted up a major arm of the Dust trafficking ring, which is worth celebrating, I guess. Just know you and your team will get your asses handed to you in the morning, regardless. This is bull, Malcolm, and I am beyond furious with you. Good night." Mallack disconnected the call.

Symone looked at Malcolm and said, "Well, that ended terribly."

Malcolm sighed. "Yep, and believe me, it's not over yet. That was just the opening act."

"Malcolm, how the Frimas did you think of that?"

"Well, chalk it up to knowing how to take care of my people and minimize the damage we might incur for our *mistakes*, right?"

"Right." Symone looked at her stripe and said, "Well, it's 21:30, briefing won't happen for another eight or so cycles."

"Yep, that sounds about right. We should probably get some sleep," Malcolm reasoned.

"Yeah, we probably should," Symone agreed. "Or…"

Malcolm looked at Symone, and she stared into his deep brown eyes, right eyebrow cocked, smirk on her lips. It was a bona fide sign that sleeping was the last thing on their minds.

25

The Calm Before

Malcolm was surprised and terrified. It was 04:28. A debrief had never started this late past the rising. He fully expected to sit in his favorite chair next to Alexia and Symone in the conference room, with the director, Stephanie, Dax, and the Analyst up front. The Elite had never been assembled in Mallack's office before. And from his memory, her office was one of the few places where audio and video could be disabled. He felt this would be a discussion unlike any other his boss had held with his team.

AI had delivered additional chairs into Mallack's office to accommodate the team before they got there. Daisy looked at Malcolm, and her eyes communicated all she wanted to say to him. Symone looked at Alexia, then Malaysia. Standing at the window, Karl admired the skyline. He then turned and looked at Malcolm. Malcolm was standing at the wall where Mallack's holoscreen hung. He held his face down organizing his thoughts, rehearsing his lines in his head. Regardless of his prep work, he fully expected he would botch this conversation.

Symone cut through the silence. "Everybody okay?"

"Nope," Malaysia summed. No one else said a word. Symone felt the apprehension weighing down on the team like her aura when she powered up. Symone glanced at Malcolm once more, reflecting on the events of the past twelve cycles and the newfound passion they shared all night. She also remembered Malcolm's statement that the previous night's phone call was only the beginning of their pending reprimand.

Symone sent Malcolm a message on his stripe. He looked at his stripe and read, "Just tell the truth. We got your back. Well, except for Daisy."

Malcolm grinned and returned, "Daisy is sitting on G, waiting on O to throw us under the bus."

Symone chuckled and responded, "Sitting on G, waiting on O, that's a new one!"

Karl noted the back and forth between them and asked, "What's funny?"

Malcolm returned, "Oh, nothing. We're just thinking about how this meeting will go."

Karl walked from the window and toward a seat, speculating aloud, "I suspect we're all about to get suspended."

"That's being nice. We might all get demoted," Daisy reacted, fearing a repeat of past agencies. "The guide is clear that we violated a ton of rules. Mallack can hand us black notices today if she wants to."

"Don't catastrophize, Daisy," Alexia volleyed. "That's my job. She's right, Malcolm. The Company could break us up if they wanted to."

"We're not going to let that happen," Malaysia reassured. "We did the right thing last night, and Mallack will understand that."

"And if she doesn't?" Daisy asked.

"Then we make her," Symone stated confidently.

Everybody looked at her, then looked at Malcolm. Malcolm looked at them and smiled. "Don't look at me. She said it."

"It's like they're twins, I swear," Alexia quipped.

The Elite nodded as Symone and Malcolm looked at each other, and both of them shrugged their shoulders and said, "Well...," then chuckled.

At that moment, Director Mallack finally walked into her office. Those who were sitting in their seats stood at attention. She saw the six and said, "Oh, good, you're all here. Sit down, all of you." She hurried to her desk, pulled her chair out, and sat down.

Malcolm noticed that Stephanie, Dax, and the Analyst were not with her. Dread filled the pit of his stomach. "Where's Stephanie, Dax, and the Analyst?" Malcolm asked as he and the others sat down.

"This conversation is not for them. AI, all communications disabled. Director override."

"Acknowledged, Director Mallack. All communications, including audio, video, and stripes in this room, are disabled." Everyone's stripes turned gray, and the holoscreens on the wall and at Mallack's desk showed error messages.

"Aww crap," Alexia muttered.

"Damn right, 'aww crap,'" Mallack reacted. "Malcolm, you lied to me last night." Malcolm was about to respond, but Mallack held her hand up as she sat down. "I don't want to hear it. I know a well-rehearsed load of bull when I hear it. So, give it to me straight. What possessed you to take down an arm of Dust?"

The room was so quiet Malaysia could see the breath entering and leaving everyone's nostrils. Symone couldn't take the silence and broke it again. "Malcolm and I went to the spot to talk to Dredge. He told us that to get the drive he made for the Collector, we had to save his daughter, who was kidnapped by Dust, and make a trade."

"So, you went to save his daughter from Dust. Okay, but why did that require all of you to be there? And how was the bench order lifted if you didn't have the drive?"

Malcolm responded, "He gave us the drive before we went to save Lana."

"Wait, what?" Mallack looked dumbfounded. "You had the drive before going to Genesis Landing?"

"Yes, Director. Dredge gave us the drive, and we decided to save his daughter and everyone else Dust had kidnapped before they shipped them all off to Akan-knows-where."

"So, you roped your entire team on this unauthorized mission? How did you get past Intelligence? How'd you convince them all to meet you in Genesis Landing?"

"Well," Malaysia broke her silence, "Alexia and I were there with Malcolm and Symone to watch what we thought would be the drop."

Mallack's voice dropped, "You were at the drop? Despite being benched?!"

"Yes," Malaysia's eyes widened, reminding Mallack that she had directed her to watch them prior to it. "We provided surveillance just in case the Collector had set a trap. We didn't know what they were walking into, so when they called us..."

"...we didn't hesitate to assist them. We didn't want them to be ambushed," Alexia continued. "The Collector's good at isolating people. You know this from the Crawler and Duncan. So, we didn't want them to fall victim to another Collector kidnapping."

Mallack scratched her head. "That still doesn't explain how you got past Intelligence."

"To be honest, it wasn't that difficult," Malcolm said. "Once I gave Dax the drive, he went straight to work on cracking it. By giving him the drive, your bench order was lifted, allowing the team to act freely without being monitored. Intelligence wouldn't have had reason to watch us."

Karl tagged himself in, "When Symone told me what was going on, I didn't hesitate. I walked out of the building, and no one was the wiser."

"Symone and I waited for another cycle and some change to not raise any other suspicions," Malcolm concluded. "Dax had no clue what was going on, and we preferred it that way because we knew this was not on the books."

"For the record," Daisy wanted to clear her name, "when they told me, I wanted to tell you, Mallack. I told them that we should tell you several times." Malcolm rolled his eyes as the Daisy-throws-everyone-under-the-bus train began rolling down the track like clockwork. But Daisy shocked everyone when she said, "But he and the rest of the team were right. We couldn't tell you what was happening."

Everyone looked at Daisy with bewilderment.

"Why not?" Mallack demanded.

"Yeah, Daisy, why not?" Malaysia echoed. She and the team leaned forward to hear Daisy's explanation to Mallack.

"Because there wasn't enough time to clear this op with you, Director. Had we tried to clear it the right way, UPD would have tied you up with so much red tape that Lana and the rest of the hostages would have been shipped away. Dust probably has many ties to some of the same people we rubbed elbows with at the Power Party. There's no telling how politics would have played a role in tying our hands. And Lana would have been dead or worse, and Dredge would have given up that drive for nothing."

Malcolm's jaw dropped. Symone noticed Malcolm's reaction and wished she could have sent him a message through her stripe.

Mallack seemed unfazed by Daisy's assessment of the Elite's call to take down Dust. "So, let me get this straight. You didn't want Malcolm or Symone to be ambushed in Leicester, but you also went to a meet-up in Genesis Landing that could have been a trap, too? How could you have known that Dredge wasn't setting you up? What if the drive was fake? What if the Collector wanted to lure you into another skirmish with her Elite? Have you ever considered her reason for sending you to Dust?"

Alexia replied, "We considered all of that, Director. But Malcolm's gut told him that this was the right decision, that Dredge was telling us the truth, and his daughter's life was in danger. And after we debated, and Symone reminded us of our responsibility to the city, we had no choice but to do something, even if it was a trap."

Mallack wouldn't budge. "That still doesn't give you any excuse to keep me out of the loop. A message, a hint, something to let me know what you guys were doing. Do you all realize what you've put me through? The phone calls I've taken, the times I've gone to bat for you, covered for you, Frimas, lied for you, to keep this team together? The numerous sleepless nights I'm experiencing because I can't stop the Chancellor, senators, commissioners, or chiefs from calling me? The times the Company has questioned our decisions? And yet, here we stand again, you all having done something stupid that I have to take the hits for. I'm beginning to wonder whether I can count on you all to have my back when it matters the most."

The team stared at Mallack like wounded puppies. Everyone reflected on the countless missions they had gone on, the lives saved, the struggles overcame both externally and internally, the teammates lost, and Duncan still in the hands of the Collector. They couldn't fathom that their leader, their director, felt this way toward them. Even Alexia couldn't express herself, seeking words to combat this verbal attack but feeling absolutely deflated. Her anger boiled so hot that it produced silence in her for the first time in ages.

Malcolm's mind ran at a million miles a minute, deeply bruised by Mallack's lack of trust in him and his team, crushed by her growing disappointment in them and her hypocrisy through not telling the team her intentions and shifty decision-making. The rest of the team looked at him, then looked back down, feeling that this would probably be the end of the Elite.

Symone cut her eyes toward Malcolm. *Malcolm, say something. Anything. Fight!*

"Mallack," Malcolm said, "with all due respect, that is the biggest load of bull you've ever said to us."

"Excuse me?" Mallack gasped.

What did I just do?

Alexia's eyes widened. Malaysia shifted in her seat. Daisy worried about her job security. Karl straightened up. And Symone swooned. *Let's go! Get her!*

Frimas, we're going to get suspended anyway, Malcolm concluded. *Take your shot, Malcolm. You got this!*

His blood boiled, adrenaline rushed through his veins, and his stomach fluttered like a nervous kid in the principal's office. Malcolm threw all of his arguments out of his head and followed his gut, unleashing his heart onto Mallack with the precision of a wordsmith. "You heard me. You've been my director for seven years. And in that time, we have been through the best and worst times of city defense. We've been through personnel changes, laws changing, losing friends, and countless battles won and lost. And all the while, you have never, in the history of my time here, *never* expressed a lack of trust in us, *in me*, this deeply. Now, maybe the Collector has gotten to you, maybe your bosses are calling for your head, maybe city officials are trying to pull your strings, I don't know. But what I don't appreciate is you wondering whether we have your back because the feeling, quite frankly, goes both ways."

Malaysia and Alexia looked at Malcolm, then at each other with amazement. Malaysia thought, *Malcolm just found his balls!*

Karl said, "Malcolm, maybe you should—"

"No, not this time, Karl," Malcolm interrupted. "Now, lately, Mallack, you have made some hasty decisions yourself. You pushed us to go to the Power Party despite Alexia's objection, for which I carry some of the blame because I didn't listen to her, either."

Alexia bowed her head and smiled, humbled that Malcolm acknowledged her wisdom. Malcolm continued, "You didn't let us figure out who gave us the intel on Jackson Santana and Emma Leslie. Then you benched the team and made just Symone and me go after Dredge after we told you that the Collector thrives on isolating people. You talk about wondering whether we have your back, but have you considered whether we feel you have ours?"

Mallack felt cornered. Malcolm rightly estimated Mallack's sudden change in tactics. She had pushed her chips in with the Analyst's Affinity Theory, recalling what the Analyst told her about not disclosing their efforts in bringing

Malcolm and Symone as close together as possible. She decided to continue traveling down that rabbit hole to keep up appearances.

"You know full well I have your backs," Mallack said. "But you have to understand what you all did and what this means for the rest of the division."

Symone had been performing mental gymnastics and pieced together every part of yesterday's events. She ascertained Malcolm's true intentions from start to finish. "We know what we did, Mallack. Don't you hear us?" Symone intervened. "We knew that everything we did was going to violate the rules, so we did everything we could to make it to where no one could say that we were operating under the direction of the Company."

"That's right," Malaysia jumped in. "Alexia and I met Malcolm and Symone for a *late lunch* in Leicester after we were benched but before their meeting. The fact that the restaurant was near the meet up between them and Dredge was merely a coincidence. We stayed, but we were not there in an official capacity."

"Dredge gave us the drive, which was the mission you sent us on," Symone tagged back in. "Once we had the drive, we did what we were ordered to do and brought it back to Intelligence."

Karl continued, "And once Intelligence cleared the bench order, we all went out to celebrate in Genesis Landing. Granted, Genesis Landing isn't the greatest place to go to celebrate anything. But that was our choice."

"Exactly," Alexia agreed. "And we didn't want to go someplace with a lot of noise."

"We couldn't have known that we were going to run into a bunch of dudes in the middle of the street who got mad at Malcolm and Symone for just being in the wrong place at the wrong time," Daisy surprisingly added.

"So, you see, Mallack," Malcolm concluded, "everything we did last night, we did with you in mind. We knew you would get some phone calls from UPD and the like, but we also knew that by keeping you out of the loop, you would have...."

"...plausible deniability," Mallack finished.

Malcolm breathed a sigh of relief, "Yes. That way, we could say that we saw a situation unfolding and had no choice but to intervene. UPD got the credit for it, not the Company, and the world keeps spinning."

Mallack pushed her rolling chair back from her desk and looked out at the Elite, supremely impressed with her unit. She stared at each of them and said, "Well done, very well done. I didn't see it that way."

"Mallack, what's really going on here? What aren't you telling us?" Malcolm pressed.

Malaysia was eager to hear what Mallack's answer would be, knowing that the Affinity Theory was her primary motivation for her decisions. She hoped that maybe Mallack would see the error of her ways and course correct right now.

"Listen," Mallack deflected, "the pressures of this seat are extremely high, and I allowed it to get the better of me. I'm not just responsible for this unit but for every unit in this division. You guys are not the only ones I have to think about. That's why we have rules in place, to try to minimize any schisms between us contractors and the Chancellor's office. You all know that tensions are worsening between the powered and unpowered people if you let the politicians narrate how things are going in Uri City. So, any misstep we take, someone will try to use it to argue that we shouldn't exist, despite all the great work teams like you do for them. It's only a matter of time before this incident gets blasted in the news and turned against us. Now, I'm getting calls from everyone to suspend all of you indefinitely."

"But," Malcolm retorted.

"But," Mallack resigned, "I don't have any grounds to do so. You didn't do anything that would give cause for suspension, and you did take down an arm of a trafficking ring. That cannot be overlooked."

"So, what does this mean?" Malaysia asked.

"This means you all are dismissed. Get out of here, and don't let this happen again."

Daisy blurted out, "That's it?"

"That's all," Mallack said as everyone looked at Daisy.

"But—" she tried to continue, but Alexia swiftly delivered green mist to Daisy's lips to shut her up.

"Thank you, Director," Alexia stated. "We're going to leave now." She shot out of her seat and pulled at Daisy's arm to move her out of the office. Everyone else got up from their seats and proceeded in a line out of Mallack's office.

"Malaysia, a word?" Mallack asked.

Malcolm and Symone noticed Mallack's request for Malaysia to stay and looked at each other but didn't say anything. They kept moving forward while Malaysia stayed behind and closed the door.

"Yes, Director?" Malaysia volleyed.

"What are your thoughts? I know you have some, am I right?"

"Tons, Director. Are you playing mind games with us or something?" Malaysia shot. "You pretend to be angry with us, but you won't tell the team the truth about what you're really after."

"You know I can't do that," Mallack reasoned.

"Yes, you can and *should*. You're tearing at the threads of this team and losing their trust in you in the process. Frimas, you're starting to lose mine."

"We just have to hold on a few more days. Once we have Duncan's location, we'll get him back, and you all will defeat the Collector and his goons. Then all will be revealed, and we can move on from this."

"Yeah, you might move on from this, but I can almost guarantee you that if you keep this up, the team is going to move on from *you*," Malaysia held no punches.

"Listen, did you see any improvement from them powers-wise?"

"Honestly, no, Director. They've gotten closer. Something's changed between yesterday and today between them, but I don't know if it affected their powers yesterday. You'll have to watch the tape to find out."

Mallack got irritated, "Your job was to...."

"...observe, I know. But I couldn't watch them and rescue the hostages at the same time. We did what we had to do and completed the mission, Director. The battle wasn't with Dredge, so I have nothing to report."

"Okay, okay," Mallack gave up. "You can go."

Malaysia started walking away, then turned to face the Director again. "You know, Malcolm is right about one thing – you're hiding something, driven by some ulterior motive. And whatever that thing is, you better hope it doesn't get one of us killed."

Malaysia walked out of the office, leaving Mallack alone once more. She wrestled with her feelings but resolved to stay the course. She knew what was at stake, recalling the Collector, her army, and how easily Duncan had been captured. She would not allow her emotions to jeopardize her mission.

Malaysia walked down the corridor, and when she turned to go to the quarters, she ran into Malcolm and Symone, who were waiting for her to leave Mallack's office. "Malaysia, everything okay?" Malcolm asked.

Without flinching, she said, "No, Mallack's out of control, and I don't know how much more she can take before she pops like a cork."

"Tell me about it. Any reason why you think she might be cracking under pressure like this?" Symone inquired.

"If you ask me," Malaysia rationalized, "she's got some special project she's working on that she won't tell anyone about, and somehow it includes us. And it's possible that we're screwing it up."

"Special project?" Malcolm perked up as they walked to the quarters together.

"Yes. She wanted to know if I had seen anything out of the ordinary with us yesterday since I have the power to see everything, and I told her no. Then I told her that whatever she has going on, she needed to get it together before she ends up losing us as a team. After today, I know she has one more time to treat us like that, and I'm definitely going to start looking for another defense to contract with."

Malcolm stood before Malaysia and said, "No way, you wouldn't leave like that."

"Malcolm, you know me. I don't ask for much, just to be appreciated for what I do. If neither she nor the Company appreciates me, I'll find someone else who will. It's not that hard for me. Frimas, I can work for myself, even."

Symone listened and understood where she was coming from. Malcolm told Malaysia, "Well, I know you will do what's best for you. But before you ever decide to leave the Company, just make sure you talk to me about it first, that's all I ask."

"You better pick up the phone," Malaysia quipped. They walked silently to the quarters and opened the door. Alexia, Karl, and Daisy were inside the commons. Malaysia walked to the commons and sat down in a recliner.

Malcolm and Symone walked to the kitchen. Malcolm pressed buttons on the pad on the countertop and asked for juice. "Symone, you want something?"

"Just some water," she answered. Malcolm tapped on the keys. His juice rose from the countertop opening. A moment later, Symone's water rose near her. They grabbed their glasses and drank from them, standing side-by-side. Malcolm felt the urge to pull Symone closer to him but kept his hands to himself while Symone placed her hand on Malcolm's back and gently rubbed him. "So, what are we going to do now?"

Malcolm said, "Well, we're still waiting for Dax and Stephanie to crack the drive. And though I'd love a training session right now, I don't think I'd be able to think straight if you followed me in there."

"Mmm hmm, I'd probably handle you easily now that you've seen and tasted my assets," Symone joked.

Malcolm chuckled while reminiscing on Symone's remarkable physique. "Is that a challenge, *Miss Watson*?"

"I mean, I'm ready for whatever, whenever. The question is, can your pride handle yielding to me?"

"Last I remember, you were the one yielding to me."

"That's only because you beat me in a race and made me."

"Well, how about we take our battle to the streets instead of going to a training room."

"What, you wanna scrap outside?"

Malcolm laughed, and Alexia perked up to pay attention to what they were saying.

"Oh, no, not like that. There's an arcade about ten minutes from here. Let's run through there and go head-to-head on everything in it. The loser has to do whatever the winner wants her to do."

"You're talking like you already know who's going to win, Mal," Symone recalled his line the last time they went head-to-head.

"Ooh, I wanna go!" Alexia jumped up.

Malcolm and Symone's thoughts were in-sync. They both thought, *Man, I don't want anyone else to go, but I also don't want anyone to feel iced out or left behind until we decide to tell everyone what we are. I should say okay.*

Malcolm broke the awkward silence, "Sure, come along."

"Where are we going?" Karl asked.

"To the arcade," Alexia replied.

"Oh wow, I haven't been to an arcade in a while!" Malaysia cheered.

"That sounds like a real treat!" Daisy imagined.

"Yes, let's all go!" Symone agreed. "We all could use some fun."

"So true. We'll eat and play, give us a little break before Intelligence cracks the drive," Malcolm reasoned. "Come on, let's get out of here so I can break Symone's heart and bruise her ego."

The team heckled Symone, and she returned, "Oh, no, no, let's be clear on whose pride is about to be shattered." The team heckled Malcolm. As everyone rose from their seats and began to leave the quarters, Malcolm and Symone looked at each other and smiled, thinking, *How did I get so lucky?*

About fifteen minutes later, the Elite arrived at The Stadium, a virtual arcade filled with a vast array of simulators from every game genre. The bright strobe lights broke the darkness of the room, and the music reverberated throughout the gigantic arena, interrupted by the sounds of the holoscreens that displayed what players saw through their VR visors.

Malcolm said, "Okay, so let's eat first so Symone can get her strength up, and then let's go to war."

"Mmm, yes, food," Karl reacted. He speed-stomped to the dining area and quickly found a table for everyone. The crew followed him and sat down. They ordered a variety of appetizers, entrées, and drinks and bantered with each other.

"So, wait, Daisy, let's talk about what happened in that room. Like, you were a totally different person in there today, defending us like that!" Alexia recounted.

"I mean," she said while swallowing her food, "I know we were wrong, but I saw the looks on those hostages' faces last night. We did well, getting them out of there and back to their homes safely. Dust deserves to live under the jail for what they put those people through."

"Yeah, but we just knew you were going to throw us under the bus," Malaysia remarked.

"Yeah, yeah, I know you guys think that I'm a stickler for the rules—"

"Because you *are*," Malaysia snapped back playfully.

"Yeah, I am. But I'm not a fool, either. I only act like this because I'm scared. You all know my history. I've lost jobs because I didn't always follow the rules and rubbed my bosses the wrong way. So, I try to do everything right and not cost myself another opportunity to do what I do best. Still, I think we did the right thing."

"Really?" Symone asked. "I didn't know that."

"Well, yeah, that's my story," Daisy said. "Besides, I didn't want to get in trouble with Malcolm."

Malcolm cleared his throat, "Wait, with me?"

"Yes, you. You know how you get when someone crosses you. I didn't want to end up on your bad side."

"Wait, how does he get again? I forgot," Symone was taking notes. Malcolm rolled his eyes.

"Oh, he won't talk to you, answers questions quickly, basically treats you like the plague."

"Oh, so that's not just when something's bothering him. That's his default," Symone laughed as she pressed Malcolm's shoulder and smiled at him.

"Yeah, girl, you're getting him down to a science now," Alexia said.

"What y'all are not going to do is pick on me," Malcolm retorted. "I do that so that I don't say what's on my mind and end up hurting somebody's feelings."

"What, like today?" Karl spoke up. "Brother, what you did in there with Mallack?" Karl clapped his hands a few times.

"Yes, let's give it up for Malcolm Bennett, who found his nuts today and put them on the table!" Malaysia cheered as everyone started clapping.

"The Frimas, man!" Malcolm laughed.

"Yo, brother, I've never seen you take on Mallack and stand up for us like that before. I think you were ready to get fired at that point, talking, 'that's the biggest load of bull I've ever heard in my entire life,' man, I was like, 'Ohhhh-hhhh!'" Karl exaggerated.

"Yes, that speech was gold!" Malaysia declared.

"Man, y'all are wilding!" Malcolm giggled. "What's crazy, though, is how we tag-teamed that whole thing. I said something, then Symone, then Malaysia, then Symone again, then you, Karl, then Alexia, and then you, Daisy. You guys are teaching me something that seven years of battles with the Company haven't. And I'm mad it's taken me this long to realize it, so I have Symone to thank for helping me see it. We really are a team, a family. And we improve each other everywhere, not just in the field. At that moment with Mallack, I felt, no, I *knew* that you all had my back, no matter the outcome. That's why I spoke up. And Mallack was getting on my nerves."

"Well, Malcolm, we will always have your back. No matter what happens, you'll never have reason to doubt that. Our team, our family, all seven of us, we got each other's backs. You taught us that, and I'm just glad to hear that you believe it," Alexia revealed.

"Thanks, guys," Malcolm said as he raised his glass and drank from it. "Alright, let's finish this last bit of food here and get to destroying some souls!"

"See, you keep talking like you're about to mop the floor with me. Don't get your feelings hurt today," Symone bantered.

"Hmm, sorry, I couldn't hear you between me chewing and this wall of bull you keep building," Malcolm joked.

"Hurry up so I can beat your ass already!" Symone's competitive streak was building up as she enjoyed their interaction.

They all finished their meals and walked away from the dining area onto the arena floor. For two cycles, the Elite bounced from one simulator to another, going head-to-head in some and teaming up in others. They shared joyous victories and agonizing defeats. Symone could be seen at times reveling in her strength and at others wallowing in sorrow, while Malcolm seemed unfazed either way, enjoying watching Symone's mood swing like a pendulum. Malaysia continued to monitor their interactions while defeating every game she played and racking up unreachable, unparalleled high scores. Daisy made sure not to break machines by tapping buttons too fast, while Karl enjoyed playing strength games, and Alexia played multiple simulators at once. The Elite took over the Stadium and bathed in this moment of childlike wonder and joy.

At one point, Malcolm was standing near a railing. Malaysia walked up to him with a bag of prizes in one hand, a huge green cup in another, and a pair of kiddie shades over her eyes. "Hey, Malcolm!"

"Damn, Malaysia! It looks like you've had a Frim of a time!"

"You know I never miss!" she agreed as she stood beside him. "I didn't know how much I needed this. Such a great time!"

"You're so right."

"So, talk to me. How are things with you and Symone?"

Malcolm answered, "You know, things are going really well, better than I ever expected."

"What do you mean?"

"We haven't said anything official to each other, but I think it's safe to assume we are together," Malcolm reasoned.

Malaysia's eyes grew wide as she noticed Malcolm's body integrity shift. She pulled the sunglasses off and inquired, "Did something happen yesterday?"

"Yeah, something happened. Multiple times, actually," Symone admitted gleefully to Alexia while smacking on some candy she won from the rewards room. They were talking near the dining area. "Oh Akan, Malcolm is amazing!" Symone's eyes shined red.

"Aaah, girl, look at you! That's a wholly different glow you're giving off," Alexia cheered. "So, give me details! How did this happen?"

"I mean, after Karl left, Malcolm came in the quarters and came to my room, and it was like, he just took charge. He knew what he wanted and who he wanted it from. But he was such a gentleman. He was so focused on taking care of me, completely satisfying me. And he knew what I wanted, too, *and* exactly how to give it to me. Just thinking about it gives me chills."

"Uh huh," Alexia reveled, tempted to peek at Symone's mind to get a more personal recount of last night's experience.

"I've been with plenty of women, but I have never felt anything like what I feel for her. It's like I've known her my whole life, like I didn't know what I was missing before she came along and showed me what it was. And I still don't know, but she either has it or is it," Malcolm relayed to Malaysia.

"Malcolm, you're usually not this emotionally expressive. She's definitely changed you."

"I agree. Something's definitely wrong with me, right?"

Malaysia laughed as she pressed into Malcolm's shoulder. "No, silly. You like her, and she likes you. It's beautiful, and it's about time! You deserve a win. And she's a great catch!"

"When we get past all this stuff, or Frimas, maybe in between, we should go on a double date," Malcolm suggested.

"Frimas, yeah, we should!" Malaysia agreed. "My man has been dying to meet you, and we just never put anything in the books."

"I think Malcolm would enjoy us all hanging out with each other," Symone told Alexia. "It's crazy, I expected him to be an ogre, but he's a really great, open-minded guy, so easy to get along with. And unpredictable."

"Well, hopefully, you two go the distance. I'm really happy for you guys."

"Thank you, Alexia! I probably wouldn't be here had you not told me to spar with him."

"I'm sure you would have figured that part out all alone. But I am glad to know I'm part of you guys' origin story!"

"I mean, you were the one who told me to figure it out," Malcolm said to Malaysia. "Thank you for being my closest friend."

Malaysia heard those words, and her heart churned. *I should tell him. This isn't fair or right. Screw it, I'm going to tell him!*

"Malcolm, I need to tell you something," Malaysia started.

"What's going on? Everything okay?"

"Well—"

Everyone's stripes buzzed and lit red. They read the message, "ELITE: Dredge's drive has been cracked. Report to Intelligence immediately to receive the Collector's message."

"Dredge was right. Of course, it's going to be a game. Why wouldn't it be a game?" Malcolm gritted his teeth. "What were you going to tell me, Malaysia?"

"Oh," Malaysia resigned. "It can wait. Let's go."

"You sure?"

"Yeah, we're one step closer to getting Duncan back. This isn't that important. We can talk about it later tonight."

"Okay, well, let's round everybody up and get back to base."

"Okay." Malaysia sighed internally. *The director is right. We cannot let the Collector win. After the mission. We'll tell them after the mission.*

26

Exposed

The Elite sat in Intelligence, ready to receive the next piece of the Collector's puzzle.

"Alright, Dax, play the message," Stephanie told him.

"Yes, ma'am." Dax pressed play on his countertop, and the unit watched the holoscreen in front of them. The screen scrambled, then displayed the Collector in her black garb, fully masked, sitting at her desk.

Three seconds of silence, then, "Is it on? Okay, ahem," she cleared her throat. "Great rising, or midday, or evening, or night, whenever it is that your team finally decodes Dredge's drive. Before we get to the particulars, I want to first tell you thank you so much for helping him out. Dredge is a terrible decision maker, and he just doesn't know when to get out of his own way. His daughter didn't deserve to get caught up in all that, and I knew you would set your personal grudge against me aside and do the right thing for him and his little girl. You guys are truly amazing, which proves that I know you all very, very well."

"My Akan, why is she like this?" Alexia yelled.

"No idea," Malaysia responded.

The Collector continued. "Again, many thanks to you. We both know by now that Dust is a terrible group, and although you didn't stop them completely, you definitely sent a message to their leader that you, well, I, have my eyes on them, and I've put them on notice that they'd better get their acts together, else they will have to answer to me."

Malcolm blurted out, "I knew it!"

The message played on. "Your generosity and courage will not go overlooked. Now, let's get to the matter at hand. I have someone you want, and you have something I need. So, in the continued spirit of trades, I am making this offer to you.

"I had Dredge build this beautiful piece of technology that came straight from this mind of mine, and on it, you will find the location of your friend Ammo. He won't tell me his name, and of course, none of my friends or techies can get his personal information from his stripe thanks to your people. You have always had the best technology that makes it impossible for anyone to know who you really are. Constantly scrubbing demographics off the grid, your true identities hidden from the world so that we can't find you and, well, wipe you off the board in your sleep."

"I got a bad feeling about this," Daisy felt in her gut.

"It got me thinking, 'Hmm, how amazing would it be if I could somehow get my hands on the identities of the Company's powered? If I know who they are, that would be more valuable than any power I could ever swipe from anyone.' Then I thought, 'Oh, I have Ammo, and I know that the Elite want their boy back.' And it hit me!"

"Ah wow," Symone figured it out.

"What if I make a trade? Yes, I give you your boy in exchange for the information on every single powered individual employed by Uri City's Company? Yes! That would make me the single most powerful person in the city and allow me to bend you all to my will, knowing that at any given moment, I could expose you all and have all your enemies hunt you in your sleep!" The Collector shivered and bellowed, "Ooh, the thought of that alone is making me orgasmic!"

"This bitch!" Alexia screamed in rage, and her eyes glowed green.

"So, here is the deal. Ammo is housed at a currently undisclosed location. I am a fair person, and I believe in giving people choices, so here are yours. Place the drive in a console in your unit, and it will give you Ammo's location while I am data mining all your personnel files for the names and faces of your defenders. It won't take me long to get what I need no more than it will take you long to extract the information you need to find your boy. Now, you can choose not to place the drive in. You could probably find some other way to get the information you want off the drive without compromising the Company. But Dredge ensured me that by the time you get the information any other way, I will have plenty of time to take your boy's power and kill him. And we'll be back to square one all over again. As this message is playing, a clock has begun, of which you now have less than ten cycles to make your decision. If, at the end of ten cycles, you have not placed the drive in your system and I don't have my data, Ammo dies.

"So, that's all I got. I thank you once again for helping my boy Dredge out with Lana. They are really sweet people, and you were so thoughtful by getting him out of that mess for me. Well, the clock ticks. Don't take too much time debating on what you will do. Else, Ammo, well, he'll have one more piece of ammo in his body than he wanted. Okay, bye!"

The holoscreen went blank.

"Are you kidding me?" Karl muttered.

The team looked around at each other. Malcolm was flustered like the rest of them. The rage built up in his chest created a laser-like focus in his mind. "Dax, how long would it take you to extract the information from the drive?"

Dax put his hand to his face and rubbed his chin. He quickly tabulated an estimated time, "Even with the head start we've had prior to the countdown, it would take two days, Malcolm, I'm sorry. Dredge is one intelligent son of a bitch."

"So," Alexia said, "let's find him and get him to crack this thing."

"That wouldn't help us," Stephanie regretfully informed the team. "Dredge built this drive with a level of sophistication that renders even him unable to bypass the locking mechanisms in time. If Dredge could be trusted, he should be working for us."

Symone gasped. "You're telling me that the only way we can get Duncan's location in time is by inserting that drive into a console in this place?"

"Yes. Our initial scans show that Dredge built a code within it that allows the drive to recognize our machines. It literally cannot work anywhere else off-site. No other holoscreen anywhere on Uretha can reveal his location, just ours here. And it has to be connected to the server. If it doesn't recognize a transfer of accepted data, it will not give up Duncan."

Alexia detoured, "Okay, before we argue this all out, can we first talk about the fact that the Collector really did have us do her dirty work for her?"

"No crap!" Malcolm shot out. "Malaysia, you were right when you said she's laying to waste her enemies until she's the last one standing. I told you all, we're being directed, and now we know why. Symone, you were right all along."

"What do you mean?" Symone asked.

"The Collector is building her army. And now she has us right where she wants us. If we give in to her, she will have a master list of every powered person in the Company and pick and choose whose powers she wants."

"Y'all, this lady is playing us, and it's working," Malaysia said.

"You're not suggesting that we give her what she wants, are you?" Stephanie worried.

"We can't just sit here and do nothing while Duncan's life hangs in the balance. He's one of us," Malaysia explained.

"But one life shouldn't cost us the entire division. You're talking about a couple hundred defenders, not to mention our UCs," Dax chimed in.

"The man's got a point," Karl said.

Alexia was surprised. "You're agreeing with him?"

"I didn't say that," Karl lifted up a hand and tilted his head slightly. "I just said he has a point. We're weighing one person's life over the entire Company in Uri City. We are deciding right now whether Duncan's life is worth us giving up the entire Company to our nemesis."

"For me, it's a no-brainer. Duncan is family."

"But it's not that simple, Alexia," Daisy argued. "We're talking about the Company. The Collector is an enemy. If we give our enemy our most prized secret – our identities – we're giving her the ability to wipe us off the board one by one. Just like we said, we're doing her dirty work for her. She has us pinned in a corner, but I don't think the answer is simply giving it up to her."

"It hasn't been that simple since we've been dealing with her," Malcolm said. "This whole time, she's been a mile ahead of us, and once again, she has us stuck with an impossible choice. I don't want to leave Duncan behind, but I also don't want to give the Collector what she wants. We don't know what her motives are—"

"You're right about that," Symone interrupted. "I still think she's building an army, but we don't know why. We don't even know if that's really what she wants. For all we know, this, us spinning our wheels, is more what she wants than anything else."

"This is insanity," Malaysia said as she planted her clasped hands on her head. "Malcolm, what are we going to do?"

Malcolm crossed his arms and slammed his back into the back of his seat. He rocked the chair for a minute while everyone waited for his response. He reasoned that a decision of this magnitude should not be left up to him, and instead should be made by the director of the division. He replied to Malaysia, "Call Mallack."

Dax tapped on keys and called Director Mallack. "This is Mallack."

Dax stated, "Director, this is Intelligence. I have the Elite unit with us."

"Okay. What was the Collector's message?"

Malcolm answered, "Long story short, the Collector wants us to trade Duncan's life for the identities of the entire Company's defenders. And we have less than ten cycles to make the call. The drive is too sophisticated to secure Duncan's location. If we don't give her the information, she will take his powers and kill him. What do you want us to do?"

Mallack got quiet. About thirty seconds later, she replied, "Malcolm, I leave the decision up to you."

Stunned, Malcolm blurted, "The Frimas?"

"Malcolm, you said that trust goes both ways. You were right. So rather than make a hasty decision, I am entrusting this decision – to save your teammate or protect the Company – to you. Whatever you decide, I back you and your team 100%. We will support you and give you whatever you need to get the job done."

Malcolm felt his heart beating out of his chest as he agonized over the heavy burden laid on his shoulders. He catastrophized, feeling that the ramifications of this decision would echo throughout the Company for decades. But he also could not leave Duncan behind knowing that he did nothing to try to get him home.

He took a deep breath and replied, "We're going to get Duncan back."

Alexia did a fist pump and let out a silent cheer. Symone smiled, Daisy stared in terror, and Malaysia and Karl let out a collective sigh.

Malcolm went into planning mode and began, "Here's what we're going to do. Send out an emergency call to every defender and UC in the Company. Tell them to return to base. Tell them to not ask questions, and that this is not a drill. We need them back here immediately. Abort all missions and bring them home."

Stephanie nodded, "Okay."

"Once they're all here, we will insert the drive in a console here in Intelligence. Extract the information you need to get Duncan's location. Once you have it, disconnect the drive. We will live with whatever she's extracted and plan accordingly. If you can't get the information on Duncan by the time the Collector's data mined all our information, then she deserves it all, and we need to find Dredge after this and give him a job."

"Copy that," Dax responded.

"Once we have all the information we need, team, we'll reconvene in the conference room and go over what the plan is to make sure we get this right. The mission is Duncan. But should the Collector make an appearance, killing her will instantly become top priority. Because this has got to stop."

"That's what I'm talking about," Alexia reacted as her eyes lit green.

"Alright, Stephanie, make the call."

Stephanie sighed and said, "Dax, do it."

Dax tapped on the keys, and the holoscreen revealed Dax's screen which prompted him to make a live voice recording. He pressed the record button and said, "Attention, all defenders, all undercover operatives, from all units. Whisper Protocol has been initiated. All defenders, all undercover operatives, from all units, report to the Company immediately. Whisper Protocol has been initiated. Abort all missions and return to base immediately. This is not a drill." He sent the message to every defender and undercover operative.

"Whisper Protocol?" Symone questioned.

"Whisper Protocol is the Company's panic button. If WP is initiated, everyone assumes that the Company has been compromised, and all hands are on deck to face whatever has come upon us. We only use it in case of emergencies, and, well, this is an emergency," Dax explained. He tapped on keys, and a map displaying all of Uri City appeared. On it, several blue dots were scattered across the map, representing every Company defender and UC. Within moments, the dots all started converging to the Highgarden District, where the Company called its base home.

"How long before the last person gets here?" Malcolm asked.

"I'd say about ninety minutes give or take traffic," Stephanie reported.

"Okay," Malcolm declared as he stood up and began walking toward the door. "Stephanie, call us when everyone is here and accounted for."

"Copy that, Malcolm."

Symone rose to meet Malcolm at the door. "Hey, Malcolm, are we sure this is the right call?"

"Honestly, no, I'm not sure at all. But I do know that we have to save Duncan. It's the only call we have that can guarantee us a shot at getting him back."

"I agree," Karl overheard them. "This was the best call, and it was smart of you to get everybody back here."

"Figured that if we know whose information gets extracted, we can provide them and their associates with protection until further notice. Minimize the damage as much as we can."

"Okay, so what do we do until then, Malcolm?" Malaysia asked.

"Well, I'm going to the quarters and laying my head down. I'm tired."

"That sounds like a good idea, actually," Alexia said.

"Come on, y'all, let's chill out for a little bit, and once Intelligence is finished, we'll kick back into gear again," Malcolm suggested.

The team left Intelligence and walked together to the quarters. Malcolm made a beeline to his residence. Alexia followed suit. The rest of the team sat in the commons.

A cycle went by. Symone went to Malcolm's residence and slid open the door. She found Malcolm sitting on his couch, his head leaning on the wall, knocked out, the news anchors on the holoscreen keeping him company and watching over him as he slept. She saw the news anchors discussing the round-up of Dust in Genesis Landing and thought, *Mallack was right, didn't take them any time to start talking about it.*

Symone walked to the couch, sat down, then curled her body on it while laying her head on Malcolm's lap. Malcolm was slightly jostled out of his sleep and noticed Symone lying on him. He placed his arm on her shoulder and fell back asleep. Symone felt a sense of peace that she hadn't felt in a while as she drifted off to sleep, too.

In the meantime, Malaysia, Daisy, Karl, and Alexia were gathered in the commons. Daisy had long sensed Malcolm and Symone getting closer together, and she decided now was a good time to confirm her suspicions. "Have any of you noticed Symone and Malcolm have gotten really, really close lately?"

"Girl, you're late," Alexia replied from the kitchen. "Everybody noticed that. Isn't it beautiful?"

"But he's her mentor," Daisy analyzed.

"So? There's no rule against it," Malaysia countered.

"And besides, they're perfect for each other. They're both smart, savvy, competitive, and quirky. It's like destiny meant for them to get together," Alexia offered.

"And it hasn't caused any problems in the field. Like, none. They are both extremely focused," Karl added. "I told Malcolm a while back that I didn't want him to lose focus on us as a team. It seems like the closer they have gotten, the more focused he's gotten. She's made him better."

Malaysia concurred. "Right? The more they connect, the stronger they're getting in every way. Malcolm's speaking up more, being more of a leader to us all. And his powers, he's harnessed more of it than ever before."

"And Symone," Alexia diagnosed, "even she has gotten stronger with hers. I swear she's going to burn down the training room one day."

Daisy wouldn't let it go. "Guys, you don't think it's a bad look, though? He's supposed to be training her. The Company can't think this is a good idea if they're getting close like that. I mean, are they hooking up?" she protested.

"I don't know," Malaysia lied, "but even if they are, we all can agree, they're not worse for it."

"My goodness, first we're pulling unauthorized jobs, now we're hooking up with subordinates," Daisy sounded dumbfounded. "What's next, we're going to usurp the Company and run it ourselves?"

"Daisy, you really need to lighten up a little," Karl tried to calm her down. "You are literally the only person who thinks about rules and morals as if they can't be flexible. I know you're scared that you're going to get kicked out of the Company, and your drive to live by your morals and the rules governs the decisions you make. But life is much more beautiful when you allow yourself space to live outside the lines from time to time."

Daisy sighed. "I don't get it. You might be right, that Malcolm and Symone are better and all that. But it still doesn't justify them hooking up while he's mentoring her. That just feels wrong to me."

"Well, just remember that they are still very much a part of this team, and whatever they're doing, it's working. And we're all better for it," Malaysia capped the conversation. "Don't try to fix what isn't broken."

"Whatever," Daisy surrendered.

Alexia walked to the couch and sat next to Malaysia. She whispered, "For real, it is okay, right?"

Malaysia quickly answered, "Who's going to break them up? You?"

"Frimas naw," Alexia smiled and laughed. "I like this version of Malcolm infinity percent better."

"Exactly."

About twenty more minutes went by, and the Elites' stripes buzzed and lit red. "ELITE: All defenders and UC's have returned to base and are accounted for. Report to Intelligence."

Malcolm slowly shook off the sleep from his head and lifted his arm up to read the message. He gently shook Symone, "Hey, Symone. Wake up."

"Huh? Oh, is it time?" Symone groggily asked.

"Yeah, it's time. You ready?"

Symone slowly got up and responded, "No, not really. But are we ever?"

"Good point." Malcolm pulled Symone's head slowly toward his, kissed Symone's forehead, then her lips. "Let's go."

Symone shivered in delight and answered, "Okay."

They got up from the couch and walked out to the commons. The others were waiting on them. Karl asked, "You ready?"

"Let's get it," Malcolm replied.

They rose and left the quarters and returned to Intelligence. Every desk with a holoscreen had a technician manning it, a full house unlike anything the Elite had seen before.

Malaysia commented, "All hands on deck, huh?"

Dax and Stephanie, standing in the middle of the floor, turned around when they heard Malaysia's voice. Dax said, "Everyone's here. Are you sure you want to do this, Malcolm?"

"Frimas naw, I'm not sure. But here we are. Call the director."

Dax contacted the director. "This is Mallack," she answered.

"Director, this is Malcolm. The team is assembled in Intelligence. Every defender is accounted for. We're ready to insert the drive."

"Malcolm, are you sure you want to do this?" Mallack asked.

"Yes, Director, we're sure. We're going to get Duncan back and beat the Collector down. This is how we're going to do it."

"Okay, Malcolm. On your order."

Malcolm looked at everyone, then at Dax. "Dax, give me the drive."

"Here you go," Dax complied. He placed the drive in Malcolm's hands.

Malcolm looked at everyone again, then said, "Dax, Stephanie, you ready?"

"100%," Stephanie confirmed.

Malcolm breathed two big sighs. He walked up to the main console in front of the holoscreen, and then tapped keys on it. A small hole opened in the countertop and lit up white. Malcolm said, "Okay, here we go." He inserted the drive into the hole, and the drive lit up yellow. The holoscreen in front of everyone displayed two progress bars, one for the Collector's data mine and the other for Duncan's location. A countdown to the start of the process also showed underneath the bars.

"7, 6, 5, 4, 3, 2, 1, start!"

The data mine began, and Stephanie, Dax, and the Intelligence Unit maxed out their computing power and typing speed to extract Duncan's location from the drive. Stephanie declared, "Come on, guys, don't let that bar get to 100%."

The bars appeared to be in a race. Dax said, "We can beat it, but we'll have to divert all energy in the building to this unit, Malcolm."

"Do it," Malcolm ordered.

Dax swiftly tapped on the keys and diverted all energy from HQ to Intelligence. The lights flickered as the computing power surged even more, pushing the progress bar for Duncan's location way ahead of the Collector's data mine bar. Everyone in the room felt tension rise within them as they rooted for Intelligence to beat the Collector's drive. Thirty seconds later, Duncan's bar reached 100%. Stephanie yelled, "Pull it out, Malcolm!"

Malcolm pulled the drive out of the console, and the lights returned to full power.

"Is that it?" Malaysia asked.

"Yeah, that's it," Dax confirmed. The technicians all cheered and celebrated their feat.

Stephanie stated, "We got all the data for Duncan's location pulled from the drive. We have to find Dredge and make an honest man out of him."

"What makes you say that?" Daisy asked.

"No," Alexia interrupted their moment, "before you two get nerdy, what do we know about Duncan? Where is he?"

"Right, okay, give us about two minutes to piece this together. Team, get to work," Stephanie said.

"Meantime, what did the Collector pull from us?"

"Okay, to find that out, I'll have to run a diagnostic of our personnel files and break down Dredge's tech to determine what the drive pulled. I don't know how long that's going to take."

"Ugh, all this waiting, I'm ready to stomp somebody's ass," Karl clenched his fists.

"No kidding!" Malcolm agreed.

"Okay, almost there," Dax reassured, "alright, here is the data we pulled." Dax scanned the information and let out an exasperated sigh. "Oh no, Malcolm, um."

"What?" Malcolm asked despondently.

Stephanie hung her head down and answered Malcolm's question. "It's a message."

"Get the Frimas out of here! Another message?!" Alexia screamed.

"You have got to be kidding me. The Collector played us. Again!" Malaysia exclaimed.

Malcolm closed his eyes and sat down. Defeat settled in his chest, recognizing that he had fallen once again for the Collector's chess move, except this time, the entire Company was now in jeopardy. Rage, fear, indecision, sadness, none of these emotions could fully capture the emptiness that his soul felt in that moment. He could barely hear Stephanie calling out to him.

"Malcolm. Malcolm. Malcolm? Malcolm! Malcolm!!!"

"What?" he soullessly asked.

"What do you want me to do?"

Malcolm sighed and waved his hand. "Play the damn message."

Stephanie played the message. The Collector showed up again, same black garb, same black mask, same undisclosed location, same desk from before. "So, here we are! Thank you so, so much for your cooperation! I have been waiting for such a long time to get this information from the Company, and now I am confident that I will have everything I need to achieve what I set out to do so many years ago. I won't be long this time. I know you're anxious to save your boy. But I am a sucker for a good game. I hope you'll play with me!

"On the map, I have six locations, one for each district in Uri City. I've stashed your boy away in one of these locations. I will give you two days to figure out where he is. Here's the catch: you can only choose one of these places to find him. If you choose incorrectly, I will blow up where he is, and that will just cause unnecessary damage to buildings and people, and nobody wants that.

"Here is my riddle. Once you solve it, you'll know exactly where he is, and I'm sure we will have a lovely time scrapping with one another. Again, you have two days to find him. If you don't, I will take his powers, kill him, dump his body, and blah blah blah, you know how these diabolical speeches go. Have a great day!

"Oh wait, the riddle! Silly me! Okay, so here it is. 'It is the place where it all began.' Good luck!" The screen went blank.

Alexia screamed. Malaysia tried to calm her down. Karl tried to reason with her, but once Daisy chimed in, a full-on argument ensued. The chaos that erupted in the room could have been televised as their anger, rage, and sadness fueled the fire that was spilling over into verbal in-fighting between them.

Malcolm, though, couldn't hear a thing. He was utterly stunned and couldn't bring himself to say a word. He resigned to sulk in silence. He got up and walked out of Intelligence.

Symone barely noticed his absence given the pandemonium swallowing the room whole. Once aware, she asked, "Hey, where's Malcolm?" No one could hear her as they verbally sparred with one another. With no one there to calm the storm, Symone realized that the team had become unhinged. They needed their leader at a time when he needed them more. *They're going to tear themselves apart if Malcolm doesn't do something. What would he do right now?*

Symone then remembered that Malcolm had told them what they would do once they got the information from the drive. She stood up and walked in the middle of the aisle. She levitated, smoldered her eyes, reddened her locs, and auraed her body. Everyone silenced themselves and stared at Symone. Her voice boomed, "Elite, go to the conference room, now! Malcolm's orders."

She then levitated out of Intelligence. Malaysia, dazed by Symone's redirect, said, "What the Frimas?"

27

Revelation

S ymone waited while the elevator shuttled her from the Elite Grand to the training floor, where Symone assumed Malcolm went. She had no words to offer. She already knew what to expect when she saw him. She remembered the angst, the rage, and the fury she felt when she heard the smug narration with which the Collector delivered her message to the Elite. She realized she now had a true enemy, someone who epitomized Bashko and was capable of more chaos than anyone she had ever faced. She recalled how divided the Elite had become in Intelligence and felt like the Collector, despite not truly knowing what her endgame was, was winning big. *What the Frimas does the Collector want?*

The elevator door opened to the training floor, and Symone walked to Malcolm's room. She opened the door and found Malcolm throwing shards of metal in the air and turning them into ash with a twist of his fingers. AI responded to Symone's presence and said, "Symone Watson, codename Starburst, entering training room. Modifying room to meet powered state."

"Malcolm, you okay?" Symone asked.

Malcolm threw another shard in the air and twisted his fingers to turn it into ash. He then turned around to face Symone. She observed the look of devastation, sorrow, and defeat in his slightly discolored face. His eyes read internal fury. Symone stood next to him and said, "Talk to me."

"I don't know what to say," Malcolm mumbled, barely audible to her. He walked away from her and stood at the wall. Symone slowly followed him.

"Try," she pushed gently.

Malcolm pressed his back against the wall and slid down to the floor, fatigue mixed in with dread hitting him like a hoverbus. He placed his arms on his knees and slumped his head downward in between his arms. He then lifted his head back up against the wall and searched for words to express everything he was feeling but couldn't bring himself to say anything.

Symone slid down the wall next to him and mirrored him. She didn't move. *Pushing him won't get him to say anything more.* She chose instead, until he told her otherwise, to just be there. Malcolm felt Symone's silent, powerful presence, and he leaned his head onto her right shoulder, eyes closed. A semblance of comfort began to surround his hurting heart.

She remembered a time when she, her mother, and her father would race to the roof of their home at night and lay atop it to watch the stars. She recalled those moments being some of the best she ever had with her family because the stars were amazing to gaze upon, and her parents took advantage of those moments to talk with her about anything. She hoped that by recreating that, she would give Malcolm a similar feeling of peace that may get him to express himself just a little bit.

She rolled her left palm and concentrated her energy. She created tiny specks of dazzling, brilliant light and lifted them to the sky. Little by little, the air above began to mimic a starry night. She silently delivered a message to AI to dim the lights in the room with her stripe. She then said, "Malcolm, open your eyes."

Malcolm opened his eyes, then looked up, and he gazed upon the impressive display of luminaries scattered through the air. He was awestruck. Tears welled up in his eyes, and the dam of his heart broke under the pressure.

Symone lay flat on the floor to stare at the ceiling. "Come here, Malcolm," she patted the floor, motioning Malcolm to lie with her. He slowly lay next to her and stared at the ceiling, too. They stargazed silently for three minutes.

Malcolm's emotions swirled as he ruminated on his recent disappointments – Duncan's near-miss at the DD Corporation, the beatdown in the parking garage, losing the Crawler's powers, Duncan's capture – and felt that they all paled in comparison to the colossal mistake of putting the entire Uri City Division of the Company at risk for a riddle. He choked up and silently declared, "I failed."

"What?" Symone asked.

"I failed."

"How so?"

"I made the wrong decision. I compromised the Company. I let the Collector play us again. And we're no closer to getting Duncan back than we were a half cycle ago. Mallack put her trust in me, and I blew it. And now we're all in danger. And for what? For what?"

Symone wanted to counter his thoughts to make him feel better. But she remembered something her mother did once during one of their stargazing conversations.

"What was the wrong move you made, Symone?" her mother asked.

"What?" a teenage Symone asked.

"What was the wrong move you made?"

"Um, I went left when I should have gone right?"

"And why did you go left?"

"Because I assumed he was going to swing at me, and I was afraid of getting hit."

"And why were you afraid of getting hit?"

"Because I didn't want to get hurt."

"Why don't you want to get hurt?"

"Because if I get hurt, I might lose."

"And yet, you lost anyway. Symone, if you're going to win, you can't go into the arena trying to not get hurt. To do so is to second-guess your instincts and move left when you knew you should have gone right. You have to trust that you can handle the pain that comes with trusting your gut."

"You're right. Win or die."

"Well, don't die, but yes, 'win or die.'"

Symone leaned into Malcolm's headspace.

"What was the wrong decision, Malcolm?" Symone calmly asked, still staring at the stars.

Malcolm sniffed, "What?"

She slowly, softly repeated, "What was the wrong decision?"

Malcolm sniffed again, turned his head, and replied, "Um, to save Duncan."

"Why was saving Duncan the wrong decision?"

He turned his head back toward the stars. "Because the Collector didn't tell us where he is." He started to beat himself up again.

"No, but," Symone countered, "what *did* the Collector do?"

Malcolm stared at the stars. He recalled the Collector's message and fast-forwarded to the end of it when she said, "It's the place where it all began."

"She gave us a clue," he explained.

"That's right, she gave us a clue. How did you compromise the Company?"

Malcolm followed Symone's logic. "I didn't compromise the Company. I pulled everyone in knowing the danger that was coming. And once we know whose data was extracted, we will protect him with the full force of the Company."

"How did the Collector play us, Malcolm?" Symone continued.

"We're playing her game, she's been playing us since day one, but until we know what she truly wants, we have no choice but to play her game and minimize the damage she does," Malcolm rationalized.

"Why did Mallack put her trust in you?"

"Frimas, why not?"

"Exactly, Malcolm." Symone sat up to look at Malcolm. "She knew that you would make the best decision for Duncan and the Company. And that's exactly what you did. The Collector pissed you off. Frimas, she pissed us all off because of how smug she is. But she's doing all of this because she knows that she is under our skin. We cannot let her win. We cannot let her tear us apart. We have to be better than her, we have to be smarter than her. Just because we're playing her game doesn't mean we have to play it her way. We are the Elite, and you, Malcolm, Kingdom Come, you are our leader."

Malcolm thought about what she said and reacted, "You're right."

Symone replied, "I know. And right now, your team needs you." She grabbed his hand, "We need you to lead us. Now, you are allowed to crack under pressure. We all do, and this one hurts. So, take the time you need to get your mind right. When you're ready, we'll be in the conference room like you ordered us to be, waiting for you," she patted his chest, "to tell us what's next. I'll see you upstairs. Enjoy the view." Symone stood up and walked away.

Malcolm turned to face Symone and said, "Miss Watson?"

"Yes, *Mister Bennett*?" Symone sarcastically responded.

"Thank you."

"You're welcome." Symone left the room. AI responded accordingly.

Malcolm stared at the stars and swooned. *I think I'm in love. How did she do that, and how did that work? Okay, Malcolm, let's focus. What's next?*

Symone returned to the Elite Grand and walked to the conference room. She entered to find the Elite gathered as instructed. She slowly closed the door. Malaysia asked, "How is he?"

"Shaken up, but he'll be alright. I told him to take his time coming up here," Symone replied.

Alexia ran up to Symone and hugged her tightly. "I'm sorry for how I acted in Intelligence."

"It's okay, Alexia," Symone assured her while squeezing Alexia back. "We're all stressed right now. The Collector is a real bitch, and she's pissed us all off. The main thing is that we stick together, no matter what. She wants to bust us up. We can't give her that."

"Agreed," Malaysia said. "So, any idea on what to do now?"

"Wait for Malcolm," Symone answered. "That's all I got."

"Okay, then," Karl replied. "Sit with us, Symone."

Malaysia, Symone, Karl, Daisy, and Alexia waited at the table.

And waited.

And waited.

And waited.

Half a cycle went by. Karl was napping, Alexia was levitating random things from her pockets, and Daisy was rapidly reading a book from her stripe. Symone stared at the ceiling, and Malaysia bounced a ball off the wall repeatedly. All but Karl wondered where Malcolm could be and whether someone should go looking for him. But nobody dared say anything, trusting that Malcolm would show when he was ready.

"We should have put a movie on or something. Ugh, this is boring," Symone admitted while twirling in her chair.

"You got that right," Alexia agreed and dropped the lint, gum wrapper, and lip gloss on the table all at once. "I am so bored right now. We should have met in the commons."

Malaysia chuckled. "Well, it's not like we can't watch anything while we wait, so, what do you want to watch?"

"Something funny, please! I need a good laugh right now," Alexia suggested.

"Got it." Symone pulled up a catalogue on her stripe and connected her stripe to the holoscreen in front of them. A comedy started playing. Daisy stopped reading her book to watch, and everyone, except Karl who was still sound asleep, was entertained by the banter between the characters in the movie. For the next half-cycle, they got lost in the holoscreen, forgetting for a moment the struggles they faced over the past several days and giving themselves a reprieve from the emotional damage they incurred just a cycle before.

Malcolm walked toward the conference room. He shook and patted his head twice, confident that his mind was focused and that he was ready to march on. He entered the conference room and noticed the ladies all having a good laugh.

"Malcolm!" Alexia yelled, eyes wide.

"You alright?" Malaysia asked.

Malcolm sighed, "Yeah, I'm good. Just needed a moment to process my feelings, apparently." He looked at Symone and nodded in approval of her tactics to get his head back in the game.

Symone paused the movie then asked, "Okay, so, Malcolm, what's the play? Karl, wake up!"

Karl snorted loudly, then said, "I'm up, what's up?"

"Malcolm's here. We're getting ready."

"Okay. So, what's the play, Malcolm?" Karl asked.

"Well, the Collector gave us locations in all of the districts." Malcolm walked over to the console near the holoscreen and tapped keys to connect to the data pulled by Intelligence. A map of Uri City showed on the screen, and six dots representing the six locations provided by the Collector blinked yellow. "Highgarden, Meridian, Genesis Landing, Leicester, the Underbelly, and Midtown. Now, the clue she gave us was 'it is the place where it all began.' Any ideas of what that could mean?"

"Maybe it means something about the origin of the city? You know, where the city began?" Daisy started brainstorming.

"Okay, so that would be at Genesis Landing. But then the location itself doesn't make sense because Genesis Landing sprawled from the edge, not from the center, where the Collector's spot is," Karl analyzed.

"Alright, so it's not a history. Maybe Midtown? It's the seat of government?" Alexia offered.

"The seat of government has moved so many times in Uri," Malaysia remembered. "At one time, it was in the Underbelly before that district became the Underbelly. I think Midtown's only like fifty years old."

"That's true," Symone concurred. "I remember my grandpa talking about that a lot, how the Underbelly suffered when the seat of government moved since Uri didn't feel the need to take care of the district like that anymore."

"Gotta love that gentrification, right?" Alexia quipped. "Pretty soon, Leicester will be next while they try to turn the Underbelly into the new Meridian."

"Let's stay focused," Malcolm interrupted. "Any other ideas?"

"How about our first battle with the Collector? That was in Genesis Landing, right?" Malaysia tried.

"That's true. But the locations don't match up. None of our battles with her, or any of the interactions, not in Meridian at the Hi-Fi, not Leicester with Dredge, fit." Symone shrugged her shoulders.

Malcolm sighed, "Alright. Let's team up with Intelligence on this. We need a quantum surge in data analysis. Daisy, you are our resident encyclopedia, go to Intelligence and work with them until you guys can come up with a solution to this. Rule nothing out, come up with as many options as you can, and let's reconvene in the rising. Right now, this is where things stand. We can't do anything until we know exactly where Duncan is. I already thought this through, and we can't do a go-to-all-locations-at-once move because she'll see right through that and blow him and possibly another one of us up. Plus, we know how the Collector likes to isolate her victims. We can't risk sending teams of us given the data breach and the Collector's unpredictability. We have to play the Collector's game. But we will play it our way, the smart way, and make sure that we win."

Symone smiled. "Okay, Malcolm."

"Until then, we're here in the building until Intelligence clears us from the data breach. Take my advice and get some rest, all of you. We've ridden a rollercoaster today. Try to take it easy."

"Yes, sir," Malaysia responded.

"What are you about to do, Malcolm?" Alexia asked.

"I'm going to go talk to the Analyst real quick to just touch bases with him, then head back to quarters and go to sleep."

"Okay. Listen, we're all proud of you, and stand by you 100%. It was the right call," Malaysia assured Malcolm.

"Thanks for having my back," Malcolm felt his heart swell with pride. "I'll see you all soon."

Malcolm walked out of the room. His mental and emotional exhaustion made it difficult to march to the Analyst's office, thinking that he needed a drink and a nap, but he dragged himself there anyway.

He entered the Analyst's office. The Analyst turned toward Malcolm and shouted, "Yes! You're here! It's about time! I'm so glad, I have so much to share with you!" He clapped his hands three times and jumped out of his seat to make his way to the desk in the middle of the office.

"Oh, okay," Malcolm said hesitantly. "What do you have?"

"So much!" The Analyst tapped on the console and pulled up Malcolm's demographics and displayed them on the holoscreen at the front of the room. "Malcolm, in the past few weeks, you have undergone a rapid transformation unlike anything we have ever seen. Malcolm, you're not Elite anymore. You are way beyond it!"

"Wait, what do you mean 'beyond?' How can anyone be beyond the Elite level?" Malcolm was shocked.

"Malcolm, we've been studying you since Sentinel Bank, and your powers have evolved to a level never recorded in the Company. The Elites register at 3.0 and above. And no one has ever reached 3.99. Malcolm, you're at 4.3.

Malcolm's jaw dropped as he sat down next to the Analyst. "What? That's impossible!"

The Analyst stared Malcolm dead in his eyes. "I thought so, too, but I ran the numbers too many times to count. And the answer is the same every single time. There's literally no category for where you're at right now. And there seems to be no limit to where your powers can go. You're doing things that you've never done, and you're using your powers much faster and more effectively than ever before. Right now, I do not think there is anyone else on the planet who can match you."

"Let me get this straight," Malcolm shook his head and tried to make sense of what he was hearing. "You're telling me that I, me, Malcolm Bennett, went from some average Elite to the supposedly most powerful being on Uretha in a quarter?"

The Analyst pounded his right palm on the countertop. "That's exactly what I'm saying, Malcolm."

"This doesn't make any sense. Nothing's changed with me. I haven't trained any differently. I haven't eaten anything differently. There's nothing about me that's changed. Unless Akan has imbued me with some special power out of nowhere, there's no reason I should be evolving like this."

"It is truly remarkable! Malcolm, you're spinning blades and flying. You're catching powers and throwing them back at people. You moved an entire sidewalk to build a barricade! And your potential/kinetic ratio is off the charts. You've lowered your kinetic percentage well below 40%."

"Insane," Malcolm looked at the screen, mesmerized by what the Analyst reported.

"Truly remarkable! The closer you and Symone get, the more powerful you're becoming! Oops!" The Analyst just realized that he said something he wasn't supposed to say and hoped that Malcolm did not catch it.

But he did. Malcolm rapidly shook his head and pounced on what the Analyst said, "Wait, what do you mean by that?"

"By what?"

Malcolm turned to face the Analyst. "What you just said, 'the closer you and Symone get,' what did you mean by that?"

"Oh, nothing, just that you two seem to be getting closer. And you're getting stronger. That's all."

"No, Analyst, that's not all. What are you not telling me?" Malcolm calmly demanded.

"Nothing, Malcolm, I'm not telling you nothing," the Analyst stammered.

Malcolm didn't buy it. He stood up, got in the Analyst's face and said, "Analyst, I am not going to ask again. It has been too long of a day, I am pissed beyond pissivity, and I do not have time for games. Now, give it to me straight. What is it about Symone and me that you think has an effect on my powers?" He grabbed the Analyst's shirt and pulled him into his face.

The Analyst lifted his hands up and pleaded, "Okay, okay! It's the Affinity Theory!"

"What the Frimas is the Affinity Theory? The short version," Malcolm released the Analyst.

The Analyst, fully aware of what Malcolm was capable of, explained, "Okay, well, some asheologists believe that powers can evolve through the interaction of two people. The closer they become, the stronger they become. We believe that you and Symone are the first in recorded history that may actually be evolving just by how close you are to each other."

"You're telling me that I'm evolving because of how close I am to her? Like, proximity?"

"No, not just proximity. Your relationship with her. It's making you stronger, Malcolm. Her, too."

Malcolm couldn't believe what the Analyst was telling him. "Wait, her, too?"

"Yes, see, look at her demographics." The Analyst tapped on the console and threw Symone's demographics and statistics on the holoscreen. "See, she's much stronger than she was when she first met you. She, too, has evolved beyond Elite, rising from 3.0 to 4.2 in the time that she's known you and been involved with you."

"I knew it! I knew she was affecting me somehow! But wait, how do you know about us being involved?" Malcolm was growing more frustrated with each piece of information the Analyst offered. "Just how much have you been watching us, Analyst?" he growled.

"Please don't get upset," the Analyst pleaded. "I was sworn to secrecy and told to monitor both Symone and you to see how your involvement correlated to your evolution."

"Sworn by whom?" Malcolm questioned.

"Director Mallack."

"You're kidding me!" Malcolm yelled and flailed his arms.

"We had no choice, Malcolm! The Collector's army is, well, *was* too strong for you guys, and we needed to find a way to beat her crew. This miracle was dumped into our lap, and we had to take advantage of it. So, we monitored you, and each time you two had a moment, we recorded the moment and then noted how you unleashed your powers."

"I can't believe this!" Malcolm sat down. "Wait, 'we monitored,' who else knows about this?"

"I don't—"

"Who else?!"

"Malaysia!"

Malcolm jumped out of his seat and walked away in disbelief. He waved his hands around his head, squatted, then stood back up and turned to face the Analyst again. "So, Malaysia's been spying on us this whole time? The secret conversations with Mallack, that's what they were talking about? About Symone and me? You're telling me that Mallack pushed Symone and me together to ensure we became as powerful as possible so we could stop the Collector? So Mallack's been behind this the entire time?" Malcolm's heart started beating out of his chest. "Symone is going to flip out!"

"Malcolm, you can't tell her."

"The Frimas you mean?! I don't have a choice!" Malcolm exclaimed. "Symone has a right to know about this! I've always known that the Company makes decisions about us without really telling us. But I never anticipated they'd do something like this. She has a right to know!"

"But—"

"No," Malcolm slammed his fist into the countertop, his force planting a permanent imprint of it in the countertop, "it's your butt that got us here in the first place, Analyst! I knew that she's been affecting me. I even asked you indirectly about it once before, and you *never* gave me a response. Just something about having to do more analysis. You should have come clean! You're always the one who wants to share with us how we're evolving and wanting to know why. But you've *always* included us in your thought processes. You've never hidden anything about our evolutions from us. You should have been straight with us from the jump, Analyst! My Akan! Now, I've got to tell this girl what you've done and pray she doesn't melt this place down."

Malcolm stormed out of the Analyst's office. The Analyst slumped in his chair and banged his head on his desk. *What have I done? Mallack will kill me, if Malaysia doesn't do it first."*

Malcolm raced a couple steps forward, then held onto the wall with his left hand to catch his breath and placed his right hand on his chest to stop his heart from breaking his rib cage. His mind spun as his worst fears began to capture him. He thought about the times Symone walked with him side-by-side, the conversations they shared, the first time he caught that she was into him, how many times they'd touched each other, their kisses in the training room, their sexual experience the night before. Everything was becoming a soup in his mind as he pondered how many times the director asked him how things were going with Symone, when Karl and Duncan ambushed him, or when Malaysia would ask about how things were going between them.

I can't tell her. She's going to think the absolute worst. But I can't keep this from her, not with all that "don't take my choice away from me" stuff she preaches. Akan, why, why did they do this? And Malaysia was in on it, too?! I can't believe it. I don't know what to do. I don't want to do this. What if she believes that this, that "us," was all a scheme? Aargh, this is too much. I don't know what to do. I gotta get out of here.

Before Malcolm could find a place to continue unraveling in solitude, Symone came walking down the corridor looking for Malcolm. She saw him leaning against the wall and ran up to him. She asked, "Hey, Mal, are you okay?"

Malcolm heard her voice, and his heart shattered as she leaned on him to lift him off the wall. He could barely get the words out of his mouth, but he replied, "We need to talk Symone."

"Okay, come on, I got you, it's okay. Let's go somewhere and talk."

"The roof," Malcolm offered, figuring that would be the safest place to unleash a bombshell that would set her off.

"Okay."

Malcolm got up and found the strength to walk to the elevator. Symone grew concerned. "Is everything okay, Malcolm?" Symone asked.

"I honestly don't think so, Symone."

"You're scaring me," she revealed as they entered the elevator.

"I'm scared, too."

"Crap, okay."

The ride to the roof felt like it took ages. Symone felt a vice in the pit of her stomach, worried that Malcolm was about to drop an atomic bomb on her. She looked at him, and he couldn't face her, keeping his face down despite seeing Symone from the corner of his eye. He projected that this was about to be the end of them and did not know what he could say or do to stop his fear from materializing.

They arrived at the roof. Sunset was just about to take over the horizon. The view of Highgarden was breathtaking, but it could not take away the dread and doom that had consumed Malcolm's heart.

Symone couldn't make sense of Malcolm's actions and lack of communication. Her mind raced. *Is it Duncan? The Collector? More bad news? Did somebody say something to the Director? Is he in trouble? Is he about to call us off? What the Frimas is upsetting him this much?*

Malcolm and Symone took several steps forward on the rooftop. "Okay, Malcolm, what is it?" Symone asked as she stopped walking.

Malcolm stopped, turned around, and gave Symone the biggest hug of his life. He then backed away from her. She prepared herself for the worst, and with her battle-ready, low voice, she inquired, "Are you about to break up with me?" Tears began to well up in her eyes.

"No, no," Malcolm reacted quickly. "That's the last thing I want."

Symone breathed a sigh of relief. "Okay, so what is it then, Malcolm?"

"Okay, um," Malcolm started pacing and moving his arms as he explained, "so I went to the Analyst, and he told me that I have evolved way beyond anything anyone has ever seen before. And he said that you have, too, way beyond expected."

Confused, Symone reacted, "That's good, right?"

"Yeah, it's actually great. But he said that we evolved because we're together. He said something about the Affinity Theory and that because we're together, we've gotten stronger."

"Okay, so, what's wrong with that, Malcolm?"

Malcolm choked up in fear. In that moment, Malcolm decided, *Tell her just enough to get the point across. Don't say anything about Malaysia. I'll let her tell Symone on her own.* "Well, Symone, they've been watching us since Sentinel Bank, the Analyst and Director Mallack. They put us together to make us strong enough to beat the Collector's army."

Symone's head shuddered, and she blinked rapidly as she received the news. She paused, then said, "Wait a minute, they put us together?"

"Yes. Mallack and the Analyst saw what they saw, and they made a play to make us powerful enough to beat Streak, Hex, Sonic, and whoever else is on the Collector's squad."

"So, you're telling me that the only reason we're together, you and me, is so that we can beat the Collector?"

"Well, no, that's not the only reason," Malcolm answered.

Symone locked her hands together and placed them behind her head. She looked up to fight back the tears in her eyes, not wanting to show emotion despite the sadness, rage, and disgust smoldering within her. And Malcolm sensed every single burning degree. "But it is *a* reason, and it's the reason why they probably made you mentor me." Symone started pacing the floor. "This whole time, everybody was asking how things were between you and me so they could keep tabs on how close we were, taking notes! They *wanted* us to get close!" She dropped her arms to her side. Symone's eyes burned, and her hair started to glow.

Malcolm could sense her pain through his pores as he noticed Symone's left side facing him. "Symone, I am so—"

Symone turned her head slowly toward Malcolm as she scoffed, "Oh, don't you dare. Don't you say it. Damn it, were you in on it, too? Saw me as your ticket to getting stronger? Is that why Mallack got you to get close to me? Talk to me during our trainings? Share your heart with me? Frimas, that's why you sparred with me when you wouldn't spar with anyone else, ever. Made me fall for you. You screwed me just to take down the Collector! Is that all I am to you people, to the Company, a means to an end?!"

"Symone—"

Symone gritted her teeth and growled, "Don't say my name! The Frimas! That's all the Company does, isn't it? Take people's choices away from them! Did anyone ever think, 'Hey, let's tell Symone what's going on so she can decide whether she wants to do this?' No, it's 'let's keep secrets!' And now everybody's going to think that I screwed my way to the top, just like I told you before! Malcolm, how could you do this to me?!"

"I was just as in the dark as you!" Malcolm tried to explain.

Symone couldn't hear anything he had to say, feeling disillusioned. Her entire world as she knew it shattered before her eyes. "You know what, I can't even face you right now. I gotta get out of here."

"Symone, wait," Malcolm grabbed Symone's arm. Symone twisted her arm quickly to release herself from his grip, then charged her hand and pointed a levitating star at him. Malcolm held both hands up, realizing that he wasn't cloaked or uniformed and that Symone could fry him at any moment.

"Don't ever touch me again." Symone blasted into the darkening sky in defiance of the Whisper Protocol, angry that she allowed herself to be played. Malcolm sighed heavily and fought back tears as his deep fear of rejection materialized.

He stared at her as she disappeared like a twinkling star. *This always happens to me. This is why I don't get close to people!* He slowly walked back to the elevator and thought aloud, "Mallack." He punched the button for the Elite Grand. His sadness turned to rage, and once the elevator door opened, all he saw was red. Malcolm stormed to Mallack's office and barged in the door.

"Malcolm?" Mallack sat at her desk, looking at the holoscreen atop her desk.

"So, this was your plan the whole time, Mallack? Put Symone and me together so we can be powerful enough to beat the Collector?"

"Careful, Malcolm," Mallack began to remind Malcolm of her rank.

"Screw you, Mallack!" Malcolm yelled. "You left us in the dark, playing games with us this whole time, putting Symone and me on missions together to push us closer so we can get stronger. You put us in jeopardy so you could fulfill this Affinity Theory bull! Who put you up to this? The Company? Is that why you've been acting so strange? So, the Company could test their theory out on us?"

"Sit down, Malcolm," Mallack said.

"I think I'll stand, thank you," Malcolm replied.

"Fine. Malcolm, the Company put you and Symone together because you are the best mentor in Uri City. They had no idea what you two could become. I became aware of this Affinity Theory through the Analyst who, after conversing with Symone and you about how you two got stronger after *just looking* at each other at Sentinel, thought that you two were evolving at a radical rate. He brought that to me, and I let it play out despite my feelings about supervisors getting romantically involved with their supervisees. And, despite how crappy I have felt keeping you in the dark, you must admit, it's working."

Malcolm grabbed the top of one of the chairs in front of Mallack's desk and squeezed it to channel his ever-brewing anger, fighting the urge to turn the chair into dust. "That does not excuse you from keeping this from us, from me! You've been sitting on this and analyzing Symone and me without our knowledge. You even had Malaysia spy on us for you! That's beyond foul, Director!"

"Malcolm, just because you're my right hand does not mean you get to know everything that's happening."

"Maybe not, but this, Director, you're not just messing with people's powers. You're messing with our lives. This Affinity Theory, us getting stronger together, you had no right to keep this from us. If the Analyst believed that we were growing stronger due to our relationship, he should have told us. We could have used that and gotten stronger because – news flash – we want to be stronger! When he told you about the theory, you should have told us because we want to be stronger! Knowing Malaysia the way I do, when she told you that she wanted to tell us, you should have let her because we want to be stronger! What you underestimate about us, Director, is that we want to crush the Collector just as badly as you do. If we had known that getting closer was elevating our evolution, we would have taken that and run with it. Instead, what you've done is damn-near guaranteed that the Collector will win."

"How do you figure that, Malcolm?" Mallack inquired, pensively rocking her chair back and forth a couple of times.

"Because unless we find a way to fix this, or by some miracle, Symone can overlook the fact that you took her choice away from her, our team just dropped from six to five, and one of your strongest allies has just abandoned her post with no incentive to return."

"She left? Even with the Whisper Protocol?" Mallack was surprised.

"Who was going to keep her here? Certainly not me! Frimas, she thinks I was involved in the deception."

"Malcolm, seriously," Mallack reasoned, elbows on her desk with her hands clasped, "what would you have done if you were in my position, knowing that the key to beating your enemy was to keep your allies in the dark?"

Malcolm stood straight up, "I would have done the same thing I've always done, Director. I would have trusted my team and told them the truth. You tell your team the truth and face the fallout *together*. Malaysia was right. You'll be lucky to have a team once this is all over. This was a foul call, Mallack." Malcolm turned to leave.

"Where are you going?"

"I've gotta explain to my team that we are a man short indefinitely and cuss out my best friend for leaving me in the dark under your direction. When I thought my day couldn't get any worse, the night said, 'Hold my beer.' Good night, Director."

Malcolm walked out of the office and went to the quarters. Mallack quickly sent a message through her stripe to Malaysia. "Malcolm and Symone know about the Affinity Theory."

Malaysia's arm lit blue. She read the message and felt a slight jolt in her stomach. "Ah crud," she said as she sat in the commons on the couch. Malcolm came through the quarters' entrance. Malaysia saw him, and their eyes locked. Malaysia could read the anger coursing through his body. She stood up and lifted her arms to her side, palms slightly raised as she said, "Malcolm, I know you're upset."

"Malaysia," Malcolm said with a low rumble, "I can't right now. I thought I could, but I can't. Right now, I need to lie down before I rip this building in two."

"Malcolm, I wanted to tell you."

"Yeah, but you didn't. And right now, that's all I got for you. Good night." Malcolm walked to his residence, leaving Malaysia in the commons alone. She slumped down on the couch. Malcolm walked into his bedroom and collapsed in his bed, his pounding mind no longer having the energy to run or think. He mustered up enough brain cells to consider sending Symone a message but not enough to actually do it before falling asleep.

Symone, meanwhile, had flown all the way to the Underbelly and landed atop her apartment rooftop. She sat on the edge of the building and crumpled. She had been crying the entire flight and sobbed silently as she ruminated about her relationship with Malcolm. She replayed every instance of their talks, his touch, their fights with and against each other, their walks, their banters. She couldn't bring herself to believe that it was all for naught, but she felt played when she thought about their lovemaking.

Was it all so that he could get stronger? Did he play me so he could become Uri City's most powerful defender? I can't believe I fell for this. How did I fall for this? I should have just left him alone. I should have taken my fight with him, packed my bags, and left as I told myself to. I should message him and tell him we're through.

She thought about the message, but just as she was about to send it, a call from Alexia buzzed through her stripe. She didn't answer it and continued sobbing silently. She then recalled the ribbon that Malcolm had created from her star. She lifted her shirt and untied the ribbon. She balled it up and thought for a moment to destroy it with the heat of her star power.

Just then, another call came through her stripe. She answered, "Hi, Mom," Symone fought through the sobbing.

"Hi, Symone! I haven't heard from you in a few days, so I wanted to check in. How are you?"

Symone sniffled and replied, still holding onto the ribbon, "Not that great, to be honest."

"Oh? Baby, what's wrong?"

"I think I made a mistake, Mom, and now I don't know what to do."

There was silence. Then, "What was the mistake, Symone?"

Symone let out a whimper, clenched the ribbon in her fist, and fought through her tears.

28

Where It All Began

The corridor was quiet. Despite the Whisper Protocol, the Elite Grand Hall still felt like a ghost town since almost everyone was in their quarters. Daisy had gotten enough sleep for the night, and her heart and mind were amped, ready to take on another twenty-six cycles. She walked the corridor to reconvene with Intelligence to help them solve the Collector's riddle and find Duncan's location before time expired. Daisy had racked her brain before she went to bed, but she couldn't come up with a solution that made any sense.

She entered Intelligence and found a pair sitting at their desks on the third row down, scanning data. "Any luck?" she asked them.

"No, nothing that would pinpoint an exact location with confident certainty," one of them replied. He continued, "We've looked at affiliation, known associates, past murders, powers stolen, and nothing fits."

"Without any other demographics or history on the Collector, we're grasping at straws," the other added. She followed up, "We even expanded to look at city history like you guys had suggested earlier and still came up with nothing. None of the districts were birthed in the locations she listed. None of the locations have any connection to the other. They're all distinct, serving different purposes, owned by different people, and none of them is the 'first' of anything or is a birthplace of something."

Daisy sifted through her thoughts as she remarked, "Wow, this has truly left us all puzzled."

"Yes. Stephanie and Dax called it a night and went to their quarters. We were hoping to find something to give them come rising, but I don't think we're going to."

Daisy sighed and asked, "Can you guys set me up over here?"

"Sure! Kevin?"

"I got you right here." Kevin motioned for Daisy to sit at a desk next to him. She walked down to meet him. He tapped a few keys on his holoscreen and patched Daisy's holoscreen to their database. Daisy sat down and scanned the information they had gathered over several cycles. She confirmed what they told her, and after about fifteen minutes, Daisy sat back and wondered what they missed.

Daisy minimized the data and gazed at the map, analyzing the six blinking yellow dots representing each district's location. She zoomed in on each location to see the names and blocks of the streets they indicated and found nothing that fit. "This is hopeless," she sighed. She sat back in her chair and zoomed the map out again, feeling taunted by the yellow blinking dots. Daisy kept staring at the dots, then at the city streets, alternating between the two.

Dots, lines.

Dots.

Lines!

Connect the dots!

She asked Kevin, "Hey, can you remove the map and leave the dots on the screen and stop them from blinking?"

"Sure thing," Kevin complied. He tapped on the countertop and removed the map, leaving just the now-frozen yellow dots. Daisy stared at the dots again. She whipped out a mini holoscreen from her left back pocket and transferred the dot pattern to it. She then opened a drawing application and drew a line from the Midtown district's dot to every dot in the other districts. She saved the picture and began another one, this time drawing a line that connected Highgarden to Midtown, followed by the Underbelly, Leicester, Genesis Landing, and finally Meridian. Next, she drew a line from Meridian to Midtown, then to Highgarden, and proceeded to draw a curved line resembling a sickle that connected Highgarden to the Underbelly, Leicester, Genesis Landing, and back to Meridian.

Next, she drew a line from Highgarden to the Underbelly, a line from Meridian to Midtown, a line from Genesis Landing to Leicester, and then from the Underbelly to Midtown to Leicester.

She then drew another picture that started from Leicester to Midtown, Highgarden, and Meridian. She then drew another line from the Underbelly to Midtown to Genesis Landing. Finally, she drew a line from the Underbelly to Highgarden, a line from the Underbelly to Midtown to Meridian, and then a line from the Underbelly to Leicester to Genesis Landing.

She took the symbols she drew and transferred them to her holoscreen. She asked Kevin, "What do you know about the Chioro?"

"I don't know anything about it, but Gamola over here knows a ton."

Gamola looked over and said, "What's up?"

Daisy said, "Come over here. Look at these and tell me what you see."

Gamola stood up and walked to Daisy's holoscreen. She examined the symbols on the screen and responded, "These are Chioro symbols, representing some of the Divines of Akan."

"I knew it!" Daisy exclaimed as she fist-pumped twice. "Do you know specifically what they represent?"

Gamola responded, "The first one, that looks like a star, it's the symbol of harmony. The Chioro believe that 'all things are connected together.' The second, it's twin fire, synergy."

"What does that mean?" Daisy inquired.

"Well, the Chioro say that 'everyone is drawn to another,' like a balance between dark and light. You can't have one without the other."

"Okay, the third?" Kevin asked. He leaned in, fascinated by Gamola's explanations.

Gamola traced the symbol on the holoscreen with her finger. "The third one is supposed to be a glass chalice, the symbol for vitalization. 'Give to one another so that no one lacks.' The fourth, the one that looks like a 'W,' it's the symbol for light, 'Rise above the darkness and help each other see the way.'"

"This is good. I need to write all this down," Kevin reacted.

"I can repeat it later," Gamola replied, "if you don't fall asleep on me like you did the last time. Anyway, the fifth is a symbol for the warrior. The Chioro say, 'Fight for love, fight for peace, fight for freedom.'"

"And the last one?" Daisy pointed at it.

"This one is the symbol of renewal, regeneration, rebirth. Some have also said it's the symbol of origin. The Chioro call it 'Sankofa,' which basically means to know where you're going, you need to know where you've been, 'go back to the place...'"

"'...where it all began!'" Daisy's eyes lit up. "Okay, so these dots, they're drawing this symbol. Put the map back up, please!"

Daisy could barely contain her excitement as Kevin put the map back up and drew the lines that composed Chioro's origin symbol. "Okay, the way the symbol is drawn, I would assume that the location in the Underbelly is the 'place where it all began.'"

"How do you know that?" Kevin asked.

"Look at the shape. The three lines all flow from that location. Zoom in there. What is that place again?"

Gamola answered, "You're not going to believe this. It's an old Chioro sanctuary that was destroyed decades ago and never rebuilt. No one dares to go there because we believe to tread on those grounds would bring about curses."

"The Collector picked the perfect location. No one would think to look there. It's gotta be where Duncan is!" Daisy assumed.

"That's amazing, Daisy!" Gamola cheered. "You have to tell the team at once, you can't sit on this!"

"Absolutely not, I am on my way!" Daisy warped out of Intelligence in a blur and barreled her way into the quarters where everyone was resting.

Kevin said to Gamola, "That was amazing! How do you know all this stuff?"

"I read up on all this stuff a long time ago. There's three more Divines, but she got what she needed, and hopefully we can finally find Duncan and bring him home!"

"True that!" Kevin agreed as he lifted his hand up. Gamola hi-fived him, and she returned to her seat. They turned their chairs, and Kevin notified Stephanie and Dax of Daisy's discovery while Gamola computed data on Duncan's probable location.

Daisy ran to the residence atrium and squealed, "Everybody, wake the Frimas up! I think I found Duncan!" Then she remembered that the room were soundproof. She sent an alert to everyone's stripe. Three seconds later, a loud horn could be heard in everyone's residence.

Malaysia rose from her couch in her residence, slid the door open, and walked out to the commons. "What did you say?"

"I found him, Malaysia, I found Duncan!"

"No way! That's great!"

Malcolm jumped from his bed and saw the message. He slipped into a pair of sweatpants and stormed out of his room and said, "You're kidding! Where is he?"

Just then, Karl and Alexia walked out of their residences, and everyone followed Daisy to the commons. Daisy began, "Okay, so I looked at the dots and realized that they when they connected, they made these symbols from Chioro culture. Barely anyone really practices it anymore, at least here in Uri City, but the texts are worth taking a look at because—"

"Daisy, land your plane!" Alexia interrupted.

"Right, sorry, anyway, take a look at this." She threw on the holoscreen the symbol atop the map of Uri City. "This is the Chioro's origin symbol, 'the place where it all began.' The Collector's clue is leading us to the Underbelly."

Malcolm stared at the symbol and the location it pointed to. "Okay, I see it, it's an arrow pointing straight at the Underbelly," Malcolm responded.

"Yeah, I actually didn't see it that way, good point. So, the location in the Underbelly is an old Chioro sanctuary that everyone believes is cursed. It's the only logical place where the Collector would have him, Malcolm."

Malcolm stared at the map. He asked, "How sure are you, Daisy?"

"100%, Malcolm, this is where Duncan is, I am sure of it. Wait, where's Symone?" Daisy and the others looked around and realized that Symone wasn't there.

"Maybe she's in her room, I'll go get her." Alexia started going toward the residences, but Malcolm pressed her shoulder and stopped her.

"She's not in there. She left a while ago," Malcolm revealed despondently.

"Wait, we're under Whisper Protocol. Why would she leave?" Daisy asked.

"An emergency came up with her, and she had to handle it, Whisper Protocol be damned," Malcolm covered for her. "She'll be back when she's ready. Right now, let's focus on the task at hand. Daisy, incredible job, this is amazing what you pulled off. Why the Collector decided to get all spiritual on us is beyond me. But it's solved, and now we have a location. We got about five more cycles before rising, so get whatever rest you can, because tomorrow, we go hard to get Duncan back. See you all in the rising. Again, great work, Daisy."

Daisy grinned, "Thank you, Malcolm!"

Malcolm walked away and back to his residence while the rest of the team stayed behind. When he closed the door, Daisy asked, "Okay, so for real, why is Symone not here?"

"I don't know," Alexia responded. She looked around to make sure Malcolm wasn't around. "I tried reaching out to her a few times when I didn't see her here nor anywhere else in the building. She never picked up."

"I think I know," Malaysia muttered, recalling the fact that Malcolm and Symone knew about the Affinity Theory. "Malcolm and Symone might have broken up."

"You're kidding!" Alexia yelled.

"Shhh! Alexia, geez!" Malaysia said lowly.

"I'm sorry," Alexia whispered. "But seriously? They broke up? Already?! Why?"

"Yeah," Karl chimed in. "Why would they break up?"

Everybody sat down at their typical spots in the room. Malaysia summarized, "Well, the Company's been spying on them and wanted them to get close so they could get strong enough to beat the Collector's army."

"What's wrong with that? Sounds like a win-win to me. They had the Company's blessing to be in a relationship, Frimas, what was the problem?"

"They didn't tell them. I told the director she should have told them—"

"Wait," Karl interrupted, "you knew?"

"Yeah," Malaysia admitted as she buried her head in her palms, "and I told her this was a bad idea. She didn't listen, and Malcolm found out somehow. Probably told Symone, and Symone got pissed off."

"I told you them hooking up was bad," Daisy pulled an I-told-you-so.

"It *wasn't* bad, though," Alexia countered. "They were good together, Frimas, *are* good together. But I bet Symone thinks Malcolm was in on the secret and only got close to her to get stronger. Frimas, that's what I would think. Wait," she paused, "is that what happened? Did *he* know?!"

"No, no, Malcolm didn't know."

"Why didn't you tell him, Malaysia?" Karl asked.

"I tried, but I chickened out once we got the Collector's message. It doesn't matter now. Hopefully they can patch things up. We're going to need them both. I can guarantee Duncan's not going to be there alone, and we can't beat the Collector without them."

"Without question," Karl agreed. "The Collector's going to send her squad there to finish the job. 'Where it all begins?' That doesn't sound like the start of a fairy tale."

"True. Alright, let's get some rest. We'll talk more about everything in the rising." Malaysia and the others went to their residences and did their best to shake their nerves and get a little more rest.

Malcolm lay in his bed, staring at the ceiling trying to drift back to sleep. His left hand rested on his stomach, while his right hand sat behind his head. His mind spun around, squarely focused on Symone and the look of utter disgust on her face as she received the news of the director's ploy. He thought about how everything they had been through together in the past several weeks seemed to crumble before his eyes. *Did they really push us together? I know everything that I felt, everything I said, was real. I can't believe that I was made to like her. No, that was all me, one hundred percent. I should say something to her. But I should also give her space, let her deal with this however she wants to. Right?*

Malcolm lifted his arm up, thinking he should send Symone a message asking her if she was okay, but he argued himself out of doing it and put his arm back down. He reminded himself that despite his feelings toward her, he had to focus on the next mission and prepare his team for whatever they were about to face in the next twenty-eight cycles. He closed his eyes and wrestled with his thoughts for a cycle before finally drifting back to a semblance of sleep.

A cycle after the rising, Malaysia was in the kitchen making breakfast for everyone. Alexia was in the commons. Karl was in his residence, and Daisy was away in Intelligence. Malcolm walked out of his residence and through the commons. He locked eyes with Malaysia, and she looked at him but didn't say anything. He didn't say anything to her as he walked to the counter and tapped keys to get himself a glass of water. The glass rose from the hole. Malcolm grabbed it and drank from it. He looked at Malaysia and said, "I'm still mad at you."

"I know," Malaysia answered.

"Okay. Thanks for breakfast."

"Gotta eat. We got a lot to do today."

"No doubt about it."

Malaysia cracked a smile, surprised yet grateful that Malcolm hadn't iced her out completely.

02:30. The team met in Intelligence to prepare for their rescue mission. Stephanie and Dax stood at the holoscreen console up front, ready to provide intel and analysis, and the Elite sat at their respective desks ready to game plan.

"Okay, Stephanie," Malcolm began, "start us off."

Stephanie looked across the room and noticed Symone hadn't made it in yet. "Wait, are we not going to wait for Symone?"

"We're not sure whether she's going to be here, and we don't have time to waste. Let's get started."

"Okay." Stephanie tapped keys on her mini holoscreen. The big screen displayed what appeared to be a sheet of paper with scrambled letters across it. "First things first, we still have not been able to determine what information the Collector mined out of here. All we know so far is that the data she extracted was massive."

"How soon before you can tell us what she extracted?" Daisy asked.

"I'd say long after the mission ends when we can dedicate more resources to the cause."

"Okay," Malcolm responded. "So that means that the Collector could have anyone's information on them, and we're unsure exactly what she can do with that information. The Whisper Protocol is in place to keep us safe until the all-clear." Malcolm turned to face his team. "Therefore, none of you are obligated to go on this mission. So, before we proceed, does anyone want out?"

The team all looked at Malcolm with a stink eye, implying, "How could you ask that?"

"Alright. Stephanie, continue."

"Yes, sir." Stephanie raised her hand from her mini holoscreen, and it raised a holographic blue-neon projection of the ruins of the Chioro sanctuary in the Underbelly. "This is the site where, thanks to Daisy's work last night, we assume Duncan is being held hostage. We did a scan of the area, and it is being heavily guarded by a cloaking device that shields it from any type of visual analysis. We cannot see into that space. So, all we have to go on are blueprints of the sanctuary taken from the archives at Public Records in Midtown.

"The sanctuary is split into three parts. The inner sanctum is located about two-thirds of the way inside the sanctuary itself."

"We should assume Duncan will be housed there," Karl said.

"Right. The sanctum is surrounded by a colonnade where worshippers would gather and perform rituals. You can expect a ton of hiding places there. The colonnade is surrounded by the open outer courtyard. Because of the damage done, there's no roofing on the outer courtyard, which means—"

"We might be sitting ducks should she decide to have snipers atop buildings somewhere," Malaysia finished.

"Yes."

Dax continued, "Now, these ruins have basically been untouched for at least one hundred years. So, it is unclear how structurally sound the grounds are. From history, a ritual went terribly wrong and caused all sorts of damage that resulted in what the sanctuary is today. Using your powers carefully will be important simply because you don't want a column to come crashing down on your head."

Malcolm stood up and faced the team. He reasoned, "Since we know that the Collector's MO is to separate and conquer, and she doesn't mind putting on a show for the world to see, we are going to retain the assistance of UPD to help with the search."

"Malcolm, are you sure that's wise?" Daisy inquired.

"Most definitely." He sat on the countertop and crossed his arms as he continued, "The more firepower we have at our disposal, the more of a chance we stand of getting Duncan back. We'd ask one of the Super teams to assist us, but with the Whisper Protocol, we can't endanger the lives of anyone else. Hopefully, UPD doesn't say no. We will use them to secure the perimeter and patrol the outer courtyard. They won't go into the colonnade nor the inner sanctum."

Malaysia tagged herself in. "Remember, our primary objective is to rescue Duncan. Whether he has his powers or not, he is the priority. We get him, and we get the Frimas out of there, no questions asked."

"She's right," Malcolm continued. His arms became more animated as he explained, "Now, if the Collector or any of her crew shows up, we are to exercise extreme prejudice. If you have a shot, you take the shot. But you do not fight alone. If you find yourself isolated, do not, I repeat, do not engage. You get the Frimas out of there until you find somebody else to either fight with or run with, but do not fight alone. We will live to fight another day."

Stephanie added, "Additionally, Double-W has been studying film and analyzing the power patterns of Streak, Hex, and Sonic. They were finally able to outfit your uniforms and cloaks with protections specific to their powers. You won't be completely immune from their assaults, but you will be able to withstand them longer and more effectively. We're hoping it will push them to fight harder than they have in the past without you losing your advantage over them. Just remember that your cloaks will still not last forever, so at some point, you will either have to beat them or abandon the fight."

Malcolm said, "Nice! We will split into three teams. Daisy, Alexia, you will lead the search for Duncan on the ground. You will take the UPD with you into the courtyard. Daisy, sweep the area once you get to the colonnade but do not engage without Alexia."

"Roger that," Daisy confirmed.

"Malaysia and I will be the eyes in the sky. We will call out for any unusual activity, keep the skies clear of any signs of trouble, and call out patterns, particularly a means of escape for you all once Duncan is secure."

"Copy that," Malaysia agreed.

"Karl, you will be on standby in the outer courtyard. Once Daisy and Alexia have confirmed Duncan is secure, you will meet with them and help clear a path for them in case there's an ambush. If you have to smash the rest of the ruins to bits, you do what you gotta do to get everyone out of there."

"No doubt," Karl pounded his right fist into his left palm.

"Remember, team, the mission is Duncan. Nothing else matters. We do not know what the Collector's intent is sending us here, but we do know that Duncan must survive. He's family, and whatever we have to do to bring him home, that's what we're going to do. So stay sharp."

"Malcolm," Alexia raised her hand, "are we going to talk about Symone? We need her on this, where is she? Why isn't she responding to our calls?"

"Look, guys," Malcolm rubbed his hand through his textured hair, sighed, then replied, "Symone has a code. She has repeatedly told me, 'Don't take my choice away from me,' and that's what she feels the Company did to her. She's angry, and I don't blame her. Like any of us here, we are not held by gunpoint to stay here or do this job. So, she made her choice. She's not here. We made our choice. We are still here. We have to assume that Symone is not going to be here and operate without her. We don't have time to wait on her since we don't know if the Collector is going to kill Duncan despite having her intel. We gotta move. We can keep reaching out to her, but we leave at sunset, with or without her. Agreed?"

"Understood," Alexia nodded.

"Okay, team," Malcolm stated, "get ready. Stephanie, Dax, get with UPD and make them give us assistance. We'll meet in the quarters a cycle before sunset and move forward from there. Dismissed."

Malcolm stood next to Malaysia and told her, "I'm going to talk to the director to let her know our game plan, then head down to the training room to get some reps in."

"Okay. Hey, are you going to reach out to Symone?" Malaysia asked.

"I don't think I should. Should I?"

"Malcolm, you know better than that."

"You're right. After I meet with the director, I'll reach out," Malcolm sighed.

"Good."

The Elite walked out of Intelligence, and as they were about to go to the quarters, they all saw a familiar face walking toward them from the elevator. Symone had returned, and the team could tell that she was not herself. Her face looked ashen and steely, showing no emotion. She looked drained, but she confidently walked toward them as if looking for a fight.

Malaysia said to Malcolm, "Malcolm, talk to her."

Malcolm walked ahead of the team and toward Symone. He stood next to her, and Malcolm's heart and mind filled up with a billion things to say.

I'm sorry.

I wish I had known.

Are you okay?

Can I fix it?

What can I do to make things right?

How can I help make things better?

I care about you so much, I was so worried about you.

I'm so glad to see you.

Symone's heart swelled, and her mind raced.

Malcolm, I'm so hurt.

Can you hug me?

Did you really not know?

I'm so sorry for how I acted.

I still want you.

You mean so much to me.

Why didn't you reach out to me?

Can we start over?

What can I do to make it right?

You hurt me.

Let's talk.

Malcolm landed on, "Are you okay?"

Symone answered truthfully, "No."

Malcolm asked, "Do you want to talk about it?"

Symone lied, "No."

Malcolm inquired, "Can you fight?"

Symone looked unfazed. "Yes."

"Okay. Malaysia and the others will catch you up, and I'll see you soon."

"Okay."

Malcolm walked away and proceeded to Director Mallack's office. Symone slightly turned to watch Malcolm walk away. She then stepped forward to meet with the rest of the team. Alexia rushed Symone, bear hugged her, and said, "I was so worried about you, are you alright?"

"You know, I'm not sure," Symone admitted. "But I got Daisy's message last night, and I am ready. How are we going to get Duncan back?"

"We'll explain everything in the quarters," Malaysia replied.

29
Ready

Malcolm knocked on Director Mallack's office door. "Come in," Mallack answered.

Malcolm entered and saw Mallack seated at her desk. He walked to his favorite seat and sat down. "Director, we're prepped for our mission to rescue Duncan."

"That's great," Mallack replied. "What's the play?"

Malcolm provided a rundown of their objective. "At sunset, we will leave from here to go to the Chioro sanctuary. Once we land, Malaysia and I will perch atop the building across the street from the ruins while Karl, Symone, Daisy, and Alexia walk with UPD into the outer courtyard. Daisy and Alexia will enter the colonnade, and Daisy will scan the inner sanctum. She'll return to Alexia, they will enter the sanctum together, and once they've secured Duncan, Karl and Symone will meet with them, and they will exit the sanctuary together. All contingencies are in place in case the Collector or any of her army shows up. Exercising extreme prejudice on all of her party."

"Good work, Malcolm, it's a solid plan. Are you sure, though, that it shouldn't be Symone and you entering the courtyard?"

Malcolm wanted to say a curse word given Mallack's Affinity Theory plan, but he maintained his composure and decorum. "I am. Malaysia will need help with keeping the sky and ground clear around the perimeter along with UPD. The way I've evolved, it will be easier to build barricades and exit routes from a perch than on the ground. With Symone back, they will have enough firepower to withstand any onslaught they may encounter."

"Okay. Listen, Malcolm," Mallack changed subjects and addressed hurting Malcolm the night before, "I feel awful for keeping the Affinity Theory and our experiment from you and Symone."

Malcolm raised his palm and shook his head. "You don't have to apologize to me or anything, Director. You did what you felt was best. I don't agree with your decision, but you were within your purview to do what you felt was in the best interests of yourself and your superiors."

Mallack leaned forward and placed her hands on her desk. "No, Malcolm, I wasn't acting with my superiors in mind. I did it with you all in mind."

"I don't understand."

"Well, after the Crawler got his powers taken, I saw an opportunity to crush the Collector, and I ran with that. You were right last night, though. I wish I had trusted you, Symone, and the whole team with the theory and given you a chance to decide what to do with it."

"Director, I know that trust is a valuable commodity around here. It may do you well to give us just a little more of it. We will do anything for you, but you've got to trust that, regardless of the enemy we face."

"You're right, Malcolm. And that's why you'll make a great director. Very, very soon."

Malcolm looked puzzled and asked, "What are you talking about?"

"Well, the Company has been watching you, Malcolm, and they are convinced that you're doing an incredible job leading this team, even with everything that's been going on with the Collector. I got a call from HQ this rising, and there appears to be a post opening up in Brilliance."

"Brilliance, Director?" Malcolm chuckled. "I don't think I'd want to take that position. That would feel like a step down for me. Nothing bad ever happens in Brilliance."

"Oh, no, it wouldn't be for you. It would be for me," Mallack revealed. "Brilliance is my home, and I've been clamoring to get back there, but I didn't want to go back into the field. So, I've bided my time, ten long years. And I finally have a chance to go back there and run the Brilliance Division. Someone would need to take my place here, and I think that person should be you."

"Really?" Malcolm questioned.

"Well, given everything you've gone through for the past seven years to get where you are, all your accomplishments have surely put you at the top of the list of candidates."

Malcolm was stunned. "Boss, I don't know what to say."

"Don't say anything right now. After you've rescued Duncan, take some time, think about it, and get back to me. Whatever decision you make, I stand by you and your team 100%. You've earned it, Malcolm, my complete trust, that is."

"Thank you, Director," Malcolm grinned.

Mallack switched gears again. "How is Symone?"

Malcolm responded, "She's a shell of herself. But she said she can fight. The team is briefing her now. I trust her, she'll be good to go."

"Have you talked to her?"

"Not yet. Was waiting until after I talked to you, once I figure out what exactly to say to her."

"Just tell her the truth, Malcolm. That's really all you can do at this point."

"I know."

"Okay, go, you're dismissed."

"Thank you, Director." Malcolm got up and left Mallack's office. Standing in the corridor, he wondered whether he should go straight to the quarters and talk to Symone, or go instead to the training room and get his reps in. He opted to walk to the elevator and train instead of dealing with his emotions right then. He pressed the down button and got a message on his stripe that read, "Talk to her, Malcolm," from Mallack.

He entered the elevator and pressed "T" for training. As the door closed, he received another message that stated, "Talk to her, Malcolm," from Malaysia. The elevator rushed to the training floor, and a third message came through Malcolm's stripe. It read, "Are you going to talk to Symone?" from Alexia. Malcolm thought, *You all really want me to talk to this woman?*

Malcolm thought to send her a message, but quickly reconsidered once the elevator doors opened. He walked out of the elevator and into the corridor leading to his training room. He considered one more time messaging her and decided not to. He went inside the training room and ran through a couple simulators, focusing on the mission at hand and preparing for what he needed to do to ensure Duncan's survival.

About a cycle and a half later, Symone was in her residence, standing straight up with her arms crossed at her chest, staring out of her bedroom windows at the bustling skyline. Her heart was still reeling from the shock of the Affinity

Theory plan executed by Director Mallack and the Analyst. She wondered whether she was too hard on Malcolm but was not yet ready to address it or her feelings about it. She dug into her pants pocket and pulled out the ribbon. She played with it as she replayed the conversation she had with her mother the night before and wrestled with her mother's almost-psychic insight. A knock at her door interrupted her thoughts. She balled the ribbon up and placed it back into her pocket.

"Symone? Can I come in?" Alexia requested.

"Yeah, come in," she answered.

Alexia walked in and made her way to Symone's bedroom. She stood in the doorway, "How are you?"

Symone turned to face Alexia. "I'm okay," she responded. "Just thinking about the mission."

"Don't lie," Alexia's eyes lit up green, reminding Symone of her ability to read minds. She walked into the bedroom and sat down on Symone's bed. "What are you really thinking about?"

"Right, I don't know how I keep forgetting about that," Symone said as she sat down next to Alexia. "I'm just trying to stay focused. But that really hurt last night."

"I can't imagine what you're going through," Alexia sympathized. "It's so strange for Mallack to have kept that from you like that."

"It's infuriating," Symone admitted. "That's why I'm trying not worry about it right now, because I don't want to become a liability for the team tonight."

"I understand," Alexia sighed. She sat farther back into Symone's bed and crossed her legs. "Well, I'm here if and when you're ready to talk about it. I just want to know you're good, mission be damned."

"Thank you, Alexia," Symone responded. She turned to face Alexia and crossed her legs, too. "I'm just so stunned. Like, is the Company really this heartless? Putting people in relationships just to make them powerful pawns in their wars? Who does that?"

"I don't know, Symone. I don't think it's that simple. Like, I could be wrong, but I just don't see the Company being that cold. If Mallack was trying to make you or Malcolm or both of you stronger, I think she made that call on her own, you know?"

"How do you figure?" Symone inquired.

"Well, if what Malcolm, Malaysia, and Daisy told me about the Company is true, the Company really doesn't spend a lot of time telling the director what to do. A lot of the decisions the directors of the divisions of the Company make are guided by what the cities they're contracted to want from them. I really do believe that Mallack made her decisions based on the phone calls she was receiving from the Chancellor and senators and chiefs and whoever else has her on speed dial, especially since we got our asses kicked by the Collector over and over."

Symone understood. "Yeah, that makes sense. Still, I just wish she had said something to me, to us, about it. How do we know she didn't decide to put me on the team with that in mind?"

"Well, the truth is, we may never know the answer unless somebody asks her."

"True." Symone shook her head and continued, "Wait, how do you know what I'm talking about? Wait, never mind, I keep forgetting, sheesh!"

Alexia didn't read Symone's mind, but she let her believe that's how she knew about Malcolm and Symone, forgetting that Symone might not know about Malaysia being ordered to spy on her and wanting Malaysia to be the one to tell her. "Exactly. But listen, regardless of what Mallack did, I know her intentions were good. And can we be honest? You've gotten stronger since you and Malcolm have gotten closer. We all see it, and we know you feel it. So, Mallack got it right, don't you think?"

"My mom said the same thing last night," Symone revealed.

"Really? What did she say?"

"Well, she said that all my years of training and fighting and winning have led to this moment, this whole quarter, and that I've wanted for so long to get stronger. Though I might not be happy with the method, the outcome is still the same, and I'm 'shining like the star you're meant to be,'" Symone raised her hands in the air.

"She's not wrong, Symone. You've become one of the strongest defenders in Uri City. And this city – not just us, not just Mallack, not just the Company – the city, Symone, Uri City needs you."

"That was really good," Symone sighed. "Seriously, though, thank you. I needed to hear that."

"You're welcome," Alexia responded. She crawled over to Symone and gave her a big hug. Symone fought the urge to stain Alexia's shirt with her tears. "So, are you going to talk to Malcolm?"

Symone released Alexia. "I don't know. I don't think it's the right time. I'm still mad at him. Plus, we got this mission, and I don't want to make things worse right now. Maybe after we get Duncan back."

"Okay, I'm going to hold you to that, though." Alexia stood up. "You need to talk to him."

"I hear ya. I'll talk to him."

Alexia left the room, and Symone stood back up and looked outside her window. She wrestled with her lingering lack of trust in Malcolm. She still was unsure whether he had a hand in Mallack's decisions. She wanted to confront him on it, but she also did not want to become nor create a distraction that would put the team at greater risk of failing their mission. Reminded again of what her mother said last night, Symone asked herself, "What do I want?" She lay back on the bed and surrendered to its softness, trying to release the tension and rage coursing through her body. She closed her eyes and shed a single tear. She then summoned the strength she was accustomed to immersing herself in and boxed her emotions up and placed them on a shelf in the corner of her mind.

While the Elite stitched itself back together, across town, another team leader was getting ready for her team's next assault on the Company's Elite. In the green-lit hallways of her lair, the Collector pranced her way to a training room that she and her followers used regularly to enhance themselves. She placed her palm on the reader, and the door unlocked. The training room mimicked the Company's training rooms, right down to the striped lights in the walls and the cloaking along the whole room. Standing at the other end of the room was a bald, gargantuan figure at least seven feet tall, whose massive, rugged figure looked like he was carved out of a mountain. He punched a punching bag slowly, methodically, grunting each time he landed a blow on it. Left, right, left, left, right, right, left, right. The Collector slowly walked up to him, her steps flowing in the rhythm of his beating pattern.

She tapped his shoulder and said, "Hi there! Just wanted to check on you and see how you're doing."

He stopped, dropped his arms, and turned slowly to face her. His head basted in sweat, eyes white as snow. He smiled and bellowed, "I've never felt better."

"Good, because it's time," the Collector declared.

He breathed a deep sigh of relief and returned, "Finally. All this training has bored me long enough. What is my assignment?"

"Just as we discussed before. The Company's Elite."

He looked at the Collector with slight concern. "The Elite, you say? Boss, are you sure I'm ready? Have I trained long enough?"

The Collector waved her arms. "Are you kidding me? This is what you were born for! Your destiny awaits tonight. Show them, show the world, who you are and what you are made of!"

His eyes lit red then purple. The ground shuddered, and his eyebrows began to glow.

"Yes, it is time." He rapidly punched his right fist into his left palm three times, sparks flew from his hands, and the punching bag base levitated off the ground.

The Collector shivered from a tingle rolling through her spine. She let out a small moan, then said, "Come, let's get you suited up, and we'll bring the rest of the team in to hash out the details for tonight." The Collector placed her right palm on his back and motioned him out of the room.

Cycles went by, and Malaysia, Alexia, Karl, Daisy, and Symone all waited in the commons for Malcolm to return. No one dared ask him where he was or what he was doing, feeling that he probably needed time to get his mind right before reconnecting with the team. Malaysia couldn't take the waiting anymore, though. She said, "I'm going to reach out."

"Oh, thank Akan," Alexia responded. "I wanted to, but I didn't want to be the one, if that makes sense."

"Gee, thanks," Malaysia quipped. She sent a message, "Malcolm, we're ready when you are. We're in the quarters."

Malcolm stood on the rooftop watching the skyline as the suns were racing to pass the horizon. He felt the buzz of his stripe and read the message. He returned, "I'll be down in a few minutes."

Malaysia felt the buzz on her stripe and read the message. "He said he'll be down in a few minutes."

"Good deal," Karl responded as he lay his head back on the cushion of the couch he sat on.

Malcolm paced the rooftop as he ruminated on the task at hand, his team, his feelings about Symone, and Mallack's surprise announcement. *So much has changed, is changing. I don't think things will ever be the same again. This whole quarter has been nothing but chaos. Since that night with the incident at that battery lab, everything has just unraveled. And being with Symone hasn't made things any easier. We've gotten closer, and we have definitely gotten stronger. But is she a distraction now? Maybe I should just leave her alone. She already thinks I had something to do with Mallack's plan. Maybe that's what we needed, maybe this will stop the chaos. But was it really chaos? Or am I creating a problem that doesn't exist? See, this, this is why I don't like getting close to people. It's just too much to deal with. Frimas, and now Mallack might leave? Ugh, I don't know what to think. Let's just focus on this mission, get Duncan back, and close the book on this once and for all.*

Malcolm made a call. "Hello?" a woman's voice answered.

"Hi, Ma," Malcolm responded.

"Oh, Malcolm, it's so good to hear from you, my son!"

"Listen, I don't have a lot of time. Can you get Dad on the line, too?"

"Sure, I'm patching him through now."

A moment later, Malcolm's dad said, "Malcolm! What's up, junior?"

"Hey Dad. I just wanted to tell you that I am about to go on an extremely dangerous mission, and if I don't make it out alive, I wanted to tell you both that I love you both very much and thank you for everything you've ever done for me."

"Oh, Malcolm, we love you, too. We are trusting and believing in Akan that you will make it through, just as he's gotten you through every other mission you've ever been on. We love you!" his mom replied.

"That's right, son, we love you, and we know you will make the right decisions to complete your mission and get out alive. Go do what you gotta do, and call us when you're back home," his dad declared.

"Yes sir, I love you both. Later." The line disconnected. Malcolm took one last look at the skyline, took a deep breath, then turned around and walked to the elevator and said, "Let's get it."

Back in the quarters, the team looked at the clock as it read 12:45. Malaysia said, "Alright, crew, we have to assume Malcolm's on his way. Let's get ready. Meet back here in fifteen."

Everybody got up and went to their residences to put on their uniforms and cloaks. Daisy walked up to Malaysia and asked, "Hey, is Malcolm okay?"

"I hope so. He's got a lot to deal with right now, but if I know him right, he's probably said, 'Let's get it,' at least once, so he should be. Suit up."

"Yes, ma'am," Daisy responded.

Weapons and Wardrobe prepared each person an enhanced uniform and cloak. The Elite opened their closets and saw two buttons in their uniform compartment. Everyone took the buttons – one the uniform, the other the cloak – and snapped them together. They then stripped themselves down to their undergarments and gym clothes. They placed the buttons on their chests near their hearts, and the buttons quickly spun to lock themselves in place. They then tapped the button once, and their stripes lit yellow to confirm the docking sequence. AI confirmed their identities to ensure that the right person had each button, and their stripes lit white. They then double-tapped their buttons, and their uniforms began to envelop their bodies from the chest all over.

As everyone finished their preparations, Malcolm entered the quarters. He noticed the team wasn't in the commons and figured they were getting their uniforms on. He walked toward the residences just as everyone began walking out of theirs back to the commons. Malaysia noticed Malcolm and said, "It's about time! Worried we were going to have to leave without you."

The team stopped when they all saw Malcolm. Malcolm marveled at the team's enhanced uniforms and said, "Alright, Elite! Weapons and Wardrobe got us new uni's, huh?"

"They did, and they are amazing!" Alexia wowed.

Daisy's uniform was modified to cover her legs entirely, and the red had silver speckles riddled all over it. Malaysia's uniform maintained purple as the primary color, but now the black only showed up on the belt and around her collar. Alexia's blue stripes in her green uniform now ran in the front and back instead of the sides, running up each leg and flowing to her neck. Karl's black and gold looked as rugged as a boulder. And Symone's color scheme was flipped, where now the star and stripes were crimson, and the rest of the uniform was gold with crimson speckles.

Malcolm stopped himself short of staring at Symone's new color scheme and the enhancement that covered her hair loc-by-loc. "Well, let me get mine on, and then we'll get started. I'll meet you all in the commons."

They all walked toward the commons as Malcolm walked to his residence. Symone noticed Malcolm's hesitance in gawking at her, and she yearned to be near him. Just as Malcolm was about to enter his residence, she called out to him, "Malcolm?"

Malcolm stopped, turned around, and resisted the urge to sense her presence and power. *Don't take that from her.* "Yeah, Symone?"

Symone had so much to say and summed it up to a simple sentence, "When this is over, we have a lot to talk about."

Malcolm held a relieved sign in his chest. "You're right. So, let's make sure we win."

"Okay," Symone answered. She turned and walked to the commons as Malcolm turned and entered his residence to retrieve and install his uniform and cloak. He did the same as the others, and his uniform and cloak enveloped him as he donned all black with blue and silver stripes across the sides. He marveled at himself in the mirror and repeated his admiration of Weapons and Wardrobe's craftsmanship.

He walked out and met his team. "Okay, let's go over the plan one more time. Daisy, start us off."

Daisy said, "The location is an old Chioro sanctuary with three sections – the outer courtyard, the colonnade, and the inner sanctum. We believe the inner sanctum is the most likely place Duncan will be located."

Alexia continued. "We are split into three teams – Daisy and I are on the ground and will lead UPD and Karl and Symone into the outer courtyard. UPD will secure the perimeter and set up shop in the courtyard. Daisy and I will explore and secure the colonnade. Daisy will then enter the sanctum and make visual confirmation on Duncan. She will then return to me."

"After I return to Alexia, we will enter the sanctum and secure Duncan," Daisy finished.

"Team Two is Karl and me," Symone recalled. "We will stand at the boundary of the colonnade and the courtyard. Once we receive confirmation of Duncan being secure, Karl will enter the sanctum while I stand in the colonnade."

"I will stand with the three and provide ex-fil support to get everyone out of the sanctum and into the colonnade," Karl continued. "We will then continue our ex-fil through the colonnade to the outer courtyard."

"Team Three is Malcolm and me," Malaysia stated. "We will keep the skies clear and scan the area for any anomalies or enemy enforcements. Once we make visual confirmation that you are in the outer courtyard, Malcolm will provide support to create a pathway for us all to escape. Karl will take the lead, UPD will follow behind, and Symone will take the rear."

"If at any time we run into enemy fire, we exercise extreme prejudice, but our primary objective is to get Duncan and to get out. We live to fight another day," Alexia echoed.

"Remember," Malcolm concluded, "we do not have visuals due to a barrier that is covering the sanctuary. If at any point one of you find what is creating that barrier, smash it to bits. But don't focus on looking for it. Keep your focus on getting Duncan and getting out."

"Copy that," Malaysia said.

Malcolm summoned a little more energy to say to his team, "Okay, team. Usually, I have some great motivational speech to give us, but this time all I have is this: let's get our brother back, whatever it takes. Symone said this back when we were with Dredge, 'what's the point of having these powers if we don't use them when people need them the most?' This is exactly that time. Every skill we've ever learned, every enhancement we have, every training, every battle, it has led us to this moment. We don't fully know what we're going to face out there tonight, but whatever it is, we will face it together. And without a doubt, we will all get out of there alive. Let's get it."

"'All I have is this,' he says," Malaysia joked. "Sounded like a motivational speech to me, and it was great. Let's go, team!"

Everybody rose from their seats. Malcolm stood next to Symone for a moment and wanted to say something to her. *I am so glad you're here.* He chose not to instead and walked to the kitchen.

Focus, Symone, she summed, staring at her man and how delicious he looked in his uniform. She walked toward the quarters entrance.

Malaysia and Karl watched their interactions. Karl whispered, "They're gonna get us killed, aren't they?"

"Nope, not on my watch," Malaysia replied. "I'm gonna talk to Malcolm. You think you can handle talking to Symone?"

"Please," Karl replied, "If I can talk to you, then Symone is child's play."

"What's that supposed to mean?"

"If you have to ask, then you'll never know." Karl walked away.

"Whatever," Malaysia dismissed him.

The team walked out of the quarters and toward the elevator. Director Mallack, Stephanie, Dax, and the Analyst met them as they stood at the entrance to Intelligence. Mallack said, "Elite, good luck. Bring Duncan home."

"Yes, ma'am," Malcolm responded.

The Collector, meanwhile, sat in an executive chair in her complete uniform, in a white-lit room with an unassuming woman in a black pencil dress sitting across from her in a lounge chair.

"Ammo is in place now?" the Collector inquired through her stripe.

"Yes, Ammo is in place. He is locked in the platform now," Streak said as she stood in the inner sanctum of the ruined Chioro sanctuary. The building took on the darkening luminance of the sky and was riddled with broken glass, rubble, dust, and brick. Streak turned to look at Ammo, whose hands were firmly secured in a box that stood about three and a half feet off the ground and was about the size of a desk. He was located in the middle of the sanctum which was a vast circular room that could easily seat one thousand guests.

"Fantastic," the Collector cheered. "And the team?"

"Everyone is in place, waiting for the Elite to show up."

"Now, remember, for this to work—"

"I know, I remember, they all must enter the sanctum. Don't worry, their plan to get Ammo out of here will easily get disrupted."

"Exactly. We cannot fail. We've come too far. How is our subject?"

"He's anxious. But I believe he is ready to go to battle and will give the Elite a run for their money."

"That's what I love to hear! Everything is going according to plan!" the Collector beamed.

Streak grinned. "You have this funny way of making the most dangerous plans sound like a theme park ride."

"What's the point of living if you're not going to have fun along the way? This is going to be a fantastic time! You're in for a real treat. Get ready, the Elite are coming to you. Have fun, and remember, live to fight another day. Don't be a hero, none of you."

"Understood, boss," Streak cut the communication.

The Collector sat back, inhaled and exhaled deeply, then said to her guest, "Tonight is going to be a show for the ages, wouldn't you agree?"

The unassuming female stroked a small lynx in her lap and replied, "Absolutely. I'm delighted to be here to witness greatness tonight."

"Great! Let's sit back and wait our turns to party. Are you hungry? Want something to eat?"

Streak relayed to Hex and Sonic, "Alright, the Elite are enroute. Everyone, get into position and wait for my signal to strike. Remember the mission and play the game right."

"Copy that," Hex acknowledged.

"Ready," Sonic signaled.

The Elite got off the elevator and entered the parking garage. They marched to the to three hovercars Intelligence prepped for them, one for each pairing. Malaysia and Malcolm entered their car first, followed by Alexia and Daisy, then Karl and Symone. Malaysia and Malcolm's car autopiloted and led the way out toward the Underbelly.

Malaysia sat across from Malcolm, and Malaysia seized the opportunity to get into Malcolm's head and pull any latent distractions or feelings out of him.

"Okay, Malcolm, so let's get this over with."

Oh man. Great. "Get what over with?" Malcolm asked.

"You're mad at me, right? So, let's have at it."

"Ugh, do we really have to do this now, Malaysia?" Malcolm pleaded.

"Yes, because I don't want to ride in silence knowing you got things on your mind. So, what's up?"

"Fine," Malcolm growled. "We might die tonight, so I guess I should get this off my chest. I'm just pissed at you because you didn't tell me what was going on with you and the director. You're my girl, Malaysia. With everything we've been through, I just didn't expect you to be in on this big 'Affinity Theory' secret. Especially to the point where you were asking me questions about Symone and me, watching us and reporting what you were observing to the director on the regular. That just wasn't right."

"I know, Malcolm," Malaysia admitted, "and I felt terrible about it once I knew what the observations were all about. I originally thought Mallack just wanted to make sure you weren't mistreating Symone and hindering her training. But once she and the Analyst told me about the Affinity Theory, I told her right then that she should have told you and Symone what her plan had been. Now looking back on it, I should have told you and let Mallack be mad with me."

"You made the best decision, Malaysia. You gave Mallack a chance to make things right. That's the Malaysia Jones I know."

Malaysia sighed. "Believe me, Malcolm, I was going to tell you yesterday. I got caught up in my head about beating the Collector and panicked. Once you walked in the quarters and told me you knew, I knew I had screwed up."

"I know," Malcolm agreed. "By then, I had just finished talking to Mallack, after talking to Symone, after talking to the Analyst—who I had to pry the information out of to begin with."

"He just can't hold water, can he?" Malaysia joked.

"No, he cannot. I was so pissed with Mallack, but it hurt like Frimas to tell Symone. She thinks I knew the entire time and was only trying to hook up with her to make myself stronger."

"For real? She said that?"

"Yes, and that mess hurt. But I can't fault her for feeling like that. I'm her superior, and the Affinity Theory was actually affecting us both. It makes sense that she would strongly consider that possibility. I didn't know what to say or do. That, and she was about to blast my body apart."

Malaysia leaned forward and asked, "So, what does that mean for you two?"

"I honestly don't know. I don't think Symone would want anything to do with me after this. It seems to me that her whole 'don't take my choices' thing might be a deal breaker for her. If she thinks I took her choice – to be with me, to get stronger, to be on this team – away from her, she may have no problem cutting ties and moving on."

Malaysia displayed shock. "Moving on? From what, the Company?!"

"The Company, me, everything. Symone's gotten stronger, obviously. She can do whatever she wants to do with her powers. She doesn't have to stay with us. And, like I told Mallack, our boss just gave Symone ammunition to move on without hesitation."

"I don't know, Malcolm," Malaysia questioned. "I don't think it'd be that simple for her. I don't think Symone wants to call it quits. Not with the Company, and for sure not with you."

"For real?" Malcolm was puzzled.

"Come on, Malcolm. Symone is not going to just give you up because of this. Sure, she's angry. But once you two talk for real, I think you'll see – as will Symone – that this, you two, are worth fighting for, worth keeping together. Forget the Affinity Theory. Everybody in the unit sees you two are a perfect fit. The way you two are around each other, challenge each other, care about each other, crave each other. Face it, you two belong together. She makes you better, and you make her better. Affinity Theory be damned. Mallack didn't set you two up. The Company didn't push you two together. The Analyst didn't matchmake you. You two did that all on your own, and it would be insane for you not to fix this."

Malcolm looked at Malaysia and replied, "And you said I was the one with the motivational speaking skills?"

Malaysia laughed as she patted Malcolm's knee. "All I'm saying, Malcolm, is that you two deserve each other, and I think you owe it to yourselves to try. Screw that stupid theory. Go get your girl. Well, *after* we beat the Collector down."

Malcolm responded, "Yes, ma'am."

Malaysia sighed. "Are we good? For real?"

Malcolm sat back and nodded his head. "We're good, Malaysia, always."

Karl, meanwhile, stared at Symone, and while the silence was comforting, it was also tense and cold. Karl waded in feet-first and bellowed, "Symone, you don't seem like yourself."

"Is it that obvious?" Symone shrugged.

"Not to most people. But definitely to me," Karl replied as he pointed to himself.

Symone looked down, then lifted her head and looked at Karl. "I'm just trying to stay focused on the mission."

"What's got you distracted?"

Symone wondered where the questioning was coming from. "Why do you want to know? Did Mallack put you up to this?"

Karl didn't flinch. "Put me up to what?"

Symone huffed and responded, "Look, if this is Mallack's way of doing a status update on her Affinity Theory bull, just save it."

"What are you talking about? What's the Affinity Theory? What does Mallack have to do with any of this?"

"Dammit, Karl," Symone countered, "Mallack's plan, the Company's plan, to make me stronger."

Karl leaned forward. "What plan?"

"Mallack came up with this plan to push Malcolm and me together so that our powers would get strong enough to fight the Collector's enemies. Apparently, the closer we got together, the stronger we became. And I am so pissed about that."

"How come?"

"Because they didn't tell me. In all the meetings I had with Mallack, Malcolm, the Analyst, even in Orientation, no one ever came to me and said, 'We think we can make you stronger by putting you side-by-side with K.C.' It's like I never got a say in the matter."

Karl navigated the conversation like a skilled therapist, mirroring her words and guiding her to the next logical question. "They didn't tell you, and you never got a say in the matter. That bothers you because?"

"Because I should have been able to decide for myself whether this was what I wanted."

"I see, so because you didn't get to choose to get stronger, didn't get to choose to get close to Malcolm, didn't get to choose to be on this team, you're upset. You didn't choose any of these things? You didn't have a say in any of this at all?"

"Well," Symone was confounded by Karl's reframe. "Um."

"Because I remember distinctly that you came on board with the Company without coercion, just like the rest of us. When they told you that you were Elite, you didn't fight it. When you trained to fight all of us, you made that decision on your own, despite Malcolm's typical training regimen. You had your sights on Malcolm the day you met him. And you and he had an attraction to each other that defied any limitations anyone could have set on you, including his own, explicit or implicit."

Symone held her head down as Karl's reasoning began to set off explosions in her rationale. "Yeah," she responded.

"How did the director take your choice from you?"

"She just didn't tell me that she and the Analyst were watching me."

"Symone, they're always watching us. You know that. That, too, is one of the first things they teach us in Orientation. But they rarely interfere with our lives. So, you were never pushed toward Malcolm. That happened all on its own. The Company never took your choice from you. *You* chose Malcolm. And choosing him *made* you stronger. Mallack and the Analyst made an assumption and decided to *back up* and watch you two more closely. But they didn't push you two together. You two chose that.

"Besides," Karl rubbed his chin, "they're not the only ones who took a choice from somebody."

Symone perked up, "Wait, what do you mean?"

"You remember when Malcolm told you he didn't want to fight you? You pushed and pushed, and he kept telling you no, explaining why he didn't want to get in the training room with you. And while his excuses have always been dumb, they were still his choices. What did you do?"

Symone realized for the first time she contradicted herself. Silence washed over her as the guru continued to dismantle her now-weakened mantra. Karl patiently waited for Symone to answer him, knowing he had her dead to rights.

"I took his choice from him."

"Right," Karl slowly articulated her reply, "*you took his choice from him.* But, Symone, look at what that did *for* him. You gave him the push he needed to become more than he's ever been before. And you two, and this team, have become better than we've ever been. It's not always about a choice being taken. Sometimes, fate knows what we need to become the best versions of ourselves. But if we stay locked in our narrow approaches to life – don't take my choice away from me, for example – we will never bathe in the beauty of what life can do to us, can do *for* us."

Symone's eyes welled up. "You're right, Karl."

"Screw the Affinity Theory, whatever that is. You and Malcolm are an incredible match. Everyone sees it. Everyone knows it. Mallack and the Company will make decisions about us without us knowing all the time. But they do that because they want us to be our best in defense of the city. Don't let their work distract you from your personal growth, your relationships, or your ability to fight for Uri City. You may not know everything that's going on. But remember, you always have a choice to fight for yourself, for peace, for love, for freedom, for your team, and for your people. Let that be your guide, and regardless of the circumstances, you'll never go wrong."

Symone rose up and hugged Karl. She then fought through her tears to tell Karl, "Thank you."

Karl hugged her back and said, "You're welcome, Symone. Now, let's focus and get ready to beat the Collector down and get Duncan back. And when we get back, go talk to Malcolm."

"Okay."

The Elite rushed to the destination in the Underbelly, awaiting the execution of their rescue mission and praying for a relatively quiet night, despite the sinking feeling in their souls that they were in for an unparalleled fight for survival.

30

We Go Through Them

Darkness covered the sky, broken up by the moons above and the lights below. K.C. and the Eagle landed their hovercar atop a building across the street from the ruined Chioro sanctuary. The Eagle stepped out of the car and onto the pad first, then K.C. They quickly walked over to the edge of the roof and perched there. The Eagle immediately scanned the landscape below and looked for any crack in the barrier that may give her some insight into what the team would be walking into. All she could see was a shimmering white domed luminescence that covered the entire courtyard and an empty, abandoned street in front of it.

"Well, it looks like getting any visual is a bust. I can't see through it with any frequency or wavelength switch," the Eagle reported.

"They prepared for you," K.C. responded. "Maybe if there's a way that I can pull the screen apart, you can get a peek in."

"That could work," the Eagle agreed. She pointed toward their left, "Meanwhile, UPD is arriving from the west."

They observed four buses of the Uri City Police Department roll up on the sidewalk adjacent to their building across the street from the sanctuary. Once they parked, the officers, all dressed in black battle gear and heads covered with helmets and face shields, filed out of their buses and stood on the sidewalk awaiting orders. Their captains stood before them and waited as Enchantra and Blitz pulled up behind them and parked their hovercar. They exited and walked toward the captains. "UPD?"

"Yes, ma'am, Captain Banks, and this is Captain Stewart," Banks pointed to the other captain. They shook Enchantra and Blitz's hands. "You're with the Company?"

"That's right. I'm Enchantra, and she's Blitz."

"Good to meet you. Got fifty of our best special ops at your disposal, awaiting your command."

Blitz looked around at the fifty, then looked back at the captains. "Good, waiting for our last two team members to arrive. Once they're here, we will enter the sanctuary from the gateway there. We'll need you to secure the perimeter and watch the outer courtyard."

They started walking toward the Chioro sanctuary entrance as Captain Stewart acknowledged Blitz's command. "Understood. We'll keep ten of our forces out here on the sidewalk to cover the entrance while the rest enter the courtyard and set up shop."

Banks continued, "We have UPD Dispatch on standby if we need additional units, and an evac plan has been prepared in case we need to escape. Given the size of the courtyard, damage taken should be minimal, but considering who we're up against, we don't want to take any chances, either."

"That makes sense. K.C., do you agree?"

"Copy that," K.C. concurred.

The Mammoth and Starburst pulled up behind Enchantra and Blitz's hovercar. They exited, and the Mammoth asked, "Everyone ready?"

"Yes," Blitz answered. "K.C., the team's assembled."

"Okay, T-minus two minutes, and we go."

"Two minutes?" Eagle asked.

"Yes, I'm going to try to tear through the screen now." K.C. looked at the dome and thrust his hands forward, feeling for the screen's particles. He could sense them crawling around like ants scrambling on the ground. He concentrated and placed the backs of his hands together, and as he felt the particles, he energized himself and began separating his hands from each other, feeling intense resistance fighting against him. He grunted and struggled, but he tore a hole through the screen. He said, "Eagle, now, see what you can see!"

The Eagle quickly looked through the hole K.C. created. She saw a part of the outer courtyard and switched to infrared to look for thermal signatures. She found none.

"Anything?" K.C. grunted.

"No, nothing yet. I'm looking for the colonnade now." The Eagle kept looking and switched to X-ray to determine where the colonnade was. She zoomed in and said, "I don't see anything suspicious in the colonnade. I can't see past the colonnade, though."

"Okay," K.C. said. He let go of the screen, and it swiftly resealed. He let out a couple of breaths and a sigh. "Enchantra, you are clear. Move in. Remember, team, the objective is Ammo. Get him and get out."

"Copy that. Banks, your men follow Blitz and me. Mammoth, Starburst, cover the rear. Let's go."

Banks declared, "Alright, squad, follow the Elite. Let's move."

Enchantra and Blitz led the UPD, who formed a double line behind them, into the outer courtyard of the Chioro sanctuary. Five men on each line split and stood on the sidewalk evenly spaced to guard the entire length of the sanctuary footprint. The Mammoth and Starburst walked in afterwards.

The outer courtyard was a thousand feet of heaps of rubble entangled in the roots of dead trees, bushes, and gardens. The dome's luminescence provided the team's only light source. Captain Stewart ordered the team, "Squad, give me five men every 200 feet to spread our forces across the courtyard." The remaining forty officers turned on night vision visors, activated their flashlights attached to their hand blasters, split themselves on either side of the courtyard, and methodically marched forward to scan the area of any traps or hidden soldiers. They stepped on broken glass, rocks, snapped twigs, and other pieces of debris but remained calm and focused. Enchantra, Blitz, and the captains motioned toward the colonnade entrance. Starburst and the Mammoth moved to the middle of the courtyard and continued monitoring the perimeter, waltzing each other back-to-back.

Recognizing how dark the area was, Starburst told the team, "I'm going to send a star upward to give us some light."

"Copy that," K.C. signed off.

Starburst lifted her right hand, created a star the size of a disco ball, and launched it above them. She pulled it back to suspend it about thirty feet in the air, and it lit up the entire courtyard. The team turned off their flashlights and adjusted their visors since their visibility greatly improved.

Enchantra, Blitz, and the captains arrived at the colonnade entrance. "Okay, your men continue to monitor the situation out here. Blitz and I are going in."

"Are you sure you don't need any backup in there?" Banks asked.

"Yes, sir," Blitz responded. "If we engage anything in here, keep the perimeter secure, as you'll be our best way out of here."

"Affirmative," Stewart said. "Come on, Banks. We'll stand at the entrance and guard."

"Roger that. Good luck in there," Banks said.

"Thank you, Captains. Blitz, let's move."

"Let's do it."

Captains Banks and Stewart kept their blasters drawn at the ready and faced the courtyard, their backs against the wall of the colonnade entrance. Enchantra and Blitz entered the colonnade, a relic of a tabernacle. Broken tables, demolished stone benches, chandeliers crumpled on the ground, torn veils and sheets, and years of dust and cobwebs littered the floor. Blitz fought the urge to run straight to the inner sanctum's entrance, recalling how much their carefulness mattered. Darkness enveloped them the more they infiltrated the colonnade. They inched closer to the sanctum door. Enchantra could feel anxiety and panic filling her core and, as K.C. taught her years ago, channeled it to energize herself further should the moment to attack presented itself.

"Am I the only one creeped out right now?" she admitted.

"Nope, definitely not the only one," Blitz assured her.

"Okay. This is some next-level creepy stuff. Why did she pick this place?"

"'Where it all began' was the Collector's clue. Maybe one day we'll find out what began here and crack what she meant by that."

"Stay focused, ladies. Get to the sanctum," the Eagle shifted their conversation.

"Right. We're in the middle of the colonnade. We are opening the sanctum's door now. Blitz, do your thing," Enchantra commanded.

"On it." Blitz charged herself up and blasted away from Enchantra as Enchantra focused on and swung open the inner sanctum's double doors using telekinesis. Blitz ran straight through the entrance and rapidly scanned the room: a vast circular dome with several broken windows and rubble of severely damaged and worn stone benches, lamps, chandeliers, and tables. On the opposite end of the sanctum was a pulpit with several broken chairs, destroyed tables, torn veils and shrouds, and damaged stairs. Standing in the middle of the sanctum was Ammo, with his hands firmly locked and secured in the table in front of him that shimmered gold from the cloak surrounding it.

"Guys, I have eyes on the prize. The sanctum appears empty, with no one here to engage. Running back to Enchantra now."

"Yes!" K.C. whispered while flexing his left arm in approval.

Blitz sped out of the sanctum and back to Enchantra in the colonnade. "Let's go; Ammo's in there."

"Let's get it," Enchantra echoed K.C.'s catchphrase. They marched quickly into the sanctum and said, "Ammo!"

Ammo lifted his head and opened his eyes. His heart leaped for joy and relief. He screamed, "It's about damn time! Get me out of this thing!"

Enchantra and Blitz ran about 150 feet to Ammo, fighting back tears and emotional exhaustion. Enchantra examined the box Ammo was locked in and inquired, "What is this? You can't blast yourself out of it?"

"No, I can't," Ammo resigned. "Somehow, they've disabled my powers with this thing, and I can't shoot myself out."

"You still have your powers?" Blitz inquired as she also looked at the box, trying to understand what it was.

"Yeah, I'm still fully me," Ammo assured them. "The Collector didn't take my powers."

As they scanned for a way to free Ammo, Enchantra asked, "Do you know what the Collector wanted?"

"Not at all," Ammo replied. "They kept talking about destiny, but none of it made sense."

"Okay, well, we're gonna get you out of here."

"Ladies, what's going on?" K.C. investigated.

Enchantra answered, "Ammo's arms are attached to a black box table that has several slots for something to go into. We're looking for a way to unlock him, but there are no buttons on it. I can't lift it with my mind because it's cloaked."

"Okay, Mammoth, you're up, get in there and get Ammo out of that table."

"Copy that," the Mammoth said.

The inner sanctum doors suddenly shut. Enchantra and Blitz looked up as they heard the loud bang of the doors. Enchantra tried reopening the door with her mind, but a purple shield blocked her power. She stared at the door and said, "They're here. K.C., the Collector's team is here." Just then, several henchmen ran out of the back of the inner sanctum and made their way toward Enchantra and Blitz.

At the same time, just as the Mammoth took a step forward, several henchmen ran out of the colonnade and into the outer courtyard, armed with blasters to match the UPD. The Mammoth planted his feet and noticed the henchmen getting into formation. He yelled, "Captains, fall back!"

The captains split – one on the left and the other on the right – and ran back to the front of the line before the henchmen could cut them off from their unit. Banks told the henchmen, "Everybody, blasters down! Don't move, on your knees, hands on your heads. This is your only warning!"

Twenty henchmen split on either side of the courtyard next to the colonnade, and finally, Hex appeared from the colonnade. He said, "We meet again, Elite!"

"It's Hex!" Starburst declared.

The henchmen in the sanctum filed in a single line just as another familiar foe appeared before Enchantra, Blitz, and Ammo. Her hair glowed as electric current flowed from the strands. "Okay," Streak growled. She stretched each arm, rolled her shoulders and neck, and then flicked her hands. Blue sparks flew from her fingertips. "Let's do this. Attack!"

"Streak's here, guys!" Blitz narrated.

"K.C., we gotta move," the Eagle reasoned.

"You're right, except we got company, too," K.C. said. He had turned around and saw Sonic and his backup. The Eagle turned around and noticed who they were up against.

K.C. quickly announced, "Okay, everyone, this is what we signed up for. Exercise extreme prejudice. Get Ammo, and get out, whatever it takes. If we can't go around them, we go through them!"

Enchantra said, "Blitz, I'll stand here and guard Ammo and use my telepathy while you run through them."

"Copy that," Blitz acknowledged. Without hesitation, she rabbited through the henchmen as they tried to pin her down but could not see her. She tripped, punched, and kicked them one by one. Streak stepped toward Enchantra and Ammo. She threw lightning bolts at Enchantra, and Enchantra picked up stones to block her strikes and tried launching them at Streak to no avail as she incinerated each one. Enchantra pulled down a piece of the weakened and damaged roof and crashed it into Streak, striking her dome and pinning her to the ground.

"That should keep her for about thirty seconds," Enchantra recognized. She turned around to look at the table to see if there was anything she could do to get Ammo out of it. "Ammo, do you know anything about this table?"

"Not at all. They all look like the same arm holders I'm in." Ammo examined the tables and slots to see if anything was distinctive about them. "Wait, what's this next to this slot? It's etched in. Can you see it?"

Enchantra looked at the etching and saw a familiar symbol. "Is that a star?"

"It looks like it. What about the others?"

Just then, Blitz took down the last henchman and sped toward Enchantra and Ammo, only to get popped by a lightning bolt from Streak. It sent her crashing forward. Enchantra said, "Blitz!" She then turned around and saw Streak blow the roofing off her body and stand back up. Enchantra picked up more pieces of rubble and tried throwing them at Streak, but she dodged them all. She then threw lightning bolts at Enchantra. Enchantra ran behind the black box and conjured a spell to guard them against Streak. She created a ball in her hand, then lifted her hands in the air, expanding the ball and enveloping Ammo and her inside. She hoped Blitz would be able to speed away until she could figure out what she needed to do next. Streak threw a couple more lightning bolts at the ball, and they bounced off it.

"Ugh!" Streak yelled out. She released two lightning whips from her hands and flung them at the shield. The whips bounced off the prism. "You can't hide in there forever!"

Hex and his henchmen marched forward. The henchmen started shooting their blasters at the officers, who found places to perch and shot back at them. Starburst flew into the air, but she suddenly hit what felt like a ceiling. Hex had placed a shell above her, preventing her from ascending higher. The Mammoth sped forward and tried to hit Hex, but he, too, ran into a shell, knocking him backward. Hex had created a box shell, pushing the spell to encase everyone within it. The Mammoth tried knocking the shell down with his fists. Starburst threw stars at the invisible wall and couldn't break through it. Hex pushed his hands toward each other, and the box began shrinking, pushing everyone in the box toward the middle of the floor. The officers lost their hiding spaces and vantage points. As they became exposed, the henchmen opened fire and injured some of the UPD team. Starburst flung a shield up to prevent Hex's crew from shooting the officers, then lowered to the Mammoth and said, "We gotta do something!"

"Right." The Mammoth banged on the ground a few times, creating a hole the size of his massive foot. He said, "I didn't think so. Blast him from under his feet. The box is only five-sided."

Starburst quickly slammed her hand into the hole the Mammoth created and shot a star in Hex's direction. It tunneled under Hex's barrier. Once the star reached Hex's feet, Starburst snapped her fingers, and it exploded, launching him into the air and breaking his concentration. The invisible walls shimmered white then disappeared.

"Okay, let's help these officers with these punks, then deal with Hex," the Mammoth instructed.

"Copy that," Starburst acknowledged. She climbed while he rushed forward. Starburst threw several stars at Hex's help and knocked several of them down. The Mammoth grabbed two guys, crashed them into each other, then threw one into the wall while throwing the other into a couple other henchmen. UPD began to gain ground, and Captain Banks said, "You two, get to your people; we can handle this."

Starburst and the Mammoth headed toward the colonnade entrance but were knocked out by pieces of courtyard debris thrown at them by Hex. "Not so fast," Hex said as he stood up. "We're not done here."

Starburst and the Mammoth quickly recovered and got up. They turned around to face Hex, and then Starburst said, "Mammoth, get to the sanctum. I got this!"

"Are you sure?"

"Whatever it takes! Get in there!"

"Okay," the Mammoth replied as he ran into the colonnade.

Starburst faced Hex and summoned her inner K.C., "Let's get it."

K.C. and the Eagle saw no way around or through Sonic and his henchmen. The Eagle quickly devised a plan. She touched Malcolm's back and whispered, "Step backward."

"What?" he asked, eyes locked on Sonic.

"Trust me. Just step backward."

K.C. and the Eagle took seven steps backward as Sonic and his team took seven steps forward. They reached the edge of the building, and K.C. inquired, "Eagle, what is your plan?"

"Hold onto me."

"What?"

The Eagle clutched K.C. by his side and rolled them off the roof. Sonic and his henchmen rushed to the edge of the building to figure out what had just happened. K.C. and the Eagle plummeted to the ground, and the Eagle quickly unholstered a pistol from her side. She instinctively tapped keys, and the pistol loaded a grappling hook. She aimed for the roof's edge and fired, and the hook pierced and lodged in the wall. K.C. and the Eagle felt the resistance, and their descent slowed. They lowered to a safe distance, and the Eagle released the rope from the gun. They landed on their feet, and she holstered her weapon.

K.C. shivered from excitement and admitted, "I'm so attracted to you right now. Let's do that again."

The Eagle laughed as she said, "Boy, bye! We gotta move!"

While they marched forward, sound waves bounced off the ground. Sonic wasn't giving up without a fight, and he landed in front of them. He then launched sound waves from his face, pushing both K.C. and the Eagle backward. They planted their feet to resist the waves. The UPD standing outside saw them and began shooting at Sonic. Their blasts bounced off Sonic's cloak but distracted him enough to cause him to stop his waves. He turned to face the UPD while K.C. and the Eagle stumbled forward from the sudden missing resistance. Sonic started screeching at the UPD, and they all dropped their weapons from the shrill in their ears. K.C. and the Eagle stood up, and the Eagle whipped out her gun and shot Sonic in the upper back. His cloak protected him from the bullet, but he still fell forward. He then turned around and sent that same screech to them. K.C. and the Eagle looked at each other, nodded, then looked at Sonic. The Eagle whipped out her gun again and shot Sonic straight in his chest, and K.C. pulled a rock off the ground and fashioned it into a stone bat. K.C. ran toward Sonic and took one of the biggest swings of his life, landing a mighty blow at Sonic's head. Sonic careened to the ground about twenty feet away.

The Eagle walked to K.C. and expressed gratitude as she pointed to her ears, "Thank Akan for these upgrades, right?"

"Got that right. Didn't hear a thing, did you?"

"Not a thing. It did feel weird at first, the nanites filling my ears. But it did the trick."

The Mammoth made it to the entrance of the sanctum, and he tried to knock the door down, but he couldn't break through the purple barrier. "Enchantra, Hex has the door barricaded. I can't get through it. Can you break it down?"

"Kinda busy at the moment, but I'm trying," Enchantra replied as the ball protecting them weakened the more Streak struck it with her whips. Enchantra concentrated on the barrier and began speaking a reverse spell to take down the barrier. She uttered, "Dispulsion," and the barrier lost its purple hue and disintegrated. "Try getting in here now, Mammoth!"

He noticed the purple hue vanish, and he banged the doors open and rushed to assist the team. He was immediately struck with a lightning bolt that made him stumble. He saw Blitz finally get up from her previous tumble. Blitz rushed to get behind Streak and landed a blow on her head from behind. Streak fell forward, and Blitz quickly ran under Streak and punched her upward. As Streak bent backward, Blitz rose above her, bringing her clasped fists down like a tomahawk onto Streak's head and then delivering a kick to her back.

Streak was dumbfounded as she crumpled to the ground and tried to regain her composure.

The Mammoth ran into the bubble guarding Enchantra and Ammo and hailed, "Ammo, good to see you, buddy! Okay, what are we looking at?"

Enchantra stated, "This box can't move because of the cloak, and it's cloaked from the inside. Can you move it?"

The Mammoth pressed his body against the table and tried with all his might to push it, but it would not budge. "Ugh, no, I can't move this thing."

"Crap!" Ammo declared.

"Wait, what are these holes?" The Mammoth examined the table and the inserts all over them. "What are these markings? Wait, is that my symbol?"

Streak got up and sent out a pulse of electricity from her body that Blitz sped away from. To avoid the shockwave, she ran onto the wall and then back toward Streak. Anticipating Blitz's return, Streak put her hands together and fired three bolts in succession. They struck Blitz's cloak, causing her to roll backward. Blitz quickly regained her composure and spun around Streak rapidly, creating a dust storm from all the debris around them. Streak was blinded by the storm. Blitz used this to run into the bubble.

"Guys, Streak isn't budging. What are we going to do?" Blitz asked.

"You see these markings? They're our symbols, aren't they?" the Mammoth asked Blitz.

She stared at them and exclaimed, "Yes, see that bolt? That's me!"

"I bet we have to stick our hands in these things to unlock Ammo," the Mammoth reasoned.

"Ugh, I pray the Collector comes out here. I can't stand her!" Enchantra replied. "Fine, so we just stick our arms in, and it unlocks him?"

"It seems that way," Blitz replied.

"Okay, let me recreate the bubble so Streak doesn't decimate us." Enchantra created another bubble from her mind and expanded it around them.

Streak recreated the whips and latched them onto Enchantra's bubble just as Enchantra created the second layer. She surged her energy to shock the bubble, damaging it. Bolts began to seep into the bubble as they formulated their plan to get Ammo out of the box.

"Guys," Ammo said, "maybe you shouldn't do this? Maybe that's what the Collector wants, then she'll have all of us, and that's game over."

"We don't have a choice. Besides, it's just one arm. Most of us will still be free to fight with our other hand regardless of what this is supposed to do. It's not going to chop our arms off, is it?"

"Unless she's got some really strong cloak-removal technology, I doubt that highly," the Mammoth said. A bolt almost hit the Mammoth's cloak. "Come on guys, let's do this."

The Mammoth stuck his arm in first, and his arm locked, the circle on the table around his arm and his symbol lighting up green. "Okay, you two, get in here."

"Actually, Enchantra, you stay out and keep us guarded until the others get in here," Blitz cautioned Enchantra as she stuck her arm in her designated spot. The circle around her arm and her symbol lit up green.

Starburst and Hex stared each other down, and then Hex mumbled a spell that created two shields, one for each hand. Against the backdrop of UPD and Hex's henchmen still trying to overpower one another, Starburst rushed Hex and fired off several gatlings of stars his way. His shields blocked them. She came within two feet of him and tried to overpower him with punches and kicks. He stopped them with his shield. She flew over him and threw a star at his head. He didn't compensate for the move and was slammed into the ground with the star. She then rolled on top of him and punched him twice, then powered her hand and hit him with a heat smack. She then blasted a star at him, and the momentum launched her into the air. She made a move for the door to the colonnade, but Hex twisted his hands, causing Starburst to be abruptly constricted. He launched her into a pillar and slammed her to the ground. Hex got back up and squeezed his hands, which further constricted her. Starburst started to heat up, the aura around her and nanites covering her hair changing from red to yellow to correspond to the change as she summoned the energy to overpower the restriction.

A gunshot rattled off and hit Hex in the head. The bullet bounced off the cloak, but Hex rolled to his side and lost concentration on his constriction spell. Starburst made a large star and quickly launched it Hex's way. K.C. immediately saw the star, grabbed it, changed into a hot rope, and bound Hex with it, then pulled the rope via manipulation to launch him to the opposite side of the room. Hex crashed through the wall.

K.C. jogged over to Starburst and inspected her. "Star, you okay?"

Starburst quickly got up and said, "Yes, I'm fine."

"Starburst, Eagle, K.C., we need you guys in here ASAP," Enchantra exclaimed. "The only way to free Ammo is to unlock the table by placing our arms in it. Hurry!"

"Let's move," the Eagle responded. The three moved into the colonnade and through the door to the inner sanctum.

Streak saw them coming through the door. "Finally," she smiled behind her visor. She threw lightning bolts their way, and K.C. immediately caught and dissipated them before they could hit either of the Elite.

"I'll keep her busy. You guys get inside the bubble," K.C. instructed.

"It's about time you got here. I was starting to worry that Sonic and Hex had taken you down. That would have been a huge disappointment," Streak stalled.

"Less talking," K.C. declared as he swung his bat and ran toward Streak. Streak sent bolts through her hands toward K.C. He lifted his hand and collected the bolts into a ball of electricity as he continued marching toward her. He ran past the bubble, tossed the electric ball in the air, and smashed a line drive toward Streak. It blasted her cloak and launched her backward. She flipped over, landed in a three-point stance, lifted her face, and stared at K.C., electricity flowing through her eyes behind her visor.

Starburst and the Eagle entered the bubble and saw the table. "Okay, where do we fit?" the Eagle asked.

"Look for your symbol and place your arm in the slot," Enchantra said as she held the bubble together.

The Eagle saw her bird and inserted her arm in the slot. Starburst saw her star and did the same. Both their circles and symbols lit green.

"Enchantra, get in here. K.C., we're ready. Get inside the bubble!" the Mammoth commanded.

Enchantra entered her slot, and her symbol and circle lit green. Enchantra's concentration on the bubble faltered, and it began to splinter. Streak threw a shockwave at K.C., and he used the shockwave's pulse to slide backward toward the bubble while also collecting the energy from the shockwave. He then threw it back at Streak and entered the bubble. Just as he entered, the bubble shattered. He saw Ammo and said, "Ammo, you're alright!"

"Less talking! Get in here and bust me out!" Ammo yelled, anxious to be free and use his arms again.

"Right, okay," K.C. ran to the table and found the last slot. He placed his arm inside, and the circle and symbol lit green. All the symbols and circles then lit white, and Ammo's arm circles and symbols lit white also. The table made a mechanical whirring sound, then unlocked them all out of the box. Ammo could feel his cybernetics fully operational once again for the first time in days. Excited to be free, he blasted his arms out of the box, destroying his side of it as he lifted away and flipped in the air.

"Fi-nal-ly!" Ammo yelled as he landed on his feet. "Ugh, this feels good! Can we please beat somebody down?!"

"With pleasure!" Enchantra declared.

The Elite – The Mammoth, Blitz, Enchantra, K.C., Starburst, Ammo, and the Eagle – back together again, assumed battle positions, facing Streak and ready to strike.

Streak looked at them and marveled, "Well, looks like the band is all back together now." Streak secretly sent a message to Hex and Sonic through her stripe that read, "They are free. Move now!"

"Guys," Blitz recalled, "the mission is Ammo and leave, remember?"

"She's right, you all. Let's get the Frimas out of here," the Eagle declared. "Fight another day."

"Right, let's move out," K.C. said.

The UPD in the colonnade surrounded Hex and prepared to apprehend him. Once he received the message from Streak, he instantly broke from the chain K.C. bound him with, floated swiftly to the entrance of the colonnade, then whisked his hands forward and pushed a purple energy storm that launched the remaining UPD forces across the courtyard and into the ruins. Outside, UPD tried to surround Sonic, and he stood up and sent out a concentrated cry that blasted out the windows everywhere and instantly shocked the officers, knocking them unconscious. Sonic's henchmen came down from the building and started to follow Sonic inside, but Sonic stopped them, saying,

"Keep them surrounded and make sure they don't come in." Sonic ran into the courtyard and saw Hex. He said, "You good?"

"Of course! Let's go! We don't want to miss the grand finale," Hex responded.

"What do you mean? We are the grand finale!"

As the Elite turned to exit from the sanctum, Sonic and Hex emerged from the sanctum entrance.

"Ah Frimas," the Eagle said.

K.C. looked at them, then turned and looked at Streak from behind, moving their way. He then looked at his team to the left and right and said, "Well, if we can't get around them...."

"...we go through them," Starburst finished, looking at K.C.

They reassumed their battle positions, and K.C. said, "Let's get it."

Starburst and Ammo turned to face Streak and made their way toward her. The Eagle requested, "Enchantra, give me a lift to that staircase in the corner!" Enchantra used her telepathy to boost the Eagle in the air and carry her to the top of a spiraling staircase. The Eagle caught the railing, flipped over it, and then positioned herself to launch a rifle assault on their enemies. Blitz sped to the outer wall, while K.C., the Mammoth, and Enchantra advanced toward Hex and Sonic.

Sonic told Hex, "Create the barrier." Sonic unleashed a soundwave that pushed against K.C., the Mammoth, and Enchantra as they tried to move forward and launch an attack. It gave Hex enough time to recite a barrier incantation. A purple shell surrounded the entire inner sanctum and encased everyone inside.

Enchantra examined the barrier while battling against the soundwave and said, "That's next level. We're not going to be able to cut through that so easily. They mean to trap us in here, guys!"

The Eagle set up and whipped out a foldable rifle. She propped the rifle on the railing, loaded it with a custom round, and aimed it at Sonic. She fired it, and it hit his chest. The bullet disintegrated on contact with the cloak but dealt major damage to it, stopping Sonic from broadcasting his signal. The Mammoth was the first to cut through the momentum. He speed-stomped the ground, jumped, and bear-hugged Sonic, tossed him upward, and then slammed him into the wall. He punched him several times, and Sonic then released a soundwave to push the Mammoth off him.

Enchantra lifted several pieces of debris off the ground and hurled them toward Hex. Hex countered by blasting them with energy storms. K.C. took advantage of his being distracted and took a piece of the inner sanctum roof and turned it into an encasement that surrounded Hex, trapping him in a five-foot diameter cylindrical dome. Enchantra quickly recited an incantation that trapped Hex inside the circular zone so that neither he nor his powers could leave the circle.

Enchantra ran up to K.C. and said, "Good, that should keep him occupied and on the sidelines."

Meanwhile, Streak was just getting started. She charged herself and sent a surge of electricity toward Ammo and Starburst. Ammo rolled to his right and shot off two cannon bursts toward her. The electricity broke his munitions. Starburst hurled two stars at Streak, and Streak slowed each star's momentum to a halt with electric bursts of her own. The stars imploded, and Starburst flew through the implosions and punched Streak in the face, knocking her backward. Ammo followed suit and fired multiple shots trying to overload Streak's cloak. Streak used her hands to create an electric barrier to block the incoming shots. Starburst fired a barrage of shots at Streak, and the combined efforts of the two attackers began to irritate Streak. Streak screamed, "Enough!"

She charged up and prepared to swiftly deliver a surge, but just as she was about to unleash a wave of electricity at them, Blitz rolled up behind her and suddenly grabbed her. Blitz's cloak lit up in response to the electric wave Streak had summoned. She lifted Streak high off the ground and yelled, "Now, Eagle!"

The Eagle took her shot, and it banged Streak in the head just as Blitz released her and let her go, and Ammo and Starburst unleashed the biggest barrage they could muster. They launched Streak into the air, and she crashed into Hex's barrier and slid down, unconscious from the team effort.

The Mammoth planted his feet to withstand Sonic's pulse. Enchantra and K.C. saw that the Mammoth needed help. Enchantra noticed a broken chair beside Sonic and telepathically lifted it, swiftly knocking Sonic in the back of his head. Sonic stopped screeching, and the Mammoth rushed toward Sonic again. Sonic was about to unleash another soundwave, but K.C. quickly noticed Sonic preparing for him and shifted the ground underneath him. Sonic lost his balance, and it gave the Mammoth enough time to grab Sonic by the throat and lift him in the air. The cloak shielded Sonic from the Mammoth's chokehold, but K.C. took a piece of stone and morphed it into a malleable wrap. He then summoned the wrap to enclose Sonic's head. Once it sealed, K.C. summoned the wrap to expand like a marshmallow so that Sonic could not blast it apart with his soundwaves but could still breathe.

The Mammoth then carried Sonic to a pillar about ten feet away from them and instructed K.C., "Tie him up." K.C. took another piece of stone, stretched it to form a rope, and the Mammoth used it to bind Sonic to the pillar.

The Elite stood around the room and looked at each other. They realized that they had succeeded in taking down the Collector's unit. K.C. said, "We did it, team!"

"We did, we actually did!" Blitz responded. "I can't believe it!"

The team came together in the middle of the floor where the damaged black box stood. They hi-fived and fist-bumped each other.

K.C. shook Ammo's hand and then pulled him in for a hug. "Good to have you back, brother!"

"It's good to be back. You losers missed me?" Ammo joked.

"You have no idea. We were about to hold auditions for your spot," Enchantra bantered.

Ammo laughed, "Whatever. Nobody can replace all of this."

"That sounds like the Ammo I know. Welcome back, man!" the Mammoth cheered.

They then looked up and around and saw that the barrier still stood.

"Okay, why is the barrier still up?" Starburst announced.

"K.C., think you can break through that?" the Mammoth replied.

K.C. lifted his hands to see if he could feel the sanctum's structure but was unsuccessful. "It's like a void. I can't feel anything. Eagle, what do you see? Enchantra?" He put his hands down.

The Eagle looked at the barrier and saw swirling symbols racing back and forth through the ceiling, the walls, and under the floor. She said, "This is a highly complex spell, K.C."

Enchantra saw the same thing and agreed. "She's right. This is a complicated incantation. There's an object holding this spell together. And unless we find and destroy that object, we are stuck here."

"And the only person who knows what that object is, is stuck inside that tomb you built over there," Ammo reasoned.

"Not necessarily," a familiar voice countered, booming through the sound system within the sanctum's walls.

K.C. shuddered in frustration. "The damn Collector."

"That's right, K.C.! By the way, your codename is ridiculous. You should really consider changing it. Kingdom Come, really? Are you an agent of Akan or something? Anyway, I see you made relatively quick work of my three. I'm very impressed by your teamwork. It's always fascinated me how well your powers work in concert. Seeing it in action once again – really, it's legendary stuff. I can see why they call you 'the Elite.'"

"Tell us how to get out of here, Collector!" Enchantra rattled off.

"Temper, temper, Enchantra. Really, you should consider anger management. As I was saying, your powers have intrigued me for a long time, and I know it's nearly impossible to take your powers from you, especially since your cloaks, well, shield you from me. So, rather than steal yours, I found suitable alternatives."

"What the Frimas does that mean?" Blitz said.

"Well, Blitz, I took *your* powers from other people. I found people with powers just like yours who had less sophisticated cloaking devices, if they had any at all, and, as the name you guys keep calling me implies, 'collected' them. And I decided, as a gift to you all, I would showcase your powers to you. Think of it as a final training exercise from me to you."

A door to the right of them slowly parted.

"Elite, meet, well, my Elite!"

The seven-foot gargantuan from the Collector's training room emerged, dressed in a red nanotech suit with black stripes and a red and black visor. He walked toward them and marveled, "How fitting that this place will be your burial ground."

K.C. stared at the juggernaut's uniform, and his mind snapped as he recognized the same uniform he wore in his nightmares. His dreams flashed before his eyes as the very person he had witnessed commit countless atrocities one night after another stood right in front of him. *No way! What the Frimas?! They were visions! So, that wasn't me! Thank Akan that wasn't me! So, then, maybe if we defeat this joker, then nothing in my visions will actually happen! Let's go!*

"Well, Uri City Division of the Company's Elite, I bid you farewell. Oh, I almost forgot! To break the barrier, you will have to kill him. He is what's holding the barrier up. Please try not to make too much of a mess of things. I really do love the sanctuary."

The team turned to face the Collector's warrior, gathered themselves, and resumed their battle positions. "Alright, so it's one of him, seven of us, and he has all our powers. We can take him, right?" Ammo asked.

K.C. fought feverishly to shake the déjà vu and declared, "We have no choice." He looked at Starburst, who was standing next to him. "Win or die."

Starburst looked back at him, grateful she had her visor on so K.C. couldn't see her smile. "Win or die," she returned and nodded.

The Collector's warrior slowly stepped forward again and stated, "You can call me Trent Salazar."

"Why are you telling us your name?" Blitz asked Trent.

"So you'll remember who killed you before you die."

"So lame. Let's fight already," Enchantra reacted.

31

The Elite Vs. Trent Salazar

K.C. Starburst. The Eagle. Blitz. Ammo. Enchantra. The Mammoth. The seven locked their minds in, ready to engage Trent Salazar, their only way out of the dome. K.C. felt an uneasiness within him, reconciling his desire to complete the mission with what he might have to do to finish it. He looked to the left, seeing Starburst, Ammo, and the Eagle, and to his right, Enchantra, Blitz, and the Mammoth. He picked up a piece of the black box Ammo destroyed, morphed it into a bat, and took the first step forward. The others followed suit.

"This is your one and only warning, Trent," K.C. advised. "Stand down."

"I refuse," Trent declared.

"Here we go," Enchantra stated. K.C. started running, and the others mimicked him as Starburst charged her hands, Ammo cocked his arms, K.C. started swinging his bat, the Eagle cocked her pistol, the Mammoth pounded his right fist into his left hand, Enchantra lit her eyes, and Blitz shuffled her feet.

Trent made the first move. He telepathically grabbed Blitz and the Mammoth and swiftly pulled them toward him. He lit and thrusted his hands into each of their chests, then blasted them with star power. The blasts hurled them away. He then grabbed them again, pulled them toward him again, and struck them again.

K.C. stopped running and immediately scanned the ground Trent stood on. He dropped the bat, threw his arms in front of him, palms up, and curled his fingers, feeling the particles that made up the ground. He slowly raised his hands, and a circular wall emerged from the debris, beginning to entomb

Trent. Starburst rose high and launched a star into the well. The team heard an explosion within it.

Trent created a shield with his telepathy and trapped the explosion within it, then released it into the walls of his cage, blowing it to bits. He emerged from the smoke and dust, exchanged his hands for cannons, and fired multiple shots at K.C., Blitz, the Eagle, and Ammo. The four rolled, jumped, and dodged the cannon fire, ducking behind objects that were only nanoseconds later blown apart by the blasts. The Eagle ran atop the pulpit and hid behind one of the massive thrones. She whipped out her bow, nocked a percussion grenade arrow in the drawstring, then assumed the launch position, pulled the string taut, and launched the arrow toward him. Trent sensed the arrow coming toward him, dodged it with lightning speed, and ran at the Eagle. She didn't see him coming. He grabbed her, head-butted her, threw her backward, and then thrust his hands forward, launching two stars at her. They struck her chest, and the Eagle soared across the pulpit.

Starburst flew toward the Eagle, caught her midair, and said, "Gotcha!" Starburst landed on the ground and released the Eagle.

"Thank you," the Eagle reacted.

"No problem. Go back to your perch on the staircase and try to get a better shot while we distract him."

"Understood," the Eagle replied. She ran back toward the sanctum entrance to get back to the staircase. Starburst hurled stars at Trent as she flew to engage him. Trent felt the energy of Starburst's stars and stopped their momentum. He then sandwiched them together, created a star of his own, and hurled them both at Starburst. She dodged the first one but didn't see the second one and was pummeled by the explosion, reversing her trajectory. She crashed into the purple ceiling.

Blitz got up, dashed toward him, and launched a series of punches into his chest. Trent was shocked by the barrage, but he quickly gained composure and began fighting back at the same speed, and Blitz was caught off guard. Trent blocked her punches and punched back, landing a blow to her chest. He then roundhouse kicked her in the face, caught her head on her right side as she began to tumble and spun her, then caught her head again on the left side, heated his palm, and blasted her with a star. She flew back, only to then get caught telepathically by Trent again, pulled toward him, and with his hands exchanged for cannons, shot in the chest with cannon fire. She sailed through a pillar and crashed toward the entrance of the sanctum.

K.C. felt for metal shards around the room and began lifting them from the ground. He pulled them all toward him and then thrust his hands forward, commanding the shards to attack Trent. Trent saw through the assault and quickly dodged each shard, then sped toward K.C. Anticipating Trent's move, K.C. quickly moved to his left and stabbed his bat into Trent's stomach. Trent suddenly bent forward. K.C., while still holding onto the bat, swung his right leg behind Trent and tripped him from behind, flipping Trent backward and onto the ground. K.C. then took his bat and attempted to tomahawk Trent, but Trent rolled over. Trent pushed himself off the ground and grabbed K.C.'s torso from the side. K.C. tumbled but did not fall over; instead, he dropped the bat and elbowed Trent in the head. Trent fell backward, and K.C. punched Trent twice in the head, then kneed him in the chest. The Mammoth saw that K.C. was gaining momentum and joined him. K.C. spun around Trent, grabbing his arms from behind and stretching him out as the Mammoth pummeled Trent with several punches to the chest.

Trent used telepathy to pull K.C.'s hands off him, then lifted K.C. off the ground and flipped him over himself, and the Mammoth grabbed K.C., spun him around, and tried to kick Trent before Trent stopped the Mammoth's foot telepathically. Trent then exchanged his hand for a cannon and shot the Mammoth in the chest. The Mammoth absorbed the blow, grabbed Trent's arm cannon, and threw him over his head. Trent spiraled through the air, stopped himself telepathically, and then hurled a star at both K.C. and the Mammoth. K.C. caught the star, shaped it into a net, and launched it back at Trent. Trent was shocked as the net enveloped him. K.C. strained his fingers and brought them in close to tighten the net. While still airborne, Trent could feel the heat of the net burning his cloak and its particles moving at an incredible speed. He manipulated the net, tearing it apart, and transformed some of the pieces into ropes, which he then used to lasso K.C. and the Mammoth. He then set the ropes off, and they exploded, knocking K.C. and the Mammoth on their backs.

Starburst recovered from the ceiling crash and, like a hawk, clutched Trent and crashed them into the ground below. She hit him with several heated palms and fists to the head. Trent finally grabbed her hands, but she created a tiny star and blew it up to make him let her go. She then placed her hands on his chest and launched a star into it, blasting herself upward and him about six inches into the ground. The Eagle saw this as an opportunity to shoot at Trent and readied her rifle. Trent got up from the hole, and Starburst launched herself downward. She cocked her right hand back, and as she thrust it forward, Trent exchanged his hand for a cannon, and her hand slid into his cannon, stopping her momentum. He then shot a cannon pulse, sending her flipping into the sky. She quickly gathered herself and landed on the ground. She threw star after star at him as they circled each other in the middle of the sanctum. She then hurled toward him and threw a barrage of punches and kicks to shut him down.

The Eagle trained her eye and prepared to take the shot. Trent could sense that the Eagle was about to make her move. The Eagle took her shot, but Trent used his hyper speed to race toward Starburst, catch her, and throw her in the path of the projectile. Starburst was hit in the stomach, and she recalled the moment she was shockingly hit while training with the Eagle weeks prior. The shot threw her into the ground as the Eagle looked up and was horrified. She retrained her eye, and Trent was nowhere to be found. She looked up again, and suddenly Trent appeared next to her. He grabbed her by the throat and lifted her in the air. She struggled to free herself from his grip.

Ammo slid from behind a pillar and launched several cannon shots at Trent. Trent released the Eagle and began blocking Ammo's projectiles, breaking them molecularly before they could reach him. The Eagle fell to her knees and palmed the landing of the staircase. Ammo relentlessly fired shot after shot. Trent collected the cannonballs one by one then heated them up rapidly. He threw them back at Ammo, and Ammo barrel rolled away as the blasts exploded on the ground. Enchantra took advantage and began hurling anything her eyes could see at Trent. Cinder blocks, pieces of shrapnel, parts of benches, torn veils, bricks, pillar ruins – she threw everything she could. Trent blocked them all, rendering Enchantra's assault useless. She ran closer to him and telepathically grabbed him, stretching his arms wide and lifting him in the air. She then felt Trent telepathically resist her power. She strained her mind and her hands to keep him stretched. The ground suddenly shifted underneath her, breaking her concentration slightly as she attempted to regain her footing. Trent took advantage and crashed Enchantra into the roof, then hurled her flat on the ground.

K.C. witnessed Enchantra fall and told the Eagle, "Get off the staircase now!" The Eagle summoned the strength to jump over the stair railing and barrel rolled on the ground. K.C. then manipulated the staircase and turned it into a solid metal ball, moving a couple of the stairs Trent was standing on. He lost his footing and fell, slipping into the ball that K.C. was creating. K.C. then sealed the ball shut, and it crashed to the ground.

K.C. wobbled as he stood up. He said, "Elite, everybody, get up. We don't have much time before Trent breaks through that."

The Mammoth collected himself and stood next to K.C. Blitz stood up in the middle of the sanctum, coughing a couple of times before regaining her composure and walking toward them. Ammo ran up, while Enchantra stood and backed up, keeping an eye on the ball. The Eagle, gun in hand, did the same, backing up with her eyes on the steel chamber. Starburst got up and levitated towards the team.

"Okay," K.C. began. "Trent is beating us down."

"No crap!" the Eagle reacted as they huddled. "He's all of us for real!"

"Right, and he's using the same divide and conquer strategy we've seen the others use before. We gotta do this together as one."

"Right," the others agreed.

"He may have all these powers, but he won't be able to think through which to use if we disorient him. When he breaks from the ball, whatever we do, we stay planted right here and shellshock the Frimas out of him."

"Copy that."

The team trained on the ball. They watched as the graphite gray container suddenly started glowing red with orange cracks breaking forth. The team assumed battle positions. Enchantra placed her hands in front of her, Ammo cocked his arms, the Eagle trained her pistol, and Starburst built a star in front of her. Suddenly, the ball split into several pieces and separated like a cracked egg. Trent stood unfazed by the trap. He lifted his hands upward, then slowly swung them in front of him, controlling the pieces of the shell to place them in front of him. He manipulated the shell pieces, turning them into throwing stars the size of frisbees. He flicked his fingers, and the pieces soared toward the Elite. Enchantra and Starburst formed shields in front of the team, and the shards disintegrated in the shields. Enchantra and Starburst then pushed their shields toward Trent, and Trent used manipulation to part the shields and walk past them.

Enchantra took advantage of Trent being slightly distracted and bound him with a quick spell. Before Trent could understand what was happening, K.C. manipulated the ground under Trent, turning the stone into a mix of quicksand and wet cement. Trent sank to his knees, and then K.C. hardened the stone, trapping Trent's legs and preventing him from easily speeding away. Trent struggled to decide which power he needed to overcome the Elite's play. Blitz seized the opportunity and dashed around Trent, kicking up a dust storm that kept him from being able to see anything going on. Trent couldn't see and began adjusting his vision to reorient himself. The Mammoth emerged from the dust storm behind Trent and suddenly grabbed Trent's hands to make sure he couldn't escape.

"Okay, guys, take him down!" the Mammoth yelled.

The Eagle, Starburst, and Ammo took aim at Trent, and with everything they had, they blasted Trent's head, firing shot after shot as the Mammoth jumped to safety to ensure that he himself wasn't taken down. They pummeled him with a light and steel show for fifteen seconds before K.C. said, "That's enough."

They disengaged, and the dust settled, revealing Trent lying unconscious from the barrage. The Elite looked around and saw that the purple cage around the sanctum still held, unfazed by their assault.

They walked to Trent and stood over his body. Ammo said, "I guess he's still alive."

"So, what do we do?" the Eagle asked. "Do we kill him?"

"Yes, let's get out of here," Ammo quickly replied as he cocked his left arm and aimed it at Trent's head. "Just give me the word, K.C."

Blitz jumped in and pulled Ammo's cannon to the side. "No, wait, we can't just kill him like this."

"Why not? He's the enemy!" Ammo resisted Blitz's reasoning.

"Because he's disarmed. We're not killers. That's not who we are or what we do," the Mammoth said.

"But you heard what the Collector said," Ammo objected as he pulled his arm back from Blitz. "This is the only way to get out of here!"

"Yeah, but Ammo, come on," Starburst interjected. "We can't just off the guy. We're defenders, not assassins."

"K.C., what do you think? He's the key, right?" Ammo pleaded.

K.C. thought about it for a moment. Then he answered, "Are we sure he's the only way to get out of here?"

"That's what the Collector said," Blitz answered.

"Exactly," K.C. said. "That's what *the Collector* said." Everybody thought for a moment while K.C. continued. "It's what the Collector wants. Put us in an impossible situation and make us become something we are not. Be a pawn in her game. Why does she want us to kill this dude?"

They all pondered the question while the Eagle quickly answered, "Who knows."

"I don't think he's the only key to get out of here. Enchantra, this is an incantation, right?"

Enchantra looked up and said, "Yes, a very powerful incantation that Hex pulled off."

"Is there anything that can break an incantation like this?" K.C. asked.

Enchantra thought for a minute, then responded, "Actually, yes. Now that I remember, an incantation is typically attached to a phrase the spellcaster knows. If we know the spell and the phrase, we can bring down the wall."

"And we don't have to kill Trent," Blitz reasoned.

"Bingo," K.C. responded. "Go get Hex, and let's get the spell from him."

The team left Trent lying on the stone and walked to Hex near the sanctum entrance. Hex was still trapped in the cylindrical dome built by K.C. and Enchantra. K.C. said, "Okay, once you remove the spell, bind him as quickly as possible, Enchantra."

"I understand," she acknowledged. She waved her hands and said, "Dispel." The green circle around the cylinder dissipated, and K.C. dismantled the cylindrical dome. Hex tried to look past the dust to screen his surroundings, but Enchantra immediately raised him up and stretched him wide. The team surrounded him, weapons drawn, daring him to try something.

K.C. said, "Alright, Hex, tell us how to get out of here. What was your incantation—"

Hex scoffed. "I'm not telling you a thing. You think we didn't prepare for this?"

"Here we go," Ammo retorted. "Let me guess, 'destiny,' right? I told y'all that's all her team kept blabbering about."

"That's right, and one thing about our boss is that she always knows what she's doing."

"Well, right now, all of us will die if we don't find a way out of here, and you are holding the key. Tell us what we want to know!" K.C. yelled.

"Not a chance," Hex responded with a smug smile. "We'd rather die than give up anything to you."

"This isn't getting us anywhere," Starburst stated.

"Got that right," the Eagle agreed.

While the team reckoned with Hex's kamikaze declaration, Hex silently relayed a message to Streak through his stripe. "Wake up, Streak! Trent is down, and they're trying to find another way out of here."

K.C. said, "Maybe I can pull the wall apart?"

"You can try," Enchantra responded, "but I don't think it will be that simple. You said you couldn't feel anything, a 'void,' remember?"

K.C. closed his eyes and began feeling for the particles within the purple wall. He said, "I can feel the ground next to it, but I can't feel it or the wall behind it. Let me try harder."

On the opposite side of the sanctum, Streak still sat on the ground with her back against the wall. The buzz from her arm jostled her from unconsciousness. She shook her head a couple of times and batted her eyes to wake herself up. She looked down and read the message from Hex. A burst of adrenaline hit Streak, and she became more alert and oriented. She stared at the Elite and recognized she had the element of surprise on her side. She studied the barrier, touched it with her hands and sent a wave of current through it.

K.C. could sense the electric current flowing through it and said, "Wait, I can feel something. It's getting stronger, more intense."

"Can you pull it?" the Eagle inquired.

"I don't know, it's fast, moving all over."

The team looked at the wall and noticed it was turning yellow and white. The Mammoth said, "K.C., look! Is this you?"

K.C. opened his eyes and saw the wall changing. "No, that's not me!"

The current hovered directly above the Elite. Streak mouthed, "Boom."

A gigantic lightning bolt fell from the ceiling and blasted the entire team. Everyone's backs hit the turf. Streak placed her hands palm-down at her side and used electricity to blast herself upward and float toward the team. Streak noticed that Sonic was still bound to a pillar and his powers disabled by the sound barrier around his face. As she began to charge her hand to free him, Starburst quickly regained her composure and launched a star from her hand toward Streak. Streak deflected it with lightning bolt, then sent several strikes toward Starburst. Starburst levitated from the ground, and the bolts missed her and struck the ground. Starburst rushed to meet Streak in the air. Streak lowered herself to the ground and delivered several bolts toward Starburst. Starburst created a shield to deflect the bolts, smashed the shield into a ball, and then launched the ball toward Streak. Streak created a whip and flung it at Starburst, binding her. She then shocked her, dealing damage to her cloak.

Ammo was the next to recover, getting on one knee, aiming his right arm cannon, and delivering several pulses toward Streak. Streak was hit by three of them, knocking her off balance and causing her to release the whip. Starburst landed on the ground, hovered to meet Streak, punched her in the face, and then kneed her in the stomach. Streak flipped over but recovered easily by somersaulting and tomahawking Starburst with her foot to her head. Starburst and Streak fell together, and Streak rolled backward, got back up, then aimed her hand toward Sonic's face and delivered a powerful strike to his face, splitting the barrier from his head. It was enough of a break for Sonic to unleash a powerful sound wave that finished the job and, consequently, jolted the rest of the team from their slumber. Sonic then screeched to break the pillar and free himself from the bond that held him there.

K.C. woke up and realized that the Collector's team was reassembled and ready for round two. "Everybody, get up. Alright, here's what we're going to do. Enchantra, you're the only one who can figure out this incantation thing, so you take Hex, create one of those bubbles you made earlier, and get the incantation and password. Meanwhile, the rest of us will hold the line here, protecting her until she succeeds."

"But K.C.," Enchantra hesitated, recalling the Analyst's assessment of their opponents' power advantage, "what if I can't get him to give it to me?"

"Then you make him! You can do this! I have faith in you!"

Enchantra nodded, "Okay." Enchantra levitated Hex, and they rushed to the ruins of the staircase. She rolled her hands together and created a crystal-looking bubble, then quickly raised her hands in the air, enclosing Hex and her within its expansion.

Trent grunted and shook out of his slumber. He reoriented himself to the sanctum and remembered what was happening. He quickly shifted the ground around him and rose from the stone pit. The rest of the team noticed the bright red figure rising from the ground. "Guys," the Eagle replied. "The giant woke back up."

K.C. quickly issued instructions. "Alright, crew. Blitz, Mammoth, you hold Trent off for as long you can. Ammo, Eagle, Sonic is your guy. Starburst and I will take down Streak. Ammo, Eagle, help Blitz and the Mammoth once you're done. Leave nothing to chance. Let's beat these jokers!"

Inside the bubble, Enchantra pondered how to persuade Hex to reveal the spell to her. She thought of trying a compliance spell but dismissed the thought since Hex still wore a cloak she couldn't break through. *The only way I'm going to get it out of him is by getting inside his head, but I've never broken through a cloak before. No time to think, just have to do it.*

Enchantra levitated Hex and concentrated on his mind, instantly feeling mental resistance from the cloak as the nanites fought against her wavelength and frequency manipulations. Enchantra grimaced but soldiered on, eyes glowing deep green, knowing this was the only way to free her friends from the Collector's trap. As she worked, she couldn't tell that Hex was working to free himself from Enchantra's bind. Hex mumbled, "Omree, matrox, unidesh, akjoni," several times, and the casing cracked. Before Enchantra could ascertain his plot, the bind exploded into several green pieces, and Hex flung his hands forward. The energy changed from green to purple, and Hex launched the pieces toward Enchantra. She quickly put up a shield, and the shards bounced off the shield and hit the bubble. Hex started to float away to escape the bubble. Enchantra realized that he was trying to escape and desperately raised her hands in the air and released a green wave from her body that latched onto the bubble. Hex banged his hands on the bubble and couldn't get through it. Enchantra breathed a sigh of relief as Hex said, "So, you've performed a barrier incantation yourself, huh?"

"Yes, that's right," Enchantra answered as she breathed heavily, exhausted from her energy expenditure. "And the only way out is through me."

"Unwise, my friend. You are no match for me. You're not worthy of fighting me."

"Shut up and give me the incantation!" Enchantra replied as she reached out telepathically and began to pull Hex her way. Hex resisted, conjuring three energy needle daggers and launching them in her direction. Enchantra rolled to her left to dodge the first two, grabbed the third, and threw it back to him. She then picked up some of the ruins within their purview and threw them his way. He stopped them and threw them at her. She flipped backward twice. She then rolled her hands to create an energy storm ball, and Hex did the same. They threw ball after ball toward each other, bursts appearing each time their storms collided with each other. Enchantra took a slab of the stone floor Hex stood on and sandwiched him between it and the barrier. Hex plummeted to the ground and was shaken by the assault. Enchantra walked toward him, but then she felt her arms and legs tighten and squeeze together, Hex telepathically restricting her movement. She fought to break his bind while Hex broke a piece of a ruined pillar and tried to crash it into her head. She felt the pillar coming and captured it with her mind, sent it past her head, and split it into several pieces. She broke free from Hex's bind. Hex stood up, placed his hands together, and launched an energy storm at her. Enchantra couldn't compensate and was hit directly in the chest. She flew to the opposite side of the bubble and slid to the floor, writhing in pain despite her cloak taking the damage.

Outside the bubble, Blitz and the Mammoth began their stand against Trent. Blitz raced to meet Trent and threw a barrage of attacks at him. Trent compensated and fought Blitz at the same speed. They traded punches, blocks, kicks, and jabs while kicking up a dust storm, making it difficult to see who was where. The Mammoth picked up cinder blocks and threw them in the dust storm, hoping to land a shot on Trent. Trent sensed the blocks, stopped them with his mind, and let them drop. He then punched Blitz in the face, grabbed her right leg, and flipped her up into the air. He switched his right hand to a cannon and shot three blasts at the Mammoth, landing one in his chest. He then, as Blitz was still in the air, launched a star into her chest and launched her across the floor. She quickly recovered in a three-point stance. Blitz noticed the Mammoth stumble and asked, "Are you okay, Mammoth?"

"Yeah, I'm good. What are we going to do?"

Blitz responded, "I'm coming to you. Grab my hand and hold on tight!"

"Wait, what? Whoa!" Before the Mammoth could rationalize Blitz's command, he was traveling near the speed of sound, holding on for dear life to Blitz's hand as their cloaks intertwined to bind them together. They spun around Trent, and Trent trained his eyes to track Blitz's movements.

Blitz ran away from Trent, spun around, and then told the Mammoth, "I'm going to let you go; you give Trent all you got!"

Blitz ran toward Trent, then suddenly stopped and let go of the Mammoth's left hand. Their cloaks instantly unbound, The Mammoth swung his right fist, and with all his might, he caved in Trent's chest. Trent soared across the sanctum, crashing into the purple barrier and kicking up dust and debris as he slid to the ground.

Meanwhile, Sonic wasted no time and screeched at Ammo. Ammo hadn't been outfitted with the upgraded cloak, so Sonic's sound disoriented him. Ammo quickly found a column, stood behind it, and found relief by the sound void it created. The Eagle stood behind another column and fired multiple shots from her pistol. The wave Sonic created crushed the bullets before they struck him. The Eagle switched her eyesight and looked at Sonic to determine the weak points in his sound assault. Sonic realized he might have an advantage on Ammo and began walking up to him. Ammo could hear the sound getting worse, the ringing in his ears intensifying. Ammo saw another column about twenty feet behind him.

He told the Eagle, "I'm going to dash to that column over there. Cover me!"

The Eagle locked onto the weak spots in Sonic's attack and said, "I got you. Go now!" The Eagle whipped out her bow and nocked three arrows within its drawstring. She stretched the bow and released, the arrows whizzing through the voids of the sound wave and, as they got within five feet of Sonic and exited the void, exploded near him. The explosions distracted Sonic as he turned around and blasted the Eagle. She struggled to move forward, the sound waves so intense that it felt like hurricane-force winds blowing against her. She stood before a broken pew and knelt to keep from flying away. Ammo took advantage and ran to the other column. He then switched out his right hand and released about thirty tiny remote, camouflaged percussion grenades, figuring that the sound wave didn't touch the ground. Sonic intensified the sound even more and began walking toward Ammo again. He didn't notice the grenades that rolled toward and circled him on the ground.

Ammo counted, "5, 4, 3, 2, 1, boom!"

The grenades exploded like firecrackers and popped Sonic's feet. He stopped screeching and jumped from one spot to another, trying to keep his composure. The Eagle felt relief and didn't waste time. She exploded from the ground and rushed toward Sonic. Ammo did the same. The Eagle reached Sonic, seized his arms, and yelled, "Ammo, now!"

Ammo jumped in the air, exchanged his hands for cannons, and released a barrage of cannon fire at Sonic's head. The Eagle kneed Sonic in the back, pushing him forward, and the cannon fire berated Sonic. He wobbled, then crumpled to the ground.

"Come on," Ammo said, "we gotta help Blitz and the Mammoth."

While Ammo and the Eagle raced to help their teammates, Enchantra got up from the edge of the bubble while Hex levitated and quickly flew over to meet Enchantra on the ground. Enchantra created a green wall before him, and he crashed into it. He then took the wall of energy and swirled it in his hands, then released it. Hex swirled his hands, and several purple glowing circles arrayed him like a rainbow. The centers of the circles began to glow white with a purple haze. They blasted energy ropes that latched onto Enchantra's arms, legs, torso, and neck. They then began to reel her in closer to Hex. Enchantra resisted, sliding slowly on the ground as she tried to dig her heels in. Enchantra's eyes glowed deep green, and she manifested green blades before her. With her mind, she swung the blades and cut herself free from Hex's grips. She then tossed the blades at Hex. He dodged them both.

Enchantra realized she was running low on mental and physical stamina and couldn't keep up with his pace. *We will trade shot after shot all night long if we keep this up. I gotta distract him. I've never tried this in the field before. Akan, I better not mess this up. Let's get it!*

Enchantra closed her eyes, then whispered the word, "Multiply." She opened her green glowing eyes, and suddenly, Enchantra began showing up in multiple places at the same time. She released ten of herself in front of Hex. One of them charged at Hex and began fighting him head-on, and Hex was unsure what to do, not one for hand-to-hand combat. The others rose to the ceiling and began throwing green lassos at Hex, binding him one-by-one. Hex pushed the first Enchantra away from him with his mind. The others then lifted their right hands in the air while holding onto their lassos with their left. Hex decided to dispel them all at once, concentrating his energy on the ropes. The ropes began to change from green to purple while the Enchantra clones held onto the lassos like their lives depended on it. Hex then released a wave of energy through the lassos, and each of the Enchantra clones pointed their hands at the barrier, and just before Hex's wave reached them, they each whispered a word that he couldn't hear. His energy reached them, and they all exploded at once, their energy knocking into the barrier.

Enchantra lay on the ground wounded and dazed. Hex walked over to her and placed his foot on her chest. He knew he had won and declared victoriously, "In what universe did you think you could beat me? As I said, you are not worthy."

Hex raised his hand toward Enchantra's body and yelled, "Petrify!" Nothing happened. Hex looked confused. He raised his hand again and yelled, "Petrify!" Nothing happened. He backed away from Enchantra and waved his hands around, causing only the air and dust around him to stir.

Enchantra stood up, walked over to Hex, looked him directly in his visor, and said, "In what universe? This universe." She grabbed him, headbutted him, and then punched him in the stomach.

Hex doubled over and coughed. "How? How did you disable my powers?"

Enchantra created energy lassos, bound Hex's arms, legs, torso, and neck, and stretched him wide. "Okay," Enchantra said. "I'm gonna take a quick break, and then I'll break your cloak. I'm a little tired. Should have brought a snack or something, sheesh."

Streak and Starburst had been fighting each other well before K.C. had issued instructions to the team. Starburst lifted off the ground and blasted Streak with a continuous heat ray. Streak created an electric shield that deflected the heat. K.C. ran past Starburst and forged his way to Streak. Streak took her right hand and threw bolts at K.C. He stopped them, pooled them, and then threw them back at Streak to no avail. Streak rolled to her left, and Starburst's array shot passed her. Streak then pounded the ground with her palms and sent lightning bolts through the ground, blasting upward at K.C. and Starburst. They both flipped backward and rolled to a three-point stance, then exploded and met Streak. K.C., Starburst, and Streak traded punches, jabs, knees, kicks, and blasts. K.C. threw a punch that Streak caught with her fist, then shocked his hand to pop his arm backward, kicked him, and blocked Starburst's kick with her left hand, then double-tapped her stomach with a punch and a shock. K.C. spun around, lowered himself to the ground, stretched his leg, and tripped Streak. Meantime, Starburst stumbled backward, but created a star and popped Streak in the left thigh. Streak fell on her back but rolled to her left to recover.

Streak took three steps back and charged up. She released a shockwave of electricity, and Starburst dashed in front of K.C. and created a heat shield before the blast could force them away. K.C. stared at the wall of heat, and an idea sparked in his head.

"Star, create the biggest star you can in front of Streak. She will try to one-up you but don't fall for it. Just keep building the star until I tell you to stop."

"Are you sure?"

"Trust me."

Starburst left the shield up as she and K.C. took about twenty steps backward. Star then pulled the heated wall toward her and used that energy to start a star. The nanites covering her locs changed from yellow to white as she built the star and expanded it. Streak saw Starburst's energy and charged up even more, then released a wave of electricity at the star. K.C. concentrated and pooled the electricity with his right hand at the contact point between Streak and Starburst's attacks to make it appear that Streak was fighting against Starburst's power. At the same time, K.C. took apart one of the thrones in the pulpit and repurposed the pieces to become metal vines. Starburst began to strain as she held the star in place.

"K.C., the star is becoming unstable," she said to him.

"Just a little longer. You can do this."

The vines slowly made their way to Streak, who was oblivious to the stealth trap K.C. was setting because of the challenge posed before her eyes. She pushed more power, more electricity, convinced she would outduel Starburst. The vines finally reached Streak, and K.C. clenched his left fist. The vines quickly grasped Streak and stretched her out. Streak was shocked and yelled, "What the Frimas?!"

K.C. then instructed Starburst, "Throw the star at Trent!"

Starburst looked around and noticed that Trent had recovered from the blow the Mammoth delivered, and he and Blitz, Ammo, and the Eagle were engaging with him across the room. She followed the order and hurled the star at Trent, signaling to the rest of the team, "Everybody move!"

The four Elite looked back and saw a huge ball of light Starburst hurled toward them. "Heads up!" the Eagle yelled. Everybody rolled away while Trent looked in shock. The star struck Trent's hands as he prevented it from making direct contact with him. Starburst flew toward the team as Trent dissipated the star. The Eagle continued firing percussion grenades from her pistol. Ammo switched to electromagnetic pulses to slow Trent's movements by sending tiny shocks to his cloak. He fired as many of them as he could get off. Trent lifted off the ground and used telepathy to push them all, including Starburst, farther backward, then pulled them into him and launched stars at each of them. They fell backward from the blasts they absorbed.

Starburst swiftly ascended, hoping that Trent didn't notice. Trent's frustration grew, and he ripped a huge slab of turf and turned it perpendicular to make a wall. He then pinned Ammo, the Eagle, the Mammoth, and Blitz to it. They struggled and couldn't free themselves from his telepathic grip. He then created four stars in front of him, then manipulated them into lances. He raised his hand to lift the lances, aiming at their heads, ready to deal a heavy amount of damage to their cloaks and render them unconscious.

Starburst swung around, flew behind Trent, and shot a gatling to distract him. Trent turned around and hurled the stars at Starburst while dropping the other four and the wall to the ground. Blitz took advantage of the opportunity and rushed at Trent, head-butting him in the back and pushing him forward while Starburst dodged his lance attack and shot a continuous heat stream at Trent. Ammo shot cannon strikes at him, and the Eagle took her pistol and fired grenade after grenade at Trent. The Mammoth took several large strides, then leaped high into the sky, tomahawking Trent in the head. He then quickly jumped out of the way to avoid the blast radius of his teammates. They dealt massive damage to his cloak, and Trent could sense he was losing the upper hand. He blasted off to the ceiling, built the biggest star he could comprise in a five-second span, and plummeted to the ground, setting off an explosion that blasted everyone backward and to the ground.

Moments before that explosion, K.C. was wrapping things up with Streak. Streak attempted to blast herself out of the ropes, but when she let out a bolt of electricity, the electric current flowed through her cloak and dealt damage to it. K.C. said, "No, not this time." He then amplified the pool of electricity he had collected from her previous assault and made it five times more powerful by exciting the particles and pushing them closer together. He then released the electric ball, and it struck Streak, dealing an incredible amount of damage to her cloak. K.C.'s trap turned Streak into a battery, and the electricity flowed through the vines, overloaded the nanites in her cloak, and depleted its integrity to zero. Her cloak shimmered and dissipated into thin air. Streak screamed in frustration.

K.C. walked over to her and punched her in the face to knock her unconscious. He replied, "This time, stay down." The explosion occurred, and K.C. looked back and rushed to help his team with Trent.

Back in the bubble, Enchantra got up from her break and concentrated on Hex's cloak again. She focused her energy and felt the nanites once again resisting her. She strained to find a point of weakness within the cloak. She could hear the nanites as if they were speaking to her. She stopped straining to push at them and instead silenced her mind to listen to the wavelengths and frequencies they danced to. She walked up to Hex and touched his head with both her hands. The frequencies and wavelengths resisted her touch, and she heard them hum. Her mind hummed back. And the more they hummed, the more she hummed. The cloak began to fall into a trance, and Enchantra could sense that she was gaining control of the frequency the cloak sang to. She hummed more, and the cloak responded, their melodic sound becoming harmonious. Enchantra hummed more, and her vocals changed to a three-part harmony. The cloak shimmered from head to toe every two seconds. Enchantra's harmony changed to five-part, and the cloak shimmered faster. Enchantra's harmonic soundwave intensified, and the cloak shimmered even faster. Enchantra then shrieked, and a green pulse took over the cloak. The cloak couldn't hold up any longer, completely unraveled by Enchantra's hypnotic serenade. It exploded and dissipated into thin air. Enchantra opened her eyes and couldn't believe what she had accomplished.

She cheered, "Oh, Akan! I did it! I did it! Oh, this is exciting, yes!"

Hex couldn't understand what had just happened. "How the Frimas?"

"Remember, *this universe*," Enchantra recalled. "Now, let's see what the incantation and password are!" She tapped into his mind, searching his memory up to the point where he created the barrier.

When the sanctum turned purple, Hex said, "Omree, matrox, unidesh, akjoni," raised his hands in the air, then said, "Cassandra."

Enchantra released Hex. "Hey, who is Cassandra?"

"Another time, Enchantra," Hex bellowed.

"Wasn't expecting you to be so cordial with your response," Enchantra smiled.

The Elites got up from the blast, groaning and writhing in pain, but their cloaks still held firm. K.C. ran over to the Eagle and asked, "You good?"

"Yeah, I'm good. Everybody, you alright?"

"All good, just shaken up," the Mammoth answered.

"Still good," Blitz declared.

"All good," Starburst stated.

"Good to go," Ammo said.

"Do you see Trent?" K.C. inquired. "Anyone got eyes on him?"

The Eagle adjusted her eyesight to clear the dust from her eyes. She couldn't see Trent anywhere. A bubble similar to Enchantra's appeared at the epicenter of the blast. The Eagle pointed at it and said, "I think Trent trapped himself in a bubble."

"Let's move," K.C. said. Everyone crept closer to the epicenter. As they drew near, they noticed that dust seemed suspended in the air, and debris from their battle and the ruins of old were floating everywhere.

"Are you guys noticing this?" Starburst analyzed.

"Yeah, this can't be good," K.C. declared. Suddenly, the temperature of the sanctum rose sharply, and some of the debris in the room started changing colors. "Guys, I think Trent is about to try something insane. We can't afford to wait any longer for Enchantra. We're going to have to do something."

"Yeah, but what, K.C.?" the Mammoth asked as the Elite stood side by side. "Everything we've done, he's countered. I don't think this guy can be killed, especially if he's cloaked. We can try overloading it, but—"

Blasts of star power shot from Trent's bubble, nearly knocking the Mammoth in his head.

"Everybody fall back!"

The Elite backed up about thirty feet, dodging any shots from the bubble. They began losing their footing as Trent lifted them from the ground, too. The Eagle declared, "He's messing with everything in here. This is Enchantra's world."

"It's mine, too," K.C. reasoned. "Look, the ground is sifting. If we don't act soon, Trent's gonna kill us all."

"K.C., can you manipulate the bubble?"

Before he could answer, all six of the Elite were hit with cannon fire at the same time. They stumbled and were hit again. They took a defensive stance. Starburst levitated and created a shield to give themselves a chance to devise a plan of attack.

"Is the room shrinking?" Starburst asked.

The Eagle scanned the room's square footage and realized, "Yes, he's crushing the room."

Enchantra looked at the floor below her and realized that Trent must be doing something outside her bubble, and she didn't have any more time to waste. She concentrated her mind and yelled, "Omree, matrox, unidesh, akjoni! Cassandra!"

The rest of the team looked up, and suddenly the purple hue of the room glowed white for three seconds, then shattered and dissipated. Enchantra had taken the barrier down.

K.C. said, "Excellent! Enchantra did it! Let's get the Frimas out of here!" As the team tried to get up, Trent's manipulations and telepathy got worse, and the sanctum walls began crumbling. The roof splintered into a million pieces and floated upward. The Eagle looked through the gaping hole in the sanctum wall and noticed that Trent's powers were extending beyond the sanctuary and into the streets and edifices of the Underbelly.

"K.C.," the Eagle declared, "we can't let Trent get away with this. He's going to flatten city blocks."

The bubble Trent resided in rose from the blast epicenter. Enchantra deactivated her bubble and was nearly hit by a blast from Trent's bubble. She called to her team, "Hey, where are you guys? Are you alright?"

"Enchantra," Blitz yelled. "We're on the other side of the bubble and Starburst's wall."

"Oh, Akan," Enchantra yelled. She created a shield to protect herself from Trent's blasts. "He's created a nexus, guys. Nobody in or out. He's going for the death blow. All his powers are combined in that thing. What are we going to do?"

"K.C.?" the Mammoth asked.

"Enchantra," K.C. asked as they began to crane their necks, watching the nexus rise, "you can't do anything?"

"No, K.C., I don't know how he learned a nexus command, but once it starts, nothing can stop it, not even him."

K.C. thought to himself, *Okay, if this is how it ends, then so be it.*

"Everybody, get out of here. The mission is Ammo, and you can complete it now. I'll stay behind and take him down—"

"Shut up, Malcolm!" Starburst retorted. "This isn't one of those movies where you make a final speech, and we leave while you make the sacrifice play. How do we stop him? How do *we* stop him?" She pulled his arm.

"Okay, okay. Um," K.C. pondered, then asked, "Enchantra, do you have one more bubble in you?"

"I think so," Enchantra returned.

"Alright, I'm going to pull Trent down here. When I do, Enchantra, put us in a bubble one more time. Starburst, place a shield before us to keep Trent from shooting us. The ground keeps shifting under us, so Enchantra, keep us steady. Eagle, scan the bubble and look for a weak point we can exploit. Ammo, Blitz, on those weak points of his bubble, I will need you to hook them with lines. Mammoth, on our signal, keep the nexus pinned to the ground for as long as you can. Starburst, you and I will build a planet when that happens."

"Build a planet?" Starburst asked.

"Remember your training," K.C. recalled.

"Oh, right, okay, I'm ready!"

"Okay, Elite, let's get it!"

Back in the courtyard, Captains Banks and Stewart, along with the UPD forces, were huddled together in the center of the area, surrounded by Sonic and Hex's henchmen, weapons drawn against them. They worried about the Elite but were not in a position to do anything to help them, not even to call for backup. Suddenly, the UPD and the henchmen heard a loud bang and looked up. They saw a massive ball of fire and light begin to rise from the sanctum.

Captain Banks asked Captain Stewart, "What the Frimas is that?"

The henchmen tried to focus on keeping the UPD surrounded, but they were also nervous, unsure whether the ball was a friend or a foe. A fireball shot from Trent's nexus crashed into the courtyard, blasting some of the henchmen nearest the colonnade walls from their posts. The other henchmen saw them, and then they looked up and saw more fireballs headed their way as Trent's powers grew more unstable and out of control. Not knowing it was Trent, the henchmen broke their positions and walked backward toward the sanctuary entrance, blasters at the ready. Captain Stewart noticed it and realized they, too, needed to defend themselves against whatever this was.

"Alright, troops, gather yourselves, get your weapons, and light that ball up!"

More fireballs rained down on the courtyard, and the UPD fell back, seeking cover behind any available object, preparing for what was to come. Captain Banks got on his stripe and tried to contact the Elite. "This is Captain Banks, can anyone from the Company copy?"

The Elite heard him, and K.C. responded, "Go ahead, this is K.C.!"

"K.C., is this you or the enemy?"

"Definitely the enemy!"

"Affirmative, we'll provide you with backup. Our men are standing at the ready."

"Fire at will, Captain!"

"Copy that! On my mark," Captain Banks declared to his team, "3, 2, 1, light 'em up!"

The UPD and the Collector's forces emptied their clips to stop Trent from decimating them. Trent only became more agitated and erratically rained down on them and the Elite.

K.C. concentrated his mind on the particles that made up the nexus and could feel their rapid, unstable pace. The ground underneath him shifted, and he requested, "Hold me up, Enchantra." She stabilized his footing as he sensed the nexus, which at this point was fifty feet in the air.

"Any higher, and he will approach the cloaking and try to break it to set himself free from this place," Blitz examined.

K.C. stretched his hands out as Starburst created a shield to protect him from the blasts Trent sent him. He grabbed the nexus and began to pull it down. Enchantra, holding K.C., used her telepathy to wrap a lasso around the nexus and helped. K.C. looked at her and smiled, then looked back at the nexus as they worked together to pull it down. Trent resisted them, and they felt him pull them upward. They said, "No!" and continued pulling the nexus down.

Fifty, forty-five, forty, thirty-five, thirty, twenty-five, twenty feet.

"Enchantra, now, bubble us!"

Enchantra quickly yelled the word "Encasement," and a bubble appeared before her hands. She threw her hands up, and the bubble swallowed the Elite and Trent inside. Trent tried to leave the bubble and banged against the ceiling. His bubble turned red and shook violently. The temperature rose again, and their cloaks recognized the toll his energy was taking on them. Streaks of fire and energy continued to berate the team, saved only by Starburst's shield.

"Guys, our cloaks' integrity won't be able to hold out much longer; we've been in battle too long," Blitz announced as she noticed her cloak was holding at 15%.

"Eagle, now, scan it!" K.C. commanded.

"Already done. He's got four weak points underneath the shell that will make good anchor points. Enchantra, go with Blitz and set the hooks."

Enchantra created a telepathy shield, and Ammo released four hooks and gave them to Blitz. "Do your thing, Blitz!"

Enchantra and Blitz scurried underneath Trent's nexus. "You ready?"

"Yes," Blitz answered. The Eagle transferred the anchor points to Blitz's visor. Enchantra released the shield, and Blitz ran as fast as she ever had, then ran atop the nexus itself. Trent scrambled to keep up as the Eagle instinctively shot percussion grenades at the nexus with her bow to distract him. Blitz ran revolutions around the nexus as she planted the first and second hooks. Trent tried to blast her with a shot of heat, but Enchantra caught it before it could hit her. She placed the third hook and kept spinning around Trent's world. Finally, she planted the last hook and jumped off the nexus. Trent tried to hit her once again but missed by a thin hair as she hurdled over Starburst's heat shield. Enchantra levitated back behind the shield. K.C. then manipulated the debris under Trent and created four heavy-duty ropes that latched onto the hooks.

"Enchantra, drop the bubble! Mammoth, go!"

Enchantra dissipated the bubble, and the Mammoth emerged from the shield and grabbed the ropes as Trent tried to leave again. The Mammoth pulled with all his might, yelling as his biceps flexed and his feet planted. Trent heated the ropes, and the Mammoth's cloak responded at his hands. The Mammoth began to slide as the ground shifted again. Enchantra held him steady.

K.C. manipulated the ground right next to Trent while pooling shots Trent was taking at him to push him face to face with the nexus. Starburst rose, shielding herself from Trent's blasts, and stood face to face with the nexus. K.C. looked at Starburst, and Starburst looked at K.C. They understood the assignment, and Starburst slapped the nexus with both hands and released a wave of energy that began to encapsulate the nexus. K.C. felt Starburst's energy, the same energy he sensed many weeks prior, the energy he craved, the energy he could control. K.C. slapped the nexus and then began converting the energy into planetary matter. The nexus began to harden. Trent tried to blast through, and neither Starburst nor K.C. budged. They concentrated their focus, and the Elite looked beyond the heat shield with wonder as K.C. and Starburst combined their abilities again. Within moments, the fire from the nexus had died down, the storm of telepathy ceased, and Trent was now entombed in a silver ball of rock that started sprouting grass.

The Mammoth pulled it down, and it settled on the ground.

K.C. and Starburst landed and knelt on the ground, and the others came to them.

"Wow, guys, that was incredible!" Enchantra declared.

"Absolutely, my Akan, I still can't believe my eyes," the Eagle cited.

K.C. and Starburst breathed heavily. They dropped their visors, looked at each other, and smiled as the Mammoth approached them. The Elite breathed a sigh of relief as they had taken down Trent and effectively saved Uri City from destruction.

"Okay, guys, can we go home *now*?" Ammo whined.

K.C. rolled from his knees and sat down. "Copy that, brother. Let's get UPD in here and—"

Suddenly, the team heard a deafening splinter behind them. Trent cracked the tomb like an oversized egg. He wasn't done yet. He was determined to emerge from the planet and complete his mission. The team turned around and saw fissures cracking along the rock's surface, red fire bursting from the seams.

"Frimas," the Mammoth lamented, "he won't back down. What do we do?"

K.C. thought about it. "Captain Banks, are you okay?"

At this point, the UPD had regained control of the courtyard as the Collector's henchmen had run away when the Elite had encased Trent in Enchantra's bubble. "Yes, we are all clear in here. The Collector's men have all fled."

"We need you and your men to enter the colonnade and find the generator powering the cloak now!"

"Copy that! UPD, we're entering the colonnade. Ten of you stay out here and cover our rear. The rest of you, come with Stewart and me. We're searching for a cloak generator. Let's go, move, move, move!"

Captain Banks, Captain Stewart, and the UPD got into formation and entered the colonnade to look for and destroy the cloak.

K.C. said to Enchantra, "I need your help. Levitate me. Starburst, come with me!"

"Where are we going?" she asked.

"Up! Just send me up!" K.C. yelled. He used his senses to grab the planet, and as Enchantra levitated him upward, K.C. and the planet went upward, too. "Mammoth, Ammo, Eagle, break the chains holding Trent!"

Without hesitation, the Mammoth grabbed a chain and tugged at it. Blitz assisted by pulling with him. Ammo and the Eagle aimed their weapons at the hooks and fired multiple shots until they all broke.

Starburst followed and caught up with K.C. "What are we going to do?"

"Encapsulate the planet one more time," K.C. said.

"Okay," Starburst complied. She slapped her hands on the cracking shell and once again created a star around Trent's planet. They had gotten seventy-five feet in the air, and Trent's star hit the cloak and could not move any higher. Enchantra was losing focus, drained from battle. K.C. could sense he was falling out of Enchantra's range.

"Somebody, help Enchantra stay awake. You can do this!"

The Mammoth grabbed Enchantra and sat her on his neck. "You got this, Enchantra, just a little while longer."

"Okay, I can do this," she whispered as blood began to flow from her nose. She concentrated with the might she had left to keep K.C. in the air.

K.C. requested, "Captain, have you located the generator?"

Captain Banks had searched the colonnade and was now searching five rooms near the back right side. His team searched room one and got nothing. They entered the second room, but still nothing. Captain Stewart and his team started with room five and found nothing, but then they saw a massive generator humming lowly in room four. Stewart declared, "We located the generator!"

"Destroy it now!" K.C. demanded.

"UPD, fire at will!"

The twenty officers, accompanied by Captain Stewart, fired at the generator, causing it to spark several times before it exploded. The barrier surrounding the sanctuary shimmered yellow, then dissipated.

K.C. said, "Okay, Enchantra, one last push, send me up!"

Enchantra's eyes batted several times as she concentrated on sending K.C. higher. Starburst followed at his side, the star power from her hands still flowing around Trent while his shell kept breaking apart. Once they had ascended approximately three hundred feet in the air, K.C. focused intently on the energy of the star. He then said to Starburst, "Catch me."

"What?"

K.C. looked at the star, stretched his hands wide, curled his fingers, and closed his eyes. Malcolm remembered what it felt like to be connected to Symone's body, the energy that flowed from her body to his, and the fire within his veins during their most intimate time together. He still could not explain how he felt her inside him, but at this moment, the star power flowing through his hands, he could feel Symone engulfing him again. K.C. connected himself with the star and the planet as white light flowed from his hands. He opened his eyes, and Starburst could not believe what she was witnessing.

Enchantra had no more energy in her, and she collapsed on top of the Mammoth, letting K.C. go in the process. The Mammoth noticed she slumped and swiftly pulled her off his shoulders, cradling her gently. He then looked up and said, "Frimas, K.C.!"

K.C. drew in a deep breath, contemplating the action he wanted Starburst's star to perform. He levitated five feet away from the star. Starburst was awestruck. *He's flying!*

White light flowed from his hands and surrounded the star. K.C. curled his hands in front of him. The energy, the star, and Trent's nexus connected. Then K.C. exploded his arms as wide as the east is from the west, and the star, the energy, and Trent's nexus separated like a completed dismantled machine. Trent floated in the middle of the dissection in his red and black uniform. He stared around, trying to understand how the nexus was broken.

K.C. could sense the nexus reforming and realized there was no way to halt the process in time to save Trent. He said, "I'm sorry, brother," then slammed his hands together. The energy, the star, and Trent's nexus slammed back together and exploded into a billion sparks, creating a fireworks show that the residents of the Underbelly stared at with wonder, fear, and confusion. K.C. closed his eyes and descended from the sky.

Starburst stared in wonder at the light show, trying to comprehend how K.C. was able to pull that off. "Hey, how the Frimas did you—" she asked, only to look and see he was falling. "Oh shit!"

"Yeah, come get me!" K.C. replied. Starburst rushed and caught him, and they floated down together to the rest of the team.

"Is it over?" Blitz asked.

K.C. landed with Starburst and said, "Yes. It's over."

"Thank Akan!" Ammo yelled. "I am exhausted!"

"Who are you telling?" the Mammoth agreed. "Poor Enchantra missed the light show. She's out cold. It's time for us to head home."

K.C. lay flat on the ground. "I'm gonna lie here for a minute first, then we can go home," K.C. said. His entire body was on fire. "I can't move."

The Elite looked around the sanctum, noting the carnage they unleashed to secure their teammate and brother-in-arms. The Eagle noticed something was off. "Hey, where are Streak, Sonic, and Hex?"

Starburst looked up and around and noticed the same thing. She responded, "You know what, I don't even care at this point. If they got away, good for them. They didn't want any more of us. And I for sure don't want any more of them."

K.C. said, "Not 'win or die' not wanting to fight anymore." He chuckled, then said, "Ow, shouldn't have laughed on that one," as he grimaced in pain. Starburst knelt next to him and placed her hand on his chest.

The Eagle said, "Alright, I'm going to summon the hovercrafts here. They can fit through this big hole we created."

K.C., Starburst, the Mammoth, the Eagle, Blitz, Enchantra, and Ammo. The seven Elite of the Uri City Division of the Company had just taken down their biggest challenge and completed the most crucial component of their mission: live to fight another day.

32

Final Debrief

Malcolm opened his eyes for the first time in two days. The exhaustion and fatigue coursing through his body and mind left him paralyzed. He granted himself the permission to rest until his body agreed that rising from his bed was the appropriate course of action. He barely remembered getting to his bed in the quarters after returning from battle. He rolled his head to see what time it was. The clock read 02:43, and the three suns danced in the sky. Malcolm rolled his head back straight and stared at the ceiling. He was overjoyed now that the team was whole again. He thought about how well they fought together to save the city from a disaster. He wondered how Symone was doing and where things would stand now that things seemed to be at peace.

Malcolm batted his eyes a couple of times, then reasoned that it was time to get out of bed. He commanded his body to rise, and his entire body strained to sit upright, tension and pain reminding him of the battle before. He groaned but mustered up the energy to sit up straight. He rolled his shoulders, craned his head from side to side, breathed a deep breath, released it, and then crashed back onto the bed on his right side. His body said, "Not yet." And he responded, "You're right." He closed his eyes and began to slip back to sleep again.

Malcolm felt a buzz in his left arm. His stripe was going off. It was a call from Malaysia. He answered it and croaked, "Hello?"

"Ew, you sound like you're still asleep."

"I was. What's up?" Malcolm asked.

"Mallack is ready to debrief. She said three days were enough, and it's time to close the file."

"Wait, three days?" Malcolm looked at the clock and noticed the time was different, reading 1:57 now.

"Uh, yeah, you've been out cold, Malcolm."

"Okay, alright, I'm on my way. Let the rest of the team know."

Malaysia was sitting in the conference room with the rest of the team in their chairs, waiting on him, the director, Intelligence, and the Analyst. "We're all here, Malcolm, waiting on you, sleepyhead. Throw something on and get in here before Mallack does."

"Alright." Malcolm's mind said, "Get up," but his body still was not getting the message, and he strained to get up and out of bed. He sat up straight, dragged his legs to the edge of the bed, planted his feet onto the floor, and managed to stand up, groaning and grimacing the entire time. He limped to the closet and grabbed a shirt and a pair of sweatpants. He struggled but managed to get them on. He found a pair of tennis shoes and laced them up. He walked out of his residence, and after about three minutes of strained walking, he pushed through the conference room doors and saw his team. He looked across the room, noticing each chair was filled, especially Duncan's.

"There he is," Karl reacted. "For a minute, I thought we would have to put you in the Infirmary for real."

"That might not be a bad idea," Malcolm answered, believing that if his body kept this up, he might need to spend a week there.

"No kidding!" Alexia said as she massaged her temples. "Probably the only person not feeling anything is Karl. They put a hurting on us."

"Yeah. Good for us we outdid them and can live to tell the tale," Daisy commented.

"True that," Duncan said. "I owe you guys so much for getting me out of there."

Malcolm made eye contact with Symone as he walked to his usual seat beside her. Symone grabbed and rubbed her neck. Malcolm pulled his chair back, stood in front of it, then pulled the seat forward and sat down. Symone asked, "You good?"

Malcolm shrugged, "I guess so. You?"

She turned her head to face him, "Yeah, I'm good."

Malcolm stared at her and thought, *Still just as gorgeous as the first time I laid eyes on you*, then smiled. Symone cut her eyes and said, "What?"

Malcolm returned, "Nothing. Just really glad to see you."

Symone quickly looked around and volleyed, "Who, me?"

"Yes, you," Malcolm chuckled.

Symone smiled and stated, "Well, thank you! I'm glad you're awake finally."

"How come?"

Symone had enough words to share with Malcolm that could fill a dictionary. She could only find, "I'm glad you're okay, Malcolm."

Director Mallack opened the conference room door. Following behind her were Stephanie and the Analyst. "Good," Mallack said, "the team's all awake and here. Let's get this started." Director Mallack, Stephanie, and the Analyst pulled their chairs from the wall in front of the holoscreen and sat down. "Give me your take on the mission."

"Malcolm and I arrived first, canvassed the area, and saw no threats," Malaysia began. "UPD arrived on the scene, Alexia and Daisy arrived next, gave UPD orders, and Karl and Symone arrived last."

"UPD split up, leaving ten outside the screen while the other forty broke up into two and stretched their forces to cover the entire courtyard," Alexia continued. "Daisy and I entered the colonnade once UPD cleared the courtyard while Karl and Symone stayed on standby."

"We moved into the colonnade and approached the sanctum door. Alexia opened it telepathically, and I stormed in and made visual with Duncan, then ran back to her," Daisy reported. "We entered together and observed Duncan with his arms locked in a box with six other slots. The box was cloaked and couldn't be moved. The door closed, and we were locked in with Streak and her henchmen."

"Same thing happened in the courtyard with Hex and his henchmen," Symone continued. "Karl was summoned to get into the sanctum to help get Duncan out of the box, but we got tangled up with Hex for a good bit."

"Same time that Sonic approached us on the roof," Malcolm added. "Malaysia grabbed me and got us off the roof, and Sonic followed. We were able to take him down thanks to the upgrades to our cloaks, keeping the sound waves from blowing our eardrums."

"We were able to get in front of Hex, so I went to help the ladies with the box Duncan was stuck in," Karl narrated. "I tried moving the box once I got in there, and nothing worked. Daisy was able to decipher that there were symbols next to the slots on the table that represented all of us, and we told everyone to get inside to unlock the box."

"Malaysia and Malcolm helped me take down Hex, and we entered the sanctum," Symone chimed in. "We held Streak back long enough to get all our arms in the slots, and the box made some mechanical noises, and Duncan blew himself out of the box."

"Yeah, and then we kicked Streak, Sonic, and Hex's asses," Duncan championed. "We were going to leave at that point, but then the room turned purple."

"Hex put a barrier up, and the Collector made her speech. Then Trent Salazar stepped in from the right of the sanctum. He was the Collector's super soldier. He had all our powers in him," Malcolm remarked.

"In him? Frimas, he was a master of them," Alexia commented. "He was destroying initially. Malcolm had to regroup us into a team formation to pummel him finally. The Collector said that the only way to get out of the room was to kill him, but we couldn't do it once we had him down. So, we had to find another way to bring the barrier down. Malcolm helped me remember that an incantation spell has a password, and since Hex put the barrier up, we could get the password from him."

"We proceeded to pull Hex from the dome we trapped him in," Malcolm said, "but doing that enabled him to wake up Streak, who then freed Sonic. I told Alexia to place Hex and herself in a bubble and get the incantation and password from Hex while we held the rest of them off. Trent woke up, and I told the team to split into pairs – Symone and me with Streak, Daisy and Karl with Trent, and Duncan and Malaysia with Sonic. I figured once we took down Streak and Sonic, we could help with Trent and keep him occupied long enough for Alexia to get what she needed out of Hex."

Alexia beamed. "I battled with Hex and was able to trick him with a nullification spell that disabled his powers and trapped him in the bubble. And then, guys, I broke through his cloak! I broke through his cloak!"

The team ooh-ed, wowed, and clapped their hands in amazement. Alexia bowed her head forward and said, "Thank you, thank you! Anyway, I broke his cloak, read his mind, and got the incantation and password. I saw the ground shift and knew I needed to exit the bubble."

"Duncan and I took down Sonic, then went to help Daisy and Karl with Trent," Malaysia continued.

"We tricked Streak and subdued her. Symone went to help them while I disabled Streak's cloak, then went to help. At that point, Trent trapped himself in a, wait, what did you call it, Alexia?" Malcolm tried to recall.

"A nexus," she returned.

"Right, a nexus. All of his powers were unraveling at once. Alexia said the incantation and password, then came out of her bubble. The wall disabled, and Trent started to rise, his impact radius widening the higher he got. We combined our forces to pull Trent down, anchor him, and Symone and I turned the nexus into a planet. We thought it would be enough, but Trent tried to break through it, so Alexia lifted me up, and Symone came with me. We asked UPD to find and disable the cloak covering the sanctuary, and once they did, we blew Trent up."

Daisy wrapped it up. "Some UPD officers sustained significant injuries, but no one was killed. The Collector's big three left before we could re-apprehend them. We called our crafts over and came back to base. Duncan's back. Mission complete."

Director Mallack stood up and said, "Excellent job, all of you. Your synopsis is consistent with the footage, so this will be an open and shut case. Stephanie, you're up."

As Mallack sat down, Stephanie stood with us and said, "First, congratulations on completing the mission. Duncan, it is so good to have you back!"

"Thank you, Stephanie," Duncan responded.

"Before I continue, I would like the Analyst to give his battle synopsis. Analyst?"

The Analyst, surprised, cleared his throat, then stood up and said, "Right, um, okay, look at the holoscreen in front of you." The screen shimmered and displayed a series of numbers. "As we had discussed a few battles back, you all had been fighting with the Collector's big three using extremely low potential/kinetic ratios. I'm happy to report that a preliminary analysis has determined that their ratios significantly increased while yours decreased. You have effectively put the Collector and her forces on notice. The Elite are not to be trifled with."

"Hey, now!" Karl banged his left fist on the table and let out a whoop.

"How did they escape the room without us knowing?" Daisy redirected.

"Who knows," Malaysia answered. "Our focus was on Trent, so we didn't pay the others any attention."

"That was some slick work Streak did, given those vines I trapped her in. Hex must have pulled them off her. But, Alexia, wasn't Hex nullified?" Malcolm asked.

"Absolutely was," Alexia answered. "And that spell was good for at least a cycle, so I don't know how he could have gotten her out of it or them out of the room."

"Maybe Trent released them before we obliterated him?" Symone offered.

Malcolm snapped his finger and said, "You know, you might be right. He probably used telepathy to free them."

"Right," the Analyst pulled them back on focus. "Regardless, you guys definitely have upgraded and become stronger than you once were a quarter ago. I can't wait to speak to you soon one-on-one about what I have on your demos and stats."

"Thank you, Analyst," Stephanie said. The Analyst sat back down in his seat.

"Stephanie, can you tell us who Trent Salazar was?" Malaysia asked.

"Right, so we pulled all the information we could on Trent Salazar. We found thirty-seven of them in Uri City, and all of them are present and accounted for except for one."

"Really?" Daisy asked.

"Yes." Stephanie pulled up data on the holoscreen for everyone to examine. "This Trent Salazar grew up in the Underbelly but had no data trail. Literally dropped off the grid twenty years ago, and there's barely any data we can use to trace him to anyone."

"So, Trent didn't die. Instead, he was just hanging out on a random street corner when the Collector approached him with a destiny speech. He then received all our powers, all as part of an attempt to what? Make a statement to us?" Karl reasoned.

"With the Collector, we will never know. But one thing is for sure. This was not an accident. Everything the Collector does is on purpose. We will continue to run data for Trent Salazar. But we're not optimistic that we'll find anything given, once again, all the other Trent's are accounted for and are not connected to the Collector or this battle."

Malcolm sighed. "Okay. Well, what about the data mine? Were you able to determine what the Collector extracted from us?"

"Well, yes." Stephanie looked down.

"Well, what was it?" Alexia pressed.

"So, we thought that the huge mine of data was because of the Collector trying to stream multiple files from as many people in the Company as possible. But," Stephanie said.

"But what?" Malaysia quipped.

"But the Collector didn't pull multiple files. She only pulled seven files. Seven names."

"Us, right?"

"Yes," Stephanie lamented. "I had Dax deep dive into figuring out what exactly she pulled off you guys, and this is where it gets weird," Stephanie commanded the holoscreen through her stripe to show what information was gathered by Dredge's drive. "For all of you, she pulled one specific piece of information: your digital fingerprint."

The team looked at each other with confusion. "Wait," Daisy started, "that's all she pulled? Our fingerprints?"

"Yes, that was it—"

"That explains the box," Malaysia reasoned. "The box Duncan was in. She needed our fingerprints to create that box to get him out. But why go through the trouble of having us help Dredge just to obtain our fingerprints and use them to break Duncan out?"

"Right, it's like all the Collector wants to do is play mind games, but for what? To prove she can reach out and touch us whenever she wants?" Daisy added.

"Well, that's just it," Stephanie continued, "In addition, she did a deeper data extraction on one of you."

"On whom?" Malcolm asked.

"You," Stephanie spoke directly to Malcolm. "She pulled your file, Malcolm."

Everyone turned to look at Malcolm as he asked, "Me? Why me? What did she pull?"

"Everything, Malcolm. She has your entire file, from the day you started at the Company to about a week ago. She has all your information. She has everything we've ever recorded – all your battles, your trainings, wins, losses, medical history, demos, stats – she has it all."

The team all looked dumbfounded. Malcolm nodded once and replied, "So, what now? Do I go into hiding?"

"Frimas naw," Malaysia replied.

"That's right," Symone chimed in. "Let the Collector try you, and we'll fry her."

"Damn right," Duncan agreed.

"Listen, Elite," Mallack responded as she stood up. "The Collector has pushed you. And you pushed back and reminded her exactly who you are and why the Company chose you. She has proven herself to be one of the biggest threats to the city, but you showed her why this city is in good hands and that the Company will not go down without a fight. We may not know what her endgame is, or why she's doing all this elaborate scheming, but whatever it is, you seven will be ready and give her a run for her money.

"You did an excellent job, from initiation to execution. Give yourself a pat on the back and take the rest of the week off. You've earned it. I am so very proud of all of you. Dismissed."

"Hey now, a whole week?" Alexia cheered as she stood up. "Exciting! Nobody call me, I will not respond!"

"Malcolm, a word?" Mallack requested.

Malcolm said, "That's why I haven't gotten up yet. Um, Symone, see you later?"

"Oh, um, sure," Symone replied. She stood up, slid her chair under the table, and walked behind Daisy out of the conference room.

As everyone else left, Malcolm stood up and walked toward Mallack. "Yes, ma'am?"

"Malcolm, I just wanted to reiterate how proud I am of you and the leadership you demonstrated with your team."

"It wasn't just me, boss. Everybody did their part and made our rescue plan work. Especially Alexia. I didn't know she broke a cloak!"

"Just as shocked as you are. That's next level."

"Indeed."

"But still, none of this would have worked had you not led them well. You are the glue that holds this team together."

"Thank you, Director. So, now what?" Malcolm crossed his arms.

"Well, like I said, take the rest of the week off. If I were you, I'd start with making up with Symone."

Malcolm looked stunned. "Wait, what?"

Mallack didn't hold anything back. She looked Malcolm in his eyes and shared, "Malcolm, look, the Analyst didn't say anything about it, but I am saying it to you. I've seen the tapes. I've observed Symone and you working together. It's like poetry, you two. From the Sentinel Bank to the Power Party, your training sessions, rescuing Dredge's daughter, and now with Trent, you two have a chemistry that defies logic. It is like watching twins finish each other's sentences. Your relationship with each other, whatever it is, has made you two the most powerful force in the Company, if not the city. You two are each powerful on your own, but together, you are indomitable. And I know that you know that whatever the next big threat is, you will need each other to beat it. So, go make up with her. Even if she decides to leave the Company, you owe it to yourself to clear the air."

"You're right," Malcolm agreed. "Thank you, Mallack. For everything."

"You're welcome, Malcolm. Dismissed."

Malcolm walked out of the conference room and traversed to the quarters. He made a beeline to his residence and fell back into his bed. Now that Trent was defeated, Malcolm felt for the first time in years that he could finally close his eyes, unafraid of what he would see as he slumbered.

A couple of cycles went by. Symone was in the elevator. She had pressed "T" for the training floor and was looking forward to blasting dummies to bits. She meditated on her ambivalence toward staying with the Company, reminded of what Karl had said to her in the hovercraft a couple of nights prior. She believed that staying on with the Company would best serve her until she had gotten to the point of maxing out her demos and stats, and she wanted to know more about the Affinity Theory and what made Malcolm and her so special. But she still did not like the feeling that a mysterious puppet master was pulling her strings and making things happen beyond her control or comprehension. But she resigned that she would not allow that to bother her to the point of giving up on the opportunity to fight for the city and get stronger along the way.

As the elevator moved along the shaft, Symone reflected on Malcolm, how deeply she cared for him, and the immense joy he had brought into her life. Still unclear about his lack of involvement in the Affinity Theory, she tried to reason that she should leave him alone. But she couldn't shake how perfect he felt to her. Her mind quickly raced from their initial meeting to the Sentinel Bank, from her chance encounter with him in the training room to their walks around the building and the city. She dwelled on their training sessions, the kisses they shared, the passionate love they made, and every single time he brought a smile to her face. She decided that regardless of what had happened with Mallack, she wouldn't just let him go. There was something special about him, and she couldn't, nor wouldn't, shake it. She wanted it. She wanted him. And, as her mother told her, the only person standing in her way was, in fact, her, Symone Watson.

The elevator rang, and the doors revealed the training room floor. She walked to her room and placed her palm on the reader to unlock the door. The palm reader lit white for approval, and the door opened. When she stepped on the floor, the room's AI stated, "Symone Watson, codename Starburst. Room adjusted to meet powered state."

Symone walked deeper into the room. She asked the room, "Play 'Say Goodnight' by Madam Reila." AI responded by playing the melody by the late singer. Symone began to levitate, powering her hands, when the training room door swung open. The bright light from the hallway cast a silhouette, and Symone squinted to see who was entering the room. AI answered her question.

"Malcolm Bennett, codename Kingdom Come. Modifying room to meet powered state." The walls hummed.

Symone landed and stood still, staring at Malcolm. Malcolm looked at her, admiring her beauty while bracing himself for what he thought might be a dangerous assault.

"Hi," Malcolm said.

"Hi," Symone responded.

"We need to talk. Mind if I join you?"

Symone thought about his request for a minute. She then instructed the room, "Suit me up." A crimson nano-suit shot out of the wall and bonded to her body, enveloping her whole. She looked at the suit and said, "Okay, so we're shooting out different colors now? This is new!" She double-tapped her chest, and her cloak shimmered around her.

Symone charged her hands, and two stars levitated at her sides. Symone stared intensely at Malcolm through her visor. Malcolm took his chain from his neck and morphed it into a ball-and-chain. He cracked a wry smile and said, "Suit me up." A black nano-suit shot out of the wall and bonded to his body. He double-tapped his chest, his cloak shimmered around him, and he charged at her.

The door to the training room sealed shut.

Epilogue

The Analyst ran the numbers on his holoscreen one last time to make sure he wasn't crazy, and the data was indeed accurate. His eyes jumped from one number to another. The Analyst was mesmerized, a little kid at Jubilee. He grabbed his mini holoscreen from his desk and laid it on the countertop. The data downloaded onto the mini holoscreen, and he picked it up and jumped out of his seat. He made a call to Director Mallack.

"Yes, this is Mallack."

"Great rising, Director! Are you available right now? I have something exciting to show you!"

"I'm in my office, but hurry. I have a meeting in twenty minutes with the Chancellor."

"I'm on my way." The Analyst disconnected the call and raced out of his office to Director Mallack's. He pushed the door open and placed his hands on his knees to catch his breath.

Mallack sat in her usual chair staring at her holoscreen and typing information. She saw the Analyst struggling to breathe and asked, "Are you okay?"

"Oh, yes, most definitely! Just give me a minute," the Analyst answered.

"Please, sit down, Analyst," Mallack offered as she used her hand to point to one of the chairs in front of her desk.

"Thank you," the Analyst stated as he reached for the chair and sat down.

"What do you have for me?"

"Right," he returned. "Director, I'm going to show you a series of numbers, and I want you to tell me what you see."

The Analyst typed on his holoscreen and uploaded his information to the big holoscreen on the right side of Mallack's office. It was a 7x8 grid. The far left was grayed out, while the other six columns were patterned with numbers, then blanks. Each number/blank pair was columned to represent Power Level, Affinity, and Skill.

"Alright, these are the numbers from before, and these are the ones after." The Analyst pressed a button, causing the previously greyed-out numbers to appear, all of them higher than the ones displayed to their left.

"Okay," Mallack stated, "so the numbers to the left are an original state, and the numbers to the right are what happened afterward. I'm assuming we're talking about the Elite, which is what the grayed-out names are to the left?"

"Yes." The Analyst pressed a button, and the Elite's names appeared on the grid's left side.

"Okay, and these numbers are what happened over the quarter, I'm guessing. Did their battle with Trent and the Collector's team boost them?"

"No, Director. These numbers are not a reflection of their last battle."

Mallack looked confused. "I don't understand."

"Well," the Analyst reasoned, "I looked at their demos and stats from their fight with Trent, and I noticed that, except for Duncan, all their stats started from a significantly higher point than before. So, I wondered when exactly these changes took place."

"What did you determine?"

"I was able to pinpoint exactly when the shifts occurred." The Analyst displayed a timeline on the holoscreen.

"What is this?"

"This is a timeline of the shifts in the Elite's powers. Symone was the first to shift. Then Alexia. Daisy was next. Then Karl. Then Malaysia. And finally, Malcolm. And each time one of them shifted, Symone shifted with them."

"What do you mean, Analyst?"

The Analyst pressed another button, and another timeline appeared parallel to the first. "This is a timeline of Symone's training spars with the Elite. Symone's stats began to evolve each time she fought one of them. I didn't think anything of it outside of Symone just getting stronger. But upon further investigation, I was able to determine that each time Symone fought one of them, her opponent got stronger, too. They may not have known or felt it, but they shifted after they engaged in battle with her. And over time, those shifts became more permanent."

Mallack stood up and placed her hands on the table, and reacted, "So, what you're saying is that—"

"—the Affinity Theory isn't just a theory anymore," the Analyst beamed.

Mallack was not convinced. She looked at the numbers and the timelines and shook her head. "But how is this possible?" she asked.

"What do you mean? The numbers don't lie, Director." The Analyst pointed at the screen.

"But, if that is the case, why hasn't Malcolm enhanced the strength of any of his teammates? Or Malaysia? Or even Alexia? If the Affinity Theory is the answer, then as the team got closer together over time, they all should have made each other stronger. Malcolm and Symone are the only ones, as far as I know, who have been – or are – in a relationship. So, the Affinity Theory should have applied to just them, not the rest of the team. Maybe the Affinity Theory isn't the answer."

The Analyst felt a singe of disappointment, but his curiosity overrode it immediately. "What are you thinking, Director?"

Mallack cradled her chin with her right hand. "I'm thinking, instead of the Affinity Theory making our Elite stronger, maybe it's Symone. Maybe she is the reason. Maybe she is the key."

The Analyst's eyes widened. "If that's the case, Director, what do we do?"

Director Mallack alternated her gaze between her holoscreen and her stripe, then turned back to the Analyst.

A low, bellowing voice echoed in the room. "Director Mallack, what can I do for you?"

Mallack, maintaining a straight face, stared at Symone's avatar on the holoscreen. She returned, "We need to talk."

Minutes later, Symone walked the corridors of the Grand Hall, worried about what Mallack wanted with her. *I don't think I've done or said anything to make her want to speak to me today. But I did make a huge stink about the Affinity Theory. Maybe she wants to talk to me about that. She might want to demote me. Well, girl, whatever Mallack wants, let's just get this over with.*

She opened the doors to Mallack's office. She noticed the Analyst in one of the chairs in front of Mallack's desk, Mallack standing at her window, and the demos and stats on the screen. Confused but confident, she asked, "You wanted to see me, Director?"

The door to Mallack's office sealed shut.

End

Acknowledgements

Every second of every day, I cannot believe that I actually wrote a book! But I would be a fool to think that I did this all by myself. Without these people in my life, Malcolm, Symone, and the world of the Affinity Saga would not exist.

First, I truly thank my Savior and Lord Jesus Christ. This book wouldn't exist without Him giving me the wherewithal to make this happen. He orchestrated all of my steps, and I am forever grateful for His love, grace, guidance, patience, and care throughout this process. He is the reason that I live, move, and have all being, and this book is but a tiny demonstration of his power and might over my life.

To you, the reader of this book, I thank you for going along the journey with me! Trust me when I say, I wrote this book for you, and the journey of the Defenders of Uri City has just begun, so buckle up!

I thank my beta readers Malikah Grant and Azalea Valaine, who took my initial thoughts and helped me understand how to craft a better story without losing the heart of my message. You two were so pivotal and offered the best guidance I have gotten on making Uri City come to life. Your fingerprints are all over this book, and I am grateful for your assistance in ways that will impact the rest of the series.

I thank my editor Bookbright E, who was the first person post-completion of the book to lay eyes on it and give me not just a polished revision, but the most positive feedback about the story. Your encouragement never went overlooked.

To my cover artist Lesia T. who knocked the artwork out of the park, I thank you for capturing Malcolm and Symone flawlessly!

I also thank S.M.R. Burton, whose book group *Wrevenge of the Nerds* was so vital in the eleventh hour to inspire me to finish the mission and get this book finished. Everyone in the group is so encouraging, inspiring, and motivational, and they helped me stay focused on my goals. For that, I am grateful.

I thank my children, Marie and Allison, who always asked for updates on how the book was going, offering word and sentence changes when appropriate, listened to every song from the playlist and offered more tracks, and encouraged me to finish so they can see the story be told on Netflix one day.

I am incredibly grateful to Lavona Gantt, who lit a fire under me in late 2021 in a cell-sized office and inspired me to bring the Affinity Theory to life. Your encouragement and your insight reminded me of the storyteller I am, and without question, Malcolm, Symone, the Collector, the Defenders, Uri City, and Uretha would not exist without you cheering me on from the sidelines. You're a rockstar, and this project is the proof.

Last, but certainly not least, I thank my wife, my great love, and my best friend, Nicole. You sat up with me every night and listened to every word and correction, questioned motives, helped me tease things out, and celebrated every win. Your contributions to the Affinity saga are plastered all over the book, and your criticisms and praise are evident throughout the story. I am so thankful for your love, your support, and your grace. You are freaking amazing, and there aren't enough words to capture just how much. I love you, so much, and I thank you for loving me the way you do.

I love you all! Blessings!

www.ingramcontent.com/pod-product-compliance
Lightning Source LLC
Chambersburg PA
CBHW031152310726
48969CB00001B/51